W9-AED-113

Great Sea Stories

Great Sea Stories

The Cruel Sea
Nicholas Monsarrat

The Ship
C. S. Forester

Dive in the Sun
Douglas Reeman

Sundial

The Cruel Sea
first published in Great Britain in 1951 by Cassell & Co. Ltd

The Ship
first published in Great Britain in 1943 by Michael Joseph Ltd

Dive in the Sun
first published in Great Britain in 1961 by
Hutchinson & Co. (Publishers) Ltd

This edition first published in Great Britain in 1979 by:
Sundial Publications Limited
59 Grosvenor Street
London W.1.

In collaboration with:

William Heinemann Limited
15–16 Queen Street
London W.1.

and

Martin Secker & Warburg Limited
54 Poland Street
London W.1.

The Cruel Sea © 1951 by Nicholas Monsarrat
The Ship © 1943 by C. S. Forester
Dive in the Sun © Douglas Reeman 1961

ISBN 0 904230 96 1

Printed and bound in Great Britain at
William Clowes & Sons Limited
Beccles and London

Contents

The Cruel Sea

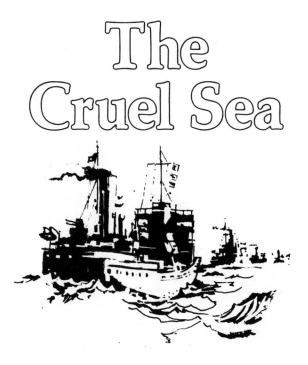

NICHOLAS MONSARRAT

To
Philippa Crosby

Author's Note

All the characters in this book are wholly fictitious. If I have inadvertently used the names of men who did in fact serve in the Atlantic during the war, I apologize to them for so doing. Where I have mentioned actual war-appointments, such as Flag-Officer-in-Charge at Liverpool or Glasgow, the characters who are portrayed in such appointments have no connection whatsoever with their actual incumbents; and if there *was* a W.R.N.S. officer holding the job of S.O.O.2 on the Clyde in 1943, then she is not my 'Second Officer Hallam'. In particular, my Admiral in charge of the working-up base at 'Ardnacraish' is *not* intended as a portrait of the energetic and distinguished officer who discharged with such efficiency a similar task in the Western Approaches Command.

BEFORE THE CURTAIN

This is the story – the long and true story – of one ocean, two ships, and about a hundred and fifty men. It is a long story because it deals with a long and brutal battle, the worst of any war. It has two ships because one was sunk, and had to be replaced. It has a hundred and fifty men because that is a manageable number of people to tell a story about. Above all, it is a true story because that is the only kind worth telling.

First, the ocean, the steep Atlantic stream. The map will tell you what that looks like: three-cornered, three thousand miles across and a thousand fathoms deep, bounded by the European coastline and half of Africa, and the vast American continent on the other side: open at the top, like a champagne glass, and at the bottom, like a municipal rubbish-dumper. What the map will not tell you is the strength and fury of that ocean, its moods, its violence, its gentle balm, its treachery: what men can do with it, and what it can do with men. But this story will tell you all that.

Then the ship, the first of the two, the doomed one. At the moment she seems far from doomed: she is new, untried, lying in a river that lacks the tang of salt water, waiting for the men to man her. She is a corvette, a new type of escort ship, an experiment designed to meet a desperate situation still over the horizon. She is brand-new; the time is November 1939; her name is H.M.S. *Compass Rose*.

Lastly, the men, the hundred and fifty men. They come on the stage in twos and threes: some are early, some are late, some, like this pretty ship, are doomed. When they are all assembled, they are a company of sailors. They have women, at least a hundred and fifty women, loving them, or tied to them, or glad to see the last of them as they go to war.

But the men are the stars of this story. The only heroines are the ships: and the only villain the cruel sea itself.

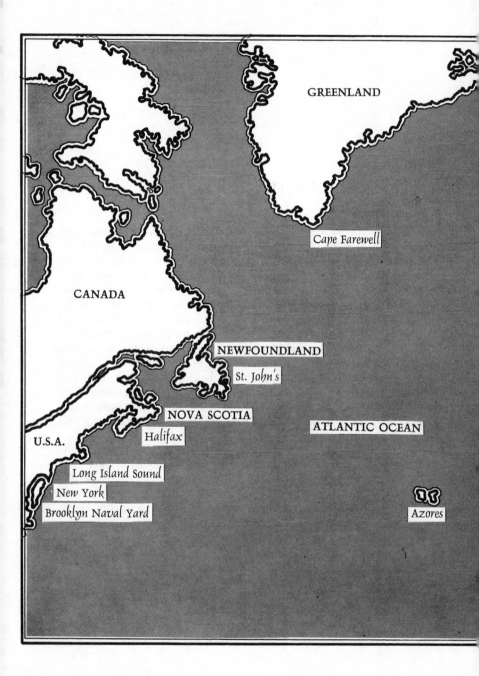

GREENLAND

Cape Farewell

CANADA

NEWFOUNDLAND

St. John's

NOVA SCOTIA

ATLANTIC OCEAN

U.S.A.

Halifax

Long Island Sound

New York

Brooklyn Naval Yard

Azores

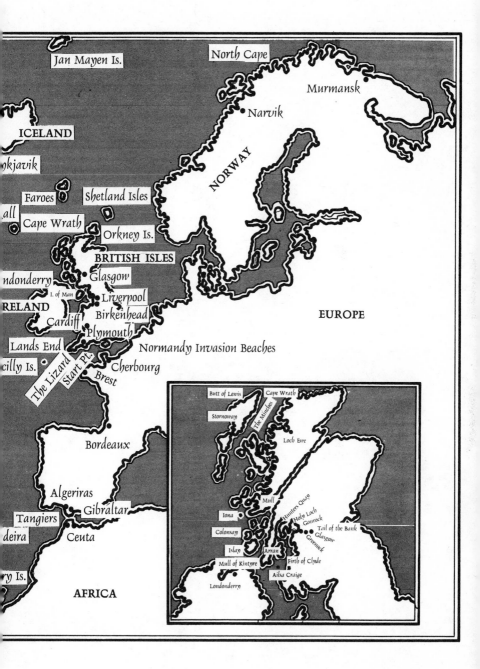

PART ONE

CHAPTER 1

1939: LEARNING

Lieutenant-Commander George Eastwood Ericson, R.N.R., sat in a stone-cold, draughty, corrugated-iron hut beside the fitting-out dock of Fleming's Shipyard on the River Clyde. Ericson was a big man, broad and tough, a man to depend on, a man to remember: about forty-two or -three, fair hair going grey, blue eyes as level as a foot-rule with wrinkles at the corners – the product of humour and of twenty years' staring at a thousand horizons. At the moment the wrinkles were complicated by a frown. It was not a worried frown – if Ericson were susceptible to worry he did not show it to the world; it was simply a frown of concentration, a tribute to a problem.

On the desk in front of him was a grubby, thumbed-over file labelled 'Job No. 2891: Movable Stores'. Through the window and across the dock, right under his competent eye, was a ship: an untidy grey ship, mottled with red lead, noisy with riveting, dirty with an accumulation of wood-shavings, cotton-waste, and empty paint drums.

The file and the ship were connected, bound together by the frown on his face. For the ship was his: he was to commission and to command H.M.S. *Compass Rose*, and at this moment he did not wholly like the idea.

It was a dislike, a doubt, compounded of a lot of things which ordinarily he would have taken in his stride, if indeed he had noticed them at all. Certainly it had nothing to do with the ship's name: one could not spend twenty years at sea, first in the Royal Navy and then in the Merchant Service, without coming across some of the most singular names in the world. (The clumsiest he remembered had been a French tramp called the *Marie-Josephe-Brinomar de la Tour-du-Pin*; and the oddest, an East-Coast collier called *Jolly Nights*.) *Compass Rose* was nothing out of the ordinary; it had to be a flower name because she was one of the new Flower Class corvettes, and (Ericson smiled to himself) by the time they got down to *Pansy* and *Stinkwort* and *Love-in-the-Mist*, no one would think anything of *Compass Rose*.

Those were trivialities, anyway. Perhaps the real trouble had to do with this precise moment of history, the start of a war. Ericson had been just too young to be closely involved in World War I: now he was secretly wondering if he were not too old to play a worthwhile part in the second round of the same struggle. At the moment he had, as his novel responsibility, a new job, a new ship, and a new crew. In theory he was proud of them all; in practice, he was unsure of the ordeal and concerned about his fitness for it.

He felt remarkably out of practice . . . Ericson had been axed from the Navy in 1927, after ten years' service: he had been on the beach for two hard years, and then spent the next ten with the Far East Line, feeling himself lucky all the time (what with the Depression and Britain's maritime decay) to have a sea-going job at all. He loved the sea, though not blindly: it was the cynical, self-contemptuous love of a man for a mistress whom he distrusts profoundly but cannot do without. Far East Lines had been a tough crowd: progress was slow, with the threat of dismissal always poised: in ten years he had only had command of one ship, an old two-thousand-ton freighter slowly pounding herself to bits on the Dutch East Indies run.

It was not a good introduction to responsibility in war. And now here he was, almost masquerading as Lieut.-Commander G. E. Ericson, with one of His Majesty's ships-of-war to commission, a crew of eighty-eight to command, and a hundred things in the realm of naval routine to re-learn, quite apart from having a fighting ship to manoeuvre and to use as a weapon.

A fighting ship . . . He raised his eyes from the interminable office-boy job of checking stores, and looked at *Compass Rose* again. She was odd, definitely odd, even making allowances for her present unfinished state. She was two hundred feet long, broad, chunky, and graceless: designed purely for anti-submarine work, and not much more than a floating platform for depth-charges, she was the prototype of a class of ship which could be produced quickly and cheaply in the future, to meet the urgent demands of convoy escort. Her mast, contrary to Naval practice, was planted right in front of the bridge, and a squat funnel behind it: she had a high fo'c'sle armed with a single four-inch gun, which the senior gunnery rating was at that moment elevating and training. The depth-charge rails aft led over a whaler-type stern – aesthetically deplorable, but effective enough at sea. Ericson knew ships, and he could guess how this one was going to behave. She would be hot in summer – there was no forced-draught ventilation, and no refrigerator – and cold, wet, and uncomfortable at most other times. She would be a natural bastard in any kind of seaway, and in a full Atlantic gale she would be thrown about like a chip of wood. And that was really all you could say about her – except that she was his, and that, whatever her drawbacks and imperfections, he had to get her going and make her work.

The crew he was less worried about. Both the discipline and the habit of command instilled by the Royal Navy died very hard: Ericson knew that he had them still. All things being equal, he could handle those men, he could make them do what he wanted – if he knew himself. The flaw might be in the material he would have to work on: in a rapidly expanding Navy, a new ship's company was likely to be a scratch lot. The advance guard of a dozen key-ratings had already arrived, to take charge in their various departments – gunnery, depth-charges, Asdic, telegraphy, signalling, engine-room. As a nucleus, they were satisfactory: but the numbers might be made up, and the gaps filled, by anything from professional hard-cases just out of Detention Barracks to green 'hostilities-only' ratings fresh from the farmyard. And his officers – a First Lieutenant and two subs – could make a hash of anything he might want to do with the ship . . .

Ericson frowned again, and then stopped frowning. Whatever his doubts, they were not to show: that was a cardinal rule. He was a seaman: this was a seaman's job, though it didn't feel like it at the moment. He bent to his desk again, wishing he could develop some sort of a taste for paper-work: wishing also that his First Lieutenant, whose work incidentally should have included the file in front of him, were a slightly more reassuring character.

CHAPTER 2

Lieutenant James Bennett, R.A.N.V.R. (The 'A' for Australia), First Lieutenant of H.M.S. *Compass Rose*, strode round the cluttered upper deck as if he owned every rivet of it, with Petty Officer Tallow, the coxswain, following him at a disrespectful distance. Bennett looked tough, and knew it, and liked it: everything about him – the red face, the stocky figure, the cap worn at an unusual angle – all proclaimed the home-spun sailorman with no frills and no nonsense. That was the picture he had of himself, and with luck it was going to carry him through the war: certainly it had got him his present job, aided by fast talking and a selection board preoccupied with more important things than sifting claims about past exploits.

Chance had found him in England at the outbreak of war, instead of clerking in a shipping office in Sydney: his commission in the Volunteer Reserve was undeniable: the rest had been easy – an anti-submarine course, an interview in London, and the job of First Lieutenant in *Compass Rose*. It wasn't *all* that he wanted – too much paper-work, for a start, though the subs would take care of that as soon as they arrived; but it would do until something better turned up. And meanwhile he was First Lieutenant of this little crap-barge, and he was going to act the part.

'Coxs'n!'

'Sir?'

Standing by the four-inch gun, Bennett waited for Tallow to catch up. It took a little time, for Petty Officer Tallow (seventeen years in the Navy, three stripes, due for Chief P.O. any moment now) was feeling disgruntled. This certainly wasn't what he had volunteered for – a fiddling bloody little gash-boat instead of a proper ship (his last ship had been *Repulse*), a First Lieutenant like something out of the films, and Christ knows what sort of a ship's company due to join next week. But Tallow, like the Captain, was a product of the Navy, which meant, above all, acceptance of the current job and the current circumstances: only in the subtlest ways (and none of them destructive) would he indicate that this sort of thing was *not* what he was used to.

As Tallow came up: 'This man,' said Bennett heavily, pointing to the rating who was working on the four-inch gun, 'is smoking during working hours.'

Tallow restrained a sigh. 'Yes, sir. Not working proper routine yet, sir.'

'Who says not?'

The seaman under discussion surreptitiously disposed of his cigarette, and bent to his task with extraordinary concentration. Tallow tried again.

'I was going to leave it until we had the full ship's company aboard, sir.'

'That makes no difference,' said Bennett briskly. 'No smoking except during stand-easy. Understand?'

'Aye, aye, sir.'

'And don't you forget it.'

Jesus, thought Tallow, what sort of a country is Australia ... Following once more in the First Lieutenant's wake, he sank a little deeper into resignation. This bastard was all wind, and the only other officers were two green subs (he'd had a glance at the scheme of complement). Barring the Captain, who was OK, it looked as if he'd have to carry the bloody ship himself.

CHAPTER 3

The door of the dockside hut flapped open, letting in a ferocious draught. The Captain looked up, and then turned in his chair.

'Come in,' he said. 'And shut the door very firmly.'

The two young men who stood before him were, physically, in strong contrast with each other, though their uniforms, with the single thin wavy stripe on the arm, gave them a surface similarity. One of them, the elder one, was tall, black-haired, thin-faced: he had a watchful air, as though feeling his way in a situation which only needed a little time to fall into its proper category, alongside hundreds of other situations which he had dealt with competently and effectively in the past. The other one was a simpler edition altogether: short, fair, immature – a very young man in a proud uniform, and not yet sure that he deserved the distinction. Looking at them, Ericson suddenly thought: they're more like father and son, though there can't be more than five or six years between them ... He waited for one of them to speak, knowing well which of them it would be.

The elder one saluted and said: 'Reporting for *Compass Rose*, sir.' He proffered a slip of paper, and Ericson glanced at it.

'You're Lockhart?'

'Yes, sir.'

'And you're Ferraby?'

'Yes, sir.'

'First ship?'

'Yes, sir,' Lockhart answered, as the natural spokesman. 'We've just come up from *King Alfred*.'

'How long were you training there?'

'Five weeks.'

'And now you know it all?'

Lockhart grinned. 'No, sir.'

'Well, that's something, anyway.'

Ericson looked at them, more closely. They were both very smart: number one doe-skin jackets, gloves, gas-masks – they might have stepped straight out of the *Manual of Training*. They had talked of this question of dress, on the long journey up from the South Coast to the Clyde: their orders had been endorsed 'Report to Admiral Superintending Contract-Built Ships', and it had seemed to politic to dress the part ... The Captain, in his old serge working-jacket with the faded gold lace, seemed theatrically shabby by comparison.

After a pause, Ericson asked: 'What was your job in peacetime?'

'Journalist, sir,' said Lockhart.

The Captain smiled, and waved his hand round the room. 'What's the connection?'

'I've done a lot of sailing, sir.'

'M'm ...' He looked at Ferraby, 'What about you?'

'I was working in a bank, sir.'

'Ever been to sea?'

'Only across to France, sir.'

'We might find that useful ... All right – take a look at the ship, and report to the First Lieutenant – he's somewhere aboard. Where's all your gear?'

'At the hotel, sir.'

'It'll have to stay there for a bit – we won't be sleeping on board for a week or so.'

With a nod, Ericson turned back to his desk. The two young men saluted, somewhat uncertainly, and made for the door. As Ferraby opened it, the Captain said, over his shoulder:

'And by the way, don't salute me indoors when I haven't got a cap on. I can't return it. The proper drill is for you to take your cap off when you come in.'

'Sorry, sir,' said Lockhart.

'It's not vital,' said Ericson. They could hear the friendliness in his voice. 'But you might as well get it right.'

When they had gone, he paused for a moment before returning to work. Journalist . . . bank-clerk . . . trips to France . . . sailing . . . It didn't sound very professional. But they seemed willing, and the older one, Lockhart, had some common sense, by the look of him. You could do a lot with common sense, at sea. And you could do precious little without it . . . He picked up his pencil again.

CHAPTER 4

Lockhart and Ferraby walked across the dock and then paused, looking up at the ship. They saw her with different eyes. Lockhart could, to a certain extent, appraise her lines and her design: to Ferraby she was entirely novel, in every detail, and this, like a lot of other things, worried him. He had been married only six weeks: saying goodbye to his wife two nights previously, he had confided once more his uncertainty, his doubt about what he had taken on. 'But darling,' she had said, with that loving smile which he found so moving and so beautiful, 'you can do *anything*. You know you can. Look how happy you've made *me*.' It was illogical, but it was very comforting all the same. Everything about their marriage was like that. They were just getting over their shyness together, and finding the process singularly sweet.

Ferraby had said goodbye to a new wife: Lockhart had said goodbye to nothing. He had answered 'Journalist' to the Captain, but he was not at all sure he deserved the title. He was twenty-seven: for six years he had scratched a living, freelancing in and around Fleet Street: it had taught him a lot, but it had not given him an ounce of security or a moment's freedom from worry. He was not even sure that that was what he wanted, in any case. He had no parents living, he had no ties: the only woman he had taken leave of had said: 'Why ever didn't we do this before?' as he climbed out of bed and into his uniform, in the cold London dawn. That had been symptomatic of his whole life: uncertain, impermanent, shifting in emphasis and intensity. He had joined up because there was a war: he had joined the Navy because he knew about ships – small ships, anyway – and could navigate. Now he felt happy, and free, and confident; and he liked the change.

Ferraby, pointing, said: 'What's that wire thing tacked onto the mast?'

'Some radio gadget, I suppose ... Let's go aboard.'

They crossed the rough plank that served as a gangway, and jumped down onto the deck. Here and there it was still rimed with frost, and a hundred things were lying about it – oil-drums, tool boxes, welding-gear, oddments of equipment. There was loud hammering from a dozen places, and somewhere up in the bows a riveting-machine was making a prodigious racket. Lockhart led the way aft, and they looked at the depth-charge gear – a replica of what they had worked on at the training-establishment: then they went below, and presently found themselves in the cabin-space. There were only two cabins, one with a single berth labelled 'First Lieutenant', and a tiny wardroom: the whole thing was cramped and full of awkward corners.

'This is going to be damned crowded,' said Lockhart presently. 'You and I share a cabin, I suppose.'

'I wonder what the First Lieutenant's like,' said Ferraby, looking at the label on the door.

'Whatever he's like, we'll have to put up with him. He can make or break this ship, as far as we're concerned.'

'How?'

'Just by being bloody, or the reverse, as the fancy takes him.'

'Oh ... I liked the Captain.'

'He *loved* you ... Yes, he's all right. The good R.N.R.s are really good.'

'A lot of them don't like us.'

'Us?'

'The R.N.V.R.'

Lockhart smiled. 'Two years from now, *we'll* do the picking and choosing ... Don't you worry about the V.R., my lad. It's going to be *our* war, in the end. That's the only way they'll be able to man the ships.'

'You mean, we'll actually get commands?'

Lockhart nodded, abstractedly. He was examining the wardroom pantry, which was inordinately small.

A raucous voice over their heads shouted: 'Below!' The noise rang round the empty wardroom.

'What a rough man,' said Lockhart.

After a pause the shout was repeated, on a higher note.

'Is that us?' asked Ferraby uncertainly.

'I fear so.' Lockhart walked to the foot of the ladder, and peered upwards. 'Yes?'

The red face framed in the companionway was not reassuring. Bennett was glaring down at him.

'What the hell are you hiding down there for?'

'I'm not,' said Lockhart.

'Weren't you told to report to me?'

'After looking round the ship, yes.'

'Sir,' prompted Bennett unpleasantly.

'Sir,' said Lockhart. He could almost feel Ferraby's harassed expression behind him.

'Is the other sub down there too?'

'Yes – sir. We didn't know you were aboard.'

'Don't wear a green coat with me,' said Bennett obscurely. 'Come up here – and double up.'

Confronting the two of them at the top of the ladder, Bennett looked at them closely. He was frowning, and the rough Australian accent was prominent.

'It's your job to find out where I am,' he began sourly. 'Names?'

'Lockhart,' said Lockhart.

'Ferraby,' said Ferraby.

'How long since you were commissioned?'

'A week,' said Lockhart. And added: 'Temporary Probationary.'

'I can see that,' said Bennett disagreeably. 'It sticks out like a——' he produced a colourful simile. 'Ever been to sea before?'

'In small boats,' said Lockhart.

'I don't mean ——ing about in yachts.'

'Then, no.'

Bennett turned to Ferraby. 'You?'

'No, sir.'

'Wonderful ... Which of you is senior?'

'We passed out together,' said Lockhart.

'Jesus Christ, I know that! But one of you is senior, one of you is ahead of the other in the Navy List.'

'We're not in the Navy List yet.'

Bennett saw Lockhart staring at him, sizing him up, and he did not like it.

'You're not out of the egg yet, by the sound of it.'

Lockhart said nothing.

'Well, we'd better find out what you *can* do,' said Bennett after a pause. 'Have you been round the ship?'

'Yes.'

'How many fire-hose points are there?'

'Fourteen,' answered Lockhart promptly. He had no idea what the right answer was, but he was quite sure that Bennett didn't know either. Later, if Bennett checked up, he would climb out of it somehow.

'Very clever,' said Bennett. He turned to Ferraby. 'What sort of gun have we got?'

'Four-inch,' said Ferraby after a pause.

'Four-inch what?' asked Bennett roughly. 'Breech-loading? Quick firing? Mark IV? Mark VI? Fixed ammunition?'

'Four-inch – I don't know,' said Ferraby miserably.

'Find out,' snapped Bennett. 'I'll ask you next time I see you. And now both of you go back to the hut, and start checking C.B.s.'

'Yes, sir,' said Lockhart. He turned to go, as did Ferraby.

'Salute,' said Bennett.

They saluted.

'I'm the First Lieutenant around here,' said Bennett. 'Don't you forget it.'

.   .   .

'An engaging character,' said Lockhart on the way back. 'I can see we're going to get on like a house on fire – and I hope the bastard fries.'

'What are C.B.s?' asked Ferraby in a forlorn tone.

'Confidential books.'

'Why couldn't he say so?'

'He had a reason.'

'What reason?'

Lockhart smiled. 'It's a process of *impressement*.'

'French?'

'The French do it better ... Vulgarly speaking, the motto is "Bull-dust baffles brains". I must say he's quite a performer.'

'It's not what I expected,' said Ferraby.

'You're the sub-lieutenant around here,' said Lockhart, mimicking brilliantly. 'Don't you forget it.'

'But which of us *is* senior?'

'I think I'd better be.'

CHAPTER 5

With nightfall, a grateful quietness returned to *Compass Rose*. The noise of hammering died, the bustle subsided: the last workman hurried across the gangway towards the waiting tram – this was before the unending urgency of night-shifts: the single watchman who remained, huddled under his canvas shelter on the quarter-deck, cursed the cold breeze which blew the charcoal fumes from his brazier directly into his eyes. The ship rocked gently to the stirring of the river: queer shadows fell on the deck, and moved, and were still again.

Now the huge activity of the Clydeside ebbed to nothing: the river, lined with silent half-finished ships, deserted shipyards, and cranes stationary against a spectral sky, resolved itself into a backwash of the war. It was the end of one day – no better, no worse than other days: the ships a little nearer completion, the jobs advanced a single stage towards their end – and towards other jobs, in an unending series which would test patience more than skill, and endurance more than both of them. The Clyde had done this sort of thing before: now, in 1939, it was going to do it again, as a matter of course, without heroics. But this moment was only the beginning; poised on the verge of a six-years' effort, there was still space to relax, and time to sleep at night.

The nightwatchman, an old pensioner, grumbled and scratched and fell into a doze. He'd had his war – the last one: it was someone else's turn now. Good luck to them: but they mustn't expect miracles from everyone. Miracles were for young chaps: for the old, a decent rest, a decent sleep, were nothing to be ashamed of.

.   .   .

In a public house in the noisy part of Argyll Street, near the railway station, Petty Officer Tallow and the senior engine-room rating, Chief E.R.A. Watts, were drinking up before going off to their lodgings. They had been there since eight o'clock that evening: they had drunk seven pints of beer apiece: it had made not an atom of difference either to their diction or their bearing, save that Tallow was now inclined to perspire and Watts' eyes were a trifle bloodshot. They were there partly because there was nothing else for them to do – they didn't care for cinemas, and their lodgings were dirty and uncomfortable: partly because they liked the place, and could not have felt more at home anywhere. There was a great deal of noise in the bar. Tallow and Watts drank and talked in low grumbling tones. They had been grumbling, as well as drinking, since eight o'clock, and had mellowed very little in the process.

'She'll not be a happy ship, I can tell you straight.' Watts was a Scotsman, grey-headed, bald, nearly through with his time in the Navy: his accent and Tallow's, broad Scots and full-flavoured Lancashire, blended in rough harmony. 'There's not the makings of it. I'm not saying the skipper's not OK, but that Jimmy's a bastard. He was round my engine-room tonight, blethering about a watchkeeping bill – and me with the bloody main shaft still opened up. Sooner I get my ticket, and settle down on the pension, the better.'

'There'll be no ticket while the war lasts,' said Tallow. He took a pull at his glass tankard, and wiped his mouth. 'If you're warm, you're in – for the duration.'

'Well, there'll be shore-billets,' insisted Watts. 'Something easy, back in barracks – that'll just suit me. The ship's too small for my liking.'

'She'll be lively enough,' agreed Tallow. 'By God, you could hoist the whole outfit aboard *Repulse*, and not feel the difference.'

Watts laughed. 'I hope yon *Repulse* will be handy, if we run into trouble.'

'We're likely to do that, by the way they're talking. Beats me how they can expect ships of that size to put up any sort of protection for a convoy. It took destroyers all their time, last war.'

'There'll be tactics,' said Watts vaguely.

'They'll need a sight more than tactics, to come out on the right side. What've we got in the way of armament? One bloody little four-inch pop-gun, and a couple of rows of depth-charges. They'll make rings round us.'

'What gets me is the accommodation,' broke in Watts, reverting to an earlier complaint. 'We're all mixed up together, *and* there's not enough room anyway. There's stokers messing alongside seamen – you know well enough they don't like that, either of them. The fo'c'sle's about six feet by four, there's no canteen, no refrigeration, no forced draught. You can't go from the messdecks to the bridge without getting wet through, and the galley's right aft so that everything will be stone cold by the time we eat it. Whoever designed that ship must have been blind drunk.'

'Wish the bastard had to sail in her.' Morosely, Tallow took a final swig at his tankard, and then looked across to the bar as 'Time' was called. 'What about it? One for the road?'

'Not for me. I've got to work tomorrow.'

Outside, Argyll Street was noisy with people coming out of the pubs and stumbling about in the blackout. It was very cold: at the street corner a raw wind made them turn up their coat-collars and put their hands deep in their pockets. As they made their way to their tram-stop:

'Heaven help sailors,' said Watts piously. 'Man, it'll be bitter at sea tonight.'

'We'll know that soon enough,' said Tallow. 'A couple of weeks from now we'll be crying our eyes out for Argyll Street, wet or fine. You just wait.'

. . .

Lockhart and Ferraby were both tired. They had spent most of the day in the dockyard hut, checking lists of stores and charts and confidential books with periodic, maddening directives from Bennett to break off and do something quite different. The list of stores was interminable: the charts covered every ocean in the world and there was, at the bottom of the box, a chart of the Black Sea. Lockhart, contemplating this, had murmured: 'What a long war it's going to be,' and Bennett, overhearing, had countered: 'It'll be a bloody sight longer unless you stop nattering and get on with it.' Later they had been sent back on board *Compass Rose*, to start on the accommodation plan – undeniably the First Lieutenant's job: the working day had finished at six, with a sharp order from Bennett to be back in the hut by half past eight next morning. As they had an hour's tram-ride from their hotel to the shipyard, it would mean a very early start to the day.

Now, after late dinner, they were both lying in bed in the hotel room they shared on Sauchiehall Street: Ferraby staring at the ceiling, hands clasped behind his head, Lockhart smoking and thumbing·through the *Manual of Seamanship*. Outside, the crude noises of Glasgow at night gradually diminished.

Presently Ferraby stirred and, leaning over on one elbow, asked: 'What are you reading?'

'The Bible – our Bible,' answered Lockhart. 'There's a lot in it which has to be squared with the actual facts.'

'You mean, the First Lieutenant?'

Lockhart laughed. 'Oh – him . . . He's feeling his way, the same as we are, only he's making more noise about it.'

'He's certainly doing that.' Ferraby lay back again. 'I wonder if I could get my wife up here?'

'Good idea. We won't be living on board for some time. Why not ask about it?'

'Ask who?'

'Bennett, I suppose. Or the Captain.'

'Bennett would say "no" . . . I was just getting used to being married.'

'It must be very satisfactory,' said Lockhart, without irony.

'It's more than that.' Shyly enthusiastic, Ferraby could not disguise the true focus of his thoughts. 'It's meant everything to me, the last few weeks. I don't know how I could have got through otherwise. She's so – when you marry a person——' he floundered, and then made an effort. 'Haven't you ever felt as if you must have someone you can trust absolutely – someone you can tell everything to, without – without ever feeling ashamed. Someone who's the other half of yourself.'

'No,' said Lockhart after a pause. 'I don't think I've ever needed that.'

'That's what it's been like for me. For both of us, I think. That's why it's so rotten to be separated.'

'Well, see if you can get her up here.' Lockhart closed his book, and stubbed out his cigarette. 'There's no harm in asking, anyway. After all, the Captain's wife is here.'

'That's different.'

'Not necessarily. Try it, and see what happens.' Lockhart switched out the light, and lay back. 'Oh God, why do we have to get up so early?'

'There's a terrific lot to do.'

'Yes, I suppose so . . . Goodnight.'

'Goodnight.'

'And don't let it get you down.'

'It's all so different from what I expected.'
'It'd be damned funny if it weren't.'

. . .

Downstairs, in the lounge of the same hotel, Bennett was withholding his custom from a grim-looking tart he had picked up at the bar. He couldn't *quite* make up his mind – and, in the meantime, he felt like a nice chat . . . The room was crowded, noisy, and very hot. Above Bennett's sweaty red face, his cap still maintained its informal angle.

For the fifth or sixth time the woman tipped her glass and said: 'Here's fun, dear!' She had a face like a ruined skull, white and lined: her tight black skirt strained at its seams, overdoing the candour of the flesh, repellent in its allure.

'Cheerio!' said Bennett, as before. He drank, and stared at his glass.

'Ever been in Australia?'

'No,' said the woman. 'Can't say I have. Long way from here, you know.'

'Too right, it's a long way! Might be the other side of hell for all the chance I have of seeing it.'

'You'll get back all right. Soon as the war's over.'

'Can't be too soon for me.' He sipped his beer moodily.

'Don't you like Scotland? . . . Bonny Scotland,' she added as an afterthought. She was clearly a Cockney, and the Scottish inflection, borrowed from the music-halls, had a grotesque unreality. ' "Glasgie belongs to me" – you know what the song says.' She drank elegantly, finger crooked, and set down her glass as if ashamed of using so crude an instrument.

'Oh, Scotland's all right,' said Bennett after a pause. 'But you know how it is——' he waved his hand round the bar, knocked over a tankard, and drenched his coat and trousers with beer. 'Oh, ——it!' he exclaimed loudly.

'Naughty!' said the woman mechanically.

Bennett mopped himself vigorously. 'Waste of a good drink,' he said. And then: 'Scotland's all right. But it's not Sydney, by a long way.'

'I suppose not,' said the woman. She crossed her legs delicately. 'Have you got a girl, back in Australia?'

'Sure,' said Bennett, 'rafts of them.'

'The girls I left behind me, eh?'

'Something like that.'

'Well,' said the woman, a trifle edgily, 'tonight's my busy night.' She picked up her bag from the counter.

'Don't go,' said Bennett, making up his mind. 'Have another drink.'

'No, thanks.'

'I'll see you home, then.'

'It's a long way,' said the woman. 'Fourpence in the trams.'

'We'll get a taxi.'

'My! – Going the pace, aren't you?' She got down from her stool at the bar and stood looking at him, judging his mood. 'What happens when we get there?'

'I'll see you're all right.'

'I've met sailors before,' said the woman.

'Not Australians.'

'No,' she admitted. 'You're the first Australian I've met, socially speaking.'

'It'll be a treat for you.' Bennett heaved himself off his stool, and took her arm. 'Well, here we go.'

The woman nodded to the barman. 'So long, Fred.'

'See you again,' said the barman. 'Goodnight.'

'I'll see to the goodnight myself,' said Bennett. 'That's my little bit of the job.' He crammed his cap over one eye at a jauntier angle still, and added, with a singular leer: 'It's not so little either, I can guarantee.'

'Are you really an officer?' asked the woman on the way out.

. . .

The Captain sat reading a bad thriller picked up from the bookshelf in the lounge of the stuffy hotel on Kelvinside: opposite him, Mrs Ericson was knitting. She was a plump, placid-faced woman of about forty: she always knitted during the evening – pullovers and mufflers for her husband, cardigans for herself, odd garments for odd relatives and their new babies. It sometimes seemed to Ericson that she had been sitting opposite him and knitting, without a break, for nineteen years on end. This was the picture of her he always visualized, when he thought of her at sea or when he was coming home on leave: he warmed to it readily, but its reality often made him impatient and irritated by the time his leave was up and he was due to go to sea again.

They were quietly happy together: they never quarrelled. He was, he supposed, a good husband and father, and she was the female counterpart: certainly he had never looked more than twice at any other woman. But now, as so often before, he was conscious of the familiar impatience as they sat in silence together. He must have been long enough ashore ... Grace was a dear girl, but this time his leave had lasted over two months, and the ship and the sea were beginning, as always, to pull him away from her and everything she stood for. It was not unfaithfulness to her: it was faithfulness to the other love, the tough professional one which was stronger than any human tie.

They had never talked of this, save laughingly when they were newly married. She had come to accept the order of priority, and, being a sensible woman, she had ceased to worry about its deeper implications. For a few days of each leave she gave him all that he wanted – the warm welcome, the tenderness, the occasional shaft of passion, the softness after hard ordeal; then, matching his mood, she faded into the placid background of their lives and, perhaps symbolically, picked up her knitting again. She counted herself happy, and, as a sailor's daughter herself, she was proud of her husband's professional skill and standing. Sea-going was indeed a family matter. Their only son, now seventeen, was apprenticed to the Holt Line of Liverpool and was at sea, somewhere in the Atlantic, at that moment.

It was of their son that she presently spoke, while the clock ticked towards eleven and the shoddy lounge gradually emptied of visitors.

'George,' she began.

Ericson laid down his book, without regret. 'Yes, dear?'

'I've been thinking about John.'

'He'll be all right,' said the Captain after a moment.

'Oh, I don't mean *that*.' Rarely did they talk of the chances of life and death at sea, and since the beginning of the war they had not mentioned the subject at all. They knew that they both had much to lose, and Grace Ericson most of all. 'But,' she went on, 'with both of you away nearly all the time, the house is going to seem lonely.'

'He'll get his leave, the same as I do, dear.'

'That may be a long time coming, and in the meantime I'll be all alone.'

'Well . . .' The Captain shifted in his chair, to cover a faint embarrassment. He had a picture of Grace knitting, alone in an empty house, for weeks on end, and it did not worry him as much as it should have done. To make up for this lack of feeling, he added with special warmth: 'You really ought to get someone to live with you. Some sort of companion.'

'There's Mother,' said Grace thoughtfully.

The Captain paused. There certainly was mother, and mother was a different matter altogether: a grim quarrelsome old lady who, on her infrequent visits to the little house on the outskirts of Birkenhead, had done nothing but complain the whole time and had spoilt her only grandson outrageously into the bargain. The nearest he had ever come to a clash with Grace was when her mother had taken it on herself to rearrange all the furniture in their sitting-room, and he had called it 'Damned cheek' and put it all back again. That had been a wonderful scene. But he did not want it repeated. And certainly he did not want Grace's mother as a permanent part of the household when he came home on leave.

He temporized. 'It's an idea,' he said, 'but I don't know whether it would really suit you. Two women living together all the time . . . It's your house, you know,' he concluded rather lamely, feeling her eye on him. 'You don't want to forget that.'

'Why should I forget it?'

'Your mother likes her own way a bit, doesn't she?'

'She's the same as most of us,' said Grace equably. 'She'd be company for me, I *do* know, own way or not. But, of course, if you don't want me to have her, I'll say no more about it.'

'You must please yourself,' he said, without enthusiasm. He realized that, compared with her, it would affect him very little – perhaps for a week or so every three or four months: he still could not bring himself to welcome the idea. 'It's likely to be a long time till I see Birkenhead again, and John the same, I shouldn't wonder. You know I don't want you to be alone all that time.'

'I'll see about it,' she answered vaguely. She was gathering up her knitting preparatory to going to bed: it was a serious business – patterns, spare needles, wool, spectacles, and the square of silk in which she wrapped the current piece of work. 'We don't want to decide in a hurry. You've plenty to think about already, haven't you?'

'Yes,' said the Captain.

'Are you pleased with the ship, George?' she asked as they rose.

'Yes,' he said. 'The ship'll be all right.'

CHAPTER 6

They were a fortnight camping out in the crowded dockside hut before they moved into the ship, and another three weeks before she was ready to sail; altogether, five weeks of concentrated work and preparation. It sometimes seemed to Ericson that there would never be any end to the new problems and questions which cropped up every day. He had to handle them all himself, or at least to decide how they were to be handled: the two subs were willing enough, but green as grass, and Bennett, he found, had less experience than his manner led one to expect, as well as a great deal less energy . . . Everything connected with the ship seemed to be the Captain's province: ordering stores and ammunition, interviewing dockyard and Admiralty officials, settling the last of the alterations and additions with the contractors, mastering technical details about the hull and the machinery, arranging the accommodation on board, answering signals, checking lists, reporting the progress and state of the ship. He had to make two or three trips to the Naval Headquarters in Glasgow before he found that Ferraby, quiet and conscientious, could be counted on to relay any message accurately and to come back with the right answer. But this did little to dispose of the work that piled up, day after day, in the hut alongside *Compass Rose*.

Gradually, however, he had his reward: gradually there came to be less noise on board, less space cluttered up with tools and dockyard equipment, less untidiness, less oil and dirt. The workmen thinned out, until only a thin trickle of them mounted the gangway every morning: stores were stowed, cabins carpeted, the messdecks fitted with their cots and lockers. *Compass Rose* took on, at last, the shape and feeling of a ship; it was time to transfer aboard her, and they were all glad to do it.

But when the main draft of the crew – sixty-odd men – arrived from Devonport Barracks, they lost little time in echoing, with choice variations, Petty Officer Tallow's strictures on their accommodation. The messdecks were small, and intolerably crowded: the hands were all lumped together – seamen, stokers, signalmen, telegraphists: they had to take their meals in the sleeping-spaces, and read or write letters with other men jammed up against them on either side. And if it was like this in harbour, what was it going to be like at sea, with the ship rolling her guts out and everything wet through as well . . . Lower-deck wit, which flourishes (in the true English tradition) on discomfort and adversity, had plenty to play with; the first few days in *Compass Rose*, before the hands were acclimatized, produced as crisp a crop of invective and blasphemy as was ever crammed into a space two hundred feet long and thirty-three broad.

Ericson was conscious of this feeling of discontent, as he surveyed the muster of hands at the commissioning ceremony. It was not that they looked sullen or mutinous: simply disinterested and perhaps a little cynical, not seeing the point of dressing up so smartly (and being ticked off for wearing a dirty jumper) just to commission a funny little sod of a ship like this. It must be his first care, he realized, to alleviate the discomfort on board: he had thought of improvements in ventilation, and in the cooking arrangements, already, and an energetic captain could do a lot with a new ship at the experimental stage, as long as the shore-side co-operated. And the job itself, with its prospect of a tough ordeal, might do much more than alleviate, by giving the crew a conscious pride in hard living and fighting. That was the thought that struck him most strongly, as the bosun's pipes sounded the 'Still', and the spotless ensign and the commissioning-pendant were broken out. *Compass Rose*, with a new coat of paint, looked clean and workmanlike: she had her numbers painted on her bows, she was nearly ready to move . . . As he started to read the Articles of War a moment later, his firm clear voice matched the first stirring of his pride in the ship. She might be 'only a corvette', not much better than a deep-sea trawler, but she could make a reputation at any level, and that was going to be his target from now on.

. . .

Meals in the cramped wardroom never seemed to progress beyond the sort of constrained artificiality which marks a public banquet attended by people who are complete strangers to one another. The Captain was usually preoccupied with the last job or the next one; he sat in silence at the head of the table, staring straight ahead or occasionally jotting down a note. Ferraby, naturally shy, was still finding his way and never volunteered either a direct statement or a direct question: and Lockhart, who was the most articulate of the four, struggled through successive monologues which only rarely inspired any kind of answer. Bennett's contribution lay in the realm of eating . . . He had formed an attachment for the crudest item in the wardroom store-cupboard, tinned sausages, which he knew colloquially as 'snorkers': they made an almost daily appearance on the menu, either at lunch or dinner, and the recurrent exclamation – 'Snorkers! Good-oh!' – with which he greeted them, sounded the knell of appetite. Then he would sit down, rub his hands, help himself liberally to Worcester sauce, and go to with a will. In fishing circles he would have been described as a coarse feeder.

The leading-steward, a morose man named Carslake, watched this performance with a sardonic eye. Clearly, he had been used to better things. He was not alone in that.

If Bennett talked at all, it was in a bombastic, contradictory whine which disposed of a subject almost before it had been introduced. One mealtime encounter which he had with Lockhart had an unusual sequel. The latter, talking about the ship's life-saving equipment, had remarked that in very cold weather one might have a better chance of survival swimming in the water, supported by a life-jacket, than sitting wet through in an open boat exposed to the wind. Bennett, his mouth full, interrupted roughly:

'Rot! Wait till the first time you're fished. You'll change your mind bloody quickly.'

'But,' said Lockhart mildly, 'how do you know that? You can hardly have been torpedoed yet.'

Bennett glared, but did not answer. Later, when the Captain had left the wardroom, he said to Lockhart:

'You talk to me like that again, and I'll crown you.'

After a pause Lockhart said levelly: 'That would get you into a great deal of trouble.'

'Just watch it, that's all!' Baulked of an easy surrender, Bennett's tone changed. He rubbed his hands together. 'Now – who's going to stand me a drink? Ferrabee!'

'Yes,' said Ferraby. 'Of course. Er – please help yourself.'

'Do we have to stand him drinks?' asked Ferraby later, when Bennett had gone to his cabin. 'He never stands them to us.'

'We don't have to stand him anything,' answered Lockhart with decision. 'It's just a racket. Next time, pour him a drink and give him the chit-book to sign at the same time. That'll hold him.'

Ferraby shook his head. 'He'll make it up somehow. You know what he's like.'

Ferraby spoke with some bitterness: he had indeed found out what Bennett was like, to his cost. A few days earlier, since it seemed likely that *Compass Rose* would not be sailing for at least a fortnight, he had asked permission to send for his wife: she could stay at an hotel in Glasgow and he could see her on alternate evenings, when he was not Officer-of-the-Day. It would involve no sort of complication and he would not be dodging his fair share of the work. Bennett, however, had turned the request down, in a particularly offensive exchange.

'Wife?' he said, when Ferraby approached him in his cabin. 'Didn't know you had one. How long have you been married?'

'Six weeks,' said Ferraby.

Bennett smirked. 'Time you gave it a rest, then.'

Ferraby said nothing. Bennett affected to consider the matter, frowning down at his desk. Then he shook his head. 'No, Sub,' he said, 'I don't like the idea. There's too much work to do.'

'But when the work's over——' began Ferraby.

'You've got to concentrate,' said Bennett crisply. 'What's the good of you slipping off for a honeymoon every time the bell strikes? It'll take your mind off the ship.'

Ferraby swallowed. He hated the conversation, but he persisted bravely. 'All I want to do——' he began again.

'I know bloody well what you want to do.' The crude leer on Bennett's face was sufficient commentary, but he clinched it more crudely still. 'You've quite enough to do without sleeping ashore every other night, and coming back clapped out. You'd better forget it.'

It was something which Ferraby did not forget ... When he told Lockhart about it he was pitifully distressed.

'I don't mind so much having it turned down,' he said. 'But to talk like that about it ... It's – it's beastly!'

Lockhart shook his head. 'You might have guessed it. He's that sort of man.'

'I hate him!'

Lockhart tried to steer him away from the emotional aspect. 'You know,' he said, 'I don't believe it's even necessary for you to get permission for this sort of thing. They can't possibly stop your wife coming up here. Ask the Captain about it.'

'But even if she were here, Bennett could stop me going to Glasgow to see her.'

'Not on your days off duty.'

'I bet he could.'

Lockhart nodded. 'Yes, I bet he could too. He'd find some way, especially if you asked the Captain after being refused permission.' He smiled at Ferraby across the wardroom table. 'Better forget it, as that bastard said. There'll be other chances later.'

       . . .

When the duty Petty Officer appeared in the wardroom doorway, cap in hand, to say that *Compass Rose* was 'ready for Rounds', Lockhart, who was Officer-of-the-Day, stood up, and followed him out of the wardroom and up the ladder towards the fo'c'sle, and the last job of his 24-hour turn of duty. Evening Rounds were part of the daily routine which, established stage by stage, was already changing *Compass Rose* from a shipyard item into a working ship-of-war.

In establishing this routine, Petty Officer Tallow, as coxswain, had had a great deal to do: more, indeed, than he would normally have needed to take on with a First Lieutenant who knew his job properly. But, seeing that the First Lieutenant was Bennett, there were a number of gaps which someone else had to fill if the ship were to function properly: unobtrusively, by a hint here and there or by direct action, Tallow saw that they were accounted for.

The Officer-of-the Day's Rounds every evening, a short tour through the messdecks and along the upper decks to check the mooring-wires and see that the ship was properly darkened, marked the end of a daily programme which covered every phase of the ship's life in harbour. The hands fell in at 6.30 every morning, and washed down the upper deck – a cold job in winter, with daylight barely established: Colours were hoisted at eight, then there was breakfast, and then the day's work proper began – mostly, at this stage, cleaning, and stowing stores. At 10.30 Stand-Easy and Up-Spirits – the issue of a tot of rum to every man on board. After that, work continued until four, when liberty-men went ashore and the duty watch settled down to their evening on board. Letters came down to the wardroom for censoring soon after dinner: Rounds were at nine o'clock, and Pipe Down at ten. The men who had all-night leave could stay ashore till 6.30 next morning.

The coxswain's particular responsibility, the ship's canteen, where duty-free cigarettes and tobacco were on sale, had already been established: Tallow ran it from his own minute cabin aft, being practically crowded through the porthole in the process. His other special duty, the rounding up of defaulters, was also under way, beginning with an odd breach of decorum which caused Ferraby, who happened to be Officer-of-the-Day, a good deal of embarrassment. He was routed out of the wardroom at nine o'clock one evening, after noises from the upper deck had warned him that one of the returning liberty-men was making a considerable disturbance. At the top of the ladder he found Petty Officer Tallow, and by his side a sullen-looking stoker swaying slightly on his feet.

'Stoker Grey, sir,' began Tallow grimly: and then, to the culprit:

'Tenshun! Off caps! Stoker Grey, sir. Urinating on the upper deck.'
'What!' exclaimed Ferraby, genuinely shocked.
'Urinating on the upper deck, sir,' repeated Tallow. 'Just came back
on board. The quartermaster reported him.'
Ferraby swallowed. He was inclined to be out of his depth, and it was
his first defaulter as well.
'What have you got to say?' he asked after a moment.
Stoker Grey swayed forward, and back again, and muttered
something.
'Speak up!' barked Tallow.
Grey tried again. 'Must have had a few drinks, sir.'
'It's absolutely disgusting,' said Ferraby. 'I never heard of——'
'Sorry, sir,' muttered Grey.
'Keep silence!' said Tallow.
'It's disgusting,' repeated Ferraby weakly. 'You ought to be ashamed
of yourself. First Lieutenant's report, Coxswain.'
'First Lieutenant's report,' echoed Tallow. 'On caps! About turn!
Quick march.'
The man shambled off. Presently, a heavy thud resounded along the
iron deck.
'Better keep an eye on him,' said Ferraby.
'I'll do that, sir,' said Tallow bleakly.
'I hope there won't be too much of this sort of thing.'
'You know what beer is, sir.'
'But still——' began Ferraby. Then he left it at that. War, it was clear,
was not for the squeamish.

.   .   .

Two days before Christmas, the Captain went up to Glasgow for a
final visit to Headquarters: he returned with a fresh sheaf of papers
which he studied for some time in his cabin. Then he went down to the
wardroom, where the others were assembled.
'Sailing orders,' he said briefly as he sat down. 'We go down river the
day after tomorrow – and in case you've forgotten, the date will be
December the twenty-fifth.'
'A nice present,' said Lockhart in the pause that followed.
'I hope so . . . Here's the rough programme, anyway.' He consulted a
sheet of paper in his hand. 'We'll be towed down to the oiling berth,
about five miles down river. We'll oil there, and then steam the rest of
the way down to Greenock. There we stay at anchor for about a
fortnight, taking on stores and ammunition, and adjusting compasses.
Then we go out on our full-power trials, probably down to Ailsa Craig
and back: we'll test the guns and the depth-charge gear on the way.
That takes us to——' he looked at the programme again '——to January

12th. Then if everything's all right, we go north to Ardnacraish for our working-up exercises.'

'How long will they take, sir?' asked Bennett.

'The programme says three weeks. It won't be less, and if we don't put up a good show they can keep us there as long as they like. So it's up to us.'

'Do you hear that, Subs?' interjected Bennett unnecessarily. 'We don't want any mistakes from either of you.'

Ericson frowned slightly. 'We don't want any mistakes from anyone, whether it's me or a second-class stoker.' It was the first time the Captain had been heard to correct anything Bennett said: momentarily Lockhart found himself wondering if it had happened before, in private, and whether the Captain were actually as blind to the situation in the wardroom, and elsewhere, as he seemed to be. If he really had a critical eye on Bennett, then there was hope for the future ... 'Well, there it is,' Ericson continued: 'we have to be ready to move in forty-eight hours from now.' He raised his voice, and called: 'Pantry!'

Leading-Steward Carslake, who had been listening attentively outside, waited a decent interval before appearing in the doorway: 'Yes, sir?'

'Gin, please – and whatever anyone else wants.' And later, over the second round of drinks, he said: 'I think we'd better have a wardroom party tomorrow night. We may not get another chance for some time.'

CHAPTER 7

At ten o'clock on Christmas morning, waiting on the cold wind-swept fo'c'sle for steam to come to the windlass, Lockhart was conscious of a slight headache. He had drunk more than usual at the previous night's party: it would scarcely have been tolerable otherwise. Mrs Ericson had presided, and done it rather well; but the rest of the company had been comparative strangers to one another – some officers off another corvette, a couple of dockyard officials, a friend of the Captain's from Naval Headquarters; and Bennett, coming in at about ten o'clock with a bedraggled-looking woman clearly picked up in the nearest hotel, had struck an unfortunate note. The sense of well-being, and the accompanying slight haze, induced by a dozen pink gins, had come as an essential relief; but Lockhart felt he was paying for it now. A biting wind, varied with an occasional drift of snow, was no cure for a hangover.

In the apportioning of jobs and stations on board, the fo'c'sle had been allotted to him as the senior sub-lieutenant, together with the two most interesting assignments – gunnery, and chart-correcting. Ferraby, with the second choice of everything, was put in charge aft: he was responsible for the depth-charges, and in harbour he would have to deal with correspondence, the crew's pay, and the wardroom accounts as well. Certainly, thought Lockhart, he himself had come off best: it couldn't be helped, but it was bad luck on Ferraby having all the finicking little oddments while everyone else had the glamour. Stamping up and down the fo'c'sle, wishing that his job (of which he had only the vaguest outline) were not so directly under the eye of the bridge, he found himself wondering once again how Ferraby – shy, inexperienced, defenceless – was going to meet the trials that lay in the future. He could be helped to a certain extent, but in the last analysis it depended on his own resources, and they were patently meagre.

The leading-stoker in charge of the windlass turned a valve, and there was a heartening hiss of steam followed by a clanking noise. 'Ready, sir,' he called out.

'Right.' Lockhart walked to the bows and, trying to disguise the fact that it was largely a process of trial and error, set to work on the task of casting off the spare mooring-wires and reeling them in. From the tug alongside, a man with a large red reassuring face watched him: ready, he felt, to correct any mistakes and deal with any crisis. He might well be needed.

When 'Hands to stations for leaving harbour' was piped, Ferraby walked disconsolately aft to the quarter-deck, prepared to execute as best he could an order he barely understood. 'Single up to the stern-wire,' Bennett had said, and left it at that – though not forgetting to add, by way of farewell: 'And if you get a wire round the screw, Christ help you!' To 'single-up' presumably meant to cast off all their mooring-lines except the last one needed to hold them to the quay; but only a process of elimination would tell him which one was the stern-wire, and he hardly felt equal to the effort of concentration.

He felt, in fact, confused and wretched. All that he had read about the Navy, all that he had learned at the training establishment, all the eagerness which had driven him to enlist on the day war broke out – all these were being destroyed or poisoned by his present circumstances. He had been immensely proud of getting a commission: he had been ready to accept without question, as an unbreakable bond, the whole of the rigid discipline and the tradition of service which he had read or learnt about: but there had been no one like Bennett in the textbooks, and Bennett, it seemed, was the reality behind the fine phrases ... He had known perfectly well, also, that he would be miserable as soon as he was separated from his wife: that was another thing he had been prepared to endure with a good heart; but the ache of separation was a high price – almost an impossible price – to pay for submitting to the present oafish tyranny. If the Navy were really Bennett, and Bennett's manners and methods, then he had been cheated and betrayed from the beginning.

He had slipped out of last night's party to telephone his wife in London. Waiting in the draughty dock-office for the call to come through, the eagerness of anticipation had almost choked him; but as soon as he heard her voice, with its soft hesitant inflection, the eagerness had ebbed away and he was conscious only of the miles between them and the weeks and months that might still keep them apart. This moment was their goodbye: there was nothing else in prospect. And it was for this that he was treated like a backward child or ordered about like a convict ...

But for her sake, and for his own, he had done his best.

'Hallo,' he started. 'Hallo, darling! Can you hear me?'

'Yes,' she said. 'Oh, how wonderful! Where are you?'

'Same place. I wanted to wish you a happy Christmas.'

'And to you ... What are you doing?'

'Having a party.'

'Oh ...'

'Not a very good one. A horrid one, really. I wish I could be with you. Are you taking care of yourself?'

'Yes, darling. Are you?'

'Yes.'

'Are you in the ship?'

'No. In the dock-office. What are you wearing?'

'The striped house-coat ... Oh darling, I wish you were here. Is there any chance?'

'I don't think so. I'm afraid not.'

'Can't I come up, then?'

'It's too late.'

'Why? What's happening?'

'I ...' Some phrase about careless talk pricked him, and he hesitated. 'I can't really tell you.'

'Is the ship ready?'

'Yes.'

'Oh ...'

The wires hummed between them. They were not doing well. He said again: 'This is just to wish you a happy Christmas,' and then suddenly he could not endure it any more and he said: 'I must go, I'm afraid ... Goodbye ... Take care of yourself,' and rang off. He had stood in the dock-office, utterly defeated, for at least five minutes before he could bear to go back to the ship; and once on board he had slipped into his cabin, without a word to anyone, and lain down on his bunk, and felt the successive waves of wretchedness flood in, with nothing to check them and no hope to drive them out.

Now, on this queer Christmas morning, Ferraby stepped onto the quarter-deck repeating 'Single up to the stern-wire' as if it were some pagan incantation. The six hands of the after-party, under their leading-hand – Leading-Seaman Tonbridge – were fallen in by the depth-charge rails, waiting for his orders.

As he came up, Leading-Seaman Tonbridge saluted and said: 'Take off the breast-rope, sir?'

'Just a minute.' Ferraby looked at the moorings. There were four separate ropes – two leading aft, one leading forward, and one, a short one, going out at right angles to the ship's side. He hesitated, while Tonbridge, a tough, self-reliant young man who knew it all by heart, adjusted the thick leather gauntlets which all the mooring parties wore. Then Ferraby had a sudden idea – a purely Bennett-idea which he was almost ashamed to use. He nodded to Tonbridge, and said, simply: 'Single up to the stern-wire.'

Tonbridge said: 'Aye, aye, sir,' and then, to the nearest seamen: 'Take off those wrappings,' and then, to the hands waiting on the jetty: 'Cast off breast-rope and spring.' Men moved: the wires splashed in the water, and were hauled in: the moorings quickly simplified themselves, to one single rope running aft. It was as easy as that.

With a sudden surprised flicker of confidence, Ferraby turned to the voice-pipe that led to the bridge. His ring was answered by the signalman. He said: 'Singled up aft. Tell the First Lieutenant.'

He felt humbly pleased with himself. He had cheated, but now, as far as moorings were concerned, he knew the right answer and he need not cheat again.

Down in the Captain's cabin, Watts, the Chief Engine-room Artificer, was reporting to the Captain about the engines under his charge. There could be no mistaking Watts, or the job he was busy on – his white overalls were stained and splashed with grease, and his hands incredibly grimy. After working most of the night on a refractory valve, he was tired, and his face grey and lined.

'She's ready to move, sir,' he said, without much enthusiasm. 'As ready as I can make her, that is, with twenty dockyard-mateys climbing all over her. I've had her turning over at ten revs for the past hour. She's a little rough yet, but it'll settle itself.'

'What about the steering engine?' asked Ericson. Earlier, there had been trouble over this, and they had been waiting for replacements.

'Seems all right now, sir.' Watts scratched his bald head, leaving a smear of grease like a painted quiff on his forehead. 'There's a lot of loose stuff in the steering-compartment – wires and dry provisions and such – it'll have to be secured when we're properly at sea. But I've tried the engine out a dozen times, hard a-port to hard a-starboard, and she's smooth as you could wish. And if we want to steer by hand, it's simple enough – too simple, mebbe.' He sniffed. He had no very high opinion of

the machinery in his charge, which had few refinements of any sort and
was scarcely more complicated than the stationary steam engine, run on
methylated spirits, which had been his first real toy. Corvettes, it was
clear, were going to be turned out simply and economically, like pins or
plastic ashtrays: as such, they hardly deserved a Chief E.R.A. to look
after them.

'All right, Chief,' said Ericson. 'We'll leave it at that. You know the
programme: we'll be towed down to the oiler and then steam the rest of
the way. I've allowed two hours for oiling: the tide's flooding all the
afternoon so there's no hurry.'

'Two hours should do us, sir. What about the revs, then?'

'That's something we can only settle finally when we've been running
for some time.' Ericson looked at one of the many slips of paper on his
desk. 'I see the builders' recommendations are: Slow Ahead, 35 revs:
Half Ahead, 100 revs. We'd better try that, to start with. If it's too fast,
or too slow, I'll give you the alterations on the voice-pipe.'

'Aye, aye, sir.' Watts, preparing to leave, summoned the vague and
rare outlines of a smile. 'Funny sort of Christmas morning,' he
commented. 'Makes you think a bit.'

'It won't be the last, Chief.'

'D'you think it'll be as long as the other war, sir?'

'Longer, probably.' Ericson stretched out his hand, and rang the bell
to the bridge. 'That's what we've got to be ready for, anyway.'

Watts, leaving the cabin, shook his head in doubt. His favourite
Sunday paper had said that the war would be over in a year, and, on this
Christmas morning, he wanted very much to believe it.

The rating who answered the Captain's bell and presently stood
before him was Leading-Signalman Wells, the senior of the three
signalmen who made up *Compass Rose*'s communications complement.
He was rather older than his rank suggested; and Ericson, looking over
his Conduct Sheet a few days previously, had discovered why. Wells had
been a full Yeoman of Signals up to two months previously: then he had
been disrated, and sentenced to eighteen days detention, for (in the
bleak words of King's Regulations & Admiralty Instructions) 'conduct
prejudicial to good order and naval discipline in that he (*a*) was absent
over leave 76 hours and 35 minutes, (*b*) did return on board drunk, (*c*)
did resist the duty Petty Officer detailed to supervise him, and (*d*) did
destroy by fire nine signal-flags, value 27s.' Reading between the lines, it
must have been a lively occasion. But the implications were not
encouraging, however much allowance one made for extenuating
circumstances which could only be guessed at – a birthday party that got
out of hand, a woman too acquiescent, a wife unfaithful: the odd
part was that Wells looked the least likely candidate for this sort of
escapade.

He was small, with a quick decisive manner and an air of competence: he kept a firm hand on his department, and Ericson had already found him helpful with suggestions, as well as absolutely dependable. Now, as he stood waiting in the cabin, cap neatly tucked under his arm, signal-pad ready, pencil poised, he was a heartening picture of a highly-trained, wide-awake signalman – the sort of man worth his weight in gold to any ship. Ericson hoped that this picture would prove to be the true one: the other story – the one in the Conduct Sheet – would mean, in a ship the size of the *Compass Rose*, endless trouble and endless waste of energy before it was brought under control.

'I want to send a signal about our leaving,' Ericson began. 'Take this down, and send it off by telephone from the dock-office.'

'Yes, sir,' said Wells. He prepared to write.

' "To Flag-Officer-in-Charge, Glasgow," ' the Captain dictated, ' "from *Compass Rose*. Sailed in accordance with your 0945 stroke twenty-three stroke twelve. Estimated time of arrival at Greenock, sixteen hundred hours." '

Wells read the signal back when he had written it down, and then said: 'Should we repeat it to Flag-Officer, Greenock, sir? They'll have to give us an anchor-berth as soon as we arrive.'

'Yes,' agreed Ericson, conscious, as happened quite often nowadays, that his memory of naval procedure was rusty and needed constant prodding. 'You'd better do that ... We'll fly our pendant-numbers going down river, of course.'

'Yes, sir,' said Wells. 'Pendant-numbers, pilot-flag, and Under Tow signal. I'll see to all that, sir.'

When the Leading-Signalman withdrew, Ericson sat on in his cabin, waiting for the First Lieutenant. By the normal routine, Bennett should report the ship 'Ready to proceed', just as the Chief E.R.A. had reported that his engines were ready to move; but though it was already past their sailing time, Ericson did not want to issue a reminder until it was absolutely necessary. He was by now aware that in Bennett he had got a bad bargain, a lazy and largely ignorant young man who should never have been given his present appointment; but he had not yet made up his mind whether to ask for a replacement, or whether Bennett could be trained to do his job properly, and he wished to give him every chance. The added complication – that Bennett bullied Ferraby constantly, and was in a state of imminent collision with Lockhart – was another thing that time might or might not solve. He did not want to step in unless the efficiency and well-being of the ship were seriously threatened; and it had not got to that point yet.

At ten minutes past their appointed sailing time, he pressed the bridge-bell, and was answered by the signalman of the watch.

'Bridge, sir!'

'Is the First Lieutenant there?'

'He's on the fo'c'sle, sir, talking to Mr Lockhart.'

'Ask him to come to my cabin.'

'Aye, aye, sir.'

Presently, Bennett knocked on the door, and came in. He was wearing a bridge-coat, with the collar turned up in a vaguely dramatic manner.

'You wanted me, sir?'

'Yes,' said Ericson. 'Are we ready to move, Number One?'

'Yes, sir,' said Bennett cheerfully. 'Any time you like.'

'You should come and tell me. I can't guess at it, you know.'

'Oh ... Sorry, sir.'

'Are all the hands on board?'

'Er – I reckon so, sir.'

A singularly cold blue eye regarded him. 'Well, are they or aren't they? Didn't you have it reported to you?'

'There was only the postman, sir. I know he's aboard.'

'What about the mess-caterers? What about the Leading-Steward? – he went shopping for me. What about the berthing-party?'

Bennett looked as nearly crestfallen as Ericson had yet seen him. It was a cheering sight. 'I'll check up, sir.'

Ericson rose, and reached for his cap and binoculars. 'Find out, and come and tell me on the bridge. And next time, remember that you report to me that the ship's ready to sail, with all the crew on board, at the proper time. That's part of your job.'

Bennett recovered swiftly. 'I'd better detail Ferraby to——'

'You won't detail anybody,' said Ericson, as brusquely as he had ever spoken so far, 'unless you want to change jobs with them.'

He left the cabin without another word, leaving Bennett to make what he liked of this substantial warning for the future. It might be what was needed to pull him up short; in any case, it was a move in the right direction. Then, as Ericson mounted the ladder towards the bridge, the small annoying scene faded from his mind and was swiftly replaced: he was aware only of an intense personal satisfaction that all the months of waiting, all the worry of fitting-out and commissioning, and all the loose ends of departure, had now been disposed of, and that *Compass Rose* – his own responsibility, almost his own invention – was ready at last for her maiden trip.

It was not particularly impressive, that first tow down river to the oiler, save for one odd accompaniment to it which Ericson, like many other people on board, found moving. As *Compass Rose* edged outwards from the quay and gathered way, with a tug at either end, Petty Officer Tallow at the wheel, and Lockhart with his fo'c'sle-party neatly fallen in by the windlass, a small cheer broke out from the knot of dockyard workers lining the quayside. It was ragged, it was uncoordinated and unrehearsed: it was all the more impressive for this rough spontaneity. Other men from other yards left their work to wave to *Compass Rose* as she passed down river – men who had built ships, were building them now, and would build countless others, pausing in their jobs to speed on her way the latest product of the Clyde. The moment of farewell was not prolonged: it was too cold to stand about, and the dusting of snow that overlay the quays and docks and berthing-slips lining the river was a sharp reminder of the wintry day. But the gesture, repeated many times on their way towards the open sea, remained in the memory: the last message from the fraternity of men who built the ship, to the sailors who would live and work and fight aboard her.

.   .   .

Five hours later, *Compass Rose*, under her own power, left the last narrow section of the river and nosed her way down stream towards the Tail-of-the-Bank, the naval anchorage off Greenock. The early winter dusk was beginning to close in, hiding the far reaches of one of the loveliest harbours in Britain: the line of hills surrounding it turned from purple to black shadow, the lit buoys and the shore lights came up blinking to challenge the twilight. It was now very cold, though the wind had died earlier that afternoon. Their berth had been signalled to them, and identified on the chart; they still had a few hundred yards to go before they dropped anchor, and the Captain, with leisure to look about him, was studying the other ships which crowded the broad sweep of the Clyde Estuary.

There were many of them – a battleship, a smart new cruiser, half a dozen destroyers, an aircraft-carrier, scores of mine-sweepers; beyond them, in the merchant-ship anchorage, was line upon line of ships collecting for a convoy, dominated by two huge liners in the grey wartime dress of troopships. At the back of the bridge, Ericson could hear Leading-Signalman Wells giving a running commentary on the ships in company – a commentary which revealed, as could nothing else, the sense of family which informs the Royal Navy. ('The battleship's the *Royal Sovereign* – we were at Gib. with her, last spring cruise – there's the old *Argus*, one of the first carriers ever built – that must be the Sixth Destroyer Flotilla – wonder what they're doing here – that's one of the new Town Class cruisers – didn't know they were in commission yet . . .') The pilot, a bluff Clydesider, said suddenly: 'Just coming on the bearing now, Captain!' and Ericson returned to the business of anchoring. The telegraph clanged for 'Stop engines', and then for 'Slow astern': he called out 'Stand by!' to Lockhart on the fo'c'sle; and a minute later, as the ship gathered gentle stern-way, his shout of 'Let go!' was answered by the thunderous roar of the cable running out. *Compass Rose* lay at anchor, her first journey accomplished. The time, he was pleased to note, was three minutes past four: the dividing dusk was now upon them, and the air had a bitter edge to it, but the ring of shore lights and the scores of craft in company seemed to be bidding him and his ship welcome.

CHAPTER 8

Now came a further pause in their progress, easier to endure with patience because it was more directly geared to their sea-going preparation. They were fourteen days at Greenock, some of them spent at anchor, ammunitioning and storing and doing harbour-exercises, others devoted to their sea-trials and the preliminary gunnery and depth-charge tests designed to prove their weapons. They could hardly have had lovelier surroundings in which to try out their ship: in the grip of a hard winter which whitened even the foothills with snow and gave to the higher peaks a serene, unassailable purity, the Firth of Clyde, especially when approached from seaward, had a breath-taking beauty.

But they had not a great deal of leisure for looking about them, nor inclination either, however attractive were their surroundings: their eyes were now turning inwards, towards the ship and their task in her. It was astonishing how, isolated at her anchorage or slipping in and out on her various trials, *Compass Rose* was already coming alive as a ship, a separate unit with a developing personality. The process of eighty-odd men shaking down together was well advanced, and now it was moving towards the next stage – the welding-together of these men into a working crew, the tuning-up for action. This was true not only of the wardroom, though here it was strongest since the wardroom supplied the directive influence: it was true of all of them – they were beginning to concentrate, beginning to feel that they and the ship had work to do, and that it was worth doing.

Wishful thinking might exaggerate this process, and fo'c'sle backchat, designed to show that *Compass Rose* was the worst abortion of a ship that ever put to sea, might seem to deny it; but it was there all the same – a strong and subtle feeling of dedication. It was being helped, from outside, by the first convoy reports and rumours – some true, some exaggerated – and by the landing of Merchant Navy survivors at nearby Gourock, from which it was clear that there must have been a number of U-boats already at sea, in full operational trim, on the day that war was declared. This, then, was going to be *Compass Rose*'s battle: it really existed, it was worth taking on, it had to be won, and the sooner they were ready for it the better.

Lockhart was specially conscious of the beginning of this feeling when they went out on their gun-trials, at the end of their first week at Greenock. The trials were simple enough: they fired a few rounds from the four-inch gun on the fo'c'sle, and tested the two-pounder aft, and the light machine-guns on the bridge, which completed an armament modest enough by any standard. 'God help us if we run into the *Scharnhorst*,' said an imaginative seaman. 'We'll just have to creep up behind and ——her ...' – But among the guns'-crews which he had been working up in harbour, and especially in a leading-seaman called Phillips who was the gunner's-mate – the rating responsible for the cleanliness of the guns and the stowage of ammunition – Lockhart was aware of an encouraging interest. Most of these guns'-crews were amateurs, of course – the 'hostilities-only' ratings who survived the derision of the regulars to become a huge majority in the Navy: but they learned fast, and here and there an obvious instance of intelligence and enthusiasm marked one of them down for a higher rating, as soon as the necessary training had been completed. Phillips, who was also in charge of the fo'c'sle-party, was big and slow-moving, a two-badge leading-seaman with considerable influence in the messdecks: and it was he who, during the gun-testing, had made a remark which caught Lockhart's attention.

The loading-number, the man responsible for ramming the shell home, had missed his swing and left the shell half in and half out of the breech: the whole rhythm of firing was lost, and it was thirty seconds or so before the shell could be extracted and put in again properly. Phillips, who was No. 1 on the gun, turned round from his sights and said ironically:

'If you do that in action, my lad, and they land a couple of fourteen-inch bricks while we're fiddling about, clearing the gun, *I'll never forgive you.*'

Lockhart enjoyed the studied understatement. Obviously, Phillips was beginning to think ahead, to the time when *Compass Rose* would be fighting instead of practising: he had seen, behind a piece of carelessness which was merely annoying, a mistake which might be fatal, and it was an encouraging symptom of a kind of interest which would pay a rich dividend in terms of efficiency and effectiveness later on.

Ferraby, isolated aft among his depth-charges, was having less success in working up to the necessary standard of competence. His key-ratings were all right – Wainwright, the torpedo-man, who saw to the settings and actually dropped the charges, and Leading-Seaman Tonbridge, who was in general charge of the depth-charge crews, were both energetic and dependable; but most of the rest of his men fell far below this standard. Much of the work aft consisted of reloading the depth-charge throwers at high speed – a heavy job involving skilful team-work; and for it he had a motley collection of off-watch stokers and telegraphists, who did not take kindly to working on a wind-swept upper deck, like any common seaman, when their natural lair was a warm boiler-room or a cosy W/T office ... Many of them, too, were undeniably stupid, of the calibre of that Stoker Grey who had been the ship's first and (so far) most unconventional defaulter; and Ferraby, none too sure of himself at the best of times, was hardly the person either to drill them into efficiency or to take a tough line when they were wilfully slack.

The result was what might have been expected. There were mistakes, delays, failures: there was surprise when things went right, and a disgruntled indifference when they went wrong. Left to himself, Ferraby might have gained confidence and gradually worked his department into a going concern; but Bennett, sensing the weak point and welcoming an easier target than Lockhart, was continually wandering aft and, leaning over the rail above the quarter-deck, destroying whatever self-sufficiency Ferraby might have built up by a stream of comment and counter-orders. Ferraby grew to dread the daily depth-charge practices which were the rule when they were in harbour; it seemed hardly worth while giving preliminary instruction, and then setting the drill in motion, when at any moment the hated red face would top the rail above him, and the raucous voice call out: 'Ferrabee! The settings should be put on *before* the lashings are taken off!' or, more simply: 'Ferrabee! That's no bloody good at all – start it again!' He had no one to complain to, nor, in the last analysis, any solid ground for complaint: he *did* make mistakes, and the depth-charge crews *were* slack and inefficient, and so, it seemed, it was going to continue, until he himself was superseded or *Compass Rose* was sunk.

For all his zest for supervision, Bennett was not enjoying himself nearly as much as he had expected. Riding a dumb kid like Ferraby was all very fine, he found, but it was about the only compensation in a job which was steadily proving a bit too serious altogether ... He had managed to farm out nearly every piece of work which should normally fall to the First Lieutenant, but still the inescapable oddments remained, and he found them irksome – particularly things like keeping up-to-date the Watch Bill, as various ratings changed their jobs or acquired fresh experience. Added to his failure to make any sort of impression on Lockhart (though he hadn't finished there yet, by a long way), and a suspicion that the Captain was a good deal less impressionable than he had seemed at the beginning, these awkward factors were in process of spoiling what had looked like an agreeable billet. Bennett couldn't make up his mind whether to chuck it now, and get something better – there were scores of soft jobs going begging, and snug niches to be filled, at this formative stage of the war – or to hang on a little longer and see if things improved. That would be one way of qualifying for a command, and a command was clearly the only thing to have, if you wanted to enjoy yourself at sea; but sweating out a year or so as First Lieutenant might be too high a price to pay for it. Soon he would have to make his choice: in the meantime, there was Lockhart to be kept in view as a long-range target, and Ferraby to supply the essential comic relief.

Of them all, the Captain, with most to worry or distract him, was the least unsure of himself and of the future. He was beginning to like the ship, simply for her 'feel' and her performance, quite apart from the proprietary pride which was always in the background: she had shown herself easy to handle, and though she was ludicrously slow in comparison with a destroyer – or indeed with any other warship he had ever heard of – she was highly manoeuvrable and could turn the corners adroitly. That speed of hers, of course, might rank as much more of a handicap in the future: the bare fifteen knots which was the most the Chief E.R.A. could coax out of her was slower than a good many merchant ships, and only a knot or so above the general speed in convoy – when, supposedly, she ought to be whistling round performing the prodigies of valour and skill set out in the Fleet Signal Book. At fifteen knots, she was liable to qualify as a pekingese of the ocean rather than as a greyhound.

The other major snag, from his own point of view, had already shown itself: that was, her behaviour at sea. In any kind of seaway at all, *Compass Rose* rolled abominably: she had given an appalling demonstration of it on one of their first trips outside harbour, when, running down to the Isle of Arran in a very moderate sea which should not have bothered her at all, she had achieved a forty-degree roll and, apart from other damage sustained to movable gear below decks, had put one of her boats under water and nearly lost it altogether. High up on the bridge, hanging on grimly while *Compass Rose* swung through a drunken, eighty-degree arc, Ericson had found himself wondering what it was going to be like when they met real Atlantic weather and had, perhaps, to hold their course and speed through it . . . This light-hearted frolic was not the best augury for that future.

But that was a test which need not yet be met: and on the day when *Compass Rose* turned homewards after her final trials and began the smooth run up the sheltered Firth of Clyde, Ericson was conscious only of an exhilarating satisfaction. The ship went forward at an easy ten knots, with the flood tide adding a couple more: the winter sunset, a lovely red and orange, made the bracken on the surrounding hillsides glow like fire. Moving through the still evening, parting the cold keen air with a steady thrust, the ship seemed to have a living purpose of her own, a quality of strength and competence: and Ericson found it hard to exclude from his voice, as he gave the helm orders that would lay a course through the defence-boom, the eagerness that possessed him. For

Compass Rose was clear: her engines and her armament were all in order: in a few days they would go north for their final working-up, and then she would be ready.

.   .   .

That evening, in his cabin, Ericson signed for the ship and formally took her over from the builders. He was well content: there had been a good many flaws to start with, as was natural with a new ship of a new design, ranging from navigation-lights that could not be seen, to the usual crop of weeping rivets; but one by one they had all been set right, and he could find no more to complain of. Now it was his responsibility to say so, in unmistakable terms.

The shipyard representative, a small brisk man whose badge of office – a bowler hat – he was reluctant to part with for more than a few seconds at a time, laid the printed form of release in front of him, and after reading it through Ericson put his signature at the bottom. Then he sat back.

'That's that,' he said. 'And I'd like to thank you for all you've done for us. It's been a great help.'

'Glad to hear it, Captain.' The small man snatched up the paper, folded it, and thrust it in an inner pocket, all in one swift movement, as though he feared Ericson would change his mind. 'I hope she'll not disappoint you, and you'll have good luck in her.'

Ericson nodded. 'Thanks ... How about a drink?'

The small man shook his head and then, rather surprisingly, said: 'Aye.' When the drinks had been poured he raised his glass formally and said: 'Not too late to wish you a Happy New Year, Captain.'

Ericson drank to it in silence. So much depended on *Compass Rose*: in fact everything depended on her – perhaps even the bare fact of their survival through 1940. But that evening, when the ship at last was his, he did not want to share this thought with anyone.

CHAPTER 9

On her way north to Ardnacraish, *Compass Rose* spent her first night at sea.

She was lucky in her weather: when she slipped through the boom during the late afternoon it was raining heavily, with the promise of a hard blow as well; but by the time they had passed the odd, conical mass of Ailsa Craig, and turned northward again, the sky had cleared and the wind gradually dropped to nothing. Later still, the bright moonlight gave them a visibility of several miles, and by midnight they were ploughing along at a steady twelve knots, with the mass of land to starboard as clearly discernible as if it had been full daylight. *Compass Rose*, with no sea to bother her and only a long gentle swell to surmount, had an easy motion: the pulse of the engine, and an occasional vibration from forward, served as reminders that she was now on passage instead of swinging round her anchor in harbour, but apart from that the night was as peaceful and as free from stress as any they had yet spent.

Lockhart, muffled against the keen air in a kapok suit and sea-boots, shared the middle watch – from midnight to four a.m. – with Bennett: it passed without incident or interest save that at two o'clock they met a south-bound convoy and were fiercely challenged by one of the wing escorts, and that Bennett spent most of the watch dozing inside the Asdic-hut, leaving Lockhart to keep the look-out and write up the deck-log every hour. He did not mind: indeed, he would have taken it as a compliment if he had not known that it sprang from pure laziness and not from any particular confidence in his ability. But the brief period of authority, when the ship was handed over to him as his personal charge, was helpful to his self-confidence, apart from its value as a first experience of watch-keeping. He had been wondering just how sure of himself he would be, when the moment came for him to handle *Compass Rose*: now he knew, and the answer was reassuring.

Ferraby and the Captain came up together at four o'clock, to take over the morning's watch: Lockhart was amused to note that Bennett handed things over with an air of weighty responsibility, as if he had been on tip-toe throughout the entire four hours and would, even now, hardly dare to close his eyes . . . For the first couple of hours Ericson dealt with everything there was to be done, leaving Ferraby to watch him, or stare at the horizon, and occasionally to check a buoy or a lighthouse on the chart inside the Asdic-compartment: but towards six o'clock, when they were set on a straight, trouble-free course which would need no alteration for thirty miles or so, he decided that he'd had enough of it. He had been on the bridge from dusk until midnight – about eight hours altogether – the previous evening, and he badly needed sleep.

He yawned, and stretched, and called Ferraby, who had wandered to the wing of the bridge.

'Think you can take her now, Sub?' he asked. 'This is our course for the rest of the watch, and there's nothing in the way. How about it?'

'All right, sir. I – I'd like to.'

'You can get me on the voice-pipe if anything turns up. Just watch out for those fishing-boats, and if you have to alter course, go to seaward of them rather than inshore. But you'd better call me if there are a lot of them about.'

'Aye, aye, sir.'

'All right, then . . .' He stayed for a few moments, watching the hills still looming clear to starboard, and the flashing light, which had been their mark for changing onto a new course, now just past the beam, and then he said: 'She's yours, Sub,' and turned to go. His sea-boots rang on the bridge ladder, and died away, and Ferraby was left to himself.

He had never known such a moment in his life, and he found it difficult to accept without a twinge of near-panic. The whole ship, with her weapons and her watchful look-outs and her sixty-odd men sleeping below, was now his: he could use her intricate machinery, alter her course and speed, head out for the open Atlantic or run straight on the rocks . . . He felt small and alone, in spite of the bridge look-outs and the signalman and the Asdic rating who shared the watch with him: he was shivering, and he heard his heart thumping, and he wondered if he could bear it if they met a convoy, or if some accident – like the steering-gear breaking down – brought on a sudden crisis. He wasn't really fitted for this: he was a bank-clerk, he was only twenty, he'd been commissioned for exactly eight weeks . . . But the minutes of uncertainty passed, as *Compass Rose* held her steady course and nothing happened to disturb it: she was, it seemed, a going concern, and possibly he knew *just* enough to supervise her without some catastrophic blunder which nothing could retrieve.

Presently he began to enjoy himself.

Leaning over the bridge-rail, he could see the whole fore-part of the ship clear in the moonlight: above him, the mast rolled through a slow, gentle arc against the dark sky: astern, their wake spreading and stretching out behind them was bounded by a thin line of phosphorescence which gave it a concise, formal beauty. He felt himself to be in the middle of a pattern, the focal point of their forceful advance: here was the bridge, the nerve-centre, with its faint glow from the binnacle and the dark motionless bulk of the two look-outs marking each wing, and here was himself, who controlled it all and to whom all the lines of this pattern led. Sub-Lieutenant Ferraby, Officer-of-the-Watch – he grinned suddenly to himself, and felt, for a moment, almost heroic. No one in the bank would believe this. But he must write and tell Mavis about it, as soon as he could. She *would* believe it.

The half-hourly relief of the bridge personnel interrupted this train of thought, setting the seal on his responsibility.

'Port look-out relieved, sir!'

'Very good.'

'Starboard look-out relieved, sir!'

'Very good.'

And up the voice-pipe from the wheel-house, where the quartermasters were changing over: 'Course North, ten West, sir – engine half-ahead – Able-Seaman Dykes on the wheel!'

'Very good.'

At that moment he would not have been anywhere else in the world.

Presently the signalman of the watch, who had been standing by his side staring through his binoculars, straightened up and said: 'Flashing light to starboard, sir.'

When Ferraby found the light he counted the flashes carefully. 'That's our next lighthouse,' he said, when he had made sure of it. 'It's still a long way ahead, though.'

The signalman stamped his feet on the grating that ran the length of the fore-bridge, and said tentatively: 'Bit cold up here, sir.'

It was the first remark he had volunteered since they came on watch, and Ferraby looked at him out of the corner of his eye. He knew him by sight already: his name was Rose – a young, newly-joined rating, younger even than Ferraby and only just qualified as an ordinary signalman. He was something like Ferraby in manner, too: shy, unsure of himself, ready to believe most of what he was told in totally new surroundings. Earlier, at the change of the watch, Ferraby had heard Leading-Signalman Wells handing over to him, using an encouraging, almost fatherly tone which must have been reassuring to a boy standing his first night duty. 'Now you don't need to get rattled,' Wells had said, 'you know the challenge, and the reply, and that's about all there's likely to be, when we're routed independently. But if we meet anyone, and there's a signal, sing out for me straight away, and I'll be up to give you a hand.' The contrast between this friendly backing, this verbal arm-round-the-shoulder, and the sort of thing he himself had to endure from Bennett, had been so marked that momentarily Ferraby had found himself wishing that he could be an ordinary signalman, with Wells to help him, instead of a sub, with a tough First Lieutenant bullying him all the time. But he was not so sure of that feeling now, after half an hour in charge of the ship. If only it could always be like this . . .

He said: 'Yes, it's damned cold,' and feeling the need to lead the conversation, he added: 'What's it like below?'

'Warm enough, sir,' answered Rose. 'But it's very crowded. And the walls' – he corrected himself hurriedly – 'the bulkheads sweat all the time. Makes everything wet through. It takes a bit of getting used to.'

'Is this your first ship?'

'Yes, sir.'

'How long have you been in?'

'A month, sir. Just the training.'

'What were you before you joined?'

Rose hesitated, and then answered: 'I helped with a van, sir.'

A van-boy . . . A van-boy, and now a signalman in a ship that might go anywhere in the world and meet God-knows-what hazards . . . There was enough of a parallel between Rose's change of status, and his own, for Ferraby to be conscious of a strong fellow-feeling with him. But was that a relationship which was encouraged by the Royal Navy? He shied away from the thought, and, hunching his shoulders which were stiffening with cold, said: 'I wonder if we could get some tea?'

'There's some cocoa on in the galley, sir,' Rose volunteered. 'Shall I ask the bosun's-mate?'

'Yes, do.'

The cocoa, when it came up, was sweet and strong and very comforting. They drank it together, side by side under the cold sky, while beneath their feet the ship lifted gently to the swell, and the sea fell back from her cleaving bow and turned outwards in a mile-long furrow, and their track was lost in the darkness astern.

. . .

Later in the watch, a cluster of lights low in the water told Ferraby that they were running into another bunch of the fishing-boats which were all round the coast that night. This fleet of them lay directly on *Compass Rose*'s course, and he wondered if he ought to call the Captain: but his spell on the bridge had given him plenty of confidence, and on an impulse he bent to the voice-pipe and spoke his first helm-order.

'Port ten.'

The quartermaster's voice answered him. 'Port ten, sir ... Ten of port wheel on, sir.'

'Midships.'

'Midships ... Wheel's amidships, sir.'

'Steady.'

'Steady, sir ... Course, north, twenty-five west, sir.'

They held the new course for five minutes, till the fishing-boats were abeam and well clear of them. Then he brought the ship back on her former course, and was just about to make a note of the manoeuvre in the deck-log when from the Captain's voice-pipe there came a sudden call:

'Bridge!'

'Bridge, sir,' answered Ferraby.

'What were you altering for, Sub?'

'A fishing-boat, sir,' he said, compromising with the strict truth. 'We're clear of it now.' His surprise made him add: 'How did you know, sir?'

He heard the Captain chuckle. 'The steering-engine makes a lot of noise down here ... Everything all right?'

'Yes, sir. The next light's coming a-beam now.'

He waited for a comment, but none came, and presently a slight snore told him that he need not wait any longer. Obscurely, he felt rather proud of that snore. It was the most definite compliment he had had so far in the ship.

. . .

It grew lighter: the sky imperceptibly paled: to the eastward, the land took on a harder outline, and beyond the nearest hills others began to come into view, their snow-summits waiting to catch the first shafts of the sun. Matching the sky, the sea round them paled also, turning from black to a livid grey; and a distant lighthouse, which had been beckoning them towards the horizon, struggled against the coming of daylight and faded till its beam was a faint, wan flicker against a mist of rising land. The whole length of the ship gradually emerged, from a dark outline into a three-dimensional and solid structure, with frost glistening all along the upper-works: on the bridge, figures and then faces came up sharp and clear – lined faces, grey with cold and fatigue, but relaxing now as the dawn cheered them.

Below, the ship stirred and came to life, welcoming or accepting the end of the watch. The smoke from the galley-chimney thickened, and bore with it a coarse and cheerful smell of frying: feet rang on ladders and along the iron deck: from a hatchway aft, the grey bristly face of Chief E.R.A. Watts peered at the daylight as if scarcely believing in it. The first night at sea was over.

Just before eight, Lockhart came up to the bridge to take over the watch. He had had nearly four hours' sleep and was feeling fresher than he had expected.

'All alone?' he asked, when he had had time to look round him.

'Yes,' answered Ferraby. He could not resist elaborating. 'I took the last two hours myself.'

Lockhart smiled. 'Is that so? And to think that I slept peacefully through it all . . .' He looked at the nearest point of land. 'How far have we got?'

Ferraby, showing him their position on the chart, asked: 'Are you taking over? Where's Number One?'

'Eating breakfast,' said Lockhart tonelessly. 'Snorkers. Good-oh.'

For a moment they stood side by side in the cold morning air. The sun was now just under the rim of the hills; it was a lovely morning. Still steady, still as tranquil as the day, *Compass Rose* ploughed northwards past magic islands. Lockhart sniffed the faint breeze. 'Fun, isn't it?' he said.

'Yes,' said Ferraby. 'Yes, it is.'

CHAPTER 10

Vice-Admiral Sir Vincent Murray-Forbes, K.C.B., D.S.O., R.N., sat at his desk in the Operations building overlooking Ardnacraish harbour, playing despondently with a silver paper-knife engraved: 'Presented to

Lieut.-Commander V. Murray-Forbes, r.n., on relinquishing command of H.M.S. *Dragonfly*. From the Ship's Company, October 1909.
Good luck.' He did not see the engraved sentences: indeed, he had not
read them for many years; but they had a direct connection with his
despondency, and especially the date, which was incontrovertible. It
was something he carried with him always, like an unlucky charm; for it
meant, by inference, that he was in his sixtieth year, and was too old to
go to sea again.

The Admiral looked what he was: an old sailor, and surely due for
retirement after a life-time of distinguished service in the Navy. It was a
lined face, strong, tremendously wrinkled round the eyes: the broad
stretch of gold braid on his sleeves was impressive, and the rows of
medal-ribbons seemed no more than the face deserved. The D.S.O. was
Jutland, the K.C.B. represented a long and brilliant serial story, from
C.-in-C. China to C.-in-C. Home Fleet and then to a notable shore
appointment: the rest of the ribbons signified that he had managed to
stay alive a long time in various odd parts of the globe. Too long, indeed,
for his present peace of mind: the year 1918, when he was captain in
command of a destroyer flotilla, had been the peak of his fighting days,
and now this new war had come too late for him to start them all over
again. For though he had managed to defer his overdue retirement, it
had not been for the reason that he had hoped.

They would not send him back to sea. 'NOT REPEAT NOT TOO OLD', he
wrote in firm capitals on the signal-pad in front of him, and then, as
firmly, scored it out again. But the defiant scrawl represented something
which could *not* be scored out. Three months earlier, after intensive
wangling, he had very nearly brought off the sea-appointment that he
craved for; but fifty-nine years could not be gainsaid, and the Sea Lord
who was his personal friend had had to pass him by. Instead – 'A most
responsible job,' they reassured him: 'a very important one, where your
experience will be vital.' So the only sphere where he really wanted to
use that experience – afloat – was finally closed to him: the best answer
they could give him was Ardnacraish, destined to be the training-base
for every new escort in the Western Approaches command. It *was*
important – damned important – but it wasn't what he wanted; and
now he looked at Ardnacraish and, with his eyes still turned back to that
sea-going appointment, he cursed it roundly.

Ardnacraish might have returned the compliment, though with less
justice: what the Admiral had done to it had had the over-riding
sanction of war. But certainly there had been changes ... If you took a
small Scottish fishing village of two hundred inhabitants in the remote
Highlands, with one inn, three shops, a slip-way, and a small landlocked
harbour: if you decided that it had to be turned into a naval training-
base, and transported there everything necessary for its establishment –

huts, storerooms, sleeping-quarters, gear and equipment of every sort: if you set up a signal tower and a radio station, laid a defence boom, deepened the harbour, and put down a line of mooring-buoys: if you drafted in a maintenance and training staff of seventy officers and men, and organized an additional floating population of two or three hundred sailors at a time from visiting ships – if you did all this, you got a certain result. It would probably be the result you wanted: but you could hardly expect a sweet unspoiled Highland village to be a residual part of it.

Ardnacraish had been lovely: it would be lovely again, when the alien visitation was over; but now it was a place for a job, a utilitarian necessity, and as such it was patchwork, ugly, and unrecognizable.

But it was his responsibility . . . The Admiral looked out of the window at the harbour, across an intervening line of corrugated-iron roofs which housed the Asdic and signal departments. There was, as usual, a brisk wind blowing: he could hear it rattling the ill-fitting doors of the other offices in the building, and he could see it ruffling its way across the harbour and sending small vicious waves slapping against the mooring-buoys. There were no ships in, at the moment, except the oiler and the tug attached to the base: the last one had left two days previously, and they were waiting for the next arrival, due that afternoon. She was to be a brand-new type, and the first of her class: a corvette – theatrical name, but an honoured one in naval history. He had her training programme ready for her, and she would start straight away.

It was a stiff programme, though an experimental one still, since convoys themselves were as yet in the embryo stage, and one hardly knew what the escorts would have to contend with. But there were certain things which all ships had to do and to be, whatever job they were intended for: as a fundamental basis, they had to be clean, efficient, and alert. In this, almost everything depended on their officers, and, judging by the last war, there were going to be some pretty odd officers before the thing was over. This ship, he noted, had an R.N.R. captain, which meant, at any rate, a seaman in command . . . The others, amateurs, might be worth anything or nothing.

The Admiral frowned. He would soon find out what they *were* worth, and what the ship was worth too: that was his job. He might be too old to take one to sea, but he was still a firm judge of what a ship should look like and how she should behave; and however long the war lasted, and whatever the urgency, no ship would leave his command which did not meet this life-long standard.

There was a knock on the door, and a signalman entered.

The Admiral looked up. 'Well?'

'*Compass Rose* entering harbour now, sir. Lieutenant Haines said to tell you.'

'Has he signalled her a berth?'

'Yes, sir.'

The Admiral got up, and walked across to the window again. A ship was just entering the narrows, moving very slowly, edging sideways to off-set the cross-wind: as he watched her, she lowered a boat which began to make for one of the central mooring-buoys. His eyes went back to the ship, and he appraised her carefully. She was small, smaller than he had expected: rather chunky, but not ungraceful if you discounted the clumsy-looking stern and the mast plumb in front of the bridge. She looked clean – and so she damned well ought to be, fresh from the builders – and the hands were properly fallen in fore and aft, in the rig-of-the-day. She was flying her pendant-numbers, and a brand-new ensign. One gun on the fo'c'sle – a pom-pom aft – depth-charges – nothing much else . . . Something like an overgrown trawler. But she'd have to do more than trawler's work.

He watched her securing to the buoy, neatly enough, and then he turned to the signalman.

'Send a signal. "*Compass Rose* from Flag-Officer-in-Charge. Manoeuvre well executed." Then tell Lieutenant Haines to call away my barge. I'm going aboard now.'

CHAPTER II

For three weeks they worked very hard indeed. From the moment that the Admiral's barge approached in a wide, treacherous sweep right under their stern and almost caught the Captain unawares, the ship's company was in a continual state of tension. If they were not out exercising with the submarine, they were doing gun-drill or running through Action-Stations in harbour: if they were not fighting mock fires or raising the anchor by hand, an urgent signal would order them to lower a boat and put an armed landing-party ashore on the nearest beach. In between times, relays of men attended drills and lectures ashore: sometimes, with half the crew thus absent and their normal organization unworkable, a fearsome directive from the Admiral would set them to some manoeuvre which necessitated every available man tackling the nearest job, irrespective of his rating.

Stokers would find themselves firing guns, seamen had to try their hand at hoisting flag-signals: telegraphists and coders, gentlemanly types, would take on the crude job of connecting up filthy oil-pipes from the oiler. 'Blast the old bastard!' said Bennett sourly, when some crisis or other found him hauling on a rope instead of watching other people do it: 'I'll be cleaning out the lavatories next.' Lockhart wished it might be true ... The three weeks' ordeal was exhilarating, and profoundly good for the ship, as far as training was concerned; but there were occasions when they all felt due for a holiday, and none too sure that it would arrive in time.

There were no holidays now: this was the time for winding up, for tuning to top pitch: they would have no other chance. Little by little the process advanced: the rough edges were smoothed off, the awkwardness of apprenticeship overcome and then forgotten. It was a progress they all acknowledged, and welcomed: their ship was coming alive, and for that reason she was a better place to live in, a surer weapon to use. There would come a time, they began to realize, when alertness and a disciplined reaction to crisis might save all their lives; if the price, now, were over-work and sometimes over-harshness, it was worth paying the score, and forgetting it as soon as it was paid. No weariness, no boredom, no grudge against authority, was worth setting against this ultimate survival.

The measure of their progress was nowhere more apparent than during the trips they made to sea, on exercises with the submarine attached to the base. The main purpose of these trips was to try out the Asdic gear – the anti-submarine detector which was their main weapon – and to perfect the team-work between the Asdic operators, the depth-charge crews, and the Captain, which would be a vital element in their future effectiveness. In those early days, the Asdic set was an elementary affair, not much more than a glorified echo-sounder, working horizontally all round the ship, instead of vertically down to the sea-bed; but it was still a weapon of precision, it could still produce results if it were properly used. And certainly the hunts themselves, with a real moving, elusive quarry to outwit, instead of the synthetic target that they practised on ashore, were the most exciting part of their training.

At first they had very little success. Bennett, Lockhart, and Ferraby all took turns at manoeuvring the ship during a hunt, and they all found the same inherent handicap – there were too many things to think about at the same time. The ship had to be handled, sometimes in bad weather which set her rolling like a metronome: the submarine had to be found, and held during the run-in: the Asdic operators had to be controlled, and chivvied back onto the target if they showed signs of wandering: the engine-revolutions had to be altered, the correct signals hoisted, the depth-charge crews warned, the right button pressed at the right moment. And if they forgot one of these little things, the whole attack collapsed and had to be written off as a failure, a foolish waste of time attended by a deplorable publicity ... It was no wonder that, during the preliminary exercises, each of them in turn developed stage-fright, and did their best to cover it by a mixture of bluff and pretended indifference. Bennett, naturally, was by far the best at this: to listen to him, nothing moving below the surface had a chance of survival when he was Officer-of-the-Watch, and precious little on top.

But gradually they improved: they learned various tricks and idiosyncrasies of the ship and the Asdic set, they learned to anticipate what a hunted submarine would do next, they learned when it was safe to guess and when it was essential to make sure before moving in any direction. Their wits sharpened, and their applied skill too. And finally there came a day when in the course of six successive 'runs' *Compass Rose* picked up the submarine each time and held it right down to the mock 'kill': when indeed, the submarine, surfacing at the end of its last encounter after trying every device and every evasion, signalled to them: 'You're too good. Go away and try it on the Germans.' At that moment of small triumph, it seemed a very good idea – and anything else a waste of energy. The time was very near when they would outgrow the schoolroom altogether, and insist on trying their armour on the adult world. They were confident that that armour would take a lot of denting. Even Chief E.R.A. Watts, when straightly tackled, would admit that *Compass Rose* was running sweetly enough, and that his engines, at least, were proving themselves robust, tireless, and dependable. From Petty Officer Tallow there was now less talk of the glories of the *Repulse*: on a smaller scale, *Compass Rose* had won his affection.

.   .   .

There was one thing which did not improve, though they were busy enough to be able to ignore it most of the time: the situation in the wardroom. Ericson, watching his officers at work, was satisfied enough with their progress, from the professional angle: it was off duty, when they were isolated on board (there was nothing for them to do ashore, even when they braved the winter cold in search of distraction), that the bickering and the ill-humour started up again, taking the place of their working co-operation. It came to a head on one occasion, and he was forced to recognize it and to take action: he did so unwillingly, since discipline necessitated his admonishing the wrong man, but with the best will in the world he could not ignore a direct clash between Bennett and the other two.

It started with Ferraby: most things did; he was now established as the vulnerable element, the weak link that betrayed the rest of the chain. He tried hard enough, he was still eager to make a success of it: but that eagerness was blunted and poisoned all the time by the knowledge that, whatever he did, Bennett would find fault with it. Given any sort of encouragement, and an occasional word of approval, he might have measured up to the new standard of effectiveness which *Compass Rose* as a whole had reached – he was not stupid, by any means, he was adaptable and enthusiastic, he wanted above all to give of his best. But since this giving always met with the same reception, since whatever he did was wrong, and the fact was pointed out to him in the crudest terms, it was no wonder that he slipped deeper and deeper into a miserable hesitation. He grew to loathe and to fear that rough voice, which might at any moment call out 'Ferrabee!' and then pick to pieces whatever he was trying to do; and hesitation, loathing, and fear were not a compound which was of any use either to himself or to the ship.

Lockhart saw what was happening, and did his best to stand in the way of Bennett's rougher attacks: it was this effort to shield Ferraby that led to an open rupture. It took place in the wardroom, one night when Ferraby, as Officer-of-the-Day, had come below again after evening Rounds. Though he had been up to the bridge, he had forgotten to check their anchor-bearings – a pure formality in this case, since there was no wind and in their sheltered harbour it would take a tidal wave to make *Compass Rose* drag her anchor; but Bennett, seizing the occasion as usual, had made it the subject of a prolonged and brutal tirade which Ferraby accepted without protest. When he was finally and contemptuously dismissed, and had left the wardroom, Lockhart, who had been a spectator, muttered something not quite under his breath. Bennett, who was standing by the sideboard pouring himself a drink, swung round.

'What did you say?' he snapped.

Lockhart came to a decision. 'I said,' he repeated more distinctly, 'why don't you leave him alone? He's only a kid, and he's doing his best.'

'It's not good enough.'

'It would be if you gave him a chance.'

Bennett slammed down his glass. 'That's enough,' he said roughly. 'You keep out of it. I don't have to argue with you.'

'You don't have to argue with anyone,' said Lockhart moderately. 'But can't you see that it's no good going on at Ferraby like that? It only makes him worse instead of better. He's that sort of person.'

'Then he'd better change, pretty quickly,' sneered Bennett.

'He's doing his best,' Lockhart repeated.

'He's not. He's been no bloody use ever since I stopped him dipping his wick at Glasgow, and that's been the trouble all along.'

Lockhart looked at him for a moment, and then said, with all the dispassion he could muster: 'What a horrible man you are.'

Bennett suddenly stiffened, his whole body rigid with fury. 'Who the hell do you think you're talking to?' he shouted. 'By God, you'd better watch out, or I'll land you in hell's own trouble! I'll see you stay a sub-lieutenant for the rest of the war, for a start.'

Lockhart, who had had the one extra drink which took him over the border-line of discretion, looked pointedly at the two rings on Bennett's sleeve, and said:

'I'm not sure I want to be a lieutenant after all.'

Bennett, now nearly beside himself, walked across the wardroom and stood over his chair. 'One more crack like that, and I'll report you to the Captain.'

'Try it,' said Lockhart. He was beginning to feel fatalistic about the outcome of the scene: it might be suicidal to keep on, but if he knuckled under now it would cancel out the whole stand he had made. 'Try it,' he repeated. 'The Captain's not *such* a bloody fool. I bet he knows how you treat Ferraby, at all events.'

'He knows I treat Ferraby like that because Ferraby's a lazy bastard who's no bloody use to anyone.' Bennett focused a venomous look on Lockhart's face, daring him to counter-attack. 'And that's about true of you, too.'

'It's not,' said Lockhart, stung out of his control at last. He abandoned caution. 'We both do a damned sight more work than you, anyway.'

After which, there was really nothing to do but put on his cap and follow Bennett up to the Captain's cabin. The respectful gaze of Leading-Steward Carslake, who had been an enthralled audience and who now came out of the pantry to watch the tense procession go by, was sufficient commentary on the seriousness of the clash. It seemed that only some vital exercise of authority could resolve it.

But the subsequent encounter in the Captain's cabin was an odd one, and less conclusive than either Bennett or Lockhart had expected. Ericson listened while Bennett put his case – fairly enough, since he was on impregnable ground; but even on the admitted facts he could not really decide how to deal with it. He had been expecting something of the sort for quite a long time, and now here it was: Lockhart had been a fool not to keep his temper, Bennett had been his natural unpleasant self – and he, as Captain, had to find the right answer, with a strong bias towards the maintenance of discipline. But what sort of discipline did he want to maintain?

The ideal solution was to tell Lockhart to behave himself, and Bennett not to be so tough; but that did not quite square with King's Regulations, and it was the letter of the law that had to be appeased. The next best thing was to find some negative ground on which to settle the matter, and he had an opening when Lockhart, in answer to a question about the origin of the row, said:

'I think Ferraby gets a rough deal, sir.'

'It's not your concern whether someone else gets a rough deal or not,' Ericson cut in briskly. 'You've got your own job to do without worrying how the First Lieutenant treats his officers.'

'I realize that, sir.' Lockhart, standing formally to attention, was still sensitive to atmosphere, and he guessed the Captain's dilemma; but having come so far he did not want the whole situation to melt away in vague generalizations about minding one's own business. 'But if you think a friends of yours is being unfairly treated, the natural thing to do is to try and help him.'

'Is it?' said Ericson ironically. 'I should say that much the best plan was to keep clear of it, and let him work out his own salvation. Then we don't get this sort of argument, and——' he looked grimly at Lockhart, 'argument between you and the First Lieutenant is something I'm not going to stand for.'

'I know that, sir. I got a bit worked up, and——' he was about to say he was sorry, but somehow he could not bring himself to form the words. Instead he finished: 'I'm not trying to get out of the consequences. But I do think that this sort of treatment——' he gestured towards Bennett, 'is having an appalling effect on Ferraby. He just hasn't an ounce of self-confidence left.'

Bennett, without looking at him, said: 'I don't want any lectures on how to treat Ferraby.'

Ericson glanced from one to the other – from Lockhart's serious, determined face, pale under the electric light, to Bennett's flushed self-confidence. Privately, he thought there's no solution really – they're just two unmixable people. Then he caught sight of his own face between them in the mirror: it was tough, square, a competent barrier between two opposing forces. He looked, in fact, a lot more convincing than he felt; he knew he was not handling this thing well, and it had to be handled perfectly, to dispose of it without a hang-over. The trouble was that he was dog-tired. The cabin, with its port-holes closed since 'darken ship' was piped five hours ago, was now stuffy and airless: they had had a long day at sea, and there was another one tomorrow. The Admiral's habit of slipping aboard 'to see how things were getting along', without any more notice than the sight of his barge leaving the quay, was proving a constant source of irritation. Tonight, Ericson had not a great deal of energy left, and none at all for this sort of domestic upheaval.

But he made another effort, seeking to deal with the thing in black-and-white terms, without subtlety, disregarding the gross cleavage that lay in the background.

'Now look here,' he began, 'this has gone far enough, and it's not going to go any further. It's bad for you, and it's bad for the ship.' He looked at Lockhart. 'I'm not going to have you interfering like this in things that don't concern you. Do you understand?'

'Yes, sir,' said Lockhart. On this basis, he was now ready to let it go: he had not won, but neither had Bennett – unless there was something more to come.

Apparently there was nothing more. 'Remember that, then,' said the Captain. 'I don't want to hear any more complaints about you, or I shall have to take some action – action you won't like. Now just forget about the whole thing. There's plenty to do, without this sort of scrapping.'

He stopped, and turned away: it seemed to be their dismissal. Bennett opened his mouth to speak, unable to believe that the matter was thus disposed of: what about the insolence, what about Lockhart's cracks, what about the denial of authority? He could not leave it like this. But he did not want to start things up again with Lockhart listening: it needed a less formal approach. He said:

'May I have a word with you, sir?'

Ericson, who had been expecting it, said: 'All right, Number One.' He nodded to Lockhart, who turned and left the cabin. 'Well,' said Ericson, a shade less cordially, 'what's the trouble?'

'Sir,' said Bennett, 'I think Lockhart got away with it.'

Ericson, disregarding the temptation to answer: 'I quite agree with you,' which would have been nearer the truth, said: 'You've got to make allowances, Number One. He's a very new officer, and I think we've all been working pretty hard. It *was* a bit rough, I know, but I don't think it will happen again.'

'I've had a lot of trouble with Lockhart,' said Bennett aggrievedly. 'I hoped you'd pull him up, sir. He needs stamping on, good and hard.'

Ericson looked at him, tense and sweating in the close cabin, and thought: one of these days someone is going to hit you, and that means a court-martial, all because you're a tough character and have to show it all the time. He remembered a first mate rather like Bennett, back in the old days in the Far East Line: foul-mouthed, ready with his fists, never giving an inch of ground or a word of praise. He'd ended by killing his man – a Chinese seaman foolish enough to argue about some bad food. He'd got off with manslaughter, but that had been the end of him. On a less dramatic plane, Bennett might go the same way – or push someone else to it. There *were* people like that, doomed by their own intransigence, damned by their crudity: it was bad luck that one of them had landed up in *Compass Rose*.

He said, shortly: 'I want to avoid having to stamp on people as far as possible, Number One. There are other ways of getting them to work properly.' He felt like adding something about Ferraby, and the need to treat him less roughly, but perhaps Bennett had had enough hints for one evening. Instead he said: 'Give Lockhart a fresh start, and see what he makes of it,' and then he turned away with a finality which even Bennett's thick skin could not resist. This was a scene which might go on for ever: he had had enough of it.

When Bennett had gone, his face registering the protest which had scarcely been allowed to come to life, much less to develop properly, Ericson walked out of his cabin, parted the thick blackout screens at the entrance to the companionway, and stepped on to the upper deck. The fresh air, though bitterly cold, came as a welcome relief: the night was clear, the little harbour easily seen, the small waves slapping against the ship's side an endless accompaniment to their vigil. He looked up at the sky: wispy clouds round the moon promised some wind later, but tomorrow's weather seemed as secure as their anchorage. Round him the familiar shipboard sounds were reassuring: the hum of the dynamos, the noise of a gramophone from the fo'c'sle, the clumping of the quartermaster's sea-boots as he made his rounds farther aft – all these were part of a life and a moment he savoured to the full. Night in harbour, after a hard day's work: there should be nothing to beat that.

But he was not *quite* satisfied: the recent scene with Bennett and Lockhart had left a bad taste. There had been too many loose ends, though if he had tried to deal with them in detail it would have been far more serious for Lockhart. And then there was Ferraby, adrift in circumstances he scarcely comprehended, as vulnerable as a baby that never grew any bigger or any cleverer ... He shrugged, and turned back to his cabin, glad to leave it all till tomorrow. There was only one real cure, anyway: they had to stop fighting each other, and fight the enemy instead.

.   .   .

Soon it was their last week at Ardnacraish, the end of their apprentice-ship: the tuning-up process came to its full flower, and with it an access of confidence which reached all but the most unimpressionable elements.

Professionally, they were sure of themselves: they knew their ship, they knew their jobs in her. Now, no matter what they were asked to do, no matter how the Admiral or his staff stalked them, no matter what odd signals made Leading-Signalman Wells suck his teeth and Bennett start swearing and shouting, they felt they could cope with it. There were occasional mistakes, lacerating to the dignity – as when one of the fo'c'sle-party broke the wrong shackle on the cable and dropped the anchor and six feet of chain neatly over the bows and into thirty feet of water; but these were odd set-backs in a continuous process, small pebbles in the stream. All in all, they had made a success of Ardnacraish; even Ferraby, now that Bennett seemed to be holding his hand and moderating his voice, was beginning to improve; unexpectedly buoyant, he took a fresh lease and tried once more to fit himself in ... *Compass Rose*, eight weeks from the day she was commissioned, was now a working proposition.

During the final week they had been joined by another corvette, the next off the assembly line. Her name was *Sorrel*, and her captain, Ramsay, was an old friend of Ericson's; her arrival was a cheerful occasion, adding to the amenities of what was, in essentials, a bleak corner of the world. When they went out on trials with the submarine, *Sorrel* and *Compass Rose* hunted as a team, and this was another advantage, adding interest to exercises which were beginning to pall: they took it in turns to attack the submarine, while the spare ship stood off and passed cross-bearings, advice, and, occasionally, the ribald comments of the more successful performer. It was a useful foretaste of what could happen in convoy, when any number of escorts might join in a hunt, and would have to learn to do this, and make an effective contribution, without getting in each other's way.

. . . .

Compass Rose's final exercise before she left was, appropriately, a practice-shoot at night.

At dusk they said goodbye to *Sorrel*, who was returning to harbour, and then for an hour they cruised about off the south end of the island, waiting first for the tug which was to tow their target for them, and then for the coming of night. It was one of those evenings that show the Scottish Highlands at their superb best: by luck, their *envoi* from the peaceful world had a loveliness which they carried with them for many months afterwards. Sunset gave them a gold-and-red-streaked sky: dusk gave them a subtle-coloured backcloth for the islands surrounding them – Mull and Iona and Colonsay: darkness itself came down from the hills in deep purple shadows which, reflected on the water round the ship, turned it to a sombre, royal hue. Then, in the deepening night, the hills were shut out altogether: the single light which marked the harbour entrance still stood guard for them, ten miles and more away, but that was the only element that bound them to the land. Alone on a dark noiseless sea, under a sky already pricked by the first stars, *Compass Rose* circled and lifted to the swell and waited for her rendezvous.

Up on the bridge, the waiting was focused down to a few alert men: the Captain at the front of the bridge, Lockhart, who was Officer-of-the-Watch, beside him, Leading-Signalman Wells leaning against his lamp and staring through his binoculars, the two look-outs on the two wings completing the pattern. It was very cold: they felt it on their faces, they felt it on their stiff hands, they felt it in their legs and thighs as they stamped their feet. The canvas screens round the bridge were no protection: on their high platform, the waiting figures were simply part of the ship, bare to the weather, open to the sky.

Suddenly Leading-Signalman Wells, intent on something which had caught his eyes on their beam, straightened up.

'There she is, sir. Red eight-oh.'

The vague blur to port resolved itself: under the growing moon, the tug emerged as a hard shape on the horizon, and the towed target as a black blob astern of her.

Wells spoke again. 'Calling us up, sir!' He turned swiftly to the signalman of the watch, Rose, at the back of the bridge. 'Take it down . . . "*Compose Rose* from *Basher*".'

'What a singular name for a tug,' said Lockhart.
'Gives you fair warning,' said the Captain. Lockhart smiled to himself. Now and again the Captain came out with a remark like that, disproving his professional inhumanity. It was the more refreshing for being so unexpected.

The dimmed signal lights winked to each other across a mile of still water.

'Signal, sir!' said Wells presently. 'From the tug: "My course and speed, two-seven-oh, four knots. Length of tow, three hundred feet. Ready for you".'

'Right,' said the Captain. 'Make to them: "On our first run we will close from four thousand yards and fire three rounds. Please signal hits".'

The lamps winked again, flickering across the darkness as if glad to find each other.

'Reply, sir. "If any",' said Wells, without expression.

'Humorist,' said the Captain briefly. He bent to the voice-pipe. 'Starboard twenty. Steer north.' and then, to Lockhart: 'Sound off Action-Stations. We'll start this from the beginning.'

The alarm-bells, faintly and shrilly heard from below, set in motion a stirring, the length and breadth of the ship, which quickly filtered up to the bridge. Figures appeared on the gun-platform, crowding round the gun: Petty Officer Tallow confirmed his presence at the wheel: the voice-pipe from the quarter-deck reported that Sub-Lieutenant Ferraby had the depth-charge party closed up. As on so many occasions during the past three weeks, *Compass Rose* quickly came to life, filling in the gaps in her readiness, crowding the upper deck with men who no longer blundered about or impeded one another as they moved, but who made swiftly for their stations as if they had been walking about in full daylight. The hours of drilling and practice were paying a dividend already: if the future were to call upon it at a crucial moment, it was there, ready and available.

Lockhart's position at Action-Stations was on the fo'c'sle, in charge of the gun: he had no sooner got there, clattering up the ladder in the darkness, and Leading-Seaman Phillips had reported that the gun's-crew was closed up, than he felt *Compass Rose* tremble as she increased speed: the wind of their advance struck cold on his face, prompting him to action. They loaded and stood ready, while the ship ran on over the dark water and the range shortened: then from the bridge came the shouted order: 'Target bearing red four-five – range three thousand – open fire!' and from that moment the responsibility was his. *Compass Rose* had no refinements in the way of gunnery: in action, as now, it was to be a matter of shouting, and then local control from the gun-platform itself. Lockhart set the range, and waited until the gun-layer, straining his eyes against the darkness, reported that he had found the target: then he gave the order:

'Shoot!'

He had never seen the gun fired at night: close to, the effect was almost stupefying – a violent crash, and then a great burst of flame and smoke which momentarily blinded him and made him gasp. Through his binoculars he watched for the fall of shot, and presently it came: a tall spout of water, a plume of spray phosphorescent in the moonlight, in line with the target but well short of it.

'Up four hundred – shoot!'

Again the crash of the explosion, again the burst of flame, and the waiting for the shot to fall. This second time, accustomed to the noise, Lockhart could hear the shell whistling and whining away into the darkness after the first report. Now they were over the target: the range must be closing quicker than he had thought, or else the first shot had been a bad one, fired as they rolled.

'Down two hundred – shoot!'

That was a good bracket – the spout of water was just short of the target. But that was the last round allowed to them ... The cease-fire gong sounded, and he called out: 'Check, check, check!' to confirm it. Then he stood back as the gun was cleared, and smelt the reek of cordite, and heard Phillips mutter: 'The next one would have sunk 'em,' and felt suddenly excited and pleased with himself. The noise and the flames and the sense of crisis were wildly novel to him: he had never done anything like it before, but it did seem – it *really* seemed – as if he had done quite well ... As if to confirm this, the Captain leant over the edge of the bridge above him and said: 'Not bad, Lockhart. Get ready for the next run.' The sound of Bennett disagreeably clearing his throat in the background need not, he felt, be given any weight as a comment.

The second run was, by contrast, a resounding failure: it would not have frightened a rowing-boat. Their first shot fell short – so short, indeed, that Lockhart knew that the gun-layer had lost his head and fired on the forward roll, with the gun pointing downwards. The second was for some reason right out of line: he could, at a stretch, blame that on the quartermaster, who swung the ship off her steady course at the critical moment. The third fall, which was to make amends, Lockhart did not even see: they might never have fired it at all, for all the evidence they had, though probably it had gone far over and been obscured by the target. And that was the end of that run ... The noise and activity now seemed a great deal less dramatic, and the reflective silence from the bridge a positive insult. He said under his breath to Phillips: 'We'll have to do better than this,' and Phillips answered determinedly: 'We'll do that, sir,' and started a blasphemous harangue of the gun's-crew, man by man. Lockhart, applying the principle of limited liability, walked casually out of earshot. He had delegated his authority, and it seemed to be in effective hands.

The harangue must have been a good one, for their last run was by far the best. One sighting shot, a little short, and then 'Up two hundred – shoot!' and two hits plumb at the base of the target. The tug, impressed, flickered a message to them, and this time the Captain said: 'Good shooting, Lockhart,' and there was no repressive cough from Bennett. '"Sink me the ship, Master Gunner",' Lockhart quoted aloud, slightly over-elated: ' "Sink her, split her in twain: Fall into the hands of God, not into the hands of Spain".' 'Sir?' said Phillips interestedly. 'Poetry,' said Lockhart. 'Sponge out, secure the gun, and then ask the leading-steward to give you seven bottles of beer.' He had never felt better in his life: at that moment, standing on the gun-platform while the crew worked and chattered in the darkness, he would have shaken hands with Bennett or joined the Navy for a twelve-year stretch.

.   .   .

It was past midnight when they entered harbour: since it was the last exercise in their programme, and the morrow was a genuine holiday, the late hour did not matter. *Compass Rose*, moving very slowly through the harbour entrance, was like a grey ghost slipping back to its lair, at some dead hour before the cock crew and ghosts must walk no more. The defence-boom had been kept open for them, but nothing stirred as they slid by it and went gently up towards their buoy. The moon was still high, and every outline was clear: the bay had a silvery rim to it, marking the limits of their refuge, giving it a containing margin. They moved past the oiler, past the sleeping *Sorrel* with her shaded stern-light, and then, foot by foot, up to their mooring.

Standing in the eyes of the ship, torch in hand, Lockhart called out directions to the bridge, while the beam of the torch sent odd wavering reflections of the water along their hull. *Compass Rose* inched her way forward and came to a stop, her bows overhanging the buoy: Lockhart bent his shaft of light downwards, picking out the white face of the rating perched on the buoy, and the wire, with the spring-clip at the end, snaking its way down to him. Then he turned and called out: 'Hooked on, sir!' to the bridge: and they were at rest, and his part in the day was over.

A few minutes later the moorings were properly secured: the telegraph-bell, faintly heard, which meant 'Main engine finished with', set the seal on their arrival. The slack of the cable ran out noisily, starting up a hollow echo from the cliffs, and Leading-Seaman Phillips, speaking out of the darkness to no one in particular, said: 'I bet that wakes the Admiral.' There was a small ripple of laughter from the fo'c'sle-men: Lockhart wondered if Phillips had already drunk his beer. Then he took a last look at the moorings, and said: 'All right – that'll do,' and followed his party across the dark fo'c'sle and down the ladder. He was stiff and tired; but the last day had been the best, and *Compass Rose*, swinging to her buoy and peaceful under the moon, was something he unaccountably loved.

CHAPTER 12

Once more, Vice-Admiral Sir Vincent Murray-Forbes sat at his desk in the Operations building overlooking the harbour. Now he was writing a report: it was one of hundreds of reports, on ships and men, which he was to write, month in month out, until the end of the war: on ships destined to be sunk or to survive, on men marked for killing, or for honour at the King's own hands. He did not know what lay in store for these ships or these men: it would not have made an atom of difference if he had been writing an epitaph on men due to be drowned tomorrow. He was concerned only with facts; and of these he had mustered a great many during the past three weeks.

'H.M.S. *Compass Rose*,' he wrote, in an old-fashioned, somewhat laborious long-hand, 'completed her programme of training on February 2nd 1940, and may be regarded as having passed out satisfactorily. The ship has been well worked up, and is clean and generally efficient. Further attention should be given (*a*) to fire-fighting, which was below the requisite standard of speed, and (*b*) to the drill for abandon ship, which did not go smoothly on the only occasion on which it was tested. But with these reservations, the organization of H.M.S. *Compass Rose* now meets the high standard necessary to a ship engaged in the exacting task of convoy escort.'

He consulted a batch of reports from his staff. 'Gunnery,' he wrote, as a sub-heading, and underlined it. 'The single four-inch gun which is the sole major armament of this class of ship will only be adequate if constant attention is given to gun-drill and to ammunition-supply. H.M.S. *Compass Rose* did well in her various gun-trials, and the night-shoot was successful, both as regards the handling of the ship and the actual firing. Anti-aircraft shooting, conducted with a towed streamer-target, was less successful: it is recommended that more provision be made for anti-aircraft gun-control, possibly by loud-speaker operated from the bridge.'

'Asdics,' he went on, and underlined again. 'On her arrival, H.M.S. *Compass Rose* was inadequately trained in this branch, and the Anti-Submarine Control Officer and the Asdic ratings were clearly in need of intensive practice. When this had been provided, her efficiency improved rapidly, and she developed an effective anti-submarine team. Communication between the bridge and the depth-charge parties aft is still inadequate in this class of vessel: attention is drawn to my No. 242/17/1/40, addressed to Admiral Superintending Contract-Built Ships (repeated to C.-in-C. W.A.) in which various improvements are suggested.'

'Depth-Charge Organization,' he wrote. 'Only constant practice will bring the depth-charge crews up to the high standard of efficiency necessary in this branch. Time-tests of re-loading and firing were generally disappointing, and it is emphasized that speed and accuracy may be vital here when the ship is in action.'

He added three short sub-headings: 'Engine-room Branch: satisfactory.' 'Telegraphy and Coding: adequate.' 'Signal Branch: excellent.' Then he took a fresh sheet of paper.

'H.M.S. *Compass Rose*. Reports on Officers,' wrote the Admiral, and referred again to his notes. 'Lieutenant-Commander George Eastwood Ericson, R.N.R.: Commanding Officer. This officer exhibited a high standard of seamanship, and showed himself expert at ship-handling. I judged him to be a conscientious and determined officer who, when he has gained more experience in this new class of ship, will extract everything possible out of his command. His relations with his subordinate officers appeared satisfactory, and it was clear that he inspired their confidence and would be followed by them without hesitation.'

'Lieutenant James Bennett, R.A.N.V.R.: First Lieutenant and Anti-Submarine Control Officer,' wrote the Admiral. 'This officer has a remarkable self-confidence, and with more experience and application his executive capacity may come to match it. He tends to rely too much on his junior officers implementing his orders (and in some cases issuing them themselves). In the initial stages there were serious flaws in the internal organization of H.M.S. *Compass Rose*, doubtless due to this officer's inexperience. A downright, forceful personality who should make a good First Lieutenant when he learns to set an example of self-discipline.'

'Sub-Lieutenant Keith Laing Lockhart, R.N.V.R.: Gunnery and Navigation Officer,' wrote the Admiral. 'I was impressed by this officer's competence, in novel surroundings and in a position of responsibility, when backed by very little practical experience. His gun's-crews were well worked up, and he seemed to inspire confidence in the ratings in his division. He should develop into a good type of officer, very useful in a ship of this class. He should pay more attention to the regulations governing dress for officers when on duty.'

'Sub-Lieutenant Gordon Perceval D'Ewes Ferraby, R.N.V.R.: Depth-Charge Control and Correspondence Officer,' wrote the Admiral. 'This officer lacks both experience and self-confidence, and appeared hesitant in giving orders. There is no reason why he should not develop into a useful officer, but he must learn to trust his own judgement, and to give the ratings under his charge the impression that he knows what he wants from them. His department improved during the latter stages of H.M.S. *Compass Rose*'s course of training.'

The Admiral drew a thick line under his report, and blotted it neatly. Then he added, at the bottom: 'Addressed, Commander-in-Chief, Western Approaches: copies to Flag-Officer-in-Charge, Glasgow: Admiralty (C.W. Branch): H.M.S. *Compass Rose*.' Then he sat back, and rang for his secretary.

CHAPTER 13

Ericson, at ease in his cabin, read his copy of this report with some satisfaction and a good deal of amusement. The Admiral had come well up to standard, by way of farewell: it was a perfect picture of Number One, despite the limits of official phraseology, and he liked especially the crack about Lockhart and 'dress regulations' – Lockhart having mislaid his cap on one crucial occasion and greeted the Admiral with something between a wave and a bow. Then, as he folded the sheets of paper again, there was a knock on the door, and Leading-Signalman Wells came in, a sealed envelope in his hand.

'Secret signal, sir,' said Wells, in not quite his normal inexpressive voice. 'The signal boat just brought it aboard.'

Ericson ripped open the envelope, and read slowly and carefully. It was what he had been waiting for.

'Being in all respects ready for sea,' said the pink slip, 'H.M.S. *Compass Rose* will sail to join convoy A.K. 14, leaving Liverpool (Bar Light Vessel) at 1200A February 6th 1940. Senior officer of escort is in H.M.S. *Viperous*. Acknowledge.'

Ericson read it through again. Then:

'Take this down,' he said. '"To Commander-in-Chief, Western Approaches, from *Compass Rose*. Your 0939 stroke four stroke two acknowledged." And send it off straight away.'

So they went to war.

PART TWO

CHAPTER 1

1940: SKIRMISHING

The war to which they went had hardly settled down, even in broad outline, to any recognizable pattern.

The liner *Athenia* had been torpedoed and sunk, with the loss of 128 lives, on September 3rd, the first day of the war: the first U-boat sinking, to offset this ruthless stroke, was on September 14th. Thus, at the beginning, the pace was hot – forty ships were sunk during that first September, and two fine warships, *Courageous* and *Royal Oak*, both went to the bottom before the turn of the year; but the pace did not last. The casualties had been mostly independent ships which happened to be at sea when war was declared; like the *Athenia*, they were in the wrong place at the wrong time; but with the growth of the convoy system this chance ill-fortune could be avoided, and ships and shipping companies were quick to see that any effort to remain in convoy, instead of straggling behind or charging proudly ahead of the pedestrian field, was worth while.

The U-boats were on the offensive – that was their role – but it was not a co-ordinated attack, nor even a very efficient one. Probably there were not more than a dozen of them at sea, at any one time, during this stage of the war, and so they hunted alone. They hung about off the coasts of Scotland and Ireland, and in the Bay of Biscay, on the look-out for stray ships which they could pick off at leisure; it was a series of individual forays – sometimes successful, sometimes a waste of time: the co-ordination and the control were to come later, and in the meantime the whole thing was unpredictable and rather amateurish. Britain was short of escorts, Germany was short of U-boats: the Atlantic was a very big ocean and, in winter weather, the finest hiding-place in the world. It was indeed like a game of hide-and-seek, played by a few children in an enormous rambling garden, with the light sometimes fading and the grown-ups calling out directions intermittently. And if some of the children were vicious and cruel, and pinched you when you were discovered, that was nothing unexpected in a nursery world.

Such was the battlefield of the Atlantic, when 1940 dawned. The danger was there, but the two sides were hardly engaged: the U-boats lurking always, but playing their luck instead of their skill. To join this untidy battle, *Compass Rose* sailed early in the year.

CHAPTER 2

Their first convoy was a bloodless skirmish, as were many others in that
momentary lull; but it was a useful foretaste of what was to come, as well
as a proving of the ship in weather worse than they had yet met.

The sun was out as they sailed down into Liverpool Bay, on that fine
February morning, to meet their convoy: it had pierced the early mist,
melted the frost of their cold night passage, dried out their clothes with a
cheerful warmth. Ericson knew the port well – he had lived there for ten
years, and had sailed in and out of it scores of times: he looked for the
familiar landmarks with an affectionate eagerness. As usual the first
sight of land was the tall Blackpool Tower, away to the north: then the
Bar Light Vessel, riding uneasily in the jumble of tide-ripped water that
marked the entrance to the River Mersey; and then, faintly glimpsed in
the mist and smoke up river, the twin spires of the Liver Building, in the
heart of the city. Somewhere there, in a little house on the Birkenhead
side, Grace was undoubtedly knitting ... He had a moment's pang that
they should be so near to each other and yet be unable to meet; and then
he forgot it altogether. Five miles ahead of them, their ships were coming
out; they were led by a destroyer – an old V. and W. Class which must be
Viperous – already giving them the 'interrogative' on her signal-
lamp.

While Leading-Signalman Wells was replying, first making *Compass
Rose*'s number and then taking down a long signal about the organization of the convoy, Ericson studied the line of ships coming towards
them. They were of all shapes and sizes: tankers, big freighters, small
ships which would surely have been better off in the coasting trade than
trying the hazards of an Atlantic passage. Some were deep-laden, some
were in ballast and uncomfortably high out of the water: they steamed in
single file from the narrow Mersey channel: their pendants flew bravely
in the sunshine, they seemed almost glad to be putting to sea again ...
That could hardly be true, thought Ericson with a smile, remembering
the tearful goodbyes, the hangovers, the feeling of 'Oh-God-here-we-go-
again' which attended every sailing; but there was something about the
file of ships – forty-six of them – which suggested a willingness to make
the voyage, a tough confidence in the future.

There were U-boats in the way of that voyage, of course – or so it was said, because most ships and most men in that convoy had yet to meet one: there was, at any rate, a threat to use U-boats. Thus, as well as being important for these ships to sail to Boston and New York and Halifax and Rio, it was essential, as a simple matter of principle as well, that they should get through. The Atlantic had never been specifically a British ocean; but it was even less a German one, and now was not the time for it to change its nationality.

Ferraby, hanging about at the back of the bridge (it was not his watch) was more stirred by the sight of those ships than he had ever been before. He liked everything about this convoy: he liked its air of purpose as it cracked on speed after the cautious passage down-channel: he liked individual ships – particularly the tough and shapely tankers: he liked the men on board who waved cheerfully to *Compass Rose* as she passed down the line towards the tail of the convoy. This sort of thing – this moment of significance and determination, this comradeship, this sea-brotherhood – was what he had had in mind when, at the training establishment, he had volunteered for corvettes: there had been times when it had seemed impossible of attainment, when he was convinced that he was going to be fobbed off with a third-rate drama of pretence and frustration: now he knew that all his wishes were coming true.

Here were the ships, assembling for their long uncertain voyage: here was *Compass Rose*, appointed to guard them: here was Ferraby himself, a watch-keeping officer – or practically so – charged specifically with a share of that guardianship. His pale face flushed, his expression set in a new mould of determination, Ferraby surveyed the convoy with pride and a feeling of absolute proprietorship. *Our* ships, he thought: *our* cargoes, *our* men ... None would be surrendered, of this convoy or of any other, if it depended on any effort of his.

Ferraby's eyes were new, and took a good deal on trust: other eyes – Ericson's among them – were not, and to them, it must be admitted, the convoy was somewhat more impressive than the escort, which reflected perfectly the pinched circumstances of the Royal Navy at this stage. To shepherd these forty-six ships through waters which were potentially the most treacherous in the world, there had been provided one fifteen-year-old destroyer, of a class which, though valiantly manned and valiantly driven, was really far too slight and slender for the Atlantic weather: two corvettes – one a pre-war edition of crude design, the other *Compass Rose*; a trawler, and a rescue tug which already, in the sheltered waters of Liverpool Bay, was bouncing about like a pea on a drum. Five warships – four and a half would be nearer the truth – to guard forty-six slow merchantmen was not a reassuring prospect for the experts on either side ... But there it was: the best that could be done. And since there were no more ships to be had, something else would have to fill the gap: skill and

luck must somehow bring about what a rational probability could not
hope to effect.

                        .   .   .

Compass Rose was kept busy all that afternoon. It meant a long day for
the Captain, who had been on the bridge since first light; but certainly
he could not leave it now, when there was really no one else who could be
trusted to handle *Compass Rose* in close company with other ships. So he
stayed on, wedged in a corner of the bridge, drinking successive cups of
tea and giving endless helm-orders, while they worked through the
various tasks which *Viperous* had set them. First they had to see that all
the ships had sailed, checking their names and numbers against the long
list which had been signalled to them: then they had to round up the
stragglers and coax them into a closer formation: then – most trying of
all – they had to pass a verbal message over the loud-hailer to each of the
forty-six ships, and, since it concerned an important alteration of their
course during the night, make absolutely sure in each case that the
instructions had been understood.

Over and over again they repeated that message: first the Captain,
then Lockhart (who had the afternoon watch), then Leading-
Signalman Wells, then the Captain again. Some ships were deaf, and
needed endless repetitions: some were foreign, and had to summon a
man from the depths of the stokehold to take the message: some were
having their afternoon sleep, and doubtless thought the booming voice
was all part of the same bad dream.

'God Almighty!' said Ericson at one point, when five minutes' hailing
of a big tanker had produced nothing more than a vague salute from a
man in bowler hat on the bridge: 'You'd think they *wanted* to get lost
tonight. Try them again, Sub.'

'Hallo, Number Thirty-Two,' Lockhart called wearily through the
loud-hailer. 'Hallo, Number Thirty-Two. I have a message for you.
Take it down, please.'

The tanker ploughed on, while *Compass Rose* kept jaunty pace with
her, like a pekingese harbouring designs on a greyhound.

'Can we use the siren, sir?' asked Lockhart. 'They don't seem to hear
the human voice.'

'We'll use the gun in a minute.' Ericson grasped the wire and blew a
prodigious blast on the siren. The man in the bowler hat walked to the
wing of the bridge and stared at them.

'Number Thirty-Two – I have a message for you!' Lockhart called out
swiftly. 'Take it down, please.'

The man on the tanker cupped his hand to his ear.

'Oh God, the bastard's deaf,' said Lockhart despairingly, forgetting
that the hailer was still switched on. The crisp comment boomed across

the intervening thirty yards of water, and evidently found its mark: the man took his hand down and shook his fist at them instead.

'You've hurt his feelings, Sub,' said the Captain.

'Mistake, sir – sorry.' Lockhart was indeed considerably taken aback by what he had done, and when next he spoke he tried to make amends by assuming a winning tone: through the loud-hailer, it sounded revolting, like a dance-band crooner wooing the customers. 'Message for you, Number Thirty-Two. Important alteration of course. Please take it down.'

In answer, the man on the tanker raised a megaphone and shouted to them. Faintly over the water came the words:

'Don't be so bloody rude. I'll report you to the Board of Trade.'

Then he went inside and shut the door of the bridge-shelter firmly behind him. They had to wait until the change of the watch brought a new man to the bridge, before they could attract any further attention at all.

. . .

That first night with the convoy was a restless affair which gave them very little sleep. They were still organized on a two-watch basis – that is, the Captain and Ferraby alternated with Bennett and Lockhart, four hours on and four hours off. It was a trying arrangement at the best of times, hard on the endurance and the temper: even if they could fall asleep as soon as they came off watch, they had to wake and dress and climb up to the bridge again, almost before they had turned over. But this was not the best of times, and *Compass Rose* far from a restful place when they were off duty. The wind was rising, and the Irish Sea with it: the ship responded to the movement with a deplorable readiness, rolling and thumping as if she were being paid for her travail by the hour. In the noisy turmoil between-decks, sleep was barely possible, even to men already dog-tired.

There were other things. An aircraft, flying low over the convoy, brought them needlessly to Action-Stations at two o'clock in the morning: one of their ships, straggling in the rear (where *Compass Rose* was stern-escort), needed constant chivvying to keep her in touch with the main body. Their progress was dishearteningly slow: Chicken Rock Light, at the south end of the Isle of Man, was their mark for so long that at times it was difficult to believe that they would ever leave it behind, and reach the open sea. Altogether, the first night at their appointed job was not reassuring: if it could be as trying as this, with no enemy to fight and only a few odd incidents to contend with, what would it be like when they met the real ordeal?

There was no answer to this question, not that night, nor at any time during the next seventeen days, which was the duration of the trip. But soon, in any case, they forgot to wonder about it: they had enough to

deal with, in the simple course of nature. The second day saw them make
more tangible progress, northwest between Scotland and Northern
Ireland; and nightfall gave them, as their last sight of land, the lovely
rain-washed hills of the Mull of Kintyre, and Islay away to the north.
Then they turned due westwards, to the open sea and the teeth of the
wind, and the deep-sea voyage had begun. As a final introduction to it,
U-boats were reported in the area immediately ahead.

They never met those U-boats, which were doubtless thankful enough
to stay submerged and escape the fury of the weather; for it was the
weather which was the most violent enemy of all. For eight days they
steamed straight into a westerly gale: five hundred miles at a grindingly
slow pace, buffeting through a weight of wind which seemed to have a
personal spite in every blow it dealt. The convoy was dispersed over
more than fifty square miles: the escorts were out of touch most of the
time; it was impossible to establish any sort of 'convoy speed' because
they were no longer a composite body, just a lot of ships making the best
they could of the vile Atlantic weather. The big ships in the van slowed
down, till they had almost lost steerage way, and tried to preserve some
sort of order; but the smaller ones still straggled away behind, virtually
heaving-to at the height of the gale and often having to steer many
degrees off their true course, simply in order not to batter themselves to
pieces. On the eighth day *Viperous*, which had had a very bad time and
had lost two men overboard, signalled 'Convoy disperse – proceed
independently': in the circumstances, the signal had an irony which they
were scarcely in the mood to enjoy.

The escorts collected: *Viperous* with damage to her bridge-
superstructure, the old corvette minus one of her boats, *Compass Rose*
intact but rolling villainously, the trawler riding well, the tug tossing
about with a ludicrous, almost hysterical violence as she tried to keep
pace with the rest. They had a rendezvous with the incoming convoy,
and they found it – somehow: in the wilderness of wind and rain, with
visibility hardly more than five hundred yards at any time, they found
the single pin-point in mid-Atlantic which brought them up with the
ships they were waiting for. It was navigation of a very high order: it had
been *Viperous'* responsibility, and Ericson, with years of experience
behind him, found himself watching *Viperous'* bridge rolling through a
sixty-degree arc, and wondering, somewhere between amazement and
deep admiration, how on earth her Captain had managed it. Taking
sights and fixing their position, under these conditions, was very nearly
impossible: somehow it had been done, and done with the absolute
accuracy of fleet-manoeuvres in calm weather.

They turned for home, with the new convoy of thirty-odd ships which,
in the better weather to the westward, had managed to preserve a
reasonable formation. But now, with the fierce wind behind them, it was

more uncomfortable still; and another U-boat alarm involved 'evasive routine' which took them many miles off their proper course and kept them nearly two days extra at sea. Aboard *Compass Rose*, conditions were indescribable. She rolled furiously, with a tireless malice allowing of no rest for anyone. Cooking was impossible, even had they not exhausted their fresh meat and vegetables many days previously: the staple diet was tea and corned beef, at breakfast, lunch, and dinner, for nearly a fortnight on end. Everything was wet through: some water had come down a ventilator and flooded the wardroom: forward, the messdecks were a crowded hell of saturated clothes, spare gear washing about round their feet, food overturned – and all the time the noise, the groaning slamming violence of a small ship fighting a monstrous sea. There seemed no end to it. *Compass Rose*, caught in a storm which could take hold of her bodily and shake her till the very rivets loosened: a storm which raged and screamed at her and never blew itself out until they were in the shelter of the land again: *Compass Rose*, adrift on this malignant ocean, seemed doomed to ride it for ever.

. . .

Bennett, disliking the experience they were all sharing, said so with honest persistence. He was now the most vocal of the wardroom, complaining with an ill-temper coloured by a real uneasiness: the rotten ship, the lousy convoy, the bloody awful weather – there were the sinews of an unending dirge which was really grounded in fear. Like the others, he had never seen weather like this, nor imagined it possible: he knew enough about ships to see that *Compass Rose* was going through a desperate ordeal, but not enough to realize that she was built to survive it, and would do so. He doubted their safety, and doubt was translated by a natural process into anger. He had, too, made a fool of himself over working out their position – so much so that the Captain, taking the sextant from him, had said: 'Leave it, Number One – I'd rather do it myself': it had not helped matters.

He should have done something about getting the mess cleared up in the fo'c'sle, but he couldn't be bothered. He should somehow have organized at least one hot meal a day, even if it were only warmed-up tinned beans: the galley fire was unusable, but with a little ingenuity it could have been done in the engine-room. This, again, was more trouble than he was prepared to take. Instead, he sulked, and shirked, and secretly longed to be out of it.

Not much more of this for him, he decided: there were other ways of winning the war ... It was all so tiring, too: if he hadn't been able to hand the watch over to Lockhart, and get forty winks now and again, he'd have been out on his feet.

Lockhart was desperately tired, and rather numbed, for nearly all that voyage. His thin wiry body was not built to withstand the cold: he was not yet accustomed to staying awake and alert, when every nerve under his skin was crying out for sleep; and bitter cold and wakefulness were all that the present offered. Bennett might shirk his watch, spending most of it inside the Asdic shelter: he himself could not do so. Four hours on, and four off, for seventeen days at a stretch – that was his share: and the hours 'on' were an unending strain, trying his eyes and his tired body to the limit. And when he stumbled down the ladder at the end of his watch, there was little relief to be had: tea and corned beef in the shambles of the wardroom, with water washing about all over the place and the furniture lashed together in one corner, and then the effort to sleep, wedged in his bunk against the endless rolling of the ship, with the light left burning in case of an alarm, and the thought, nagging all the time, that he must get up and face the wind and the sea again, within a few hours. When he *did* face it again, and felt the gale whipping and tearing at his face and clothes, and *Compass Rose* lurching under his feet as if the world itself were drunk, it was with a body from which every instinct save a dumb endurance had been drained.

There was one night he remembered especially, towards the end of the trip, when the wind had veered to the north and the gale was at its height. A gigantic sea was running at them from the beam: *Compass Rose* would rise to it as if she were going up in a lift, balance herself uneasily at its peak, and then fall away into the trough of the wave with a wicked sideways roll. Sometimes the next wave, towering up in its turn, would catch them as they lay there sluggishly and beat down on them before they could rise. That was the moment when the heart quailed: when solid tons of water fell with a thunderous drumming on the bridge and the upper deck, and the spray flew over in clouds, wind-driven and cutting. The storm was indeed incredibly noisy: the water crashed and thudded against their side, the wind howled at them out of the blackness as if it had a conscious intention of terror. Round them was nothing but a waste of sea, a livid grey whipped up here and there to white foam; and then beyond it, like a threatening wall, the surrounding dark, the chaos and flurry of the night.

With Bennett dozing inside, Lockhart was clinging to the rail in one corner of the bridge, staring through misted binoculars at the single merchant-ship on which he was keeping station. He was wet through, and cold to the bone: his feet inside the sodden sea-boots squelched icily whenever he moved: from the pinched skin of his face the water ran down, riming his eyes and lips with salt. He felt little resentment against Bennett, who should really be doing this job: he had a general disgust that someone nominally his senior should be content to evade responsibility at a moment like this, but he was really feeling too remote from personalities to care. For him, the world had resolved itself into a storm, and a small blur to leeward of *Compass Rose*: the blur was a ship which he must not lose, and so, for hour after hour, he nursed *Compass Rose* in her station, altering the engine-revolutions, edging over when the blur faded, and away again when it loomed too large.

He was roused at one point from this tremendous concentration by someone nudging him, and he turned round to see a figure in the darkness beside him.

'Who is it?' he asked. It could hardly be Bennett.

'Coxswain, sir,' said a voice.

'Hallo, Coxswain! Come to see the fun?'

'Just for a bit of air, sir.'

They both had to shout: the wind caught the words on their very lips and whipped them away into the night.

'I brought a mug of tea up, sir,' Tallow went on. And as Lockhart took it gratefully, he added: 'It's got a tot in it.'

Tea and rum ... When Lockhart bent down to shelter behind the rail, and took a sip, it ran through him like fire: it was the finest drink he had ever tasted. He was oddly moved that Tallow should have taken the trouble to make tea at two o'clock in the morning, add a tot of his own rum, and negotiate the difficult climb up to the bridge with it. He could not see Tallow's face, but he divined a sympathy in his manner which was nearly as warming as the drink.

'Thanks, Coxswain,' he said when he had finished it. 'I needed that.' He raised his binoculars again, confirmed that *Compass Rose* was still in station, and relaxed slightly. 'What's it like below?'

'Terrible, sir. Couldn't be worse. It'll take us a week to get straight after this lot.'

'Not much longer,' said Lockhart, though he did not feel that very acutely. 'Two or three days, and we'll be in shelter.'

'Can't be soon enough for me, sir. Proper uproar, this is. A lot of the lads wish they'd joined the Army instead.'

They talked till the end of the watch, shouting at each other against the storm. Lockhart was glad of the company: it was a tiny spark of warmth and feeling in a furious and inhuman onslaught. They would need a lot of that, if the Atlantic were going to serve them like this in the future.

. . .

Physically, Ferraby was in a worse way than any of them. He had been acutely sea-sick during most of the voyage, but he never gave in to it: always, when it was time for him to go on watch, he would drag himself up the ladder, his face the colour of a dirty handkerchief, and somehow last out the four hours on the bridge. Then he would stumble below again, and force himself to eat, and be sick once more, and lie down on his bunk, waiting for sleep to blot out the clamour of the storm, and his misery with it. Often sleep would not come, and he lay awake throughout his time off watch. Those were the worst moments of all, when doubt as to whether he could go on with this job pressed on his consciousness like a living weight of guilt.

Towards the end, the strain nearly proved too much for him. This was particularly so when he had to go on watch at night, after an hour or so of sleep snatched in the stuffy heaving cabin. He would get into his sea-boots and duffle-coat, listening to the sounds of the storm outside, and the thud of water hitting the side of the ship and the deck overhead. Then he climbed slowly up the ladder, tired beyond belief, fearing the wind and the misery waiting for him up on the bridge: watching the square of dark sky at the entrance above him, to see if the gale were passing. He was very weak, and without any will except to last out this watch, and the next one, and a few more until they made harbour. Once, he stopped halfway up the ladder, and found himself crying. 'Mavis,' he said – and went on, as if his wife had answered him from somewhere up above.

He bore his ordeal alone, bravely: his set white face invited nothing save the kindness of ignoring it. He did not give in, because to fail to go on watch, to confess his defeat, would have been worse than any sea-sickness, any fatigue, any wind or rain or fury. There was no way out that was not shameful; and that was no way out.

.   .   .

The Captain carried them all.

For him, there was no fixed watch, no time set aside when he was free to relax and, if he could, to sleep. He had to control everything, to drive the whole ship himself: he had to act on signals, to fix their position, to keep his section of the convoy together, to use his seamanship so as to ease *Compass Rose*'s ordeal as much as possible. He was a tower of strength, holding everything together by sheer unrelenting guts. The sight of the tall tough figure hunched in one corner of the bridge now seemed essential to them all: they needed the tremendous reassurance of his presence, and so he gave it unstintingly, even though the hours without sleep mounted to a fantastic total.

He was tired – he could not remember ever having been so tired – but he knew that he was not too tired: there were always reserves . . . It was part of the job of being Captain, the reverse side of the prestige and the respect and the saluting: the tiny ship, the inexperienced officers, the unbelievable weather – he had taken these on as well, and they would not defeat him. So he dealt with everything that came, assuming all cares out of an overflowing strength: he was a professional – the only one among amateurs who might in the future become considerable assets to him but at the moment were not very much help – and the professional job, at sea, was not without its rewarding pride. It had to be done, anyway: he was the man to do it, and there was no choice and no two answers.

They grew, almost, to love him, towards the end of the voyage: he was strong, calm, uncomplaining, and wonderfully dependable. This was the sort of Captain to have: *Compass Rose* could have done with nothing less, and *Compass Rose*, butting her patient way homewards under the blows of the cruel sea, was lucky to have him.

.   .   .

No voyage can last for ever, save for ships that are sunk: this voyage ran its course, and presently released them. There came an afternoon – the afternoon of the sixteenth day – when the horizon ahead was not level, but uneven; not the pale grey of the sky, but the darker shadow that was the land. The foothills of Scotland came up suddenly, beckoning them onwards: their rolling lessened as they came under the lee of the northern coastline: presently, towards dusk, they were in shelter, and running down towards the home port that promised them rest and peace at last. It was difficult to realize that the worst was over, and that *Compass Rose*, on a steady keel, could become warm and dry again: it was difficult to believe in the relaxation that had been so relentlessly denied them. It must be an illusion, or a swindle: probably the Irish Sea would open up at the other end, and they would find themselves in deep water once more, fighting another round of the same exhausting battle. They had been on trial for so long that the acquittal did not seem to ring true.

So the first convoy ended. It had been a shock – the more so because of the doubt, in the background, as to how they would fare in action with U-boats, if action were added to so startling an ordeal. But they did not think of this straightaway: that night, tied up alongside the oiler after seventeen days of strain, they were all so utterly exhausted that a dead and dreamless sleep was all they were fit for.

CHAPTER 3

It seemed that they were to be stationed permanently at Liverpool, and there they settled down, as part of the Liverpool Escort Force which was gradually being built up. The centre of naval activity was Gladstone Dock, down river and away from the town: it was already crowded with destroyers and sloops, and the corvettes which were now beginning to leave the shipyards in substantial numbers. The forest of masts, the naval parties moving on the dockside, and the huts and store-rooms put up for their use, were all heartening symptoms of a growing escort strength; but they were matched by a steady increase in the number and size of convoys, which made demands on the naval potential almost impossible to meet. It was clear that many chances would have to be taken with the safety of merchant-ships, for a long time to come.

Among the corvettes to arrive at Liverpool was *Sorrel*, who, delayed at Ardnacraish by some clash with the Admiral which she was not particularly ready to discuss, joined her sister ship soon after their second convoy.

Ericson was not notably pleased that *Compass Rose* was based on Liverpool; in fact he was inclined to resent the fact, without being too sure why. The theory was admirable: they came in from a convoy, and there was Grace, knitting away in her little house across the river and waiting for him. But it was an undeniable distraction, at a time when he wanted to concentrate exclusively on the ship: and, in some indistinct way, it seemed to be cheating – he had embraced a hard life and an exacting job, and here now was another embrace, to make things pleasant after all ... He could not have said why he found that wrong, and certainly he never hinted anything of the sort to her; but it was a fact that he preferred to live on board when they were in harbour, and was faintly irritated at having to find excuses for doing so.

The man it suited most was Tallow: his home also was in Birkenhead, just over the river from Gladstone Dock, and he had no false notions as to the relative comforts of *Compass Rose* and No. 29 Dock Road ... It was a home he shared with his widowed sister Gladys, who had kept house for him ever since her husband died, four or five years previously: whenever he came back on leave, his room was waiting for him, and a cheerful welcome as well. Gladys Bell (Bell had been a postman) worked in a Liverpool office, supplementing a tiny pension: she was fortyish, plain, good-natured, and she and Tallow got on very well together, in an undemanding sort of way. He had hoped that she would marry again, even though he would lose thereby; but there had never been any sign of it, and by and by the idea ceased to worry him. If a decent widowhood suited her, it certainly suited him.

When he went round to the house on their second night in harbour, and walked into the tiny gas-lit kitchen with a 'Well, Glad!' which had been his greeting ever since she could remember, her plain sallow face lighted up at the surprise. She had not seen him for six months.

'Bob! Where've you sprung from, lad?'

'We're in for a bit,' he said, 'It's our home port – couldn't be better.'

'Well, that's nice.' Her mind darted immediately to the larder, wondering what she could give him on his first night ashore. 'Have you had your tea?'

'Tea?' He smiled mockingly. 'Have you ever known me have my tea on board, when I can get your cooking just by crossing the river?'

There was a hesitant cough behind him in the doorway.

'Oh,' said Tallow awkwardly. 'Brought a friend, Glad. Chief E.R.A. Watts. Same ship.'

'Come into the front,' she said, when they had shaken hands and mumbled to each other. 'This kitchen's not fit to be seen.'

In the front parlour, she lit the gas: the overcrowded room sprang to life, as if the hissing noise had been a stage-direction. (It was the best part of the shabby old house, carefully cleaned and cherished: the creaking wing-chairs were comfortable, the mahogany table sat four-square and solid in the middle, the ornaments were mostly souvenirs brought home by Tallow himself, from Gibraltar and Hong Kong and Alexandria. Lace curtains gave them a genteel privacy, at the cost of three-quarters of the available light: from the mantelpiece, Tom Bell the postman regarded them importantly, as if he carried registered letters for each one of them.)

Gladys turned from the flaring gas-light, and looked at the two men with pleasure. They were both very smart – spotless jackets, gold badges, knife-edge creases to their trousers: she found herself wondering, not for the first time, how they managed to keep their clothes so nice, in the cramped quarters on board.

'How's the new ship?' she asked her brother.

The two men exchanged glances, before Tallow answered:

'She'll never live to be old, I'd say.'

Watts laughed, scratching his bald head. 'That's about the size of it, Mrs Bell. We've had a rare trip, I can tell you.'

'Was it rough?'

'Rough as I've ever known it,' said Tallow. 'We were chucked about like – like——' He sought for a suitable simile, and failed. 'Remember I wrote you how small she was? I didn't tell you the half of it. We were standing on our heads most of the time.'

'What about those submarines?'

'*We* were the submarine, I should say.' Watts, warming to the friendly atmosphere, chipped in with a readiness rare to him. 'Never got our heads above water for days on end. Must be the new secret weapon – the corvette that swims under-water.'

Gladys clicked her lips. 'Well, I never . . . You must be ready for a bit of a rest.'

'I'm ready for a pint,' said Tallow with alacrity. 'How about it, Glad? Anything in the larder?'

She shook her head. 'I wasn't expecting you, Bob. Why not walk round to the Three Tuns while I'm getting the tea?'

Tallow cocked his eye at Watts. 'What d'you say?'

Watts nodded. 'Suits me.'

'Half an hour,' said Gladys firmly. 'Not a minute more, otherwise it'll spoil.'

'What are you going to give us?'

'Never you mind.'

They collected their caps, and made for the door gradually, like boys preparing to play truant and pretending to do something else. She watched them amusedly as they sidled out. Men ... But it sounded as if they'd earned it. She went through to the kitchen and made ready, happily, to welcome them back as they deserved. Later, in the cosy parlour with a big fire going, they all enjoyed themselves: the two men talked of the trip, and of other trips, while she sat back and listened to them, and threw in an occasional comment. She did not like the sound of *Compass Rose*; but when she said so, bluntly, they were curiously quick to put in a good word for the ship, to make excuses for this and explain away that. Men, again ... But it was good to have them there, and to know that they were relaxed and happy, after the hard times.

. . .

As soon as they got in at the end of their first trip, Ericson applied for another officer to be appointed to the ship; it was clear that there was far too much work for a First Lieutenant and two subs to handle, leaving out of account the chance that accident or illness might make them more short-handed still. He presented a good case, arguing the matter first with a faintly supercilious staff officer who seemed to think that corvettes were some kind of local defence vessel, and then incorporating his arguments in a formal submission to the Admiralty: it must have been an effective document, since Their Lordships acted on it within three weeks. Sub-Lieutenant Morell, they said, was appointed to *Compass Rose*, 'additional for watch-keeping duties'; Sub-Lieutenant Morell would join them forthwith.

Morell arrived, fresh from the training establishment, accompanied by an astonishing amount of luggage: he was a very proper young man, so correct and so assured that it appeared fantastic for him to grace anything so crude as a corvette. In peace-time he was a junior barrister, a product of the other London which was so great a contrast to the bohemian world that Lockhart knew and worked in: Lockhart, indeed, could only imagine him in black coat and pin-stripe trousers, moving from his chambers in Lincoln's Inn to a sedate lunch-party at the Savoy, or later, impeccably tail-coated, squiring the least impulsive of the season's débutantes to Ciro's or the Embassy. He was grave, slow-moving, and exceedingly courteous: in his brand-new and beautifully-cut uniform he seemed far better suited to a diplomatic salon than to *Compass Rose*'s rough-and-ready wardroom. He was a living reproof to the solecism of displaying emotion. He was, inevitably, an Old Wykehamist.

He and Bennett could hardly be expected to mix. On the first evening, at dinner, Morell watched, with an expression of disbelief which Lockhart found ludicrous, as Bennett greeted the tinned sausages with his usual salute, tucked his napkin under his chin, and fell to on this deplorable dish. Morell offered no comment, but it was clear that the scene had made an impression: later, when he and Lockhart were alone in the wardroom, he remarked: 'I understand the First Lieutenant comes from one of the Dominions,' with an absence of expression which was itself the best substitute for it.

'Australia,' answered Lockhart, himself non-committal.

'Ah ... I have met one or two Australians – usually the victims of confidence tricksters. We can never persuade them that in London they are likely to encounter people with sharper wits than their own.'

'It's amazing how people still fall for that sort of thing.'

'It is not amazing,' said Morell, after reflection. 'But it is, at least, continually strange ... Do we often have tinned sausages for dinner, by the way?'

'Very often.'

'Whether this war is long or short,' said Morell, after reflecting again, 'it is going to *seem* long.'

That was the only comment he made which could have been construed as any kind of criticism. But in spite of this discretion, he must have come into early collision with Bennett: next afternoon, when work was over, he sought out Lockhart and asked him, with some formality, for guidance.

'The First Lieutenant used an expression which is novel to me,' he began, 'I wish you'd explain what it means.'

'What was it?' asked Lockhart, with an equal gravity.

'He said – ah – "Don't come the acid with me".' Morell screwed up his eyes. '"Come the acid" ... I must confess I have not heard that before.'

'What were you talking about?'

'We were discussing the best way of dismantling the firing-bar on the Asdic set.' He paused. 'That's not too technical for you?'

'No,' said Lockhart. 'But it may have been too technical for Bennett. He's been trained in a rough school.'

'That may well be the case ... So "coming the acid" ...'

'It means that you probably corrected him without wrapping it up enough.'

Morell smiled: it was the first time Lockhart had seen him do so. 'I could hardly have been more diplomatic.'

'You must have overdone it, then.'

The other man sighed. 'How strange to meet Scylla and Charybdis in Atlantic waters ... Perhaps I should explain the allusion. There were——'

'Do not,' said Lockhart, with a fair approximation of Bennett's accent, 'come the acid with me.'

'Ah!' exclaimed Morell. 'Now I understand.'

They both laughed. Lockhart was glad that Morell had joined them: he promised to enliven the wardroom, though with little intention of so doing, and the wardroom could do with all the enlivenment possible.

. . .

Lockhart himself had his own collision with Bennett soon afterwards. A new Admiralty Fleet Order decreed that sub-lieutenants over twenty-eight years of age, with three months' sea service to their credit, were eligible for a second stripe, if they got the necessary recommendation from their commanding officers; but when, at the due time, he put in his application through the usual channels – Bennett – he met such a barrage of scorn and sarcasm that he could hardly keep his temper.

'Jesus Christ, Sub!' said Bennett. 'You must be round the bend. Who's going to recommend you for lieutenant, after a couple of convoys?'

'I hope the Captain,' answered Lockhart evenly. 'It's within the regulations – it's on age as well as sea-time.'

'Think you're fit to take my job, eh?'

Lockhart said nothing.

'Well, I don't,' Bennett went on after a pause. 'Not for a hell of a long time, either.' He fingered the sheet of paper, on which Lockhart had set out his application in the formal language the occasion demanded. 'I can't sign this bloody thing,' he said peevishly. 'It's much too early. Let it stand over for a bit.'

'I want it to go to the Captain,' said Lockhart stubbornly.

'Well, I don't.'

'You can't refuse.'

'I can do any——thing I like,' Bennett flared up. 'You bloody kids make me sick, putting in for promotion before you've hardly got your uniforms. I suppose Ferraby 'll be along next, wanting my job too.'

'One thing at a time,' said Lockhart, angry in his turn. 'That's *my* application. It's in accordance with the A.F.O. Are you going to put it through?'

Bennett tried to stall. He really had no authority to hold up the application: he was simply extracting the maximum unpleasantness out of it. He said: 'I'll see about it. There's no rush.'

'I want it to go to the Admiralty before we sail again.'

'What makes you think the skipper will recommend you?' sneered Bennett. 'Been doing a bit of crawling?'

'No more than you,' said Lockhart curtly.

The wrangle, far from edifying, continued on these lines till Bennett, with a singular ill-grace, agreed to forward the application. In the end it went through, with Ericson's recommendation, and Lockhart got his promotion. Thereafter Bennett addressed him always, with thick irony, as '*Lieutenant* Lockhart'. But that did not matter at all: he was a step farther on his way, and the way itself was beginning to seem clearer.

CHAPTER 4

The first few convoys followed the pattern of their initiation. They still worked with *Viperous* as leader of the group, which had been strengthened by *Sorrel* joining it: they were still, as a fighting escort, untried by the enemy. There were submarines about – other convoys kept running into them – but so far their luck had held: the log recorded no shot-in-anger, only a succession of comments on the weather. This, at least, continued to put *Compass Rose* to the test: whatever the season, it seemed that the Atlantic could never wholly abandon its mood of violence.

But the longer days of spring and early summer did, in fact, afford them some relief: watch-keeping by day was certainly less of a strain, whatever antics the ship was going through. They were now divided into three watches, four hours on duty and eight off: Bennett and Lockhart were both on their own, and Morell and Ferraby shared the third watch together. The eight hours off duty were so great an advantage, bringing them fresh to their watch, that it was almost impossible to believe that they had once done without them. Certainly the new arrangements suited Ericson, who could now sleep most of the long day and be available, comparatively rested, at any time during the night. Of his watch-keeping officers, he found that Bennett was all right as long as nothing unexpected happened: that Lockhart was completely trustworthy, and not afraid to call him in good time to deal with any crisis: and that Morell and Ferraby, between them, added up to something like a dependable pair of hands and eyes. He could hardly expect more, from this cheerfully amateur collection.

But the nights were still a strain and a challenge to them all, whether the enemy were near or far. 'Darken Ship' was piped at sunset each day: from that moment, no glimmer of light must show either in the convoy or among the escort – the faintest gleam might beckon a submarine which otherwise would have no suspicion that ships were in its area. That moment when they drew the covers on was always significant: usually there had been some sort of U-boat warning during the day, and if other convoys were running into trouble it must, sooner or later, be their own turn. Thus there would be a feeling throughout the ship, each time dusk fell, that they were approaching uncertainty again, extending the chances of action: from then on, at any moment, there *might* be a U-boat sniffing the air a few miles off, there *might* be a torpedo track, there *might* be a bang close by them – or even in their own guts. The canvas-screens were drawn across the entrances, the lights were dimmed inside, the galley-fire damped down: *Compass Rose*, steaming through the cold evening air towards a horizon barely distinguishable from the sky, became a grey shadow clinging to other shadows which she must not lose. In thick weather, when the moon was down, to keep their correct station on the convoy as it hurried through the essential darkness was a strain on the attention and the eyesight which left them, at the end of their four hours, exhausted and blinking with fatigue. But if they lost the convoy, or got grossly out of station, the price was not simply a red face in the morning: it might be a U-boat piercing the gap they had left, and lives and ships on their conscience.

There were other cares at night, complicating a plain effort of seamanship. The current orders were that escorts were to zigzag, so that they could move faster and lessen the chance of being hit themselves; it was a sensible precaution, and one they all approved of, but a zigzag on a pitch-black night, with thirty ships in close contact adding the risk of collision to the difficulty of hanging onto the convoy, was something more than a few lines in a Fleet Order. Lockhart, who now kept a permanent middle watch – midnight to four a.m. – and on whom the brunt of the dark hours fell, evolved his own method. He took *Compass Rose* out obliquely from the convoy for a set number of minutes: very soon, of course, he could not see the other ships, and might have had the whole Atlantic to himself, but that was part of the manoeuvre. Then he turned, and ran back the same number of minutes on the corresponding course inwards: at the end, he should be in touch with the convoy again, and in the same relative position.

It was an act of faith which continued to justify itself, but it was sometimes a little hard on the nerves. He once had a nightmare, and later evolved a fairy story, in which *Compass Rose*, steaming towards the convoy again on the inward course, never met it: she went on and on, over a blank dark sea which presently paled with the daylight, and there was never a ship in sight ... And once the Captain had come up, when they were at the very limit of the outward leg and out of touch with the convoy, and had looked about him as if he could scarcely believe his eyes.

'Where are they, Lockhart?' he asked with a certain grimness.

Lockhart pointed. 'There, sir ... We're on the outer zigzag,' he added, to justify a blank horizon. 'We'll meet them again in seven minutes.'

Ericson grunted. It was not a reassuring sound, and Lockhart, counting the minutes, wondered what on earth he was going to say if this time his nightmare came true. When at last the ships came up again, black and solid, he had a surge of relief, which he felt the Captain was aware of.

'Zigzagging on time?' said Ericson curtly.

'Yes, sir.'

'Check your course each time you alter. Don't leave it to the quartermaster – he might make a mistake.' Then he walked off the bridge without further comment. That was what Lockhart liked about the Captain: if he trusted you, he showed it – he didn't fiddle about in the background, pretending to do something else, and all the time watching you like a nursemaid. And he was quite entitled to be worried, and to ask questions when he felt like it: if they did lose the convoy, whichever one of them was responsible, it was, as far as the official record went, the Captain's fault.

What Lockhart found especially annoying was handing over his watch to Bennett. By tradition, the First Lieutenant had the morning watch – four a.m. to eight: Bennett followed the custom as far as the actual time went, but in other respects he scarcely justified his position. It was mortifying to cling onto the convoy all through the middle watch, keeping exact station and a fast, accurate zigzag, and hand over *Compass Rose* in a pin-point position at the end of it; and then to hear, as he left the bridge, Bennett saying: 'Signalman! See that ship there? Tell me if we start to lose her,' and then settling down inside the Asdic hut. One of these days, thought Lockhart, they might all forfeit their lives, simply because Bennett had a dislike of fresh air. But it was hardly a matter he could complain of, officially. It would have to wait till the Captain took notice of it.

. . .

At this stage – still unwarlike, still a tame apprenticeship – they found hardest to bear the monotony of rolling, with, as an occasional variant, the shuddering crunch with which *Compass Rose* greeted a head sea. The rolling affected every single thing they did, on watch or off. Often they had to cling to the bridge-rail for hours at a stretch, and cold, while the ship disgraced herself with a tireless forty-degree roll; and then, off-watch and supposedly resting, they had to eat their meals with the food continually slopping into their laps, and the wardroom furniture creaking and sliding and occasionally breaking adrift altogether and hurtling across the room. They were always being hurt, in spite of a continual watchfulness: doorways hit them as they were leaving their cabins: they were thrown out of their bunks as soon as sleep relaxed their tense care, and all round them on the floor would be books and papers and boots and clothes, which some especially violent roll had released from control.

It was tremendously exhausting, this never being able to rest without something going wrong, something hitting them, something coming adrift and breaking, or making a noisy clatter for hour after hour. There was a damnable rhythm about the movement: they got tired of it, they got tired of always hanging onto something, they got tired of paying for a moment's forgetfulness with bruised legs and shoulders, cut lips, wrenched ankles. But they could not escape it: it was an inherent element in going to sea in corvettes. Sometimes, up on the bridge, they would watch *Sorrel* being chucked about like a cork, and the spray going over as she punched her way through a rough sea, and they would think how tough she looked, and what a pretty picture, handsome and determined, she made. It was a pity that the reality, in *Sorrel* as in *Compass Rose*, was so infinitely unpleasant.

One of their convoys, about this time, was a classic in this respect. After nine days on the outward trip, they had turned for home, with some hope of making a quick passage and getting back in less than a week. It did not work that way ... The gale which sprang up did more than scatter the convoy: it kept every single ship in it hove-to for two days on end, waiting for the weather to moderate. In those two days, *Compass Rose* covered eighteen miles – sideways, and due south: she spent them in company with a small merchant-ship which had engine trouble and asked for someone to stay with her. For all the forty-eight hours, *Compass Rose* circled very slowly round the derelict, taking three hours to complete each circuit, moving with agonizing slowness against the mountainous seas and rolling, rolling, rolling all the time as if she wanted to tear her mast out.

They lost one of their boats, which went clean under a huge wave and never came up again: they lost some oil-drums which were stowed aft: they lost their patience many times, but patience had to return, and sweat it out to the end ... When the storm finally blew itself away, they spent another twenty-four hours hunting for the convoy and reassembling it. They were at sea for twenty-two days on that trip: at the end, *Compass Rose*, and her crew with her, looked as if they had all been through the same tidal wave, emerging in tatters at the end of it.

.   .   .

They found, on all their convoys, that the food soon became intolerably coarse and dull. *Compass Rose* carried enough fresh meat, bread, and vegetables for five days: after that, their diet was the same dreary procession of tinned sausages, tinned stew, hard biscuit, and tea. (The tinned stew came in an ornate container labelled 'Old Mother Jameson's Farm House Dinner'. Said Morell, surveying the dubious mixture on his plate: 'I must remember *never* to go to dinner at Mrs Jameson's).' It was enough to support life, and that was all one could say about it: since they ate these horrible meals in a wardroom which was sooner or later flooded out or, at the best, ran with sweat throughout the voyage, the pleasures of the table in *Compass Rose* never threatened to seduce them from their duty.

They found, all the same, that there were times when they could still relax – that some moments at sea were enchanting. Now and again, an afternoon watch on the bridge would prove so perfect a way of passing the time that it seemed almost ludicrous for them to be paid for it. The convoy was in formation, and not menaced by U-boats: the hot spring sunshine poured down from a flawless sky: the brave ships advanced in line leaving behind them, like *Compass Rose*, a broad white sparkling wake that meant a smooth passage and a day nearer home. On the bridge, there was nothing to do but check the change of course as they zigzagged, and keep an eye on *Viperous* in case she woke early from her afternoon siesta: for the rest, it was warmth, cool clean air, a steady ship under one's feet, and an occasional sound – a gramophone, the swish of a hose, the clang of an emptied bucket – to prove that *Compass Rose* carried nearly ninety men on this prosperous voyage.

They found that some nights, especially, had a peaceful loveliness that repaid a hundred hours of strain. Sometimes, in sheltered water, when the moon was full, they moved with the convoy past hills outlined against the pricking stars: slipping under the very shadow of these cliffs, their keel divided the phosphorescent water into a gleaming wake that curled away till it was caught and held in the track of the moon. It was then that the watches went pleasantly, with the night air playing round the ship like the music of Prospero's Isle: Morell and Ferraby would talk idly of their homes, or Lockhart and Wells, sharing a later watch, would make it go swiftly in reminiscence and conjecture. These magic nights, unmarred by fatigue or any alarm, were very few: when they were granted, their sweetness remained for long afterwards. Once or twice, Ericson, coming up to the bridge in the early hours of the morning, would find it, and the whole ship, so peaceful and so softly lapped by darkness, that it was hard to recall the purpose of their voyage. *Compass Rose*, afloat on a calm sea, seemed to shed every attribute save a gentle assurance of refuge.

They found, to meet those other nights which were so brutal and so prolonged, that they were toughening up. They became cunning at anticipating what the next big sea would do to the ship, and expert at avoiding its consequences: to hang on as they moved from place to place, to wedge themselves so that even the relaxation of sleep would not dislodge them, to keep themselves warm, and their clothes waterproof – these were lessons which the harsh school drove home until they were ingrained. Even the lack of sleep was less damaging now: they developed the facility of snatching odd moments of it whenever possible, and for the rest they could, if need be, stay awake for an astonishing number of hours without losing the edge of alertness. The process of accepting the hard necessities of their life meant that much of their normal feeling was blunted: Lockhart, finding himself one evening discarding the volume of essays he had bought before sailing in favour of the crudest and most trivial of the current magazines, thought, with faint alarm: hell, I'm getting as bad as Bennett . . . But it was, in a sense, true, and necessary as well: the time for sensibility was past, gentleness was out-dated, and feeling need not come again till the unfeeling job was over.

They found, above all, that one part of every trip could be actively enjoyed: the last day of it, when they were in sheltered water and getting ready for their return to harbour. Now was the time when, running down the Irish Sea and making the last turn for home, they set to work to tidy up the ship after the chaos of the voyage; portholes were opened to the cleansing breeze, wet clothes stripped off and hung out to dry, the furniture and the tables and stools in the messdecks released from their lashings and set out properly. The sun gleamed on the saturated decks, and dried them off swiftly, leaving a rime of salt: round the bows, the porpoises and the seagulls played, crossing and recrossing their pathway as if clearing a way of welcome for them.

The convoy, the line of ships they had been guarding for so long, began the last mile of its journey, up river to the docks; deep-laden, crammed to the decks with cargo, immensely worthwhile, it struck a note of thankful pride as it was safely delivered. The escorts parted, steaming in single file past their charges and farther up river. For them, at last, here was the haven where they would be; peace alongside the oiler, the mail coming aboard, hot baths, clean clothes, rest and sleep after many days and nights had denied them all these things.

CHAPTER 5

Suddenly it was time for their first spell of leave: six days, for half the ship's company and all the officers save one, so that *Compass Rose* could have her boilers cleaned and a few small repairs carried out. It was their first break since the ship was commissioned, five months previously; they felt that they had earned it, and Ericson, while not encouraging them in this view, privately admitted that they were right.

He himself, sitting opposite Grace in a comfortable armchair for six successive evenings, could not get used to the stillness of the house. Aboard *Compass Rose* there was always something stirring: even when she was in harbour, there were engine-room fans and dynamos going all the time, there was the quartermaster clumping round the upper deck, there were signals coming down, and the noise of Morse from the W/T office, and the wardroom radio doing its best to cheer the lonely-hearted sailors, cradled in the deep of Gladstone Dock. Here there was nothing, save the click of Grace's knitting needles and the rustle of coal in the grate. Her mother had postponed her visit, though she might descend on them in the near future: John, their son, was away at sea – Ericson still had not managed to meet him since *Compass Rose* was commissioned, even though they went in and out of the same port. So, in the silent house, they sat opposite each other. To Grace, it was nothing out of the ordinary: to Ericson himself, it was an unsettling contrast with what must be his true habit of life.

There were other things he could not get used to. It was a woman's house, soft and rather frilly: the cushions multiplied on the sofa, the ornaments were brittle and inescapably gay, the tablecloth was a lace affair that caught against his hands whenever he moved them. He felt out of place: he felt as if he were somehow breaking training, at a time when a hard austerity was the essential choice. Sleeping with Grace in the big double-bed upstairs had an indulgence, an added warmth, which he did not really want to enjoy. She was his wife, but to lie with her, even in passive sleep, had a sensual element which betrayed his instinct for celibacy.

If she was aware of this subtle withdrawal, she gave no sign: for very many years she had taken things at their face value, her husband included, and a war was not the time to question what lay below the surface of any reasonable relationship.

'You're restless, George,' she said, one night when he had tossed and turned till past midnight, and finally woken her from a comfortable dream. 'Can't you get to sleep?'

'It's the bed,' he answered irritably. 'I can't get used to it.'

'I thought sailors could sleep anywhere.' Between waking and sleeping, her common sense had a fugitive quality which occasionally betrayed her into flippancy. Ordinarily, she would never have made so derivative a comment.

'This one can't.'

'Shall I make some tea?'

'No thank you.'

Now that he had woken her, he wanted nothing except that she should go to sleep again, and leave him to his isolation. The longer they talked, in this intimate setting, the deeper he was involved in a softer world which might destroy his resolute spirit. Even in peace-time, he had sometimes resented this recurrent surrender: sea-going was really a job for a single, tough man. Now, in war, relaxation seemed a form of treason ... The odd, over-dramatic thoughts continued to pursue him, as Grace turned over and went to sleep again. He had never felt quite like this before: perhaps he was worrying too much, perhaps he *did* need a spell of leave after all. But that didn't mean letting everything slip.

Tomorrow he would go down to the ship again. Just to look around, just to see how she was getting on.

. . .

Bennett was talking to a woman in a hotel bedroom. She was the usual woman – infinitely tainted, infinitely practised, hard as nails; it was the usual room. The hotel stood, or rather lay in wait, at the back of the dock area; it was dedicated to a fornication so incessant and so transitory that there were often more people passing up and down the stairs than using the bedrooms. It was like a dirty hive, serving a machine-made sexuality, emitting a drone of love ... If Bennett had known that the building housed, at that particular moment, four members of *Compass Rose*'s crew besides himself, it would probably have struck him as a form of insubordination. He would not have considered that he himself was in the wrong place.

Now he untied his tie before the tarnished mirror, while behind him the bed-springs creaked as the woman composed herself for the encounter. While thus occupied, they made the conversation appropriate to the moment.

'Did you have a nice voyage, dear?'

'Lousy,' said Bennett briefly. 'Gets worse every time. I reckon I'm going to quit.'

'You can't do that, can you?'

'I'll find a way. They can't keep me cooped up in a little crap-boat like that for ever.'

'It must be funny on a boat – a lot of men all jammed up together. What d'you talk about?'

Bennett, who was taking off his trousers, paused. 'What do you think?'

'Love, eh? Love all the time, I suppose.'

'Something like that.'

'They say sailors are all the same.' The woman, whom no violence and no crudity incidental to her trade could now surprise, sketched a sentimental sigh. It was a minor triumph of artifice over conviction. 'There was a bit in the *Mirror* about it the other day – how they were always on the look-out for pen-pals.'

'First I've heard of it,' said Bennett. He leered. 'They're always on the look-out for something, but they don't want to use a pen in it.'

The woman smiled mechanically. For her, no indecent jokes were new, or funny, but they seemed to entrance the customers. One man had nearly fallen out of bed, telling her about a friend of his who got cramp on the job and had to be carted off to hospital, with the girl beside him on the stretcher. For the life of her, she couldn't crack a smile about that one ...

'Well,' said Bennett, turning to the bed, 'this is what I've been waiting for.'

'My!' said the woman, almost immediately. 'You *are* passionate, aren't you! Sure you're not French?'

'There's only one thing French about me,' said Bennett, and roared with sudden laughter.

The woman smiled again. Very comical ... 'I'm sure you must be French,' she insisted. 'They say they're too bloody passionate to live.'

'You can't hold onto it for ever,' said Bennett explanatorily. 'I've been carrying this lot around for four months.'

'It all adds up, doesn't it?' said the woman vaguely. 'Careful now ...'

. . .

Morell, who had very much wanted a quiet evening at home, said: 'Of course, darling. Where would you like to go?'

Elaine Morell did not answer immediately. There were so many lovely places and they had only five days to cover them ... Of course, she could go anywhere she liked, whether he were here or not, but it was nice to make the most of him while he *was* here – he looked so sweet in his uniform, even though the single thin stripe was a bit depressing. She pulled a face at herself in the dressing-table mirror, adjusted a curl at the nape of her neck, and said:

'You decide, darling. It's your leave, after all.'

Morell, lounging behind her on the quilted bed, wondered if that were quite true. He wondered, indeed, whether anything really belonged to him, where his wife was concerned: he found her so incredibly lovely and persuasive that all his will, all his competent judgement, could be swamped on the instant, and he would surrender the most cherished project at a flick of her fingers. The world saw him as a grave young man, with a capable brain, developing judgement, and a future in the law; it did not see, it could not guess, how his marriage had proved a sensual solvent for this whole fabric.

She was a minor actress, on the fringe of the West End stage: she was not appearing at the moment – the war seemed to have made her so very busy in other ways ... When Morell had married her, it was almost as if he were playing a part himself, so incongruous did the combination of himself and this glamorous creature seem: the incongruity had been solved by his ceasing, for all intents and purposes, to be himself at all, when he was with her. He spoke to her as he spoke to no one else, with a tender diffidence which none of his friends would have recognized or credited: he listened to her talking, and answered her, as if the brittle chatter of her lovely mouth had been his lordship's address to the jury. He also did exactly as he was told.

At this moment, for instance, he was desperately tired: it would be the third night running they had gone out to dine or to dance, and he wanted peace, he wanted Elaine to himself. But from the beginning she had proclaimed that she wished to show him off everywhere, and so it had been a procession of cocktail parties, restaurants, and nightclubs: even on his first evening, they had not returned home to their flat until four in the morning. Of course, she had made it up then, made it up with a cunning intensity which had, after three months without her, swamped and overthrown his senses. It seemed that she had felt that too. 'Darling,' she had said, with that murmur in her throat which could stir something inside him, even in a moment of satiety, 'Darling, you must go away more often, or something – that was terrific!'

In the face of so fierce a welcome, how difficult to refuse her anything; and if he did refuse her (though this was a thought for secrecy), how quickly that fervour might dry up ... She was beautiful – not in a remote fashion, but with a face which beckoned, a mouth formed only for kissing, and a body so soft, so shapely, and so glowing that its only conceivable purpose was to fuse with the sinewed imprint of a man's. She had, for Morell, a sensual pull which two years of marriage had never assuaged: her moving limbs induced in him an almost insane urgency, her body seemed to flicker for his delight. Even, as now, to watch her dressing, perfuming her neck and shoulders, adjusting a brassière to encase her flawless breasts, was intolerably exciting ... Whenever she wanted, she could promote this frenzy: whenever she did not want, the frenzy was there in a yet more desperate degree.

Of course she demanded too much, of course she betrayed the cool man he had imagined himself to be. But a single glance of hers, a single movement, squared the account, making it natural and essential to please her, and boorish to do otherwise. And, once again, if he *didn't* please her, if he failed to follow her lead in anything, it became dangerous, it was more than he dared. There were so many other people ...

One of these other people indeed had telephoned, on Morell's first evening at home. From her bath Elaine had called: 'Answer that, darling – I'm wet,' and when he lifted the receiver a man's voice, against a background of music and other voices, had broken in immediately:

'Elaine? There's a swell party here, but we need that beautiful body – how about coming over?'

Morell said, rather foolishly: 'Hallo?'

'Oh, sorry,' said the voice. 'Who's that?'

'Morell.'

'*Who?*'

'Morell.'

'Oh – yes.' An odd laugh. 'Sorry, old boy, I didn't know you were back.'

'I'll tell my wife you called,' said Morell. 'Who is it speaking?'

'Doesn't matter – forget it. G'bye.' He sounded rather drunk, but not as drunk as all that.

That evening, once again, they danced till very late, in a nightclub so hot, so noisy, and so uninhibited that it might have been part of a zoo. It was very crowded. Elaine seemed to know a great many people, among them half a dozen Air Force pilots who came up in a solid procession to ask her to dance. At one point, clinging to Morell in the twilight of the dance-floor, she had stroked his sleeve and murmured: 'Darling, how long before you get promoted?' and he had ceased to be proud of her head on his shoulder, and felt rather foolish instead. But, as usual, she drove all that away, as soon as they were home: in bed at last, erotic with alcohol, she swamped and sucked him of fervour till the fatigue of love became an aching reality, and sleep the only drug to ease it.

It was his leave, after all.

. . .

With Mavis, Ferraby spent a wonderful and tender period. She was now living with her mother, and the circumstances – a cramped, suburban house at Purley, a lack of privacy at meals and in the evenings – were not ideal; but it was so lovely to see her again, so lovely to *be* somebody, to be considered and deferred to, after the brusque contempt of *Compass Rose*, that the drawbacks were forgotten. The freedom from constraint, and the fading out of the hatred at close quarters, were tangible blessings; and in their private times together, the return to tenderness proffered so startling a contrast that, to begin with, he could scarcely believe it.

'He must be absolutely beastly!' said Mavis indignantly, when Ferraby had told her something of Bennett's manners and methods. 'Why do they allow it?'

'It's discipline,' said Ferraby vaguely. He did not really believe this, nor had he, for very shame, told her the full story; but he did not want the shadow to stay where it had fallen. 'The First Lieutenant's meant to run the ship really, and that means the officers as well.'

'But he needn't be so horrid about it.'

'He's like that.'

'They oughtn't to allow it,' she said again. 'I'd like to give him a piece of my mind.'

Dear Mavis, so sweet and attractive in slacks and the blue Angora jersey, with her little face screwed up in anger and sadness . . . He kissed her, and said: 'Let's forget about it. How about going for a walk?'

'If you're not too tired.'

He looked at her, and smiled. 'Why should I be too tired?'

She blushed, not meeting his eye. 'Gordon Ferraby, you're a disgrace . . . You know quite well what I meant.'

He felt very masculine as he took her arm.

But the mention of Bennett's name must have started a train of thought which remained with him. That night he dreamed of *Compass*

Rose in a storm, and of Bennett shouting at him and refusing to let him issue the right helm-orders, so that they were in danger of running ashore: he woke up, yelling at the top of his voice and sweating with panic, just as the ship drove through smoking breakers towards a line of rocks . . . Mavis, putting her arms round him, was appalled at the feel of his wet trembling body and at the idea, which each shudder communicated, of an emotional turmoil greater than he could bear: when he apologized for the noise he had made, it was as if he were excusing some hopeless deformity for which he deserved all the pity in her heart.

'I must have been dreaming,' he muttered hoarsely. 'I'm sorry, darling.'

'What was the dream about, Gordon?'

'The ship.'

'Tell me.'

'I've forgotten.' But after a moment he did start to tell her, while she held him close and listened with misgiving and with a new understanding compassion flooding through her: for in the end he told her everything – his fears and failures, the guilty doubt of his fitness for the job, the true story of the last few months. It was easier in the dark, with her head on his shoulder, and, as usual with her, there was no shame in confession; indeed, it was she who was the more moved when he had finished, who suffered his own fear of returning after the leave was finished, and felt it as her own miserable dilemma. Above all, she was shaken by the revelation, which nothing in his cheerful letters to her had even hinted at. This was not the man she knew and had married: what had they done to him?

They talked far into the night. There was little she could give him save the assurance of her own confidence: it sounded pathetically inadequate, against the wretched background he had sketched for her. She remembered for long afterwards a single stubborn sentence of his, which he repeated whenever she suggested that he might ask for a different job: 'I can't give up something I volunteered for.' She could not persuade him either that the job was proving infinitely harder than he had imagined, and might thus be honourably abandoned, or that Bennett was so horrible a complication that the whole basis of his engagement was changed. Somewhere deep inside him, an obstinate self-destroying will was at work, forbidding him to surrender.

For some reason, after that night, she hoped that she would have a child as soon as possible.

.   .   .

Lockhart, having lost the toss, stayed aboard as duty-officer. It would be his turn for leave next time, and in any case he found that he did not mind being left behind: it was the sort of rest he needed, and in his spare time he occupied himself much as he would have done on leave – reading, listening to the radio, unwinding the tight coil of the past few months. *Compass Rose*, with her boilers blown down and no fans working, was cool and silent: it was odd to feel the ship, hitherto so active and alive, sinking back into a suspended laziness which matched his own. There was very little to do, and nothing that demanded any sort of concentration on his part: he saw the hands fall in after breakfast, and told Leading-Seaman Phillips what had to be done in the way of sweeping and painting: he opened the mail, in case there was anything urgent: he despatched the liberty-men ashore, clean and tidy, at four o'clock; and he went round the ship at nine in the evening, to see that all was secure for the night. Meals were something of a picnic: both the leading-cook and Carslake, the leading-steward, were on leave, and his welfare was in the hands of the second steward, Tomlinson, who had once had a coffee-stall in the Edgware Road and whose methods were better suited to a quick turn-over in saveloys and hot pies, cash only and no back answers, than to the gentler world of the wardroom. But since, being alone, Lockhart had revived his peace-time habit of reading all the time he was eating, the slap-dash service and the indifferent food did not greatly worry him.

They were tied up alongside *Viperous*, which was also boiler-cleaning: it was the first time he had been able to examine a destroyer in close detail, and he took advantage of their neighbouring position to go aboard several times. His opposite number, also left on board for the leave period, was a young R.N. sub-lieutenant who, though aware of his inferiority of rank, could hardly take an R.N.V.R. lieutenant seriously: Lockhart was amused to watch the struggle between his natural respect for a two-ringer and his natural contempt for an amateur. There was nothing amateur about *Viperous*, certainly: the rigid R.N. atmosphere, allied to the almost professional glamour of a destroyer, was a potent combination. *Viperous* and *Compass Rose* might be doing the same job, and they might share the same hardships; but there was no doubt which of them was the elder brother, with an elder brother's unchallenged status. Their relative positions in the hierarchy, however, now seemed to matter less than they had done at the beginning. Lockhart was coming to believe in corvettes, as were many other people; they were the smallest ships regularly employed on Atlantic convoys – the trawlers and tugs had been withdrawn as unsuitable – and sea-going in corvettes was already appropriating a toughness and a glamour of its own.

He had one or two visitors during the leave-period. Among them was Lieut.-Commander Ramsay, the Captain of *Sorrel*, who came aboard one morning and put his head round the wardroom door.

'Anyone in?' he asked loudly. He was a cheerful individual, red-faced and stocky, with a rolling West Country accent: reputed to be a

disciplinary terror in his own ship, he appeared to shed it as soon as he
crossed the gangway.

'Hallo, sir!' Lockhart put aside his newspaper. 'Come in.'

'Is your Captain on board?'

'No, he's on leave still. Will you have a drink?'

'Aye. Gin, please . . . I see you got that second stripe. How's that First
Lieutenant of yours?'

Lockhart grinned. 'Bearing up.'

'Makes you hop about a bit, doesn't he?'

'He – er – maintains a stiff discipline, yes.'

Ramsay smiled in his turn. 'One way of putting it . . . Here's luck.'

They gossiped for some little time, mostly about their own escort
group and the job that corvettes were doing: they both betrayed the
half-humorous resignation which seemed inevitable when those who
sailed in corvettes were talking shop together. Ramsay related in detail a
mishap to *Sorrel* which had occurred on the last convoy – a huge wave
had broken right *over* her bridge, smashed two windows in the
charthouse, and bent the rail nearly a foot out of the true. *Compass Rose*
could not quite match that experience, Lockhart decided after rummag-
ing in his memory, though there was a morbid interest in trying to do so
on her behalf . . . Ramsay, when he rose to leave, said, out of the blue:

'Maybe you'll get a First Lieutenant's job yourself, one of these days.'

The remark made Lockhart both pleased and thoughtful for some
time afterwards. It was an idea which had never even occurred to him;
now that he examined it, it did not seem so fantastic as it might have, at
the beginning of the year.

His principal other visitor was Ericson himself, who slipped aboard
one day towards the end of their leave, and walked round the ship with
an air so suspicious and so proprietary that Lockhart found himself
imagining half a dozen things he had either done wrong, or failed to do
at all. But the Captain seemed to be satisfied that *Compass Rose* was
coming to no harm: he stayed to have lunch on board and, as if to mark
the difference between this occasion and the normal times when the ship
was working, he dropped all formality and proved himself very good
company on a new and level plane. He was especially interesting when
he talked about his own apprenticeship in the Navy, and the quick
learning which the war had now made necessary, compared with the
wearisome year-to-year grind of peace-time sea-going and the desperately slow promotion which rewarded it. Lockhart had the impression that Ericson was now becoming convinced of something –
perhaps the capability of amateurs like himself – which before he had
rejected out of hand . . . Altogether, it was one of the most pleasant meals
he had ever had in *Compass Rose*: it left him with a feeling of respect,
almost of hero-worship, for Ericson, which a little earlier he would have

dismissed as a surrender of individuality. Some of his peace-time convictions, it seemed, were being rubbed off: if the ones that took their place were as natural and as unforced as this new regard, it did not matter at all.

CHAPTER 6

On the evening of their return from leave, Lockhart, Morell, and Ferraby were all in the wardroom when Bennett stumbled down the ladder and entered the room. He was undeniably drunk, and most of his trouser buttons were undone: the general effect was so unpleasant that it was difficult to include him in their company without exhibiting a strong reaction. For some moments he busied himself at the sideboard, while they watched him in silence; then he turned round, glass in hand, and focused his eyes on each of them in turn.

'Well, well, well,' he said with foolish emphasis. 'Good little boys, all back from leave at the proper time . . . How did you tear yourself away?'

No one answered him.

The full glass slopped over his coat as he gestured drunkenly. 'Matey lot of bastards, aren't you?' He eyed Lockhart with confused belligerence. 'What's been happening while I've been away?'

'Nothing at all.'

'I suppose you were slipping ashore the whole time.' He took an enormous gulp of whisky, coughed, and only just held onto it. His eyes moved unsteadily round to Morell and Ferraby. 'And as for you married men – married——' he lost the thread of what he was going to say, but unfortunately started again. 'You had a wonderful time. Don't tell me.'

'It was very pleasant,' said Morell after a pause.

'I bet you left a bun in the oven, both of you,' said Bennett thickly. Then suddenly he turned a grey-green colour, and lurched out of the room. They heard him stumbling up the ladder, and the clang of the lavatory-door behind him.

'Now what on earth does that peculiar phrase mean?' asked Morell, when he had gone.

Lockhart, considerably embarrassed, said: 'I shouldn't worry about it if I were you.'

'But what?' Morell insisted.

Lockhart explained, as delicately as he could, the reference to pregnancy. It could not be made to sound in the least delicate, and the reaction was what he had expected. Ferraby flushed vividly and looked at the floor: Morell lost his normal air of indifference and for a moment his face had a startling expression of disgust and anger.

'What a monstrous man he is!' he said in the uncomfortable pause that followed. 'How can we get rid of him?'

'I've an idea he might get rid of himself,' answered Lockhart, glad of the change of subject. 'He didn't like that last convoy at all. I wouldn't be surprised if he gave this job up.'

'How could he do that?' asked Ferraby, in a voice so subdued and spiritless that it was almost a whisper.

Lockhart gestured vaguely. 'Oh, there are ways ... If I were he, I think I should get a duodenal ulcer. For some reason the Navy takes them very seriously – if they suspect anything like that they put you ashore straightaway, in case something blows up while you're at sea.'

'One of us had better tell him,' said Morell after reflection. 'I wouldn't like him to be in any doubt as to how to go about it, just for want of a word of advice.'

'I should say he knows,' remarked Lockhart.

'How wonderful if he did go,' said Ferraby, in the same small voice. 'It would make such a terrific difference.'

'Funnier things have happened.'

'But not nicer,' said Morell. 'Not in my experience, at least.'

.   .   .

By one of those coincidences that occasionally sweeten the crudest circumstances, Lockhart's forecast came exactly true. The very next day, at lunch, Bennett, who had been eating with his accustomed fervour, suddenly clapped his hands to his stomach and gave a realistic groan.

'Jesus Christ!' he said, in a voice suppressed by tension and mashed potato. 'That hurt!'

'What's the matter?' said Ericson, looking at him with non-committal interest.

'Hell of a pain ...' Bennett gave another groan, yet more heart-rending, and doubled up across the table. His hands were still clasped to his stomach, and his breath came heavily through clenched teeth. It was difficult, for a variety of reasons, not to applaud the occasion.

'Better lie down,' said Ericson. 'Take it easy for a bit.'

'Jesus, it's agony!'

'Perhaps you have a bun in the oven,' said Morell suavely. He raised his eyebrows as he saw Lockhart struggling with laughter.

Bennett levered himself upright, and tottered towards the door. 'Reckon I'll lie down,' he mumbled. 'It may pass off.' He went through the doorway towards his cabin, moaning with great clarity.

'Bad luck,' observed the Captain.

'Most moving,' said Morell. 'I imagine there's nothing we can do to help him.' The remark was so clearly a statement of non-intention that Lockhart could hardly stop laughing out loud.

Ericson looked round the table suddenly. 'What are you all grinning at?' he demanded.

'Sorry, sir,' said Lockhart, who was the most uncontrolled offender. 'I was thinking of something.'

Morell frowned, with a wonderful air of disapproval. 'It hardly does you credit, at a time like this,' he said stiffly. 'If the First Lieutenant is in pain, I should not have thought you would be able to laugh at anything else.'

Ericson looked from one to the other, started to speak, and then let it go. They were behaving rather badly: but he himself was conscious of a certain lightening of the atmosphere, now that Bennett had taken himself off, and it was hardly honest to check the same feeling in other people ... The only drawback to the slightly farcical occasion was the possibility of Bennett's really being ill: for *Compass Rose* was at twelve hours' notice for steam, and likely to sail the next day.

His foreboding was accurate enough. Bennett complained of pain all that afternoon: he went off to the Naval Hospital the same evening, and he did not return. When Ericson summoned Lockhart to his cabin next morning, he had on his desk two signals which did not go well together. One was their sailing orders, for four o'clock: the other was about Bennett.

'The First Lieutenant won't be back for some time, Lockhart,' Ericson began. 'He's got a suspected duodenal ulcer.'

'Oh,' said Lockhart. He felt inclined to laugh at the way it had all fallen into place so neatly, and then he had a sudden thought which brought him up sharply. Something else was falling into place, something that concerned him intimately, something for the bright future. He waited for the Captain to speak, knowing what he was going to say, almost fearing to hear it in case it should be less than he hoped.

Ericson was frowning at the two signals. 'We sail this afternoon, and we'll have to go without him. There's no chance of getting a relief by then, either.' He looked up. 'You'll have to take over as Number One, and organize the watches on that basis.'

'Yes, sir,' said Lockhart. His heart, to his secret surprise, had raced for a moment, as if to mark a violent pleasure. First Lieutenant ... It could be done, and it would have to be – he wouldn't have another chance like this one for a very long time.

'I'll help you with it,' Ericson went on. 'You should be able to carry on until a relief arrives.'

'I can carry on anyway.'

'Can you?' Ericson looked at him again. Lockhart had spoken with a kind of informal resolution which was a new thing in their relationship.

'Yes, sir.'

'All right,' said Ericson after a pause. 'I'll see ... Do your best this time, anyway.'

Lockhart walked out of the cabin with that precise determination.

. . .

The first convoy, with the new job to do, was a challenge, and Lockhart took it on happily. As far as watch-keeping was concerned, it gave him an easier run: he now had the morning watch, from four a.m. until eight, and in this early part of the summer that meant almost four hours of daylight watch-keeping, instead of the strain and difficulty of a totally dark middle watch. But there were many other things which went with his promotion, added responsibilities which must always be borne in mind: from the first afternoon, when after a final check-up with Tallow he reported *Compass Rose* 'ready to proceed', he was never clear of the routine interruptions which the proper execution of his job entailed, and never free of worry lest he had forgotten something. He did not mind, because he was professionally and personally interested, as well as immensely eager to make a success of it; but on that convoy, as on many others still to come, he worked harder than he had ever done before.

In essence, he had to present the Captain with a going concern, a smoothly-run ship which would not fail him in any trial. In harbour it involved one range of responsibility, concerned mostly with discipline, topping up stores and ammunition, and the organization of working-parties so as to keep the ship clean and efficient: at sea it took on a more vital quality, closer to the war and with less margin for error. Weapons had to be tested daily: parties detailed to deal with the odd things that went wrong: watches had to be changed or strengthened, the messdecks visited twice a day to see that they were tidied up and as dry as possible – otherwise life on board became even more grossly uncomfortable than it need be: at nightfall, *Compass Rose* must fade into the twilight with no light showing, no weapon out of order, and no man on board in any doubt of what he must do, whatever the circumstances. It was a full programme; but he was strengthened by Ericson's backing, which was strong and continuous, and pleased also by the reaction of Morell and Ferraby. They gave him a cheerful co-operation: freed from Bennett's heavy-handed regime, and wanting above all to make a success of the substitution, they went out of their way to help him through the first uncertain period.

For they *were* free of Bennett: he faded away into a dilatory background of hospital boards and recurrent examinations, and they never saw him again. Lockhart's promotion was confirmed, not without some misgivings, by Western Approaches Command; and the new officer who arrived to fill the gap, one Sub-Lieutenant Baker, was junior

to Ferraby and, if his hesitant air was anything to go by, likely to remain
so. The new team assembled and settled down, making of *Compass Rose* a
different ship altogether. The wardroom was now a pleasant place
where they could relax and feel at ease, without a morose and critical eye
singling them out for comment: after six months of suspicion and the
most oafish kind of tyranny, it made for a happy freedom which they did
not want to abuse. The same feeling spread throughout the ship,
filtering down to the lower deck, where Bennett's crude methods had
aroused the most resentment and the strongest reaction in terms of idling
and shirking: the idea that Lockhart, though no fool, was a better man to
work for, produced, as it often does, more work and not less. There were
of course, to start with, one or two efforts at taking advantage of the more
reasonable rule, notably by liberty-men who returned on board late and
produced elaborate excuses for doing so; but after one conspicuous
offender, claiming to have been involved in a boarding-house fire, had
been informed by Lockhart (who had taken the trouble to find out) that
the night in question had been the first one for four months on which the
Liverpool Fire Brigade had not been called out, and had then been sent
to detention by the Captain, the number of men ready to 'try it on'
showed a steep decline.

Ericson, observing the general improvement, was pleased with his
experiment. He had gone to a good deal of trouble to get Lockhart's
appointment confirmed, in the face of a stubborn sort of disbelief ashore,
and the trouble was worth while. Both he and *Compass Rose* had gained
something which might be even more valuable in the near future.

. . . .

There was one job of Lockhart's which had been his ever since he had
joined *Compass Rose* and had admitted, in a moment of inattention, that
one of his great-uncles had once been a surgeon at Guy's Hospital; and
that was the job of ship's doctor. So far it had involved him in nothing
more than treating toothache, removing a splinter from a man's eye,
and advising, with no sort of experience to guide him, on a stubborn case
of lice-infestation: all the serious cases went to the Naval Hospital
ashore, and as yet nothing in this class had ever occurred at sea.
Vaguely, he realized that this would not always be so: other corvettes
had had casualties to deal with, after ships in convoy had been
torpedoed, and sooner or later he himself would be faced with an
experience he was little fitted for. It was a thought he shied away from,
because he had a real doubt as to how he would meet the ordeal: nothing
in his life, not even a casual motor accident, had brought him in contact
with blood and violence, and he feared a reaction which might be
ineffective or foolish. 'Fainting at the sight of blood' – the stock phrase
sometimes occurred to him, with a discomforting twinge of anxiety.
Suppose that was what happened, suppose he could not help it . . . The

job of doctor was the only one on board which, in moments of introspection, he wanted to relinquish.

But so far it had been a sinecure: so far, their most challenging medical problem had been sufficiently beyond his scope for him to be justified in rejecting it.

The occasion had been the start of a convoy, when the line of ships was forming up after the slow progress down river. A nearby tanker had started signalling to *Compass Rose*, and Wells, receiving the message, passed it onto the Captain.

'From the tanker, sir,' he said. ' "Have you a doctor on board or can you give medical advice?" '

Ericson looked at Lockhart, who was also up on the bridge. 'How about it, Number One?'

'I'll have a crack at it, sir,' said Lockhart. 'I can't do much harm at this distance.'

'All right.' He turned to Wells. 'Make to them: "Medical advice available. What are symptoms?" '

There was a pause, while the lamps flickered again. Then Wells, reading the reply, suddenly said: 'Oh!' in a startled voice. It was the first time Lockhart had ever seen him surprised, and he wondered what could be coming. With no sort of expression, Wells gave the 'Message received' signal, and then said:

'Reply, sir: "Tight foreskin".'

There was a reflective silence on the bridge.

'Sir,' said Lockhart, 'I honestly don't know.'

'Does you credit,' answered Ericson. It was one of those remarks he occasionally made, which endeared him to Lockhart as something more than a good Captain. 'I don't think we have any experts on board, have we?'

'No, sir,' said Lockhart.

' "Afraid we cannot help your patient",' Ericson dictated to Wells, ' "Will ask destroyer, which has a doctor". Send that off... Fine start for a twenty-one day convoy,' he said thoughtfully. 'That'll teach him not to go to *that* address again.'

The subsequent exchange of signals with *Viperous* was of a kind which does not figure in the official log: at the end of it, Lockhart had less inclination to continue his medical career than ever before. Later, in mid-Atlantic, they enquired after the casualty, and received the answer: 'Patient enjoyed a good night.' 'We know that,' was Morell's dry comment. 'It was the original trouble.'

And then, suddenly, being the doctor wasn't funny any more.

.   .   .

Dunkirk, that fabulous flight and triumph, was their signal for joining battle: from then onwards, almost every convoy they escorted suffered some sort of attack, either from U-boats or aircraft, and the loss of ships began to be an inevitable part of their sea-going. Dunkirk, as it was bound to, made a great difference to the balance of things in the Atlantic: the operation itself drew off many ships, destroyers and corvettes alike, from regular convoy-escort, and some of them were lost, others damaged, and still others had to remain in home waters when it was over, to be on hand in case of invasion. The shortage of escorts at this stage was ludicrous: even with the arrival of fifty obsolescent destroyers which America had now made available to the Allies, convoys sailed out into the Atlantic with only a thin token screen between them and the growing force of U-boats. When, after Dunkirk, the Royal Navy turned its attention to the major battle again, it was to find control of the battlefield threatened by a ruthless assault, which quickened and grew with every month that passed.

There was another factor in the altered account. The map now showed them a melancholy and menacing picture: with Norway gone, France gone, Ireland a dubious quantity on their doorstep, and Spain an equivocal neutral, nearly the whole European coast-line, from Narvik to Bordeaux, was available to U-boats and, more important still, as air-bases for long-range aircraft. Aircraft could now trail a convoy far out into the Atlantic, calling up U-boats to the attack as they circled out of range: the liaison quickly showed a profit disastrous to the Allies. In the three months that followed Dunkirk, over two hundred ships were sent to the bottom by these two weapons in combination, and the losses continued at something like fifty ships a month till the end of the year. Help was on the way – new weapons, more escorts, more aircraft: but help did not come in time, for many ships and men, and for many convoys that made port with great gaps in their ranks.

It was on one of these bad convoys, homeward bound near Iceland, that *Compass Rose* was blooded.

. . .

When the alarm bell went, just before midnight, Ferraby left the bridge where he had been keeping the first watch with Baker, and made his way aft towards his depth-charges. It was he who had rung the bell, as soon as the noise of aircraft and a burst of tracer bullets from the far side of the convoy indicated an attack; but though he had been prepared for the violent clanging and the drumming of feet that followed it, he could not control a feeling of sick surprise at the urgency which now possessed the ship, in its first alarm for action. The night was calm, with a bright three-quarter moon which bathed the upper deck in a cold glow, and showed them the nearest ships of the convoy in hard revealing outline; it was a perfect night for what he *knew* was coming, and to hurry down the length of *Compass Rose* was like going swiftly to the scaffold. He knew that if he spoke now there would be a tremble in his voice, he knew that full daylight would have shown his face pale and his lips shaking; he knew that he was not really ready for this moment, in spite of the months of training and the gradually sharpening tension. But the moment was here, and somehow it had to be faced.

Wainwright, the young torpedo-man, was already on the quarter-deck, clearing away the release-gear on the depth-charges, and as soon as Wainwright spoke – even though it was only the three words 'Closed up, sir,' – Ferraby knew that he also was consumed by nervousness . . . He found the fact heartening, in a way he had not expected: if his own fear of action were the common lot, and not just a personal and shameful weakness, it might be easier to cure in company. He took a grip of his voice, said: 'Get the first pattern ready to drop,' and then, as he turned to check up on the depth-charge crews, his eye was caught by a brilliant firework display on their beam.

The attacking aircraft was now flying low over the centre of the convoy, pursued and harried by gun-fire from scores of ships at once. The plane could not be seen, but her swift progress could be followed by the glowing arcs of tracer-bullets which swept like a huge fan across the top of the convoy. The uproar was prodigious – the plane screaming through the darkness, hundreds of guns going at once, one or two ships sounding the alarm on their sirens: the centre of the convoy, with everyone blazing away at the low-flying plane and not worrying about what else was in the line of fire, must have been an inferno. Standing in their groups aft, close to the hurrying water, they watched and waited, wondering which way the plane would turn at the end of her run: on the platform above them the two-pounder gun's-crew, motionless and helmeted against the night sky, were keyed ready for their chance to fire. But the chance never came, the waiting belts of ammunition remained idle: something else forestalled them.

It was as if the monstrous noise from the convoy must have a climax, and the climax could only be violent. At the top of the centre column, near the end of her run, the aircraft dropped two bombs: one of them fell wide, raising a huge pluming spout of water which glittered in the moonlight, and the other found its mark. It dropped with an iron clang on some ship which they could not see – and they knew that now they would never see her: for after the first explosion there was a second one, a huge orange flash which lit the whole convoy and the whole sky at one ghastly stroke. The ship – whatever size she was – must have dis-integrated on the instant; they were left with the evidence – the sickening succession of splashes as the torn pieces of the ship fell back into the sea, covering and fouling a mile-wide circle, and the noise of the aircraft disappearing into the darkness, a receding tail of sound to underline this fearful destruction.

'Must have been ammunition,' said someone in the darkness, breaking the awed and compassionate silence. 'Poor bastards.' 'Didn't know much about it. Best way to die.' You fool, thought Ferraby, trembling uncontrollably: you fool, you fool, no one wants to die ...

From the higher vantage-point of the bridge, Ericson had watched everything; he had seen the ship hit, the shower of sparks where the bomb fell, and then, a moment afterwards, the huge explosion that blew her to pieces. In the shocked silence that followed, his voice giving a routine helm-order was cool and normal: no one could have guessed the sadness and the anger that filled him, to see a whole crew of men like himself wiped out at one stroke. There was nothing to be done: the aircraft was gone, with this frightful credit, and if there were any men left alive – which was hardly conceivable – *Sorrel*, the stern escort, would do her best for them. It was so quick, it was so brutal ... He might have thought more about it, he might have mourned a little longer, if a second strike had not followed swiftly; but even as he raised his binoculars to look at the convoy again, the ship they were stationed on, a hundred yards away, rocked to a sudden explosion and then, on the instant, heeled over at a desperate angle.

This time, a torpedo ... Ericson heard it: and even as he jumped to the voice-pipe to increase their speed and start zig-zagging, he thought: if that one came from outside the convoy, it must have missed us by a few feet. Inside the Asdic-hut, Lockhart heard it, and started hunting on the danger-side, without further orders: that was a routine, and even at this moment of surprise and crisis, the routine still ruled them all. Morell, on the fo'c'sle, heard it, and closed up his gun's-crew again and loaded with star-shell: down in the wheel-house, Tallow heard it, and gripped the wheel tighter and called out to his quartermasters: 'Watch that telegraph, now!' and waited for the swift orders that might follow. Right aft, by the depth-charges, Ferraby heard it, and shivered: he glanced downwards at the black water rushing past them, and then at the stricken ship which he could see quite clearly, and he longed for some action in which he could lose himself and his fear. Deep down in the engine-room, Chief E.R.A. Watts heard it best of all: it came like a hammer-blow, hitting the ship's side a great splitting crack, and when, a few seconds afterwards, the telegraph rang for an increase of speed, his hand was on the steam-valve already. He knew what had happened, he knew what might happen next. But it was better not to think of what was going on outside: down here, encased below the water-line, they must wait, and hope, and keep their nerve.

Ericson took *Compass Rose* in a wide half-circle to starboard, away from the convoy, hunting for the U-boat down what he presumed had been the track of the torpedo; but they found nothing that looked like a

contact, and presently he circled back again, towards the ship that had
been hit. She had fallen out of line, like one winged bird in a flight of
duck, letting the rest of the convoy go by: she was sinking fast, and
already her screws were out of water and she was poised for the long
plunge. The cries of men in fear came from her, and a thick smell of oil: at
one moment, when they had her outlined against the moon, they could
see a mass of men packed high in the towering stern, waving and
shouting as they felt the ship under them begin to slide down to her
grave. Ericson, trying for a cool decision in this moment of pity, was
faced with a dilemma: if he stopped to pick up survivors, he would
become a sitting target himself, and he would also lose all chance of
hunting for the U-boat: if he went on with the hunt, he would, with *Sorrel*
busy elsewhere, be leaving these men to their death. He decided on a
compromise, a not-too-dangerous compromise: they would drop a boat,
and leave it to collect what survivors it could while *Compass Rose* took
another cast away to starboard. But it must be done quickly.

Ferraby, summoned to the quarter-deck voice-pipe, put every effort
he knew into controlling his voice.

'Ferraby, sir.'

'We're going to drop a boat, Sub. Who's your leading hand?'

'Leading-Seaman Tonbridge, sir.'

'Tell him to pick a small crew – not more than four – and row over
towards the ship. Tell him to keep well clear until she goes down. They
may be able to get some boats away themselves, but if not, he'll have to
do the best he can. We'll come back for him when we've had another
look for the submarine.'

'Right, sir.'

'Quick as you can, Sub. I don't want to stop too long.'

Ferraby threw himself into the job with an energy which was a drug
for all other feeling: the boat was lowered so swiftly that when *Compass
Rose* drew away from it and left it to its critical errand the torpedoed ship
was still afloat. But she was only just afloat, balanced between sea and
sky before her last dive; and as Tonbridge took the tiller and glanced in
her direction to get his bearings, there was a rending sound which
carried clearly over the water, and she started to go down. Tonbridge
watched, in awe and fear: he had never seen anything like this, and never
had a job of this sort before, and it was an effort to meet it properly. It had
been bad enough to be lowered into the darkness from *Compass Rose*, and
to watch her fade away and be left alone in a small boat under the stars,
with the convoy also fading and a vast unfriendly sea all round them; but
now, with the torpedoed ship disappearing before their eyes, and the
men shouting and crying as they splashed about in the water, and the
smell of oil coming across to them thick and choking, it was more like a
nightmare than anything else. Tonbridge was twenty-three years of age,

a product of the London slums conditioned by seven years' Naval training; faced by this ordeal, the fact that he did not run away from it, the fact that he remained effective, was beyond all normal credit.

They did what they could: rowing about in the darkness, guided by the shouting, appalled by the choking cries of men who drowned before they could be reached, they tried their utmost to rescue and to succour. They collected fourteen men: one was dead, one was dying, eight were wounded, and the rest were shocked and prostrated to a pitiful degree. It was very nearly fifteen men: Tonbridge actually had hold of the fifteenth, who was gasping in the last stages of terror and exhaustion, but the film of oil on his naked body made him impossible to grasp, and he slipped away and sank before a rope could be got round him. When there were no more shadows on the water, and no more cries to follow, they rested on their oars, and waited; alone on the enormous black waste of the Atlantic, alone with the settling wreckage and the reek of oil; and so, presently, *Compass Rose* found them.

Ferraby, standing in the waist of the ship as the boat was hooked on, wondered what he would see when the survivors came over the side: he was not prepared for the pity and horror of the appearance. First came the ones who could climb aboard themselves – half a dozen shivering, black-faced men, dressed in the filthy oil-soaked clothes which they had snatched up when the ship was struck: one of them with his scalp streaming with blood, another nursing an arm flayed from wrist to shoulder by scalding steam. They looked about them in wonder, dazed by the swiftness of disaster, by their rescue, by the solid deck beneath their feet. Then, while they were led to the warmth of the messdeck, a sling was rigged for the seriously wounded, and they were lifted over the side on stretchers: some silent, some moaning, some coughing up the fuel oil which was burning and poisoning their intestines: laid side by side in the waist, they made a carpet of pain and distress so naked in suffering that it seemed cruel to watch them. And then, with the boat still bumping alongside in the eerie darkness, came Tonbridge's voice: 'Go easy – there's a dead man down here.' Ferraby had never seen a dead man before, and he had to force himself to look at this pitiful relic of the sea – stone-cold, stiffening already, its grey head jerking as it was bundled over the side: an old sailor, unseamanlike and disgusting in death. He wanted to run away, he wanted to be sick: he watched with shocked amazement the two ratings who were carrying the corpse: how can you bear what you are doing, he thought, how can you touch – it...? Behind him he heard Lockhart's voice saying: 'Bring the whole lot into the fo'c'sle – I can't see anything here,' and then he turned away and busied himself with the hoisting of the boat, not looking behind him as the procession of wrecked and brutalized men was borne off. When the boat was in-board, and secure, he turned back again, glad to have escaped some part of the horror. There was nothing left now but the acrid smell of oil, and the patches of blood and water on the deck: nothing, he saw with a gasp of fear and revulsion, but the dead man lying lashed against the rail, a yard from him, rolling as the ship rolled, waiting for daylight and burial. He turned and ran towards the stern, pursued by terror.

In the big seamen's messdeck, under the shaded lamps, Lockhart was doing things he had never imagined possible. Now and again he recalled, with a spark of pleasure, his previous doubts: there was plenty of blood here to faint at, but that wasn't the way things were working out ... He had stitched up a gash in a man's head, from the nose to the line of the hair – as he took the catgut from its envelope he had thought: I wish they'd include some directions with this stuff. He had set a broken leg, using part of a bench as a splint. He bound up other cuts and gashes, he did what he could for the man with the burnt arm, who was now insensible with pain: he watched, doing nothing with a curious hurt detachment, as a man who had drenched his intestines and perhaps his lungs with fuel oil slowly died. Some of *Compass Rose*'s crew made a ring round him, looking at him, helping him when he asked for help: the two stewards brought tea for the cold and shocked survivors, other men offered dry clothing, and Tallow, after an hour or two, came down and gave him the largest tot of rum he had ever seen. It was not too large ... Once, from outside, there was the sound of an explosion, and he looked up: by chance, across the smoky fo'c'sle, the bandaged rows of wounded, the other men still shivering, the twisted corpse, the whole squalid confusion of the night, he met the eye of Leading-Seaman Phillips. Involuntarily, both of them smiled, to mark a thought which could only be smiled at: if a torpedo hit them now, there would be little chance for any of them, and all this bandaging would be wasted.

Then he bent down again, and went on probing a wound for the splinter of steel which must still be there, if the scream of pain which the movement produced was anything to go by. This was a moment to think only of the essentials, and they were all here with him, and in his care.

It was nearly daylight before he finished; and he went up to the bridge to report what he had done at a slow dragging walk, completely played out. He met Ericson at the top of the ladder: they had both been working throughout the night, and the two exhausted men looked at each other in silence, unable to put any expression into their stiff drawn faces, yet somehow acknowledging each other's competence. There was blood on Lockhart's hands, and on the sleeves of his duffle-coat: in the cold light it had a curious metallic sheen, and Ericson looked at it for some time before he realized what it was.

'You must have been busy, Number One,' he said quietly. 'What's the score down there?'

'Two dead, sir,' answered Lockhart. His voice was very hoarse, and
he cleared his throat. 'One more to go, I think – he's been swimming and
walking about with a badly-burned arm, and the shock is too much.
Eleven others. They ought to be all right.'

'Fourteen ... The crew was thirty-six altogether.'

Lockhart shrugged. There was no answer to that one, and if there had
been he could not have found it in his present mood: the past few hours,
spent watching and touching pain, seemed to have deadened all normal
feeling. He looked round at the ships on their beam, just emerging as the
light grew.

'How about things up here?' he asked.

'We lost another ship, over the other side of the convoy. That made
three.'

'More than one submarine?'

'I shouldn't think so. She probably crossed over.'

'Good night's work.' Lockhart still could not express more than a
formal regret. 'Do you want to turn in, sir? I can finish this watch.'

'No – you get some sleep. I'll wait for Ferraby and Baker.'

'Tonbridge did well.'

'Yes ... So did you, Number One.'

Lockhart shook his head. 'It was pretty rough, most of it. I must get a
little book on wounds. It's going to come in handy, if this sort of thing
goes on.'

'There's no reason why it shouldn't,' said Ericson. 'No reason at all,
that I can see. Three ships in three hours: probably a hundred men all
told. Easy.'

'Yes,' said Lockhart, nodding. 'A very promising start. After the war,
we must ask them how they do it.'

'After the war,' said Ericson levelly, 'I hope they'll be asking us.'

CHAPTER 7

They sailed on eleven convoys that year: sometimes to Iceland,
sometimes to Gibraltar, sometimes to the pin-point in mid-Atlantic
which was their rendezvous with the incoming ships. As winter drew on,
the weather took a natural turn for the worse: but once the appalling
discomfort and the tiredness were accepted, they grew to welcome the
rising wind and the falling glass, for the respite of another kind which
these brought. For at least they provided cover for the convoy: a black
night with a stiff sea running, was a form of insurance against attack
which they were ready to pay, for as long as was necessary. At that time,
U-boats had not reached the stage of development when they could fire

torpedoes at almost any level: and the bad weather, in any case, made the ships hard to find and harder to hit. At the beginning, they never thought that they would welcome an Atlantic gale: as time went on, no other sort of weather suited them so well.

But the wind did not always blow, the moon was not always obscured by cloud. There were many repetitions of that first losing convoy: the tally of survivors gradually mounted, the total of ships lost pursued a steady upward curve. Something, it was clear, would have to be done about this question of survivors, if it was to be worth while fishing them out of the water; for corvettes, which were detailed for the bulk of this rescue work, were really ludicrously inadequate for the job. They needed a doctor, or at least a qualified Sick Berth Attendant, to see to the wounded and the exhausted men: it was futile, it was senseless to risk the ship in picking them up, only to have them die on board, from shock or burns or oil-poisoning which could not be properly treated.

Corvettes needed other things for this work, too: spare clothes, spare blankets, a proper sick-bay, drugs to ease pain. They even needed more canvas, for sewing up the dead. A lot of such things, which had not been foreseen, were now emerging into grisly reality.

It was on this note of inadequacy, this scrambling waste of effort and courage, that nineteen-forty drew to its close. Another, more memorable note, was struck, too, just before the end. On Christmas morning they saw a ship, loaded with iron ore, break in half and sink in less than one minute: she went down like a stone in a pond, leaving nothing save an oily scum and four men on the surface of the water. This was the record so far, out of many quick kills: it still had power to shock. But then all the losses, the deaths, the scale of slaughter, still startled and moved them.

They should have known that things were just warming up.

PART THREE

CHAPTER I

1941: GRAPPLING

They started the new year with a piece of domestic drama which in its untidiness and its inherent futility somehow reflected the wider battle. The centre of the storm was a small able-seaman by the name of Gregg. Gregg was one of the fo'c'sle-party, in Morell's division: the latter knew little about him save that he was quiet and dependable, and had never been in any sort of trouble during the whole of the fifteen months he had been in *Compass Rose*. It was therefore something of a surprise when Gregg failed to return on board at the end of their stay in harbour, and was not to be found by the time the ship left on her first convoy of the year. They sailed without him, after leaving with the shore authorities sufficient particulars to ensure that he would not be stranded on the dockside when he returned. The post-mortem and the clearing-up would have to wait; all that was involved now was the nuisance of being short-handed – the trouble in store, like the other details and duties of life in harbour, was shelved, while the sea claimed all their attention.

But certainly the trouble was there when they got back home. Absence without leave was sufficiently serious: to miss one's ship completely was in a higher scale of crime altogether, since if one did so, and the ship was involved in any kind of action, one was liable to a charge of desertion in the face of the enemy as well. Ericson, surveying Able-Seaman Gregg when he was brought up at Captain's Defaulters, on the morning after their return to harbour, waited with some interest to hear what he had to say. He might conceivably have some legitimate excuse which would disentangle him altogether – though it was hard to see what this could be. Alternatively, there might be something which would lessen the seriousness of the charge. Ericson hoped for this extenuation, since Gregg was a decent kid who had not been in trouble before: otherwise the thing might involve sending him to detention, and he would probably be permanently spoilt.

The crisis broke when Gregg refused to say anything at all.

The evidence on one side was simple: he had left the ship one afternoon, he had missed her when she sailed, he had reported back on board the morning she returned to harbour: the absence-without-leave for seventeen days was not disputable. But when Ericson asked for an explanation, he was met by a shake of the head, and a muttered 'Nothing to say, sir,' which brought him up short.

'You must have something to say,' said Ericson sharply. He looked at the small sandy-haired figure in front of him, and tried to analyse the man's expression. It was not quite apologetic, it was not quite shy, it was certainly not rebellious; it had a sort of submissive determination which was, in the circumstances, rather brave ... 'I want to know why you left the ship,' Ericson went on, 'and what you've been doing while we've been at sea. You've got to account for yourself – otherwise you'll be in serious trouble.'

They all stared at Gregg: the Captain, Lockhart, Morell, and Tallow who had marched him up to the table. The expressions on the ring of faces varied: the Captain, as judge, was non-committal, Morell looked puzzled, Lockhart wore his First Lieutenant's disciplinary frown, and Tallow exhibited the professional disgust of a man who had no patience with defaulters and not the smallest belief in their excuses. In the middle of it all, braving the storm, Able-Seaman Gregg preserved his unblinking air of reserve. 'When did you last see your father?' thought Lockhart inconsequently, and frowned yet more determinedly still. This sort of thing was no longer allowed to be funny.

'Well,' said Ericson after a pause. 'I'm waiting.'

'Nothing to say, sir,' repeated Gregg in the same flat tone. Tallow drew in his breath with a sharp hiss, and Ericson, hearing it, was somehow reminded of the whole weight of tradition, the machinery of Naval justice, that lay behind this moment. Soon he would have to apply that tradition, balancing the see-saw of crime and punishment, and the idea seemed wasteful and futile, when all it boiled down to was himself and a forlorn able-seaman who would not try to save his own skin.

He wanted to find the real reason that lay behind it, and he wanted to rescue Gregg from a situation which, with the best will in the world, must always be weighted against him. He tried again.

'That's just silly,' he said reasonably. 'I don't know what you're trying to cover up, but I shouldn't think it's worth it. You know that I can send you to detention for this?'

'Yes, sir,' mumbled Gregg.

'I don't want to do that, because you haven't been in trouble before and your divisional officer tells me you're a good worker. But unless you give me an explanation I haven't any alternative.' He paused. 'How did you come to miss the ship and what have you been doing the last seventeen days?'

There was still no answer. Gregg looked stolidly out in front of him, his eyes just below the level of Ericson's chin, maintaining the foolish contest of wills which could only have one end. The noises of the ship and the dockside seemed suspended, waiting for the scene to resolve itself. To Lockhart it seemed, fancifully, that this might never happen, that Gregg need never answer, that they might wait there for ever, till they all grew old and the war was over and no one cared any more ... Perhaps Ericson had something of the same feeling, for he straightened up suddenly and said:

'Stand over.'

'Stand over,' repeated Tallow, with the tiniest edge of doubt in his voice. And then, with more force: 'On caps!' he continued automatically. 'About turn! Quick march!'

When Gregg was out of earshot, Ericson turned to Morell.

'I'll see him again tomorrow,' he said. 'In the meantime, you'd better have a talk with him and try and find out what it's all about. I don't want to send him up without knowing what's behind it.'

'Yes, sir,' said Morell.

'Is he married?'

'Yes, sir.'

'Ask him if there's anything wrong there ... Coxswain!'

'Sir?'

'Stand Gregg over till tomorrow morning.'

'Aye, aye, sir.'

'Next case.'

But when Morell saw Gregg later that day, down in his cabin, he took a different line. There was less need for formality here, and less occasion for care in what one said: he could treat Gregg as he would have treated a witness in court, a witness who knew something but might have to be wheedled or bullied or tricked into revealing it. With no one listening, and no record to keep, the relationship of officer to rating could be stretched a long way outside the normal pattern.

'The Captain's doing his best for you,' Morell said shortly, when Gregg once more repeated his stubborn, 'nothing-to-say' formula. 'Probably a damned sight more than you deserve, but that's nothing to do with me. What he's trying to get at is, what made you suddenly walk ashore and miss the ship. Why won't you tell him?'

'I don't want to say, sir,' said Gregg, with the same finality as before.

'You'd rather have a month's detention?'

Gregg's expression changed to a sulky frown, but he said nothing.

'That's what it would mean, you know,' Morell went on. 'It'll be a black mark against you for the rest of your time in the Navy, it'll always be there, on your conduct sheet.'

'I'm only in for the war, sir.'

'Well, how long do you think that's going to last? You want to get on, don't you? – you don't want to stay an able-seaman for two or three more years? How can you be recommended for leading-seaman if you do this sort of thing, and then refuse to say anything about it?'

'I don't know, sir.'

'You'd better talk, Gregg.' Morell changed his tone. 'What's it all about? Where did you go to? Did you go home?'

After a pause: 'Yes, sir,' said Gregg, swallowing. 'I went to London.'

'Well, that's something ... Is there anything wrong there?'

'Not now, sir.'

'Was there?'

'Yes.'

'What?'

The obstinate, blank look returned. 'I don't want to say.'

'You know I won't repeat it to anyone.'

'You'll repeat it to the Captain,' said Gregg shrewdly.

'I don't have to. And that's only two people, anyway: it won't go any further.'

Gregg shook his head. He was wavering, but he still could not face whatever it was that filled his mind. 'It will, if I say it up at the table. It'll be all over the ship then.'

Morell frowned. 'What you say at Defaulters *doesn't* go all over the ship. You know that perfectly well ... Now let's get this straight. There was some trouble at home?'

'Yes, sir.'

'With your wife?'

'Yes.'

'What sort of trouble?'

Gregg gestured, rather pathetically. 'The usual.'

'How did you hear about it?'

'Someone wrote – a pal at home.'

'And you went off home to try to fix it up?'

'Yes.'

'Why didn't you tell me?'

No answer.

'You see what it's got you into,' said Morell hardly. 'What the hell do you think your officers are for, if not to help you when this sort of thing happens?'

'I didn't know, sir ... I wanted it kept a secret.'

'How can it be a secret, when you're absent without leave for seventeen days?'

'But no one knows about it still, sir – only you.'

'But you're going to tell the Captain,' said Morell.

'I don't want to do that. I'd rather go to cells, and have done with it.'

'Don't be a bloody fool,' said Morell. 'I don't say you'll get off, but it might make a lot of difference. He's a human being, you know.'

'But I can't tell it all up at the table,' said Gregg desperately. 'Not with all of you listening.'

'We don't have to be listening. You know you can see the Captain privately, if it's a family matter, don't you?'

'Yes, sir.'

'Well?'

Gregg came to a sudden decision. 'I'd like to do that, sir.'

'Why didn't you say so this morning?'

'I didn't think of it.'

'You'd have saved yourself a lot of trouble. And been a lot more popular.' Morell stood up. 'All right – I'll arrange for you to see him this afternoon.'

Gregg looked scared. 'What do I say, sir?'

'You tell him exactly why you went home, and what happened when you got there.'

'And it won't go any further?'

'No.'

'And I'll maybe get off?'

'I don't know. Probably not altogether. But it'll give you a better chance than simply refusing to speak. That can only have one end, can't it?'

'Yes.' Gregg smiled suddenly. 'Thanks a lot, sir.'

'There's nothing to thank me for.' It was time to return to normal, time to drop the curtain again. 'You're not clear yet, not by a long chalk. Now get back to work. I'll send for you when the Captain wants to see you. And this time, tell him the truth – everything – and don't waste any more time.'

It was doubtful if Gregg could have brought himself to tell his story, even now, if he had not been coaxed and persuaded up to the very last moment. But Ericson, forewarned by Morell of what was at the heart of the trouble, was at special pains to make it easy for him. With Gregg in his cabin he gave ostentatious orders that he was not to be disturbed: he made him sit down, he gave him a cigarette, and he led off his questions as if taking it for granted that Gregg would have no embarrassment about telling him everything. And when the man still hesitated, sitting on the edge of his chair, stiff and sweating in his number-one suit with the gold badges, Ericson suddenly leant forward and said:

'You're married, Gregg, aren't you?'

'Yes, sir.'

'Did you go home to see your wife?'

Gregg's eyes flickered upwards once, and then down again. His voice was not much above a whisper. 'Yes, sir.'

'You'd better tell me about it,' said Ericson. 'You want to tell somebody, don't you? – apart from the trouble you're in over it?'

He looked away as the other man struggled to answer. But the lead
was enough, the balance was tipped: now at last, up in the quiet cabin,
with the sun filtering through the porthole and the muted sound of water
running against the hull, Gregg told his appalling story.

It had begun with a letter, waiting for him when *Compass Rose* got back
from her last trip: a letter from a pal.

> *Dear Tom* [it said], *Of course it's none of my business, but I've been up
> and down the old street once or twice, thinking of calling on Edith and
> asking how you're getting along, and then I haven't liked to go in because
> she's got company already. Dear Tom, there's a lot of talk about it, a car
> outside the house at all hours, they say he's a traveller for one of the big
> firms. I seen him once saying goodbye, they were laughing. I didn't like it,
> Tom, I thought I'd write and tell you. If I done wrong I'm sorry, you
> know me, always putting my foot in it. Keep cheerful, you better ask for a
> bit of leave and straighten it up, it all comes of these chaps being in a
> reserved bloody occupation, shooting's too good for some, yours till the cows
> come home.*

'I had to go, sir,' said Gregg, twisting his hands together. At that
moment there was more than certainty in his voice: something like
defiance. 'I had to go, straightaway. When you get a letter like that . . . I
wasn't due for leave even next time it came round, and that was three
weeks ahead. I had to see what was going on. We've only been married
six months.'

And so he had gone, without a word to anyone, that same afternoon:
slipping ashore with the liberty-men, catching the last London train
from Lime Street station, arriving about eleven at night, getting the bus
out to Highgate.

'What happened then?' asked Ericson, when the pause had stretched
to unbearable limits.

'It's a little house, sir,' said Gregg, 'a nice little house. It used to be my
mother's – she left it to me. When I walked up from the bus-stop, it was
just like the letter said.' The defiance was gone now, swallowed up in
misery: he was reliving the horrible moment. 'When I got to the house,
the car was outside the door, and – and there was a light on upstairs.'

Gregg paused, and frowned: the imprint of emotion on the smooth
round face was very moving. 'See what I mean, sir? Downstairs, it was
dark.'

'Yes,' said Ericson, 'yes, I see.'

For a moment Gregg hadn't known what to do, he'd been so taken
aback, so horrified, so sick with it. He had stood in the dark street,
looking from the car up to the light, the terrible bedroom light. 'I didn't
need telling any more, sir: there was enough to bet on, there . . . I waited
a long time, thinking what to do, and then I thought, well, give her a

chance, she's only a kid really, and lonely by herself, so I walked up the path whistling a bit, and I made a lot of noise opening the door and going inside ... You see, I love her, sir,' he said, with simple determination, as if only he knew about love. 'We've been married just the six months.'

But now there was a long silence which Ericson could not break, so clearly pitiful was the feeling behind it: the word 'love' must have struck a hopeless note of memory. When Gregg started again, it was as if the key had now changed to something darker, more horrible still: as if this part of the story, which he had not yet shared with anyone, had a special forbidden quality which made them both guilty, teller and hearer alike.

Gregg's wife had called out when she heard the door go: scared, she sounded, and there was a lot of moving about ... She said, 'Who is it?' and he answered 'Tom', and there was whispering which made him feel angry and sick at the same time. He had switched on the light in the hall and waited, knowing quite well what they were doing and what the whispering meant; they were wondering if it could be bluffed out, what the evidence was, how much he had seen and guessed. But evidently they soon decided that it was hopeless, for now a man's voice spoke quite loud, and when Edith called out 'I'm coming down,' it had a sulky note of defiance.

'I still didn't know what to do, sir – I couldn't make sense of it at all. She'd always been so different, there'd never been anything like this. We were only married a couple of leaves back – you read the banns for us, here on board.' Ericson suddenly remembered that this was so: he could even recall, with a queer distaste, having read: 'Edith Tappett, spinster, of the Parish of Highgate, London', and wondering what a girl with so unromantic a name could be like. Now he knew: now they both knew ... 'Pretty soon she came down,' Gregg went on, speaking rather fast and looking at the floor. 'She hadn't got dressed, even then: she was all anyhow, in her dressing-gown. There was stuff on it, sir – I could see.'

Ericson thought: that's something he'll never forget: what a horrible thing to have in one's mind, for ever and ever ... But Gregg was hurrying on, leaving one scene for another yet more terrible, as if his choice were so rich and so wide that he need not stay long over one aspect of it.

'She'd had a bit to drink, sir – I could tell that. But that wasn't enough for her to talk the way she did. You'd have thought it was *my* fault. "I've got a friend," she said, "I wasn't expecting you" – just like that. And when I said: "Friend? – what do you mean, friend?" she said: "There's no need to shout, Tom, you don't want any trouble, surely?" And then she called out: "Walter", and after a minute the man came down the stairs. *He* didn't care,' said Gregg, with fury and misery in his voice, 'he walked down the stairs doing up his coat ... A big flashy chap, well-dressed, full of himself – you could tell he did this sort of thing every day of the week.' Gregg looked up and then down again, flushing remembering a deep humiliation. 'He was twice the size of me, sir. I couldn't even – I couldn't——' His voice tailed off into an empty realm of cowardice and despair, where only his defeat, his still-raw shame, was real.

'Never mind that,' said Ericson quickly, as if there were no significance in the pause, the moment of abasement. 'Tell me what happened next. What did your wife say?'

'You should have let me know, Tom,' was what his wife had said. 'How was I to tell you'd be back?' And then she had actually introduced them, and the man had said, 'Ah, the sailor home from the sea,' and Gregg had told him to get out, and the man had answered: 'We don't want any unpleasantness, thank you.' It was all part of a topsy-turvy nightmare in which Gregg could not get his bearings at all. 'After he'd gone, we had it out properly, but I couldn't get her to see it straight at all.' Gregg's voice still held some of the astonishment of that moment. 'She said she'd got used to – to love, sir, with me, and she couldn't do without it. She said it had been going on for two months. She said that this chap had talked her into it, but she wasn't really sorry, only on my account. She said it was the war, and lots of people did it . . . She acted like a different person. In the end we just went off to bed. She was with me that night, sir, though – though I could hardly touch her at first.'

There was now a much longer pause, almost as if Gregg had finished putting his side of the affair and were waiting for the verdict. But that could not be the end of the story, thought Ericson, looking down at his desk: it was horrible enough, and it excused a good deal as far as Gregg's behaviour went, but it only accounted for two days – three at the outside – and he had been away for seventeen . . . He waited, wanting to prompt the other man but unable to find a way which would not sound brutal or indifferent: he had been moved by the recital – horrified, even – and he did not want it to seem as if he considered it of no account, or was brushing it aside in favour of a strict, immovable justice. But presently Gregg took up the story again, without any reminder: perhaps he had merely been collecting his thoughts, perhaps there was worse to come.

'That was the first day, sir,' he said, 'and I stayed two more, just to make sure – I'd still be back in time to catch the ship, and that way it didn't seem it would be so bad.' He looked swiftly at the Captain, aware that he was taking a lot for granted, but the latter made no sign: the verdict, the judgement was to come at the very end . . . 'She was just like she used to be in the old days,' Gregg went on: 'she stopped talking about the other chap, she didn't say anything more about these funny ideas, she seemed to have forgotten all about it, except when I spoke about it at the end. But before I left I asked her what was going to happen, and she promised faithfully to give it another try. So I went off to catch the early train——' Ericson could tell there was yet another climax coming, another stroke of pain, from Gregg's swifter, shorter breathing, and the way his words came faster and faster, 'and I missed it because of the traffic, and I came back, thinking I'd spend the day with her and catch the train in the evening, and she wasn't there – the house was empty, and she'd taken her case as well.'

This time Ericson was afraid that Gregg was going to break down altogether: his voice came to a sudden stop, and his mouth, working and trembling uncontrollably, seemed on the point of puckering into tears. It was a moment of surrender: he looked young and capable and smart in his uniform, and then, above the neatly-rolled collar and the clean white flannel, his defeated face destroyed the picture utterly. Without a word Ericson went to his cupboard, poured out some whisky, and handed the glass to Gregg: because it was so unusual a thing to do, so far outside the normal, it was capable of being a failure and a mistake. For a moment Ericson wondered if, at a later date when Gregg had forgotten the worst of this matter, he might translate the occasion into different terms: perhaps boasting cheekily in the messdecks: 'Trouble? Not *me*! The skipper gave me a tot of whisky and told me to come back any time ...' But no, it would not be like that. The giving of the whisky seemed to surprise Gregg into an effort of control: as he sipped it, looking round the cabin and out through the sun-lit porthole, his mouth and face firmed again, and he prepared to go on. What he had said, and what he had still to say, was desolate, but not too desolate for ordered speech.

It was possible, he had thought, that his wife might be at her mother's, over at Edgware; even though she had said nothing about going, she was in the mood for impulsive action. So to Edgware he went, by bus, only to draw another blank. 'She wasn't there, and she hadn't been there for weeks. I could see her mother thought it was funny, but I wasn't answering any questions. Then I went to see my pal, the one that wrote the letter, but he'd gone back after his leave and they didn't know anything. So I left it, and went home again.'

He had been alone in the empty, silent house for a week. As he dismissed it thus, in a single sentence, Ericson tried to visualize what it must have been like: the waiting, the loneliness, the suspicion, the knowledge of betrayal. 'I had to stay, sir, in case she came back,' he said, and Ericson could not, for pity, deny the claim. 'I'd have gone looking for her, but I didn't know where to look – there was the whole of London. And then I got an idea, I should have thought of it before. There was a married friend of hers, woman I never cared for, over the other side of London, down White City way. I thought she might be staying there, so I went over, and asked at the house. She said the wife *had* been there, a few days back, but had gone away again, she didn't know where.' The story was pouring out now, unchecked by any reserve: in the silent cabin the words and sentences, clumsy and ill-formed, yet flowed with an eloquent readiness towards their cruel end. 'I thought she was telling lies, there was something in the way she looked, so I hung about a bit, watching for the car, and then I turned into the first pub I came to, for a pint and something to eat, and there they were, the two of them, sitting down and drinking port.' He swallowed. 'She was laughing, and then she looked up and said: "Look who's here".'

Ericson thought he was going to stop, as he had stopped many times before, but the whisky had done its work – or perhaps it was the story itself, which could not be delayed at so crucial a point.

'I asked her what she was doing there, instead of being at home,' Gregg went on immediately, 'and she said there was no harm in having a drink. Then I said: "Where've you been the last week?" and she said: "Staying with Else" – that's this woman. I said I wasn't going to stand for it, and the man said: "What you need is a drink." I said: "I don't want a drink from you – if this goes on I'm going to see about a divorce." I didn't really mean it, I just wanted to give him a scare. He said: "You've got no evidence." So I said: "How about you coming down the stairs that night?" and he said: "I was just saying goodnight to Mrs Gregg – it was quite innocent." I said: "How about that stuff on her dressing-gown, then?" and he said: "Reckon we must have spilt the milk," and then he winked at her and she laughed like a – like a rotten tart.'

What an accurate description, thought Ericson: how can he want her now, how can he feel anything but hatred and disgust? But in Gregg's voice there was neither of these: when he said 'rotten tart' he was not condemning, he was mourning what he and she had lost. There was no trace of rationality in it, no balancing of right and wrong: there was simply the incalculable instinct of love, of what people feel – or feel that they should feel – when they undertake to bind themselves to other people. Even now, it seemed, Gregg did not question the validity of that binding: the bargain might be bad, but it was a bargain still – and all this sprang from 'love', a word in a book, a scene in a film, a foolish core of determination in a man's brain.

Gregg was continuing, with quiet assurance. 'I was going to say something to him about that, sir, but then he said: "You needn't worry, anyway, I'm off to the States next week, big buying job." And the wife said: "First I've heard of it, Walter, when are you going?" and he said: "Thursday – I'll come round to say goodbye," and I said: "Like hell you will – you don't come near the house again." It was funny, sir, he didn't try to argue the toss about that, he just said, "Have it your own way, then"; I think what I said about the divorce must have rattled him a bit, but perhaps he'd had enough of it anyway. Then he stood up and said to the wife: "Thanks a lot, see you again one of these days," and she said, very surprised: "Do you mean goodbye, Walter?" and he walked off, and by and by she started crying and I took her home.'

At that, Gregg paused and looked at Ericson, as if judging how he would receive what he was going to say next: he was near the end now, and he must, in spite of his earlier indifference, have felt it necessary to justify himself while he had the chance. Ericson was careful to keep his expression as non-committal as possible: even now, there was no verdict to be given, no comforting words to forestall the threat of discipline. This was still a private hearing, out of the main stream, with the normal course of events held in suspense.

Gregg seemed to gather himself together. 'That was the Friday, sir,' he said. 'I'd been adrift ten days already, and this chap didn't leave till the next Thursday, six more days.' He swallowed again. 'I still couldn't go, sir, I still couldn't leave her, even now it wasn't safe: he might change his mind and come round to the house, and if he didn't, I knew she'd be off to meet him if she got half a chance . . . So I thought I'd stay on, and keep her there with me: I was in the rattle anyway, whatever happened, and there was only one way to make sure she didn't see him. Even then it was touch and go. We went to the pictures once, and she got up to go to the Ladies, and after a bit I went out myself, and I just caught her as she was going out through the front entrance. After that, we stayed at home all the time . . . She used to cry a lot: she was always on at me, wanting to go out – I was afraid to go to sleep, towards the end, and then I locked up all her clothes and hid the key where she couldn't find it.' He passed his hand over his forehead. 'But one night – it was the Wednesday, the night before this chap left – she waited till I was asleep and broke the cupboard open and got dressed, and then something woke me up, and she tried to run for it, and I got to the door first and she was screaming and pulling at me, I thought she'd go mad . . . I stayed awake all that night, to make sure, and then in the morning she saw it was too late, and she kind of gave up and I knew it was all right to leave . . . I wasn't going to talk to her at all about it, I wanted to forget it and start afresh; but when I was saying goodbye she said: "Will you be in trouble?" and I said yes, I would and she said: "I'm in trouble too, Tom," and then she said she was going to have a baby.'

Ericson looked at the floor. There was only one question to be asked, and not for a million pounds could he have asked it. But then suddenly Gregg asked and answered it for him, in one swift brave stroke.

'The kid'll be mine, sir, and that's all there is to it.'

Love again, thought Ericson, with wonder in his heart: love the unfailing cure, no matter how hideous the deception, how vile the betrayal . . . Now that the story was done, he wanted to dispose of it as quickly as possible: it was clear that Gregg could not be punished for something which had tried him too high, which he was simply not equipped to deal with, and there was a wise provision for mercy available in such cases. But in spite of his willingness to spare Gregg any further ordeal, there was one point to be made; and it must be driven home at once, if only in fairness to other men who, caught in the same circumstances, did not take the law into their own hands but stayed within the framework of discipline. He turned in his chair.

'Thank you for telling me this, Gregg – I shall think it over before your case comes up again tomorrow. At the moment there's only one thing I want to say, but it's something you ought to remember.' He summoned an incisiveness he did not wholly feel. 'Your officers aren't there just to run the ship and give orders – they're there to help you as well. In a case like this, if you'd come to me as soon as you got that letter I could have given you special leave, and then you wouldn't have had to break ship. And we could have arranged for someone to visit your wife, while you were away.' He smiled – very briefly, for it was not a smiling moment: the miserable face opposite him was the only proper measure of its quality. 'Just remember that the Royal Navy has a routine for *everything*, whether it's for going into battle, or for taking a shell out of a gun when it's jammed and may explode, or for helping in domestic trouble like yours. It's usually the only workable routine there is, the best available, because the Navy looks after its own.' He saw that for some reason Gregg was near to tears again, and he broke off: the point had been made, and he could not bring himself to hammer it further home. 'That's all for now. Ask the First Lieutenant to see me.'

When Gregg had gone, Ericson sat for a long time in thought. On one point, thought was straightforward. Gregg's story would have to be checked – that could be done on the spot, in London, as a matter of routine – and if it were true, he could legitimately let him off altogether: even though Gregg had done wrong, even though women and marriage and emotion should not play a part in war . . . But he knew that the story *was* true – and it was here that thought strayed uncontrollably: there had been no acting in that anguish, no lies behind the pitiful story. Some women were worthless, and some were getting bored with the war: when the two things coincided, no result, however mean or sordid, should ever come as a surprise.

CHAPTER 2

Presently the turn of the year was left behind, and the lengthening days that marked the spring brought them one respite at least – easier nights at sea. Morell's middle watch, indeed, was now the only one which passed in complete darkness; and soon, as spring gave way to early summer, even he was allowed a partial relief from the strain of hanging onto the convoy and guessing at black shadows for four hours on end. During the last half-hour of his watch, towards four o'clock in the morning, there would be a faint lifting of the darkness in the east: through his binoculars the horizon would lose its vagueness and take on a harder outline, and the ships that lay in his line of sight began to abandon their gloomy neutrality and grow into three-dimensional figures again. By the time Lockhart came up to relieve him, at the change of the watch, it was possible to distinguish in detail the upper-works of *Compass Rose* and the faces of the men up on the bridge: when they said good morning to each other, it was a matter of recognition and not guess-work. And then, within half an hour, it was the dawn, and the start of another day – a day farther out into the Atlantic, or a day nearer home. Lockhart would survey the calm collection of ships, and perhaps drop back a mile or so to encourage the stragglers: the Captain would come up, grey and bristly from an uncomfortable night in his berth in the wheel-house, and look about him and sniff the air, and then wander from side to side of the bridge, sextant in hand, ready to catch the last stars before they died with the sun; and finally, to mark the end of the night, Tomlinson the young steward sidled up and collected the sandwich plates and the derelict cocoa cups, the debris of the night's picnic.

That was the simple outline of dawn, as it came to *Compass Rose* on dozens and scores of mornings; but many dawns had more to them than this. Often, tragically, daybreak was the time for counting heads, for closing gaps in the ranks, for signalling to *Viperous* the tally of survivors and the total of the dead. For now, with 1941 advancing, they were a year older, and so was the war; and the further it progressed the deeper they seemed to be involved in failure and set-back.

The tide was now set and running strongly against all Allied shipping: over a full two-thirds of the Atlantic the attackers had the initiative, and they held onto it and gave it ruthless force and effectiveness. It was like a dark stain spreading all over this huge sea: the area of safety diminished, the poisoned water, in which no ship could count on safety from hour to hour, seemed swiftly to infect a wider and wider circle. In the background the big ships skirmished and oc-casionally came to blows: the *Hipper*, the *Scharnhorst*, and the *Gneisenau* emerged on raiding forays, the *Hood* was sunk by one prodigious shot at eleven miles' range, and then, in a swift counter-stroke, the destruction of the *Bismarck* squared the account. But these were dramatic surprises, highlights of a ponderous and intermittent warfare: plying to and fro ceaselessly, the convoys fought their longer and bloodier battle against a multiplying enemy.

The enemy was planning as well as multiplying. At last, the U-boats were co-ordinating their attack: they now hunted in packs, six or seven in a group, quartering a huge area of the convoy-route and summoning their full strength as soon as a contact was obtained. They had the use of French, Norwegian, and Baltic ports, fully equipped for shelter and maintenance: they had long-range aircraft to spot and identify for them, they had numbers, they had training, they had better weapons, they had the spur of success ... The first concerted pack-attack sank ten out of twenty-two ships in one convoy: the monthly record of sinkings mounted – fifty-three in one month, fifty-seven in another. The U-boats gradually extended their operations further westward, until there was no longer, in mid-Atlantic, a safe dispersal-area for the convoys; neither from Britain, Canada, nor Iceland (which had now been drawn fully into the strategic pattern) could complete aircover be provided, and the escorts themselves were limited in their endurance. So the stain spread, and the ships went down. There were counter-measures: patrolling aircraft extended their range, a number of merchant-ships were provided with fighters launched by catapult, and the quality of the weapons in the escorts improved slowly: to mark this improvement, one month in the middle of 1941 saw seven U-boats sent to the bottom – the highest total of the war. But seven U-boats was not enough: there were still too many of them hunting and striking, and not enough escorts to screen the convoys: there was still a vast margin which could only be covered by luck and human endeavour, and neither of these could match the standard and the pace of the enemy, or stop the slaughter.

Of this slaughter, *Compass Rose* saw her full share. It was no longer a surprise when the alarm-bell sounded, no longer a shock to see the derelict humanity that was hoisted over the side after a ship went down: it was no longer moving to watch the dying and bury the dead. They developed – they had to develop – a professional inhumanity towards their job, a lack of feeling which was the best guarantee of efficiency: time spent in contemplating this evil warfare was time wasted, and rage or pity was something which could only come between them and their work. Hardened to pain and destruction, taking it all for granted, they concentrated as best they could on fighting back and on saving men for one purpose only – so that they could be returned to the battle as soon as possible.

. . .

Ferraby and Baker, the two juvenile leads, shared the first watch, from eight until midnight. Following the contemporary corvette fashion, they had both grown beards: in some curious way it made them look younger instead of older, and also rather unconvincing, like the naval personnel in a provincial revival of *H.M.S. Pinafore*. ('Nice drop of horticulture you've got there,' a visitor to the wardroom had said, surveying the effect: the remark had earned, from Morell, the highest raised eyebrows of the war so far.) Baker, who had arrived on board a year previously, as a shy young man with a vague background in accountancy, had shed none of his diffidence in the intervening period: he and Ferraby were alike in many ways – in their automatic acceptance of authority, no matter how flimsy its basis, in their lack of confidence, in their fear that sooner or later the test of war would reveal their shortcomings ... When they talked together, it was on a level plane of protective humility, as men talk when, in an outer office, they are waiting to be interviewed for a job they do not think they will get: it is no good showing off to each other, because neither is worth impressing, and raised voices or a cock-sure attitude may be overheard, and lead to their disqualification before they have even faced the boss ... But latterly, Ferraby had secured an appreciable lead: he was now a father, and when the two of them were together he exhibited the first stirrings of paternal consequence.

'Did you mind it being a girl?' asked Baker one night, when, as usually happened at sea, the conversation turned to the gentler background of home. 'Or did you really want a boy?'

'It didn't seem to matter what it was, as long as *she* was all right,' said Ferraby frankly. 'You get so worried towards the end ... Of course she had her mother there, to look after her, but all the same I was glad when it was over.' Even now, he could not think of that night, just before the end of his last leave, without acute discomfort: Mavis's cry as she woke suddenly, about midnight, the frantic telephoning, the ambulance that would not come, the agonized waiting past dawn, past midday, past half another night ... To see Mavis and the baby together, next morning, two heads on the pillow instead of one, had made up for most of it; but it could not wholly kill the force of memory. 'It was a bit of luck I was on leave when it started,' Ferraby went on. 'Otherwise I don't know what I'd have done, thinking about it happening while we were at sea.'

'My turn for leave next,' said Baker, reacting to the cherished word. 'Two more convoys, I should say – about six weeks.'

Six weeks ... That started, in Ferraby, a fresh train of thought which he was not ready to share with Baker, or with anyone else. Six weeks was a long time in the Atlantic, at this stage, when the next six hours – or six minutes, for that matter – might bring them disaster. There were so many U-boats on the hunt; sooner or later, he was sure, one of them was going to get *Compass Rose* in its sights. Ferraby was never free of that fear nowadays: it was as if, when Bennett left, he had to exchange one tyranny for another, as if the fear of Bennett would only give way to the fear of being torpedoed. Of all of them on board, Ferraby was the least hardened to what was going on: he could not forget the nodding head of the dead man, that first time they had picked up survivors, he could not forget the recurrent alarm, the inevitable attack, the slim chance of survival. Even now, as he talked to Baker or looked at the ship they were stationed on, he was uncomfortable and nervous, preoccupied with what the next few moments might bring: it was getting towards midnight, the end of their watch, and this was the time when things so often happened – the bang, the flare from a torpedoed ship, the explosion in the heart of the convoy. And if they did not happen in the first watch, they could happen in the next one, the middle – and that was worst of all.

At midnight, every night at sea, Ferraby was free to go below, and turn in, and sleep undisturbed till breakfast-time: he had never found this possible save at the very beginning and the very end of a voyage, when they were in safety and shelter. There was something in the very act of lying down below the water-line which tortured his imagination: it seemed quite impossible that *Compass Rose* would not be torpedoed during these dark hours, and that the torpedo, when it struck, would not rip its way into the very cabin where he lay ... Night after night, when they were out in the deep of the Atlantic, these thoughts returned to him: he would lie there, while the ship rolled and groaned and the water sluiced past a few inches from his bunk, sweating and staring at the bulkhead and the rivets that bound the thin plating together. That plating was all that stood between him and the black water: he waited in terror for the iron clang, the explosion, the inrush of water, the certainty of being trapped and choked before he could make a move. One terrible night he *had* managed to get to sleep, even though there had been warnings of a submarine pack in their vicinity: after an hour of sweating nervousness he had dozed off, and then, between waking and sleeping, he had heard a monstrous explosion that seemed to come from within the ship itself, and as he leapt from his bunk the alarm-bell clanged, followed by a rush of feet, and he had felt a surge of blinding panic as he raced for the ladder and the open sky.

Out on the upper deck, where at last he gasped the free air, the scene now was like a scene from hell. One of the escorts had fired a snow-flake rocket – a big flare which could illuminate a two-mile circle and was meant to limelight any submarine that might be on the surface: its yellow brilliance now hung over the wild water, showing him the convoy straining against the storm, and *Sorrel* racing off to starboard, hunting and guessing, and then, quite close to them, a ship, badly listed, already on her way down. Even as he watched her, there was a sudden gush of flame from her funnel, and she seemed to fall apart: a filthy waft of burnt oil and paint and steam came towards them, the very smell of death, and she was gone, quenched by the sea. Ferraby leant against a stanchion, physically sick: that ship might have been *Compass Rose*, and the men now trapped and drowned might have been their own crew, and the place where the torpedo had struck, his own cabin. For many nights

after that, he could not bear to go below after he came off watch: he
would wander about the upper deck, or curl up in a corner at the back of
the bridge, or in the alley-way by the wheel-house: wakeful till dawn,
fingering his safety-light and his blown-up life-jacket, waiting in taut
apprehension for their turn to come. He had seen other men like this,
rescued survivors who would not go below again even to snatch a meal,
and he had wondered at their fear and their obsession. Now he
wondered no more.

But this was something he could share with no one – and especially not
with Mavis, who must now never know the extent of his terror and his
danger. They had taken a small house outside Liverpool, and he saw her
every time *Compass Rose* was in harbour: the recurrent meeting and
separation and goodbye were sweet and harassing at the same time, not
helping him at all ... More and more, the war was making demands on
him beyond his capacity, presenting a bill which his bankrupt spirit
could not meet.

CHAPTER 3

Lockhart had come to rely on Ericson, and to admire him unstintingly in
the process. He was everything a Captain should be: the centre of calm
on the bridge, whatever was happening, a fine seaman who could
handle *Compass Rose* with absolute assurance, a tireless personality who
took infinite pains over every part of his job, whether it was rounding up
stragglers, or fixing their position at sea, or cherishing their paintwork
when they came alongside the oiler. He seemed irreplaceable: it was
therefore something of a shock when he was suddenly put out of action,
and Lockhart had to take the ship himself for the last five days of a
convoy. Ericson was thrown out of his bunk one night when *Compass
Rose*, at her most captious, achieved a forty-five degree roll, and he broke
a rib: the slightest movement gave him intense pain, and it was out of the
question for him to appear up on the bridge. Lockhart signalled the
casualty to *Viperous*, and with a good deal of misgiving took over
command for the rest of the trip.

He had of course no choice in the matter, though that did not make it
any easier. But once the initial challenge was met, the preliminary awe
overcome, he found that he was enjoying himself: he was playing a new
role, and it seemed to be within his range ... Of course it was ludicrous,
really: the idea of a free-lance journalist called Lockhart roaming the
Atlantic in entire charge of a 1,000-ton ship and a crew of 88 men would
have raised a laugh in any pre-war Fleet Street bar. But this was no
longer pre-war, and the mould was different: he had had eighteen

months of training for this moment, eighteen months of watching Ericson and imbibing, unconsciously, the function of command, and when the moment came it seemed not much more than an easy step upwards, with an extra tension to mark the occasion and a certain humorous surprise to spice it. That was one of the best things about the Navy – in wartime at least: it taught you quickly, it taught you well, it taught you all the time: suddenly you woke up with a direct responsibility for a valuable ship and a section of a convoy and a lot of men, some of them your friends, and it seemed as if you were simply turning another page of a book you knew by heart already.

When Ericson, grumbling between the bouts of pain, took to his bunk, *Compass Rose* was nine hundred miles west of the Irish Channel, butting along as stern escort to a slow convoy which had already had its fill of head winds and U-boat scares. But then the luck changed: the wind dropped, and they made their five-day approach to land without any further warnings and not a single genuine alarm. Lockhart reorganized the watches so as to leave himself free of any set hours: being new to the job, and not having Ericson's developed confidence, he stayed awake far longer than he need have done and spent, up on the bridge, an average of two-thirds of every day. He had to be ready for surprises, and the safest way to do that was to be on the spot at all the likely times ... Now and again he went down to report to the Captain, who would repeat, on each occasion, the same insistent questions: was the convoy closed up, was *Compass Rose* in her proper station, were there any U-boat warnings, had Lockhart taken his sights carefully and worked out their position, what did the weather look like? The only question he never asked directly was: 'Are you worried about what you're doing?' and Lockhart was grateful for the implied confidence. The nearest Ericson got to such a query was when he remarked, going off at a tangent:

'I don't suppose you thought this could ever happen, a couple of years ago.'

Lockhart smiled. He was standing in the middle of the Captain's cabin, still muffled against the cold outside, his sea-boots and duffle-coat making an odd contrast with Ericson's elegant dressing-gown.

'A couple of years ago, sir,' he answered, 'my only command was a five-ton yawl, rather pretty, mucking about in the Solent.'

'How big a crew?'

'*She* was rather pretty, too.'

'Get back on the bridge,' said Ericson, 'before my temperature goes up.'

Thank God for a good Captain, thought Lockhart as he made his way up the ladder again: for a good *man*, too, a man to respect and to like, whatever the circumstances. During the last few months, their relationship had developed a great deal, on welcome lines of friendship:

close to each other all the time, and liking the success of the arrangement, they had come to ration their formality, confining it to the
necessary public occasions and leaving the rest on an easier plane.
Lockhart still called the Captain 'sir', in public or private, because that
was the way he felt about it; but the two of them, trusting each other's
competence and viewing the whole thing as an effective partnership,
had come a long way since Lockhart first stepped into the Clydeside
dock-office, a year and a half previously.

The easy voyage drew to its close, with no more disturbing incident
than when an Iceland trawler, southbound, tried to cut at right angles
through the convoy in semi-darkness, and had to be headed off from so
daring a project. In the narrows between Scotland and the north of
Ireland, the convoy split, some ships making for the Clyde, others
southwards to Cardiff and Barry Roads, and the main portion to
Liverpool Bay. Going down the Irish Sea and closing the Liverpool
coastline meant, for Lockhart, a sharpening of the tension, like the last
part of a training course which concludes with a formidable test-paper.
In these confined waters, much could happen if anything went wrong
with their navigation or if they failed to stay alert: there was a
treacherous coast-line to be watched, and a great deal of shipping
moving up and down it, as well as the usual sprinkling of off-shore
fishing-boats, some with lights, some without, and all of them trailing
nets of unknown length and complexity. Fishing-boats, indeed, were a
hazard of a special character. The Admiralty had for centuries been
receiving claims from imaginative fishermen who, as soon as they saw a
ship-of-war within five miles of them, immediately shook their fists at
heaven and swore blind that their nets had been overrun and torn to
ribbons. Their Lordships had even introduced a 'Fishing-boat Log' as a
counter-measure: whenever fishing-boats were sighted at sea, their exact
position was to be noted down and an estimate given of their distance
away. It did not always do the trick, but at least it sorted the brazen
claims from the merely frivolous.

Lockhart was on the bridge for the whole of the last night, checking
their course, making sure of the various buoys and lights as they were
sighted, leaving nothing to chance: he understood now how immensely
tiring Ericson must have found it at the beginning of their commission,
with untried, inexperienced officers as his sole help, and a ship whose
performance and handling were, even for a professional seaman, largely
a matter of guesswork. When dawn came round again, and found the
convoy safely past the Isle of Man and heading east for Liverpool and
home, Lockhart was conscious of an immense relief, and wearily
thankful that, except for the business of docking *Compass Rose* (which he
was still nervous about), the hardest part of the trip was over. The sun
drying out the decks and the seagulls playing triumphantly round the

bows seemed a reflection of this holiday mood. He had had nothing
spectacular to cope with; but it had all been new, and if anything had
gone wrong there could have been no more public demonstration of his
shortcoming.

The holiday, however, had been declared too soon. He was just
thinking of going below to shave and change, leaving the easy final
watch to Baker, when he saw *Viperous* heading for the stern of the
convoy, moving with the high speed, enormous wash and unnecessary
air of drama which were the things he most envied in destroyers . . . She
cut between the last two ships of the wing column, turned in a flurry of
foam, and edged up alongside *Compass Rose*.

'Switch on the loud-hailer,' said Lockhart quickly. He had no idea
what was coming, but there was likely to be a conversation involved.
From the destroyer's bridge he saw binoculars raised and turned his
way: at a lower level, the two crews leant over their respective rails,
and, recognizing their friends here and there, exchanged the repartee
appropriate to a home-coming.

From *Viperous*, the loud-hailer boomed out suddenly, carrying a
pleasant, deep voice with the brisk inflection of authority.

'How's your Captain?' it asked.

Lockhart raised his microphone. 'About the same,' he answered. 'It
hurts a good deal – he's still turned in.'

'Give him my best wishes . . .' There was a short pause. 'We're due for
leave today, and I want to get in early to see about our pay. Do you think
you can lead the convoy in? The Bar Light Vessel's about nine miles
ahead.'

'Yes,' said Lockhart. It wasn't a moment for hesitation, though he had
very little idea of what was required of him. 'Yes, I can do that.'

'The commodore's just signalled them to form single file,' the voice
went on. 'Take station ahead of him as soon as they've done that. When
you get up to Gladstone Dock, make the usual arrival signal – thirty-
eight ships, convoy B.K. 108. I'll explain about us.'

'Yes, sir,' said Lockhart, recalling the need for formality. *Viperous*'s
captain, the senior officer of the escort group, was a young commander
with a forceful reputation.

For a moment longer the two ships kept level pace. 'All right,' came
the voice from *Viperous*. 'I'll leave you to it. But don't let them go too fast
– the harbour-master doesn't like it.' Somewhere deep within the
destroyer the engine-room telegraph clanged, and she suddenly jumped
forward, throwing out a bow-wave like the slicing of a huge cream cake.
'We will now,' said the disappearing voice, authoritative to the last,
'give you our impersonation of a greyhound of the ocean.' And *Viperous*
drew swiftly away, leaving *Compass Rose* as if standing still, and Lockhart
pondering the superiority of destroyers over all other ships. If only one

could press a button like that aboard *Compass Rose*, and leave the fleet
behind ...

But he had more to do than yearn for better things. The convoy was
forming into single line, ready for the narrow passage up river, and he
had at least six miles to make up before he was in station at the head of
the column. *Compass Rose* could not rival *Viperous'* swift get-away, but she
did her best: the hull throbbed as the revolutions crept upwards, and
presently they were passing ship after ship on their way to the front of the
convoy. Lockhart noticed, without paying much attention to it, that the
sun had gone in and that it had turned suddenly colder; but he was not
prepared for what followed after. They were just drawing level with the
fourth ship of the convoy, and he had sighted the Bar Light Vessel,
marking the entrance to the river itself, about two miles ahead of them,
when the Bar Light Vessel disappeared; and as he stared round him,
unwilling to believe that visibility could have deteriorated so swiftly, the
convoy disappeared also, sponged out like chalk from a slate. It was fog,
fog coming down from the north, fog blowing across their path as thick
as a blanket and blotting out everything on the instant.

Lockhart leaned over the front of the bridge, momentarily appalled.
The fog enveloped them in great thick wafts of vapour, cold and acrid;
he could see the tip of their gun-barrel, twenty feet in front of him, and
nothing more at all – no sea, no ships, not even *Compass Rose*'s own stem.
It was like moving inside a colourless sack, isolated and sightless – and
then suddenly he heard the other occupants of the sack, a wild chorus of
sirens as the convoy plunged into the fog-bank. It had taken them by
surprise, when they had just crowded into a single compact line: many
ships were less than their own length from the next one ahead of them,
and the convoy was telescoping like a goods train when the brakes are
applied. Now, unsighted, moving blindly in the raw and luminous air,
they were doing the only thing left to them – making as much noise as
possible, and praying for the fog to lift.

Lockhart's moment of panic did not last. *Compass Rose* had been in fog
before, and he had admired Ericson's calmness and sure control of the
situation: now he simply had to follow that example. There was a
temptation to sheer away from the convoy, and take an independent line
altogether, but that had to be resisted: in a fog, one had to trust other
ships to hold their course, and do the same oneself, otherwise it was
impossible to retain a clear picture of what was going on. One single
ship, losing its nerve and trying to get out of trouble in a hurry, could
destroy that picture, and with it the whole tenuous fabric of their safety,
and bring about disaster.

At the moment all the ships were comfortably to starboard, and he set
to work to plot, inside his head, the varying notes of their sirens. The
nearest one, with the deep note, was a big tanker they had been passing

when the fog came down: the ship ahead of her made a curious wheezing sound, as if some water had got into her siren. The commodore's ship, at the head of the column, had another distinguishable note; and above them all the authoritative voice of the foghorn on the Bar Light Vessel, two miles ahead, supplied as it were the forward edge of the pattern. Beyond that foghorn they could hardly go in safety, for there the channel narrowed to a bare fifty yards: if the fog did not lift, and the convoy had to anchor, it must be done within a time limit of not more than twenty minutes.

Lockhart had the picture in his head, for what it was worth: and beside him in the raw air of the bridge the others – Morell, Baker, Leading-Signalman Wells, the two look-outs – tried to contribute their own quota of watchfulness and interpretation. For the sounds were deceptive – they all knew that well: it was possible that a siren which seemed to be coming clearly from one side was being reflected off the fog-bank, and came in fact from some unknown area of danger. *Compass Rose* ran on, over the oily water, with the ghostly company beside her keeping a distance and a formation which could only be guessed at: the rest of the convoy seemed to recede, while the four sounds Lockhart was especially on the alert for – the big tanker, the ship ahead of her, the commodore, and the Bar Light Vessel – succeeded in even rotation, with *Compass Rose* as the fifth element in the pattern. As long as that pattern held, and the fog blew over or dispersed, they were safe.

Suddenly he raised his head, and was conscious of Wells jerking to attention at the same time. A new siren had sounded, an intruder in the pattern, and it seemed to be coming from their port bow – the side away from the convoy, the side that had been clear. 'Ship to port, sir?' said Wells tentatively, and they waited in silence for the sound to come again. One – that was the tanker: two – the ship ahead of her: three – the commodore: four – a prolonged wail from the Bar Light Vessel. Then *five* – a wavering blast, nearer now, coming from that safe space to port which had suddenly assumed an imminent danger. Lockhart felt his scalp lifting and prickling as he heard it. It might be anything – a ship coming out, a stray from the convoy, an independent ship creeping along their own path: but it was *there*, somewhere in the fog, somewhere ahead of them and to port, steaming along on God-knows-what course and getting nearer with every second that passed.

He gripped the front of the bridge-rail and stared ahead of him. He knew without turning round that the others were watching him: he was the focus now, *Compass Rose* was in his grip, and her safety and perhaps all their lives depended on what he did next. Their own siren sounded, tremendously near and loud, and then the safe four in succession, and then the damned fifth – nearer still, dead ahead or a little to port. He said: 'Slow ahead!' surprised at the calmness of his voice: the telegraph clanged, the revolutions purred downwards to a dull throbbing, the slop and thresh of their bow-wave died to a gentle forward rustling. But the tension did not die: he felt himself taut and sweating as *Compass Rose* ran on, nearing the edge of the known pattern and nearing also the fifth ship, the doubtful element that could wreck them all. If the commodore did not give the signal for anchoring he *must* do something – either stop dead, or take a wide sheer to port, away from the crowd and the danger: they could not simply run on, swallowing up the safety margin, surrendering foot by foot their only security. He heard Morell by his side cough: the damp air mingled with the sticky sweat under his hair, so that drops ran down his forehead: their own siren boomed out suddenly, just above their heads: he had a quick vision of what might lie a few second ahead – the crash, the grinding of wood and metal, the wrecked bows, the cries of men trapped or hurt in the messdecks: he felt all the others watching him, trusting and yet not trusting, hoping that he could meet this inexorable crisis – and then suddenly the port look-out called out: 'Ship to port, sir!' and forty yards away, in the fog that suddenly cleared and the sunshine that suddenly broke through, a small coaster slid past them and down the side of the convoy. He felt a great surge of relief as the last wisps of fog blew away, showing him the lines of ships still intact and the Bar Light Vessel riding clear on the smooth water. As suddenly as the danger had come, it had been taken away again. It was a full reprieve: he had done his best, and the best had been good enough, and now *Compass Rose* steamed on with the rest of them, towards the familiar landmarks of home.

An hour later they were in the thick of the Mersey traffic, leading the slow and stately progress up river to the convoy anchorage. The long line of ships stretched behind them, deep-laden, travel-stained, proud and yet matter-of-fact: ships they had guarded for many days, ships they knew well by sight from this and earlier convoys, ships they had cursed for straggling or admired for skilful handling. It was another convoy – Lockhart had lost count by now, but perhaps it was their sixteenth, perhaps their twentieth; another great company of ships, safe home with hundreds of men and thousands of tons of supplies, after running the gauntlet of the weather and the worst that the enemy could do. Perhaps pride *was* the key-note, pride and a sober thankfulness: the supplies were needed, the men were precious, and their own *Compass Rose* was a well-loved hostage to fortune ... Wells said suddenly: 'Commodore calling up, sir!' and there was silence on the bridge as he took and acknowledged the message from the big freighter that led the convoy. Then Wells turned from the signal-lamp.

'From the Commodore, sir. "Nice to see those Liver birds again. Thanks and goodbye."'

Lockhart looked up river, towards the great gilded birds that topped the Liver Building in the heart of Liverpool. He shared the commodore's sentiment, down to the last tip of their wings ...

'Make: "They look bigger and better every time. Goodbye to you",' he dictated to Wells. He waited while the message was despatched and then, with a curious sense of disappointment, he gave the helm-order which took *Compass Rose* in a wide sheer away from the convoy and towards their own berth at the oiler. The job was done, the release was official, but to part company now was like surrendering a foster child one had learned to love ... Earlier he had been worried about manoeuvring *Compass Rose* up to the oiler, but now he took her alongside with a careless skill, as if he had done it every day for the past year. After the weight of the last few days, after the ordeal of the fog, there seemed nothing that he could not do. When finally he gave the order: 'Finished with main engines', and went down to report to Ericson, he felt at least ten years older, and triumphant in his maturity.

CHAPTER 4

There was the life at sea, crude, self-contained, sometimes startling: there was the tender life of home, when leave came round: and there was the medium world of life in harbour, when they rested from one convoy and prepared for the next one. Of the three, harbour routine gave them perhaps the most vivid sense of being one unit of a complex weapon engaged in a huge and mortal battle.

Gladstone Dock, where nearly all the Western Approaches escorts roosted, had developed in two years into a vast, concentrated hive of naval activity. Strategically, the Battle of the Atlantic was controlled from the underground headquarters in Liver Buildings: down in Gladstone Dock, and in other smaller docks grouped along the waterfront, the ships that fought the battle, the crude pawns that did the work, lay in tiers, three and four abreast along the quayside, salty, shabby, overworked, overdriven; fresh and wet from the encounter, resting thankfully, or waiting for the next tide to take them out again ... They looked workmanlike, without much elegance, but tough and dependable: they were close packed, stem to stern, their masts reaching for the sky, their level fo'c'sles towering over the jetty – the jetty which was itself crowded with sheds and training-huts and an untidy jumble of gear and spare parts and oil-drums and newly-delivered stores. But it was the ships which drew and focused the eye: the lean grey destroyers, the stocky sloops and corvettes, the trawlers that swept the fairway – this was the whole interlocking team that had the battle in its hands. Here in Gladstone Dock was the hard shell for the convoys, the armour of the

Atlantic: it did not shine, it was dented here and there, it was unquestionably spread thin and strained to the limit of endurance; but it had stood the test of two brutal years, and it would hold as long as the war held, and for five minutes longer.

The men who manned these ships were cast in the same mould. For sailors, the Battle of the Atlantic was becoming a private war: if you were in it, you knew all about it – you knew how to watch-keep on filthy nights, how to surmount an aching tiredness, how to pick up survivors, how to sink submarines, how to bury the dead, and how to die without wasting anyone's time. You knew, though not in such detail as your own particular part of the job, the overall plan of the battle, and the way it was shaping. You knew, for example, that at this moment the score was steadily running against the convoys; you knew by heart the monthly totals of sinkings, the record and the quality of other ships in other escort-groups, the names of U-boat commanders who had especially distinguished themselves by their skill or ruthlessness. The whole battle was now a very personal matter, and for sailors involved in it there was a pride and a comradeship which nothing could supplant. For they were the experts, they were fighting it together, they had learnt what it took from a man, and the mortal fury which, increasing from month to month, tested whomever was sucked in, from the highest to the lowest, down to the fine limits of his endurance.

This was especially true of the men who sailed in corvettes, the smallest ships loose in the wild Atlantic at this desperate stage: when they foregathered in harbour after the tough convoy, the triumphant attack, the miserable loss and slaughter, they were very conscious of their calling ... They read about themselves in the newspapers, they quoted the ludicrous headlines which lagged so far behind the truth: but deep within himself each man knew that the public reputation, the corvette label, was a reflection of something which, when isolated at sea, always confronted him with a mixture of triumph and horror, which was a stark and continuous challenge, which really did take a man to survive ... When a sailor said: 'I'm in corvettes,' he might be alert for the answering: 'That must be tough – I believe they roll their guts out': but whatever the answer, whatever the scale of sympathy or incomprehension, the truth kept him company, and in his private mind he could be proud of it.

Alongside each other, in harbour, one wardroom visited another: a taste of someone else's gin and a new angle to flotilla gossip enlivened the set routine and the waiting for action. But there was little to distinguish between the men themselves: whatever the ship, they were the same kind of people – amateurs who had graduated to a professional skill and toughness. When Ericson looked round his own wardroom, he saw in theory a journalist, a barrister, a bank-clerk, and a junior accountant;

but these labels now were meaningless – they were simply his officers, the young men who ran his ship and who had adapted themselves to this new life so completely that they had shed everything of their past save the accent it had given them. It was the same in other ships: all the corvettes were officered on these lines: the new experimental craft had taken their men to school with them, and had developed swiftly and evenly into units remarkable for their dependability and essential to the struggle. It was no wonder that, when they met and relaxed between convoys, these young men all exhibited, like a brand-name, the disdainful confidence of the elect. To sail in corvettes was a special kind of test and a special distinction, and none could know it better than themselves.

It coloured – it was bound to colour – their feelings for other men who were not in the battle. During her time in harbour, *Compass Rose* had many contacts with the shore staff, who supervised the continuous programme of gunnery and Asdic training which filled most of the working days between convoys; and there were many visitors on board – experts of all kinds to check their equipment, signalling and engineering staff, liaison characters, religious performers: men with excellent reasons for coming aboard, and men with none at all save a militant thirst and the chance of slaking it at any one of a dozen floating bars ... There was indeed a very wide range of callers, and it was fair to say that most of them were welcome, since most of them were hard-working, helpful, genuine, and wistfully honest when they proclaimed their longing to go to sea instead of sitting out the war in an office job ashore. But there were others, nibbling and sipping at the outside of the real core; professional callers, who could be counted on to come aboard at eleven in the morning with some transparent excuse, anchor themselves in the wardroom with a glass in one hand and the bottle convenient to the other, and stay there with so established an air that the final choice lay between closing the bar or asking them to lunch ... Some of them acted a part, and the talk would run on their eagerness to go to sea, if only they could shake off this infernal catarrh; others did not even bother to do this, and exhibited only the complacency which went naturally with a soft job, plenty of spare time, and a prescriptive right to scrounge free drinks for several hours a day. When one was recovering from two or three weeks of vile weather at sea, with perhaps a rough convoy thrown in, and the memory of men gasping out their lives in the very wardroom where one sat, it was particularly hard to be civil to a man who seemed to regard the whole thing as an agreeable frolic, and his own soft role in it as the reward of a natural talent.

For the most part their reaction, even among themselves, was silence, a tacit contempt which could hardly find expression without acknowledging what they thought of their own job. But sometimes this contempt overflowed. There was one occasion aboard *Compass Rose* when, lunch having been delayed for a full hour by a determined stayer who would not take even the broadest hint that the morning gin-session was over, they sat down at the lunch table in a state of frustrated impatience. Ericson was ashore, and Lockhart, sitting at the head of the table and helping himself to nearly-congealed steak-and-kidney pie, voiced the general feeling when he said:

'That man really is the limit. He comes aboard every single day we're in harbour, and I don't suppose he does a stroke of work while he's here.' He looked at Morell. 'What did he do for us this morning?'

'He had eight gins,' answered Morell evenly. 'Apart from that, he said our gun was very nice and clean.'

'Flotilla Gunnery Officer!' exclaimed Lockhart savagely. 'I'd like to take that gun and——'

'Quite so,' said Morell. 'But I claim the right to pull the trigger.'

Ferraby, picking at his food at the bottom of the table, broke in. 'Don't you remember him at *King Alfred*?' he asked Lockhart. 'He was there the same time as us. He said he was going into Coastal Forces.'

Lockhart nodded. 'I remember his face vaguely.'

'You've had plenty of time to refresh your memory,' said Morell.

'What makes me specially angry,' went on Lockhart, 'is his general attitude – the way he looks at the war. He comes aboard here, drinks our gin, doesn't pretend to be the slightest use to us, and then talks about the war and the Navy as if they were both some kind of racket, specially invented to give him a soft job.'

'That's probably exactly what the war has meant for him,' said Morell. 'There are hundreds of people like that, you know: they don't see the point of it, they don't *want* to see the point of it – they get themselves a nice easy job, with a bit of extra pay attached, and the longer the war goes on the happier they are. They're not fighting, or helping to fight, because they don't see the thing as a fight at all. It's simply a little cosmic accident which has given them a smart uniform and the chance to scrounge cigarettes at duty-free prices.'

'But how many people do see it as a fight?' Baker did not often join in wardroom discussions, but this time he seemed to have nerved himself to take part. He looked round the table, rather hesitantly. 'We all feel pretty close to it here, I suppose, but even so——' he floundered for a moment, 'even when we're at sea, it's difficult to feel that we're there because we've got to win the war and beat the Germans. Most of the time it's not like being in a war at all – it's just doing a job because everyone else is doing it, and if it were the French instead of the Germans we'd do it just the same, without asking any questions.'

'I know what you mean,' said Lockhart after a pause. 'Sometimes it *is* like being caught in a machine, a machine which someone else is working and controlling.' He hesitated. The true answer was of course that one should have taken sufficient interest in politics before the war to understand what the war was about, and to feel a personal and overwhelming desire to win it; but for someone like Baker, barely out of his teens and with the narrowest of interests, the criticism would have been harsh. His trouble was not lack of interest, but immaturity. 'But all the same,' he went on, 'we *are* in it, and we *are* fighting; and even if we don't consciously give it a melodramatic label like "fighting for democracy" or "putting an end to fascist tyranny", that's precisely what we're doing and that's the whole meaning of it.'

Morell looked at him curiously. 'You really feel that, don't you?'

'Yes.' Then, conscious that the others were looking at him with an equal curiosity, Lockhart relaxed, and smiled. 'Yes, I'm a very patriotic character. It's the only thing that keeps me going.'

There was a knock at the wardroom door, and the quartermaster came in.

'Gunnery Officer, sir,' he said formally.

'Yes?' said Morell.

'The officer who went ashore awhile ago just came back, sir.'

'Oh God!' said Lockhart involuntarily.

'He asked me to give you this, sir.' The quartermaster held out an envelope. 'Said he forgot about it.'

'Thank you,' said Morell. He took the envelope, and slit it open with a knife. An imposing-looking sheet of foolscap fell out. Morell glanced at it, and his face assumed a ludicrously startled air. 'Good heavens!' he muttered. 'It's not possible.'

'What is it?' asked Lockhart.

'An amendment to the new Flotilla Gunnery Orders that came out yesterday,' answered Morell. 'Our friend has justified his existence at last.'

'Anything important?'

'Oh yes. In fact it's fundamental . . .' Some element of control in his voice made them all look up. 'I will read it to you. "Flotilla Gunnery Orders",' he read out, his inflection infinitely smooth. ' "Amendment Number One. Page two, line six. For 'shit' read 'shot'." '

.   .   .

Among the many ships which they encountered regularly at Liverpool were some manned by men of the Allied navies, men who had either escaped in the ships themselves and made their way to Britain, or had been recruited on their arrival and drafted to a British ship which had been turned over to them. There were, among others, several Dutch minesweepers, a Norwegian corvette, and a French submarine chaser of so dramatic a design that it was difficult to tell, at a first glance, whether she was sinking or not. Such ships, and such men, set a curious problem:

the problem of whether to take them seriously, and count on them as honest and effective allies, or to discount them altogether and treat them as an unexpected piece of decoration, acceptable as long as they did not get in the way of more serious preoccupations but hardly to be rated as ships of war and men of action.

The trouble was that they varied: sometimes they were convincing, sometimes not. The 'foreign' ships were of course essentially self-contained: isolated in a strange country and cut off from their own defeated peoples, their officers and men had a wary reserve in dealing with strangers which was difficult to break down. One wanted to understand them, to make allowances, to sympathize with their position; but there were so many other things to think about that the curious, the almost tender complication of appreciating an exile's feelings was too much trouble altogether, unless one were in an exceptionally sympathetic mood ... Sometimes it did seem worthwhile, when they could be persuaded to talk freely; for many of them had exciting stories to tell of how they came to be fighting for the Allies, stories so very much more significant than simply signing on the dotted line and stepping into an R.N.V.R. uniform: stories of drama and intrigue when their countries were on the verge of defeat, of escape seen as the only salve for honour, of taking desperate decisions under cover of a passive acceptance, of fighting and eluding, of breathing suddenly the free air of England ... They all shared this basic excitement, in many and varied forms, and they shared also a sadness, a looking backwards towards what they had left behind; but even in sadness they varied, even here there were degrees of plausibility.

The Dutch and the Norwegians seemed essentially serious and dependable: they too had this backward glance – many of them had heard nothing of their friends and families since their countries had been cruelly overrun in 1940 – but they matched it by a forward look as well, a positive effort to regain and re-establish what they had lost, a fighting-back towards home and peace with honour. Their ships always made a remarkable impression, because the men themselves seemed to have remarkable qualities; by cutting themselves off from their homes they had cleared the ground for a single-minded effort, and this effort, involving the seamanlike virtues of cleanliness, patience, and courage, was reflected in all they did and most of what they said. By chance, it was Ericson who summed up this feeling, after spending an evening in one of the Dutch minesweepers in Gladstone Dock.

'I like those Dutchmen,' he said to Lockhart next morning, when they were walking round the upper deck during Stand-Easy. 'They take the whole thing seriously – everything's related to war, or if it isn't they don't want to hear about it. Even when I said it was a pity Princess Juliana had had three daughters in a row, instead of a son, their captain got terribly red in the face and said: "If you think we don't fight for daughters, I smash you. Come outside." Of course,' added Ericson reasonably, 'we'd had a few glasses of Schnapps – but he was quite determined about it ... That's the kind of man I like to have minesweeping in front of a convoy: not these bloody Frogs, all yearning for home and missing the corners.'

For the Frenchmen were different: that was something which could not be denied. It happened that Lockhart went aboard the French ship on a good many occasions, to take advantage of the food (which was exquisite) and the chance of talking French; and he could not help being aware of a dubious quality, a fugitive relaxation which seemed to infect the whole ship. It was not that their basic allegiance was in question, but that they had been defeated by events and were not wholly convinced that France could now be rescued from her degrading situation. They talked of General de Gaulle with respect, but they seemed always to leave a margin for events to deteriorate: if de Gaulle failed, they were going to shrug it off – *faut pas penser, faut accepter* – and put their money on a different horse, even the one labelled Laval and running in the colours of collaboration ... They were no longer proud, as the Dutch and the Norwegians were proud: they talked much more of their homes and their families, much less of the job they were doing: they longed openly for home, home on any terms, home by surrender if it could not be regained by victory: at times it seemed that their mainspring was not *la patrie* but *l'amour* – a four-letter urge which, by an odd coincidence, seemed to render them impotent ... It was a pity; Lockhart, who had lived in Paris and admired all things French, found it profoundly sad; but it was a manifestation of the Gallic spirit in adversity which could not be disguised.

In the course of an argument the captain of the French ship, somewhat less than sober, said to Lockhart one night: 'You don't really trust us, do you?' He used the tone of voice, the bitter inflection, which seemed to add: 'We do not mind, because you are a barbarous nation anyway.' But the stain was there, and was thus acknowledged; and the charge of Anglo-Saxon insensibility could not wipe it out, nor pretend that it was the product of a simple misunderstanding.

There were, as yet, no Americans officially upon the scene: their two years' profitable neutrality had not yet been ended by the galvanic shot-in-the-arm of Pearl Harbor. But here and there they were to be met: flyers relaxing at Liverpool between trans-ocean trips, and sailors in the anonymous middle reaches of the Atlantic. For they were now escorting some of the convoys, from American ports to a point where they could be taken over by the British escort: strange-looking destroyers, with long names often beginning with 'Jacob' or 'Ephraim', would appear from the mist, and spell out Morse messages very slowly and gently, for the dull British to assimilate as best they could. 'They must think we're a lot of kids,' said Leading-Signalman Wells disgustedly one day, when an exceptionally prudent American operator had tried his patience to the limit. 'It's like Lesson Number One back in barracks. And what a bloody ignorant way to spell "harbour"...' But the main reaction was a pleasant sense of comradeship: it was good to have some more ships lending a hand, at this time of strain, and the fact that the transatlantic link was being completed in this natural way, Americans handing over to British, gave the latter a grateful and brotherly satisfaction. The Americans were still out of the war; but between Lend-Lease, and this unobtrusive naval effort, they were certainly doing their best round the edges.

Others were not. There are degrees of neutrality, just as there are degrees of unfaithfulness: one may forgive a woman an occasional cold spell, but not her continued and smiling repose in other men's arms. Even in the grossest betrayal, however, whether of the marriage vow or the contract of humanity, there could be variations of guilt: for example, one could understand, though one could not condone, the point of view of such countries as Spain or the Argentine, which had political affinities with Germany and did not disguise their hatred of England and their hopes of her defeat. They had never been married to democracy in the first place ... But it was difficult to withhold one's contempt from a country such as Ireland, whose battle this was and whose chances of freedom and independence in the event of a German victory were nil. The fact that Ireland was standing aside from the conflict at this moment posed, from the naval angle, special problems which affected, sometimes mortally, all sailors engaged in the Atlantic, and earned their particular loathing.

Irish neutrality, on which she placed a generous interpretation, permitted the Germans to maintain in Dublin an espionage-centre, a window into Britain, which operated throughout the war and did incalculable harm to the Allied cause. But from the naval point of view there was an even more deadly factor: this was the loss of the naval bases in southern and western Ireland, which had been available to the Royal Navy during the First World War but were now forbidden them. To compute how many men and how many ships this denial was costing, month after month, was hardly possible; but the total was substantial and tragic. From these bases escorts could have sailed further out into the Atlantic, and provided additional cover for the hard-pressed convoys: from these bases, destroyers and corvettes could have been refuelled quickly, and tugs sent out to ships in distress: from these bases, the Battle of the Atlantic might have been fought on something like equal terms. As it was, the bases were denied: escorts had to go 'the long way round' to get to the battlefield, and return to harbour at least two days earlier than would have been neccessary: the cost, in men and ships, added months to the struggle, and ran up a score which Irish eyes a-smiling on the day of Allied victory were not going to cancel. From a narrow legal angle, Ireland was within her rights: she had opted for neutrality, and the rest of the story flowed from this decision. She was in fact at liberty to stand aside from the struggle, whatever harm this did to the Allied cause. But sailors, watching the ships go down and counting the number of their friends who might have been alive instead of dead, saw the thing in simpler terms. They saw Ireland safe under the British umbrella, fed by her convoys and protected by her air force, her very neutrality guaranteed by the British armed forces: they saw no return for this protection save a condoned sabotage of the Allied war effort; and they were angry – permanently angry. As they sailed past this smug coastline, past people who did not give a damn how the war went as long as they could live on in their fairy-tale world, they had time to ponder a new aspect of indecency. In the list of people you were prepared to like when the war was over, the man who stood by and watched while you were getting your throat cut could not figure very high.

.   .   .

Liverpool was a sailors' town, and she went out of her way to make this generously plain. From the merchant-ships lining the quays and docks, from the escorts cramming Gladstone Dock, hundreds of men poured ashore every night, intent on enjoying their short hours of liberty: they got drunk, made disturbances, thronged the streets and the public-houses, monopolized the prostitutes, seduced the young girls, and accommodated the married women – and Liverpool forgave them all, and still offered her hospitality unstintingly. It was difficult to estimate the contribution to morale which Liverpool made, during this wartime invasion; but the happy background, the sure welcome, which continued for year after year, was a memorable help to sailors, giving them something to look forward to after weeks at sea, something which could take the sting out of loneliness as well as exhaustion.

Compass Rose, of course, came in for her share of this generosity; after being based there for eighteen months, most people on board had contacts ashore, and could be sure of the home-cooking and the blessed normality of family life, which was itself the best tonic of all. Some of *Compass Rose*'s crew had married Liverpool girls, or had brought their wives up to live there: the ship now seemed to belong to Liverpool, and as long as their luck held and she was not transferred to the Clyde or Londonderry, the two other big Western Approaches bases, they were very happy in the situation – the best compromise between war and peace which was possible.

Ericson also was glad of this permanent tie with the shore, which made for a contented crew and less likelihood of serious leave-breaking; he was even reconciled, on his own account, to the consolidation of his domestic life, with Grace as the placid background and the little house in Birkenhead as his resting-place between convoys. He did not concentrate any the less on *Compass Rose*; and the fact that Grace's mother was now living with them, and was installed in a permanent position on the left side of the fireplace, meant that he need not feel guilty about sleeping on board if the need arose. The other Birkenhead resident, Tallow (now a Chief Petty Officer), was growing positively sleek on his sister Gladys' cooking; and he was deriving a certain amount of amusement from the situation between Gladys and Chief E.R.A. Watts, who had been a persistent and welcome visitor ever since *Compass Rose* was first stationed at Liverpool. Watts was a widower with grown-up children, Gladys was a widow comfortably past the age of romantic ardour; it was a quiet affair, a placid understanding that, come the end of the war, they would settle down together and, between his pension and her modest savings, make a go of it ... When Watts had first broached the subject to Tallow, it was in such a roundabout way that the latter could hardly grasp what he was driving at: but when Watts finally muttered something about 'getting fixed up after the war', light broke through.

'Why, that's fine, Jim!' exclaimed Tallow. The two men were alone in the petty officers' mess, and on an impulse, Tallow leant forward and held out his hand. They shook hands awkwardly, not looking at each other, but there was warmth in Tallow's voice as he went on: 'Best thing that could happen for her. And for you, too. You've asked her, eh?'

'Sort of ...' Watts was still embarrassed by the display of feeling. 'We've got a – an understanding, like. The only thing is——' He paused.

'What's the trouble?'

'She was a bit worried about you. I mean, she's been house-keeping for you for a long time, hasn't she? She didn't want you to be disappointed.'

'Oh, forget about it!' Tallow smiled. 'Might get married myself one of these days – you never know. You go ahead, Jim, and I'll give the bride away, any time you like.'

'Can't see it happening soon,' answered Watts. 'Not with the war going the way it is. Longest bloody job I ever saw.'

'You're right about that ... Don't worry over me, anyway: just name the day, and I'll dance at your wedding.'

But that was not to be. For Liverpool, the sailors' town, was soon to pay for that label in the most brutal way imaginable; and a tiny part of that payment bore away with it Watts' modest hopes of happiness.

CHAPTER 5

Even far down river, at the Crosby Light Vessel, they knew that something was wrong; and as they made their way upstream at the tail of the convoy many of the crew clustered on the upper deck, shading their eyes against the strong May sunlight and looking towards the city they had come to know as home. Morell, who was standing on the fo'c'sle with the men getting out the mooring-wires, trained his glasses up the river towards the Liver Buildings: there seemed to be a lot of smoke about, and here and there a jagged edge to the skyline which he had never noticed before ... At his side he suddenly heard Leading-Seaman Phillips exclaim: 'Christ! It's copped a packet!' and then he smelt – they all smelt – the acrid tang of the smoke blowing down river, and his eyes, focusing suddenly on a big warehouse just above Gladstone Dock, discovered that it was split from top to bottom, that one half of it was a gigantic heap of rubble, that the rest was blackened and smouldering. His binoculars, traversing steadily across the city and over to the Birkenhead side, showed him many such buildings, and scores of small houses lying ruined in the centre of a great scorched circle: there were fires still burning, there was a heavy pall of smoke lying over the northern part of the city, there were gaps, whole streets missing, rows of houses mis-shapen and torn. He dropped his glasses, shocked by the scale of the destruction, the naked ruin of a city which they had left prosperous and unharmed; and then he caught the eye of one of his fo'c'sle-party, a young seaman whose wife, he knew, had recently come to live in Liverpool.

'What – what's it like, sir?' asked the man hesitantly.

'Not too good, I'm afraid,' answered Morell. 'It looks as if they've been raided several times.'

'Bastards!' said Phillips, to no one in particular. 'Look at those houses ...'

The smoke and the dirty air, the smell of destruction, blew thick and strong across the river towards them; and such was their home-coming.

From the signal station they were ordered to go straight into Gladstone Dock. 'I hope they didn't get the oiler,' said Ericson, as Wells read out the message to him. 'She'd go up like a Roman candle ...' He had been looking through his glasses at the Birkenhead side of the river,

where his own house was: the damage there was on a special scale of fury,
as if the bombers, trying for the docks, had mistaken the neat rows of
houses for the nearby quayside, and had triumphantly unloaded. Or
perhaps they had not minded what they hit ... *Compass Rose* veered
suddenly across the river, and Ericson called out, in sharp tones: 'Watch
her head, Coxswain!' and up the voice-pipe came Tallow's answering
voice: 'Sorry, sir!' and Ericson remembered that he was not the only one
who had a personal interest in what had happened at Birkenhead.
Thankfully he decreased speed, and set a course for the squat stone
entrance to Gladstone Dock. At least they would know soon, at least
they had not to wait for the uncertain mail or the chance flight of
rumour, to learn the worst.

As they came alongside the southern quay of the dock-basin, a
berthing-party of half a dozen men from the nearest destroyer ran along
to meet them and to take their mooring-wires. The first heaving-line
whipped across from ship to shore, establishing contact once more after
a fortnight at sea, and Leading-Seaman Phillips, standing high on the
fo'c'sle-head, called out:

'What's been going on?'

One of the berthing-party, a tough three-badge able-seaman, looked
up and grimaced. 'You've missed something, mate!' he shouted back.
'Eight nights on end – that's all we've had: bombers coming over every
night as thick as bloody sparrows. They've made a right mess of this
town, I can tell you.'

'Go on,' said Phillips. 'What's got it worst?'

The A.B. gestured vaguely. 'All over, I reckon – Bootle, Birkenhead,
Wallasey. And down in the town too: there isn't any Lord Street left –
they got the lot, both sides. Worst bombing of the war, the papers said. I
don't want any worse myself ... There was an ammunition ship just
alongside here, blazing all over, but they towed her out into the middle
of the river before she went up.' He gestured again, more vividly. 'Best
dose of salts I've ever had ... Give us your head-rope.'

From the bridge above them a remarkably cold voice said: 'Stop
talking and get on with those wires.' Phillips winked at the man standing
on the quay below him, and got an answering jerk of the head. They
both knew, to within very fine limits, just how long such a conversation
could go on.

Presently, when they were secure and Ericson, up on the bridge, had
rung off the engines, he turned to Lockhart.

'Number One.'

'Sir?'

'There'll be a lot of requests for special leave, probably. You'd better
cancel ordinary leave, and give it to ratings who have homes or relatives
ashore.'

'Aye, aye, sir.'

'See that these wires are squared off. I'm going ashore to telephone.'

There were a lot of other candidates for the telephone: a small procession of men, anxious to establish contact, queueing up outside the single dockside call-box, waiting patiently, not talking to each other. Ericson got through, and spoke for a moment to his wife: she sounded subdued, but at least she was there ... Ferraby, whose small house was on the outskirts of the city, had the same comforting luck: but Tallow, when it came to his turn, could not get his number at all, simply the high continuous note which meant 'line out of order'. When he was back on board, and making a hurried toilet in the petty officers' mess before going ashore again, Watts said tentatively:

'I'd like to come with you, Bob.'

Tallow, who was shaving, nodded his head. 'Yes, Jim. You come along.'

'They might just have damaged the telephone wires,' said Watts after a pause.

Tallow nodded again. 'It might be that.'

But the nearer they got to the house, after crossing the river by ferry-boat, the more they knew that it was *not* that. From the landing-stage they walked uphill towards Dock Road, slowly because of the blocked roads and the rubble and glass and smashed woodwork which was strewn over the streets; the trail of wrecked houses and the smell of newly-extinguished fires was a terrible accompaniment to their journey. They did not talk to each other, because the cruel destruction was saying it all for them: there was no need to speculate on what they were going to find, when the odds mounted with every pace they took, with every shop and little house which had been blasted to ruins. Presently, walking in step side by side, smart and seamanlike in their square-cut uniforms, they turned the last corner, or the place where the last corner should have been, and looked down Dock Road.

There wasn't a great deal left of Dock Road: the two corner houses just beside them had gone, and three more farther down, and then there was a great hole in the centre of the roadway, and then, farther down still, a ragged heap of rubble where another house had sprawled into the street. It must have been a stick of bombs, as neatly placed as the button-holes in a dress ... Tallow looked at the farthest point of destruction, sick and hurt: he said, somewhere between surprise and a fatalistic calm: 'That's the one, Jim, I know it is,' and he started foolishly to run. Watts, possessed by the same urgency, kept pace with him, and they went at a steady jog-trot down the street: past the first lot of wrecked houses, past the second, past the crater in the roadway, and up to the last shattered corner. Number 27 was half ruined by blast: so was Number 31. Number 29 had taken the full force of a direct hit.

Number 29 Dock Road ... Under the bright afternoon sunshine the wreck of the little houses seemed mean and tawdry; there was flayed wall-paper flapping in the wind, and half a staircase set at a drunken angle, and a kitchen sink rising like some crude domestic altar from a heap of brickwork. The house had collapsed upon itself, and then overflowed into the garden and the roadway: the broken glass and the rubble slurred under their feet as they came to a halt before it. It was not a house anymore, this place where, between voyages, Tallow had been so comfortable and content, and Watts had stumbled out a halting proposal of marriage, and Gladys had made a warm cheerful haven for them all; it was simply a shapeless mass slopping over from its own foundation, a heap of dirt and rubbish over which drifted, like a final curse, the smell of burnt-out fire.

Some men – a rescue-squad in dusty blue overalls – were picking over the ruins like scavengers who did not know what they were seeking.

After a moment of hesitation Tallow accosted the nearest of them, a big man in a white steel helmet.

'How did it happen?' he asked.

Scarcely looking at him, the rescue man said: 'Don't ask bloody silly questions. I'm busy.'

'It's my house,' said Tallow, without expression.

'Oh ...' The rescue man straightened up. 'Sorry, mate ... We get more bloody fools hanging round these jobs than I ever saw in my life.' He looked at Tallow with rough compassion. 'Direct hit, this one. Middle of the raids – about five days ago. You been away?'

'Yes. Just got back.'

By his side, Watts said: 'We didn't know about this.'

There was silence, while the dust stirred and settled. With an effort, Tallow put his question.

'How about the people inside, then?'

The rescue man looked away from him, and across the street. 'You'd better ask at the warden's post, down there.' He pointed. 'They see to all that.'

'But what about them?' said Tallow roughly. 'Do you know or don't you?'

This time the rescue man looked directly at him, searching for words as he stared. 'You can't expect much, mate, not after this. We got them out. Two women. Don't know their names. Ask over there, at the warden's post. They'll tell you all about it.'

'Were they dead?' asked Tallow.

A moment of hesitation; then: 'Yes, they were dead.'

On their way across the street towards the warden's post, Tallow said: 'It was probably Mrs Crossley. She used to sit with Gladys in the evening.'

Inside the warden's post, a brick shelter on the street corner, three men were sitting at a table playing cards. Two were young, and one was an oldish man with grey hair. As Tallow and Watts entered, stooping under the low doorway, one of the young men glanced up and called out in mock alarm:

'Look out, lads – the Navy's here!'

The oldish man put down his cards and said: 'Just in time for a cup of tea. Always glad to see the Navy.'

'Name of Tallow,' said Tallow briefly. 'Number 29 Dock Road.' He jerked his head back. 'You know – the one across the street. What happened?'

There was a long, shocked silence, while the three men stared at Tallow, the smiles fading from their faces, the cheerful welcome evaporating into shame. Then the old man stuttered and spoke:

'Mr Tallow – yes. That was your house, wasn't it? I'm very sorry, very sorry indeed.' He fumbled with some papers on the rough deal table, concealing his raw embarrassment. 'Mr Tallow ... I reported it to the Town Hall, of course. Two casualties – yes, I've got it down here. Mrs Bell, Mrs Crossley ... Didn't they notify you?'

'We've only just got in. Been at sea for a fortnight. When did it happen?'

'May the fifth. That's five days ago, isn't it?' He read the names again. 'Mrs Bell, Mrs Crossley. Would they be relatives of yours?'

Tallow swallowed. 'Mrs Bell was my sister. Mrs Crossley was a friend.'

The old man shook his head. 'I'm very sorry to hear it. If there's any help we can give——'

'What did they do with——'

One of the young men, the one who had greeted them so cheerfully, stood up suddenly. 'Take it easy, chum,' he said quietly. 'Here – sit down for a minute.'

'When was the funeral?' asked Tallow. He did not sit down.

'Two days ago.' The young man coughed. 'There were some others, you know. Twenty-one altogether.'

'Twenty-one? All from Dock Road?'

'Yes. It was a bad night.'

Standing in the entrance behind Tallow, Watts stirred suddenly. 'Where was it? The funeral, I mean.'

'Croft Road Cemetery.' The old man answered this time. 'It was very tasteful, I can assure you of that. The Mayor and Corporation attended. They were all together in one big grave, and the floral tributes——' He paused, and his tone altered suddenly. 'They can't have known anything, Mr Tallow. It was all over in a minute – in a second. They can't have suffered at all.'

'No,' said Tallow. 'I see that.'

'It's a sort of comfort,' said the old man gently.

'Yes,' said Tallow. 'Thank you. I'll come back in a day or two.'

Outside, the sunshine was very bright after the gloom of the warden's post. The two men stood side by side, not looking at each other, staring at the house and the men climbing over the rubble. Some children were playing in the front garden, setting up a wall of bricks and then knocking it down. A dusty and desolate peace lay over everything.

'I'm sorry, Bob,' said Watts after a pause. 'Real sorry.'

'I'm sorry too, Jim. On your account, I mean. I know how you felt. We've both lost——' Tallow straightened his shoulders suddenly. 'Well, that's that, anyway. Let's make a move.' He began to walk slowly up Dock Road, and Watts fell into step beside him. 'It's funny,' said Tallow as they were passing the jagged crater, 'but I still can't hardly believe it.' He looked up at the sky, the innocent treacherous sky. 'It doesn't make sense, really,' he went on, astonishment and pain in his voice. 'You come in from sea, feeling real glad to be back, and then you go home and find that people you thought were alive and happy, were really dead and buried while you were still two days out . . . It doesn't make sense,' he repeated vaguely. 'Jim, I think I want a drink.'

CHAPTER 6

They did four more convoys, of the rough nervous character that marked most convoys nowadays; and then, at high summer, they were given what they had been looking forward to for many months – a refit, with the long leave that went with it, the first long leave since *Compass Rose* was commissioned. They had all wanted that leave: many of them needed it badly: life on Atlantic convoys was a matter of slowly increasing strain, strain still mounting towards a crucial point which could not yet be foreseen, and it took its toll of men's nerves and patience, as surely as of ships. It showed itself in small ways – leave-breaking that had no hope of escaping punishment, quarrelling in the wardroom, an outbreak of petty thieving in the messdecks – and its only cure was a proper rest, free of routine, free of danger, free of discipline. As long as that rest was granted, they could take on the burden again, and sweat it out to the end; but without such a pause, irritation and inefficiency could gain ground at a startling pace.

Not less than her crew, *Compass Rose* herself needed the respite. It was the first substantial break in service since she had left the Clyde, nearly two years before: apart from necessary minor repairs, designs had altered, weapons improved, and personnel increased, and there was a lot to be done to bring her up to date with the newest corvettes. She was due for an entirely new bridge, roomier and better protected, with the mast tucked away behind it in authentic naval fashion: she could now have a properly equipped sick-bay, new depth-charge rails and throwers, and a superior Asdic-set that would do everything except tell them the name of the opposing U-boat. The total list of alterations and additions was a substantial one; and *Compass Rose*, sinking back gratefully in the hands of the shipyard, turned her face from the sea and settled down to a six weeks' course of rejuvenation.

With two-thirds of the ship's company on leave, and only Baker to keep him company in the wardroom, Lockhart was very conscious of this slacking-off process. He had postponed his own leave in order to see *Compass Rose*'s refit properly launched – that was specifically his job – and as he wandered round the ship, checking over what had to be done from the long complicated defect list, he felt a curious sense of disappointment to see how swiftly *Compass Rose* had ground down to a full stop. She should have held on longer than this ... A few days before, she had come in from sea as a going concern, and a good one – smart, efficient, controlled by a routine which, after two years, had no loose ends of any sort; now, at a stroke, the routine was broken, and she had relapsed into a hulk, a dead ship tied to the jetty – dirty and untidy, her boilers cold, her men gone, her main-spring run down. He could hardly believe that she could deteriorate so quickly and completely.

He watched the workmen removing great chunks of the bridge with acetylene-cutters, he watched the sparks falling on the useless gun-mounting from which the gun had been removed; he wandered aft, disconsolate, to where the welders, busy on the new depth-charge rails, had bent the old ones into fantastic and unusable shapes. He knew that *Compass Rose* would come back stronger, stronger and better than ever; but at this moment of dissolution it was sad to see a ship, which had been so taut and trim, lose the name of action over a single weekend.

There were other things during those first days of the refit which he liked even less. He could not help contrasting the disciplined and cheerful crew of *Compass Rose*, and the infinitely hard work which, day after day, they took as a matter of course, with what passed for the war-effort among the dockyard workers. Perhaps this was a bad shipyard; but good or bad, the contrast was obvious, with unpleasant implications as well. Some of them worked hard and honestly, most did not: most of them jogged along at a take-it-or-leave-it pace, talked and shirked in corners half a dozen times a day, and knocked off with so great a punctuality that when the whistle went they were already streaming across the gangway, homeward bound. Many times Lockhart interrupted card games, down in the engine-room out of sight of the foreman: there was one hardy poker school which assembled every afternoon in the Asdic compartment, locked the door on the inside, and played out time till five o'clock, deaf to everyone but the dealer ... Considering that these men led a protected life, free of discipline or compulsion, that they had their homes to go to at the end of every day, that the calls on their labour were restricted to set hours, and that they were paid a great deal more than any rating on board, it was difficult not to feel impatience and contempt at their grumbling, grudging contribution. They were among the people whom sailors fought and died for; at close quarters, they hardly seemed to deserve it.

On one occasion, Tallow came to Lockhart in a high state of indignation. 'Just come and look at this, sir,' he said, hardly able to get the words out, and led the way up to the boat-deck. Alongside the boats were the Carley floats – safety rafts each equipped with paddles, a keg of water, and a watertight tin of provisions sufficient to last for a week or so. There were two Carleys, and there should have been two tins of food: now, after a week in dockyard hands, there were none.

'Those bloody dockies!' said Tallow, allowing himself an unusual freedom. 'Stealing food that might keep a man alive after he's been torpedoed ... By God, I'd like to put some of them on a raft in the middle of the Atlantic, and let them work it out for themselves! Isn't there anything we can do, sir?'

'I'm afraid not.' Lockhart surveyed the rifled Carley floats with melancholy calm. He had learnt a lot of things during the past few days. 'We can complain, of course – I'll see the dockyard superintendent about it – but it won't bring the stuff back and it won't teach people what an appalling thing this is to do.' He looked at Tallow. 'They just haven't got the same idea, Coxswain, and that's all there is to it.'

'It's time they were taught it,' muttered Tallow angrily. 'And these are the chaps who go on strike whenever they feel like it – more pay, less work, and no cross words from the foreman. I wish they could swop jobs with us, just for one trip. They'd know when they were well off, then.'

Newspaper accounts of strikes, which they would read when they returned to harbour, made sailors, indeed, sometimes wonder what on earth they were fighting for ... It really seemed a reversal of common sense, to put it no higher, that once he was in uniform a man had to do exactly what he was told, without arguing, for an infinitesimal wage and in extreme discomfort, while the man from the house next door, in civilian clothes but with the same stake in the war, could hold the country up to ransom until he got exactly what he wanted. Sailors did not talk much about it, because they were busy and preoccupied with what they had to do, and were not very vocal anyway; but it was there in the background, tied up with the black market, with people who wangled extra food and wasted petrol which had cost men's lives on its journey to England: it was part of the whole rotten minority racket which, in moments of frustration, could induce a rage so wild that it poisoned all pleasure in the job, and all pride in its fulfilment.

. . .

Normally, Ericson would have spent a good deal of time on board during the refit: the temptation to prowl round continuously, while so many strange things were being done to *Compass Rose*, would have been irresistible. But for the first time since the war started, his leave had coincided with his son's, and he found himself eager to spend as much time as he could at home, making the most of a meeting which chance might not bring round again for a long time, and another sort of chance might destroy altogether. Young John Ericson, out of his apprenticeship, was now a Fourth Officer: the blue uniform with its single gold stripe sat oddly on his awkward, boyish figure, and Ericson, watching him covertly as he sat on the sofa which, a few years before, he had scrambled over or used as a rocking-horse, could hardly believe that the boy was now entitled to wear the man's rig. He had grown up so fast, almost while Ericson's back was turned, and, most fantastic of all, he was doing the same job as his father ...

In the evening, the family circle round the fireside had a touch of unreality about it. Ericson sat in his usual armchair, reading or talking: Grace knitted busily at one end of the sofa, and young John, miraculously adult, sat puffing a shiny new pipe at the other. Opposite Ericson, in the other armchair, the old lady did the crosswords and impressed her will on them all. Grace's mother had mellowed a little, Ericson decided, but not much: she still tried to rule the roost, she still behaved as if she were the only grown-up in a houseful of children. It was lucky that he himself was home so seldom, and that he had *Compass Rose* to retreat to when things got on his nerves. For the old lady, spider-like, was not going to move now – that was obvious: she was installed for the duration, and the household had to be regrouped round her, in a way which the captain of one of His Majesty's ships-of-war could hardly accept as natural.

Part of the unreality lay in their conversation: they talked of everything but what was uppermost in their minds, the force which had brought them all together and might separate them again at any moment – the war. Both Ericson and his son, indeed, were ready enough to talk of it, but before the women they were curiously shy: sitting round the fireside, they remembered enough of the job they were sharing to know that it could not be put into fireside words. When they did come anywhere near the subject, it was simply to chaff each other in the traditional Royal and Merchant Navy rivalry: the only things that could be mentioned about their partnership were frivolous variations on the surface – the different helm-orders, the different rates of pay, the things that mattered least of all. And then, breaking in on their talk, Grace would say: 'I'm sure it doesn't make any difference how fast a corvette can go. You all have to go along together, don't you?' And the old lady, scratching away at the evening paper, would mumble: 'What's a word of eleven letters meaning "futility"?' and the whole family would unite to solve this major problem ... So they sat on, night after night: two men, two women, closely bound, yet far apart: feeling the weight of war, and disregarding it in favour of the lightest alternative they could think of.

Once during that meeting, Ericson and his son did talk. It was towards the end of John's leave, when Ericson, moved by a hunger for close companionship which he could scarcely define, proposed a bus-ride into the country and a long walk over the Cheshire moors. The bus took them inland, through the unlovely Birkenhead suburbs and the ribbon-development that lay beyond; and then, leaving the bus, they struck north-westwards on foot, and walked towards the sea. They walked steadily for four hours, under the warm sunshine, meeting the breeze that blew in from the Irish Sea and the Atlantic itself: their isolation, in these wild surroundings, part of an England they knew and loved, brought them close together, and they talked as they might have talked at sea, sharing a watch on a calm night. They talked of the job they were doing, the matter that lay in the forefront of their minds: the things that were happening to the convoys, the ships and friends they had lost, the truth behind the statistics and the bald or misleading newspaper announcements. But it was not until the late afternoon, when they reached the north-west coast and lay on a hill-side sloping to the sea, and watched, on the horizon, a line of ships heading out into the Atlantic, that they spoke at last without reservation and without shyness, acknowledging their secret feelings.

'It's just plain murder, Dad,' said John Ericson at one point, when they touched on the happenings of the last few months, and the fearful total of sinkings. 'You can't call it anything else ... The same thing happens to convoy after convoy, only a little worse each time. How long can they go on sending us to sea, when it's an absolute certainty that half the ships won't come back?'

'Some convoys get through, John,' said Ericson defensively.

'Damn few ... Oh, we're not blaming the escorts – they do the best they can, and it's pretty good all the time. It's just that the convoy system doesn't seem to be *working*. You ought to hear our old man on the subject! We can go fifteen knots, any time we like, and yet we have to jog along at seven and eight knots, stuck in a convoy for three weeks on end, a sitting target for the U-boats.'

'You're still better off in a convoy, instead of steaming independently. The figures prove it.'

'It doesn't feel like it, when those torpedoes are flying round, and the only signal you can get from the Commodore is "Maintain convoy speed"... And watching ships and people that you know being blown up or sunk or bombed, every time you put to sea. Sometimes I feel as if——' He paused.

'What, John?'

'Are you ever afraid, Dad?' The young face, an unformed version of his own, turned towards Ericson anxiously. 'Really afraid – trembling, I mean – when you know there's going to be an attack?'

'I think we all are ...' Ericson lay on his back, staring at the blue and gold sky, speaking as casually as he could. 'I know that I am, anyway. The only thing is to show it as little as you can – because it's catching – and to try and do your job as well as you would if you *weren't* afraid.' He examined a sprig of heather with great attention. 'There's nothing much in being afraid, John: if a man tells you that he isn't, on our job, he's either a liar or such a cast-iron bloody fool that he's not worth talking to.'

'I get the needle pretty badly sometimes.'

'Well, you're not a liar, at least.'

They both laughed. There was between them now a closeness, a trusting confessional honesty, which they had never reached before.

'I think of you a lot, Dad, when I'm at sea,' John went on after a pause. He too was staring at the sky, which with the approach of evening was losing colour swiftly. On the far horizon, the line of sea and sky began to blur as the sun dipped towards the water. 'Particularly when I see those corvettes chasing round the convoy. They're so incredibly small ...'

'There's something to be said for being a small target.'

'There's something to be said for ten thousand tons of solid ship underneath you, in an Atlantic gale.'

'I think of you, too, John.' Ericson, cherishing the moment of intimacy, the first since childhood, hardly knew how to phrase what was in his mind. 'We're both doing the same job, and we know the sort of job it is, and I can't help being anxious about you. Anxious and – proud of what you're doing. When I was your age, I hadn't got anything like as far. So just take care of yourself, won't you? – I want to be able to celebrate the next Armistice properly ... We must think about catching our train, John, or your grandmother will be on the warpath again.'

John grinned as he got to his feet. 'She's a terror, isn't she?'

'She certainly keeps us all in order, yes.'

'Oh, it's all right for me,' said John, grinning again. 'I'm not the captain of *my* ship.'

.   .   .

In the garden of the small house just outside Liverpool, Ferraby played with the baby. The baby, a girl, was now six months old: pretty, gurgling, crawling unsteadily, and answering her name – Ursula – with an ecstatic bubbling noise. Ferraby loved everything to do with being a father, from wheeling the pram out in the afternoons to preparing a bath at the exact temperature: even to be woken up in the middle of the night was an acceptable part of fatherhood, establishing his connection firmly. But most of all he liked simply to be with the child, watching her, talking to her, feeling her minute fingers curling round his own. He felt no need for any more exciting kind of activity, these days: his whole leave was passing in this simple and tender fashion, and he would have chosen nothing else. But now, as he played in the sunshine, holding the warm body, touching the soft petal skin, his thoughts were far away: his thoughts were of steel and storm, the ugliest thoughts in the world.

Such moods and such thoughts came in waves, and he could not now control them. At any time of the day or night, his mind would go back to *Compass Rose*, and the way his leave was running out, and what would take the place of this respite, which must soon come to an end: sometimes, as now, the contrast between terror and tenderness, the extremes of his two lives, overwhelmed him with its futility. At one and the same time, he felt the sweetness of the present, here in the garden, and the threat of the future that lay out in the Atlantic: he felt that he could only face one of them, and it was not the future – the future was too hard and too evil, and he hated it with all his soul.

He no longer told Mavis anything of this, though sometimes he told the baby.

Now, as he sweated with his thoughts and his prophetic fear, the baby, gurgling again, crawled to the edge of the rug and fell gently onto her face in the grass. The swift wailing changed magically as Ferraby picked her up and held her close to him. Mavis, brought out of the house by the noise, checked her step and stood watching them, a smile on her face. Bless his heart . . . It was lovely to see Gordon so relaxed and so happy.

. . .

Young Baker said: 'Yes, Mother – I'd love to,' and went upstairs to put on his collar and tie. It was the fourth time he'd been out to tea with his mother that week; but she enjoyed it so much, she got so much fun out of showing him off, that it was impossible to say 'No' to her. There was nothing else to do, anyway.

As usual, he was spending his leave at home, in his mother's small house in a Birmingham suburb. For the first few days it had been fun to be fussed over, to enjoy the good cooking and the undoubted comfort of his mother's housekeeping, to be the male centre of a soft feminine flutter. But soon this had begun to pall: he could not help realizing that this was not the sort of flutter he wanted, nor quite the sort of softness either . . . Baker was nineteen years old, a shy, anxious-to-please young man whose normal instincts, as yet ungratified, were somewhat heated by his predilection for the more furtive brands of erotica: he collected the pin-up girls from *Esquire* and similar publications, he subscribed to 'art' magazines, he even possessed, hidden under a pile of shirts in his wardrobe, a series of postcards which recorded the athletic aspects of love in unusual variety. But so far, no one had appeared in support of these day-dreams: the only girls he met at home were the approved daughters of his mother's friends, selected, it seemed to him, for their inherent wholesomeness, and his only feminine contact at Liverpool was a Wren in the Pay Office, who was much too interested in her career to spare any attention for a sub-lieutenant, and met his tentative advances with a smile as thin as his single stripe . . . So he spent his time ashore, and his leave-periods, balanced between hope and despair: hope that somewhere, just around the next corner, was the girl he so much wanted, and despair when the next corner proved inevitably bare. It was so unfair: other people had girls, and did all sorts of things with them: even in the cinemas there was a maddening activity in the back row: only he, it seemed, was still waiting for the right one to come along, to ease his futile longing.

From the foot of the stairs his mother called out: 'Tom! It's time we started,' and he put on his coat and prepared to go down. Another tea-party . . . But you never knew: perhaps, this time, the girl would be there, and she would smile and they would recognize each other instantly, and somehow they would get away from the crowd, and she'd start to do the most marvellous things to him, and it would happen at last.

There *was* a girl there, as it turned out, but she was terrible: awkward, sallow, flat-chested – no sort of help at all. He could not even imagine himself kissing her . . . They sat round in a formal circle, drinking tea and eating cucumber sandwiches: Mrs Keyes, Mrs Ockshott, Mrs Henson, his mother, an old chap who was somebody's husband, the girl who was somebody's daughter, and himself in the place of honour – the young naval officer snatching a brief hour of peace between fearful voyages. The conversation, indeed, ran on something like these lines: on such occasions, his mother made obvious efforts to draw him out, and the simplest course was to play up to her and lay it on as thick as possible. It was easy to expand in this uncritical atmosphere.

'Sometimes,' he said, munching, 'it's so rough that we can't put anything on the table at all. We eat things straight out of the tin, or just go without.'

The ladies clicked their tongues sympathetically, and his mother said: 'Fancy that!' in fond horror. He caught the girl's eye fixed on him admiringly. But she was so ugly . . . She was sitting with her knees apart, he observed, exposing the kind of safety knickers which you sometimes saw in advertisements, with elastic round the thighs. No good at all . . . He took another sandwich.

'Yes,' he went on recklessly, 'I remember the steward bringing some corned beef up to the bridge for me. It was the first food I'd had for – for two days. The funny thing was, when it arrived I just couldn't eat it. Exhaustion, I suppose.'

'Fancy that!' said his mother again. And then: 'Tell us about that man who was drowning, Tom. You know – when you went overboard in the storm.'

'Oh – that ...' The girl, though still looking at him, had now closed her legs. You're welcome, he thought, and passed his cup for some more tea. 'It's nothing much,' he began, marshalling his thoughts rapidly. 'But one night, when the Captain called for volunteers——'

He made the story into a good one – almost too good, if the face of the only other man in the room was anything to go by. But the women lapped it up: and the ugly girl was positively hypnotized by everything he did and said. He enjoyed the admiration while it lasted, but on the way home he relapsed into boredom and frustration again. What did those old cows and that awful girl matter? He was just throwing the stuff away ... He really wanted to tell these stories sitting by the fireside, with a different kind of girl – *the* girl – resting her head on his knees, and looking up at him, and not minding when his hand moved gradually down under the top of her dress.

How wonderful it would be, he thought, to be married, really married.

. . .

Morell, nursing a glass of brandy, sat in the warm, subtly feminine sitting-room of the flat in Westminster, watching the clock and waiting till it was time to fetch his wife from the theatre. His uniform jacket lay on the chair opposite him, waiting also for the moment to move. But the moment, much as he wanted it, was not yet here.

The clock showed five past ten, which meant another half-hour before he could reasonably start: Elaine did not like him hanging round the theatre or her dressing-room when she was on the stage, and she was rarely ready to leave – make-up off, clothes changed – before eleven o'clock each night. (At sea, he had pictured himself waiting in her dressing-room, playing with the make-up box, talking to her dresser, until she came off stage: but it had not worked out like that.) Many times he had found himself wishing that the run of the play would come to an end, but it showed no sign of doing that: besides, the wish was purely selfish – she would have been so disappointed ... But certainly the engagement meant that he had not seen much of her during his leave: six evening shows a week, and two matinées as well, left her with very little spare time, even leaving out of account the extra appointments – lunches, dinners, cocktail parties – that seemed to go naturally with being in a current West End play.

Morell sipped his brandy, while the clock crawled towards the half-hour. His mood was morose and uncertain, in spite of the fact that they would be meeting again very soon: the trouble was that he could not count on the meeting being a happy one.

At the beginning, Elaine had seemed genuinely regretful of the time they must spend apart. 'Oh darling, what a shame!' she had exclaimed, on the night of his arrival. 'Just when you've got long leave, I've got a part in a play that's actually going to run ... But never mind,' she had continued, rubbing her face against his shoulder, 'fetch me at the theatre, and I'll make it up to you afterwards.' And later than night, when he had claimed her at the stage-door and taken her home, she did make it up to him, with all the sensual tenderness he remembered from the past. Indeed, it had been like that for three or four nights, without a shadow of hesitation on her part, so that he was immensely, violently happy. And then, and then ...

What did it amount to, exactly, the obvious deterioration? What had made her attention fade, and his happiness and confidence with it? To begin with, it had been the fault of living in a crowd: people ringing up all the time, engagements she would not cut, late parties after the play was over, parties from which he was excluded. 'But, darling,' she would say, 'it's no good you coming along. It's just theatre people, probably talking shop the whole time. You'd be bored to bits.' And when he had remonstrated further: 'Darling, I've *got* to go,' she would insist, with an edge of irritation. 'It's important – it might mean more work when this play is finished.' There was no getting past that argument: or none that she would recognize as valid.

It was no good asking questions, either. 'Oh, just a party,' she would say, when he wanted to know where she was going. 'You don't know the people – you probably wouldn't like them, anyway.' Question and answer, question and silence, question and angry protest. (But he could not help the questions: he was wretchedly jealous of every moment of their separation.) 'Oh darling, don't *heckle*!' she would answer finally, when his probing reached a foolish level of persistence. 'It's driving me mad ...' And that would be that. He wanted to explain to her where it was driving *him*, but he had begun to be afraid of any sort of emotion, any groping beyond the normality of their life together, any experiment. He had so much to lose, and it seemed clear, for some reason, that he could afford it far less than she. Each time he tried to re-establish himself, the effort was feebler, the ground more surely lost, the abject surrender more obvious.

He really had no weapons, and he had already betrayed the fact, with fatal effect upon them both.

There was something else, too, worse than all this, something he noticed quite early on in his leave: a subtle lessening of her fervour, a certain automatic response, so that he could not decide, in cold blood, whether she were genuinely moved in love, or merely a competent performer ... There had been one moment, a moment of ludicrous detachment when, close as they were, he had seemed to be observing her from an immense distance, and had suddenly found himself making up a speech in his head. 'This woman, as your Lordship will observe,' the strange words formed just behind his tongue, 'makes love with a degree of technical competence which——' but he had not been able to complete the sentence. Indeed, suddenly cold and sick, it was all he could do to complete the act of love, so as not to betray himself, and her.

There was nothing definite to go on, and nothing definite to comfort him either. Worst of all, he was no longer able to talk to her about it, to ask for reassurance and to receive it. They shared a house and a bed, they shared an easy conversation and a range of jokes; but they shared nothing below the surface – the candour and the closeness were gone, and he was afraid to challenge their passing, for fear of what he might uncover.

The clock struck the half-hour, and with a thankful readiness he rose to put on his coat. As he moved, the telephone rang.

For a full minute he let it ring unanswered. Almost certainly it was one of her friends, her intolerable friends – the women with their quick malicious tongues, the fat men with wandering hands and contracts in their pockets, the juvenile leads who were very nearly homosexuals but were willing to try anything, the stage riff-raff swelled by home-based officers on the make ... But the ringing persisted, and finally he crossed to the side table and lifted the receiver.

It was Elaine.

'Darling,' she began, speaking quickly as if knowing that he was going to object, 'I've been asked to a party, after the show tonight.'

'Oh,' he said, non-committally.

'I *must* go, darling. Readman will be there. You know – the producer.'

'All right,' he said, after a pause. He had other words ready, but he knew they would not be effective. 'Can I fetch you from anywhere?'

'No. I'll be so late, darling.'

'You know it doesn't matter. Where will you be?'

'I don't know, really.' The edge of irritation was creeping into her voice again. 'We'll probably go on somewhere. Don't you worry.'

But foolishly he persisted. 'Ring me up, then. I can come along anywhere, any time.' Oh, darling, he thought, you're my wife, and this is the last week of my leave, and I want you here, not at parties with other people. But these also were words which were not effective.

'That's so silly——' she began – and then, treacherously, she disposed of the matter in a swift series of sentences, leaving him no time to answer.

'Really it'll be too late, darling. And don't wait up for me. Get some sleep, and I'll see you in the morning. Goodbye.'
He had already opened his mouth to start another pleading sentence when he heard the telephone click. Presently the dialling tone began. He sat down again, and took up the glass of brandy, conscious only of a shattering disappointment. Then, before he had time to control the direction of his mind, he thought suddenly of two things, in swift and horrible succession. He did not know what wretched instinct presented them so vividly, but once they were there he could not drive them out again. He remembered, first, the huge bruise which he had found on Elaine's thigh, the first night of his leave. She bruised very easily; it had been rather a joke on their honeymoon, and on their first night it was still a joke. 'I knocked it getting out of a taxi,' she had answered when he asked her. 'Fine story!' he had grumbled, and then, in a different mood: 'May I bring you another taxi – pretty soon?' and she, in answer: 'The meter's ticking up already ...' A charming scene, melting into frenzy – but now he remembered only the readiness of her first answer.
The second thing he thought of made him get up and, with a clear sense of shame, go into the bathroom. Hanging behind the bathroom door was a sponge-bag, a special sponge-bag in which Elaine kept her 'things'. He leant against the wall, unwilling to put, even secretly to himself, so disgusting a question. Then he reached out his hand, and took the sponge-bag from its hook, and opened it, loathing himself, and looked inside.
What he was looking for was not there.
Of course, it was not conclusive. Once – rather a long time ago – she had said: 'Oh, I always want to be ready for you.' It could have, even now, a simple and tender explanation.
But as soon as he was back in the sitting-room, and had sat down, he began to imagine, in very terrible detail, Elaine making love with someone else.

                    .   .   .

Lockhart also spent his leave in London, though on a less emotional plane. Indeed, there were times when, if he had been offered some kind of overflow from Morell's situation, he might have taken it on just to keep his hand in. At sea, he was aware in himself of a celibate dedication to the work he was doing: a long leave ashore was inclined to probe the chinks in that armour, reminding him of a different sort of past and exposing a human weakness for sensual indulgence which he had imagined was stowed away with his civilian clothes. But, in the event, the occasion never offered, and his leave passed as a tranquil extension of the male world which the past two years had made normal for him.
He stayed in a borrowed flat in Kensington, the owner of which was

absent on some mysterious mission to America; after living for so long in
a crowd, he might well have been lonely. But on his doorstep was
London, his own fine town, shabby and bomb-damaged but with all her
offerings unimpaired: the people, the bars, the theatres, the concerts, the
simple slow walks down streets that ended at the river or the green open
parks – these were all here under his hand, and he made the most of
them, with a thankful appetite for variety.

He met a great many people – by chance, by coincidence, by
arrangement, by misfortune: of them all, he best remembered two. They
were not good examples of wartime London, and they were not the
pleasantest people he met; but they stuck in his memory, just as, at a
children's birthday party, it is the child who is sick or who loses its
temper who makes the most lasting impression – particularly on the
adults.

He met, in the Café Royal, a man who had been, for a brief and
inglorious period, his employer in an advertising agency in London.
Lockhart had taken on the job, some time in the middle thirties, when he
was broke – indeed, he would scarcely have considered it in any other
circumstances, so foolish and irksome was it from the very beginning.
His work consisted of writing advertising copy in praise of food: in
outlining the style to be aimed at, his employer, a large fat man by the
name of Hamshaw, tried to communicate his own sense of mission, and
was clearly taken aback by Lockhart's somewhat frivolous approach.
Matters proceeded uneasily for some months: more and more of
Lockhart's stuff was returned to him, marked 'too harsh', 'too stiff', 'a
softer approach, please', once even 'the reference to saliva is indelicate'.
There came a day when Lockhart's projected phrase to round off a dog-
biscuit advertisement: 'Dogs Like 'Em', was rejected in favour of 'No
more toothsome morsel has ever been offered to the canine world', and
he knew that, broke or not, his patience was exhausted.

He waited for the chance of a parting gesture, and the chance came.
On his desk one morning was a note from Hamshaw: 'Please let me have
a suitable slogan for Bolger's Treacle Butterscotch.' Lockhart considered for a moment, scribbled a line at the bottom of the page, picked
up his hat, and walked out. Not till some hours later did Hamshaw,
nosing round the copy room, light upon the farewell effort: 'Bolger's
Butterscotch – Rich and Dark like the Aga Khan'.

Even in those days, Hamshaw had been sufficiently pompous; now,
appointed to control the thought of entire sub-continents on behalf of
the Ministry of Information, he was positively Olympian. He greeted
Lockhart with a detached bow, and said: 'Ah, Lockhart – come and
share my table' as if he were offering Holy Communion to a dubious
backslider. When they had chatted warily for some time:

'A fine service, yours,' said Hamshaw with deliberation, gently massaging a ponderous chin. 'But I must confess that at the Ministry we find you – shall we say? – a little backward.'

'Backward,' repeated Lockhart non-committally.

Hamshaw nodded, popped a sandwich into his mouth, and nodded again. 'Yes. We'd like to see a little more readiness to release material – about the Atlantic, and so forth. It's very difficult to get the Admiralty to co-operate, very difficult indeed.'

'I think they take security fairly seriously.'

'My dear Lockhart, you can't teach me anything about *security*!' said Hamshaw, as if it were his own personal conception. 'I can assure you we have that *very* much at heart. What we want is more willingness to publicize what's going on, once the demands of security are met. These successes – if successes they are – are no good unless people hear about them, no good at all.'

Lockhart frowned, not seeing why he should accept this nonsense, even as a matter of social convenience. 'A sunk U-boat is sunk,' he said shortly, 'whether it's on the front page in two colours or not. The advertising afterwards doesn't affect it at all.' 'The *advertising*, as you call it,' Hamshaw looked at him portentously, alert for any disrespect, 'is valuable from the morale point of view. The national morale, which is one of our prime concerns, needs a continual supply of favourable news items to sustain it. Indeed, I think it is safe to say that the war could not be fought for one single day without the constant public inspiration which we supply. However,' he went on, perhaps aware of Lockhart's wandering attention, 'I mustn't ride off on my hobby horse, absorbing though it is. Tell me about your own work. You find it personally satisfying?'

'Something like that,' said Lockhart.

'In many ways,' said Hamshaw, staring into the middle distance, 'it is a great pity you did not stay with us. I was able to take some of my staff with me to the Ministry – those I particularly trusted – and they have all done well. You might have had a junior controllership by now – possibly even a sectional directorship.'

'God bless my soul!' said Lockhart.

'Oh, yes, there is great scope for advancement – very great scope indeed. But perhaps you are happy enough where you are.'

'Yes,' said Lockhart, 'I think I am.'

'Well, that is all that matters. It is all one war,' went on Hamshaw with frightful condescension, 'all one great cause. We realize that very fully, I assure you. We cannot all be charged with supplying the driving force for the battle – the services play an honourable part in the field itself.'

'How vulgar you make it sound,' said Lockhart evenly, as for the second time in their joint lives he picked up his hat, preparatory to flight.

'But bear with us a little longer. We *are* trying to get integrated in your war-machine.'

'Now I've angered you, somehow,' said Hamshaw reproachfully.

'Yes,' said Lockhart, 'somehow you have,' and left him to work it out. It would doubtless be dismissed as some regrettable form of war-psychosis.

Later that evening, in the bar of a Fleet Street pub, he met a fellow-journalist, by the name of Keys, whom he had not seen since the beginning of the war. Keys was considerably older than himself, a tough and seasoned senior reporter on the staff of one of the popular dailies: like Hamshaw, his natural inclinations seemed to have been stimulated and intensified by war, and where he had once been something of a sceptic about human nature in general, he was now crudely cynical about every aspect of the war, and the motives of anyone who had the remotest connection with it. With no prompting at all save the whisky at his elbow, he treated Lockhart to a diatribe of extraordinary violence, embracing the whole of Britain: indeed, not one of his fellow-countrymen escaped the lash. The politicians were feathering their nests without regard to the common good, the industrialists were selling shoddy war-material at fantastic profits, all the newspapers without exception were lying their way through the struggle, ignoring Allied setbacks and inventing successes to put in their place. The working-class were loafers to a man; and service-men, of course, were the dupes of a huge national confidence trick, if no worse ...

'There's nothing to choose between us and the Germans, anyway,' concluded Keys savagely, staring at Lockhart's uniform as if it were some kind of prison garb, shameful to anyone who wore it. 'We're both after the same thing – the domination of Europe, and the markets that go with it. The Germans are just a bit more honest about it, that's all.'

'Um,' said Lockhart non-committally. The bar was crowded, and he did not want to attract attention by an argument which was bound to be futile, and might become unpleasant. Just above their heads was a large sign, in Gothic characters, which read: 'THERE IS NO DEPRESSION IN THIS HOUSE'. It might be better to take his cue from that.

'By God!' exclaimed Keys, seeming to lash himself into a sudden fury, 'I've had to write more claptrap about the great Allied war effort, the last few months, than I would have thought possible. It's enough to turn your stomach.'

'Why do it, then?'

Keys shrugged. 'For the same reason you're wearing that uniform,' he answered, with a bitter inflection.

'I doubt it,' said Lockhart shortly.

'Don't fool yourself... There's a war, and you join up like a good little boy, because everyone else is doing it. There's a war, and my paper has to plug the patriotic angle because it would be unsaleable otherwise, and I have to turn the stuff out because I'd lose my job if I didn't. It's the same reason – the fear of not toeing the line, and of being unpopular if you don't follow the crowd like a lot of bloody sheep.'

'There are other reasons,' said Lockhart.

Keys snorted derisively. 'I suppose you're going to tell me the whole Navy's fighting for God, King and country.'

'It's an idea that lies behind a lot of what we feel,' said Lockhart without heat. 'It *isn't* just a war for right and justice, with all the merit on one side, I know, and there's enough truth in that "domination of Europe" thesis to make one think twice before accepting patriotic speeches at their face-value. But if we lost, or if we hadn't declared war in the first place, we wouldn't have a chance of establishing *any* of the things we believe in. What do you suppose England would be like, if the Germans were running it?'

'More efficient,' said Keys.

Lockhart smiled. 'I see I'm not likely to make much headway,' he said good-humouredly. He found it, for some reason, impossible to be annoyed with Keys, who had lived so long with the-news-behind-the-news that he could hardly distinguish a genuine emotion from a counterfeit one, and was quite unaffected by either. 'I'll just have to carry on in my patriotic day-dream ... It's a *real* feeling, sometimes, you know,' he went on quietly, 'and a lot of people have died for it already.'

'More fools they,' said Keys contemptuously.

'Ah, yes,' said Lockhart, 'but they couldn't know that, could they? They've only got the newspapers to go by, and you people do *such* a good job.'

Lockhart got slightly drunk that night, possibly as an antidote, and it was in a mood of detached intoxication, weaving his way down the long slope of Piccadilly towards Knightsbridge and home, that he tried to sort out his impression of the day's encounters. Of the two men, Hamshaw and Keys, he infinitely preferred the latter's approach to the war: he might be bitter and cynical about it, but at least he was not deluding himself, at least he was free of the pompous haze of grandeur with which Hamshaw had surrounded himself and the war and his role in it. War was not like that: no sacred cause, served exclusively by pledged knights, was involved; on the other hand, war was not Keys' brand of shoddy commercial dog-fight, either. There had been something in what he said, some slender basis for the idea that the fight was between equally-guilty contestants, each determined on European ascendancy; but not enough to resolve it finally into a simple and selfish struggle, with nothing to choose between the eventual winners. Keys had rationalized his own bitterness, which might spring from a dozen different causes; it might even be grounded, deep down, in the fact that he was too old to be of any practical use in the war and, being excluded for what perhaps seemed an ignoble reason, was determined to shrug off the whole business.

'We can't all be born at the same time,' said Lockhart aloud, addressing the façade of a big block of flats at Rutland Gate. But perhaps Keys wasn't as logical, as infinitely wise, as he himself was at this moment. Keys was too old for fighting: therefore, to him, fighting was a worthless preoccupation, and the war a cut-throat extension of commercial travelling.

Of course there must be something more . . . Lockhart had never been a professed patriot: even now, closely involved in the fight, he could feel no dedication save to the necessity of winning – and *then* seeing about a fair and equitable settlement. But the winning was paramount: the alternative meant disaster, for everything he stood and felt for, and subjection to a cruel, impersonal, and loathsome tyranny which would bring the curtain down on human hope.

There must be Germans, too, who felt like that: good ones, deluded, but sincere and equally concerned with the humanities: good soldiers, good sailors, good airmen who felt they were destroying a perverted English attempt at conquest. It was a pity that they had to be killed as well . . .

'I'm a German, really,' he said out loud again, pausing to rest against a convenient lamp-post. 'Nothing to choose between us . . . But my part of Germany's got to win, and then we'll start parcelling the whole thing out again.'

'Yes, sir,' said the policeman who suddenly appeared at his side. 'Have you got far to go home?'

Lockhart blinked, and focused his eyes with an effort. The figure which was now before him seemed enormous in the lamplight. 'Why are policemen always taller than I am?' he asked, complaining. 'Now, in Germany——'

'How about a taxi?' asked the policeman, with the usual all-embracing patience. 'You'll get one a little way back, in Knightsbridge.'

'A fine night for walking,' said Lockhart.

'A fine night for sleeping,' said the policeman, reprovingly. 'They're all asleep round here. We don't want to wake them up, do we?'

'Were you ever in the Navy?' asked Lockhart, with a vague idea of establishing a friendly contact.

'No, sir,' said the policeman, 'I've had no luck at all.' A taxi, coasting slowly past on its way back to town, turned neatly at a wave of his hand, and ground to a standstill beside them. 'What's the address, then?'

Lockhart gave it, and stood wavering as the policeman opened the taxi door. The annoying part about being drunk was that everyone was so much more efficient than oneself . . . He paused, with one foot on the step of the cab.

'I was walking home quite quietly,' he said.

'Yes, sir,' said the policeman.

'I don't want any trouble,' said the taxi-driver, an oldish man in a thick green overcoat. 'Navy or no Navy.'

'This is all right,' said the policeman, slamming the door as Lockhart subsided on the seat. Through the open window he added: 'You sure of that address?'

'Yes,' said Lockhart. 'Engraved on my heart.'

'All right,' said the policeman. He nodded to the taxi-driver. 'Off you go.'

'We've got to win,' said Lockhart, by way of valediction.

'Don't I know it,' said the policeman. 'But not all in one night. Leave something for tomorrow.'

'What's it like in them battleships?' asked the taxi-driver over his shoulder, about a mile farther on.

'I should think it's absolutely terrible,' answered Lockhart, who was trying to light a cigarette and disentangle his gas-mask at the same time.

'I only asked,' said the taxi-driver sourly. 'They can sink, for all I care.'

'Don't you want to win the war?' asked Lockhart, astounded.

'There's a lot of things I want,' said the taxi-driver. He gave a swift and meaning glance at his meter. 'Double fare after twelve o'clock, you know.'

'Nonsense,' said Lockhart.

The taxi-driver clapped on his brakes, and brought the cab to a standstill. 'What did you say?' he asked grimly.

'I was born in this town,' Lockhart began, with a clarity of thought which astounded even himself. 'You know perfectly well——'

It was not a satisfactory evening.

But this was not the note on which his leave ended: neither this, nor Hamshaw, nor Keys. He carried away with him a very different sort of memory. For on his last night in London he went to the theatre, to a non-cerebral musical comedy which was the only thing he could get a seat for; and there, when the lights went up for the interval, he saw a sight which stayed with him afterwards for very many months.

It was a party of R.A.F. officers from some hospital – a hospital which supposedly dealt with plastic surgery cases. The six young men in Air Force uniform were all the same: Lockhart, looking sideways along the row, received so frightful an impression of disfigurement that for a moment he thought it must be a trick of lighting and shadow. But it was no trick: the faces *were* all shattered in the same formless way, mutilated alike by wounds and by slap-dash surgical repair: puckered by scars or by burning, twisted into living caricature, lacking eyebrows, lacking ears, lacking lips and chins; greyish-yellow where fire had scorched them, livid red where they were scarred, a line of violence and pain which shocked Lockhart nearly to sickness. Between each terrible face was a fresh young one – a girl's; and the girls were all smiling and talking animatedly and looking closely into the *other* faces, without flinching, and the other faces, which were not equipped to smile, and hardly even to talk, looked back at them searchingly, with dreadful alertness ... 'They oughtn't to allow them in,' whispered a woman sitting just behind him. 'What about decent people's feelings?' Shut up, you flaming bitch, thought Lockhart, nearly saying it aloud, and then, looking down the row again towards the wounded men, as many other people were looking, drawn by the magnet of this insane ugliness: you poor bastards, he thought again, I hope you're going to be all right – in time, in a year or two ... This, and nothing else, was the war; this was the part you couldn't glamorize, or belittle, or pretend about in any way. He was glad when the lights went down again, but glad only for their sakes, for the cover of darkness which they must welcome: for himself, after the initial shock, he had felt more at home with this cruel evidence of the fight than with anything else in London. Indeed, the wounded men were a good token of the best of this city, scarred and fired in the same way: maimed for life, maybe, but talking and working and playing with what was left, and never to be daunted now or in the future.

It was the right kind of memory to take back from leave: the unsoftening kind, the dream-of-home which ran no risk of tenderizing the spirit. Lockhart took it with him thankfully.

. . .

They hardly knew *Compass Rose*, by the end of her refit: she seemed to have moved right out of the corvette class altogether, and to have graduated with unexpected honours. The new bridge was a replica of a destroyer's, with a covered chart-table and plenty of room to walk about: the sick-bay, presided over by a sick-berth attendant who had actually been a country vet at one period, was properly fitted up and stocked for most of the emergencies they had met so far. There were more depth-charges and anti-aircraft guns: there was the new Asdic-set: above all, there was now a brand-new weapon altogether – Radar.

Radar – the most formidable invention in sea-warfare – had been slow in coming to them. By now, all the escort destroyers had it, and a lucky corvette or two; but Ericson, who had applied many times during the past year for it to be fitted, had always come away discouraged. 'You haven't a hope,' the man in charge of such things at headquarters had told him, whenever he raised the question. 'There are all sorts of ships ahead of you. In fact,' said the man, who was not a smooth-spoken character, 'as far as Radar is concerned, corvettes are sucking on the hind tit. You'll just have to wait until everyone else has had a go.'

'What a pity Bennett is not still with us,' remarked Morell, who had overheard the conversation. 'The phrase would have delighted him ...'

But now at last they had it, mounted on the bridge in all its glory and promise. Radar was the one thing they needed, the one weapon which the Atlantic war had long demanded: a means of making contact at night or in thick weather with whatever lay in waiting nearby. It could detect a U-boat on the surface at a considerable distance, and show its course and speed: on its fluorescent screen Radar gave a 'picture' of the convoy or of nearby ships, a picture which simplified station-keeping at night to such a degree that it was difficult to see how they had ever done without it. There need be no more hanging-on and punishing the eyes at night, since Radar did it all: no more searching for lost ships or for the incoming convoy – there they were, clearly picked out on the screen, scores of miles away. It was going to be a help and a comfort – that they all realized; and beyond this, perhaps it would, as a weapon, even start to equalize the Atlantic score, meeting the cunning and secret attack with a delicate revealing finger, the best that science could do for man.

They were fitted with it in time to return to sea when the battle was climbing to crucial heights; in time for the worst convoy of all so far.

CHAPTER 7

The smiling weather of that late summer helped them to settle down to sea-going again, after the relaxation of their refit. It was a curious business, this tuning-up of men and machinery, and in some cases it caught both of them unawares. *Compass Rose* hit the knuckle of the jetty – fortunately, not very hard – on her way out of dock, owing to a small defect in her reversing gear; and one seaman, to his lasting shame, was actually sea-sick on the five-minute trip across the river to top up at the oiler ... But these were odd items in a quick process of re-establishment: when they picked up their convoy off the Bar Light Vessel they were already halfway back to the old routine, and by the time they were two days out, clear of land and heading in a wide south-westerly circle for Gibraltar, the ship was fighting fit again. The weather gave them a wonderful succession of sunlit days and calm nights; and conscious of their luck in sailing for hour after hour over a deep blue, mirror-calm sea, the sort of warm and lazy trip that cost a guinea a day in peace-time, they quickly made the transfer from land to seafaring. It was, from many angles, good to be back on the job again: clear of the dubious and emotional tie of land, they were once more part of an increased escort – two destroyers and five corvettes – charged with the care of twenty-one deep-laden ships bound for Gibraltar. This was their real task, and they turned to it again with the readiness of men who, knowing that the task was crucial, were never wholly convinced that the Navy could afford to let them take a holiday.

The treachery of that perfect weather, the lure of the easy transition, were not long in the declaring.

It started with a single aircraft, possibly an old friend, a four-engined Focke-Wulf reconnaissance plane which closed the convoy from the eastwards and then began to go round them in slow circles, well out of range of any gun-fire they could put up. It had happened to them before, and there was little doubt of what the plane was doing – pin-pointing the convoy, shadowing it, noting exactly its course and speed, and then reporting back to some central authority, as well as tipping off any U-boats that might be nearby. The change this time lay in the fact that it was occurring so early in their voyage, and that, as they watched the plane circling and realized its mission, the sun was pouring down from a matchless sky onto a sea as smooth and as lovely as old glass, hardly disturbed at all by the company of ships that crossed it on their way southwards. Unfair to peace-loving convoys, they thought as they closed their ranks and trained their glasses on the slowly-circling messenger of prey: leave us alone on this painted ocean, let us slip by, no one will know ...

At dusk the plane withdrew, droning away eastwards at the same level pace: up on the bridge, preparing to darken ship and close down for the night, they watched it go with gloomy foreboding.

'It's too easy,' said Ericson broodingly, voicing their thoughts. 'All it's got to do is to fly round us, sending out some kind of homing signal, and every U-boat within a hundred miles just steers straight for us.' He eyed the sky, innocent and cloudless. 'I wish it would blow up a bit. This sort of weather doesn't give us a chance.'

There was nothing out of the ordinary that night, except a signal at eleven o'clock addressed by the Admiralty to their convoy. 'There are indications of five U-boats in your area, with others joining,' it warned them with generous scope, and left them to make the best they could of it. As soon as darkness fell the convoy changed its course from the one the aircraft had observed, going off at a sharp tangent in the hope of escaping the pursuit: perhaps it was successful, perhaps the U-boats were still out of range, for the five hours of darkness passed without incident, while on the Radar-screen the compact square of ships and the out-lying fringe of escorts moved steadily forwards, undisturbed, escaping notice. *Viperous*, making her routine dash round the convoy at first light, signalled: 'I think we fooled them,' as she swept past *Compass Rose*. The steep wave of her wash had just started them rolling when they heard the drone of an aircraft, and the spy was with them again.

The first ship was torpedoed and set on fire at midday. She was a big tanker – all the twenty-one ships in the convoy were of substantial size, many of them bound for Malta and the eastern Mediterranean: it was a hand-picked lot, a valuable prize well worth the pursuit and the harrying. And pursued and harried they were, without quarter: the swift destruction of that first ship marked the beginning of an eight-day battle which took steady toll of the convoy, thinning out the ships each night with horrible regularity, making of each dawn a disgusting nursery-rhyme, a roll-call of the diminishing band of nigger-boys.

. . .

They fought back, they did their best: but the odds against them were too high, the chinks in their armour impossible to safeguard against so many circling enemies.

'There are nine U-boats in your area,' said the Admiralty at dusk that night, as generous as ever; and the nine U-boats between them sank three ships, one of them in circumstances of special horror. She was known to be carrying about twenty Wrens, the first draft to be sent to Gibraltar: aboard *Compass Rose* they had watched the girls strolling about the deck, had waved to them as they passed, had been glad of their company even at long range. The ship that carried them was the last to be struck that night: she went down so swiftly that the flames which engulfed the whole of her after-part hardly had time to take hold before they were quenched. The noise of that quenching was borne over the water towards *Compass Rose*, a savage hissing roar, indescribably cruel. 'By God, it's those poor kids!' exclaimed Ericson, jolted out of a calm he could not preserve at so horrible a moment. But there was nothing that they could do: they were busy on a wide search ordered by *Viperous*, and they could not leave it. If there were anything left to rescue, someone else would have to do it.

Four of the girls *were* in fact picked up by another merchant-ship which had bravely stopped and lowered a boat for the job. They were to be seen next morning, sitting close together on the upper deck, staring out at the water: there was no gay waving now, from either side ... But the ship that rescued them was one of the two that were sunk that same night: she too went down swiftly, and *Compass Rose*, detailed this time to pick up survivors could only add four to her own total of living passengers, and six to the dead. Among these dead was one of the Wrens, the only one that any ship found out of the draft of twenty: included in the neat row of corpses which Tallow laid out on the quarter-deck, the girl's body struck a note of infinite pity. She was young: the drenched fair hair, the first that had ever touched the deck of *Compass Rose*, lay like a spread fan, outlining a pinched and frightened face which would, in living repose, have been lovely. Lockhart, who had come aft at dawn to see to the sewing-up of those that were to be buried, felt a constriction in his throat as he looked down at her. Surely there could be no sadder, no filthier aspect of war ... But there were many other things to do besides mourn or pity. They buried her with the rest, and added her name to the list in the log, and continued the prodigal southward journey.

Six ships were gone already: six ships in two days, and they still had a week to go before they were near the shelter of land. But now they had a stroke of luck: a succession of two dark nights which, combined with a violent evasive alteration of course, threw the pursuit off the scent. Though they were still on the alert, and the tension, particularly at night, was still there, yet for forty-eight hours they enjoyed a wonderful sense of respite: the convoy, now reduced to fifteen ships, cracked on speed, romping along towards the southern horizon and the promise of safety. Aboard *Compass Rose*, a cheerful optimism succeeded the sense of ordained misfortune which had begun to take a hold; and the many survivors whom they had picked up, wandering about the upper deck in their blankets and scraps of clothing or lining the rails to stare out at the convoy, lost gradually the strained refugee look which was so hard on the naval conscience. Hope grew: they might see harbour after all ...

So it was for two days and two nights; and then the aircraft, casting wide circles in the clear dawn sky, found them again.

Rose, the young signalman, heard it first: a stirring in the upper air, a faint purring whisper which meant discovery. He looked round him swiftly, his head cocked on one side: he called out: 'Aircraft, sir – somewhere ...' and Ferraby and Baker, who had the forenoon watch, came to the alert in the same swift nervous movement. The throbbing grew, and achieved a definite direction – somewhere on their port beam, away from the convoy and towards the distant Spanish coast. 'Captain, sir!' called Baker down the voice-pipe. 'Sound of aircraft——' but Ericson was already mounting the bridge-ladder, brought up from his sea-cabin by the hated noise. He looked round him, narrowing his eyes against the bright day, and then: 'There it is!' he exclaimed suddenly, and pointed. On their beam, emerging from the pearly morning mist that lay low on the horizon all round them, was the plane, the spying eye of the enemy.

They all stared at it, every man on the bridge, bound together by the same feeling of anger and hatred. It was so unfair ... U-boats they could deal with – or at least the odds were more level: with a bit of luck in the weather, and the normal skill of sailors, the convoy could feint and twist and turn and hope to escape their pursuit. But this predatory messenger from another sphere, destroying the tactical pattern, eating into any distance they contrived to put between themselves and the enemy – this betrayer could never be baulked. They felt, as they watched the aircraft, a helpless sense of nakedness, an ineffectual rage: clearly, it was all going to happen again, in spite of their care and watchfulness, in spite of their best endeavours, and all because a handful of young men in an aircraft could span half an ocean in a few hours, and come plummeting down upon their slower prey.

Swiftly the aircraft must have done its work, and the U-boats could not have been far away; within twelve hours, back they came, and that night cost the convoy two more ships out of the dwindling fleet. The hunt was up once more, the pack exultant, the savage rhythm returning and quickening . . . They did their best: the escorts counter-attacked, the convoy altered course and increased its speed: all to no purpose. The sixth day dawned, the sixth night came: punctually at midnight the alarm-bells sounded and the first distress-rocket soared up into the night sky, telling of a ship mortally hit and calling for help. She burned for a long time, that ship, reddening the water, lifting sluggishly with the swell, becoming at last a flickering oily pyre which the convoy slowly left astern. Then there was a pause of more than two hours, while they remained alert at Action-Stations and the convoy slid southwards under a black moonless sky; and then, far out on the seaward horizon, five miles away from them, there was a sudden return of violence. A brilliant orange flash split the darkness, died down, flared up again, and then guttered away to nothing. Clearly it was another ship hit – but this time, for them, it was much more than a ship; for this time, this time it was *Sorrel*.

They all knew it must be *Sorrel*, because at that distance it could not be any other ship, and also because of an earlier signal which they had relayed to her from *Viperous*. 'In case of an attack tonight', said the signal, '*Sorrel* will proceed five miles astern and to seaward of the convoy, and create a diversion by dropping depth-charges, firing rockets, etc. This may draw the main attack away from the convoy.' They had seen the rockets earlier that night, and disregarded them: they only meant that *Sorrel*, busy in a corner, was doing her stuff according to plan . . . Probably that plan had been effective, if the last two hours' lull were anything to go by: certainly it had, from one point of view, been an ideal exercise, diverting at least one attack from its proper mark. But in the process, someone had to suffer: it had not cancelled the stalking approach, it did not stop the torpedo being fired: *Sorrel* became the mark, in default of a richer prize, meeting her lonely end in the outer ring of darkness beyond the convoy.

Poor *Sorrel*, poor sister-corvette . . . Up on the bridge of *Compass Rose*, the men who had known her best of all were now the mourners, standing separated from each other by the blackness of night but bound by the same shock, the same incredulous sorrow. How could it have happened to *Sorrel*, to an escort like themselves . . . ? Immediately he saw the explosion, Ericson had rung down to the wireless office. ' "*Viperous* from *Compass Rose*",' he dictated. ' "*Sorrel* torpedoed in her diversion position.

May I leave and search for survivors?"' Then: 'Code that up,' he
snapped to the telegraphist who was taking down the message. 'Quick as
you can. Send it by R/T.' Then, the message sent, they waited, silent in
the darkness of the bridge, eyeing the dim bulk of the nearest ship,
occasionally turning back to where *Sorrel* had been struck. No one said a
word: there were no words for this. There were only thoughts, and not
many of those.

The bell of the wireless-office rang sharply, breaking the silence, and
Leading-Signalman Wells, who was standing by the voice-pipe, bent
down to it.

'Bridge!' he said, and listened for a moment. Then he straightened up,
and called to the Captain across the grey width of the bridge. 'Answer
from *Viperous*, sir ... "Do not leave convoy until daylight".'

There was silence again, a sickened, appalled silence. Ericson set his
teeth. He might have guessed ... It was the right answer, of course, from
the cold technical angle: *Viperous* simply could not afford to take another
escort from the screen, and send her off on a non-essential job. It was the
right answer, but by Christ it was a hard one! ... Back there in the lonely
darkness, ten miles and more away by now, men were dying, men of a
special sort: people they knew well, sailors like themselves: and they were
to be left to die, or, at best, their rescue was to be delayed for a period
which must cost many lives. *Sorrel*'s sinking had come as an extraordinary shock to them all: she was the first escort that had ever been lost
out of their group, and she was, of all the ones that could have gone, their
own chummy-ship, the ship they had tied up alongside after countless
convoys, for two years on end: manned by their friends, men they played
tombola with or met in pubs ashore: men they could always beat at
football ... For *Sorrel* to be torpedoed was bad enough; but to leave her
crew to sink or swim in the darkness was the most cruel stroke of all.

'Daylight,' said Morell suddenly, breaking the oppressive silence on
the bridge. 'Two more hours to wait.'

Ericson found himself answering: 'Yes' – not to Morell's words, but to
what he had meant. It was a cold night. With two hours to wait, and
then the time it would take them to run back to where *Sorrel* had gone
down, there would be very few men left to pick up.

There were in fact fifteen – fifteen out of a ship's company of ninety.

They found them without much difficulty, towards the end of the
morning watch, sighting the two specks which were Carley rafts across
three miles or more of flat unruffled sea. However familiar this crude
seascape had become to them, it was especially moving to come upon it
again now: to approach the loaded rafts and the cluster of oily bodies
washing about among *Sorrel*'s wreckage: to see, here and there in this
filthy aftermath, their own uniforms, their own badges and caps, almost
their own mirrored faces ... The men on the rafts were stiff and cold and

soaked with oil, but as *Compass Rose* approached, one of them waved with wild energy, foolishly greeting a rescuer not more than twenty yards away from him. Some of the men were clearly dead, from cold or exhaustion, even though they had gained the safety of the rafts: they lay with their heads on other men's knees, cherished and warmed until death and perhaps for hours beyond it. Ericson, looking through his binoculars at the ragged handful that remained, caught sight of the grey face of *Sorrel*'s captain, Ramsay, his friend for many years. Ramsay was holding a body in his arms, a young sailor ugly and pitiful in death, the head thrown back, the mouth hanging open. But the living face above the dead one was hardly less pitiful. The whole story – the lost ship, the lost crew, the pain and exhaustion of the last six hours – all these were in Ramsay's face as he sat, holding the dead body, waiting for rescue.

It was a true captain's face, a captain in defeat who mourned his ship, and bore alone the monstrous burden of its loss.

Lockhart, waiting in the waist of the ship while the survivors were helped aboard, greeted him with impulsive warmth as he climbed stiffly over the side.

'Very glad to see you, sir!' he exclaimed eagerly. Everything about Ramsay – his expression, his weary movements, his reeking oil-soaked uniform – was suddenly and deeply moving, so that to have saved his life, even in these tragic circumstances, seemed a triumph and a blessing. 'We were all hoping——' he stopped awkwardly, watching Ramsay's face. He knew immediately that it would be wrong, terribly wrong, to say: 'We were all hoping that we'd pick *you* up, anyway.' That was not what Ramsay himself was feeling, at that moment. Rather the reverse.

'Thanks, Number One.' Ramsay, straightening up, turned round and gestured vaguely towards the men still on the rafts. 'Look after them, won't you? One or two of them are pretty far gone.'

Lockhart nodded. 'I'll see to all that, sir.'

'I'll go up to the bridge, then.' But he lingered by the rails, watching with hurt eyes as the remnants of his crew were helped or hauled or lifted tenderly in-board. In the middle of the crowd of men working, he was unassailably withdrawn and private in his grief. When the living were seen to, and they were starting on the dead, he turned away and walked slowly towards the bridge-ladder, his oily bare feet slurring and slopping along the deck. Lockhart was glad to be kept busy and preoccupied at that moment. It was not one to be intruded on, upon any pretext.

To Ericson, up on the bridge, Ramsay presently held out his hand and said:

'Thanks, George. I'll not forget that.' The West Country accent was very prominent.

'Sorry we couldn't be here earlier,' said Ericson shortly. 'But I couldn't leave the screen before daylight.'

'It wouldn't have made much difference,' answered Ramsay. He had turned away, and was once more watching the bodies coming in-board, and the other bodies that disfigured the even surface of the sea round *Compass Rose*. 'Most of them were caught below, anyway. We broke in half. Went down in a couple of minutes.'

Ericson said nothing. Presently Ramsay turned back to him and said, half to himself:

'You never think that *you'll* be the one to catch it. It's something you can't be ready for, no matter how much you think about it. When it does happen——' he broke off, as if at some self-reproach which he did not know how to voice, and then the moment itself was interrupted by Signalman Rose, alert at one of the voice-pipes.

'Signal from *Viperous*, sir,' he called out. 'Addressed to us. "Rejoin the convoy forthwith".'

'Something must be happening,' said Ericson. He walked to the head of the bridge-ladder, and looked down at the waist of the ship. The two rafts were cleared now, but there were still twenty or more bodies floating within a circle of half a mile round them. 'I'd like to——' he began uncertainly.

Ramsay shook his head. 'It doesn't matter, George,' he said quietly. 'What's the odds, anyway? Leave them where they are.'

He did not look at anyone or anything as *Compass Rose* drew away.

. . .

What had happened, as they discovered when they caught up the convoy, towards midday, was that another ship had been torpedoed, in broad daylight, and *Viperous* was rightly anxious to close up all the escorts as soon as possible. There could be no pause, no respite in this long chasing battle: certainly the dead had no claim – not even when, as now, they were beginning to outnumber the living. By noon of that seventh day, the tally of ships remaining was eleven – eleven out of the original twenty-one; behind them were ten good merchant-ships sunk, and countless men drowned, and one of the escorts lost as well. It was horrible to think of the hundreds of miles of sea that lay in their wake, strewn with the oil and the wreckage and the corpses they were leaving behind them: it was like some revolting paper-chase, with the convoy laying a trail from an enormous suppurating satchel of blood and treasure. But some of it – the Wrens, and *Sorrel*, and the screams of the men caught in the first ship lost, the burning tanker – some of it did not bear thinking about at all.

It was not a one-sided battle, with repeated hammer-strokes on the one hand and a futile dodging on the other, but it was not much better than that, in the way it was working out; there were too many U-boats in contact with them, not enough escorts, not enough speed or manoeuvre-ability in the convoy to give it a level chance. They had fought back all that they could. *Compass Rose* had dropped more than forty depth-charges on her various counter-attacks, some of which should have done some damage: the other escorts had put up a lively display of energy: *Viperous* herself, after one accurate attack, had sufficient evidence in the way of oil and wreckage to claim a U-boat destroyed. But as far as the overall picture was concerned, all this was simply a feeble beating of the air: with so many U-boats in their area, miracles were necessary to escape the appalling trap the convoy had run into, and no miracles came their way. There was no chance of winning, and no way of retreat; all they could do was to close their ranks, make the best speed they could, and sweat it out to the end.

Compass Rose had never been so crowded, so crammed with survivors. It was lucky, indeed, that they had the new sick-bay and the Sick-Berth Attendant to deal with their wounded and exhausted passengers: Lockhart could never have coped with the continual flow single-handed. But apart from the number of people requiring attention, they had collected a huge additional complement of rescued men – far outnumbering, indeed, their own crew. There were fourteen Merchant Navy officers in the wardroom, including three ship's captains: there were a hundred and twenty-one others – seamen, firemen, cooks, Lascars, Chinese – thronging the upper deck by day and at night crowding into the messdecks to eat and sleep and wait for the next dawn. During the dark hours, indeed, the scene in the darkened fo'c'sle was barely describable. Under the shaded yellow lamp was a scene from the Inferno, a nightmare of tension and confusion and discomfort and pain.

The place was crammed to the deckhead: men stood or sat or knelt or lay, in every available space: they crouched under the tables, they wedged themselves in corners, they stretched out on top of the broad ventilating shafts. There were men being sea-sick, men crying out in their sleep, men wolfing food, men hugging their bits of possessions and staring at nothing: wounded men groaning, apparently fit men laughing uneasily at nothing, brave men who could still summon a smile and a straight answer. It was impossible to pick one's way from one end of the fo'c'sle to the other, as Lockhart did each night when he made the Rounds, without being shocked and appalled and saddened by this slum corner of the war: and yet somehow one could be heartened also, and cheered by an impression of patience and endurance, and made to feel proud ... Individuals, here and there, might have been pushed close to defeat or panic; but the gross crowding, the rags, the oil, the bandages, the smell of men in adversity, were *still* not enough to defeat the whole company. They were all sailors there, not to be overwhelmed even by this sudden and sustained nightmare: they were being mucked about, it was true, but it would have to be a lot worse than this before they changed their minds about the sea.

There was another sort of nightmare, which kept recurring to Lockhart as he looked at the throng of survivors, and at *Compass Rose*'s seamen making their cheerful best of the invasion, and met a puzzled or frightened face here and there in the crowd. Suppose, like *Sorrel*, they were hit: suppose they went down in a minute or so, in two broken halves, as *Sorrel* had done: what would happen in there, what sort of trapped and clawing shambles would develop as they slid to the bottom? The details could not really be faced, though it was possible that other people in the fo'c'sle were occupying their spare time in facing them. Once, when Lockhart was adjusting a survivor's bandaged arm, the man said:

'Be all right for swimming, eh?'

Lockhart smiled. 'Sure thing. But you won't be doing any more swimming on this trip.'

The man looked straight at him, and jerked his head. 'You're dead right there. If anything happens to this lot, we're snug in our coffin already.'

. . .

The afternoon that they rejoined the convoy, another signal came from the Admiralty. 'There are now eleven U-boats in your area,' it ran. 'Destroyers *Lancelot* and *Liberal* will join escort at approximately 1800.'

'Two L Class destroyers – that's grand!' said Baker enthusiastically, down in the wardroom at tea-time. 'They're terrific ships. Brand new, too.'

'They'd better be very terrific indeed,' said Morell, who was reading a copy of the signal. 'Eleven U-boats works out at one to each ship left in the convoy. I very much doubt,' he added suavely, 'whether Their Lordships really intended such a nice balance of forces.'

Lockhart smiled at him. 'Getting rattled, John?'

Morell considered for a moment, 'I must admit,' he said finally, 'that this is *not* a reassuring occasion. Whatever we do, those damned U-boats get inside the screen every time. We've lost almost half our ships, and we're still two days away from Gibraltar.' He paused, 'It's odd to think that even if nothing else happens, this is probably the worst convoy in the history of sea-warfare.'

'Something to tell your grandchildren.'

'Yes, indeed. In fact, if you guarantee me grandchildren I shall recover my spirits very quickly.'

'How can he guarantee that you have grandchildren?' asked Baker who was, aboard *Compass Rose* at least, a dull conversationalist.

'If they're as stupid as you,' said Morell, with a flash of impatience so rare that he must in truth have been nervous, 'I hope I don't have any.'

They were all feeling the same, thought Lockhart in the offended silence that followed: irritable, on edge, inclined to intolerance with each other. The tiredness and strain that had mounted during the past week was reaching an almost unbearable pitch. There could be no cure for it save gaining harbour with the remnants of their convoy, and that was still two days ahead. He suddenly wanted, more than anything else in the world, to be at peace and in safety. Like the rest of them, like all the escorts and all the merchant-ships, he had very nearly had enough.

The two destroyers joined punctually at six o'clock, coming up from the south-east to meet the convoy, advancing swiftly towards it, each with an enormous creaming bow-wave. They both exhibited, to a special degree, that dramatic quality which was the pride of all destroyers: they were lean, fast, enormously powerful – nearer to light cruisers than destroyers – and clearly worth about three of any normal escort. They made a cheerful addition to the ships in company, thrashing about valiantly at the slightest scare or none at all, darting round and through the convoy at a full thirty-five knots, signalling in three directions at once, and refusing to stay still in any one position for more than five minutes at a time.

'Proper show off,' said Leading-Signalman Wells, watching them through his glasses as they sped past on some purely inventive errand. But there was a touch of envy in his voice as he added: 'All very well for them to dash about like a couple of brand-new tarts – they haven't had the last week along o' this lot.'

At dusk the two newcomers settled down, one ahead and one astern of the convoy, completing the atmosphere of last-minute rescue which had accompanied their arrival. They were doubtless well aware of the effect they had produced. But theatrical or not, their presence did seem to make a difference: though there was an attack that night, all that the circling pack of U-boats could account for was one ship, the smallest ship in the convoy. She was hit astern, and she went down slowly: out of her whole company the only casualty was a single Lascar seaman who jumped (as he thought) into the sea with a wild cry and landed head first in one of the life-boats. In the midst of the wholesale slaughter, this comedy exit had just the right touch of fantasy about it to make it seem really funny . . . But even so, this ship was the eleventh to be lost, out of the original twenty-one: it put them over the halfway mark, establishing a new and atrocious record in U-boat successes. And the next night, the eighth and last of the battle, when they were within three hundred miles of Gibraltar, made up for any apparent slackening in the rate of destruction.

That last night cost three more ships, and one of them – yet another loaded tanker to be torpedoed and set on fire – was the special concern of *Compass Rose*. It was she who was nearest when the ship was struck, and she circled round as the oil, cascading and spouting from the tanker's open side, took fire and spread over the surface of the water like a flaming carpet in a pitch-black room. Silhouetted against this roaring backcloth which soon rose to fifty feet in the air, *Compass Rose* must have been visible for miles around: even in swift movement she made a perfect target, and Ericson, trying to decide whether to stop and pick up survivors, or whether the risk would not be justified, could visualize clearly what they would look like when stationary against this wall of flame. *Compass Rose*, with her crew and her painfully collected ship-load of survivors, would be a sitting mark from ten miles away ... But they had been detailed as rescue-ship: there were men in the water, there were boats from the tanker already lowered and pulling away from the tower of flame: there was a job to be done, a work of mercy, if the risk were acceptable – if it was worth hazarding two hundred lives in order to gain fifty more, if prudence could be stretched to include humanity.

It was Ericson's decision alone. It was a captain's moment, a pure test of nerve: it was, once again, the reality that lay behind the saluting and the graded discipline and the two-and-a-half stripes on the sleeve. While Ericson, silent on the bridge, considered the chances, there was not a man in the ship who would have changed places with him.

The order, when it came, was swift and decisive.

'Stop engines!'

'Stop engines, sir ... Engines stopped, wheel amidships, sir.'

'Number One!'

'Sir?' said Lockhart.

'Stand by to get those survivors in-board. We won't lower a boat – they'll have to swim or row towards us. God knows they can see us easily enough. Use a megaphone to hurry them up.'

'Aye, aye, sir.'

As Lockhart turned to leave the bridge, the Captain added, almost conversationally:

'We don't want to waste any time, Number One.'

All over the ship a prickling silence fell, as *Compass Rose* slowly came to a stop and waited, rolling gently, lit by the glare from the fire. From the bridge, every detail of the upper deck could be picked out: there was no flickering in this huge illumination, simply a steady glow which threw a black shadow on the sea behind them, which showed them naked to the enemy, which endowed the white faces turned towards it with a photographic brilliance. Waiting aft among his depth-charge crews, while the flames roared and three boats crept towards them, and faint shouting and bobbing lights here and there on the water indicated a valiant swimmer making for safety, Ferraby was conscious only of a terror-stricken impatience. Oh God, oh God, oh God, he thought, almost aloud: let them give this up, let them get moving again ... Twenty feet away from him in the port waist, Lockhart was coolly directing the preliminaries to the work of rescue – rigging a sling for the wounded men, securing the scrambling-nets that hung over the side, by which men in the water could pull themselves up.

Ferraby watched him, not with admiration or envy but with a futile hatred. Damn you, he thought, once more almost saying the words out loud: how can you be like that, why don't you feel like me – or if you do, why don't you show it? He turned away from the brisk figures and the glowing heat of the flames, his eyes traversing the arch of black sky overhead, a sky blotched and streaked by smoke and whirling sparks; he looked behind him, at the outer darkness which the fire could not pierce, the place where the submarines must be lying and watching them. No submarine within fifty miles could miss this beacon, no submarine within five could resist chancing a torpedo, no submarine within two could fail to hit the silhouetted target, the stationary prey. It was wicked to stop like this, just for a lot of damned merchant-navy toughs ...

A boat drew alongside, bumping and scraping: Lockhart called out: 'Hook on forrard!' there were sounds of scrambling: an anonymous voice, foreign, slightly breathless, said: 'God bless you for stopping!' The work of collection began.

It did not take long, save in their own minds; but coming towards the end of the long continued ordeal of the voyage, when there was no man in the ship who was not near to exhaustion, those minutes spent motionless in the limelight had a creeping and paralytic tension. It seemed impossible for them to take such a reckless chance, and not be punished for it; there was, in the war at sea, a certain limiting factor to bravery, and beyond that, fate stood waiting with a ferocious rebuke. 'If we don't buy it this time,' said Wainwright, the torpedo-man, standing by his depth-charges and staring at the flames, 'Jerry doesn't *deserve* to win the war.' It did seem, indeed, that if *Sorrel* could be hit when she was zigzagging at fourteen knots, there wouldn't be much trouble with *Compass Rose*; and as the minutes passed, while they collected three boat-loads of survivors and a handful of swimmers, and the huge circle of fire gave its steady illumination, they seemed to be getting deeper and deeper into a situation from which they would never be able to retreat. The men who had work to do were lucky: the men who simply waited, like Ericson on the bridge or the stokers below the water-line, knew, in those few agonizing minutes, the meaning of fear.

It never happened: that was the miracle of that night. Perhaps some U-boat fired and missed, perhaps those within range, content with their success, had submerged for safety's sake and broken off the attack: at any rate, *Compass Rose* was allowed her extraordinary hazard, without having to settle the bill. When there were no more men to pick up, she got under way again: the returning pulse of her engine, heard and felt throughout the ship, came like some incredible last-minute respite, astonishing them all. But the pulse strengthened and quickened, in triumphant chorus, and she drew away from the flames and the smell of oil with her extra load of survivors snatched from the very mouth of danger, and her flaunting gesture unchallenged. They had taken the chance, and it had come off; mixed with the exhilaration of that triumph was a sober thankfulness for deliverance, a certain humility. Perhaps it would not do to think too much about it: perhaps it was better to bury the moment as quickly as possible, and forget it, and not take that chance again.

. . .

Another ship, on the opposite wing, went down at four o'clock, just before dawn; and then, as daylight strengthened and the rags of the convoy drew together again, they witnessed the last cruel item of the voyage.

Lagging behind with some engine defect, a third ship was hit, and began to settle down on her way to the bottom. She sank slowly, but owing to bad organization, or the villainous list which the torpedoing gave her, no boats got away; for her crew, it was a time for swimming, for jumping into the water, and striking out away from the fatal downward suction, and trusting to luck. *Compass Rose*, dropping back to come to her aid, circled round as the ship began to disappear; and then, as she dipped below the level of the sea and the swirling ripples began to spread outwards from a central point which was no longer there, Ericson turned his ship's bows towards the centre of disaster, and the bobbing heads which dotted the surface of the water. But it was not to be a straightforward rescue; for just as he was opening his mouth to give the order for lowering a boat, the Asdic-set picked up a contact, an under-sea echo so crisp and well-defined that it could only be a U-boat.

Lockhart, at his Action-Station in the Asdic-compartment, felt his heart miss a beat as he heard that echo. At last . . . He called through the open window: 'Echo bearing two-two-five – moving left!' and bent over the Asdic-set in acute concentration. Ericson increased the revolutions again, and turned away from the indicated bearing, meaning to increase the range: if they were to drop depth-charges, they would need a longer run-in to get up speed. In his turn, he called out: 'What's it look like, Number One?' and Lockhart, hearing the harsh pinging noise and watching the mark on the recording set, said: 'Submarine, sir – can't be anything else.' He continued to call out the bearing and the range of the contact: Ericson prepared to take the ship in, at attacking speed, and to drop a pattern of depth-charges on the way; and then, as *Compass Rose* turned inwards towards the target, gathering speed for the onslaught, they all noticed something which had escaped their attention before. The place where the U-boat lay, the point where they must drop their charges, was alive with swimming survivors.

The Captain drew in his breath sharply at the sight. There were about forty men in the water, concentrated in a small space: if he went ahead with the attack he must, for certain, kill them all. He knew well enough, as did everyone on board, the effect of depth-charges exploding under water – the splitting crash which made the sea jump and boil and spout skywards, the aftermath of torn seaweed and dead fish which always littered the surface after the explosion. Now there were men instead of fish and seaweed, men swimming towards him in confidence and hope … And yet the U-boat was there, one of the pack which had been harassing and bleeding them for days on end, the destroying menace which *must* have priority, because of what it might do to other ships and other convoys in the future: he could hear the echo on the relay-loudspeaker, he acknowledged Lockhart's developed judgement where the Asdic-set was concerned. As the seconds sped by, and the range closed, he fought against his doubts, and against the softening instinct of mercy: the book said: 'Attack at all costs,' and this was a page out of the book, and the men swimming in the water did not matter at all, when it was a question of bringing one of the killers to account.

But for a few moments longer he tried to gain support and confidence for what he had to do.

'What's it look like now, Number One?'

'The same, sir – solid echo – exactly the right size – *must* be a U-boat.'

'Is it moving?'

'Very slowly.'

'There are some men in the water, just about there.'

There was no answer. The range decreased as *Compass Rose* ran in: they were now within six hundred yards of the swimmers and the U-boat, the fatal coincidence which had to be ignored.

'What's it look like now?' Ericson repeated.

'Just the same – seems to be stationary – it's the strongest contact we've ever had.'

'There are some chaps in the water.'

'Well, there's a U-boat just underneath them.'

All right, then, thought Ericson, with a new unlooked-for access of brutality to help him: all right, we'll go for the U-boat. With no more hesitation he gave the order: 'Attacking – stand by!' to the depth-charge positions aft: and having made this sickening choice he swept in to the attack with a deadened mind, intent only on one kind of kill, pretending there was no other.

Many of the men in the water waved wildly as they saw what was happening: some of them screamed, some threw themselves out of the ship's path and thrashed furiously in the hope of reaching safety: others, slower-witted or nearer to exhaustion, still thought that *Compass Rose* was speeding to their rescue, and continued to wave and smile almost to

their last moment ... The ship came in like an avenging angel, cleaving
the very centre of the knots of swimmers: the amazement and horror on
their faces was reflected aboard *Compass Rose*, where many of the crew,
particularly among the depth-charge parties aft, could not believe what
they were being called upon to do. Only two men did not share this
horror: Ericson, who had shut and battened down his mind except to a
single thought – the U-boat they must kill: and Ferraby, whose privilege
it was to drop the depth-charges. 'Serve you bloody well right!' thought
Ferraby as *Compass Rose* swept in among the swimmers, catching some of
them in her screw, while the firing-bell sounded and the charges rolled
over the stern or were rocketed outwards from the throwers: 'Serve you
right – you nearly killed us last night, making us stop next door to that
fire – now it's our turn.'

There was a deadly pause, while for a few moments the men aboard
Compass Rose and the men left behind in her wake stared at each other, in
pity and fear and a kind of basic disbelief; and then with a huge hammer-
crack the depth-charges exploded.

Mercifully, the details were hidden in the flurry and roar of the
explosion; and the men must all have died instantly, shocked out of life
by the tremendous pressure of the sea thrown up upon their bodies. But
one freak item of the horror impressed itself on the memory. As the
tormented water leapt upwards in a solid grey cloud, the single figure of
a man was tossed high on the very plume of the fountain, a puppet figure
of whirling arms and legs seeming to make, in death, wild gestures of
anger and reproach. It appeared to hang a long time in the air, cursing
them all, before falling back into the boiling sea.

When they ran back to the explosion area, with the Asdic silent and
the contact not regained, it was as if to some aquarium where poisoned
water had killed every living thing. Men floated high on the surface like
dead goldfish in a film of blood. Most of them were disintegrated, or
pulped out of human shape. But half a dozen of them, who must have
been on the edge of the explosion, had come to a tidier end: split open
from chin to crutch, they had been as neatly gutted as any herring. Some
seagulls were already busy on the scene, screaming with excitement and
delight. Nothing else stirred.

No one looked at Ericson as they left that place: if they had done so,
they might have been shocked by his expression and his extraordinary
pallor. Now deep in self-torture, and appalled by what he had done, he
had already decided that there had been no U-boat there in the first
place: the contact was probably the torpedoed ship, sliding slowly to the
bottom, or the disturbed water of her sinking. Either way, the slaughter
which he had inflicted was something extra, a large entirely British-
made contribution to the success of the voyage.

By the time they were past the Straits, and had smelt the burnt smell of Africa blowing across from Ceuta, and had shaped a course for Gibraltar Harbour, they were all far off balance.

It had gone on too long, it had failed too horribly, it had cost too much. They had been at Action-Stations for virtually eight days on end, missing hours of sleep, making do with scratch meals of cocoa and corned-beef sandwiches, living all the time under recurrent anxieties which often reached a desperate tension. There had hardly been a moment of the voyage when they could forget the danger that lay in wait for them and the days of strain that stretched ahead, and relax and find peace. They had been hungry and dirty and tired from one sunrise to the next: they had lived in a ship crammed and disorganized by nearly three times her normal complement. Through it all, they had had to preserve an alertness and a keyed-up efficiency, hard enough to maintain even in normal circumstances.

The deadly part was that it had all been in vain, it had all been wasted: there could have been no more futile expense of endurance and nervous energy. Besides *Sorrel*, which was in a special category of disaster, they had lost fourteen ships out of the original twenty-one – two-thirds of the entire convoy, wiped out by a series of pack-attacks so adroit and so ferocious that counter-measures had been quite futile. That was the most wretched element of the voyage – the inescapable sense of futility, the conviction that there were always more U-boats than escorts and that the U-boats could strike, and strike home, practically as they willed.

The escorts, and *Compass Rose* among them, seemed to have been beating the air all the time: they could do nothing save count the convoy's losses at each dawn, and make, sometimes, a vain display of force which vanished like a trickle of water swallowed by an enormous sea. In the end, they had all sickened of the slaughter, and of the battle too.

To off-set the mortal bleeding of the convoy, by far the worst of this or any other war, *Viperous* had sunk one U-boat: a second had probably been destroyed; and *Compass Rose* herself had collected 175 survivors – nearly twice the number of her own crew. But this seemed nothing much, when set alongside the total loss of lives: it seemed nothing much, when measured against the men they had depth-charged and killed, instead of saving: it seemed nothing much, when shadowed by the stricken figure of *Sorrel*'s captain, wordless and brooding at the back of their bridge as *Compass Rose* slid into the shelter of Gibraltar Harbour, under the huge Rock that dwarfed and mocked the tiny defeated ships below.

. . .

At half past eight on the evening of their arrival, there was a knock on the door of the Captain's cabin. Ericson, sitting in his armchair with a glass in his hand and a half-empty bottle of gin on the side-table, called out: 'Come in!' in a voice from which all expression save an apathetic listlessness had vanished. He had been drinking steadily since four o'clock, in an attempt to forget or to blur the edges of certain scenes from their recent voyage. It had not been successful, as a glance at his face showed all too plainly.

In answer to his invitation three extraordinary figures entered the cabin: three tall, very fair men, all dressed alike in sky-blue suits of an excruciating cut, vivid shirts with thick brown stripes, and yellow pointed shoes. They stood before him, like a trio from some monstrous vaudeville act, looking down at the figure slumped in the chair with expressions half doubtful, half smiling: they had the air of men who expect to be recognized and welcomed, and yet are uncertain of their exact status in novel circumstances. They were like three public-school boys who had strayed, by accident, into the headmaster's side of the house.

The Captain stood up, rocking slightly on his feet, and focused his eyes with an effort. 'Who——?' he began, and then he suddenly recognized them. They were three of his late passengers, the captains of Norwegian ships, who had been living in the wardroom for the past three or four days after being picked up as survivors. The last time Ericson had seen them, they had been wearing what was left of their uniforms; now, it was clear, they had been ashore, and some Gibraltar outfitter had done his worst for them in the way of civilian clothes. It was a highly efficient disguise for men who, when properly dressed as ships' captains, could exhibit a formidable air of competence and toughness.

The tallest and fairest of them, possibly the elected spokesman, took a pace forward, and said, in a voice just over the border-line of sobriety: 'Good evening, Captain. We came back to thank you for our lives.'

Ericson blinked. 'Didn't recognize you,' he said, his voice equally blurred. 'Come in. Sit down. Have a drink.'

'Thank you, no,' said the first speaker.

'Thank you, yes,' said the man just behind him, with perverse readiness. 'I wish to drink with this brave man who stopped his ship in the middle of a fire, and gave me my life.'

'And me,' said the third man, who had the worst suit and the vilest shirt of all, 'me, I have the same wish, much stronger. And for my wife too, and my three children.'

'That's fine,' said Ericson, a trifle embarrassed. 'Let's sit down. What'll you have?'

But when they were all three provided with glasses, and had settled down on the hard cabin chairs, the conversation lagged. There had been a formal toast to their rescuer, and much repetition of the word 'Skoal!' each time they drank; apart from that, there did not seem much to say.

Ericson was too near to his brooding thoughts to switch over to conviviality at such short notice; and the three visitors, who had clearly included any number of bars in their shopping tour ashore, were further handicapped by their halting English. Ericson, with an effort, complimented them on their new and appalling clothes: there were more drinks, and more cries of 'Skoal!': and then a stone-wall silence fell, one of those silences which demonstrate instantly that all the conversation which has gone before, no matter how lively, has been an arid social artifice. Finally it was broken by the first of the three captains, who leant forward in his chair and said solemnly:

'We know that you have much to think about.'

'Yes,' said Ericson, 'I've been thinking.'

'You are sad?'

'Yes,' said Ericson again. 'I'm pretty sad.'

The second captain leant forward in his turn. 'The men in the water?'

Ericson nodded.

'The men you had to kill?' asked the third captain, completing the chorus.

'The men I had to kill,' repeated Ericson after a pause. He remembered having once seen a Russian play with dialogue like this. Perhaps Norwegian plays were the same.

'It was necessary to do it,' said the first captain decisively, and the other two nodded. 'Yes,' said the second. The third one said 'Skoal!' and drank deeply.

'Maybe,' answered Ericson. 'But that didn't make them look any prettier, did it?'

'It is war,' said the second captain.

'Skoal!' said the first.

'I wash my hands, please,' said the third.

When he came back, Ericson roused himself momentarily. 'I really thought there was a submarine there,' he said. 'Otherwise I wouldn't have done it.' He realized how foolish that must sound, and he added: 'I had to make up my mind. I've put it all in the report.'

'There is no blame,' said one of the captains.

'But there may be thoughts,' said another.

'Naturally there will be thoughts.'

'For thoughts there is gin,' said the first captain, with an air of logic.

'Skoal!' said Ericson.

It went on like that for a very long time. It was neither better, nor worse, than being alone. But when his three visitors had gone, Ericson did not relax; he simply reached out his hand for the bottle again. It was quite true that for thoughts there was gin.

It was Lockhart who finally found him, some time after midnight, leaning over the rail just outside his cabin, staring down at the water, muttering vaguely. Lockhart himself, though he had had less to drink, was in no better case as far as his private thoughts were concerned. Earlier that evening he had gone ashore with Lieut.-Commander Ramsay, *Sorrel*'s captain, to see the latter to his billet in the nearby Naval Barracks: it had been a sad, silent walk through streets and crowds whose cheerfulness was not infectious, and they had parted almost as strangers. Now Lockhart was back on board, but he felt quite unable to turn in: he had the jitters, like nearly everyone else in the ship, he was exhausted beyond the point of relaxation, his brain had too much company for sleep.

But when he came to the end of his pacing of the iron deck, there was the Captain, leaning over the rail in helpless defeat. Someone on board was even worse off than himself ... The big tough figure stirred as Lockhart approached, and turned towards him.

'Are you all right, sir?' asked Lockhart.

'No,' answered Ericson readily. 'I don't mind telling *you* that I'm not.' His tone was thick and slurring: it was the first time Lockhart had ever heard it so, and after these two years of close association it was hard to identify the surrendered voice with the competent one he knew so well.

Lockhart came close to him, and leant against the rail also. They were on the side away from the quay: before them was the harbour, ghostly under the moonlight, and ahead was the black shadow of the aircraft-carrier *Ark Royal*, their nearest neighbour, and behind towered the huge Rock of Gibraltar, the haven for which they had been steering for many days and nights. All round them the ship, at rest after her disastrous voyage, was oppressively silent.

'You've got to forget all about it,' said Lockhart, suddenly breaking through the normal barrier of reserve that separated them. 'It's no good worrying about it now. You can't change anything.'

'There *was* a submarine,' shouted Ericson in a furious voice. He was now helplessly drunk. 'I'm bloody well sure of it ... It's all in the report.'

'It was my fault, anyway,' said Lockhart. 'I identified it as a submarine. If anyone killed those men, I killed them.'

Ericson looked up at him. Incredibly, there were tears in his eyes which glittered like bright jewels starting from a mask, proclaiming his weakness and his manhood in the same revealing moment. Lockhart looked at them in amazement and compassion: how moving was that pale working face, how comforting, after their ordeal, the glistening tears of this strong man ... He made as if to speak, wanting to forestall Ericson and save him from further revelation; but the other man suddenly put his hand on his shoulder and said, in an almost normal voice:

'No one killed them ... It's the war, the whole bloody war ... We've

just got to do these things, and say our prayers at the end ... Have you
been drinking, Number One?'

'Yes, sir,' said Lockhart. 'Quite a lot.'

'So have I ... First time since we commissioned ... Goodnight.'

Without waiting for an answer he turned and lurched towards his
cabin entrance. After a moment there was a thud, and Lockhart,
following him into the cabin, found that he had collapsed and was lying
face downwards in his armchair, dead to the world.

'Sir,' said Lockhart formally, 'you'd better get to bed.'

There was no sound save Ericson's heavy breathing.

'You poor old bastard,' said Lockhart, half to himself, half to the
prone figure spread-eagled below him, 'you poor old bastard, you've
just about had enough, haven't you?' He considered getting the other
man's clothes off and somehow bundling him into his bunk, but he knew
he would never be able to do it – the helpless fourteen-stone weight
would be far too much for him. Instead he began to heave the Captain's
body round so as to settle him comfortably in the armchair, talking out
loud as he did so. 'I can't get you to bed, my dear and revered Captain,
but I can at least snug you down for the night ... You'll have quite a
head when you wake up, God bless you – I don't think I'd like to be one
of your defaulters tomorrow morning ... Get your legs out straight ...'
He eased Ericson's collar and tie, looked down at him for a moment
more as he lay relaxed in the armchair, and then moved towards the
doorway. 'That's the best I can do for you,' he murmured, his hand on
the light-switch. 'Wish it could be more, wish I could *really* cure you ...'
He clicked off the light. 'Drunk or sober, Ericson, you're all right ...'

He was already halfway through the doorway when he heard the
other man's voice behind him, vague and sleepy.

'Number One,' said Ericson, 'I heard that.'

'That's all right, sir,' said Lockhart, without embarrassment. 'I meant
it ... Goodnight.'

There was silence as he went out, silence as he climbed down the
ladder to the deserted wardroom. All round him, as on the upper deck,
the exhausted ship lay in the embrace of sleep, hoping to forget the
horrible past. Lockhart dwelt for a moment on that past, and his own
guilty part in it; then he unlocked the sideboard, set out a bottle and a
glass, and, following what now seemed an excellent example, drank
himself into insensibility.

CHAPTER 8

Morell sat at ease on a balcony overlooking the main street of Gibraltar, gravely sipping a tall glass of Tio Pepe sherry so exquisitely pale and dry that it was an honour to welcome it upon the tongue.

Below him the crowds were thickening as the liberty-men thronged ashore from the many ships in harbour. There was so much here that was new, to do and to see: the shops carried their full cargoes of silk stockings and scents, the gharries threaded their way down the narrow streets with their canopies ruffled by the breeze, and from the cafés and beer-halls the music and the laughter beckoned continuously; it was all part of the fun, part of the novel landfall. They always enjoyed their visits to Gibraltar; and now, as far as *Compass Rose* was concerned, it came as a special balm for their defeat, underlining the wonder of having survived so fearful a voyage. Morell, like the rest of them, was welcoming it all with open hands: after a week in harbour, the hot sunshine, the chance of relaxing in their white tropical rig, the swimming parties to the eastern side of the Rock, the strange faces in the street, the glamour of visiting a foreign port, still showed no signs of palling. There was nothing much on the credit side of that voyage; but if one were lucky enough to be alive at the end of it, instead of dead like most of *Sorrel*'s crew, Gibraltar seemed a particularly good place to be alive in.

They felt, too, that they themselves had a special status here. Rumours of the disaster to the convoy had spread swiftly among the personnel of the Base: it was enough to remark, in the Naval Mess ashore: 'We were with A.G.93,' for an alert silence to intervene, and for curious speculative glances to focus on the speaker. A.G.93 was a convoy with a reputation: anyone who had sailed with it ought by rights to be either round the bend, or dead. . . It was something to have earned even this dubious *cachet*, in a port which was playing so dramatic a part in the war and where the big ships, whose base it was, were earning world-wide reputations for courage and daring.

Ark Royal, for example, lay next ahead of them in the harbour below, the sheer of her bows climbing like an overhanging cliff up to the enormous flight-deck that crowned her super-structure. She was now the most hunted ship on the seven seas, the target for the bombs, the torpedoes, and the boastful lies of the enemy: with her were the battle cruiser *Renown* and the rest of 'Force H', that famous company of ships which had fought the convoys through to Malta in the face of a ferocious opposition, and could still find time to trail the *Bismarck* to her death, a thousand miles to the northward. Grouped round them in the teeming harbour were the lesser vessels – the destroyer flotillas, the Fleet minesweepers, the clutch of submarines which harassed the coastwise shipping of the western Mediterranean: across the bay in Algeciras, smugly privileged, were the spying eyes of the enemy, sheltering under the wing of Spain whose contribution to victory this was: far to the eastward were Crete and Greece, now in the throes of a bloody rout; and over all the fabulous Rock stood guard, that impregnable honeycomb of tunnels and lifts and ammunition and stores and guns, holding the Straits by the throat, and a thousand square miles of ocean in the same mortal grip.

Morell called for another glass of sherry, and sat on in his soft delectable corner of the fortress, watching the declining sun and the lengthening shadows of the evening, sipping the delicate drink in complete contentment. Presently there was vague shouting and the sound of some disturbance in a café further down the street; but he did not bestir himself to look over the balcony-rail, nor was he in the least curious about the noise. If it were anyone from *Compass Rose* in trouble, he would hear all about it in the morning; if not, they could murder each other with jagged bottle-tops, for all he cared... He wanted nothing more from this moment: no excitement, no complication, no angel in the path. They had had their ordeal, they had survived it, and it was good, very good, to be at ease at last.

CHAPTER 9

On the sixth day of their journey home, late in the forenoon watch Chief E.R.A. Watts came up to the bridge with a worried frown on his face. So far, things had been going well with their return convoy: there had been no shadowing aircraft, no scares about U-boats waiting for them, no drama of any sort. It made a nice change... But now there was a chance of things not going well at all, and it was he who had to break the news.

'Captain, sir!' Watts stood at the back of the bridge, awkwardly shifting his feet on the smooth white planking. He never came up there if he could help it, because it made him feel entirely out of place: his proper station was on the engine-room 'plate' three decks below, among the pipes and the gauges that he understood so well; this open-air stuff, with look-outs and flag-signals and water dashing past all round, was not his cup of tea at all. Even his overalls and oily canvas shoes looked funny, with everyone else dolled up in sea-boots and duffle-coats ... Ericson, who had been preparing to check their noon position, and enjoying the sunshine at the same time, turned round at the sound of his voice.

'Well, Chief? Anything wrong?'

'Afraid so, sir.' Watts came forward, rubbing his hands on his overalls. His grey creased face was full of concern. 'I've got a bearing I don't like the feel of at all. Running hot, it is – nearly red-hot. I'd like to stop and have a look at it, sir.'

'Do you mean the main shaft, Chief?' Ericson knew that his knowledge of the engine-room, sufficient for normal purposes, did not include all the technical refinements, and he wanted to get his facts straight.

'Yes, sir. Must be a blocked oil-pipe, by the look of it.'

'Any good if we slow down? I don't want to stop if we can help it.'

Watts shook his head vigorously. 'If we keep the shaft turning it's liable to seize up, sir. And I can't trace the oil-line back from the main feed unless we stop engines. It's one of those awkward corners – the after bearing, right up against the gland space.'

Ericson, struggling to give form to the sketchy picture in his mind, frowned in concentration. But the answer seemed fairly clear. If a main bearing was running hot, it wasn't getting its proper ration of oil: if the oil were continuously denied, and the melting-point of the metal were reached, the bearing and the surrounding sleeve would be welded into one, and the main shaft would be locked. That was, comparatively speaking, a straightforward piece of mechanical mystery ... For a moment he cast about in his mind for possible alternatives, but he knew there were none. They would have to do the least healthy thing in the war at sea – stop in mid-ocean, with their engine put out of commission.

'All right, Chief,' said Ericson, making up his mind to it. 'I'll send a signal, and then ring down for you to stop. Be as quick as you can.'

'I'll be that, sir.'

They were just in visual touch with *Viperous*, who was zigzagging in broad sweeps across the van of the convoy. When *Compass Rose* signalled her news, the answer was laconic:

'Act independently. Keep me informed.'

'Acknowledge,' said Ericson briefly to Rose, who was signalman of the watch. Then: 'Starboard ten. Stop engines,' he called down to the wheel-house; and *Compass Rose*, turning in a wide sweep away from the convoy, lost way and came gradually to a standstill.

Up on the bridge they waited in silence, while the convoy steamed past them, and the corvette which had the stern position altered course to pass close by, like an inquisitive terrier which does not know whether to wag its tail or bark. Down below in the engine-room, Watts and a leading-stoker called Gracey set to work on their examination of the oil-feed. It was indeed an awkward corner, jammed up against a bulkhead and barely approachable: to trace the trouble they had to pick out the suspect oil-pipe, from an array of a dozen others, and then take it to pieces in sections to find out which part of it was blocked. The engine-room was very hot: they were forced to bend nearly double as they worked, groping for the joints from opposite sides of the piping because there was not room for them to stand side by side: sections of the pipe could not be brought out and examined before other sections of other pipes had been loosened and removed. It was a full two hours before they had located the trouble – an L-shaped, curved section which appeared to be totally blocked.

Watts stepped backwards and straightened up, holding the pipe in one hand and wiping his sweaty forehead with the other. 'Now what?' he said rhetorically. 'How do we find out what's inside this?'

'Suck it and see, I suppose,' answered Gracey, who was a lower-deck comedian of some note.

'Get a piece of wire,' said Watts coldly. Some people were allowed to be funny to Chief E.R.A.s, but leading-stokers were not included in this licensed category. 'Not too thick . . . I'm going to report to the Captain.'

After two more hours of steady work they were still no further on. Whatever had got inside the pipe seemed to be stuck there immovably: it couldn't be blown out, it couldn't be pushed through, it couldn't be melted or picked to pieces. Waiting on the bridge of his useless ship, Ericson found it hard to restrain himself from storming down to the engine-room and telling them to stop loafing and get on with it; but he knew that this would have been futile, as well as unfair. Watts was doing his best: no one else on board could do better. At four o'clock with the last ships of the convoy out of sight below the horizon, Ericson had sent a signal by R/T to *Viperous*, explaining what was happening; there had been no answer beyond a bare acknowledgement and it was clear that *Viperous* was setting him a good example in trusting him to make the best of the repair and to rejoin as soon as possible.

He stood wedged in a corner of the bridge, staring down at the dark oily water which reflected the overcast sky; behind him, Ferraby and Baker, who had the watch, were idly examining the pieces of a Hotchkiss anti-aircraft gun which one of the gunnery ratings was stripping. The Asdic-set clicked and pinged, monotonously wakeful, the Radar-aerial circled an invisible horizon: the two look-outs occasionally raised their binoculars and swept through their respective arcs – forward, aft, and forward again. *Compass Rose* was entirely motionless: her ensign hung down without stirring, her vague shadow on the water never moved or altered its outline. She was waiting for two things – for her engine to start again, and for the other thing which might happen to her, without warning and without a chance of defending herself either. Who knew what was below the surface of the dark sea, who knew what malevolent eye might be regarding them, even at this moment? In the nervous and oppressive silence, such thoughts multiplied, with nothing to set against them save the hope of getting going again.

On the quarter-deck aft, some of the hands were fishing. If Ericson had told them that they were fishing in at least a thousand fathoms of water, as was in fact the case, it would probably have made no difference. Fishing – even with breadcrumb bait dangling six thousand feet above the ocean bed – was better than doing nothing, at a moment like this.

Down below in the engine-room, Chief E.R.A. Watts had come to a certain decision. It involved considerable delay, and some danger of wrecking everything beyond repair; but there was no choice left to him.

'We'll have to saw the pipe up,' he said to Gracey, at the end of another futile bout of poking and picking at the obstruction. 'Bit by bit, till we find the stoppage.'

'What then?'

'Clear it out, and then braze the whole thing together again.'

'Take all night if we do that,' said Gracey sulkily.

'Take all the war if we don't,' retorted Watts, 'get a hacksaw, while I tell the Captain.'

Watts was actually up on the bridge when *Viperous* appeared in sight again. She came storming down from the north-westwards at about five o'clock in the afternoon, her big signal-lamp flickering as soon as she was over the horizon; she wanted to know everything – the state of their repairs, the chances of their getting going again, and whether they had had any suspicious contacts or seen any aircraft during their stoppage. In consultation with Watts, Ericson answered as best he could: they had located the trouble, and would almost certainly be able to clear it, but it would probably take them most of the night to do it.

Viperous, who had stopped her swift approach as soon as she was in effective touch, circled lazily about ten miles off them while the signals were exchanged. Then there was a pause, and then she signalled:

'Afraid I cannot spare you an escort for the night.'

'That is quite all right,' Ericson signalled back. 'We will sleep by ourselves.' He put that in, in case *Viperous* was feeling sad about the arrangement. It was perfectly true that two escorts could not be spared from the convoy during the night; there could be no argument about the rightness of that decision.

There was another pause. *Viperous* began to shape up towards the northward horizon again. When she was stern-on to them:

'I must leave you to it,' she signalled finally. 'Best of luck.' She began to draw away. Just before she got out of touch she signalled again: 'Goodnight, Cinderella.'

' "Goodnight, dear elder sister",' Ericson dictated to Rose. But then he cancelled the message, before Rose started sending. The captain of *Viperous* was just a little bit too elder – in rank – for him to run the risk.

. . .

The repairs did not take all the night, but they took many trying hours of it. Watts had to cut the oil-pipe eight times before he found the exact point of obstruction: this was at the joint of the elbow, and consisted of a lump of cotton-waste hardened and compressed into a solid plug. The question of how it got there gave Watts half an hour of abusive and infuriated speculation, and left Leading-Stoker Gracey, along with the rest of the engine-room complement, in sullen contemplation of the whole system of naval discipline. But time was not there to be wasted: even as he raged and questioned, Watts was working swiftly on the pieces of piping, brazing them together again into something like the same length and curve as they had had before. The result did not look very reassuring, and once they were delayed and very nearly defeated by a section which succumbed to the heat of the blow-lamp and collapsed into solid metal: but finally the whole pipe was cleared and smoothed off, and they set to work to coax it back into position again.

Outside, dusk had come down, and then the night. With its coming they took extraordinary precautions against discovery: Lockhart went round the upper deck three or four times to ensure that the ship was properly darkened and that no chink of light would betray them: the radios in the wardroom and the messdecks were closed down, and stringent orders given against unnecessary noise: the boats were swung out, ready for lowering, and the lashings of the rafts cast off – in case, as Tallow put it morbidly, they had to make a rush job of swimming. 'And if any of you,' he added to the hands working on the upper deck, 'makes a noise tonight, I'll have his guts for a necktie ...' The situation now involved a worse risk than any stopping or loitering had done before, because this time they were quite helpless: if a torpedo passed right underneath them, they could only wave goodbye to it, and wait for the next one. As the hours passed, the tension became unbearable: this was the sea, the very stretch of water which on their outward voyage had seen so many men go to their death, and here they were, sitting on it like a paralysed duck and waiting for the bang.

But there was nothing to do but wait. Watch succeeded watch: the hands tiptoed delicately to their stations, instead of clumping along the deck or stamping their sea-boots on the iron ladder, as they usually did: *Compass Rose* floated motionless, with the black water occasionally slapping against her side: a brilliant quarter-moon hung in the mid-

Atlantic sky, showing them all the outlines of their hazard. Throughout the ship there was the same tension, the same disbelief in the future, the same rage against the bloody stokers down below who had let the engine get gummed up, and were now loafing and fiddling about ... Lockhart had it in mind to give the watch on deck, and the other spare hands, something definite to do, to take their attention away from the present danger; but everything he thought of – such as fire-drill or lowering a boat to the water-line – involved noise and probably the flashing of torches on the upper deck, and in the end he abandoned the idea and left them alone. Waiting in idleness was bad for the nerves; but the risk attending anything else might be worse still.

Ericson spent all these hours up on the bridge: there was no other station for him at such a moment, and no other choice in his mind. The look-outs changed half-hourly: cocoa came up in relays from the wardroom: the Asdic and the Radar kept up their incessant watch: curbing his immense impatience, Ericson sat on, enthroned like some wretched ragamuffin chief on the bridge of his useless ship. Mostly he stared at the water and the horizon, sometimes at the bright moon which no cloud would obscure: occasionally he watched the shadowy figures on the upper deck, the men who waited there in silent groups, collected round the guns or the boats, instead of going below and turning in. This was a new thing aboard *Compass Rose*. But he could not find fault with their prudence, he could not blame them for their fear.

There was an example of this nervous strain much closer at hand. Ferraby had not been below decks since the ship came to a stop, and now he was curled up in a blanket at the side of the bridge: he lay on his back, his hands clasped behind his head, his inflated life-jacket ballooning out like some opulent bosom; he had been there since he came off watch, at midnight, and he had never stirred or changed his position. Ericson had thought that he was dozing; but once, taking a turn round the bridge, he had noticed that the other man's eyes were wide open, and that he was darkly staring at the sky overhead. There was a sheen of perspiration at his temples. He was very far from sleep ... Ericson paused in his pacing, and looked down at the pale face.

'All right, Sub?' he asked conversationally.

There was no answer, and no sign that he had been heard. But Ericson did not persist with his question: this was a time to disregard people's reactions, to look past them without comment. The ship had been stopped, a still and defenceless target, for over twelve hours: *Sorrel* was fresh in all their minds: this was where it had all happened before. It was no wonder that, here and there, nerves stretched to breaking-point were jumping and quivering in the effort to hold on.

He walked to the front of the bridge again, and sat down without another word. Ferraby could not help what was happening to him: no blame attached to him for his raw nerves, any more than a new-born child could be blamed for weighing six pounds instead of eight. The womb of war had produced him thus. But somewhere at the back of his mind Ericson was conscious of a strange sort of envy, an irritated consciousness of what a huge relief it would be to relax his grip, to surrender the unmoving mask of competence, to show to the world, if need be, his fatigue or fear . . . Gibraltar, he thought suddenly; I gave up there, Lockhart saw it – but that had been alcohol, alcohol and guilt, nothing else. And it was not to happen again, it was not to happen now . . . Waiting in the darkness, watching the silver ripples crossing the track of the moon, he slowly tightened up again.

Only once during that night was there an interruption of their vigil, but it was an interruption which startled them all. In the stillness that followed the change of the watch, just after midnight, breaking harshly in upon the sound of lapping water, there was a sudden burst of hammering from below, a solid succession of thuds which resounded throughout the ship. Everyone came to attention, and looked at his neighbour in quest of reassurance: secretly they cursed the men working in the engine-room, for reawakening their fear and their hatred. The noise could be heard for miles around . . . On the bridge, Ericson turned to Morell, who had just taken over the watch.

'Go down and see Watts,' he said crisply. 'Tell him to stop the hammering or to muffle it somehow. Tell him we can't afford to make this amount of noise.' As Morell turned to go, Ericson added, less formally, 'Tell him the torpedo will hit him first.'

That was perfectly true, thought Morell, as he climbed down successive ladders deep into the heart of the ship; to go below the water-line at a moment such as this was like stepping knowingly into the tomb. He could not help feeling a comradely admiration for the men who had been working patiently, ten feet below the surface of the water, for so many hours on end: it was part of their job, of course, just as it had sometimes been part of his own to be up on the exposed bridge when an aircraft was spraying them with machine-gun fire; but the cold-blooded hazard involved in working below decks in the present circumstances seemed to demand a special category of nervous endurance. If a torpedo came, the engine-room crew must be an instant casualty: they would have perhaps ten seconds to get out, as the water flooded in, and those ten seconds, for a dozen men fighting to use one ladder in the pitch darkness, would mean the worst end to life that a man could devise . . . But hazard or not, they oughtn't to make so much noise about what they were doing: that was stretching their necks out too far altogether.

The hammering stopped as he slid down the last oily ladder to the engine-room itself, and Watts, hearing his step on the iron plating, turned to greet him.

'Come to see the fun, sir? It won't be long now.'

'That's my idea of good news, Chief,' answered Morell. No settled naval hierarchy could ever make him address Watts, who was nearly old enough to be his grandfather, with anything save an informal friendliness. 'But the Captain's a bit worried about the noise. Can you do anything to tone it down?'

'Pretty well finished now, sir,' said Watts. 'We were just putting one of those brackets back .... Could you hear the hammering up top?'

'Hear it? There were submarines popping up for miles around, complaining about the racket.'

There was a short laugh from the handful of men working round the oil-pipe: down there, even the funniest jokes about submarines were only just funny ... Morell looked round the circle of faces, harshly lit by the naked hand-lamp clipped to a nearby stanchion: they all shared the same look, the same factors of expression – tiredness, concentration, fear in the background. He knew them all by sight – Watts, Leading-Stoker Gracey, a couple of young second-class stokers named Binns and Spurway who were always getting drunk ashore, an apprentice E.R.A. called Broughton who was a Roman Catholic – but he had never known them quite like this: the labels and the characters he usually attached to them seemed to have been stripped and melted away, leaving only the basic men whose brains and fingers either could or could not patch up the oil-pipe before a submarine caught them, and whose faces reflected this uncertain future. There was no pettiness about them now, no individual foible, no trace of indiscipline: as they worked, Care sat on their shoulders, Time's winged chariot was at their backs (Morell smiled as the odd phrases, incongruous in the glare and smell of the engine-room, returned to him), and they knew this all the time and it had purged them of everything save a driving anxiety to finish what they had to do.

'Any signs of submarines, sir?' asked Gracey after a pause. He was a Lancashire man: he pronounced the hated word as 'soobmarines', giving it a humorous air which robbed it of its sting. Said like that, it was hardly a submarine at all, just something out of a music-hall, no more lethal than a mother-in-law or a dish of tripe. How nice, thought Morell, if that were true.

'Nothing so far,' he answered. 'The convoy seems to be quite happy, too. But I don't think we want to hang about here too long.'

Watts nodded. 'Seems like we're sitting up and asking for it,' he said grimly. 'If they don't get us now, they never will.'

'How much longer, Chief?'

'Couple of hours, maybe.'

'Longest job we've ever had,' said Gracey. 'You'd think it was a bloody battle-wagon.'

'Me for barracks, when we get in,' said Broughton. 'I'd rather run the boiler-house at Chatham than this lot.'

'Who wouldn't?' said Spurway, the smallest and usually the drunkest stoker. '*I'd* rather clean out the dockside heads, any day of the week.'

Morell suddenly realized how intensely nervous they had all become, how far they had been driven beyond the normal margins of behaviour. He said: 'Good luck with it,' and started up the ladder again. At the top, the stars greeted him, and then the black water. A small chill wind was stirring, sending quick ripples slapping against their side. Alone in the dark night, *Compass Rose* lay still, waiting.

CHAPTER 10

In the cold hour that stretched between two and three a.m., with the moon clouded and the water black and fathomless as sable, a step on the bridge ladder. But now it was a different sort of step: cheerful, quick-mounting, no longer stealthy. It was Chief E.R.A. Watts.

'Captain, sir!' he called to the vague figure hunched over the front of the bridge.

Ericson, stiff and cold with his long vigil, turned awkwardly towards him. 'Yes, Chief?'

'Ready to move, sir.'

So that was that, thought Ericson, standing up and stretching gratefully: they could get going, they could leave at last this hated corner, they could make their escape. The relief was enormous, flooding in till it seemed to reach every part of his body: he felt like shouting his congratulation, seizing Watts' hand and shaking it, giving way to his light-headed happiness. But all he said was: 'Thank you, Chief. Very well done.' And then, to the voice-pipe: 'Wheel-house!'

'Wheel-house, bridge, sir!' came the quartermaster's voice, startled from some dream of home.

'Ring "Stand by, main engines".'

Very soon they were off: steaming swiftly northward, chasing the convoy: the revolutions mounted, the whole ship grew warm and alive and full of hope again. There was no need to look back: they had, by all the luck in the world, left nothing of themselves behind and given nothing to the enemy.

. . .

At about six o'clock, with the first dawn lightening the sky to the eastwards, they 'got' the convoy on the very edge of the Radar-screen. Lockhart, who was Officer-of-the-Watch, looked at the blurred echo appreciatively: it was still many miles ahead, and they would not be in direct touch till mid-morning, but it put them on the map again – they were no longer alone on the waste of water that might have been their grave. He woke the Captain to tell him the news, as he had been ordered to: it seemed a shame to break into his sleep with so straightforward an item, which might well have been kept till later in the morning, but the orders had been explicit – and probably Ericson would sleep the easier for hearing that they were in touch again. Indeed, the sleepy grunt which came up the voice-pipe in answer to Lockhart's information seemed to indicate that Ericson had only just risen to the surface, like a trout to a fly, to take in the news, before diving down fathoms deep to the luxury of sleep once more. Lockhart smiled as he snapped the voice-pipe cover shut again. After such a night, the Captain deserved his zizz.

The morning watch progressed; towards its ending at eight o'clock the light grew to the eastward, blanching the dark water: Tomlinson, the junior steward, foraging for the cups and sandwich plates of the night's session, went soft-footed on the wet and dewy decks, like a new character in a suddenly cheerful third act. The engine revolutions were now set near their maximum: *Compass Rose*'s course was steady, aiming for the centre of the convoy ahead: Lockhart had nothing to do but stamp warmth into his feet and keep an appraising eye on the Radar-screen as the range closed and the pattern of ships hardened and took shape. It was good to see that compact blur of light, as welcome and as familiar as the deck under his sea-boots, gaining strength and edging nearer to them: they had been away from it too long, they wanted, above all, an end to their loneliness, and here it was at last, tangible and expectant, like a family waiting to greet them at the finish of a journey ... His thoughts wandered: he responded automatically as the quartermaster and the look-outs changed for the final half-hour of the watch: *Compass Rose*, breasting the long Atlantic swell and shifting gently under his feet, might have been a train rocking over the last set of points as it ran into Euston station. At the end of the platform there would be – he jerked to attention suddenly as the bell rang from the Radar-compartment.

'Radar – bridge!'

Lockhart bent to the voice-pipe. 'Bridge.'

The voice of the Radar operator, level, rather tired, not excited, came up to him. 'I'm getting a small echo astern of the convoy, sir. Can you see it on the repeater?'

Lockhart looked at the Radar-screen beside the voice-pipe, a replica of the one in the operator's compartment, and nodded to himself. It was true. Between the convoy and themselves there was now a single small echo, flickering and fading on the screen like a candle guttering in a gentle draught. He watched it for a half a minute before speaking. It was never more than a luminous pinpoint of light, but it always came up, it was persistently *there* all the time: it was a contact, and it had to be accounted for. He bent to the voice-pipe again.

'Yes, I've got it . . . What do you make of it?' Then, before the man could answer, he added: 'Who's that on the set?'

'Sellars, sir.'

Sellars, thought Lockhart: their Leading Radar Mechanic, a reliable operator, a man worth asking questions . . . He said again: 'What do you make of it?'

'Hard to tell, sir,' answered Sellars. 'It's small, but it's there all the time, keeping pace with the convoy.'

'Could it be a back-echo off the ships?'

'I don't think so, sir.' Sellars' voice was dubious. 'The angle's wrong, for a start.'

'Well, a straggler, then?'

'It's a bit small for a ship, sir . . . Do you see the ship right out to starboard – probably one of the escorts? That one's a lot bigger.'

Lockhart stared at the Radar-screen. That, again, was quite true. On the edge of the convoy-pattern, away to starboard, was a single detached echo which was probably a corvette; and it was appreciably bigger than the speck of light which they were querying. He found himself hesitating, on the verge of reporting the strange echo to the Captain, and yet not wanting to wake him up from his deserved sleep without good reason. It could be one of many things, all of them harmless: it could be a fault in the set, which was not yet clear of its teething-troubles; it could be a straggler from the convoy (though its size was against it): it could conceivably be a rain-storm. Or it could – it *could* – be something that they really wanted to see . . . After watching for a full two minutes, while the echo strengthened slightly, maintaining level pace with the convoy as before, he said to Sellars: 'Keep your eye on it,' and then, unwillingly, he crossed to the Captain's voice-pipe and pressed the bell.

When he came up to the bridge, knuckling his eyes and rubbing his stiff face, Ericson was not in the best of tempers. He had had a bare four hours' sleep, interrupted by the first convoy-report; and to have it broken into again, just because (as he phrased it to himself) there was a bloody seagull perched on the Radar-aerial and the First Lieutenant hadn't got the sense to shoo it away, did not seem to him the best way of greeting the happy dawn. He grunted as Lockhart pointed out the echo and explained how it had developed: then he looked up from the Radar-screen, and said briefly:

'Probably a straggler.'

'It's a lot smaller than the other ships, sir,' said Lockhart tentatively. He recognized the Captain's right to be short-tempered at this god-forsaken hour of the morning, but he had taken that into account when he woke him up, and he wanted to justify the alarm. He pointed to the screen. 'That's the stern escort, I should say. This thing is at least ten miles behind that.'

'M'm,' grunted Ericson again. Then: 'Who's the Radar operator?' he asked, following Lockhart's own train of thought.

'Sellars, sir.'

Ericson bent to the voice-pipe, and cleared his throat with a growl. 'Radar!'

'Radar – bridge!' answered Sellars.

'What about this echo?'

'Still there, sir.' He gave the range and the bearing. 'That makes it about ten miles astern of the last ship of the convoy.'

'Nothing wrong with the set, is there?'

'No, sir,' said Sellars, with the brisk air of a man who, at ten minutes to eight on a cold morning, was disinclined for this sort of slur, even coming from a bad-tempered Captain. 'The set's on the top line.'

'Have you had an echo like this before?'

There was a pause below. Then: 'Not exactly, sir. It's about the size we'd get from a buoy or a small boat.'

'A trawler? A drifter?'

'Smaller than that, sir. Ship's boat, more like.'

'H'm . . .' Ericson looked at the Radar-screen again, while Lockhart, watching him, smiled to himself. It was clear that his bad temper was fighting a losing battle with his acknowledgement of Sellars' competence. Behind them, the rest of the bridge personnel, and Baker, who had just come up to take over the watch, were also eyeing the Captain speculatively, alert for any decision. But when it came, it was still a surprise.

'Sound "Action-Stations",' said Ericson, straightening up suddenly. And to the wheel-house, in the same sharp voice. 'Full ahead! Steer ten degrees to starboard.'

Lockhart opened his mouth to speak, and then snapped it shut again. Taken by surprise, he had been about to say something phenomenally silly, like 'Do you really think it's a submarine, sir?' The loud, endless shrilling of the alarm-bells all over the ship, and the thud of heavy boots along the decks and up the ladder, gave the best answer of all to this foolish speculation . . . He stood by the battery of voice-pipes, conscious of more than the usual excitement as the various positions were reported to him, and he acknowledged the reports: the pattern and the sequence of this were yawningly familiar, it was all old stuff, they had been doing it, in fun or in earnest, for two whole years: but this time, this time it really might have some point to it . . .

One by one the voices pricked his eagerness.

Ferraby from aft: 'Depth-charge crews closed up!'

Morell from the fo'c'sle: 'Gun's crew closed up!'

Baker from amidships: 'Two-pounder gun closed up!'
Chief E.R.A. Watts from far below: 'Action steaming-stations!'
Tallow from the wheel-house: 'Coxswain on the wheel, sir!'

Lockhart gave a swift glance round him, and fore and aft, a final check for his own satisfaction. The bridge look-outs were at their places on the Hotchkiss guns: Leading-Signalman Wells was ready by the big signal-lamp. Grouped round the four-inch gun just below the bridge, the steel-helmeted crew stood alert, with Morell staring ahead through his binoculars and then turning back to direct the loading: far aft, Ferraby was the centre of another group of men, clearing away the safety-lashings from the depth-charges and preparing them for firing. Satisfied, Lockhart turned to the Captain, presenting the completed pattern for whatever use he chose to make of it.

'Action-Stations closed up, sir!' he called out. Then he dropped back to his own charge, the Asdic-set: the killing instrument itself, if one were needed ... Underneath them, as if conscious of her weight of tensed and ready men, *Compass Rose* began to tremble.

Ericson was watching the Radar-screen. His call for Action-Stations had been not much more than an impulse: he could even admit that it might have been prompted by irritation, by the feeling that, if he himself had to be awake, then no one else on board was going to go on sleeping. But certainly they had picked up an odd-looking echo, one of the most promising so far: it was possible that this time they were really onto something, and in that case the full readiness of *Compass Rose* was a solid comfort. Momentarily, he raised his binoculars, and peered ahead, but the morning mist lay all round the horizon and there was nothing to be seen. He looked down at the Radar-screen again, and then bent to the voice-pipe.

'Report your target.'

Sellars gave the range and the bearing of the contact. Whatever it was, it was still moving at the slow convoy speed, and they were overhauling it rapidly.

'It's gaining strength a bit, sir,' he concluded. 'Same size, but a firmer echo. Must be something pretty solid.'

That was what the picture on the Radar-screen showed. The whole convoy had emerged now: a compact square of ships, with the outlying escorts showing clearly, and the small stranger swimming along behind ... Ericson had begun to believe in it; for the first time, he felt he was watching a U-boat behaving according to the book – trailing a convoy just out of sight, perhaps after an abortive night attack, and waiting for dusk to come again, before moving up for another attempt. But what this U-boat *didn't* know about was the straggling escort left behind, the ship outside the picture which was hurrying in to spoil it. If they could just get within range before they were spotted ...

Compass Rose ran on; the whole ship was expectant, pointing towards her target, racing to find out what it was, hoping for the legal quarry. If it were a U-boat, then they were building up towards the best chance of the war so far: it was the thing they had been waiting for, the point of all their endurance; the next hour could make sense of everything. All over the upper deck, the men standing-to were cheerful in their hope: the word had gone round that they were chasing something definite, and a steady leakage of information from the Radar-room kept them up to date and fed their expectation. And on the bridge, every man who had a pair of glasses – the Captain, Wells, the two look-outs – strained towards the horizon, and the promise that might break from it at any moment.

Compass Rose ran on: the bow-wave creamed under her forefoot, the boiling wake spread behind her, whipping against the wind with rough impatience as she drove towards her prey. The sun was over the horizon now, a pale sun which melted the mist and set the waves sparkling for ten and fifteen miles ahead: a pale sun, a strengthening sun, a cheerful sun which was on their side and had come up to help them. The rigging began to whine: the trembling of the bow-plating as it thrust and divided the water could be felt all over the upper deck: by the depth-charge rails, the pulse of the screw against the racing sea made the whole after-part vibrate, on a broad monotone singing-note like a statement of intention in some formidable work of music. Chief must be giving it stick, thought Ericson with a grin of satisfaction: that'll wake up those loafing stokers, that'll shake a bit of soot down the funnel ... After last night's protracted helplessness, it was good to reverse the roles and to be launched on this swift stalking hunt.

Compass Rose ran on. 'Report your target!' said Ericson, for the fifth or sixth time: from below, Sellars' voice, excited and jubilant, confirmed the dwindling range, the certainty of a lively rendezvous. For Ericson, it was as if the whole ship were gathering itself together under his hand, getting wound up taut for the spring: it was a fanciful thought, such as he sometimes had when he was very tired or very tense: he felt the ship under him like the rider feels the horse, and he felt glad and proud of her ready response. It was for this that they had waited so long and sweated so hard ... He crossed to the compass platform, took an exact bearing from the last Radar report, raised his glasses, and stared along the line.

Almost immediately he saw it.

It was a square speck of black on the horizon: it was the conning-tower of a U-boat. Even as he looked at it, it lifted to the long swell, and he saw at its base a plume of white – the wash thrown off by the submerged hull. Far ahead of it, to complete the picture, there were some stray wisps of smoke, the tell-tale marks of the convoy which was betraying itself from over twenty miles away. Two targets, two hunters – he straightened up with a jerk, and whipped to the front of the bridge.

'Morell!' he snapped.

Morell looked up. 'Sir?'

'There's a U-boat on the surface, dead ahead. Far out of range at the moment. But be ready. We want to get a couple of shots in before she dives – if we can get near enough.' Ericson half-turned towards Lockhart: as he did so, Wells, who was standing by his side and staring through his binoculars, called out:

'I can see it, sir – dead ahead!' His voice was high with excitement, but almost immediately his professional sense pulled him back to normal again. 'Shall we send a sighting report, sir?'

'Yes. W/T signal. Warn the office.' He gathered his thoughts together. 'Take this down ... "ADMIRALTY, REPEATED TO VIPEROUS. SUBMARINE ON SURFACE TEN MILES ASTERN OF CONVOY T.G. 104. COURSE 345, SPEED FIVE KNOTS. AM ENGAGING".' He turned round again, towards Lockhart in the Asdic-cabinet. 'Number One! There's a ——'

Lockhart put his head out of the small window, smiling widely. 'I kind of overheard, sir,' he answered. 'Too far away for me, at the moment.'

Ericson smiled in answer. 'We'll need that damned box of tricks before very long. You can stand by for the quickest crash-dive in history, as soon as they see us.'

'Sir,' said Lockhart, 'let's make the most of it while their trousers are down.'

All over the ship, the next five minutes were intense and crowded. The warning of immediate action was passed to Ferraby on the depth-charges aft, and then to the engine-room. 'Crack it on, Chief!' said Ericson, crisply, down the voice-pipe: 'we've only got a certain amount of time to play with.' *Compass Rose* began to romp across the sea towards her target: under pressure from the last few pounds of steam, she seemed to be spurning the water in a desperate attempt to close the range before she was discovered. Through Ericson's glasses, the square speck of the conning-tower was bigger now: it had gained in detail, it had a variety of light and shade, it even had the head and shoulders of a man – a man silhouetted against the hard horizon, a man gazing stolidly ahead, ludicrously intent on his arc of duty. All unconscious of their fate, the little victims play, thought Lockhart, who could now see the U-boat with his naked eye, without effort: it was still too far away for an Asdic contact, but at this rate, by God, they could to a straightforward ramming job, without calling on the blessings of science ... The distance shortened: Sellars' voice rose steadily up the scale as he reported the closing range: presently a totally unfamiliar bell rang on the bridge – the bell from the four-inch gun – and Morell, with the air of a man presenting his compliments on some purely speculative occasion, said:

'I think I could reach him now, sir.'

The range was four sea-miles: eight thousand yards. It was a long shot for a small gun, it might spoil the whole thing; but surely, thought Ericson, that stolid man in the conning-tower *must* turn round, and see them, and say either 'Donnerwetter!' or 'Gott in Himmel!' and take the U-boat in a steep dive down to safety ... He delayed for a moment longer, weighing the chances of discovery against the limitation of the valiant pop-gun which was their main armament; then he leant over the front of the bridge, and nodded permission to Morell.

The roar of the gun could hardly have followed more swiftly: Morell's finger must have been hovering very near the trigger ...

It was a good shot, even with the help of Radar to do the range-finding, but it was not good enough for their crucial circumstances; the spot of grey-white water which leapt skywards was thirty yards ahead of the U-boat – the best alarm-signal she could ever have had. The man in the conning-tower turned as if he could hardly credit his senses, like a lover who has been given positive guarantees that the husband is overseas and now hears his voice in the hall; then he ducked down, as if plucked from below, and the conning-tower was empty. In the expectant silence, their gun roared again: Ericson swore aloud as this time the shot fell short, and the tall column of water unsighted them. When it fell back into the sea, and their vision cleared, the U-boat was already going down, at a steep angle, in a fluster of disturbed water.

Whatever the state of her look-outs, she must have had her crash-diving routine worked out to perfection. In a matter of seconds, the hull and most of the conning-tower were submerged: Morell got in a third shot before the surface of the sea was blank, but in the flurry of her dive it was difficult to spot its exact fall. It seemed to land close alongside: it might have hit her. She was moving to the right as she disappeared.

Ericson shouted: 'She's down, Lockhart!'

Almost immediately, Lockhart's tense voice answered: 'In contact ...'

The pinging echo of the Asdic contact was loud and clear, audible all over the bridge: Lockhart watched in extreme nervous excitement as the operator settled down to hold onto it: they could not lose it now, when the U-boat had been right before their eyes a few seconds ago ... *Compass Rose* was moving very fast, and he had to prompt the operator once as the U-boat seemed to be slipping out of the Asdic beam; the man was sweating with excitement, pounding with his fist on one edge of his chair. 'Moving quickly right, sir?' Lockhart called out, and nodded to himself as Ericson laid a course to cut the corner and intercept. He rang the warning-bell to the depth-charges aft: they were now very near, and the sound of the contact was getting blurred, merging with the noise of the transmission. This was the moment when luck could take a hand: if the U-boat chose her moment rightly, and made a violent alteration of her course, she might slip out of the lethal area of the coming explosion. There were a few more seconds of waiting, while they covered the last remaining yards of the attack; then Lockhart pressed the firing-bell, and a moment later the depth-charges were down.

The whole surface of the sea jumped as the pattern exploded: Ferraby, busy over the re-loading and harassed by the knowledge that there was a U-boat within a few yards of them, jumped with it, startled out of his wits by the noise so close to him. The columns of water shot high into the air: it seemed to all of them unfair – scarcely believable, in fact – that the shattered U-boat did not shoot up at the same time, so sure were they that they must have hit her ... As *Compass Rose* ran on, and the shocked sea subsided, they were left staring, voiceless with expectation, at the great patch of discoloured water that marked the explosion area: they were waiting for the U-boat to break surface and surrender.

Nothing happened: the ripples began to subside, and with them their foolish hopes: in anger and amazement they realized that the attack had been a failure. 'But God damn it!' swore Lockhart, speaking for the whole ship, 'we *must* have got her. The damned thing was *there* ...' 'Get back on that search,' said Ericson shortly. 'We haven't finished yet.' Lockhart flushed at the rebuke, which could not have been more public: he felt raw enough already, without the Captain giving the wound an extra scrape. He said: 'Search sixty degrees across the stern,' and bent to the Asdic-set again: almost immediately, they regained the contact, fifty yards from where they had dropped the pattern of depth-charges.

Compass Rose turned under full helm, and raced for her second attack. This time it was simpler: perhaps they *had* done some damage after all, because the U-boat did not seem to be moving or making any attempt at evasion. 'Target stationary, sir!' reported Lockhart as they completed their turn, and he repeated the words, at intervals, right down to the very end of their run-in. Once more the depth-charges went down, once more the enormous crack of the explosion shook the whole ship, once more they waited for success or failure to crown their efforts.

Someone on the bridge said: 'Any minute now ...'

The U-boat rose in their wake like a huge unwieldy fish, black and gleaming in the sunlight.

A great roar went up from the men on the upper deck, a howl of triumph. The U-boat came up bows first at an extraordinary angle, blown right out of her proper trim by the force of the explosion: clearly she was, for the moment, beyond control. The water sluiced and poured from her casings as she rose: great bubbles burst round her conning-tower: gouts of oil spread outwards from the crushed plating amidships. 'Open fire!' shouted Ericson – and for a few moments it was Baker's chance, and his alone: the two-pounder pom-pom, set just behind the funnel, was the only gun that could be brought to bear. The staccato force of its firing shook the still air, and with a noise and a chain of shock like the punch! punch! punch! of a trip-hammer the red glowing tracer-shells began to chase each other low across the water towards the U-boat. She had now fallen back on a level keel, and for the moment she rode at her proper trim: it was odd, and infinitely disgusting, suddenly to see this wicked object, the loathsome cause of a hundred nights of fear and disaster, so close to them, so innocently exposed. It was like seeing some criminal, who had outraged honour and society, and had long been shunned, taking his ease at one's own fireside.

The two-pounder was beginning to score hits: bright flashes came from the U-boat's bows, and small yellow mushrooms of cordite-smoke followed them: the shells were light, but the repeated blows were ripping through her pressure-hull and finding her vitals. As *Compass Rose* came round again, listing sharply under her full helm, the machine-guns on her bridge and her signal-deck joined in, with an immense clatter. The U-boat settled a little lower, and men began to clamber and pour out of her conning-tower. Most of them ran forward, stumbling over the uneven deck, their hands above their heads, waving and shouting at *Compass Rose*; but one man, more angry or more valiant than the rest, opened fire with a small gun from the shelter of the conning-tower, and a spatter of machine-gun bullets hit *Compass Rose* amidships. Then the counter-firing ceased suddenly, as the brave man with the gun slumped forward over the edge of the conning-tower: the rest of the crew started jumping overboard – or falling, for *Compass Rose's* guns were still blazing away and still scoring hits on men and steel. Blood overran the U-boat's wet deck, and sluiced down through the scuppers, darkly and agreeably red against the hated grey hull: she began to slide down, stern first, in a great upheaval of oil and air-bubbles and the smoke and smell of cordite. A man climbed halfway out of the conning-tower, throwing a weighted sack into the water as he did so: for a moment he wrestled to get his body clear, but the dead gunner must have jammed the escape-hatch, for the U-boat disappeared before he could free himself. A final explosion from below drove a cascade of oily water upwards: then there was silence. 'Cease fire,' said Ericson, when the sea began to close in again and the surface flattened under a spreading film of oil. 'Wheel amidships. Stop engines. And stand by with those scrambling nets.'

The wonderful moment was over.

For one man aboard *Compass Rose* it had been over for some little time. A young seaman, one of the victorious pom-pom's crew, had been killed outright by the lone machine-gunner on the U-boat; the small group of men bending over his body, in compassion and concern, was out of sight behind the gun-mounting, but they made a private world of grief none the less authentic for being completely at variance with the rest of the ship. They were, however, truly private: no one else could see them: and no one else had eyes for anything but the remnants of the U-boat's crew as they swam towards the safety of *Compass Rose*. Many of these, in an extremity of fear or exhaustion, were gasping and crying for help: still exalted by their triumph, the men aboard *Compass Rose* began to cheer them ironically, unable to take seriously the plight of people whom they knew instinctively had been, a few minutes before, staunch apostles of total warfare ... 'These are my favourite kind of survivors,' said Morell suddenly, to no one in particular: 'they invented the whole idea themselves. I want to see how they perform.'

They performed as did all the other survivors whom *Compass Rose* had picked out of the water: some cried for help, some swam in sensible silence towards their rescuers, some sank before they could be reached. There was one exception, a notable individualist who might well have sabotaged the whole affair. This was a man who, swimming strongly towards the scrambling-net which hung down over the ship's side, suddenly looked up at his rescuers, raised his right arm, and roared out: 'Heil Hitler!' There was a swift and immediate growl of rage from aboard *Compass Rose*, and a sudden disinclination to put any heart into the heaving and hauling which was necessary to bring the survivors on board. 'Cocky lot of bastards,' said Wainwright, the torpedo-man, sullenly: 'we ought to leave them in to soak ...'

Lockhart, who was standing on the iron deck overseeing the rescue-work, felt a sudden spurt of rage as he watched the incident. He felt like agreeing with Wainwright, out loud: he felt that the Captain would be justified in ringing 'Full ahead' and leaving these men to splash around until they sank. But that was only a single impulse of emotion. 'Hurry up!' he called out, affecting not to notice the mood of the men round him. 'We haven't got all day ...' One by one the swimmers were hauled out of the water: the man who had shouted was the last to be lifted out, and he had his bare foot so severely trodden on by Leading-Seaman Tonbridge, not a light-treading character, that he now gave a shout of a very different sort.

'Less noise there!' said Lockhart curtly, his face expressionless. 'You're out of danger now ... Fall them in,' he added to Tonbridge, and the prisoners were marshalled into an untidy line. There were fourteen of them, with one dead man lying at their feet: the crew of *Compass Rose* stood around in a rough semi-circle, staring at their captives. They seemed an insignificant and unexciting lot: water dripped from their hands and feet onto the deck, and above their nondescript and sodden clothes their faces were at once woe-begone and relieved, like very bad comedians who have at least got through their act without violence from the audience. No heroes, these: deprived of their ship, they were indeed hardly men at all. The crew of *Compass Rose* felt disappointed, almost tricked, by the quality of those whom they had first defeated and then salvaged from defeat. Was this, they thought, really all that was meant by a U-boat's crew?

But there was still something about them, something which attacked the senses and spread discomfort and unease, like an infected limb in a sound body ... They were strangers, and their presence on board was disgusting, like the appearance of the U-boat on the surface of the sea. They were people from another and infinitely abhorrent world – not just Germans, but U-boat Germans, doubly revolting. As quickly as possible, they were searched, and listed, and hidden below.

.   .   .

Ericson had ordered the German captain, who was among the prisoners, to be put in his own cabin, with a sentry on the door as a formal precaution; and later that morning, when they were within sight of the convoy and steaming up to report to *Viperous*, he went below to meet his opposite number. That was how he phrased it, in his mood of triumph and satisfaction: *Compass Rose* had really done very well, she had brought off something which had cost two years of hard effort, and he was ready to meet anyone halfway, in the interests of good humour. But after the testing excitement of the morning, his mood was a matter of careful balance: he was not prepared for the sort of man he found in his cabin, and he experienced, during the interview, the swiftest change of feeling he had ever known.

The German captain was standing in the middle of the cabin, peering somewhat forlornly out of the porthole: he turned as Ericson came in, and seemed to collect himself into some accustomed pattern, the only one that the world deserved to see ... He was tall, dead-blond, and young – nearly young enough to be Ericson's son; but thank God he was not, thought Ericson suddenly, noting the pale and slightly mad eyes, the contempt that twitched his lips and nostrils, the sneer against life and the hatred of his capture by an inferior. He was young, but his face was old with some derivative disease of power. There's nothing we can do with these people, thought Ericson with sombre insight: they are not curable. We can only shoot them, and hope for a better crop next time.

'Heil Hitler!' began the German crisply. 'I wish to ——'

'No,' said Ericson grimly, 'I don't think we'll start like that. What's your name?'

The German glared. 'Von Hellmuth. Kapitän-Leutnant von Hellmuth. You are also the Captain? What is yours?'

'Ericson.'

'Ah, a good German name!' exclaimed von Hellmuth, raising his yellow eyebrows, as to some evidence of gentility in a tramp.

'Certainly not!' snapped Ericson. 'And stop throwing your weight about. You're a prisoner. You're confined here. Just behave yourself.'

The German frowned at this breach of decorum: there was bitter hostility in his whole expression, even in the set of his shoulders. 'You took my ship by surprise, Captain,' he said sourly. 'Otherwise ...'

His tone hinted at treachery, unfair tactics, a course of conduct outrageous to German honour: suitable only for Englishmen, Poles, Negroes. And what the hell have you been doing all these months, Ericson thought, except taking people by surprise, stalking them, giving them no chance. But that idea would not have registered. Instead he smiled ironically, and said:

'It is war. I am sorry if it is too hard for you.'

Von Hellmuth gave him a furious glance, but he did not answer the remark: he saw, too late, that by complaining of his method of defeat he had confessed to weakness. His glance went round the cabin, and changed to a sneer.

'This is a poor cabin,' he said. 'I am not accustomed ———'

Ericson stepped up to him, suddenly shaking with anger. In the back of his mind he thought: If I had a revolver I'd shoot you here and now. That was what these bloody people did to you: that was how the evil disease multiplied and bred in the heart ... When he spoke his voice was clipped and violent.

'Be quiet!' he snapped out. 'If you say another word, I shall have you put down in one of the provision-lockers ...' He turned suddenly towards the door. 'Sentry!'

The leading-seaman on duty, a revolver in his belt, appeared in the doorway. 'Sir?'

'This prisoner is dangerous,' said Ericson tautly. 'If he makes any sort of move to leave the cabin, shoot him.'

The man's face was expressionless: only his eyes, moving suddenly from the Captain to von Hellmuth, gave a startled flicker of interest. 'Aye, aye, sir!' He disappeared again.

Von Hellmuth's expression hovered between contempt and anxiety. 'I am an officer of the German Navy——' he began.

'You're a bastard in any language,' Ericson interrupted curtly. He felt another violent surge of anger. I could do it, he thought, in amazement at his wild feeling: I could do it now, as easily as snapping my fingers ... 'I'm not particularly interested in getting you back to England,' he said, slowly and carefully. 'We could bury you this afternoon, if I felt like it ... Just watch it, that's all – just watch it!'

He turned and strode from the cabin. Outside, he wondered why he was not ashamed of himself.

CHAPTER 11

The two bodies lay side by side on the quarter-deck, neatly tucked in under the two ensigns. Ericson, clearing his throat to start reading the burial service, found his eye held almost hypnotically by the twin splashes of colour. There are two sailors under there, he thought: they lie there indistinguishable, except that ours was killed outright and theirs died of wounds and exhaustion: and there's not much to choose between the two flags either, in the use they are now put to – though perhaps the boldly-marked swastika made a smarter shroud than the White Ensign . . . He cleared his throat again, irritated and surprised at his thoughts.

'*Man that is born of woman hath but a short time to live,*' he began, hardly looking at the book: he knew the service by heart. But the gentle words affected him: as he read, he thought of the dead, and of the young seaman who was *Compass Rose*'s first casualty. He found that sad: and the German captain, standing free of escort a yard from him, found his own role sad also. His proud face was working, he was emotionally shocked out of the arrogant mould: he admitted bereavement . . . It was probably the swastika, Ericson reflected: the dead sailor from his crew would not bother him, but the 'gesture of honour' implied by the burial party and the enemy ensign would knock him out.

At Lockhart's signal to the bridge, the engine stopped; *Compass Rose* fell silent, save for the water sucking and gurgling under her counter. '*We do now commit their bodies to the deep,*' said Ericson, and paused. The pipes shrilled, the planks tipped, the neat canvas parcels slid from under the ensigns and went over the side, disappearing without trace. Close by him, he heard and felt the German captain tremble. Yes, thought Ericson, it *is* sad, after all.

He put on his cap, and saluted. The German captain, watching him, did the same. When they faced each other, Ericson saw tears glittering in the pale eyes. He nodded, and looked away.

'Thank you, Captain,' said the German. 'I appreciate all you have done.' He held out his hand awkwardly, 'I would like——'

Ericson shook his hand without saying anything. He was shy of his emotion, and of the thirty-odd members of *Compass Rose*'s crew who must be watching them.

The German captain said suddenly: 'Comrades of the sea . . .' Did he mean the two men they had just buried, Ericson wondered, or themselves, the two captains who were sharing the same experience? Perhaps it did not matter . . . He nodded again, and began to walk forward, leaving Lockhart to see to the prisoner.

But as he walked, he lost the mood of emotion and sorrow: it suddenly became false. This was no special occasion: there had been so many burials from *Compass Rose*: eighteen in one day was the record so far – eighteen before breakfast. Two was nothing; two was hardly worth turning out for . . . Those bloody Germans! he thought as he began to climb up to the bridge: first they made you lose your temper, then they made you cry. It was unsettling, it was spurious; there was something totally wrong in having them on board. One lost strength and virtue through the mere association. Prisoners are a mistake, he thought crudely: we should have used them for target practice in the water, we should have steamed away and left them whining. They would spoil *any* ship, destroy any settled habit of mind . . .

Subconsciously he knew that even this atrocious thought – the shooting of survivors in the water – had its origin in the presence of the prisoners on board, in the way in which von Hellmuth had twice thrown him off balance.

He sat down in his chair on the bridge, and began a conscious effort to get back to normal. He realized that he was very tired.

CHAPTER 12

The tiredness and the revulsion of feeling meant that he hardly talked at all about the sinking of the U-boat: after the first excitement, he became taciturn, and Lockhart, who suggested a drink in the wardroom to celebrate, found himself virtually snubbed when Ericson said: 'I don't think we ought to start drinking at sea.' But Ericson was hugging close to him his pride and pleasure in their triumph: indeed, it was the first time he had ever understood this phrase 'hugging close', and he found that it brought almost physical warmth. He did not share in the immense and uproarious excitement which pervaded the whole ship and which could initiate a ragged burst of cheering from the messdecks at any hour of the day; but in the back of his mind, as in the minds of every man on board, was a clear sense of achievement – achievement crowning 1941, crowning two whole years of trial and effort, and making up for every hated minute of them. They had worked very hard for that U-boat, they had endured every extreme of fatigue, boredom, eye-strain, cold, and crude discomfort: now, at a stroke, the slate seemed to be wiped clean, the account squared. But for Ericson, it was a private account: he did not want to share his new solvency with anyone.

Only once did he emerge from his emotional retreat. Later in the voyage, when they were near home, chance took them close alongside *Viperous*, and the flood of congratulations that came over the loud-hailer seemed to release some spring within him, unloosing a boyish sense of well-being and cheerfulness. He picked up the microphone.

'Would you like to see some Germans?' he asked *Viperous*, across the twenty yards of water that separated them. 'They're just about due for an airing ... Dig them out, Number One,' he added aside to Lockhart. 'Fall them in on the fo'c'sle.'

Presently the first of the file of prisoners began to mount the ladder.

'They're a scruffy-looking lot,' Ericson called out apologetically, as the men shambled into view, peering about them like mice leaving the shelter of the wainscot. 'I think we ought to win the war, don't you?'

PART FOUR

CHAPTER 1

1942: FIGHTING

The old year, triumphant only at its close, had achieved a level of violence and disaster which set the tone for the new. Just before Christmas, two Allied countries had sustained naval losses of shocking dimensions: Britain had lost two great ships – *Prince of Wales* and *Repulse* – in a single bombing attack, and America, at Pearl Harbor, had suffered a crippling blow which robbed her of half her effective fleet at one stroke. ('Proper uproar, it must have been,' Lockhart overheard someone in the messdecks say, and another anonymous voice answered: 'Biggest surprise since Ma caught 'er tits in the mangle ...') The attack brought America into the war, an ally coming to the rescue at a most crucial moment: but her principal war was never the Atlantic – that lifeline remained, from beginning to end, the ward of the British and the Canadian navies. America turned her eyes to the Pacific, where she had much to do to stem the furious tide of the Japanese advance: in the Atlantic, the battle of escort against U-boats still saw the same contestants in the ring, now coming up for the fourth round, the bloodiest so far.

For now the battle was in spate, now the wild and vicious blows of both sides were storming towards a climax. The U-boats had a clear ascendancy, and they used it with the utmost skill and complete ruthlessness. Germany started the year with a total of 260 of them: she added to it at the rate of 20 a month – a swelling fleet which made it possible for her to keep 100 U-boats at sea in the Atlantic at the same time. Spread in a long line across the convoy-routes, they intercepted and reported convoys as a matter of the simplest routine: this interception was combined with a perfected system of pack-attack, by which 20 or more U-boats were 'homed' onto a convoy and fell upon it, as one team, with a series of repeated blows, until its remnants reached safety. In the face of this crushing opposition, the Allied efforts seemed puny, and their counter-measures like the futile gestures of one slow wrestler caged in a ring with a dozen tormenting opponents.

In the single month of March, 94 ships were sunk: in May, 125: in June, 144 – nearly five a day: the appalling rate of loss continued around the 100 mark, every month for the rest of the year. It was the nadir of the war at sea: it was, in fact, a tempo of destruction which would mean defeat for the Allies within a measurable period of time, if it were allowed to continue. The escorts did their best, aided by new offensive weapons and by the inclusion of small aircraft-carriers – converted merchantmen – accompanying the convoys: in addition, they initiated a scheme of 'support groups', self-contained striking forces of six or eight escorts which were kept continuously at sea, ready to go to the help of hard-pressed convoys. These combined efforts showed results which were the best of the war so far: in the first seven months of the year, 42 U-boats were sunk, and in the best month of all, November, 16 of them were destroyed: this was double the rate of destruction of the previous year, but then the U-boats were doubling their successes as well ... On balance, the honours – if that was the right word for so inhuman and treacherous a struggle – were going overwhelmingly to the enemy; unless that tide could be stemmed, and turned backwards, the battle of the Atlantic was going to decide the whole war; and the Allied cause, squeezed and throttled by starvation and the denial of war materials, would collapse in ruins.

'It is,' said Mr Churchill at one point, 'a war of groping and drowning, of ambuscade and stratagem, of science and seamanship.'

It was all that. And sometimes the thing was in terms still cruder: sometimes the blood was thicker than the water.

CHAPTER 2

For *Compass Rose*, there were special times which stuck in the memory, like insects of some unusually disgusting shape or colour, transfixed for ever in a dirty web which no cleansing element could reach.

There was the time of the Dead Helmsman (all these occasions had distinctive labels, given them either when they happened, or on later recollection. It simplified the pleasure of reminiscence). This particular incident had a touch of operatic fantasy about it which prompted Morell to say, at the end: 'I think we must have strayed into the Flying Dutchman country': it was a cold-blooded dismissal, but that was the way that all their thoughts and feelings were moving now.

The ship's life-boat was first seen by Baker, during the forenoon watch: it was sailing boldly through the convoy, giving way to no man, and pursued by a formidable chorus of sirens as, one after another, the ships had to alter course to avoid collision. The Captain, summoned to the bridge, stared at it through his glasses: he could see that it must have been adrift for many days – the hull was blistered, and the sail, tattered and discoloured, had been strained out of shape and spilled half the wind. But in the stern the single figure of the helmsman, hunched over the tiller, held his course confidently: according to the strict rule of the road he had, as a sailing ship, the right of way, though it took a brave man to put the matter to the test without, at least, paying some attention to the result.

It seemed that he was steering for *Compass Rose*, which was a sensible thing to do, even if it did give several ships' captains heart failure in the process: the escorts were better equipped for dealing with survivors, and he probably realized it. Ericson stopped his ship, and waited for the small boat to approach: it held its course steadily, and then, at the last moment, veered with a gust of wind and passed close under *Compass Rose*'s stern. A seaman standing on the depth-charge rails threw a heaving-line, and they all shouted: the man, so far from making any effort to reach them, did not even look up, and the boat sailed past and began to draw away.

'He must be deaf,' said Baker, in a puzzled voice. 'But he can't be blind as well ...'

'He's the deafest man you'll ever meet,' said Ericson, suddenly grim. He put *Compass Rose* to 'slow ahead' again, and brought her round on the same course as the boat was taking. Slowly they overhauled it, stealing the wind so that presently it came to a stop: someone in the waist of the ship threw a grappling-hook across, and the boat was drawn alongside.

The man still sat there patiently, seeming unaware of them.

The boat rocked gently as Leading-Seaman Phillips jumped down into it. He smiled at the helmsman: 'Now then, chum!' he called out encouragingly – and then, puzzled by some curious air of vacancy in the face opposite, he bent closer, and put out his hand. When he straightened up again, he was grey with shock and disgust.

He looked up at Lockhart, waiting above him in the waist of the ship. 'Sir,' he began. Then he flung himself across and vomited over the side of the boat.

It was as Ericson had guessed. The man must have been dead for many days: the bare feet splayed on the floor-boards were paper-thin, the hand gripping the tiller was not much more than a claw. The eyes that had seemed to stare so boldly ahead were empty sockets – some sea-bird's plunder: the face was burnt black by a hundred suns, pinched and shrivelled by a hundred bitter nights.

The boat had no compass, and no chart; the water-barrel was empty, and yawning at the seams. It was impossible to guess how long he had been sailing on that senseless voyage – alone, hopeful in death as in life, but steering directly away from the land, which was already a thousand miles astern.

. . .

There was the time of the Bombed Ship, which was the finest exercise in patience they ever had.

It started, in mid-ocean, with a corrupt wireless message, of which the only readable parts were the prefix 'S.O.S.' and a position, in latitude and longitude, about four hundred miles to the north of their convoy. The rest was a jumble of code-groups which, even when 'reconstructed', did not yield much beyond the words 'bomb', 'fire', and 'abandon'. It must have been difficult for *Viperous* to decide whether it was worth detaching an escort for this forlorn effort of detection: there was no reason to suppose that the position given was accurate, and they could ill spare a ship for a long search; and this quite apart from the fact that the message might be false – the result of a light-hearted wireless operator amusing himself or an attempted decoy by a U-boat, both of which had happened before. But evidently *Viperous* decided that it was worth a chance: her next signal was addressed to *Compass Rose*, and read: 'SEARCH IN ACCORDANCE WITH S.O.S. TIMED 1300 TODAY.' A little later she reopened R/T communication to add: 'GOODBYE'.

The first part of the assignment was easy: it boiled down to turning ninety degrees to port, increasing to fifteen knots, and holding that course and speed for twenty-six hours on end. It was the sort of run they all enjoyed, like a dog let off a leash normally in the grasp of the slowest old lady in the world: now there was no restraint on them, no convoy to worry about, no Senior Officer to wake from his siesta and ask them what on earth they were doing. *Compass Rose* raced on, with a rising wind and sea on her quarter sometimes making her sheer widely, till the quartermaster could haul her back on her course again: she was alone, like a ship in a picture, crossing cold grey waves towards an untenanted horizon.

She ran all through the night, and all next morning: not a stick, not a sail, not a smudge of smoke did she see: it was a continuous reminder of how vast this ocean was, how formidable a hiding-place. There were hundreds of ships at sea in the Atlantic all the time, and yet *Compass Rose* seemed to have it to herself, with nothing to show that she was not, suddenly, the last ship left afloat in the world.

But when they had run the distance and reached the likely search-area, the phrase 'hiding-place' returned again, this time to mock them. It was mid-afternoon of a brisk lowering February day, with darkness due to fall within three hours: they were looking for a ship which might have been bombed, might have been sunk, might have been playing the fool, might be a different longitude altogether, and halfway round the world from this one. On a sheet of squared tracing-paper Ericson plotted out a 'box-search' – a course for *Compass Rose* consisting of a series of squares, gradually extending down wind in the direction the ship should have drifted. Its sides were each seven miles long: every two hours, the area shifted another seven miles to the north-eastward. Then he laid it off on the chart, so as to keep a check on their final position, and they settled down to quarter the ocean according to this pattern.

It was very cold. Darkness came down, and with it the first drift of snow: as hour succeeded hour, with nothing sighted and no hint of a contact on the Radar-screen, they began to lose the immediate sense of quest and to be preoccupied only with the weather. The wind was keen, the snow was penetratingly cold, the water racing past was wild and noisy: these were the realities, and the early feeling of urgency in their search was progressively blunted, progressively forgotten. Hours before, it seemed, there *had* been something about a carefully worked-out meticulous investigation of this area; but that was a very long time ago, and the bombed ship (if she existed) and her crew (if they still lived) were probably somewhere quite different, and in the meantime it was excruciatingly cold and unpleasant ... At midnight the snow was a whirling blizzard: at 4 a.m., when Lockhart came on watch, it was to a bitter, pitch-black darkness that stung his face to the marrow when he had scarcely mounted the bridge.

'Any sign of them?' he shouted to Morell.

'Nothing ... If they're adrift in this, God help them.'

It was 'nothing' all that watch, and 'nothing' when daylight came, and 'nothing' all the morning: at midday the wind fell light and the snow diminished to an occasional drift, wafting gently past them as if hoping to be included in a Christmas card. Individually, without sharing their doubts, they began to wonder if the thing had not gone on long enough: the search had taken two days already, and during the last twenty-four hours they had 'swept' nearly six hundred square miles of water. The contract could not call for very much more ... 'I've just remembered it's St Valentine's Day,' said Ferraby suddenly to Baker, during the idle hours of the afternoon watch. 'Put it down in the log,' growled Ericson, overhearing. 'There won't be any other entries ...' It was unusual for him to admit openly to any sort of doubt or hesitation: they felt free now to question the situation themselves, even to give up and turn back and forget about it.

The solid echo which was presently reported on the Radar hardly broke through to their attention at first.

But it was the ship all right, the ship they had been sent to find. They came upon her suddenly: she was masked until the last moment by the gently whirling snow, and then suddenly she emerged and lay before them – a small untidy freighter with Swedish funnel-markings. She was derelict, drifting down wind like some wretched tramp sagging his way through a crowd: she listed heavily, her bridge and fore-part were blistered and fire-blackened, and her fore-bridge itself, which seemed to have taken a direct hit from a bomb or a shell, looked like a twisted metal cage from which something violent and strong had ripped a way to freedom. One lifeboat was missing, the other hung down from the falls, half-overturned and empty. There was nothing else in the picture.

Compass Rose circled slowly, alert for any development, but there was no sound, no movement save the snow falling lightly on the deserted upper deck. They sounded their siren, they fired a blank shot: nothing stirred. Presently, they stopped, and lowered a boat: Morell was in charge, and with him were Rose, the young signalman, Leading-Seaman Tonbridge, and a stoker named Evans. As they pulled away from *Compass Rose*, Ericson leant over the side of the bridge, megaphone in hand.

'We'll have to keep moving,' he called out. 'This ship is too much of an attraction ... Don't worry if you lose sight of us.'

Morell waved, but did not answer. He was no longer thinking about *Compass Rose*: he was thinking, with a prickling of his scalp, of what he was going to find when he boarded the derelict.

I am no good at this, he thought, as they pulled across the short stretch of water that separated the two ships: no good at bombs, no good at blood, no good at the brutal elements of disaster ... When Leading-Seaman Tonbridge jumped onto the sloping deck with the painter, and made the boat fast, it was all Morell could do to follow him over the side: '*You* go,' his subconscious voice was saying to Tonbridge: 'I'll wait here, while you take a look.' It was not that he was afraid, within the normal meaning of the word: simply that he doubted his ability to deal with the disgusting unknown.

In silence he climbed up and stood on the deck: a tall grave young man in a yellow duffle-coat and sea-boots, looking through falling snow towards the outline of the shattered bridge. He said to Stoker Evans: 'Have a look below – see how deep she's flooded,' and to Tonbridge: 'Stay by the boat,' and to Signalman Rose: 'Come with me.' Then they began to walk forward: their feet rang loudly on the iron deck, their tracks in the snow were fresh, like children's in a garden before breakfast: round them was complete silence, complete empty stillness, such as no ship that was not fundamentally cursed would ever show.

It was not as bad as Morell had expected – in the sense that he did not faint, or vomit, or disgrace himself: the actual details were horrifying. The bridge had taken the full force of a direct hit by a bomb: there had been a small fire started, and a larger one farther forward, between the well-deck and the fo'c'sle. It was difficult to determine exactly how many people had been on the bridge when it was hit: none of the bodies was complete, and the scattered fragments seemed at a first glance to add up to a whole vanished regiment of men. There must have been about six of them: now they were in dissolution, and their remnants hung like some appalling tapestry round the bulk-heads, gleaming here and there with the dull gleam of half-dried paint. The whole gory enclosure seemed to have been decorated with blood and tissue: ' "When father papered the parlour", ' hummed Morrel to himself, 'he never thought of this . . .' The helmsman's hand was still clutching the wheel – but it was only a hand, it grew out of the air: tatters of uniforms, of entrails, tufts of hair, met the eye at every turn: on one flat surface the imprint of a skull in profile, impregnated into the paintwork, stood out like a revolting street-corner caricature, stencilled in human skin and fragments of bone. 'You died with your mouth open,' said Morell, looking at this last with eyes which seemed to have lost their capacity to communicate sensation to the brain. 'I hope you were saying something polite.'

He walked to the open side of the bridge, high above the water, and looked out. The snow still fell gently and lazily, dusting the surface of the sea for a moment before it melted. There was nothing round them except anonymous greyness: the afternoon light was failing: *Compass Rose* came into view momentarily, and then vanished. He turned back to Rose who stood waiting with his signal lamp, and they stared at each other across the space of the bridge: each of their faces had the same serious concentration, the same wish to accept this charnel-house and be unmoved by it. It was part of their war, the sort of thing they were trained for, the sort of thing they now took in their stride – sometimes without effort, sometimes with . . . I suppose Rose has looked at all this, and looked away again, thought Morell: I suppose he is waiting for me to say something, or to take him down the ladder and away from the bridge. That would be my own choice too . . . He cleared his throat.

'We'll see what Evans has to say, and then send a signal.'

The ship could not be got going again, but she was fit to be towed: though the engine-room and one hold were deeply flooded, the water was no longer coming in and she might remain afloat indefinitely. That was the outline of the signal which Rose presently sent across to *Compass Rose*: reading it, Ericson had to make up his mind whether to start the towing straight away, or to cast around for the missing boat and its survivors. After two nights adrift in this bitter weather, there was little chance of their being alive; but if the bombed ship would remain afloat, it would not matter spending another day or so on the search. Perhaps Morell had better stay where he was, though: he could keep an eye on things, and there must be a lot of tidying up to do.

'Remain on board,' he signalled to Morell finally. 'I am going to search for the life-boat, and return tomorrow morning.' Something made him add: 'Are you quite happy about being left?'

Happy, thought Morell: now *there* was a word . . . It was now nearly nightfall: they were to be left alone in this floating coffin for over twelve hours of darkness, with the snow to stare at, the sea to listen to, and a bridge-full of corpses for company. ' "Happiness is relative",' he began dictating to Rose, and then he changed his mind. The moment did not really deserve humour. 'Reply: "Quite all right",' he said shortly. Then he called to Tonbridge and Evans, and took them back with him to the bridge. That was where a start must be made.

Morell was never to forget that night. They used the remains of daylight for cleaning up: the increasing gloom was a blessing, making just tolerable this disgusting operation. They worked in silence, hard-breathing, not looking closely at what they were doing: the things they had to dispose of disappeared steadily over the side, and were hidden by the merciful sea. Only once was the silence broken, by Leading-Seaman Tonbridge. 'Pity we haven't got a hose, sir,' he said, straightening up from a corner of the bridge which had kept him busy for some minutes. Morell did not answer him: no one did. The place where they stood, though blurred now by shadow, was eloquent enough.

They made a meal off the emergency rations in the boat, and boiled some tea on the spirit-stove they found in the galley; then they settled down for the night, in the cramped chart-room behind the bridge. There were mattresses and blankets, and a lamp to give them some warmth: it was good enough for one night on board, if they did not start thinking.

Morell started thinking: his thoughts destroyed the hope of sleep, and drove him outside onto the upper deck – there was no comfort in the sleeping men close to him, only anger at the relief they had found: he felt that if he stayed he would have to invent some pretext for waking them up. He made his footfalls soft as he went down the ladder, he made his breathing imperceptible as he crossed the well-deck: the hand that pushed aside the canvas curtain screening the fo'c'sle was the hand of a conspirator. He took a step forward, and felt in front of him a hollow emptiness: he struck a match, and found that he was in a large mess-hall, full of shadows, full of its own deserted silence. The match flared: he saw a long table, with plates set out on it – plates with half-eaten helpings of stew, crumbled squares of bread, knives and forks set down hurriedly at the moment of crisis. None of those meals would ever be finished now: all the men who had set down the knives and forks were almost certainly dead. I am thinking in clichés, he thought, as the match spluttered and went out. But clichés were as effective as thoughts freshly minted, when the reality which they clothed pressed in so closely and was backed by such weight of crude fact.

Pursued by ghosts, he walked aft along the snow-covered upper deck. The wind whined on a strange note in the rigging: the water gurgled close under his feet: the ship was restless, needing to fight the sea all the time. There was no comfort to be found under the open sky: the deck held too many shadows, the unfamiliar shape of it had too many surprises. And suppose there were *other* surprises: suppose the ship were not deserted, suppose a mad seaman with an axe rushed him from the next blind corner: suppose he found fresh footprints in the snow, where none of them had trodden.

At the base of the mast a shadow moved. Morell gripped the pockets of his duffle-coat, his nerves screaming. The shadow moved again, sliding away from him.

He roared out: 'Stop!'

The cat mewed, and fled.

Morning came, and with it *Compass Rose*. She had nothing to report – no boats, no survivors – and Morell, in a sense, had nothing to report either. A heaving-line was passed from *Compass Rose*, and then a light grass rope, and then the heavy towing-hawser: there was no windlass to haul this on board the bombed ship, and Morell's party had to man-handle it in foot by foot, straining against a dead weight of wire which at times seemed as if it would never reach them. But finally they made it fast, and gave the signal, and the tow started.

They made less than three knots, even in good weather: it took them ten days of crawling to finish the journey. Each morning, as soon as it was light, Morell waved a greeting to Lockhart: each evening, as 'Darken Ship' was piped, Lockhart waved goodbye to Morell. Day after day, night after night, the two ships crept over the water, both useless save for this single purpose, both doomed by the umbilical tie to be any U-boat's sitting shot. When, at the mouth of the Mersey, they parted at last and Morell came aboard, it was like waking from a nightmare which one had despaired of surviving.

'Sorry to leave?' asked Lockhart ironically, as Morell came up to the bridge.

'No,' answered Morell, fingering his ten-days' growth of beard, 'no, I'm not.' He looked at the ship astern of them, now in the charge of two harbour tugs. 'I may say that the idea of the convict missing his chains is purely a novelist's conception of life.'

.   .   .

There was the time which was rather difficult to label: they mostly knew it as the time of the Captain's Meeting.

This time was on a Gibraltar convoy, a convoy in the same bad tradition as most of the Gibraltar runs: there had been a steady wastage of ships all the way southwards, and although they were now within two days of the end of the trip the U-boat pack was still with them. Ericson seemed to be showing particular interest in a ship in the front line of the convoy: often he would train his glasses on her for minutes at a time, and she was the one he always looked for first as soon as daylight came up. She survived until the last day; and then, when dawn broke after a night of disaster, she was no longer in her station, and her place in the van of the convoy had been taken by the next ship astern.

At first light the customary signal came from *Viperous*:

'Following ships were sunk last night: *Fort James, Eriskay, Bulstrode Manor, Glen MacCurtain*. Amend convoy lists accordingly.'

There was something in Ericson's manner as he read this signal which discouraged comment. He remained on the bridge for a full hour, staring silently at the convoy, before saying suddenly to Wells:

'Take a signal ... "To Escorts in company, from *Compass Rose*. Please report any survivors you may have from *Glen MacCurtain*".'

The answering signals came in very slowly: they did not make cheerful reading. *Viperous* and two other escorts sent 'NIL' reports. The corvette in the rear position signalled: 'Two seamen, one Chinese fireman.' The rescue-ship detailed to look after survivors sent: 'First Officer, two seamen, one fireman, five Lascars.'

They waited, but that seemed to be all. *Glen MacCurtain* must have gone down quickly. Ferraby, who had the watch, said tentatively:

'Not many picked up, sir?'

'No,' said Ericson. 'Not many.' He looked towards the horizon astern of them, and then walked to his chair and sat down heavily.

Presently a merchant-ship in the rear of the convoy started flashing to them. Wells took the signal, muttering impatiently to himself: evidently the operating was not up to acceptable Naval standards.

'Message from that Polish packet, sir,' he said to Ericson. 'It's a bit rocky ... "We did see your signal by mistake",' he read out, his voice slightly disparaging. ' "We have one man from that ship".'

'Ask them who it was,' said Ericson. His voice was quiet, but there was such acute tension in it that everyone on the bridge stared at him.

Wells began to flash the question, signalling very slowly, with frequent pauses and repetitions. There was a long wait; then the Polish ship began to answer. Wells read it out as it came across:

' "The man is fourth officer",' he began. Then he started to spell, letter by letter: ' "E - R - I - C - S - O - N." ' Wells looked up from the signal-lamp. 'Ericson ... Same name as yours, sir.'

'Yes,' said Ericson. 'Thank you, Wells.'

.   .   .

There was a time, a personal time for Lockhart, which he knew as the time of the Burnt Man.

Ordinarily, he did not concern himself a great deal with looking after survivors: Crowther, the Sick-Berth Attendant, had proved himself sensible and competent, and unless there were more cases than one man could cope with, Lockhart left him to get on with his work alone. But now and again, as the bad year progressed, there was an overflow of injured or exhausted men who needed immediate attention; and it was on one of these occasions, when the night had yielded nearly forty survivors from two ships, that Lockhart found himself back again at his old job of ship's doctor.

The small, two-berth sick-bay was already filled: the work to be done was, as in the old days, waiting for him in the fo'c'sle. As he stepped into the crowded, badly-lit space, he no longer felt the primitive revulsion of two years ago, when all this was new and harassing; but there was nothing changed in the dismal picture, nothing was any the less crude or moving or repellent. There were the same rows of survivors – wet through, dirt-streaked, shivering: the same reek of oil and sea-water: the same relief on one face, the same remembered terror on another. There were the same people drinking tea or retching their stomachs up or telling their story to anyone who would listen. Crowther had marshalled the men needing attention in one corner, and here again the picture was the same: wounded men, exhausted men, men in pain afraid to die, men in a worse agony hoping not to live.

Crowther was bending over one of these last, a seaman whose filthy overalls had been cut away to reveal a splintered knee-cap: as soon as he looked the rest of the casualties over, Lockhart knew at once which one of them had the first priority.

He picked his way across the fo'c'sle and stood over the man, who was being gently held by two of his shipmates. It seemed incredible that he was still conscious, still able to advertise his agony: by rights he should have been dead – not moaning, not trying to pluck something from his breast ... He had sustained deep and cruel first-degree burns, from his throat to his waist: the whole raw surface had been flayed and roasted, as if he had been caught too long on a spit that had stopped turning: he now gave out, appropriately, a kitchen smell indescribably horrible. What the first touch of salt water on his body must have felt like, passed imagination.

'He got copped by a flash-back from the boiler,' said one of the men holding him. 'Burning oil. Can you fix him?'

Fix him, thought Lockhart: I wish I could fix him in his coffin right now ... He forced himself to bend down and draw close to this sickening object: above the scored and shrivelled flesh the man's face, bereft of eyelashes, eyebrows, and the front portion of his scalp, looked expressionless and foolish. But there was no lack of expression in the eyes, which were liquid with pain and surprise. If the man could have bent his head and looked at his own chest, thought Lockhart, he would give up worrying and ask for a revolver straight away ... He turned and called across to Crowther:

'What have you got for burns?'

Crowther rummaged in his first-aid satchel. 'This, sir,' he said, and passed something across. A dozen willing hands relayed it to Lockhart, as if it were the elixir of life itself. It was in fact a small tube of ointment, about the size of a toothpaste tube. On the label was the picture of a smiling child and the inscription: 'For the Relief of Burns. Use Sparingly.'

Use sparingly, thought Lockhart: if I used it as if it were platinum dust,

I'd still need about two tons of it. He held the small tube in his hand and looked down again at the survivor. One of the men holding him said: 'Here's the doctor. He'll fix you up right away,' and the fringeless eyes came slowly round and settled on Lockhart's face as if he were the ministering Christ himself.

Lockhart took a swab of cotton-wool, put some of the ointment on it, swallowed a deep revulsion, and started to stroke, very gently, the area of the burnt chest. Just before he began he said: 'It's a soothing ointment.'

I suppose it's natural that he should scream, thought Lockhart presently, shutting his ears: all the old-fashioned pictures showed a man screaming as soon as the barber-surgeon started to operate, while his friends plied the patient with rum or knocked him out with a mallet . . . The trouble was that the man was still so horrifyingly alive: he pulled and wrenched at the two men holding him, while Lockhart, stroking and swabbing with a mother's tenderness, removed layer after layer of his flesh. For the *other* trouble was that however gently he was touched, the raw tissue went on and on coming away with the cotton-wool.

Lockhart was aware that the ring of men who were watching had fallen silent: he felt rather than saw their faces contract with pity and disgust as he swabbed the ointment deeper and deeper, and the flesh still flaked off like blistered paint-work. I wonder how long this can go on, he thought, as he saw, without surprise, that at one point he had laid bare a rib which gleamed with an astonishing cleanness and astringency. I don't think this is any good, he thought again, as the man fainted at last, and the two sailors holding him turned their eyes towards Lockhart in question and disbelief. The ointment was almost finished: the raw chest now gaped at him like the foundation of some rotten building. Die! he thought, almost aloud, as he sponged once more, near the throat, and a new layer of sinew came into view, laid bare like a lecturer's diagram. Please give up, and die. I can't go on doing this, and I can't stop while you're still alive.

He heard a dozen men behind him draw in their breath sharply as a fresh area of skin suddenly crumbled under his most gentle hand and adhered to the cotton-wool. Crowther, attracted by the focus of interest and now kneeling by his side, said: 'Any good, sir?' and he shook his head. I'm doing wonders, he thought: they'll give me a job in a canning-factory . . . Some blood flowed over the rib he had laid bare, and he swabbed it off almost apologetically. Sorry, he thought: that was probably my fault – and then again: Die! Please die! I'm making a fool of myself, and certainly of you. You'll never be any use now. And we'll give you a lovely funeral, well out of sight . . .

Suddenly and momentarily, the man opened his eyes, and looked up at Lockhart with a deeper, more fundamental surprise, as if he had intercepted the thought and was now aware that a traitor and not a friend was touching him. He twisted his body, and a rippling spasm ran across the scorched flesh. 'Steady, Jock!' said one of his friends, and: Die! thought Lockhart yet again, squeezing the last smear of ointment from the tube and touching with it a shoulder muscle which immediately gave way and parted from its ligament. Die. Do us all a favour. Die! Aloud, he repeated, with the utmost foolishness: 'It's a soothing ointment.' But: Die now! his lips formed the words. Don't be obstinate. No one wants you. You wouldn't want yourself if you could take a look. Please die!

Presently, obediently, but far too late, the man died.

.   .   .

There was the time of the Skeletons.

It happened when *Compass Rose* was in a hurry, late one summer afternoon when she had been delayed for nearly half a day by a search for an aircraft which was reported down in the sea, a long way south of the convoy. She had not found the aircraft, nor any trace of it: *Viperous* had wirelessed: 'REJOIN FORTHWITH', and she was now hurrying to catch up before nightfall. The sea was glassy smooth, the sky a pale and perfect blue: the hands lounging on the upper deck were mostly stripped to the waist, enjoying the last hour of hot sunshine. It was a day for doing nothing elegantly, for going nowhere at half speed: it seemed a pity that they had to force the pace, and even more of a pity when the Radar operator got a 'suspicious contact' several miles off their course, and they had to turn aside to investigate.

'It's a very small echo,' said the operator apologetically. 'Sort of muzzy, too.'

'Better take a look,' said Ericson to Morell, who had called him to the bridge. 'You never know ...' He grinned. 'What does small and muzzy suggest to you?'

To Morell it suggested an undersized man tacking up Regent Street after a thick night, but he glossed over the thought, and said instead: 'It might be wreckage, sir. Or a submarine, just awash.'

'Or porpoises,' said Ericson, who seemed in a better humour than he usually was after being woken up. 'Or seaweed with very big sand-fleas hopping about on top ... It's a damned nuisance, anyway: I didn't want to waste time.'

In the event, it wasted very little of their time, for *Compass Rose* ran the distance swiftly, and what they found did not delay them. It was Wells – the best pair of eyes in the ship – who first sighted the specks on the surface, specks which gradually grew until, a mile or so away, they had become heads and shoulders – a cluster of men floating in the water.

'Survivors, by God!' exclaimed Ericson. 'I wonder how long they've been there.'

They were soon to know. *Compass Rose* ran on, the hands crowding to the rail to look at the men ahead of them. Momentarily Ericson recalled that other occasion when they had sped towards men in the water, only to destroy them out of hand. Not this time, he thought, as he reduced speed: now he could make amends.

He need not have bothered to slow down: he might well have ploughed through, the same as last time. He had thought it odd that the men did not wave or shout to *Compass Rose*, as they usually did: he had thought it odd that they did not swim even a little way towards the ship, to close the gap between death and life. Now he saw, through his glasses, that there was no gap to be closed: for the men, riding high out of the water, held upright by their life-jackets, were featureless, bony images – skeletons now for many a long day and night.

There was something infinitely obscene in the collèction of lolling corpses, with bleached faces and white hairless heads, clustered together like men waiting for a bus which had gone by twenty years before. There were nine of them in that close corporation; they rode the water not more than four or five yards from each other: here and there a couple had come together as if embracing. *Compass Rose* circled, starting a wash which set the dead men bobbing and bowing to each other, like performers in some infernal dance. Nine of them, thought Morell in horror: what is the correct noun of association? A school of skeletons? A corps?

Then he saw – they all saw – that the men were roped together. A frayed and slimy strand of rope linked each one of them, tied round the waist and trailing languidly in the water: when the ripples of the ship's wash drove two of them apart, the rope between them tightened with a jerk and a splash. The other men swayed and bowed, as if approving this evidence of comradeship ... But this is crazy, thought Ericson: this is the sort of thing you hope not to dream about. *Compass Rose* still circled, as he looked down at the company of dead men. They must have been there for months. There was not an ounce of flesh under the yellow skins, not a single reminder of warmth or manhood. They had perished, and they had gone on perishing, beyond the grave, beyond the moment when the last man alive found rest.

He was hesitating about picking them up, but he knew that he would not. *Compass Rose* was in a hurry. There was nothing to be gained by fishing them out, sewing them up, and putting them back again. And anyway ...

'But why roped together?' asked Morell, puzzled, as the ship completed her last circle, and drew away, and left the men behind. 'It doesn't make sense.'

Ericson had been thinking. 'It might,' he said, in a voice infinitely subdued. 'If they were in a life-boat, and the boat was being swamped, they might tie themselves together so as not to lose touch during the night. It would give them a better chance of being picked up.'

'And they weren't,' said Morell after a pause.

'And they weren't. I wonder how long ——' But he did not finish that sentence, except in his thoughts.

He was wondering how long it had taken the nine men to die: and what it was like for the others when the first man died: and what it was like when half of them had gone: and what it was like for the last man left alive, roped to his tail of eight dead shipmates, still hopeful, but surely feeling himself doomed by their company.

Perhaps, thought Ericson, he went mad in the end, and started to swim away, and towed them all after him, shouting, until he lost his strength as well as his wits, and gave up, and turned back to join the majority.

Quite a story.

. . .

There was the time that was the worst time of all, the time that seemed to synthesize the whole corpse-ridden ocean; the time of the Burning Tanker.

Aboard *Compass Rose*, as in every escort that crossed the Atlantic, there had developed an unstinting admiration of the men who sailed in oil-tankers. They lived, for an entire voyage of three or four weeks, as a man living on top of a keg of gunpowder: the stuff they carried – the life-blood of the whole war – was the most treacherous cargo of all; a single torpedo, a single small bomb, even a stray shot from a machine-gun, could transform their ship into a torch. Many times this had happened, in *Compass Rose*'s convoys: many times they had had to watch these men die, or pick up the tiny remnants of a tanker's crew – men who seemed to display not the slightest hesitation at the prospect of signing on again, for the same job, as soon as they reached harbour. It was these expendable seamen who were the real 'petrol-coupons' – the things one could wangle from the garage on the corner: and whenever sailors saw or read of petrol being wasted or stolen, they saw the cost in lives as well, peeping from behind the headline or the music-hall joke, feeding their anger and disgust.

Appropriately, it was an oil-tanker which gave the men in *Compass Rose*, as spectators, the most hideous hour of the whole war.

She was an oil-tanker they had grown rather fond of: she was the only tanker in a homeward-bound convoy of fifty ships which had run into trouble, and they had been cherishing her, as they sometimes cherished ships they recognized from former convoys, or ships with queer funnels, or ships that told lies about their capacity to keep up with the rest of the fleet. On this occasion, she had won their affection by being obviously the number one target of the attacking U-boats: on three successive nights they had sunk the ship ahead of her, the ship astern, and the corresponding ship in the next column; and as the shelter of land approached it became of supreme importance to see her through to the end of the voyage. But her luck did not hold: on their last day of the open sea, with the Scottish hills only just over the horizon, the attackers found their mark, and she was mortally struck.

She was torpedoed in broad daylight on a lovely sunny afternoon: there had been the usual scare, the usual waiting, the usual noise of an under-water explosion, and then, from this ship they had been trying to guard, a colossal pillar of smoke and flame came billowing out, and in a minute the long shapely hull was on fire almost from end to end.

The ships on either side of her, and the ships astern, fanned outwards, like men stepping past a hole in the road: *Compass Rose* cut in towards her, intent on bringing help. But no help had yet been devised that could be any use to a ship so stricken. Already the oil that had been thrown skywards by the explosion had bathed the ship in flame: and now, as more and more oil came gushing out of the hull and spread over the water all round her, she became the centrepiece of a huge conflagration. There was still one gap in the solid wall of fire, near her bows, and above this, on the fo'c'sle, her crew began to collect – small figures, running and stumbling in furious haste towards the only chance they had for their lives. They could be seen waving, shouting hesitating before they jumped; and *Compass Rose* crept in a little closer, as much as she dared, and called back to them to take the chance. It was dangerously, unbearably hot, even at this distance: and the shouting, and the men waving their arms, backed by the flaming roaring ship with her curtain of smoke and burning oil closing round her, completed an authentic picture of hell.

There were about twenty men on the fo'c'sle: if they were going to jump, they would have to jump soon ... And then, in ones and twos, hesitating, changing their minds, they did begin to jump: successive splashes showed suddenly white against the dark grey of the hull, and soon all twenty of them were down, and on their way across. From the bridge of *Compass Rose*, and from the men thronging her rail, came encouraging shouts as the gap of water between them narrowed.

Then they noticed that the oil, spreading over the surface of the water and catching fire as it spread, was moving faster than any of the men could swim. They noticed it before the swimmers, but soon the swimmers noticed it too. They began to scream as they swam, and to look back over their shoulders, and thrash and claw their way through the water as if suddenly insane.

But one by one they were caught. The older ones went first, and then the men who couldn't swim fast because of their life-jackets, and then the strong swimmers, without life-jackets, last of all. But perhaps it was better not to be a strong swimmer on that day, because none of them was strong enough: one by one they were overtaken, and licked by flame, and fried, and left behind.

Compass Rose could not lessen the gap, even for the last few who nearly made it. Black and filthy clouds of smoke were now coursing across the sky overhead, darkening the sun: the men on the upper deck were pouring with sweat. With their own load of fuel-oil and their ammunition, they could go no closer, even for these frying men whose faces were inhumanly ugly with fear and who screamed at them for help; soon, indeed, they had to give ground to the stifling heat, and back away, and desert the few that were left, defeated by the mortal risk to themselves.

Waiting a little way off, they were entirely helpless: they stood on the bridge, and did nothing, and said nothing. One of the look-outs, a young seaman of not more than seventeen, was crying as he looked towards the fire: he made no sound, but the tears were streaming down his face. It was not easy to say what sort of tears they were – of rage, of pity, of the bitterness of watching the men dying so cruelly, and not being able to do a thing about it.

Compass Rose stayed till they were all gone, and the area of sea with the ship and the men inside it was burning steadily and remorselessly, and then she sailed on. Looking back, as they did quite often, they could see the pillar of smoke from nearly fifty miles away: at nightfall, there was still a glow and sometimes a flicker on the far horizon. But the men of course were not there any more: only the monstrous funeral pyre remained.

CHAPTER 3

The time for their long leave came round again.

Each leave was different from the last one, a development or a stultification of what had gone before. In war, nothing stood still, in any part of the field; in this war, the years were passing, eating up not only men and treasure but bearing swiftly onwards the normal tide of life as well. Nothing stood still: nothing waited for peacetime before moving onto the next chapter. The men grew older: the women loved them more, or less, or fell in love again; babies were born, cooking deteriorated, mortgages fell due, uncle died and left that funny will, mother came to live, the paint flaked off the bathroom ceiling. And sometimes, with distance and separation, it was difficult to do anything about the paint or the baby or the loving more or less: the men just had to hope, and trust, and be reassured or betrayed, and take whatever they found when they got back. Distances were too great, and the thread sometimes too tenuous, for them to play an effective part at home as well as at sea; and the sea had the priority, whether they liked it or not.

. . .

Able-Seaman Gregg's baby was not a success. He had been prepared to shut his mind to its suspect parentage: this might have been possible if the child had been attractive, or cheerful, or just plain healthy, but as it was none of these things he could not help seeing, behind the sickly and squalling infant, the image of a large man called Walter Something who had got away with murder. He had been looking forward to this spell of leave, and the chance of being with Edith and getting to know the child; but now he knew the child too well – a pale, under-developed, and undeniably dirty child which filled the house with its crying and the larger part of the kitchen with its soiled napkins. And Edith – he was now not sure whether he really knew anything about Edith at all.

He had been brought face to face with this doubt one evening when, returning to the house after a shopping expedition, he had passed a stranger on the way out – a middle-aged woman in W.V.S uniform who had given him, first a questioning glance, and then a grudging smile as he stood aside to let her go by. He had watched her doubtfully as she went off down the street, and then gone through to the kitchen. The scene was as usual – the hearth and the clothes-rack were strung with drying baby-clothes, the child whimpered in its cot; amid a smell compounded of food, urine, and scorched napkins, Edith sat by the fireside reading a film-magazine.

He threw his cap on the table. 'Who was that?' he asked.

Edith looked up. 'Who?'

'The woman.'

'Oh, her . . .' Edith shrugged elaborately. 'Some old nosey-parker from the Welfare.'

'What welfare?'

'The Borough Council. They send them round. Nothing better to do, I suppose.'

Gregg found himself, for once, wanting to sort the matter out. He sat down opposite her. 'But how did she come here, in the first place?'

Edith yawned, not looking at him. 'She started coming. To see the baby. Kind of welfare work.'

'But what did she say?'

'She said to look after it.'

'Feed it, you mean?'

'Yes. And stay with it all the time.'

'But you do stay with it, don't you?'

'Course I do. Don't go on so, Tom. I tell you she's just poking her nose.

All that about a summons . . . Cheeky old bitch – I bet no one ever tried to give *her* a baby.'

'A summons . . .' Gregg stood up again, frowning. 'Here, what's it all about?'

'There was a report,' said Edith sulkily, after a pause. 'The baby was crying one night.'

'Well, what about it?'

'They thought I'd left it alone in the house. But I was asleep, Tom, honest I was. I just didn't hear it, that's all. And someone reported it.'

'Why didn't you tell me?' he asked.

'What's there to worry about?' she said jauntily. 'They can't do anything to you. It's a lot of sauce.'

'But you don't want that sort of thing . . .' He wondered, as many times before, how much to believe; he could only guess and grope at what went on while he was away, he could only go by the probabilities . . . He walked over and looked down at the baby, which was sucking a wooden spoon. Its face was small and pinched: there were sores round its mouth: its legs were like small pale sticks on the soiled and tumbled bedclothes. I wish it could talk, he thought, not for the first time. He turned back to his wife.

'You don't leave it by itself, Edith, do you? Or go out nights.'

'Course not.'

'Wonder why you didn't hear it crying?'

'You know me when I'm asleep.'

.   .   .

Lockhart, also in London, did four things, and then seemed to come to a dead stop. He went to a concert: he called on an editor for whom he had written before the war, and sold him an article on corvettes – subject to Admiralty approval: he had a Turkish bath: and he ordered a new uniform, adorned with the small oakleaf emblem which signified that he had been mentioned in despatches. That was a two-day programme: when it was completed, he was aware that he was looking round for more, and that nothing was in prospect. It was not that he was bored – no Londoner could be bored in London; it was simply that, when he was on leave, his life seemed to lack human significance altogether. His living world was *Compass Rose*, and nothing else; away from her, he felt as if he were held in suspension, waiting for the time when he could leave the trivial shadow life and return to hard fact.

It was all wrong, of course: he ought to have been able to profit from his holiday. But there was something missing, ashore: something to make sense of the necessary interlude. It would have been nice, for example, to have someone to say goodbye to, at the end . . .

Later, however, when he caught his train at Euston, and watched the leave-takers on No. 13 Platform, he was not so sure. There was something in the universal goodbye atmosphere that seemed likely to spoil both the past and the future: the kisses, the tears, the hungry mouths groping for each other for the last time – all these must surely mean that the leave-period had been sad, with this parting in view all the time, and that the future was going to be lonely and unhappy on both sides, for the same reason. It was not difficult to see what this sadness did to a man, in terms of his contentment and his efficiency: it was a necessary part of war, but it impeded it at the same time. For sailors, there should be no ties with the land at all, if they were to produce their best when the need came to show it: the recurrent dream-of-home could only stand in the way, getting in a man's heart and eyes when both of these had to be purposeful and clear.

If I were in love with someone, like *that*——, thought Lockhart, watching out of the corner of his eye one of *Compass Rose*'s leading-stokers, whose dejection at saying goodbye to his wife was matched by the unselfconscious misery written in her face: if I felt like *that*, every time I came back to the ship, what sort of job would I do in the morning ...? But even as the thought struck him, he became aware of its inherent smugness; and presently, as the train drew out of Euston and headed for the north, he began to wonder if any rule of this sort could be applied in general terms. One man might need the tenderness of a love-affair or a happy married life to dilute the ordeal of war: it might, indeed, be the only thing which would keep him going and make his wartime life endurable. Another might only be devitalized or distracted by any break in the hard routine, and would be compelled to sign on for a sort of monastic dedication, if he were to be any use in war at all.

He himself – but even there he was not entirely sure. He had grown used to the company of women, before the war: he certainly appeared to have 'given them up' for the duration. Until now, it seemed to have been working out admirably. But just lately he had found himself wondering if some concession to humanity might not pay a dividend.

For instance, he thought, as he settled himself for the uncomfortable night-journey, there was a fair-haired W.A.A.F. sitting opposite to him, whose entrancing legs no dull grey stockings could spoil: whose shoulders would feel very square under his hand: and whose eyes, agreeably, ready to flicker in his direction even under these unpromising circumstances, might well have widened and softened, to a really heart-breaking extent, on a pillow.

The sensual day-dream merged gradually into a drowsy night-version, which lasted a long way north.

. . .

For Ericson, there were no day-dreams, and few night ones: he had found himself very tired by the time his leave came round, and he wanted to do nothing except sleep, and relax, and potter about the house until he had to return to the ship. It was a programme which Grace understood, and could adapt herself to; but the third member of the household, her mother, seemed unable to take it at its face value. It was clear that she interpreted his laziness, in some odd way, as a reflection on Grace, or on herself, or even on the quality of the housekeeping. The old woman had aged, becoming querulous in the process: from her permanent stronghold by the fireside (Used to be my chair, thought Ericson), she issued comment, criticism, and an undertone of discord which cut right across his need for a quiet life.

'He ought to take you out more,' was one theme which was always good for a triangular half-hour of discomfort when the three of them were together. 'Is he ashamed of you, or what?'

It always annoyed Ericson that she spoke as if he were a small boy allowed, on sufferance, to listen-in to the grown-ups.

'I don't want to go out, Mother,' Grace would say. 'It's quite comfortable here, thank you.'

'Of course you want to go out! You're still a young woman. What's the good of him winning all these medals if he never stirs outside the house?'

Ericson, on whose chest the blue-and-white ribbon of the D.S.C. stood out in solitary splendour, lowered his newspaper.

'You've got it mixed up,' he said tolerantly. 'They gave me a medal for the U-boat, not for parading up and down Lord Street with Grace.'

The old woman sniffed. 'It's not natural ... He ought to take you down to the ship, too. He's the Captain, isn't he?'

'Mother!' said Grace warningly.

'She's refitting,' put in Ericson shortly.

'They can still give you a nice dinner, I shouldn't wonder. It'd make a change for Grace.'

'I don't want a change,' said Grace.

'If I'm going to eat corned beef,' said Ericson, 'I'd rather eat it here than in a stone-cold wardroom.'

'What's the matter with corned beef, I'd like to know?' asked the old woman pregnantly. 'I'm sure Grace does her best to make things nice for you. Slaving away in the kitchen all day, with never a chance to go anywhere ... When your father was alive,' she said to Grace, 'he used to take me out twice a week.'

Poor old bastard, thought Ericson, raising his newspaper again: that's probably what killed him off so quickly ... It had, as usual, been a mistake to join in the conversation: it never got them anywhere, and the old woman could twist and turn and shift her ground like something in the zoo. But later, when he was alone with Grace, he returned to a point which had worried him momentarily, and he asked:

'*Do* you want to go out in the evenings, instead of staying at home?'

She smiled comfortably. 'I want to do what you want. And I know you're tired when you come back.'

He squeezed her arm, with a rare gesture of affection. 'I don't know what I'd do without you, Grace ... But your mother makes me angry sometimes, always complaining, whatever we do or don't do.'

'She's getting old, George.'

'We're all getting old,' he said irritably. 'I'm getting damned old myself. It doesn't mean I have to keep nagging away all the time, just to show I'm still alive.'

'You're different.'

'So are you.'

She smiled again. 'They say that daughters always grow up to be like their mothers, in the end.'

'Then God help me, twenty years from now!'

'Now George ... What are you going to do this afternoon?'

'Sleep.' He caught her eye, and laughed. 'I suppose you'd really like to dress up and go out calling.'

'No,' she said seriously. 'You have your sleep. You've earned it. We'll go calling when all this is over.'

. . .

Tallow and Watts sat side by side in a Lime Street pub, drinking beer and watching the dart players. The two Chief Petty Officers' caps lay peak-to-peak on the table in front of them: their two square-cut uniforms, with the gold buttons and badges catching the light, seemed far too smart and businesslike for their surroundings. The place was crowded, dingy, and uncomfortable: a near-miss in one of the big raids had removed every square foot of glass, and the windows were permanently boarded up, so that even at high noon the lights had to be burning, the air stale. Every time the door swung open, loosing a vicious draught round their ankles, a rather drunk man at the end of the counter called out: 'Mind the light – you'll have us all blown to bits!' He had been saying this virtually every night for the past year: it had involved him in arguments and fights a few times, but usually people grinned at him and said nothing. The door was on an automatic spring, and heavily curtained, in any case: it completed the pub's air of makeshift inferiority.

Tallow and Watts had spent every evening of their leave there: it was as good as any other pub in the district, and it was the one nearest to the Y.M.C.A. hostel where they were staying. Though they did not voice their thoughts, they were both in mourning for the past, and for the comforts and cheerfulness of the house in Dock Road. Then, there had been some point in going ashore, some sense in the way they spent their time: now there was just this sort of place, and a shake-down in a glorified doss-house, and a cup of tea and a meat-pie at the corner café. It was a break with the past which they still had not got used to.

For Watts, there was another break which, after the first weeks, he had never mentioned again: the way that Gladys Bell had been killed, just when things seemed to be coming straight for them. He could not pretend, even to himself, that the bomb falling on 29 Dock Road had destroyed any wild and colourful romance; but it would have been a comfortable sort of marriage, it would have been what he wanted . . . He mourned her death in the same way that Tallow had mourned when *Repulse*, his old ship, had been sunk: it had destroyed a more promising, more significant past, it was a senseless waste, it left a blank where no blank should be.

The pub door swung open, the draught stirred the sawdust on the floor, the man at the bar said: 'Mind the light – you'll have us all blown to bits!'

'Bloody fool,' said Tallow morosely.

'Round the bend,' said Watts.

They returned to their silence: drinking, not talking, watching a small man in a cloth cap placing his darts wherever he pleased, with an easy skill which brought a murmur of appreciation from the other players. Presently Watts said: 'He must have played before.' Then he stood up, and collected their empty glasses for another pint.

.   .   .

Ferraby played in the garden with the baby, but the baby was different, and Ferraby was different too.

The little girl was now eighteen months old, and starting to talk: she was also starting to have an expressive will of her own, and the will seemed to be directed against himself. It was as if the tension and the jitters, which he could not now shake off, communicated themselves to the child as soon as he touched her: it was to her mother she ran now, whenever she wanted comfort or companionship, never to him, and if he took her in his arms she would wriggle free within a few moments, and then keep a careful space between them. She would watch him, and in the small lively face would be the beginning of fear; and even as he grieved, he wondered at it. How could she sense his terrible unease? What could a shaking hand mean to a child? How was it that, as soon as they were close to each other, the small mind could feel the brush of his disquiet, the chaos of his thoughts?

He admitted the chaos; he knew, though he could not control, the nightmare direction that his mind was taking, the total preoccupation with violent death. He kept seeing, in the child's smooth and soft limbs, other bodies neither soft nor smooth – crushed bodies, burnt bodies, bodies that came apart as soon as they were lifted from the water. Under the brown curls he saw a bleached skull: under the pretty shoulders he saw a watery skeleton. He imagined death in his child, and he imagined things more terrible still in his wife.

For many weeks now he had been unable to make love to Mavis, because of an insane fear of a happening which he saw in acute detail: the fear that he might do something terrible to her body, and it would prove to be rotten, and rip apart from the crutch upwards, and never come together again.

Now, in the quiet garden, the little girl said: 'Leaf,' and pointed to the tree above their heads. Ferraby said: 'Leaf – that's right,' and reached out and gently squeezed her leg. She said: 'No,' immediately, and drew away and then stood watching him – serious, withdrawn, on guard. He said: 'I won't hurt you, love,' and she hesitated, and took a step – but it was a step backwards; and before he could help himself she had turned into a different picture altogether, and was lost to him.

He saw, in the bare pointing foot, a bony splinter sticking out from under a blanket; and in the finger that went up to her mouth he saw the finger of a man trying to make himself vomit, to rid his stomach of the oil that was poisoning him.

He turned away, and lay down, and felt his body tremble against the earth.

. . .

Morell was washing his hands in the cloakroom of a night-club when he overheard some R.A.F. officers talking about his wife. As a result of this, when he finally took Elaine home they had a furious quarrel which lasted for several days and which was still unresolved – except in the fatal sense of surrender and defeat for himself – when his leave came to an end.

The two R.A.F. officers were moderately drunk: they had come into the cloakroom a few minutes after Morell, and had not seen him as he bent over the wash-basin. But the thick speech was clear enough for him to hear every word.

'That's a lot better,' said the first voice.

'Mine's pure gin, old boy,' said the other.

'Better tell the quack in the morning.'

'He knows already . . . Who's the tarty-looking number in the red dress?'

'Actress type, old boy. Elaine Swainson.'

'Oh, her . . . Know her?'

'Used to. She aims a bit higher these days. The hat on the bedpost has to have a ton of brass on it.'

'Nice take-off?'

'They say . . . Try your luck if you want to. She might feel like slumming.'

'Isn't she married?'

'Not all that amount. Got marital thrombosis.'

'What's that, old boy?'

'Got a clot for a husband.'

There was a sound of laughter. 'That's bloody good, old boy.'

'Think I'll write a book about it . . . Are you going to have a crack at her?'

'Maybe.' There was another laugh, of a different sort. 'Lend me a quid, old boy.'

'A quid?' A snort of derision. 'More like a tenner, and don't expect any change.'

'Commercial type, huh?'

'There's a safe-deposit box under the bed . . . Come on – let's look over the stable again.'

Morell carried that conversation back to sea with him. He could remember every word, every inflexion of it; he could remember the exact smell of the antiseptic, and the look of servile discontent on the attendant's face as he slipped out without tipping him. But as well as the conversation, there was the quarrel with Elaine; and the quarrel was worst of all.

It started in the taxi on the way home, it continued at the flat; it drove him to sleep alone, on the sofa, and to suffer the most fearful night of his life. In the morning, there was no truce, and no respite for his thoughts either: she would excuse nothing, she would admit nothing, she would not even give a straightforward denial to his suspicions. It was clear that she did not give a damn either way; in the music-hall phrase, he knew what he could do with it.

The trouble was that he did not know at all. He could believe, or he could disbelieve, that she was faithful to him; but he could not say truly whether he wanted Elaine on any terms, or only on honest ones.

She knew this: it gave her a whip in either hand.

'You can think what you like,' she said disdainfully, later next morning. 'I'm sick of all this questioning, all this drama every time you come home.'

'Darling, it isn't drama.' He looked at her as she stood by the window, in her green flowered dressing-gown, with the edge of her nightdress showing above the patterned mules: after the night spent apart from her, she was specially lovely, specially desirable: her body beckoned to him, her set face over-rode the beckoning. 'But can't you see how I feel? It's natural for me to be jealous, when I hear people talking about you like that.'

'You should give me the benefit of the doubt.'

'There shouldn't be any doubt.'

'Oh, God!' She gestured impatiently: he had seen her duplicate it a hundred times on the stage. 'This is such tripe . . . Do you expect me to stay home every night, just to make you happy?'

'You would if you loved me . . . Do you love me?'

She said: 'When you behave. But I won't be told what I'm allowed to do. I won't be taken for granted.'

'You can take *me* for granted.'

She nodded to that. At first she said nothing; it was as if he had produced some cliché which had hardly been fresh the first time she heard it. Then she said: 'That may not be what I want.'

He thought, in surprise: But darling, you *married* me ...

There was something here that no longer added up. He shut his mind to what it was: he had no weapons anyway, and he had to bring her back, he could not lose her ... When he gave in, and asked for her forgiveness and appealed for her continuing love, she allowed him no more than a perfunctory acquiescence. It was clear to him – except when he blinded himself with emotion or sentiment or hope – that she did not give a damn about that either. She was in the strongest position in the world: the loved woman who need only love when she chose, and who, at the slightest crossing of her will, reverted to natural ice.

He wanted to kiss her, he wanted to take her in his arms, and then back to bed. But he did not know what the answer would be – not now, not any more. He looked away from her, and round the softly-furnished room with its overflow of cushions, its feminine accent and promise. He remembered suddenly the bridge of the bombed ship, adorned with blood and scraps of dead men. He thought: this is a slaughter-house, just like that was.

. . .

Baker, for the first time, did not spend his leave at home. He did not even tell his mother that leave was due again: he wrote that *Compass Rose* was in port for a bit, and then, when his fortnight's spell of freedom arrived, he booked a room at a small down-town hotel, and settled in there. He had no clear idea of what he was going to do, except for one point, one action – the thing he had dreamt and thought about for so long.

This leave, he *must* do it. The time for dreaming was past. Everyone else slept with women, and talked about it, and took it for granted. He had overheard a messdeck phrase which pricked his imagination: 'She gave me a slice on the mat.' He wanted a slice on the mat – not the next time they were in harbour, but this time.

On the first night of his leave he stood by the tram-stop outside Central Station, looking about him, and wondering. He realized that he knew nothing at all about what he meant to do: now that it had come to the point, he was in a panic of indecision. He ought to have asked someone, he ought to have listened properly when people were talking about it, instead of pursuing his own daydreams ... How did you pick up a woman? What did you *do*? How did you tell a prostitute from an ordinary woman, anyway? And then, did you give them the money first, or did you say nothing, and leave it on the dressing-table afterwards? Would it be expensive? Did they tell you how much it was, before you started? Did they understand how not to have babies? Could you be arrested if they found you doing it? What was it like, how did you begin, how long did it go on for?

Confused with doubt, sweating a little, but desperately determined, he started to walk slowly along the street towards the Adelphi Hotel, looking at the women as they came towards him. He had twenty-five pounds in his pocket: he wanted to be on the safe side.

. . .

When the members of the wardroom reassembled, on the last night of the refit leave, and were sharing a rather silent after-dinner drink, Lockhart said suddenly:

'I've been looking at some figures.'

'I'm sure you have,' said Morell suavely, glancing up from his newspaper. 'Please spare us the details.'

'Please don't,' said Baker.

'These are the other kind,' said Lockhart, 'and they've taken me the best part of a day to work out, from the old deck-logs. Do you know that tomorrow's convoy is the thirty-first that we've done, and that we've now put in four hundred and ninety days at sea – nearly a year and a half?'

A glum silence greeted the intelligence. Then:

'I didn't know,' said Morell. 'Now I do. Tell me some more.'

Lockhart looked at the piece of paper in his hand. 'We've steamed 98,000 miles. We've picked up 640 survivors.'

'How many have we buried?' asked Ferraby.

'I left that out . . . We've each kept about a thousand watches ——'

'And we've got one solitary U-boat, out of the whole thing,' interrupted Morell. 'Are you trying to break our hearts?' He stood up, and stretched: his face was pale and rather drawn, as if he had either had a very good leave or a very bad one. 'And tomorrow we start another convoy – and then another, and another . . . I wonder what we'll die of, in the end.'

'Excitement,' said Baker.

'Old age,' said Ferraby.

'Food-poisoning,' said Lockhart, who had overeaten.

'None of those things . . .' Morell yawned again. 'One day someone will ring a bell and say the war's over and we can go home, and we'll all die of surprise.'

Lockhart smiled. 'In the circumstances, not a bad death.'

Morell nodded to him. 'Not a bad death at all. But I don't think it will happen tomorrow.'

CHAPTER 4

Waiting on the fo'c'sle, with the two lines of men on either side and the petty officers facing him, Lockhart wondered why Ericson had decided to have Sunday Divisions, when *Compass Rose* was due to sail at eleven that morning. Usually he skipped Divisions if they were sailing on a Sunday – there was too much to do, and it was a nuisance for the hands to dress up in their clean rig when they had to get back into working clothes immediately afterwards. But possibly he wanted to smarten the ship's company up a bit, the day after their long leave ended: a formal parade, with a church service at the end, was a good way of taking a fresh tug at discipline, a method of pointing out, in simple terms, the difference between life ashore and life afloat. And perhaps, thought Lockhart, he might as well point a bit of it out himself.

'Lieutenant Morell!' he called out sharply.

'Sir?' said Morell.

'Stop those men in your division talking.'

'Aye, aye, sir.'

By agreement, Lockhart looked exceedingly bleak, and Morell unusually attentive, during this exchange, which was a purely formal expression of reproof within the naval hierarchy. His seniority over Morell was just under three weeks: enough to preserve the chain of command, not enough to make his position as First Lieutenant any sort of dividing line between them.

He heard Morell administering a rocket to the offender, and he turned away towards the bows of the ship, glancing down the lines of men whom he had just inspected as he did so. Leave or no leave, they looked smart enough: clean, polished up, fundamentally tidy and seamanlike. There was a breeze whipping across the dock, setting the signal-halyards rattling, ruffling the men's collars here and there: a cold breeze, a sharp breeze, promising a brisk start to their convoy. He wondered how many of the hands would be sea-sick tonight, after their spell ashore: it was going to be lively enough, as soon as they left the shelter of the river.

Ericson's head appeared at the top of the ladder. Lockhart called out: 'Divisions! 'Tenshun!' and saluted, formally presenting the ship's company for the Captain's inspection.

Ericson took his time as he walked up and down the lines: it was a smart turn-out, he saw immediately, and he wanted, as usual, to make it seem worth while by giving it careful attention. (He remembered overhearing a rating off another ship complaining: 'Divisions? Skipper runs past like a bloody ferret and then dives down to the gin again . . .') *Compass Rose* had been lucky in the way she had kept her ship's company together, for though it was getting on for three years since they commissioned, there had been remarkably few changes. As he walked slowly round, Ericson was reminded of this passage of time, and the movements up the scale which had taken place within the family: Wells, for instance, was now a Yeoman of Signals again, Leading-Seaman Phillips and Carslake, the leading-steward, were both Petty Officers, Wainwright a leading-torpedo-man. God knows they've earned it, he thought as he reached Ferraby's communications-division, and the latter saluted: they had made of *Compass Rose* one of the best ships in the flotilla, the one that *Viperous* seemed to choose automatically when there was anything out of the ordinary to be done. (That cut both ways, of course: it was one thing to earn the limelight by sinking a U-boat, but quite another to qualify, on that account, for all the odd jobs, all the towing and rescuing and searching that were liable to keep a ship at sea for a couple of extra nights at the end of a convoy.) These were the men, anyway, who had made *Compass Rose* what she was; the process had meant, for them, nearly three years of training and practice and learning at first hand, three years of sweating it out in wretched surroundings, three years of cruel weather, cruel dangers, cruel sights to remember.

Life in corvettes had claimed them altogether: there were times when each man was, for days and weeks at a stretch, reduced (or perhaps exalted) to nothing more than a pair of strained eyes, a pair of sea-boots anchoring him to the deck, and a life-belt snugly clamped round his waist. These were the essentials, these were what a man had to become . . . The thing that Ericson still found amazing was that the great majority of his crew, who had taken on this astonishing transformation, were amateurs: they had volunteered or been conscripted from a dozen different jobs, without a hint of the sea in them; and the original stiffening from the 'Old Navy' no longer stood out at all in the general picture.

The sea in their blood, he thought, as he acknowledged Baker's salute and turned to his division of stokers: the phrase meant something after all: it was not just a romantic notion left over from Nelson, it was not just a baritone rendering of 'Heart of Oak', with manly emphasis on 'Jolly tars are our men'. 'The sea in their blood' meant that you could pour Englishmen – any Englishmen – into a ship, and they made that ship work and fight as if they had been doing it all their lives, catching up, overtaking, and leaving behind the professionals of any other nation. It was the basic virtue of living on an island.

He was proud of them.

He completed his inspection of this last division, walked back to his place in the centre of the square, took off his cap, and after a pause began to read the Morning Service.

The noises of departure began, sounding all over the ship like repeated calls to action.

Ericson, sitting in his cabin and listening to the familiar activity intensifying as their sailing-time drew near, could follow its progress in detail. He heard the pipe for the hands to fall in: he heard them begin to move about the deck, making fast all the spare gear, getting out the fenders, running back with the wires as they were cast off from the dock-side. Another pipe sounded close by him, and with it the quartermaster's voice: 'Testing alarm-bells! Testing alarm-bells!': presently the bells themselves sounded, clanging for a full minute throughout the ship and giving him, in spite of the preliminary warning, a twinge of discomfort somewhere under his heart. Muffled in the background, Chief E.R.A. Watts' contribution began to make itself heard: the windlass clanked as it was turned over, the steering-engine ran backwards and forwards through the full arc of the rudder, and a gentle pulsing indicated that the main shaft was moving slowly, at five or ten revolutions a minute, in preparation for its long task. It would never stop turning, for the next four hundred hours at least ... Just over Ericson's head, the telegraph-bells rang in the wheel-house, and were faintly answered from the engine-room; and then, after a pause, came the last pipe of all: 'Hands to stations for leaving harbour! Special sea-duty men – close up!'

Lockhart appeared at the door of his cabin, his cap under his arm, and said: 'Ready to proceed, sir.'

Ericson took his binoculars from the shelf over his bunk, buttoned up his great-coat, and made for the bridge-ladder.

.   .   .

Down river, to seaward of the Bar Light Vessel, the convoy assembled.

There were forty-four ships, ranging from a 10,000-ton tanker to what looked like the oldest refrigerator ship in the world: another six would join them south of the Isle of Man, and another eight off the Firth of Clyde; and Baker, checking the names and numbers of the Liverpool portion from the convoy-list on the chart-table, found himself wonder-ing, not for the first time, at the immense complexity of organization that lay behind all these convoys. There might be a dozen of them at sea at the same time, comprising upwards of five hundred ships: those individual ships would come from a score of different ports all round the coast of England: they would have to be manned, and loaded at a prescribed date, railage and docking difficulties notwithstanding: they would each have to receive identical convoy-instructions, and their masters would have to attend sailing conferences for last-minute orders: they would have to rendezvous at a set time and place, with pilots made available for them; and their readiness for sea had to coincide with that of an escort group to accompany them, which itself needed the same preparation and the same careful routing. Dock space had to be waiting for them, and men to load and unload: a hundred factories had to meet a fixed despatch-date on their account: a railway shunter falling asleep at Birmingham or Clapham could spoil the whole thing, a third mate getting drunk on Tuesday instead of Monday could wreck a dozen carefully-laid plans, a single air-raid out of the hundreds that had harassed the harbours of Britain could halve a convoy and make it not worth the trouble of sending across the Atlantic.

Yet the ships always seemed to turn up: as usual, here they were, on this bright cold afternoon ... Baker, ticking off their names as Wells called them out, wondered idly who was behind the organization: was it one superman, or a committee, or hundreds of civil servants all telephoning each other at once?

Thank God it wasn't *his* worry, anyway. He had a particular worry of his own.

. . .

The convoy was 'north-about' – that is, it was routed past the coast of Scotland, between the Isle of Lewis and the mainland, through the troubled, tide-ridden water of the Minches, and then westwards from Cape Wrath towards the open sea.

They sailed past the Isle of Man, and the smug neutrals of Ireland, and the Lowland Scottish hills: the Bristol portion of the convoy joined them, and then the Clyde contingent: a day and a night passed, and they were steaming northwards through the last of the sheltered water before they made their turn westwards. But 'sheltered' did not mean much, where the Minches were concerned: this stretch of narrow sea between Stornaway and the Scottish coast was one of the wildest anywhere round Britain, an uneasy area with swirling currents, violent overfalls, and, at the northern end, the ceaseless swell of the Atlantic coiling in to set up a wicked cross-sea at any state of the tide. Ships here were never still, sailors here were never easy: *Compass Rose*, with her convoy was moving past one of the loveliest meeting-places of sea, sky, and land in the world – past a brave sea-coast with the sunlight sparkling on its fringe of breakers, past whitewashed cottages at the heads of lochs, and light-houses and beacons standing guard at their entrance, past royal purple hills with the first snow of winter already lying on their peaks: *Compass Rose* had this to look at, this to enjoy, and all that her company could think about was the prospect that the ship, harried by this wilful sea, would roll so far in one direction that she would be unable to make a recovery towards the other.

It had never happened yet; but they had already learned that, in war, there was a first time for everything.

Presently, however, when towards evening they came level with Cape Wrath, the awkward motion subsided, and the noise of their passage changed to a steady threshing as *Compass Rose* turned westwards with the convoy and headed for the main Atlantic. Just before nightfall, a rain squall blotted out the craggy and forbidding cliff which would be their last sight of land for many days.

Now they were setting out again: leaving the Island, and facing the tiredness, the nerve-strain, the huge question-mark of the journey: taking it all on again, confronting once more, with a possessive hatred, the things they had got used to, the ordeal they understood.

It was very cold within sight of Iceland: *Compass Rose*, running south-westward past the frozen coastline after delivering four ships inde-pendently to Reykjavik, had a rime of bitter frost all over her upper-works. The watch on deck, stamping their feet and blowing through numbed lips, stared indifferently at this strange island, on which the pale afternoon sun glinted as upon an iced cake left by the kitchen window-sill. It looked just as Iceland ought to look – no more, no less: it had plenty of snow, it had black cliffs and white mountains and a broad glacier. It did not seem to repay them for the many extra degrees of cold involved in approaching near enough to take a peep.

At four o'clock Ericson came up to the bridge, checked their position, and rang down for increased speed. The diversion had put them a long way astern of the main body of the convoy, and he wanted to catch up before midnight, if possible.

It grew colder still as night fell.

CHAPTER 5

The torpedo struck *Compass Rose* as she was moving at almost her full speed: she was therefore mortally torn by the sea as well as by the violence of the enemy. She was hit squarely about twelve feet from her bows: there was one slamming explosion, and the noise of ripping and tearing metal, and the fatal sound of sea-water flooding in under great pressure: a blast of heat from the stricken fo'c'sle rose to the bridge like a hideous waft of incense. *Compass Rose* veered wildly from her course, and came to a shaking stop, like a dog with a bloody muzzle: her bows were very nearly blown off, and her stern was already starting to cant in the air, almost before the wave was off the ship.

At the moment of disaster, Ericson was on the bridge, and Lockhart, and Wells: the same incredulous shock hit them all like a sickening body-blow. They were masked and confused by the pitch-dark night, and they could not believe that *Compass Rose* had been struck. But the ugly angle of the deck must only have one meaning, and the noise of things sliding about below their feet confirmed it. There was another noise, too, a noise which momentarily paralysed Ericson's brain and prevented him thinking at all; it came from a voice-pipe connecting the fo'c'sle with the bridge – an agonized animal howling, like a hundred dogs going mad in a pit. It was the men caught by the explosion, which must have jammed their only escape: up the voice-pipe came their shouts, their crazy hammering, their screams for help. But there was no help for them: with an executioner's hand, Ericson snapped the voice-pipe cover shut, cutting off the noise.

To Wells he said: 'Call *Viperous* on R/T. Plain Language, Say——' he did an almost violent sum in his brain; 'Say: "TORPEDOED IN POSITION OH-FIVE-OH DEGREES, THIRTY MILES ASTERN OF YOU".'

To Lockhart he said: 'Clear away boats and rafts. But wait for the word.'

The deck started to tilt more acutely still. There was a crash from below as something heavy broke adrift and slid down the slope. Steam began to roar out of the safety-valve alongside the funnel.

Ericson thought: God, she's going down already, like *Sorrel*.

Wells said: 'The R/T's smashed, sir.'

Down in the wardroom, the noise and shock had been appalling; the explosion was in the very next compartment, and the bulkhead had buckled and sagged towards them, just above the table they were eating at. They all leapt to their feet, and jumped for the doorway: for a moment there were five men at the foot of the ladder leading to the upper deck – Morell, Ferraby, Baker, Carslake, and Tomlinson, the second steward. They seemed to be mobbing each other: Baker was shouting 'My lifebelt – I've left my lifebelt!' Ferraby was being lifted off his feet by the rush, Tomlinson was waving a dish-cloth, Carslake had reached out above their heads and grabbed the hand-rail. As the group struggled, it had an ugly illusion of panic, though it was in fact no more than the swift reaction to danger. Someone had to lead the way up the ladder: by the compulsion of their peril, they had all got there at the same time.

Morell suddenly turned back against the fierce rush, buffeted his way through, and darted into his cabin. Above his bunk was a photograph of his wife: he seized it, and thrust it inside his jacket. He looked round swiftly, but there seemed nothing else he wanted.

He ran out again, and found himself already alone: the others had all got clear away, even during the few seconds of his absence. He wondered

which one of them had given way ... Just as he reached the foot of the
ladder there was an enormous cracking noise behind him: foolishly he
turned, and through the wardroom door he saw the bulkhead split
asunder and the water burst in. It flooded towards him like a cataract:
quickly though he moved up the ladder, he was waist-deep before he
reached the top step, and the water seemed to suck greedily at his thighs
as he threw himself clear. He looked down at the swirling chaos which
now covered everything – the wardroom, the cabins, all their clothes
and small possessions. There was one light still burning under-water,
illuminating the dark-green, treacherous torrent that had so nearly
trapped him. He shook himself, in fear and relief, and ran out into the
open, where in the freezing night air the shouting was already wild, the
deck already steep under his feet.

. . .

The open space between the boats was a dark shambles. Men
blundered to and fro, cursing wildly, cannoning into each other,
slipping on the unaccustomed slope of the deck: above their heads the
steam from the safety-valve was reaching a crescendo of noise, as if the
ship, pouring out her vitals, was screaming her rage and defiance at the
same time. One of the boats was useless – it could not be launched at the
angle *Compass Rose* had now reached: the other had jammed in its chocks,
and no effort, however violent, could move it. Tonbridge, who was in
charge, hammered and punched at it: the dozen men with him strove
desperately to lift it clear: it stuck there as if pegged to the deck, it was
immovable. Tonbridge said, for the fourth or fifth time: 'Come on, lads –
heave!' He had to roar to make himself heard; but roaring was no use,
and heaving was no use either. Gregg, who was by his shoulder,
straining at the gunwale, gasped: 'It's no bloody good, Ted ... she's fast
... It's the list ...' and Tonbridge called out: 'The rafts, then – clear the
rafts!'
The men left the boat, which in their mortal need had failed them and
wasted precious minutes, and made for the Carley floats: they blundered
into each other once more, and ran full tilt into the funnel-guys, and
shouted fresh curses at the confusion. Tonbridge started them lifting the
raft that was on the high side of the ship, and bringing it across to the
other rail; in the dark, with half a dozen fear-driven men heaving and
wrenching at it, it was as if they were already fighting each other for the
safety it promised. Then he stood back, looking up at the bridge where
the next order – the last order of all – must come from. The bridge was
crooked against the sky. He fingered his life-jacket, and tightened the
straps. He said, not bothering to make his voice audible:
'It's going to be cold, lads.'

. . .

THE CRUEL SEA

Down in the engine-room, three minutes after the explosion, Watts and E.R.A. Broughton were alone, waiting for the order of release from the bridge. They knew it ought to come, they trusted that it would ... Watts had been 'on the plate' when the torpedo struck home: on his own initiative, he had stopped the engine, and then, as the angle of their list increased, he had opened the safety-valve and let the pressure off the boilers. He had followed what was happening from the noise outside, and it was easy enough to follow. The series of crashes from forward were the bulkheads going, the trampling overhead was the boats being cleared away: the wicked down-hill angle of the ship was their doom. Now they waited, side by side in the deserted engine-room: the old E.R.A. and the young apprentice. Watts noticed that Broughton was crossing himself, and remembered he was a Roman Catholic. Good luck to him tonight ... The bell from the bridge rang sharply, and he put his mouth to the voice-pipe:

'Engine-room!' he called.

'Chief,' said the Captain's far-away voice.

'Sir?'

'Leave it, and come up.'

That was all – and it was enough. 'Up you go, lad!' he said to Broughton. 'We're finished here.'

'Is she sinking?' asked Broughton uncertainly.

'Not with me on board ... Jump to it!'

. . .

D plus four minutes ... Peace had already come to the fo'c'sle; the hammering had ceased, the wild voices were choked and stilled. The torpedo had struck at a bad moment – for many people, the worst and last moment of their lives. Thirty-seven men of the port watch, seamen and stokers, had been in the messdecks at the time of the explosion: sitting about, or eating, or sleeping, or reading, or playing cards or dominoes; and doing all these things in snug warmth, behind the single closed water-tight door. None of them had got out alive: most had been killed instantly, but a few, lucky or unlucky, had raced or crawled for the door, to find it warped and buckled by the explosion, and hopelessly jammed. There was no other way out, except the gaping hole through which the water was now bursting in a broad and furious jet.

The shambles that followed was mercifully brief; but until the water quenched the last screams and uncurled the last clawing hands, it was as Ericson had heard it through the voice-pipe – a paroxysm of despair, terror, and convulsive violence, all in full and dreadful flood, an extreme corner of the human zoo for which there should be no witnesses.

. . .

At the other end of the ship, one peaceful and determined man had gone to his post and set about the job assigned to him under 'Abandon

Ship Stations'. This was Wainwright, the leading-torpedo-man, who, perched high in the stern which had now begun to tower over the rest of the ship, was withdrawing the primers from the depth-charges, so that they could not explode when the ship went down.

He went about the task methodically. Unscrew, pull, throw away – unscrew, pull, throw away. He whistled as he worked, a tuneless version of 'Roll out the Barrel'. Each primer took him between ten and fifteen seconds to dispose of: he had thirty depth-charges to see to: he reckoned that there would just about be time to finish ... Under his feet, the stern was steadily lifting, like one end of a gigantic see-saw: there was enough light in the gloom for him to follow the line of the ship, down the steep slope that now led straight into the sea. He could hear the steam blowing off, and the voices of the men shouting further along the upper deck. Noisy bastards, he thought, dispassionately. Pity they hadn't got anything better to do.

Alone and purposeful, he worked on. There was an obscure enjoyment in throwing over the side the equipment that had plagued him for nearly three years. The bloody things all had numbers, and special boxes, and check-lists, and history-sheets; now they were just splashes in the dark, and even these need not be counted.

Someone loomed up nearby, climbing the slope with painful effort, and bumped into him. He recognized an officer's uniform, and then Ferraby.

Ferraby said: 'Who's that?' in a strangled voice.

'The L.T., sir, I'm just chucking away the primers.'

He went on with the job, without waiting for a comment. Ferraby was staring about him as if he were lost in some terrible dream, but presently he crossed to the other depth-charge rail and began, awkwardly, to deal with the depth-charges on that side. They worked steadily, back to back, braced against the slope of the deck. At first they were silent: then Wainwright started to whistle again, and Ferraby, as he dropped one of the primers, to sob. The ship gave a violent lurch under their feet, and the stern rose higher still, enthroning them above the sea.

.   .   .

D plus seven ... Ericson realized that she was going, and that nothing could stop her. The bridge now hung over the sea at an acute forward angle, the stern was lifting, the bows deep in the water, the stem itself just awash. The ship they had spent so much time and care on, their own *Compass Rose*, was pointed for her dive, and she would not be poised much longer.

He was tormented by what he had not been able to do: the signal to *Viperous*, the clearing of the boats, the shoring-up of the wardroom bulkhead, which might conceivably have been caught in time. He thought: the Admiral at Ardnacraish was right – we ought to have

practised this more ... But it had all happened too quickly for them:
perhaps *nothing* could have saved her, perhaps she was too vulnerable,
perhaps the odds were too great, and he could clear his conscience.

Wells, alert at his elbow, said: 'Shall I ditch the books, sir?'

Ericson jerked his head up. Throwing overboard the confidential
signal books and ciphers, in their weighted bag, was the last thing of all
for them to do, before they went down: it was the final signal for their
dissolution. He remembered having watched the man in the U-boat do
it – losing his life doing it, in fact. For a moment he held back from the
order, in fear and foreboding.

He looked once more down the length of his ship. She was quieter
already, fatally past the turmoil and the furious endeavour of the first
few minutes: they had all done their best, and it didn't seem to have been
any use: now they were simply sweating out the last brief pause, before
they started swimming. He thought momentarily of their position, thirty
miles astern of the convoy, and wondered whether any of the stern
escorts would have seen *Compass Rose* catching up on their Radar, and
then noticed that she had faded out, and guessed what had happened.
That was their only chance, on this deadly cold night.

He said: 'Yes, Wells, throw them over.' Then he turned to another
figure waiting at the back of the bridge, and called out: 'Coxswain.'

'Sir,' said Tallow.

'Pipe "Abandon ship".'

He followed Tallow down the ladder and along the steep iron deck,
hearing his voice bawling 'Abandon ship! Abandon ship!' ahead of
him. There was a crowd of men collected, milling around in silence,
edging towards the high stern: below them, on the black water, the two
Carley floats had been launched and lay in wretched attendance on
their peril. A handful of Tonbridge's party, having disposed of the
Carleys, had turned back to wrestle afresh with the boat, but it had
become locked more securely still as their list increased. When Ericson
was among his men, he was recognized; the words 'The skipper – the
skipper' exploded in a small hissing murmur all round him, and one of
the men asked: 'What's the chances, sir?'

Compass Rose trembled under their feet, and slid further forward.

A man by the rails shouted: 'I'm off, lads,' and jumped headlong into
the sea.

Ericson said: 'It's time to go. Good luck to you all.'

Now fear took hold. Some men jumped straight away, and struck out
from the ship, panting with the cold and calling to their comrades to
follow them: others held back, and crowded farther towards the stern,
on the high side away from the water; when at last they jumped, many of
them slid and scraped their way down the barnacled hull, and their
clothes and then the softer projections of their bodies – sometimes their

faces, sometimes their genitals – were torn to ribbons by the rough plating. The sea began to sprout bobbing red lights as the safety-lamps were switched on: the men struck out and away, and then crowded together, shouting and calling encouragement to each other, and turned to watch *Compass Rose*. High out of the water, she seemed to be considering the plunge before she took it: the propeller, bared against the night sky, looked foolish and indecent, the canted mast was like an admonishing finger, bidding them all behave in her absence.

She did not long delay thus: she could not. As they watched, the stern rose higher still: the last man left on board, standing on the tip of the after-rail, now plunged down with a yell of fear. The noise seemed to unloose another: there was a rending crash as the whole load of depth-charges broke loose from their lashings and ploughed wildly down the length of the upper deck, and splashed into the water.

From a dozen constricted throats came the same words: 'She's going.'

There was a muffled explosion, which they could each feel like a giant hand squeezing their stomachs, and *Compass Rose* began to slide down. Now she went quickly, as if glad to be quit of her misery: the mast snapped in a ruin of rigging as she fell. When the stern dipped beneath the surface, a tumult of water leapt upwards: then the smell of oil came thick and strong towards them. It was a smell they had got used to, on many convoys: they had never thought that *Compass Rose* would ever exude the same disgusting stench.

The sea flattened, the oil spread, their ship was plainly gone: a matter of minutes had wiped out a matter of years. Now the biting cold, forgotten before the huge disaster of their loss, began to return. They were bereaved and left alone in the darkness; fifty men, two rafts, misery, fear, and the sea.

. . .

There was not room for them all on the two Carleys: there never had been room. Some sat or lay on them, some gripped the ratlines that hung down from their sides, some swam around in hopeful circles, or clung to other luckier men who had found a place. The bobbing red lights converged on the rafts: as the men swam, they gasped with fear and cold, and icy waves hit them in the face, and oil went up their nostrils and down their throats. Their hands were quickly numbed, and then their legs, and then the cold probed deep within them, searching for the main blood of their body. They thrashed about wildly, they tried to shoulder a place at the rafts, and were pushed away again: they swam round and round in the darkness, calling out, cursing their comrades, crying for help, slobbering their prayers.

Some of those gripping the ratlines found that they could do so no longer, and drifted away. Some of those who had swallowed fuel-oil developed a paralysing cramp, and began to retch up what was poisoning them. Some of those who had torn their bodies against the ship's side were attacked by a deadly and congealing chill.

Some of those on the rafts grew sleepy as the bitter night progressed; and others lost heart as they peered round them at the black and hopeless darkness, and listened to the sea and the wind, and smelt the oil, and heard their comrades giving way before this extremity of fear and cold.

Presently, men began to die.

.   .   .

Some men died well: Chief Petty Officer Tallow, Leading-Seaman Tonbridge, Leading-Torpedo-man Wainwright, Yeoman of Signals Wells; and many others. These were the men who did all things well, automatically; in death, the trick did not desert them.

Tallow died looking after people: it had always been his main job aboard *Compass Rose*, and he practised it to the last. He gave up his place on Number One Carley to a young seaman who had no lifebelt: when he saw the man's plight, Tallow first reprimanded him for disobeying standing orders, and then slipped down off the raft and shouldered the other man up. But once in the water, a fierce cramp attacked him, and he could not hold onto the ratlines; even as the man he had rescued was grumbling about the 'bloody coxswain never giving them any peace', Tallow drifted away and presently died of cold, alone.

Tonbridge overspent his strength trying to round up people and guide them towards the Carleys. He had already brought in half a dozen men who were too far gone to think or act for themselves, when he heard another choking cry from the farther darkness, another man on the point of drowning. He set off, for the seventh time, to help, and did not come back.

Wainwright, having decided that it would be better if the two Carleys kept close together, set himself the job of steering and pushing one towards the other. But it was heavier than he thought and he was not as strong as he hoped; he soon lost his temper with the sea that kept forcing the rafts apart, and the cold that robbed him of his strength, and he wrestled with the task to the point of exhaustion, and died in a fierce rage.

Wells died making lists. He had been making lists nearly all his sea-going life: lists of signals, lists of ships in convoy, lists of code-flags. Now it seemed to him essential to find out how many men had got away from *Compass Rose*, and how many were left alive: the Captain was sure to ask him, and he didn't want to be caught out. He swam round counting heads, for more than an hour; he got up to forty-seven, and then he began to be afraid that some of the men he had counted might have died in the meantime, and he started to go round again.

It was much slower work, this second time, and presently, as he swam towards a dark figure in the water, a figure who would not answer his hail, the man seemed to draw away instead of coming nearer. Wells approached him very slowly, unable to manage more than one stroke at a time, resting for long pauses in between, and within a few minutes of finding that the man was dead, he died himself, calling out a total which was now far from accurate.

. . .

Some men died badly: Chief Engine-room Artificer Watts, Able-Seaman Gregg, Petty Officer Steward Carslake; and many others. These were the men whose nature or whose past life had made them selfish, or afraid, or so eager to live that they destroyed themselves with hope.

Watts died badly: perhaps it was unfair to expect him to do anything else. He was old, and tired, and terrified; he should have been by the fire with his grandchildren, and instead he was thrashing about in oily water, bumping in the darkness against men he knew well, men already dead. He never stopped crying out, and calling for help, from the moment he jumped from *Compass Rose*: he clung to other men, he fought wildly to get onto one of the Carleys which was already crammed with people, he got deeper and deeper into the grip of an insane fear. It was fear that killed him, more than anything else: he became convinced that he could stand no more, and that unless he was rescued immediately he would perish. At this, a last constricting terror began to bind his weak limbs and pinch the brittle arteries of his blood, until abject death itself came to rescue him. It had nothing about it that the death of an old pensioner should have had, and both his service and his normal spirit deserved far better than the last prayerful wailing that saw him out. But that was true of many other people, at this fearful ending to their lives.

Gregg died badly, because he clung to life with ferocious hope; and on this account he met death in a curious way. Just before the ship sailed, Gregg had got another letter from his friend in the Army. 'Dear Tom,' it said, 'you asked me to keep an eye on Edith when I got home on leave. Well ...' Gregg found it hard to believe that his wife could have gone straight off the rails again, the moment he had left her and returned to his ship; but even if it were true, he felt sure that he could fix it all up in a couple of days. Just let me get back to her, he thought: she's only a kid, all she needs is a good talking-to, all she needs is me to make love to her ... For that reason, he felt that he could not die: it was a feeling shared by many of his shipmates, and the competition to stay alive was, in out-of-the-way corners, spiteful and violent.

It took Gregg an exhausting hour to jostle and force his way to a place alongside one of the Carleys: he saw that it was hopeless to try to get on top of it, but his immense determination drove him to do all he could to see that he did not lose his place. He finally squeezed his body between the side of the Carley and the ratline that ran round it, so that he was fastened to the raft like a small parcel tied to a larger one; and there, securely anchored, he aimed to pass the whole night, dreaming of home and the wife who must surely love him again as soon as he got back ... But he had been too greedy for his life: as the night progressed, and he weakened and grew sleepy with cold, the rope slipped from his shoulders to his neck – the rope which ran, through loops, all the way round the raft, and was being drawn tight by a score of desperate men clinging to it. He woke suddenly, to find it pressing hard on his neck; before he could struggle free, the raft lurched upwards as a man on top fell from one side to the other, and the rope bit deep under his chin and lifted him from the water. It was too dark for the others to see what was happening, and by that time, Gregg's strangled cries might have been any other strangled cries, the ordinary humdrum sounds of drowning. His wild struggles only shortened the time it took to hang himself.

Carslake died a murderer's death. The small baulk of wood which floated near him during the darkest hour of the night was only big enough for one man, and one man was on it already, a telegraphist named Rollestone. Rollestone was small, bespectacled, and afraid; Carslake matched him in fear, but in nothing else, and the fact that he had not been able to get a place at one of the Carleys had inflamed in him a vindictive frenzy to preserve his life. He saw Rollestone's figure, prone on the plank of wood, and he swam over slowly, and pulled at one end of it so that it went under-water. Rollestone raised his head.

'Look out,' he said fearfully. 'You'll have me over.'

'There's room for both of us,' said Carslake roughly, and pulled the wood under-water again.

'There isn't ... Leave me alone ... Find another piece.'

It was the darkest hour of the night. Carslake swam slowly round to the other end of the plank, and went to work with his hands to loosen Rollestone's grip.

'What are you doing?' whimpered Rollestone.

'I saw this first,' said Carslake, panting with the effort to dislodge him.

'But I was *on* it,' said Rollestone, nearly crying with fear and anger. 'It's mine.'

Carslake pulled at him again, clawing at his fingers. The plank tipped and rocked dangerously. Rollestone began to shout for help, and Carslake, shifting his grip, raised an arm and hit him in the mouth. He fell off the plank, but immediately started to scramble back onto it, kicking out at Carslake as he did so. Carslake waited until Rollestone's head was clearly outlined against the dark sky, and then raised both hands, locked together, and struck hard, again and again. Rollestone only had time to shout once more before he was silenced for ever. It was the darkest hour of the night.

But the murderous effort seemed to weaken Carslake. His body, hot for the moment of killing, now grew very cold; when he tried to climb onto the plank, he found that he was too heavy and too awkward in his movements, and he could not balance properly. Presently he rolled off it, and sank back into the water, breathing slowly and painfully. The plank floated away again, ownerless.

. . .

Some men just died: Sub-Lieutenant Baker, Stoker Evans, Lieutenant Morell; and many others. These were the men who had nothing particular to live for, or who had made so fundamental a mess of their lives that it was a relief to forfeit them.

Baker, for example, found no terror in death that he had not already suffered, in full measure, during the past week. Ever since *Compass Rose* sailed, he had been wandering round the ship under a morbid load of guilt, alone with a shameful fear which the passing days had disgustingly confirmed. He knew nothing about venereal infection, and he had no one to turn to; indeed, he was only guessing when he diagnosed the swollen and painful organs, and the soiled underwear, as symptoms of what, in the happy past, he had learned to call a 'dose' – the cheerful joke of the cheerful man-of-the-world . . . But as the days went by, he could no longer be in any doubt of what had happened to him; it had meant a week of trying to avoid human contact, a week of increasing pain, a week of infinite degradation and terror. On the night that *Compass Rose* had been hit, he had already been prepared to end his life by his own hand.

In the abandoning of the ship, he had swum about for some minutes and then found a place on Number Two Carley; but the slow drying of his body after he had climbed out of the water had been horribly painful. He had fidgeted and altered his position continuously, without relief, for several hours, and finally, driven to desperation, he had slipped off the raft and into the sea again. The icy water was agreeably numbing . . . He had begun to welcome the increasing cold as it ate into his groin, and the feeling that this loathsome and hated part of his body was at last being brought under control. He died as quickly as would any other man who welcomed the cold, at a moment when a single degree of temperature, one way or the other, could make the difference between a blood-stream moving and a blood-stream brought to a dead stop.

Stoker Evans also died for love: indeed, there had been so much of it, in one form or another, in his life, that it had long got out of hand. By this stage of the war, Evans had acquired two nagging wives – one in London, the other in Glasgow: he had a depressed young woman in Liverpool, and a hopeful widow in Londonderry; there was a girl in Manchester who was nursing one of his children, and a girl in Greenock who was expecting another. If the ship went to Gibraltar, there would be a couple of Spanish women gesticulating on the quay: if it went to Iceland or Halifax or St John's, Newfoundland, some sort of loving or threatening message would arrive on board within the hour. All his money went to meet half a dozen different lots of housekeeping-bills, or to satisfy affiliation orders: all his spare time in harbour was spent in writing letters. He was rarely inclined to go ashore, in any event: the infuriated husbands or brothers or fathers who were sure to be waiting for him outside the dock-gates, were not the sort of welcome home he relished.

Evans had arrived at this deplorable situation by a fatal process of enterprise. He was not in the least good-looking; it was just that he could never take 'No' for an answer.

But recently there had been a new and more serious development. Just before *Compass Rose* had sailed, the two official 'wives' had found out about each other: the ship had in fact only just cleared harbour in time for him to escape. But he could guess what would happen now. The wives would combine against the other women, and rout them: they would then combine again, this time against himself. He saw himself in the police-court for breach-of-promise, in the dock for seduction, in prison for debt, in jail for bigamy: he could imagine no future that was not black and complicated, and no way out of it, of any sort.

When, towards three o'clock in the morning, the time came for him to fight for his life against the cold, he felt only lassitude and despair. It seemed to him, in a moment of insight, that he had had a good run – too good a run to continue indefinitely – and that the moment had come for him to pay for it. If he did not pay for it now – in the darkness, in the cold oily water, in private – then he would have to meet a much harsher reckoning when he got home.

He did not exactly surrender to the sea, but he stopped caring much whether he lived or died; and on this night, an ambiguous will was not enough. Evans did not struggle for the favour of life with anything like the requisite desperation; and that potent region of his body which had got him into the most trouble seemed, curiously, the least determined of all in this final wooing. Indeed, the swift chill spreading from his loins was like a derisive snub from headquarters; as if life itself were somehow, for the first and last time, shaking its head and crossing its legs.

Morell died, as it happened, in French, which was his grandmother's tongue: and he died, as he had lately lived, alone. He had spent much of the bitter night outside the main cluster of survivors, floating motionless in his kapok life-jacket, watching the bobbing red lights, listening to the sounds of men in terror and despair. As so often during the past, he felt aloof from what was going on around him; it did not seem to be a party which one was really required to join – death would find him here, thirty yards off, if death were coming for him, and in the meantime the remnant of his life was still a private matter.

He thought a great deal about Elaine: his thoughts of her lasted as he himself did, till nearly daylight. But there came a time, towards five o'clock, when his cold body and his tired brain seemed to compass a full circle and meet at the same point of futility and exhaustion. He saw now that he had been utterly foolish, where Elaine was concerned: foolish, and ineffective. He had run an antic course of protest and persuasion: latterly, he had behaved like any harassed stage husband, stalking the boards in some grotesque mask of cuckoldry, while the lovers peeped from the wings and winked at the huge audience. Nothing he had done, he realized now, had served any useful purpose: no words, no appeals, no protests could ever have had an ounce of weight. Elaine either loved him or did not, wanted him or could do without, remained faithful or betrayed him. If her love were strong enough, she would stay his: if not, he could not recall her, could not talk her into love again.

It was, of course, now crystal clear that for a long time she had not given a finger-snap for him, one way or the other.

The bleak thought brought a bleaker chill to his body, a fatal hesitation in the tide of life. A long time passed, with no more thoughts at all, and when he woke to this he realized that it was the onset of sleep, and of death. It did not matter now. With calm despair, he stirred himself to sum up what was in his mind, what was in his life. It took him a long and labouring time; but presently he muttered, aloud:

'*Il y en a toujours l'un qui baise, et l'un qui tourne la joue.*'

He put his head on one side, as if considering whether this could be improved on. No improvement offered itself, and his slow thoughts petered to nothing again; but his head stayed where it was, and presently the angle of enquiry became the congealing angle of death.

. . .

Some – a few – did not die: Lieutenant-Commander Ericson, Lieutenant Lockhart, Leading Radar Mechanic Sellars, Sick-Berth Attendant Crowther, Sub-Lieutenant Ferraby, Petty Officer Phillips, Leading-Stoker Gracey, Stoker Grey, Stoker Spurway, Telegraphist Widdowes, Ordinary-Seaman Tewson. Eleven men, on the two rafts; no others were left alive by morning.

It reminded Lockhart of the way a party ashore gradually thinned out and died away, as time and quarrelling and stupor and sleepiness took their toll. At one stage it had been almost a manageable affair: the two Carleys, with their load of a dozen men each and their cluster of hangers-on, had paddled towards each other across the oily heaving sea, and he had taken some kind of rough roll-call, and found that there were over thirty men still alive. But that had been a lot earlier on, when the party was a comparative success ... As the long endless night progressed, men slipped out of life without warning, shivering and freezing to death almost between sentences: the strict account of dead and living got out of hand, lost its authority and became meaningless. Indeed, the score was hardly worth the keeping, when within a little while – unless the night ended and the sun came up to warm them – it might add up to total disaster.

On the rafts, in the whispering misery of the night that would not end, men were either voices or silences: if they were silences for too many minutes, it meant that they need no longer be counted in, and their places might be taken by others who still had a margin of life and warmth in their bodies.

'Christ, it's cold ...'
'How far away was the convoy?'
'About thirty miles.'
'Shorty ...'
'Did anyone see Jameson?'
'He was in the fo'c'sle.'
'None of *them* got out.'
'Lucky bastards ... Better than this, any road.'
'We've got a chance still.'
'It's getting lighter.'
'That's the moon.'
'Shorty ... Wake up ...'
'She must've gone down inside of five minutes.'
'Like *Sorrel*.'
'Thirty miles off, they should have got us on the Radar.'
'If they were watching out properly.'
'Who was stern escort?'
'*Trefoil*.'
'Shorty ...'
'How many on the other raft?'
'Same as us, I reckon.'
'Christ, it's cold.'
'Wind's getting up, too.'
'I'd like to meet the bastard that put us here.'
'Once is enough for me.'
'Shorty ... What's the matter with you?'
'Must be pretty near Iceland.'
'We don't need telling that.'
'*Trefoil*'s all right. They ought to have seen us on the Radar.'
'Not with some half-asleep sod of an operator on watch.'
'Shorty ...'
'Stop saying that ...! Can't you see he's finished?'
'But he was talking to me.'

'That was an hour ago, you dope.'
'Wilson's dead, sir.'
'Sure?'
'Yes. Stone cold.'
'Tip him over, then ... Who's coming up next?'
'Any more for the Skylark?'
'What's the use? It's no warmer up on the raft.'
'Christ, it's cold ...'

At one point during the night, the thin crescent moon came through the ragged clouds, and illuminated for a few moments the desperate scene below. It shone on a waste of water, growing choppy with the biting wind: it shone on the silhouettes of men hunched together on the rafts, and the shadows of men clinging to them, and the blurred outlines of men in the outer ring, where the corpses wallowed and heaved, and the red lights burned and burned aimlessly on the breasts of those who, hours before, had switched them on in hope and confidence. For a few minutes the moon put this cold sheen upon the face of the water, and upon the foreheads of the men whose heads were still upright; and then it withdrew, veiling itself abruptly as if, in pity and amazement, if had seen enough, and knew that men in this extremity deserved only the decent mercy of darkness.

Ferraby did not die: but towards dawn it seemed to him that he *did* die, as he held Rose, the young signalman, in his arms, and Rose died for him. Throughout the night Rose had been sitting next to him on the raft, and sometimes they had talked and sometimes fallen silent: it had recalled that other night of long ago, their first night at sea, when he and Rose had chatted to each other and, urged on by the darkness and loneliness of their new surroundings, had drawn close together. Now the need for closeness was more compelling still, and they had turned to each other again, in an unspoken hunger for comfort, so young and unashamed that presently they found that they were holding hands ... But in the end Rose had fallen silent, and had not answered his questions, and had sagged against him as if he had gone to sleep: Ferraby had put his arm round him and, when he slipped down farther still, had held him on his knees.

After waiting, afraid to put it to the test, he said: 'Are you all right, Rose?' There was no answer. He bent down and touched the face that was close under his own. By some instinct of compassion, it was with his lips that he touched it, and his lips came away icy and trembling. Now he was alone ... The tears ran down Ferraby's cheeks, and fell on the open upturned eyes. In mourning and in mortal fear, he sat on, with the cold stiffening body of his friend like a dead child under his heart.

Lockhart did not die, though many times during that night there seemed to him little reason why this should be so. He had spent most of the dark hours in the water alongside Number Two Carley, of which he was in charge: only towards morning when there was room and to spare, did he climb onto it. From this slightly higher vantage point he looked round him, and felt the cold and smelt the oil, and saw the other raft nearby, and the troubled water in between; and he pondered the dark shadows which were dead men, and the clouds racing across the sky, and the single star overhead, and the sound of the bitter wind; and then, with all this to daunt him and drain him of hope, he took a last grip on himself, and on the handful of men on the raft, and set himself to stay alive till daylight, and to take them along with him.

He made them sing, he made them move their arms and legs, he made them talk, he made them keep awake. He slapped their faces, he kicked them, he rocked the raft till they were forced to rouse themselves and cling on: he dug deep into his repertoire of filthy stories and produced a selection so pointless and so disgusting that he would have blushed to tell them, if the extra blood had been available. He made them act 'Underneath the Spreading Chestnut Tree', and play guessing games: he roused Ferraby from his dejected silence, and made him repeat all the poetry he knew: he imitated all the characters of ITMA, and forced the others to join in. He set them to paddling the raft round in circles, and singing the 'Volga Boatmen': recalling a childhood game, he divided them into three parties, and detailed them to shout 'Russia', 'Prussia', and 'Austria', at the same moment – a manoeuvre designed to sound like a giant and appropriate sneeze . . . The men on his raft loathed him, and the sound of his voice, and his appalling optimism: they cursed him openly, and he answered them back in the same language, and promised them a liberal dose of detention as soon as they got back to harbour.

For all this, he drew on an unknown reserve of strength and energy which now came to his rescue. When he climbed out of the water, he had felt miserably stiff and cold: the wild and foolish activity, the clownish antics, soon restored him, and some of it communicated itself to some of the men with him, and some of them caught the point of it and became foolish and clownish and energetic in their turn, and so some of them saved their lives.

Sellars, Crowther, Gracey and Tewson did not die. They were on Number Two Carley with Lockhart and Ferraby, and they were all that were left alive by morning, despite these frenzied efforts to keep at bay the lure and the sweetness of sleep. It was Tewson's first ship, and his first voyage: he was a cheerful young Cockney, and now and again during the night he had made them laugh by asking cheekily: 'Does this sort of thing happen *every* trip?' It was a pretty small joke, but (as Lockhart realized) it was the sort of contribution they had to have . . . There were other contributions: Sellars sang an interminable version of 'The Harlot of Jerusalem', Crowther (the Sick-Berth Attendant who had been a vet) imitated animal noises, Gracey gave an exhibition of shadow-boxing which nearly overturned the raft. They did, in fact, the best they could; and their best was just good enough to save their lives.

Phillips, Grey, Spurway, and Widdowes did not die. They were the survivors of Number One Carley, with the Captain; and they owed their lives to him. Ericson, like Lockhart, had realized that sleep had to be fought continuously and relentlessly if anyone were to be left alive in the morning: he had therefore spent the greater part of the night putting the men on his raft through an examination for their next higher rating. He made a round-game of it, half serious, half childish: he asked each man upwards of thirty questions: if the answer were correct all the others had to clap, if not, they had to boo at the tops of their voices, and the culprit had to perform some vigorous kind of forfeit ... His authority carried many of the men along for several hours: it was only towards dawn, when he felt his own brain lagging with the effort of concentration, that the competitors began to thin out, and the clapping and shouting to fade to a ghostly mutter of sound: to a moaning like the wind, and a rustling like the cold waves curling and slopping against the raft, the waves that trustfully waited to swallow them all.

The Captain did not die: it was as if, after *Compass Rose* went down, he had nothing left to die with. The night's 'examination' effort had been necessary, and so he had made it, automatically – but only as the Captain, in charge of a raftful of men who had always been owed his utmost care and skill: the effort had had no part of his heart in it. That heart seemed to have shrivelled, in the few terrible minutes between the striking of his ship, and her sinking: he had loved *Compass Rose*, not sentimentally, but with the pride and the strong attachment which the past three years had inevitably brought, and to see her thus con-temptuously destroyed before his eyes had been an appalling shock. There was no word and no reaction appropriate to this wicked night: it drained him of all feeling. But still he had not died, because he was forty-seven, and a sailor, and tough and strong, and he understood – though now he hated – the sea.

All his men had longed for daylight: Ericson merely noted that it was now at hand, and that the poor remnants of his crew might yet survive. When the first grey light from the eastward began to creep across the water, he roused himself, and his men, and set them to paddling towards the other raft, which had drifted a full mile away. The light, gaining in strength, seeped round them as if borne by the bitter wind itself, and fell without pity upon the terrible pale sea, and the great streaks of oil, and the floating bundles that had been living men. As the two rafts drew together, the figures on them waved to each other, jerkily, like people who could scarcely believe that they were not alone: when they were within earshot, there was a croaking hail from a man on Lockhart's raft, and Phillips, on the Captain's, made a vague noise in his throat in reply.

No one said anything more until the rafts met, and touched; and then they all looked at each other, in horror and in fear.

The two rafts were much alike. On each of them was the same handful of filthy oil-soaked men who still sat upright, while other men lay still in their arms or sprawled like dogs at their feet. Round them, in the water, were the same attendant figures – a horrifying fringe of bobbing corpses, with their meaningless faces blank to the sky and their hands frozen to the ratlines.

Between the dead and the living was no sharp dividing line. The men upright on the rafts seemed to blur with the dead men they nursed, and with the derelict men in the water, as part of the same vague and pitiful design.

Ericson counted the figures still alive on the other Carley. There were four of them, and Lockhart and Ferraby: they had the same fearful aspect as the men on his own raft: blackened, shivering, their cheeks and temples sunken with the cold, their limbs bloodless; men who, escaping death during the dark hours, still crouched stricken in its shadow when morning came. And the whole total was eleven ... He rubbed his hand across his frozen lips, and cleared his throat, and said:

'Well, Number One ...'

'Well, sir ...'

Lockhart stared back at Ericson for a moment, and then looked away. There could be nothing more, nothing to ease the unbearable moment.

The wind blew chill in their faces, the water slopped and broke in small ice-cold waves against the rafts, the harnessed fringe of dead men swayed like dancers. The sun was coming up now, to add dreadful detail: it showed the rafts, horrible in themselves, to be only single items in a whole waste of cruel water, on which countless bodies rolled and laboured amid countless bits of wreckage, adrift under the bleak sky. All round them, on the oily, fouled surface, the wretched flotsam, all that was left of *Compass Rose*, hurt and shamed the eye.

The picture of the year, thought Lockhart: 'Morning, with Corpses.'

So *Viperous* found them.

PART FIVE

CHAPTER 1

1943: THE MOMENT OF BALANCE

Three out of the fourteen mirrors that lined the walls of the smoothest bar in London gave Lockhart three versions of himself to choose from. There was the looking-straight-at, and the looking-sideways-to-the-right, and the looking-sideways-to-the-left: having nothing better to do, while he waited for Ericson to keep their midday appointment, he studied, with a certain speculative interest, these three different aspects of the lean young naval officer relaxing from the fatigues of active service. The uniform was immaculate: the face was thin, but not without a significant determination: the smudges under the eyes were an understandable tribute to the rigours of the past ... Against the background of this enormously sophisticated room, with its thick carpet, shiny furniture, and general air of luxury, the face and figure were perhaps a trifle on the functional side: though there were other officers, from all three services, lined up at the bar or seated at the flanking tables, they were hardly warlike – in fact they looked as though they had been sitting where they were since the beginning of hostilities; and the women they escorted had, to an even greater degree, this same air of permanent availability. But he did not appear wholly out of place, Lockhart decided; if he could not attain the easy self-confidence of the habitués, at least he brought to his corner of the room an authoritative look, a dark-blue consequence which matched the carpet. And one more pink gin would come near to putting him in the habitué class, in any case ... He glanced around him.

'Waiter!'

'Sir?' The waiter, a very old man in a soft frilled shirt, appeared by his side.

'Another pink gin, please.'

'Pink gin, sir.'

'And waiter ——'

'Yes, sir?'

Lockhart pointed to the water-jug on his table. 'This water has some dust on it.'

The old man clicked his tongue. 'I'm sorry, sir.' He lifted the jug, examined it for a moment, and then put it on his tray. 'I'll have it changed immediately, sir.' He bent forward. 'I'm sorry, sir,' he repeated. 'It's the war, I'm afraid.'

'Oh, dear,' said Lockhart. 'In that case I don't want to make too much out of it.'

The old waiter shook his head. 'You've no idea what it's like now, sir. Cracked glasses – not enough ice – bits of cork in the sherry . . .' He bent forward again. 'We had a cockroach in the potato chips, just the other day.'

Lockhart swallowed. 'Should you be telling me this?'

'I thought I'd just mention it, sir. It's not at all what we like to give our customers, but what can we do? We just can't get the supplies like we used to. There was an American officer here only last week, complaining about the soda-water being warm.'

'Warm soda-water is a terrible thing,' said Lockhart dreamily.

'It spoils everything, sir.'

'Yes, indeed. Horrible to swim in, too.'

'I beg your pardon, sir?'

'Nothing,' said Lockhart. 'I was just thinking of something.'

'Pink gin, then, sir?'

'Yes, and make it a big one.' He looked up suddenly, and caught sight of Ericson standing at the entrance to the bar. After staring at him closely for a moment, he added: 'Make it two big ones, in fact, I think we have something to celebrate.'

Ericson caught his eye, and began to twist his way through the crowded room towards the table. There was a certain faint selfconsciousness about the big figure which Lockhart noticed, understood, and indubitably loved. This was a man to go through the war with . . . When Ericson reached his table, Lockhart stood up, and smiled broadly.

'Sir,' he said, 'congratulations.'

Ericson looked down, a trifle shyly, at the cap he was carrying under his arm. The shining gold braid on its peak proclaimed a very new promotion. 'Thanks, Number One,' he said. 'They only told me last week. The passage of time, of course.'

'Nothing else,' said Lockhart equably. 'But here's to it, all the same.' He drank off the last quarter-inch of liquid in his glass, and looked towards the bar. 'I ordered you a large pink gin.'

'That,' said Ericson, 'will do for a start.'

The drinks arrived. As Ericson nodded and raised his glass, Lockhart glanced down once again at the gold braid on the peak of the cap. He was now feeling a trifle shy himself: he had not seen the Captain for over two months, and their last dock-side parting – a strange blend of formality, raw emotion, and mutual astonishment at their survival – was not a thing to be recalled, in these or indeed in any surroundings.

'I doubt if I shall ever be a commander,' he said finally. 'The passage of time won't be enough – at least, I hope not – and nothing else will operate in my case.'

'Don't be too sure,' said Ericson. He paused. 'I was at the Admiralty most of yesterday. Things are starting to move again.'

Lockhart was suddenly attacked by a spasm of the nervousness, the near-terror, which he had not yet learned to subdue. If things were 'starting to move again', he himself must move with them: it meant the end of the hard-won interval, the end of relaxation and recovery: it meant taking the whole thing on again. He knew Ericson must have been settling his future, or at least suggesting to the Admiralty the line it might take; and he was almost afraid to learn what the future was going to be. For him, the balance between control and surrender was delicate still: his nerves, tautened and laid bare under the shock of *Compass Rose*, seemed to treat any change as if it were the end of the whole world. Even Ericson's brass-hat came into this category: it was like a secret signal, dismissing all he knew and trusted, promising nothing but change and complication. It could mean anything: it could mean loneliness, strange difficulties, goodbye ... Aware of how odd it must sound, he switched the subject abruptly, and asked:

'What else have you been doing? Did you go and see Morell's wife?'

Ericson, who seemed to follow his lead for the moment, nodded. 'Yes, I've just come from her flat.'

'How was she?'

'She was in bed.'

'Oh ... Is she taking it badly?'

'I think she was taking it very well,' said Ericson grimly. 'There was someone there with her.'

For a moment the two men's eyes met.

'Damn the war,' said Lockhart.

'Yes,' said Ericson. 'To hell with it.'

For some queer reason Lockhart suddenly felt relieved. Sex, he thought: the universal cure ... 'Tell me all,' he said: 'omit nothing ... She hasn't wasted much time, has she?'

'I shouldn't say she ever has,' answered Ericson. 'But you shall be the judge ... When I got to the flat, some sort of maid or charwoman opened the door. She said straight away that Mrs Morell couldn't talk to anyone. I didn't want to have the journey for nothing, so I said: "Will you tell her that the captain of her husband's old ship would like to see her for a few minutes?" She said she'd ask, and went off.' He paused. 'It's queer, you know I didn't imagine for a moment that anything funny was going on, even though I had to wait for a very long time. I should have guessed, really: the place smelt like a brothel, from the start.'

'I wouldn't know,' said Lockhart, primly.

'I'll give you the address, if you like ... Well, after a bit, Mrs Morell came into the room where I was.' Ericson paused again.

'Pretty?' asked Lockhart.

'Very ... She had a dressing-gown on, but she looked tidy otherwise, and damned attractive. She apologized for keeping me waiting, and sat down, and waited for me to start. I said how sorry I was about her husband, and how much we'd all liked him – the usual thing.'

'But true,' said Lockhart.

'But true ... Then I waited, in case she wanted to say something, but she just sat there looking at me. So I said, would she like to hear about the torpedoing, and what probably happened to Morell.' He paused. 'She said: "No – I don't think I'm terribly keen to hear about that. Those things are all the same, aren't they?"'

'Oh,' said Lockhart inadequately.

Ericson nodded. 'By this time I was feeling rather a fool. There she was, having obviously just got out of bed, lounging on the sofa to the very best advantage – and I must say she had a wonderful figure: not a line or a shadow on her face, beautifully made up, and about as much in mourning as the man that sank us ... It was all so unreal, when you remember what Morell was like.' He laughed shortly. 'As a matter of fact, I'd had a sentence ready in case she was too upset – something to the effect that though it was terribly sad now, later on she could be proud of the way he died and the job he was doing – but by God! that was one sentence I didn't use ... After a bit I'd had enough, so I stood up to go. I said: "If there's anything I can do, please let me know," and she – gave me a great big smile and said: "That's swell – and if you'd like a couple of tickets for the show, I'll leave your name at the box office. And mind you come round afterwards."'

Ericson sipped his drink. After a moment he continued:

'I'm not sure how I answered that one, but anyway I didn't take up the offer ... I said goodbye, and she followed me out into the hall; and just as she was opening the front door there was a lot of noise from behind us, a sort of thumping. I heard a door being opened, and then a man's voice, rather drunk, called out: "For Christ's sake throw that sailor out and come back to bed!" By that time I was in the corridor outside the flat, and as I turned back she said "Goodbye" very quickly, and shut the front door between us, and after a moment I heard her on the other side.'

'Talking?' asked Lockhart.

'No – starting to laugh.'

The ordinary sounds of the bar, which had been somehow held at bay during Ericson's recital, now seemed to break in upon them. Voices sprouted here and there: glasses rattled on the table-tops: a man and a woman giggled in chorus. Lockhart sighed gently: the sigh covered

many things, many futile and conflicting thoughts: but all he said was:
'I wonder if Morell knew about it.'

Ericson raised his head. 'She didn't strike me as the sort of woman
who would bother to keep it a secret, if she saw anything she wanted.'

'Poor old bastard ... What a waste of a good man.'

'It's a waste of a good man, quite apart from her. In fact, if you relate
his death to her at all, you poison the whole thing.'

Lockhart nodded. 'True ...' He raised his glass. 'Absent friends.'

'Absent friends.'

Immediately they had drunk, and set down their glasses, Lockhart
squared his shoulders, and said: 'And the Admiralty?'

Ericson sat back, and rubbed his hands together, as if at last ready to
share a pleasant prospect. 'Now then ... It's a new ship, Number One:
new job, new everything. They're giving me a frigate – that's the latest
type of escort. They've given me *that*' – he pointed to the gold peak of his
cap – 'so that we'll be in charge of the escort group. And they're giving
you a half-stripe.'

Lockhart genuinely startled, sat up in his chair. 'Good Lord!
Lieutenant-Commander? What will they do next?'

'There's a new Fleet Order, just come out,' answered Ericson. 'You're
the right age, and you've done enough time as First Lieutenant, and
you've got the necessary recommendation.'

Lockhart smiled. 'That's you, I suppose?'

Ericson smiled back. 'That's me ... But there's a snag. Or rather,
there could be, as far as I'm concerned.' He paused. 'I'll be senior officer
of the group, as I said. They agreed that I could have a lieutenant-
commander as First Lieutenant, to keep an eye on the rest of the group
as well as my own ship. The job's worth the step-up in rank. They said
that I could have you, if I wanted. I said I didn't know.'

Lockhart waited, not sure what was behind Ericson's last phrase. Was
it doubt as to whether he could handle the job – or had Ericson noticed
that his nerves were still shaky – or was it something else?

It was something else, something quite different. 'Listen,' said
Ericson, 'I'll be quite honest with you. You could have your own
command if you wanted it – command of a corvette, that is. They're
moving up one or two First Lieutenants already, and you could do the
job on your head. I could give you *that* recommendation too.' He was
looking, once more, a trifle shy. 'I don't know how you feel about it. If
you stay with me, it'll postpone your command for at least a year, or you
might even miss it altogether. Sometimes these things have to happen
with a rush, just at the right moment, or they don't happen at all. The
job with me – senior First Lieutenant of the group – is a good one, and
I'd very much like to have you with me; but it's not the top job for you,
and I can't pretend it is.' He laughed suddenly. 'This is all slightly

embarrassing. You'll have to make up your own mind about it. I won't make any comment, either way.'

Lockhart's thoughts, in that moment of decision, were swift and undelaying. A or B, he thought: the crossroads of the career, the choice (maybe) between fame and obscurity, living and dying. Then he thought: this is all nonsense – I don't have to weigh it up at all. We're a good team – none better – and it's a blessing that we're going to be allowed to continue. Why fool about with it, why invent a dilemma where none exists? He smiled afresh, and sat back, nursing his drink, and said: 'Tell me about the new ship.'

Ericson's glance was the full equivalent of the comment he had promised not to make: he had no need to enlarge upon it. Instead he said:

'It's a new class – frigates – and they're really something. Same size and shape as a destroyer: eight or nine officers, about a hundred and sixty men. It's got everything, Number One: turbines, twin screws, three big guns, new Asdics, new Radar. The group will probably be three frigates and four or five corvettes, so we'll have plenty to do, playing round with them and keeping them up to the mark. Ours is still building, by the way; she's on the Clyde, and we'll be commissioning her in a couple of months' time.'

'What's she called?'

'*Saltash*. They're all called after rivers.'

'*Saltash* ...' Lockhart rolled it round his tongue. It was going to be strange, getting used to a new name. 'It has a nice sound,' he said, 'but I can't say I ever heard of it, as a river.'

'It's a very small and obscure river in Northumberland,' answered Ericson. 'I looked it up. It flows into the Tyne. It's not on the map.'

'Well, it is now,' said Lockhart, almost belligerently. He snapped his fingers. 'Waiter! Bring a lot more pink gin ... *Saltash*,' he said again. 'Yes, I think we might make something out of her ...'

'It rhymes with "hash",' said Ericson tentatively.

'True,' said Lockhart. 'I'll bear that in mind all the time.'

They lunched well and, towards the end, hilariously. Once committed to a new and definite course, Lockhart felt very much better; and Ericson seemed to catch his mood and to turn, with him, away from the dark past, and to bend every hope on what was to come. Indeed, it was with something like a holiday cheerfulness that they arranged a meeting, in Glasgow, later in the month, as a preliminary to the first look at the new ship. There was much that they had left unsaid concerning the fact that they would be together again; but it seemed that they were both taking it for granted that nothing else, however promising, would have seemed wholly right, and that something in the past had already shaped the future.

If we are both content, thought Lockhart, looking across at Ericson as he drew gingerly on an unaccustomed cigar, then we are both lucky, and we can leave it so. War won't offer us much more than that ... There's a lot of gin in that thought, he said to himself wisely, and a lot of claret too; but it's a good thought, all the same, a rare thought.

'Sir,' he said, 'I've had a rare thought.'

'So have I,' said Ericson. 'Brandy or Benedictine?'

. . .

But later that week, alone, Lockhart found that the past still lived, and was not to be exorcized by the simple act of thinking and acting their next trip. Caught off his guard, he was tricked into a last, inadvertent, backward glance at *Compass Rose* which was acutely moving.

He had gone to the National Gallery in Trafalgar Square, to hear one of the 'lunch-time concerts' which were just beginning to draw the London crowds. He found the big gathering somewhat intimidating, and he sat down well at the back of the gallery, half-hidden behind a pillar. Myra Hess was playing the piano, and playing Chopin; in the perfect stillness which the audience accorded her, the lovely notes dropped like jewels, exquisitely shaped and strung, sculptures and liquid at the same time, falling straight upon the heart.

He listened unguardedly, surrendering to the music, keeping no reserve and no awareness of the outside world. She played two gentle nocturnes, and then one of the studies, one with a repeated descending passage which sounded like a terrible lament. Lockhart sat back, and the music carried him, like a child, from note to note and phrase to phrase. He drew a long breath, and suddenly he found that he was crying.

He knew, without doubt, why. He was crying, uncontrollably, for the many things which he had hoped to have forgotten. It was not only because of the weakness, the nervous frailty which was still with him, two months after the appalling ordeal: the tears were drawn from him by *Compass Rose* herself, and the wasted love and effort, and the many dead. And by others besides the dead ... Earlier in the month he had gone to see Ferraby, who was still detained in hospital. Looking down at him as he lay in bed, Lockhart had wondered, indeed, whether he would ever come out of it. Ferraby was now a ruin of a young man, thin, wasted, intolerably nervous: the face on the pillow was like a damp skull. Tied round one of his wrists was a piece of string. 'It's my string,' said Ferraby, embarrassed, and began to play with it. Then, more confidently: 'They gave it to me. It's for my nerves. They said I was to play with it whenever I felt I had to do something.' As he spoke, the hooked fingers wrenched and pulled at the string, and knotted it, and twisted it, and set it swinging like a pendulum. Then Ferraby said: 'I'm much better now, though,' and turned over on his pillow and began to cry.

He had cried as Lockhart was crying now: perhaps with the same tears, perhaps with others. Many tears could flow for *Compass Rose*: too many to be staunched, or swallowed, or ignored. Lockhart turned aside in his chair, and tried to control his moving face and lips. The music ceased: the applause filled the hall. Nearby, a girl stared at him, and then whispered to her companion. Under their prying gaze he got up, awkwardly, and walked through into one of the empty galleries. His throat was aching, but the tears, ceasing to fall, were drying on his cheeks.

All right, I was crying, he thought; what of it? Someone should cry for *Compass Rose*: she deserved it. I don't mind its being me: not with that music, not with all those people dead and the ship wasted. The music released the crying, but the crying was due anyway: I would rather cry to Chopin than to a silence, or to a drink, or to a woman. I was hearing that sad and lovely music: underneath it I must have been thinking of all those men, and Morell and Ferraby, and Tallow giving up his place on the raft: I could not help the tears. But they're finished now, and better now: it was a thing to happen once, and it is over, costing nothing, spoiling nothing, proving nothing except that the past is sad and wasteful, and that sometimes music can point directly at it and say so.

The ache in his throat eased, and he walked back, and stood in the entrance to the music gallery, leaning against a pillar. When, after an interval, the notes of the piano started again, he found that their power to unman was gone, and that he could listen, and not be moved. He found also, later, that this was for him the last moment of mourning.

CHAPTER 2

The Clyde shipyards again ... They were far busier now, Ericson realized, remembering the slow, gearing-up days of 1939, when the Clyde was just getting into its war-stride, and there was room to move and time to spare. Now things were very different: from Renfrew down to Gourock, the banks seemed to be lined and crammed with ships at every stage of construction, and the men working on them had a purposeful air, a strained eagerness to be quit of one ship and get started on the next, which had altered the whole tempo of the river. The rate of sinkings in the Atlantic had served as a progressive challenge: air-raids had sharpened the will to hit back: the news that now came out of Africa, of an army no longer barely holding its own but romping forward to victory, had been a heartening tonic, prompting the wish to join in that advance and finish the business once and for all. Now the Clyde was on its mettle: after nearly four years of it, the men toiling up and down its banks to meet the needs of the war at sea might be just about ready for a rest, but if that showed anywhere it showed in impatience and haste, not in any slackening of the output of work. That was constant, intensive, and admirable.

Saltash, the nearly-finished product of their care and skill, lay at the fitting-out wharf opposite John Brown's yard. Seen close to, the frigate appeared enormous: to Ericson and Lockhart, as they stared up from the dockside, she seemed to symbolize, dauntingly, the size and weight of what they now had to take on afresh. 'Looks like a block of flats,' said Ericson, letting his eyes move slowly from the outward sheer of the bows towering over them, past the tall superstructure of the bridge, and along the sweep of the iron deck to the square-cut stern; and indeed there was something big, solid, and ponderous about *Saltash* which seemed to match, in permanence, the long sheds that lined the wharf. Somehow, presumably, they would have to take this lot to sea . . . Viewed from the dockside, she exhibited the usual, half-bedevilled air of a ship that was not yet free of the land. Her first coat of naval grey was marred and spotted by red lead: her upper decks were grimy, and littered with the sweepings of weeks of fitting-out work: the shattering noise made by the riveters, still busy on the fo'c'sle head, was the signature tune of the whole disorder.

She was thus dirty, noisy, and confused: to the casual passer-by she seemed hardly worth looking at yet. But Ericson could no more have walked past at that moment than he could have quit the sea itself.

He led the way on board, crossing the rough gang-plank and stepping down onto a deck littered with packing-cases and empty oil-drums. Now the impression of size and complexity increased: even allowing for the confusion of fitting-out, there was clearly going to be an enormous amount to take in and to master. *Saltash* was over three hundred feet long, and she seemed to rise in mounting tiers, building up steeply in a line which climbed by way of the quarter-deck, fo'c'sle, flag-deck, bridge, upper-bridge, and crow's nest, to the wireless aerial that crowned the tip of the mast. At all levels, she was already crowded with equipment, and there were indications of much more to come: there was stowage for a huge outfit of depth-charges, there was any number of rafts and life-nets, there were dozens of ready-use ammunition lockers to serve the guns. Guns, thought Ericson, appreciatively: lots of guns, not just a gun-and-a-half like the corvettes carried: here there were three big ones, and a four-barrelled pom-pom, and a dozen Oerlikons stuck all over the upper deck like sprigs of holly. There was also, by way of refinement, a power-operated hoist from the main magazine, to keep all these weapons blazing away merrily, with no awkward pauses . . . Two big motor-boats: direction-finding apparatus: a very new weapon which threw a positive spray of small depth-charges over the side: echo-sounding gear: some equipment for dealing with acoustic torpedoes: these were what even a cursory glance found time to take in. They promised complication, and a lot of new things to learn; but they promised a formidable ship also, as soon as they were in practised use.

Ericson left Lockhart staring at some mine-sweeping equipment which was entirely novel to both of them, and made his way down to the engine-room. The succession of steep ladders that led to the lowest level of the ship became progressively more oily and dirty: by the time he had reached the engine-room itself, badly lit by make-shift 'shore lighting', Ericson's hands and the sleeves of his coat were much the worse for wear. The place, full of shadows, seemed to be a tangle of unrelated equipment: it was also cold and damp. A group of men were working on part of the oil-feed, and on the other side from them a man in white overalls and a naval cap was examining the main switch-board with the help of a torch. He turned as he heard Ericson's step behind him, and Ericson looked at him more closely. He was a small man of about forty, with thin greying hair above a solid brown face: he had an air of energy and competence, with something else added to it, a sort of ingrained deference which came immediately to the surface as soon as he saw the brass-hat and the three gold rings, and the D.S.C. ribbon on Ericson's shoulder.

'I'm the Captain,' said Ericson after a pause. 'Are you my engineer officer?'

'Yes, sir,' said the other man, somewhat warily. 'Johnson. Commissioned Engineer.'

'How do you do, Chief?' Ericson held out his hand. 'What's the state of things down here?'

Johnson swept his arm round. 'All the main machinery's in, sir. I've been here three weeks now, and of course they were working on the fitting-out long before that. They're doing the fans and dynamos now. They reckon another month before she's ready for trials.'

'What's the quality of the work, generally?'

Johnson shrugged his shoulders. 'It's a bit austerity, sir. Fourth year of the war ... But the turbines are all right – lovely job. They say they'll give us twenty-five knots.'

'Sounds promising ... What was your last ship, Chief?'

'*Manacle*, sir. Destroyer. In the Med., mostly.'

'Is this your first time in charge?'

'Yes, sir.' He hesitated. 'As an officer, that is. I've just come up from E.R.A.'

Ericson nodded to himself, in satisfaction. A youngish Commissioned Engineer, newly promoted from engine-room artificer, and ex-destroyers, sounded a likely proposition. It was probable that none of his skill would be wasted in the new job. A twin-turbine ship of 2,000 tons was no longer in the 'simple' class, as *Compass Rose* had been: she was a complicated mass of machinery which would need a high degree of attention for most of its working life ... He saw Johnson glancing uncertainly at his hands, and smiled and said:

'I got a bit dirty on the way down here.'

'I'll find you a pair of gauntlets if you like, sir.' Johnson was quickly apologetic, and ready to help. 'She's very dirty all over, I'm afraid. These dockies don't seem to care what they do to her.'

Ericson nodded again. 'You can't do much about keeping her clean at this stage, I know. Yes, get me a pair of gauntlets, and some overalls, too, if you can. I'll be doing a lot of climbing about, the next few weeks.'

'Do you want to look round here now, sir?'

'Not yet, Chief. I'll leave it till things are a bit more ship-shape.'

He paused, before ending the interview, and Johnson, hesitating, asked:

'What was *your* last ship, sir?'

'A corvette. *Compass Rose.*'

Immediately an alert look came over Johnson's face. Ericson thought: he's heard about *Compass Rose*, he probably remembers the exact details – that she went down in seven minutes, that we lost eighty men out of ninety-one. He knows all about it, like everyone else in the Navy, whether they're in destroyers in the Mediterranean or attached to the base at Scapa Flow: it's part of the linked feeling, part of the fact of family bereavement. Thousands of sailors felt personally sad when they read about her loss; Johnson was one of them, though he'd never been within a thousand miles of *Compass Rose* and had never heard her name before.

He became conscious that Johnson was still staring at him, and he said, with an effort:

'She was torpedoed.'

Johnson said: 'Yes, I know, sir.'

That was all there was for either of them to say.

. . .

When he left the engine-room, Ericson went up to the bridge: he had been saving it until the last, and this seemed to be the moment ... It was deserted, and his feet left fresh tracks in the frosty rime that covered the planking: he was struck, first, by the amount of space there was, and then by the array of equipment that lined it. There were rows of telephones, there were batteries of voice-pipes; there were special Radar-repeaters, and a big chartroom at the back, and gunnery-control instruments, and a really tremendous Asdic-set. There was an illuminated plotting-table which recorded the ship's movement electrically:

there was a wide flag-deck with a pair of outsize signalling lamps. They would need a lot of men up here at sea, he realized presently: two officers-of-the-watch, two signalmen, two look-outs, two Asdic-operators, a bridge-messenger – nine at least, even at normal cruising stations. But from this centre of control, command could be fittingly exercised ... And then, as he walked slowly to the front of the bridge, and looked down at the fo'c'sle with its two hooded guns, a feeling of futility suddenly attacked him. Certainly he could command the ship, from this wide high platform with its mass of technical aids: but what was the point of it? Look what happened to the last lot ... He shivered involuntarily in the raw morning air, and gripped the steel plating at his chest-level as if steadying himself against the shock of a breaking wave: below him, the black and greasy Clyde, meandering past their hull, was an uncomfortable reminder of the sea lying in wait outside. There had been many thoughts like this during the past two months, and he had hoped that he had begun to be free of them: he had not guessed that they would return so strongly, as soon as he stood on the bridge of another ship.

He *must* be free of them – and there was only one cure ... He straightened up, and walked across the bridge and down the ladder towards his own quarters. On the way he met Lockhart.

'Collect all the plans, and whatever else the Chief has, Number One,' he said briskly. 'We'd better learn the complete layout, for a start.'

The job must begin all over again.

. . .

The next officer to arrive, a few days later, gave Lockhart a singular shock. He was sitting in the small dock-office which had been set aside for their use, working out a rough watch-bill from the scheme of complement, when the door opened behind him, and a voice said:

'Say – is this right for *Saltash*?'

That tone, that accent ... Lockhart spun round in his chair, and then relaxed again. It was *not* Bennett, their old Australian First Lieutenant, but the two voices could not have been more alike: the one he heard now had the same broad twang, the same sharpened vowel-sounds, recalling heaven-knew-what annoyance and dislike from the past. The newcomer was a lanky, fresh-faced lieutenant, in a uniform of a curious light-blue serge: he stood in the doorway with a confident air, and then as his eye fell on Lockhart's sleeve he straightened up promptly and said:

'Sorry to interrupt, sir. I'm looking for *Saltash*.'

Lockhart, listening in fascination to his voice, gathered himself together.

'This is the right place – she's the one over there.' He pointed out of the window, towards the untidy grey hull. 'Who are you?'

'Allingham, sir. Gunnery Officer.'

'Australian?'

'Yes. R.A.N.V.R.' He looked down at Lockhart's two-and-a-half rings again. 'Are you the captain, sir?'

'No – First Lieutenant. The captain's a Commander.'

Allingham abandoned formality again, with perceptible readiness. 'Big stuff . . . But why so much brass?'

'We're going to be in charge of the escort group,' said Lockhart, somewhat austerely. Hearing the loathed accent, he was ready to dislike on sight, and readier still to resent any kind of uppishness. 'So I'll be senior First Lieutenant.'

Allingham nodded. 'Fair enough. What's the ship like?'

'Still in a mess,' said Lockhart. 'But she's going to be good.' He relaxed a trifle. 'There are lots of guns for you to play with.'

'Good oh!'

Once more the accent and the expression stabbed Lockhart's memory, an authentic, arrow-swift echo from the past, and he could not resist remarking on it.

'We used to have an Australian First Lieutenant in my first ship. His name was Bennett.'

'Not Jim Bennett?'

'I expect so.'

Allingham whistled. 'Say – he was a bit of a success up here, wasn't he?'

'No,' said Lockhart. 'I wouldn't say that.'

Allingham put his cap and gas-mask down on the table. 'But if it's the same man, he certainly was. I heard him lecturing back in Australia.'

'Lecturing?' said Lockhart blankly.

'Yes. He's ashore now, you know. Didn't he have a nervous break-down after sinking those submarines?'

'I don't know,' said Lockhart. 'You tell me.'

'Oh, he's famous, back home. Quite a character. It seems he was in this ship called *Compass Rose*, and the skipper got sick, and Bennett took her out on a convoy, and they got two submarines after a four-day battle. But he had to be on the bridge the whole time, and he cracked up after it.' Allingham paused. 'Between you and me, there was a bit of a stink in some of the papers because he didn't get a medal out of it . . . *Is* it the same man?'

'None other.' Lockhart collected his wits. 'And he goes round lecturing about all that?'

'Sure. They had him on a recruiting drive. And talking in the factories – all that sort of bull. They say it stimulates production.'

'It stimulates me,' said Lockhart equably. 'The last I saw of Bennett, he'd succumbed to a duodenal ulcer through eating tinned sausages too fast, and he left *Compass Rose* and went ashore to a hospital.'

'No submarines?' asked Allingham, surprised. 'No nervous strain?'
Lockhart shook his head. 'The submarine, like the nervous strain, was
all ours.'

Allingham laughed. 'Good old Jim Bennett. He certainly could tell
the tale.'

'He was a bastard,' said Lockhart succinctly. 'I loathed him and
everything he stood for.'

Something in his tone caught Allingham's attention. He hesitated,
and then said with a certain emphasis:

'They're not all like that, where I come from.'

'I'm beginning to appreciate that.' Lockhart smiled, and the other
man met his smile, and relaxed, turning his back on the dangerous
ground. 'They couldn't be,' Lockhart continued, 'or Australia would
have fallen to bits long ago . . .' He stood up. 'Let's forget it. Come and
look at the ship.'

. . .

Saltash's complement of officers was eight: besides Ericson, Lockhart,
Johnson, and Allingham, they had been allocated a surgeon-lieutenant,
two sub-lieutenants (one of them a navigating specialist), and a
midshipman who was to act as the Captain's secretary. It was their first
formal meeting in the big wardroom which brought, to Ericson, the
most vivid reminder of the past: there was, particularly among the
younger men, the same reserve, the same wariness, as he remembered in
the Lockhart and Ferraby of long ago, when he had watched them
feeling their way in new surroundings, trying to guess what would be
popular and what would not. But there, he realized as he looked at them
sitting round the table, there the resemblance ended: for these were no
green hands – with the exception of the midshipman, they had all been
to sea before, and they knew the best and the worst of convoy work.
Clearly, he wouldn't be taking *this* ship to sea with a couple of brand-
new subs who had never yet stood a watch, and a First Lieutenant of
Bennett's peculiar calibre . . . He waited until they were all settled in
their places, and then he tapped on the table.

'I've collected you all here,' he began, 'so that I can meet you
properly, and also get an idea of what you've been doing before you
joined *Saltash.*' He looked round the ring of watchful faces. 'Some of it I
know already: the First Lieutenant was with me in another ship, and' –
he smiled at Johnson – 'the Chief I've talked to before. As far as the rest
of you are concerned, all I've got is your names.' He looked down at the
list in front of him. 'Let's start with you, Guns – you seem to have made the
longest journey to join us. What were you doing before this?'

'Mine-sweeping, sir,' said Allingham promptly, as if well used to
being singled out on an occasion like this. 'Round the north coast of
Australia, based on Darwin mostly. Then I got a bit browned off with

that, because nothing was happening and it didn't look as if the Japs would get down our way after all, so I put in for a transfer up here.'

'Was there any mine-laying in that area?'

Allingham shook his head. 'We put up two in three years.'

'And you've taken a gunnery course here?'

'Yes, sir. I've just come from Whale Island.'

'Did they make you run about much?'

Allingham grinned. 'I don't think we ever stopped, from the time we stepped inside the gates. I must have lost pounds, myself.'

There was a ripple of laughter round the table. Whale Island, the Royal Naval gunnery school, had a reputation for tough, everything-at-the-double discipline which no one who had taken a course there ever troubled to deny.

'Well, you've got plenty of guns to practise with . . .' He looked for the next name on his list, and read: 'Raikes, Sub-Lieutenant.' He turned enquiringly to the young man at the bottom of the table. 'Where have you come from, Sub?'

'East coast, sir,' answered Raikes, the sub-lieutenant who was to be navigating officer. He was a brisk young man with a precise, rather high-pressure manner: Ericson got the impression that his peace-time job had probably involved selling some slightly unpopular household gadget, and that he had carried the necessary tricks of speech and habit with him into the war.

'Whereabouts? Harwich?'

'Yes, sir. We did convoys from there up to the Humber.'

'What sort of ship?'

'Corvette, sir. The pre-war type. Twin screw.'

'I remember them . . . You must have had plenty of practice in coastal navigation.'

'Yes, sir.' Raikes hesitated, not knowing how much Ericson knew about the east coast, or wanted to know. 'There's a swept channel for the convoys, with a buoy every five miles or so. If you miss one of them you probably run aground, or end up in a minefield.'

'How many times did that happen to you?'

'It didn't, sir.'

Ericson smiled at the forthright answer. 'Well, you'll have to rub up on the other sort of navigation now. How long is it since you used a sextant?'

'Not since the training course, sir – a couple of years. There was never any need on the east coast. But I've been practising a lot lately.'

'Good. I did most of it myself in my last ship, but I'll want you to take it over.'

The next officer on Ericson's list was the doctor. 'Surgeon-Lieutenant Scott-Brown,' he read, and found no difficulty in identifying him, even without the bright red rings on his sleeve. Scott-Brown reminded him of Morell: he had the same assured, slightly *dégagé* air, as if, without in the least disparaging the present, he felt all the time that his real background, the structure of his competent life, was elsewhere. He was large and fair: he sat solidly in his chair, giving the impression that it was he who was conducting the interview, and that Ericson was the patient whose duty it was to reveal everything. But that doesn't matter, thought Ericson: all we want is a good doctor.

He said: 'Where do you come from, Scott-Brown?'

Scott-Brown said, somewhat surprisingly: 'Harley Street, sir.'

'Oh ... This is your first ship?'

Scott-Brown nodded. 'I was in practice, sir, and then I was doing research work for Guy's Hospital, and then there were the big raids on London. They've only just released me.' He said this with no apologetic air, as if it were beyond dispute that he had not been wasting his time, before his late arrival in the Navy.

'You're something of a luxury,' said Ericson. 'We've never had a doctor before.'

'Who did the doctoring for you?'

'I did,' said Lockhart. He had been watching Scott-Brown, and he too had been reminded, like Ericson, of Morell. This man seemed patently sure of himself and of his skill, in just the same way, but the fact was a comfort, not an irritant. No more first-aid for me, thought Lockhart thankfully: not unless things go very wrong ...

Scott Brown turned in his direction. 'How did you learn the job?'

'As I went along ... I'm afraid I must have killed a lot more patients than you have.'

A brief smile showed itself on Scott-Brown's face. 'That's a very large assumption,' he answered slowly. 'I've been in practice nearly eight years.'

Once more the ripple of laughter round the table linked them all together. This might be rather a good wardroom, thought Ericson: plenty of variety, plenty of common sense, something solid and confident about it.

'We could have kept you pretty busy during the last two years,' he said: 'I don't know what it's going to be like now ...'

There were two more names on the paper in front of him, those of the second sub-lieutenant and the midshipman. Out of the corner of his eye he had been watching the latter, a tall, slim, and wonderfully innocent-looking young man who was at present fidgeting with an ashtray in the nervousness of waiting for his turn. He's almost a schoolboy, thought Ericson: in fact, that was probably exactly what he was, until a few weeks ago. Perhaps one so young could afford to wait a little longer ... He looked at the other man, the sub-lieutenant, who sat at his side.

'Vincent,' he said. 'Haven't I seen you somewhere before?'

Vincent was small, dark, and rather shy: before he spoke, he seemed to be gathering himself together, and making a tangible effort to arrange his words properly.

'I was in the same group as you, sir,' he brought out finally. 'In *Trefoil*.'

Ericson nodded slowly. 'I thought it was something like that.' His voice was normal, but within himself he had been startled by the familiar name. *Trefoil* had been a sister-ship of *Compass Rose*, for nearly two years: she had been the stern escort on the last convoy, and it was she who, blessedly wide-awake, had noticed *Compass Rose* appear and then disappear on the Radar-screen, and had reported the fact to *Viperous*. It was probable that he and Lockhart owed their lives to *Trefoil*, it was even possible that this small shy sub-lieutenant had had a direct hand in it. But he did not want to raise the subject now: it would keep for a more private occasion.

'Then we know all about each other,' he said pleasantly, 'and you know what the job entails . . . That leaves you, Holt,' he said suddenly to the midshipman. 'How have you been spending your time lately?'

The ashtray fell off the table with a clatter. Midshipman Holt blushed vividly: the colour rose to his clear face, producing an enviable air of youth and health. Heavens! thought Ericson: he must be about seventeen: I could be his father – in fact, I could damned nearly be his grandfather.

'Sorry, sir,' said Holt. He collected himself manfully. 'I've just finished the course at *King Alfred*.'

'And before that?'

'Er – Eton, sir.'

'Oh.' Ericson caught Johnson's eye, and was amused to see in it a perceptible degree of deference. Certainly Eton gave the wardroom a touch of class, a leavening of distinction for the rough sailormen . . . He took another look at Holt, and saw that, in gaining confidence, his face had taken on a lively intelligence and humour. Perhaps it wasn't simply the Eton label that they would come to remember him by.

'Did they teach you anything about the sea there?' he asked.

'Oh no, sir,' said Holt, in surprise. 'It was a very *narrow* sort of education.'

For the third time a small laugh went round the table, and again Ericson welcomed it. As soon as this kid finds his feet, he thought, he'll keep us all young – and God knows we need it . . . A pause intervened, while Ericson looked at them each in turn, and tried to sum up what he and they had learnt. Now we know where we all come from, anyway, he thought: we come from the Atlantic, the Mediterranean, the east coast of England, North Australia, Harley Street, and Eton. But the assorted backgrounds had given them a valuable range of experience: *Saltash*, providing them all with plenty to do and plenty to learn, would have a substantial fund of skill and energy to draw on.

He cleared his throat. 'Well, that will do for a start,' he said. 'We'll have a lot of hard work, getting the ship ready for sea, but I know I can rely on all of you to do your best. The First Lieutenant will be allocating the various jobs to you, as far as divisional work is concerned, and of course you have your own departments already: that is' – he looked down again – 'Allingham – gunnery: Raikes – navigation: Vincent – depth-charges: and Holt – correspondence. I don't expect we'll be ready for trials for another three weeks, so you'll have plenty of time to get things in running order.' He stood up, and signed to Lockhart to come with him. At the door he turned and said:

'We can have a less formal meeting at six this evening, if the gin's arrived.'

When the door shut behind them, a silence fell on the wardroom. Johnson was studying an engineering manual which had been open on the table in front of him: Scott-Brown, the doctor, and Raikes were lighting cigarettes: Holt was picking up, as unobtrusively as possible, the fallen ashtray. Finally, after a long pause, Allingham looked across at Vincent, the sub-lieutenant who had been in *Trefoil*, and said:

'What happened to the skipper's last ship? She was torpedoed, wasn't she?'

Vincent nodded, searching for the right words again. 'Yes. She was catching up the convoy after taking a couple of ships to Iceland: we got her on the Radar, just after midnight, a long way astern of us, and then she faded out. We waited a bit, but nothing happened, so we reported it to *Viperous* – she was senior officer of the escort – and *Viperous* went back and found the rafts in the morning.'

'It was damned lucky that someone noticed them on the Radar,' said Allingham.

'Yes,' said Vincent non-committally.

Scott-Brown looked at him. 'Was that you?'

Vincent said: 'I was Officer-of-the Watch, yes.'

'Nice work,' said Allingham. 'How many of them were picked up?'

'Ten, I think. Ten or eleven.'

Allingham whistled. 'Not so hot.'

'What's the medal he's wearing?' asked Scott-Brown.

'The D.S.C.,' said Holt, the midshipman, readily. 'And the First Lieutenant's got a mention.'

'I wonder what they were for.'

Johnson looked up from his book. 'They sank a submarine, coming back from Gibraltar. About a year ago. Took a lot of prisoners, too.'

Scott-Brown smiled. 'You've got an accurate memory, Chief.'

'She was a good ship, *Compass Rose*,' answered Johnson seriously. 'One of the best.'

'Jolly bad luck losing all those chaps,' said Holt. His young voice and 'London' accent were a curious contrast with Johnson's rough North-Country tone. 'I wonder what it's really like, being torpedoed.'

'Don't you bother with it,' said Raikes succinctly. 'They say it's not worth finding out.'

'I'm not in the least inquisitive myself,' commented Scott-Brown.

'Me neither,' said Allingham. 'I just want to see Australia again.'

'What a curious thing to want,' said Holt innocently.

Allingham looked at him for a moment, and then said: 'Young fellow, you want to buck your ideas up a bit. Didn't they teach you about Australia at that slap-up school of yours?'

'Oh yes,' said Holt. 'Convicts and rabbits.'

'Now see here——' began Allingham energetically.

'I think,' said Scott-Brown, intervening, 'that your leg is being pulled, in the best Etonian manner.'

'Oh ...' Allingham finally achieved a smile. 'Isn't there some system of flogging midshipmen in the British Navy?'

Johnson looked up again. 'It went out a long time ago.'

'I'm an old-fashioned sort of joker,' said Allingham. 'I'm thinking of bringing it in again.'

. . .

In the Captain's cabin, Ericson was saying:

'They're not a bad lot at all, Number One. They've had a good deal of experience, anyway – about two-hundred-per-cent more than *Compass Rose* started with, I should say.'

Lockhart smiled. 'Don't rub it in, sir.'

'I remember you and Ferraby coming into that dockside-hut, looking like a couple of white mice ... You know, it's funny to have an Australian in the ship again. Reminds me of Bennett.'

'Yes,' said Lockhart. 'Horrible, isn't it?'

CHAPTER 3

It was Holt who normally made the twice-a-week journey into Glasgow, to collect their secret signals from Operations and to see to the other odd jobs which attended the progress of *Saltash* towards her readiness for sea. After a couple of weeks, however, Lockhart found himself growing restless, as if he had spent long enough on board at one stretch and needed to move outside the atmosphere of routine and detail which was his particular and unending share of that progress. For a fortnight he

288 THE CRUEL SEA

had been wrestling with stores lists, alterations lists, accommodation lists, and the various complicated schemes which would keep *Saltash* in running order at sea and in harbour: he was finding it dry work, and he felt that he needed a break. He was also curious to learn what was going on in the outside world, the world that lay beyond the mouth of the Clyde which was still their closest contact with the sea: he had been away from the Atlantic for nearly four months, and the personal interest, the feeling almost of responsibility for the whole ocean, which had retreated under the deep hurt of *Compass Rose*, was now returning. It was time to be drawn into the swim again, time to find out what was going on and how the battle was faring; particularly so as they would be returning to that battle, with their brand-new contribution, in a matter of a few weeks.

At breakfast one morning, therefore, Lockhart said to Holt: 'I'll do the Glasgow trip today, Mid. I want some fresh air.'

Scott-Brown looked at him over the top of his newspaper. 'That's the one thing you won't find in Glasgow.'

Lockhart smiled. 'I want a change, anyway.'

'Sir?' said Holt. Lockhart turned to him enquiringly. 'Sir, there's a commissioned lovely in Operations ———'

'There's a *what?*'

'A Wren officer, sir.'

'I prefer that version ... What about her?'

'They say she's the prettiest girl in the Wrens. She's got everyone at Operations tied up in knots.'

'I don't think it's a Wren who's responsible for that ... What about her, anyway?'

'I just thought I'd mention it, sir.'

Lockhart inclined his head gravely. 'Thank you ... Where can one see this paragon?'

'In the Ops Room itself, sir. She practically runs the place.'

'What were you doing in Ops Room, when the signal section is miles away, and on a different floor?'

The midshipman smiled engagingly. 'Just keeping in touch, sir.'

Scott-Brown looked at him. 'How old are you, Midshipman?'

'Nearly eighteen.'

'I can't help feeling that you've got plenty of time ahead of you for this sort of thing.'

'Don't rush it,' said Raikes. 'Leave a little for when you come of age.'

'In Australia,' said Allingham, 'he'd be married by now.'

'I dare say he would be in England, if there were any justice.' That was Scott-Brown again, precise and authoritative as usual. 'But there are people who can evade their responsibilities almost indefinitely.'

'One law for the rich,' said Raikes.

'I'm not rich,' interrupted Holt.

'You are doubtless well-endowed,' said Lockhart. 'It's better really.'

'Certainly,' said Scott-Brown. 'Some say that those are the only true riches.'

Lockhart nodded. 'A lot of women think so.'

'Particularly the rather older ones, of independent means already.'

'This conversation is beyond me,' said Holt.

'Then there's hope for you yet.' Lockhart stretched. 'Well, I shall be seeing your pretty Wren, as it happens, because I'm going to Ops Room to find out who's winning the war.'

'H'm,' said Scott-Brown.

'H'm,' said Holt, on a more meaning note still.

'Cough your fill,' said Lockhart, preparing to leave. 'I've got a good deal of lee-way to make up.'

A barrage of coughing from the entire wardroom followed him down the passage to his cabin.

. . .

On this bleak March morning, the grey town was infinitely drab. Spring must come to Glasgow some time, thought Lockhart, as he made his slow way down Argyll Street, through the crowds of apathetic shoppers, and the depressed hang-dog men waiting for the pubs to open; but it's not happening yet, it simply hasn't got anything to work on . . . He remembered the weeks he had spent in Glasgow, more than three years ago, when he and Ferraby were sharing a hotel room, and, in their time off from *Compass Rose*, had walked round the town doing their best to feel that they were gay young blades giving the place a treat. Glasgow had not suited that part, any more than it now suited the idea and the promise of spring; today it had the same dour umimpressionable aspect, the same futureless air, as he remembered from 1939. Presumably something had been happening in the meantime: babies must have been born, love must have been made, money must have been lost and won; but it did not show on the grimy wet pavements, nor in the desolate, half-empty shops, and all the inward-looking pallid faces he passed in the streets denied it utterly.

One is on one's own here, he thought, staring momentarily into the window of a cheap jeweller's shop, where tray upon tray of wedding rings waited for the customers that never came, the sparks that were never kindled. If a man did not carry, within his breast, the urgency, the flicker of risky life, the touch of wilful self-conceit that turned a body into a person, then he would never catch it anywhere in these ten square miles.

But perhaps it was the war . . . At the Naval Headquarters he collected a bundle of signals and some sealed envelopes, and then went down two floors and walked along a dark echoing corridor until he came to a room labelled 'Staff Officer, Operations'. He knocked and opened the door.

.   .   .

One desk was empty: at the other was a girl. She was telephoning as Lockhart came in, and for a full half-minute, as she listened, her eyes rested on his face. He was very glad to have the enjoyment of them for so long, without interruption: they were large eyes, with long lashes, and they were the principal feature in a face of extraordinary distinction. This was not 'the prettiest girl in the Wrens', as the midshipman had phrased it – anyone could have *that* title. She was lovely: there were those eyes, and an oval face with high cheek-bones and dark hair swept upwards, and a pale and flawless skin. What have you *not* got, wondered Lockhart, as he came nearer, and saw that the eyes were grey and that her hands were slim and beautifully kept. He looked down and away, not yet prepared to hold her glance indefinitely. There was a card on her desk, with 'Second Officer Hallan' printed on it, and underneath, 'S.O.O.2'. 'S.O.O.2', he thought, without the least surprise: second staff-officer in charge of operations: she must be good. But what else could she be, looking like that, lovely, intelligent, her trim tailored uniform as becoming as any balldress ever made? I'm building this up, he thought, a trifle wildly, but by God I'm not inventing it . . . She said: 'Send it to me, please,' into the telephone, put down the receiver, made a note on a pad in front of her, and looked up again. Then she said: 'Yes?'

Lockhart swallowed. 'If it's not illegal,' he began uncertainly, 'I wanted to have a look at the plot, and see what's going on in the Western Approaches.'

'Oh.' She did not bother to look doubtful: she was simply cool and unimpressed. Probably she's got a lot of people coming in here, on any damned silly excuse . . . 'I don't think I can let you do that,' she said after a moment. 'There's a security ban on the whole thing.'

Her voice was low, the words musically pronounced as if each one were worth saying and not swallowing.

'I know that,' answered Lockhart. 'But you see . . . I was in it for the last three years, and now I've been ashore for nearly four months, commissioning a new ship, and I wanted to catch up with what's been happening.'

He might have resented having to give this long explanation, if she had not been so clearly the kind of person who was entitled to an explanation for everything. Her grey eyes now rested firmly on his, without any hesitation. Somewhere behind all this there's a woman, thought Lockhart: there must be. But she isn't on view today. Not for me, anyway.

After a moment she said: 'Which ship are you?'

'*Saltash*.'

'Oh yes, the new frigate.' She smiled momentarily: the movement gave to her mouth an opening softness which made Lockhart tremble. It's because I haven't seen a girl like this for so long, he thought: and then, hell! there's got to be *some* explanation. After a moment he heard her continue: 'Haven't you got a young man called Gavin Holt on board?'

'Yes, indeed. Our midshipman. He practically sent his love to you.'

'I practically return it . . .' But that might be too close an approach, Lockhart realized immediately: in a minute she wasn't going to like him at all. However, she went on amiably enough: 'Who's your captain? Or is it you?'

'No. Commander Ericson.'

'Oh yes. He's rather a star, isn't he?'

'Yes.'

Her eyes went down to the rings on his sleeve. 'Are you the First Lieutenant, then?'

He nodded. 'Yes.'

She frowned, for a swift moment. 'Isn't that a bit unusual? Why not a command of your own?'

'I wanted to stay with Ericson,' answered Lockhart, somewhat rebelliously.

The eyebrows moved again, a fractional and intolerable lifting. 'Scared of it?'

Lockhart flushed suddenly. Now we throw it all away, he thought. 'If I were scared of having a command,' he said, 'I'm damned if I'd tell *you* about it.'

After a moment's silence, the smile began to break in her face again, and now it reached her eyes, which were frankly drawing his.

'Sorry,' she said. The voice was soft, and a little laughing. '*Really* sorry . . . Look – if you worked in this building, with a lot of peculiar young men all scheming for a rise in rank without a rise in the amount of work they're doing, you'd become a bit suspicious yourself.'

'It isn't like that,' said Lockhart inadequately.

'I'm sure. Because I've just remembered who you are.' There was a genuine, an exquisite contrition in her face now. 'You and he were in *Compass Rose* together, weren't you?'

'Yes,' said Lockhart. 'How did you know that?'

'Someone was talking about it the other night . . . You got a submarine, too. Do I apologize again?'

'Never again . . . But does it increase my chance of seeing the plot and hearing the news?'

She nodded readily. 'I think it guarantees it. What can we tell you?'

They talked, with some degree of technicality, for nearly ten minutes: from it, Lockhart gathered a confused impression that things in the

Atlantic were slightly on the up-grade, after a bad Christmastime, that Second Officer Hallam had held her present job for four months, and that her eyes were dark rather than light grey. But he could not enjoy those eyes and that lovely face and voice for ever, and presently she said: 'I expect you're very busy with commissioning,' which was clearly her method of saying that she herself was busy anyway. He took the hint without any resentment. Once again, she was that sort of person.

And in a way, he realized, he was only living on borrowed good humour: if she had not been over-disdainful in the first place, mistaking his quality, she would not now be making these charming amends, she might never have taken as much as a single step towards him.

Even so, their leave-taking was vaguely depressing. As Lockhart got up to go, a young R.N. lieutenant put his head round the door and said: 'Are we lunching, Julie?' She smiled, and answered: 'Yes, Edward. In about five minutes.' 'Julie', thought Lockhart, on his way down the gloomy corridor. Now there's a nice name. Farther down, he thought: I can't say I've ever cared very much for 'Edward', though.

.   .   .

Certainly Lockhart was very busy with commissioning – all of them were. The crew – the West Country crew from Devonport Barracks – had arrived: there were now 172 men living aboard *Saltash*, and the task of fitting them in and organizing them into their watches was a complex and rather dull job that needed a lot of patience. At this stage most of it devolved upon Lockhart and on the coxswain, Chief Petty Officer Barnard. Barnard was the very antithesis of Tallow: Tallow had been rather slow-moving and solid, something like the North-Country accent he talked with: Barnard, was small, energetic, quick-witted, and the West-Country drawl in his speech seemed almost out of character, as if he were a brittle drawing-room actor playing, for fun, a country farmer's part. He had, also, a small yellow beard; and Lockhart, looking at it for the first time, had thought to himself: I wonder whether we ought to have that beard off – it's almost too like Captain Kettle . . . But the beard was not just another bit of theatrical nonsense: it was a genuine Western Approaches beard, nourished in the cold-weather, non-shaving routine of convoy-escort: when one got used to it, it seemed an essential part of this brisk and capable man. Barnard was obviously a disciplinarian, with a frosty eye for defaulters; but he had an engaging humanity as well, and his contribution, during those first few weeks, in binding a new and somewhat raw crew together, was invaluable.

All the wardroom was busy: some of its activity was inescapable, to be met and heard all over the ship, some of it patient and unobtrusive. The largest quota of noise and movement was undoubtedly made by Allingham, who had set to work to instil into his guns' crews something of the fiery discipline he had just picked up at Whale Island. The broad

Australian voice might be heard at any hour of the day, anywhere on the upper deck, going through the loading or the firing drill: there would be a harsh series of commands, then the click and clang of machinery, then another spate of words, usually either discontented or threatening. But there was something about Allingham's manner, a sort of fierce gusto, which made him popular with the crew in spite of his badgering tactics: the words and phrases he used might, in Bennett's mouth, have been actively unpleasant, but here there could be no resentment – Allingham was so obviously efficient, and so obviously ready to jump in and do the job himself, any time of the day, that he carried his men along with him without a hitch.

His manner was a direct contrast with that of Vincent, the sub-lieutenant who was working up the depth-charge crews. Vincent knew his job well enough, after two or three years in corvettes, but he was extremely diffident about giving the necessary orders, and his way of supervising a practice-run recalled a rather young governess whose only effective weapon was an appeal to nursery good-will. 'I'm afraid that wasn't very successful,' Vincent would say mildly: 'try to hurry it up a little, next time;' while within earshot – there were few places on board where he was *not* within earshot – Allingham was bawling: 'If you jokers are trying to break my heart by waddling round the deck like a flock of old whores on a picnic, you'll have to try a long, long time. Now GET CRACKING!'

Only the future could show which of these methods of instruction was the more efficient ... Between the two extremes, like a man keeping his head in a foreign country, Johnson was often to be seen striding round the upper deck, silent, purposeful, followed by gangs of filthy and forbidding-looking stokers, intent on rounding up the spare engine-room stores and getting them below. Sometimes he would pause to listen to Allingham, sometimes he would watch Vincent; then he would frown, and turn away, and say something brief and incomprehensible to one of his strange followers; and they would gather round whatever it was they had discovered – a drum of oil, or a set of spares – and lumber into action, claiming their own with the heavy gestures of men for whom one idea at a time was saturation-point.

In the wardroom itself, a holy calm reigned during most of the working-day. Three people were permanently installed there: Scott-Brown, who was checking over his medical equipment item by item; Raikes, the navigator, bringing the charts up to date; and Midshipman Holt, who was listing the confidential books and codes. Lockhart, putting his head round the door one morning, was struck by their industrious air: the only movement was the scratch of a pen, the rustle of a sheet of paper. Then Holt looked up, and caught his glance.

'The backroom boys, sir,' he said. There was a thunderous clatter

overhead, where Allingham was doing something very noisy at high
speed, time and time again. Holt raised his eyes theatrically. 'All the
brains of the ship are here, and yet we don't make a sound.'

'Quiet!' said Scott-Brown vaguely, without looking up from his lists.

'Me?' asked the midshipman, astonished.

'Yes, you,' said Raikes. 'If you've got time to talk, you've got time to
help me with these charts.'

'I couldn't be busier,' said the midshipman promptly. 'I'm working
my trousers to the bone . . .' He sighed a deep sigh, and bent over his task
again. There was another roar from overhead as Allingham started to
reason with his men. The bearded coxswain appeared at the doorway,
and said briskly to Lockhart: 'Request-men ready, sir.' An encouraging
odour of coffee came from the wardroom pantry.

Saltash was getting into her stride.

The Captain himself was away: he had, in fact, gone back to school.

For a fortnight he had been at Liverpool, caught deep in the toils of
something which, innocently labelled 'Commanding Officers' Tactical
Course', had proved an ordeal of the most daunting kind. The course
was intended to illustrate the latest developments of the war in the
Atlantic, and to provide a practice-ground for close study of them: there
was a series of lectures, and then, each afternoon, the officers under
instruction were installed in a large empty room, on the floor of which
was a 'plot', with models to illustrate the convoy, the escort, and the
threatening enemy. The 'convoy game' began: 'sighting reports' came
in, bad weather was laid on, ships were sunk: U-boats crowded round,
and the escorts had to work out their counter-tactics, and put them into
effect, as they would do at sea. A formidable R.N. captain was in charge:
and large numbers of patient Wrens stood by, moving the ship-models,
bringing the latest 'signals', and sometimes discreetly advising the next
course of action. Rather unfairly, they seemed to know all about
everything.

Even with the intensive lecturing, Ericson found a lot of it extraordinarily difficult to grasp. Things had moved on in the Atlantic during
the four months he had been ashore: there were new weapons, new
dangers, new schemes of counter-attack about which he knew very little.
He found that he was out of practice, too, and out of tune with the feel of
command: there was so much to think about, and to guard against, as
soon as a crisis blew up; often he could hardly remember the correct
helm-orders, or how to draft an intelligible signal . . . By reason of his
rank, he was usually chosen to be Senior Officer of the escort when they
played the convoy game; and whenever he made mistakes, he could not
help remembering that in a few weeks he was going to be leading his own
escort group to sea, and that if he made these mistakes in a real battle
they would carry a heavy price: more ships sunk, more men drowned:

perhaps another burning tanker, perhaps another *Compass Rose* – and all now to be laid directly at his door and on his conscience.

Sometimes these errors were so elementary that they appalled him. There was one occasion which remained in his memory for a long time afterwards. He had been detailed, as usual, to act as the Senior Officer of the escort: it was an action at night, and to initiate it he was given two 'sighting reports', coming in the form of two urgent signals within a minute of each other.

'Radar bearing 300 degrees, three miles.'

'Asdic contact bearing 360 degrees, one mile.'

That meant, presumably, two submarines, some distance apart and both on the same side of the convoy. He thought for a moment: then he sent signals to two of his wing escorts, telling them to investigate the contacts. When he had done so, he tried to think of what should follow, he tried to translate the picture on the floor into the reality of a convoy at sea, with danger threatening and a hundred ships to guard. Nothing happened in his brain, nothing occurred to him. The minutes went by. Presently the Wren by his side shook her head, solemn and reproachful.

'Sir,' she said, 'you *must* remember to bring up another escort, to close the gap on the starboard side.'

The gap, thought Ericson, with a feeling of extreme guilt: yes, we've had that gap before ... He looked at the girl, who was not more than twenty years old, and the sight of her young, thoughtful, and intelligent face suddenly staggered him with a sense of his inadequacy. I must be slipping, he thought, and then: *perhaps I have slipped* ... Here was a kid of twenty, who had remembered the correct move: he himself was forty-eight, and he had not. Possibly that was the whole fatal point: he was forty-eight, and there had been nearly four years of this: it might be that he was now permanently stale, permanently beyond the flexibility of mind that the job demanded. Perhaps he had had his war, as far as a front-rank contribution was concerned.

He had shaken his head at the ugly thought, but it had stayed with him, even when, towards the end of the course, he started to get the hang of things and had improved his record. He had not been able to rid himself of this depression, he had remained puzzled and daunted by the prospect of the future. It would have been bad enough anyway, after *Compass Rose*, to make the fresh start and get geared up again; but now the new tactics, the larger responsibility, and the complex problems had multiplied beyond belief the range of effort needed. Clearly, there was an immense amount to learn; clearly, he might be past the learning stage. And what sort of a Senior Officer was he going to be, when he made mistakes which, a year ago, he would not have made in his sleep?

. . . .

He allowed none of this doubt to show, when he returned to *Saltash*; and indeed, as soon as he stepped aboard the ship and felt the solid deck under his feet, be began to feel that some of his misgivings had been foolish and exaggerated. At forty-eight, he could not really be past the effort of command ... Lockhart had met him at the gangway, and Ericson had been further heartened, as they walked round the ship together, by the progress she had made while he was away. It was half past four, and the first liberty-men were just falling in on the quarter-deck: the inspection of them, before they went ashore, was efficiently and properly handled by Raikes, and the men themselves looked trim and alert. *Saltash* herself seemed almost ready to go to work: the upper deck was clear, the paintwork clean: one need no longer pick one's way through strange and encumbered territory – she had emerged as an organized ship, easy to recognize, familiar in every part. After Lockhart had given him a detailed progress-report, the two of them went down below to have tea in the wardroom, where the rest of the officers were gathered; and Ericson found it good to relax in this young company, and to join in talk which, where he was concerned, had just enough formality in it to mark him out as the Captain, and just enough freedom to show that here the others were off-duty, and on their own ground. It was a delicate and entirely natural balance which both sides understood perfectly.

'How was the course, sir?' asked Allingham, as soon as he had settled in an armchair. 'Tough?'

Ericson nodded. 'They didn't exactly make us run about, but there was everything else. I haven't worked so hard for a long time.'

'Are there any new horrors in the way of weapons?' asked Raikes.

'Well ...' Ericson considered. 'They've perfected those acoustic torpedoes that chase you up the tail, but that's rather old stuff by now. Then there's a rumour of some sort of under-water breathing apparatus for U-boats' – he broke off, and looked round the wardroom – 'this is not to be talked about, by the way – a long tube or pipe which allows them to stay submerged indefinitely.'

'Bastards,' said Raikes, without rancour.

'We'll just have to try a little harder, that's all ...' He turned to Johnson. 'We shall be starting trials in about ten days' time, Chief. Down river to the Tail-of-the-Bank, and we'll stay there till we go to Ardnacraish.'

'I seem to have heard that programme before,' said Lockhart.

'Me, too,' said Vincent. 'I wonder how that fierce old character at Ardnacraish is getting on.'

'Who is that?' asked Scott-Brown.

'The Admiral in charge of working up all the escort ships. He's done a terrific job, right through the war, but he's not exactly an angel of compassion.'

'The position doesn't really call for one ...' Ericson pondered the prospect of the future. 'How about a farewell party, before we leave here?'

'It's provisionally arranged, sir,' said Lockhart. 'At the end of next week, if that's all right with you. Chief is going to rig up a bit of fancy lighting for us, and we thought of having drinks and then some sort of supper afterwards.'

'Do we know enough people for a big party?'

Scott-Brown laughed. 'The present invitation-list is about sixty.'

'Sixty?' Ericson raised his eyebrows. 'What have you all been doing while I've been away?'

'You know how wardroom visitors add up, sir,' said Johnson, with the morose air of a man with a small bank-balance and no social ambitions at all. 'This place has been a proper hotel, sometimes.'

'Oh, there are quite a lot of deserving characters as well,' said Scott-Brown. 'We owe a good deal of hospitality, really. There are officers from the two other ships in the yard. And the builders. And people from the Base. And lots of Wrens. I've got a rough list here.'

He dug it out of his pocket, and passed it over to Ericson.

'Will the Admiral come?' asked Ericson, looking at the name at the top of the paper.

'His flag-lieutenant says, yes, he loves parties and wouldn't miss this one for the world.'

'Good.' Ericson went farther down the list. 'I suppose all these mysterious men with Scottish names are from the shipyard ... Who's Second Officer Hallam?'

'A glamour-pants from Ops,' said Holt.

'A what?' asked Ericson, startled.

The midshipman blushed. 'Er – she's a Wren from Operations, sir. The First Lieutenant asked her.'

'Pretty?'

'Absolute smash hit, sir.'

Ericson looked quizzically at Lockhart, who to his own surprise was conscious of a shade of embarrassment. 'I hope you're not weakening, Number One.'

'In no sense, sir,' answered Lockhart. 'I thought we ought to have as many people as possible from the Base. They've been rather good to us.'

'Is Second Officer Hallam in that category?'

'Yes, I think so.'

'She hasn't been good to me,' murmured the midshipman, not quite under his breath.

'Holt!' said Lockhart, in a voice accustomed to command.

'Sir?' said Holt.

'That will just about do.'

'Sorry, sir,' said Holt, not in the least put out. 'I thought you'd be glad to know.'

Lockhart opened his mouth to speak, and then wisely decided to leave it. Ericson looked at him again. Well, well, he thought: so that's how it is. About time, too. I hope she's nice.

.   .   .

Lockhart had not really expected Julie Hallam to accept the invitation to their party; and watching her installed in one corner of the rapidly-filling wardroom, he was not sure that it was a good idea, for his own peace of mind. She really was alarmingly attractive: he had not seen her since their first meeting, and everything about her – her hair, the shape of her face, her clear skin and large grey eyes – came as a new and delicious shock. He had met her at the head of the gangway, and taken her down to the wardroom, almost in silence; and there he had had to surrender her – there were still plenty of minor things for him to see to, and he wanted to be on hand to greet the Admiral. When he returned to the wardroom, he knew at once that he would never get close to her, in any effective sense.

She was sitting on the arm of a chair, and her corner of the room seemed to be everyone's favourite choice. At her side, Scott-Brown was exerting his formidable charm: there were a number of Base officers who had a clear and undeserved priority: Ericson, doing the rounds of his guests, delayed near her for a long time, talking and making her laugh. Holt was constantly attentive: the Admiral's flag-lieutenant hung over her like a decorated cliff: even the stewards, circulating with drinks and oddments to eat, seemed to reduce to Dead Slow when they were within the orbit ... I can't blame anyone, thought Lockhart: not with her looking like that. But damn it, all the same ... The party, crowded and noisy, made him remember *Compass Rose*'s modest start, with not more than a dozen people in the wardroom, and Bennett walking in with some horrible woman or other. I wonder where Julie Hallam was then, he thought: it's getting on for four years ago – she must have mets lots of people in four years: how does she manage to look lovely, beckoning, and proud at the same time ... He shook his head, and turned away, and began conscientiously to talk to people.

The Admiral, a genial and popular character, made conversation on the royal pattern: there was a series of adroit questions, two minutes' exchange of pleasantries, and then a move onto someone else. To Lockhart he said:

'Is this your first job as First Lieutenant?'

'No, sir,' said Lockhart. 'I was in another ship with Commander Ericson. *Compass Rose*.'

'Oh, yes.' The Admiral, who had a royal memory as well, sheered away from what was evidently not a party topic. 'You've been in the Western Approaches all the time, haven't you?'

'Yes, sir. Over three years.'

'A long stretch ... Is your commissioning going all right?'

'Yes, sir.'

'I hope my people are looking after you properly.'

'They've been very helpful, sir.'

'Good.' He nodded, and moved away. Presently Lockhart heard him ask Allingham: 'Is this your first job as Gunnery Officer?' He caught sight of Johnson standing by himself in one corner of the room, and made his way across.

'Enjoying yourself, Chief?'

Johnson nodded. Then he said, somewhat hesitatingly: 'This is all a bit new to me, Number One.'

That was something which Lockhart specially liked about Johnson: a few weeks ago he had been in the Petty Officers' mess of a destroyer, and he was entirely honest about the novelty of the promotion. He said: 'If you get bored, Chief, you can always blow the fuses and finish the party.'

Johnson smiled. 'I'll remember that.'

Lockhart took a small tray of food from one of the stewards, and began to go round with it, talking to people on the way. The room was now very crowded: in Julie Hallam's corner, the attendant circle was thickest of all. Like vultures, he thought ruefully, and then: no, like courtiers, with the best excuse in the world for their royal attendance ... He had a momentary glimpse of the shapely head, with its crown of dark hair, bending forward to listen to something that Holt was saying: then she vanished, and he went back to work, wishing for the first time in the war that he could be a good-looking seventeen-year-old midshipman without a care in the world.

He talked to a woman in a very large hat, who said: 'What I don't understand is, how you know where you're going when you're in the middle of the sea.'

He talked to a man in a raincoat, who said: 'We've put a lot of work into this ship. Hope you take care of her.'

He talked to a rather plain Wren who said: 'I've seen you in a restaurant somewhere.' He talked to the harbour-master, and handed round some more food, and saw the Admiral off, and went out onto the upper deck to look at the black-out: then he wrote up the Night Order Book, and had a word with Chief Petty Officer Barnard, and came back and talked to the Deputy Provost of Glasgow. Time passed: there were no signs of the crowd thinning out. Then he found himself next to the First Lieutenant of another new frigate, who said:

'I've just arrived. One of our liberty-men fell into the river. Who's that incredibly good-looking girl over there?'

Lockhart's eyes went round, for the first time for nearly two hours, to Julie Hallam, and by chance she raised her head at the same moment. Across the dozen people between them, across the nodding faces and bent backs that were nearest to her, their eyes met. She smiled directly for him, and he smiled back, and then made a comical grimace of despair, indicating the close containing circle round her. He saw her hesitate: then she said something to the people nearest to her, broke away from them, and came towards. him. He moved at the same moment, and they met under the lamp in the middle of the room, a rather hard lamp that made her hair shine and still could not rob her face of an atom of its loveliness. To be close to her suddenly was like a dagger in the heart, a melting dagger that turned on the instant to tender warmth. The smile still lingered round her mouth and eyes when she looked up and said:

'As my official escort, you haven't done terribly well for yourself, have you?'

He laughed, liking the word 'escort'. 'Such competition ...'

'And you've been busy, like a good First Lieutenant.' She glanced down at her watch. 'I must go soon, I'm afraid. We have to be back at ten.'

'Oh ... I haven't spoken to you at all.'

She smiled once more, letting her eyes move frankly over his face. After a moment she said, with a trace of shyness:

'You wouldn't believe how many people have been told that you're seeing me home.'

.   .   .

In the darkness, their footsteps were slow: spinning out the deserted streets, cherishing the black pavement as if it were a measure of fleeting time itself.

'That seems a very cheerful sort of wardroom you have there,' she said presently. 'I like Allingham, and your doctor too. And of course the midshipman is terribly sweet.'

'He makes me feel about ninety, sometimes. But it's good to have someone really young and cheerful about the place.'

'It can be infectious ... You must be very fond of Ericson.'

'I feel I want to finish the war with him, and with no one else. It's as strong as that.'

The blur of her face turned towards him, and he saw her smile. 'That's almost exactly what he said about you.'

'David and Jonathan,' he said. 'Does it sound silly?'

'I'm jealous.' He heard her laugh. 'I don't mean *jealous*. I mean that women don't often have that relationship, and if they do there aren't many first-rate things it can be applied to, like running a ship or fighting a war.'

'It's about the only personal relationship that should be allowed to operate in wartime.'

'Marriage, surely?'

He shook his head. 'No. That's a side-tracking element, a distraction. There was girl I was talking to tonight, one of your Wrens. Joan something.'

'Joan Warrender. Yes, she's getting married quite soon.'

'To a naval officer. The captain of a destroyer, in fact.'

'Well?' She sounded rather puzzled.

'I wondered how getting married fitted in with being a destroyer-captain during a war.'

There was a silence, while they traversed a cross-street and came into the shadow of a building again.

'You're rather a Puritan, aren't you?' she said reflectively.

'In that respect, yes. War has to be a matter of dedication: anything else gets in the way. You have to be single-minded, free of distraction, tough, untender – all the words that don't go with marriage. Otherwise you'll fail, and war will weed you out. It might even do worse: it might take your life, because you're not attending properly.'

'How did you get like this?' she asked after a moment. 'You're not a professional – you don't have to crucify yourself . . . What *were* you before the war?'

'Journalist . . . It's just something that grew. Perhaps it's only true for me. But there was a man in my last ship who was being torn to bits by a bad marriage – and I think one could be sapped by a good one, in the same way. It's too dangerous, too much of a hostage to give way. Better to be on your own. You've got to reach that professional standard, anyway. Muddling through at half-speed just won't do.'

Inconsequently, she said: 'You're very thin.'

'That was *Compass Rose*, mostly. And worry, and less sleep than usual for a long time.' But he did not want to talk about any of that. He said: 'You're not thin.'

After a moment she smiled, and said: 'You might at least qualify that.'

'I mean, you're not harassed or over-driven, although you're doing a harassing job. What were *you* before the war?'

'I was on a fashion magazine.'

'Oh.' He glanced round at her figure in its austere, unfeminine uniform, and they both laughed, making the dark night a companionable cloak shared between them. He said suddenly: 'And now you're S.O.O.2, and you look the way you do. You have everything, really, haven't you?'

He wondered how she would answer that, or whether she would

become, in any degree, coy or disclaiming. He need not have bothered.

'It's not a particularly successful combination.' Once more he was struck by the low clarity, the beauty of her voice in the darkness. Their steps slowed again, willingly matching each other's, as he listened to it, and to her. 'Look,' she said, 'I have this face, and I have a brain, and I can talk. But people don't really like the arrangement: they prefer things one at a time. Women are afraid of the mixture, men don't want it – they don't know what to do with it.'

'Surely they do. Look at the droves of courtiers tonight.'

'But what did the courtiers want? Me as a woman, solely, not as an individual.'

'They enjoy talking to you as well.'

'And all the time they think: Chat, chat, chat – doesn't she know that a mouth is for kissing? True?'

He laughed. 'Maybe true. You wouldn't want yourself changed though.'

Her head went up, challenging him and the dark night as well. 'Not I ... I wouldn't pretend to change, either. I won't pretend to be a plain girl with brains, to suit the women, or a pretty one without them, for you people.'

'Count me out,' he said. 'I have a weakness for organized perfection.'

After a moment, she stopped before a tall gloomy building and said: 'This is where I live.'

He did not know how to say goodbye. He remembered her phrase, 'a mouth is for kissing', but the moment was not that moment. He said: 'The walk made the party. Thank you for it.'

A shaded light falling on her face showed it serious, and heart-breakingly lovely at the same time. Its shape held him in a spell he could have prolonged for ever: its nearness transfixed him. But this was still farewell: the night that had embraced must now divide them.

'The walk was a good idea,' she said. 'Mine, too ... Would you have asked me?'

He shook his head.

She said: 'Why? Dedication to war?'

He shook his head again. 'I just thought the answer would be "No".'

'Next time ——' she began and stopped.

There was a long pause, while they eyed each other: she hesitant, even discomposed, he diverted. Finally:

'I just thought I'd leave you in the air for a moment,' he said. 'Next time, I'll certainly take a chance and stake the earliest possible claim.'

'It will be very embarrassing if you don't,' she answered, restored to her grave serenity. 'Even with Puritans, one can't make the running every day of the week.'

'My turn next,' he agreed. 'Goodnight.'

She nodded and was gone, walking quickly up some steps and through a curtained doorway. Lockhart stared for a moment at the place where she had been standing; and then he turned and went slowly down the street again. His footsteps made an endless hollow ring on the lonely pavement, but the man within him had never been farther from loneliness.

CHAPTER 4

Vice-Admiral Sir Vincent Murray-Forbes, K.C.B., D.S.O., came down to the quay at Ardnacraish as soon as *Saltash* was signalled, and put off in his barge almost before she was secured to the buoy. *Saltash* would be the five-hundred-and-twenty-first ship to pass through his hands, and she received exactly the same welcome as the previous five hundred and twenty: if the enormous amount of work which this number entailed weighed heavily on the Admiral, it did not show either in his face, which was alert and attentive as usual, nor in his scramble up the ladder, which was as energetic as it had ever been. Tremendous in gold braid, he acknowledged the piping and the salutes of Ericson and his officers, who were drawn up in a respectful semi-circle on the quarter-deck; then he walked a pace or two forward, glared round him, turned back to Ericson, and said:

'She's bigger than I thought.'

Ericson, working it out rapidly, came to the right answer and put on an expression of interest.

'Is this the first frigate to arrive here, sir?'

'Yes. Yours was the first corvette, too, back in 1939. Strange. Long time since then. Introduce me to your officers.'

The Admiral went quickly round the assembled ring. To Lockhart he said: 'You met me without a cap last time,' and to Vincent: 'You were in *Trefoil*'; the rest of them received a nod and a straight glance from under the bushy eyebrows. After that he toured the ship at a brisk pace, and then descended to Ericson's cabin, where he sat down, accepted a glass of their best sherry, and said:

'They seem a good class of ship, these frigates. We want something bigger and tougher in the Atlantic, though the corvettes have done a good job, a first-rate job.' He looked at Ericson. 'You lost *Compass Rose*.'

'Yes, sir,' said Ericson.

'It's a long war,' said the Admiral, looking as though he were ready to begin the whole thing over again if necessary. 'A damned long war. But the Huns are running, by God, they're running! Or they will be soon. This is the beginning of the end of it.' His manner changed.

'You're here for three weeks, Ericson. I needn't tell you anything about the training-course, or what I want you to do. You know the sort of standard I expect.' He looked out of the porthole. 'You'll find it a bit bleak here, as usual. We've got a cinema ashore now, and a better canteen, but that's about all there is.'

Ericson ventured a smile. 'As far as I remember, sir, there won't be much spare time anyway.'

'I should think not, by God! It's still the middle of the war ... How's that First Lieutenant of yours? Better than the last one you had?'

'He's first class, sir. We've been together for a long time.'

'Remarkable what these R.N.V.R. fellows have done. I wouldn't have believed it, at the beginning.' He drained his sherry, refused a second glass, and stood up again. 'Time for me to be moving ... You must dine with me one night. I want to hear about that U-boat.'

How does he do it, wondered Ericson, ushering him out onto the upper deck: is it a prodigious memory – or just good briefing? ... By the ladder, the piping party came to attention, headed by the coxswain. 'I've seen you before,' said the Admiral, looking at the yellow beard rather than the man. 'Barnard, sir,' said the coxswain, his West-Country accent very prominent: 'coxswain of the *Tangerine* when she was up here.' The Admiral nodded, satisfied. 'No beard then,' he said to Ericson, 'but it takes more than a beard to hide a man. Knew him straight away.'

The pipes shrilled, and the Admiral saluted and climbed over the side, all in one agile movement. With his head at a level of the rail he said gruffly: 'You start your sea-exercises at half past five tomorrow morning.' Then he disappeared down the ladder, and presently the sleek and spotless barge shot out from the side of the ship and sped towards the shore. On the way it started signalling to *Saltash* with a hand-lamp. 'All guns should be trained fore-and-aft in harbour,' came the message. Lockhart looked round swiftly, and saw, alas, that 'X' gun was trained approximately ten degrees out of the true. He walked heavily aft, calling to Allingham as he went.

.   .   .

Three weeks, the Admiral had said, and three weeks it was, with every hour counting. The time went more quickly now: for all of them except Holt, there was less to learn, more to practise and to perfect: they were simply picking up again the outlines of a known job, on a bigger and broader scale than ever before. *Saltash* steamed faster, fired more guns, detected U-boats at a greater range, and dropped more depth-charges; in the matter of degree, they were breaking new ground, in the matter of anti-submarine warfare they were not. It was the same task as it had been for the last three years; they now had better weapons to help them in it, but its essentials never altered. They must accept A, they must guard against B – and A and B were the same old characters, the weather and the enemy, waiting in the wings for yet another scene from the longest play in the world.

The days passed: the ship shook together and started to work: the men smartened up, and the time taken for each operation – for firing a gun, dropping a depth-charge, sending a signal, lowering a boat, rigging a hose – decreased gradually as the seconds were pared off. *Saltash* began to fulfil the picture in the Admiral's mind – and in Ericson's as well. A bigger and better *Compass Rose*, Ericson wanted her to be: in moments of introspection and memory, it did not seem a particularly happy thing to be aiming at, but it was the whole point of being given a new ship and more men to man her. He and Lockhart were alike in mourning the past, and in turning their backs upon it; it was made easier by a ship that came readily to hand, and by the intensive and demanding future they knew they must prepare for.

In a ship of this size, both of them were far more remote from the crew than had been the case in *Compass Rose*; the working day was no longer a matter of dealing with personalities at close range, it was simply a question of the allocation of numbers – twenty seamen to do a job on the fo'c'sle, sixteen stokers to practise oiling at sea. All that mattered was that there should be enough men available at any given moment, with a Petty Officer to detail them off by name, using his closer knowledge of their capabilities. *Saltash*'s crew was almost double the size of *Compass Rose*'s, and sometimes it seemed that they were twice the distance away as well, and twice as anonymous. There was no one like Gregg, the seaman with the unfaithful wife, there was no one like Wainwright to cherish the depth-charges, there was no one like Yeoman Wells who looked after the signalmen with a father's care; or if there *were* these characters on board, as there must still have been, they did not meet the eye, they had the permanent disguise of being names on a watch-bill or a pay-list, not individuals whose foibles had to be remembered. Perhaps it was a gain, perhaps it was a loss: when he took 'Hands Fall In' each morning, and looked down a long double line of eighty seamen whom he barely knew by sight and would not have recognized ashore, Lockhart sometimes regretted the intimate past, and the feeling, which he had had in *Compass Rose*, that this was a family matter, not a parade. But possibly the gain was in efficiency, which was always liable to be a cold-blooded matter.

I just want the whaler lowered, thought Lockhart to himself on one occasion, when he could not avoid noticing that one or two of the hands were still miserable with sea-sickness, after a day outside. I need twelve men to do it. I don't want to bother about whether they've got hangovers this morning, or whether they're in debt or in despair. I just want the whaler on the water. Twelve men, that's all I need. Bodies . . . Coxswain!

It was he who dealt mostly in this principle of numbers, not people; and he could not help being aware of the change. He could even feel guilty about it, like a man forced by circumstances to replace twelve trusted workmen with twelve mechanical grabs. The answer, of course, lay in the extra amount of work the grabs could do; but that did not salve the general wound to humanity ... Without doubt, however, that was the way the war was going: the individual had to retreat or submerge, the simple unfeeling pair of hands must come to the fore. The emphasis was now on the tireless machine of war; men were parts of this machine, and so they must remain, till they fulfilled their function or wore out. If, in the process, they did wear out, it was bad luck on the men – but not bad luck on the war, which had had its money's worth out of them. The hateful struggle, to be effective, demanded one hundred per cent from many millions of individual people: death was in this category of demand, and lower down the list, the cancellation of humanity was an essential element in the total price.

. . .

They were all together in the wardroom, after dinner, when their sailing signal arrived, marking the end of their stay at Ardnacraish. Earlier, the Admiral's report had come through; he was satisfied – no more, no less – and *Saltash* could go. The signal which translated this into action was short and to the point.

'H.M.S. *Saltash* sails for Greenock 0600 hours April 15th, and will be attached to Clyde Escort Force.'

'Damn,' said Vincent as he read the message. 'I wanted to be at Liverpool again.'

'The Clyde will do for me,' said Johnson.

'Anything will do for me,' said Holt. 'I want to see the world.'

'I must say,' remarked Scott-Brown, 'that there are worse places than Glasgow in the spring.'

'We may not see much of it,' said Lockhart, carefully non-committal. The midshipman's bright and speculative eye was on him, but he avoided meeting it. Julie, he thought: it wasn't goodbye after all ... 'But Glasgow is certainly something to have in the background.'

So, once more, they went to war.

. . .

The war to which they went, towards the middle of 1943, had reached a hard and hopeful moment. Since the new year, the escorts and convoys in the Atlantic had been neither winning nor losing: the moment of balance was at hand, with the escorts cutting back the long start which the U-boats had gained, and attaining, with tremendous effort, some sort of parity in terms of sinkings. They were still stretched thin – sometimes there were seven hundred ships at sea at one time, and a hundred escorts, which meant a huge choice of targets for the U-boats; but the thin weapon was sharp, and try as they would, the U-boats could no longer break through in any decisive sense, could not hold the bloody advantage they had gained during the past three years.

Certainly they tried desperately hard, certainly they tried everything. The wolf-pack attacks were now reaching their zenith, and occasionally they brought off a surprise and brutal success, as when seven tankers out of a total convoy of nine were sunk in a two-night battle in the South Atlantic. The enemy could now regularly keep over a hundred U-boats at sea at the same time, and the packs themselves, concentrating in any given area, could always muster anything up to twenty. Early in the year, their successes had begun to mount again, to a peak point in March when they sank a hundred and eight ships. The new acoustic torpedoes, which automatically 'homed' themselves onto the noise of a propeller, claimed many victims. But then the tide began to turn: March saw fifteen U-boats sunk, April sixteen, and May the huge total of forty-five. At this stage, evidently, the German High Command began to think it over, for the U-boats now started to withdraw from the North Atlantic convoy routes, and to disperse to other and softer areas. The attack, at long last, was running down.

It was running down because the pace was too hot; the escorts, as well as the U-boats, had been steadily crowding onto the scene, and they had at last got the full measure of what they had to deal with. They could now go all the way across the Atlantic, thanks to the new technique of oiling at sea: there were enough ships available to provide many roving escort-groups, independent of any specific convoy, and coming to the help of the ones that were hardest pressed. Above all, the escorts were learning how to find, stalk, and kill the enemy, with the smallest possible margin for failure.

It was now a very skilful war. Nothing was left to chance: gone for ever were the makeshift days when untrained and underarmed escorts put to sea with a handful of depth-charges and a couple of Lewis guns and, hoping for the best, ran straight into slaughter. Science was now king in the Atlantic: science, and skilled men to make use of it. Radar and Asdics had become phenomenally accurate: a system of interception of wireless signals from U-boats made it possible to foresee an attack almost before it had been planned: aircraft-carriers accompanied many of the convoys, to give, all the way across, the air-cover which had been so long and so fatally absent from the black stretch of water that marked and marred the centre.

Counter-attacks on U-boats had now reached a high degree of skill and co-ordination: practice and training during the time spent in harbour, carried out in concert by teams from each ship in the group, ensured that escorts knew what to do, no matter what happened, and knew also exactly what all the other ships would be doing at the same moment. There was no more improvisation, no more of the slap-dash 'it'll-be-all-right-on-the-night' feeling which had cost so many ships and men in the past. Now it was a streamlined job, a smooth essay in destruction; and the ships which went to sea to carry it out had strong and highly-organized backing from the naval bases ashore, which sent them out well equipped, well worked-up, ready for anything.

They despatched them fully armoured to a war where convoy losses were no longer inevitable, where the total frustration of an attack, and even the sinking of a U-boat, were beginning to be nothing out of the ordinary. With the tide starting at last to flow in the escorts' favour, there could have been no better moment to rejoin the battle.

.   .   .

Ericson had summoned a last conference aboard *Saltash*, at ten o'clock on the morning of their sailing day, so that he could give the captains of the seven other ships under his command a final run through their sailing orders, a final briefing on the way the escort-screen was to be organized. The whole group, comprising three frigates and five corvettes, lay at anchor off the Tail-of-the-Bank; swinging to their shortened cables in the brisk tide-way, enjoying a bright, blustering April morning which promised them lively movement as soon as they left the shelter of the Clyde. The three frigates – *Saltash*, and the two others which, fresh off the stocks, had later joined her at Ardnacraish – were brand-new; the five corvettes were old stagers, and they looked it, as did most corvettes nowadays: they had an air of shabby sufficiency, a salt-stained rusty competence impossible to counterfeit. At a quarter to ten, motor-boats began to put off from each ship in turn, all bearing, besides their coxwain and bowman, a solitary figure in the stern; and Lockhart, waiting at the head of the ladder to greet the various captains and pipe them aboard, saw them converging on *Saltash* like chickens rallying to the man with the dinner-pail.

They had to pick their way through a crowded anchorage; within his view were upwards of forty naval escorts – destroyers, sloops, frigates, corvettes, and trawlers: a battleship, a cruiser, and two small aircraft-carriers lay in an outer ring, as if to endorse the evidence of power and plenty; and farther down the river the vast concourse of merchant-ships in the convoy anchorage completed a picture of concentrated naval might.

It was, indeed, a brave sight, a promise of success coming at last within reach. But it recalled, inevitably, the stringencies of the past. 'I wish we'd had some of these ships available a couple of years ago,' said Lockhart, indicating the escorts to Raikes, who as Officer-of-the-Day was waiting on deck with him. 'It might have saved us a few rough nights.'

'Muddle through,' answered Raikes, in tones of brisk cynicism. 'If we'd had these ships then, there would have been something wrong with them, for certain – they wouldn't have floated in salt water, or something. Better to wait for nature to take its course.'

'We're not muddling through now,' said Lockhart coldly, summoning his decided views on the point. 'We weren't then, really, either. We just hadn't got the machinery for building escorts quickly, that's all.'

'Which was part of the muddle, surely,' said Raikes, uncertain whether he ought to argue about it. Lockhart, he knew, had a definite viewpoint on the subject, whereas he himself had only a vague civilian disparagement of the whole conduct of the war, summed up now and again in the words: 'If this thing was run on competitive business lines, the Navy wouldn't last a fortnight.' 'We hadn't got the ships,' he continued, 'because we were caught with our pants down.'

'That's the difference,' said Lockhart, 'between thinking war's a good thing, and thinking it's horrible. We delayed getting ready for it as long as we possibly could, because we thought it was thoroughly bad, and could somehow be avoided. We're only just catching up now.'

'Boat coming alongside, sir,' said the quartermaster, a bored eavesdropper in this conversation. He intercepted, and acknowledged, a covert signal from the coxswain of the approaching motor-boat. 'Captain of *Harmer*, sir.'

'Stand by to pipe,' said Lockhart. *Harmer* was the senior frigate, after *Saltash*, and her captain was a notorious stickler for the utmost limits of naval etiquette. Lockhart could see him now, peering up out of the corner of his eye to confirm that he was going to be properly piped aboard. On the last day of the war, he thought, they might consider piping him aboard with a mouth-organ – playing, preferably, *I'll be glad when you're dead, you rascal, you!* ... He realized that he was thinking on the lines of the cynical, the determinedly amateur Raikes, and he came to an especially stiff salute as the captain of *Harmer* started to climb on board. The latter might have a weakness, amounting almost to fetishism, for the ceremonial aspect of command, but he ran a good ship at the same time; and that, in war, excused nearly everything, from bad temper to sodomy.

Something like the same thought presently struck Ericson, as he sat at the head of the wardroom table and surveyed his assembled captains. These were the sort of men he wanted: two of them, he knew for certain, drank far more than they ought to, one was invariably unpleasant to his officers – but their methods got results, their ships *worked* ... There were seven of them, ranging from the captain of *Harmer*, an old lieutenant-commander nearer sixty than fifty, to the young, the positively baby-faced two-ringer in charge of *Petal*, the junior corvette. But in spite of a

wide variety in age, in looks, in accent and upbringing, they all had the
same aura of responsibility, the same air of knowing what it was all
about: their faces – the lined, over-accented faces of men who had often
been exhausted in the past and would often be so again – their faces all
bore, in a greater or lesser degree, the harsh stamp of command in war.

Perhaps I look like that myself, thought Ericson; and indeed he had
only to recall the face that met him in his shaving-mirror every morning
to be damned certain that he did ... But the hard lines had been hardly
earned, the look of undue and continued tension was excusable. He
himself, with the men round the table, made up a handful of the
principals in a private fight which all the participants knew, perforce, in
exhaustive detail. They were men who had become dedicated to a single
theme of war, like the Eighth Army men in the desert who had slept for
years under the same stars, grown to love the same comrades, and fought
two and three and four times over the same stretch of arid, precarious
coast-line. Like these desert fighters, the men of the Atlantic had become
remarkably expert, astonishingly specialist, with no eyes for any theatre
of war except their own. For them, even the cleansing of that other
disputed ocean, the Mediterranean, was a different sort of job from this
one; it was being carried out by another group of sailors who, though
brothers, had no connection with their own single-emblem firm. *Their*
firm was the Atlantic, and their job was the unspectacular, year-to-year
passing of ships to and fro between the New World and the Old: an
aspect of war that was hardly war at all, but more like a rescue operation
on an enormous scale – rescue of ships in peril, rescue of men in the
water, rescue of troops who needed arms and of aircraft which needed
petrol; rescue of the forty-million garrison of Britain who had to have
food and clothing to keep them alive, as they confronted, year after year,
the hostile coast of Europe.

When the newspapers called it 'the life-line', for once the newspapers
were right; and the men who had tended that life-line for nearly four
years, who had watched it being almost throttled and at last saw it
easing, included, as of right, the men who now sat round the table in the
wardroom of *Saltash* – men who were hopeful and cynical at the same
time, tired but not too tired, ready for surprises and wielding counter-
surprises of their own.

On the table before them were the tools of their trade: the convoy lists,
the sailing orders, the charts, signal-codes, lists of R/T call-signs,
screening diagrams, schemes of search, tables of fuel endurance. In this
self-contained circle, these were as familiar as the alphabet or the sound
of their own ship's bell; for months and years on end, these things had
been the interior decoration of their lives, the frieze that ran round the
inside of the head ... Ericson looked down at the list of his ships: it read
like a banner whose staff was clasped in his own hands:

'*Saltash, Harmer, Streamer, Vista, Rockery, Rose Arbour, Pergola*, and *Petal.*'

But was the staff truly and firmly in his hands? Reading the list, knowing what it meant in terms of effort and effectiveness, he was conscious, as he had been on the tactical course at Liverpool, of a certain inadequacy. There had been an undeniable break in his training, a break which the men round him had not suffered: no one else at the table had been stuck on shore for four months, no one else had had a chance to become rusty, no one else (though this was a private whisper) came fresh from losing his ship and nearly all his men ... But that was something which was *not* to show. He cleared his throat.

'You've all got the screening diagram in front of you,' he began formally. 'You see how the escort is to be stationed, on the outward journey at least: two frigates in front of the convoy – that's myself and *Harmer*: two corvettes on either side – *Vista* and *Pergola* to starboard, *Rockery* and *Rose Arbour* to port. The third frigate, *Streamer*, is in position K, and the other corvette, *Petal*, is astern of the whole outfit.'

'Tail-end Charlie, as usual,' said the captain of *Petal*, a young man entirely undaunted by his lack of seniority. 'One day I'm going to find out what the *bows* of a merchant-ship look like.'

'You'd better ask *Rockery* about that,' remarked the captain of *Harmer* caustically, and there was a general laugh round the table. A few weeks previously, *Rockery* had been squarely rammed by a straggling merchant-man whom she was trying to chivvy into greater activity, wrapping herself round the bows of the bigger ship and remaining there for some hours, as neatly centred and as prominent as a handle-bar moustache: she had only just come out of the repair-dock after the encounter.

'It wasn't my fault,' said the captain of *Rockery* rebelliously. He had the air of a man who had been repeating the phrase, at very short intervals, for a very long time, and had still to make his convert. 'She came straight at me, and I couldn't dodge.'

'Sounds like a girl in Piccadilly,' said the captain of *Petal*.

'The result was the same, too,' said *Streamer*'s captain, the one whom Ericson had earlier recalled as being unpleasant to his officers. 'He had to go into dock for repairs.'

There was another laugh round the table, a further loosening of the atmosphere of purpose which had been present at the beginning. Now just a minute, thought Ericson to himself: this is all very well, but it isn't to be this sort of meeting and I'm not going to run it like this at all: here is where we end the chatter, here is where I take a good sharp pull ... He rapped on the table suddenly.

'That's enough gossip for today,' he said, as coldly as he could. 'I want to get through this as quickly as possible, because I'm sure you all have as much to do in your own ships as I have in mine.' Disregarding the swift chilling of the atmosphere, meeting no one's eye, he continued:

'We're going all the way across this time, to St John's, Newfoundland: there'll be the usual procedure for oiling at sea – that is, you will make a "fuel remaining" signal each morning, and I will choose the time for refuelling, and the order in which you're to come alongside the tanker.' I'm laying this on a bit thick, he thought suddenly, but it's their own fault for chattering like a lot of bloody women ... He looked up, to find the captain of *Harmer* staring at him with an expression of active dislike; and after a moment the latter said:

'So far, we've always made our own decisions about oiling.'

There was a silence, while the others waited for his answer: it was clear that none of them had liked his exercise of discipline, the first essay in the strict control of his group, and were ready, if not to defy him, at least to nibble at his authority in any way they could. It was not a sulky or a disgruntled reaction, it was just that they were all conscious of knowing their jobs just as well as Ericson did – otherwise they would not have achieved their commands – and they resented any hint to the contrary. All right, thought Ericson instantly: if that's the way you want it, I'll be tough with you – the group is mine, and if it makes any mistakes, the blame is mine as well ... He suddenly put up one hand, and touched lightly the three broad rings on his other sleeve: he saw the eyes of everyone at the table follow the gesture, which could not have been clearer, or, indeed, more offensively pointed. Then he looked directly at *Harmer*, and said, in a voice he hardly recognized and with an entirely novel feeling of challenge:

'Then that is one of the things I want to change.'

The sentence, undisputed, set the tone for the rest of the session, and, though he had really had no intention of making so crude a declaration of authority, Ericson did not try to improve on it. Instead, he dealt brusquely with all he had to deal with: the signal routine, the procedure in case of attack, the half-dozen different points which had to be settled at the start of every convoy. No one at the table said anything, except to agree with him; it was as if they had decided to leave things where they were, to suspend judgement and see how the new scheme of close control worked out. But they gave no ground in the way of good humour, either; when, at the end, Ericson relaxed his formal manner and said: 'I'll see you all later, then – probably in some frightful hotel at St John's,' no one smiled or tried to meet him in any way. They too were clearly saying to themselves: if you want to be a bastard, go ahead and see how it works. ...

When they had gone, and he surveyed the empty wardroom, he had a moment of doubt as to how he had handled the meeting. He began to wonder why he had behaved like that – and then, consciously, he stopped himself wondering, and stood up, and gathered his papers together. All that he wanted, all that the situation at sea demanded, was an efficient, tightly-organized escort group: if he became unpopular in the process of getting it, it did not matter in the least.

· · ·

They sailed on the last day of April, under a ragged sky which soon clouded over to form a lowering barrier to the westward; and that first convoy – free of attack, but rough and slow and tiring – was the start of a four-months' routine, all spent on the run to and from St John's, Newfoundland. Neither Ericson nor Lockhart had ever been there before, though most of the other ships had: it was an area continually menaced by fog, and occasionally – if they were routed far northwards – by the threat of ice, and the Newfoundland coastline, with its black crags endlessly battered by the shock and surge of the Western Atlantic, was forbidding in the extreme. The entrance to St John's was a difficult one, not much more than a hole in the rocks, a narrow passage between tall cliffs with a strong tide sluicing past on the seaward side: the approach had to be at speed, and speed, with a few yards to spare on either side of the ship as she threaded her way through the gap, added a hair-raising risk to normal navigation. Ericson had never heard of a ship piling up in the narrows, in spite of the scores that went in and out every week, and certainly *Saltash* never came to any harm; but the ordeal of the entrance waited for him at the end of each trip westwards, and again when they left St John's homeward bound – a recurrent hazard, a sting in the tail of every convoy which might one day find its mark.

Once inside the landlocked harbour they were snug enough, though St John's had little to give in the way of material comfort. It had the air of being the last outpost of civilization in a wild continent: the quays were crowded with tough, salty fishing-schooners, the streets were steep and narrow, and, though it was late spring, only just free of snow: the townsfolk still trudged round in snow-boots and jerkins, fur caps and lumber-jack's shirts. In nearly every ship window was a placard advertising that the wares were 'just landed' or 'just unpacked' – frontier-phrases which were still appropriate here: many of the buildings and houses had a makeshift, impermanent air, as if it were even now uncertain whether the inhabitants could cling to the small haven which they had wrested from nature. Moving against this crude backcloth, the men in naval uniform from the British and Canadian escorts which thronged the harbour had a curious overdressed look about them, an insistence on formality which the natives were surely entitled to laugh at ... There was really nothing to do in St John's except to go ship-visiting and wait for the return journey: it was no more than a pause, in rough and simple terms, before making the outward passage of the narrows and rounding up the convoy again for its three-thousand-mile gauntlet, with the enemy ahead preparing new snares, brewing new poisons for their ruin.

For Ericson, not only the harbour entrance was difficult and trying.

Falling into the old routine, getting geared up again to the heavy
rhythm of sea-going in war, would have been hard enough in any case,
after so long ashore and with the imprint of *Compass Rose* so fresh and
cruel upon the memory: but for him it was complicated by a dozen new
tasks, a dozen additional items which went with the job of Senior Officer
Escort. He had to handle his group at sea, he had to supervise them
when they were docked: he had to keep an eye on the commodore,
on the moon, on stragglers and ships out of station, on U-
boat signals, on the fuel position, on the routing of the different
components of the convoy: he had also to continue nagging at his ships in
harbour, where the emptying of the dust-bins by the guard-corvette
seemed just as important to higher authority as the posting of *Streamer* to
the danger side of the convoy, whenever they were on passage.

It meant there was something to think about all the time, it meant
that he could never relax his grip; and the tactical side of it, when they
were in convoy, put the whole concept of escort into a higher category
altogether. One ship – a big, new ship, still at the exploratory stage –
would have been sufficient responsibility already: but now he had eight
of them, to be handled as a single weapon, a single shield for what he had
to guard: it meant that he must carry in his brain, not the manageable
plan of his own command, but another bigger picture altogether – a
picture with eight arms, eight different possibilities, eight assorted points
of strength or weakness. All of them must be considered and remembered, none must be wasted or ignored.

Each day and night of each trip could bring its own problems, and no
problem could ever be left to solve itself. If there were a suspicious
Radar-contact to be investigated, for example, he might detach *Streamer*,
the third frigate, which was usually given these roving commissions.
Detaching *Streamer* meant putting one of the corvettes in her place –
Pergola for choice, the best of the five. That made a gap on the port side,
and the port side was the moonless side, the point of danger. It must be
filled immediately: *Petal* must come up from astern. But that left the
straggling merchantman, which *Petal* had been shepherding, without
any protection. Was that to be accepted? Or should he reduce the
convoy-speed, to let the straggler catch up? And supposing there was a
threat of attack, should he bring *Streamer* back again to the close screen –
or was she doing more useful work, possibly intercepting another U-boat
before it was in touch with the convoy? But suppose *Streamer*'s contact
were an independent merchant-ship in difficulties: the job might delay
her for two or three days: should he then tell her to proceed independently, knowing that she might run short of fuel and would need to
rendezvous with the tanker which travelled with them? Could he spare
her from the screen, in any case? Was it worth leaving his own station,
now at this moment, to investigate a woolly Asdic-contact which had just

been reported ahead? If it were a U-boat, and if it attacked, and if it scored a hit, there might be survivors: could a corvette be spared to pick them up? If so, which wing of the convoy was it safer to weaken? And was that a star-shell, low on the horizon to starboard? And if so, was it from *Streamer*? And if so, did she need help? And if so, who was to give it?

Sometimes the questions seemed to come like a storm of insects, pricking and stinging him from a dozen different directions at once. But they had to be handled on this personal plane: there had to be one co-ordinating brain, no matter how overloaded it became, and one authoritative voice, even though it might have to speak swiftly and continuously for hours on end. Now, in retrospect, Ericson forgave *Viperous* every complaint or query, every testy signal, every bit of interference that *Compass Rose* had ever suffered from her: he forgave, and he copied the pattern thankfully. For if complete control had to be exercised, it could only be done on this basis of the all-seeing eye, the voice of Jove from the clouds, the thunder-clap that allowed no back answer. There was no room for hurt feelings: in fact, there was little room for feelings of any sort.

It was a regime he found himself applying within his own group; nothing else would serve, whether the rest of them liked it or not. He was aware that he was still unpopular with the other captains, or, at least, regarded warily as a man likely to stick a surprise oar in, any time of the day or night. It did not matter: it was a small price to pay for efficiency and confidence. If the relationship, within the group, was business-like and nothing more, at least it was effective, and it was showing results.

That, at least, was obvious to them all. *Saltash* was now becoming the nucleus of a strong team which, welded together gradually and exercised to the point of exhaustion, was achieving a solid sort of partnership, an improving standard. Fewer mistakes were made, fewer foolish signals sent, less time wasted. It had tangible successes to its credit, too. In May, *Harmer* shot down a reconnaissance aircraft over the Clyde Estuary: a month later, two of the corvettes, *Vista* and *Rose Arbour*, shared a U-boat between them, a quick mid-ocean kill that may have surprised both sides. It was good to chalk up this official evidence of something they all knew – that the group was an effective force, and that all the effort and the patience did not go to waste.

Other groups were doing as well, some of them better: for that was the sort of place the Atlantic was becoming, towards the turn of that crucial year. The new ships were proving themselves, the new weapons were flattering their designers; the small aircraft-carriers which were now available for many convoys were playing a steady part in spotting U-boats before they became actively dangerous. And in August of that year came a piece of news which stirred a thousand hearts, afloat and ashore; for during that month, more U-boats were destroyed than merchant-ships were sunk. For the first time in the war, the astonishing balance was struck.

It was heartening, it was wonderful – but perhaps, on reflection, it was no more than was to be expected. If it *didn't* happen at some point, if the two lines on the graph *didn't* cross, that was the time to start worrying ... For now they were beginning to be cool in killing, now nothing surprised them: winning as well as losing, they were ready to take it in their stride. In Ericson's group, as with the rest of the Clyde Escort Force, and the Liverpool contingent, and the strange fellows who sometimes came round from Rosyth on the east coast, the Atlantic had become a profession; if the Royal Navy were rising to the top of it, that was hardly a matter for comment – it would really have been extremely odd if anything else had happened.

Aboard *Saltash*, when they weighed anchor at the start of a fresh convoy, and set off down river, with the rest of the group tailing along behind them at the regulation five cables' distance – aboard *Saltash*, the gramophone which was connected to the loud-speakers on the upper deck always played the same tune. The tune was that jaunty trifle, *We're Off to See the Wizard, the Wonderful Wizard of Oz.* Lockhart had initiated its playing, as something between a joke and a tonic – but somehow the tune was serious, and the words were true. It was as if they were really going off to search a strange sea-lair, to seek once more a passage of arms with a cunning enemy who sometimes used magic ... But it was their own lair as well, and their own familiar wizard, no longer veiled, no longer fearful: now they knew him, and all about him, from the tip of his watery whiskers to the cold green gleam in his eye.

. . .

'Starboard ten.'
'Starboard ten, sir.'
'Steer one-three-five.'
'Steer one-three-five, sir.'
Saltash came round slowly in the gloom, preparing for the long leg across the front of the convoy. Lockhart, watching the dim compass-card edging away to the left, tried to work out the diameter of their turning-circle, and then gave up the calculation. Must be about a thousand yards ... A mile astern of them, he could just see the leading ship of the port column – or rather, he could see a vague smudge, darker than the grey night, and a thin white bow-wave that occasionally caught the moon: in between them, *Saltash*'s phosphorescent wake boiled and spread and faded to nothing in the calm darkness.

Within a minute or so the leader of the next column came into view on their quarter, and then the next, and the next, a whole rank of shadows, admirably disciplined and stationed; as it ploughed towards the homeward horizon, escaping notice for the fifteenth night in succession, the whole convoy was on its best behaviour. The look-out called: 'Ship fine on the starboard bow, sir!' but he called softly, for the ship was *Harmer*, keeping her distance on a parallel zigzag, and the look-out knew it, and Lockhart knew it as well. Then the helmsman said: 'Course – one-three-five, sir.' Then there was silence again, and the crisp threshing of their bow-wave, and the ghostly shadows of a score of ships slipping past under their lee, as they made their starboard leg across the van, their precise act of guardianship. Smoothly, steadily, like these shadows, the summer night with the convoy slid by.

Presently Lockhart became aware that Ericson had come up to the bridge and was standing some paces behind him, accustoming his eyes to the darkness. As usual, he waited a few moments, while the Captain glanced up at the sky, and bent to the compass-bowl, and stared at the nearest ships, and raised his glasses and looked at *Harmer*; then Lockhart turned, and said: 'Good morning, sir.'

'Morning, Number One.' The gruff voice, the phrase a thousand times used, were as much a part of Lockhart's watch as the sound of that bow-wave breaking below them. Ericson moved up to his side, leaning over the front of the bridge, and stared down at the fo'c'sle, and the seven attendant shadows which were the figures of B-gun's crew.

'Cocoa, sir? It's just been made.'

'Thanks.' Ericson took the cup from the bridge-messenger, and sipped it cautiously. 'What's the time?'

'About half past four, sir. Did you sleep?'

'A little ... Anything I haven't seen in the signals?'

'A routine one about a change of ciphers. And *Petal* came through on R/T. One of the ships was showing a stern light.'

Ericson lowered his cup, and Lockhart felt rather than saw that he had stiffened to attention.

'When was this?' he asked curtly.

'Just after I came on watch, sir. *Petal* hailed them, and they switched it out.'

'Why didn't you tell me?' The tone, infinitely cold, was no longer a novelty to anyone on board.

Lockhart frowned in the darkness. 'It solved itself, sir. I didn't want to wake you for nothing.'

'You know my standing orders, Number One.'

'I'm sorry, sir.'

With anyone else, Lockhart knew, Ericson would have already been in a rage: even now, the margin between control and anger was paper-thin. 'Anything,' said Ericson, with extraordinary force, '*anything* that happens at sea – to an escort, to a ship in convoy, to this ship – is to be reported to me straight away. You understand that perfectly well.'

'Yes, sir,' said Lockhart formally, and waited. He knew that there would be two more sentences, in the same raw tone of reproof, and that Ericson would then let it go. It was not that he was becoming set in any offensive mould; but he really did feel that he should be told of every conceivable development, no matter how trivial, and the idea that Lockhart might try to stand between him and petty interruptions – and was, indeed, perfectly capable of doing so on many occasions – was still unacceptable, and still provoked him.

The taut shadow at Lockhart's side spoke again. 'If anything goes wrong, it is my responsibility.'

'Yes, sir.'

'And I expect you, as First Lieutenant, to set an example to the other officers.'

'Yes, sir.'

There will be a pause now, thought Lockhart, and then he will relax; and after a bite he will remember that he often does trust me to an extraordinary degree, and he will want to bring all this back to normal again, and he will do so – though perhaps obliquely. The Captain would never apologize, Lockhart knew, because there was no warrant for it. He *was* allowed to make any rules he liked, in the interests of the ship or the group; the order that he was always be called, if they sighted as much as a single smudge of smoke thirty miles away, was a perfectly legitimate one, and he was entitled to give it, and to see that it was obeyed. But behind all this there were other things, threads of a different weaving that were just as strong – the past years, the imponderables of their friendship, *Compass Rose*, the two rafts . . . Ericson set down his cup, and straightened up again, and looking ahead towards the horizon said:

'It's getting to be a different kind of war, now.'

Lockhart smiled to himself, sensing the first proffering of the olive-branch, though he could not yet accurately divine the form that it would take. But all that it was proper for him to say was:

'In what way do you mean, sir?'

Ericson gestured vaguely, as a man groping towards an idea whose outline was still blurred.

'It's so much less personal than it was at the beginning,' he said slowly. 'There doesn't seem to be any room for – for individual people any more.'

'I suppose not, sir.'

'At the beginning there was time for all sorts of things – making allowances for people, and joking, and treating people like sensitive human beings, and wondering whether they were happy, and whether they – they liked you or not.' Ericson drew in his breath, as if his ideas, cloaked by darkness, were running away with him. 'But now, now the war doesn't seem to be a matter of men any more, it's just weapons and toughness. There's no margin for humanity left – humanity takes up too much room, it gets in the way of things.'

'Yes, sir.'

'It used to be a family sort of job, this. Christian names, lots of parties, weekends off if your wife could get up to see you –' he gestured – 'all that sort of thing. People could still afford to be people – in fact, they felt offended if you didn't allow them to be. That was specially true of a small ship, like *Compass Rose*. It was a very cheerful sort of wardroom we had there, wasn't it? From time to time it was serious, but mostly it wasn't, it was just a lot of friends doing the best they could with the job, and shrugging their shoulders if it went wrong, and laughing it off altogether. It was friendly – human – but it's certainly finished now. It finished with *Compass Rose*, in fact.'

'Port ten,' said Lockhart.

'Port ten, sir.'

'Steer oh-six-five.'

'Steer oh-six-five, sir.'

Ericson waited, while *Saltash* came round in a wide circle, and settled down on her new course. Then:

'I don't mean that *Compass Rose* was a bad sort of ship, or that that was a bad way to fight the war, at that stage. Far from it. I just meant that it's out of date now. The war has squeezed out everything except the essentials. You can't make any allowances now, you can't forgive a mistake. The price may be too high.'

'Yes, sir,' said Lockhart.

'Do you remember,' said the Captain reflectively, 'that kid Gregg – able-seaman – whose wife was playing him up, and who broke ship and went home to try to fix things up? That's almost two years ago now, and two years ago I could afford to let him off with a hell of a lecture, and a caution.' He shook his head in the darkness. 'Not now, by God! If Gregg came up before me now, I wouldn't listen to any of that damned rigmarole about his wife. I'd give him three months in prison for desertion, and take very good care that he stayed an able-seaman for the rest of the war. We can't afford wives and domestic trouble and sympathetic understanding any more. That sort of thing is finished with.'

'Yes, sir.'

'It's just the way the war has gone, that's all. It's too serious now for anything except a hundred-per-cent effort.' He thought for a moment. 'A hundred-per-cent toughness, too. I remember when we sank that U-boat, and I had the German captain in my cabin. He was rude to me – damned insolent, in fact – and I remember thinking that if I got just a little bit angrier, I'd probably pull a gun and shoot him.' He drew a long breath again. 'If that happened now, I wouldn't wait, I wouldn't count ten and think it over. This time I'd plug him and chuck him overboard afterwards – and everyone else who was inclined to argue the toss about it.'

'Yes, sir.'

'I know that that isn't the sort of thing we're fighting for – but we've got to win before we can pick or choose about moral issues. Get this thing over, and I'll be as sweet as you like to anyone, whether it's a German captain, or Able-Seaman Gregg, or' – Lockhart felt him smiling as he came at last to the point – 'or you.'

'I'll remember that, sir.'

'I suppose you think, Number One, that this is all wrong, and that you should never allow yourself to be deteriorated by war.'

'Yes, sir.'

'But you've become dedicated to it yourself, surely? You believe in that hundred-per-cent idea, don't you? No room for mistakes, no room for mercy – no room for love or gentleness, either.'

'Yes, I suppose so … … Difficult, isn't it?'

Saltash ploughed on, and the convoy with her, creeping steadily across the dark sea. Ahead of them, on the far eastern horizon, it was already lighter, already a whole night and a quarter day nearer home. Home, thought Lockhart. The Clyde again, the anchorage, calm and rest. Julie Hallam.

CHAPTER 5

'Julie Hallam,' said Lockhart distantly, 'I thought you were high up in the Wrens, I thought you were the strictest Wren in the world.'

'So I am,' said Julie. 'I terrorize all the others. Tell me more.'

'Then what about the feet, the toes …' He pointed. 'What could be less official, less strict? How can you justify that sort of thing?'

Julie glanced over the side of the dinghy, where her bare toes trailed in the gently-passing water. She raised one foot, and the shining drops, catching the sunlight, chased each other down her leg and fell in-board. She looked up at him again.

'Do I have to justify?' Her voice was slow, rather dreamy, as though, at this happy moment, she was hardly listening to what she was saying, and trusted him not to take advantage of it. 'What regulation am I breaking?'

He waved his hand vaguely, releasing the tiller for a moment to do so. The small boat yawed, and he pulled it back on its course again. 'Oh – good order and naval discipline generally. You're a Wren – fully naval, subject to the Articles of War, and they lay it down clearly that you must *not* dabble your toes in the water, while in any ship under my command.'

The foot splashed over the side again, and the boat rocked momentarily. 'You're rather sweet,' she said, 'when you're talking nonsense . . . On the contrary, I've suspended all the Articles of War for at least five hours. I'm on a picnic, far out of reach of the naval tentacles. I'm in very shabby slacks. My hair is down – literally. Dabbling my toes fits in perfectly with all that. Nelson would approve.'

He looked at her. 'Nelson would not approve. But your hair is very pretty that way.'

It was true. As he looked at her, half sitting and half lying on the middle thwart of the dinghy, he was deeply conscious that she had foregone nothing by assuming a holiday air. Enjoying his leisurely scrutiny, he presently decided that it was the shape of her face which was the continuing focus of her loveliness: the dark hair down nearly to her shoulders could not detract from its distinction, any more than the slacks and the yellow shirt could alter the rest of her. Rather did they proclaim it louder, as if her beauty were free to say: 'I am available in any version – take your choice!' she was elegant still, without the groomed hair, and wearing washed-out blue denim slacks instead of a tailored skirt: if the elegance were now on a totally different plane, it did not make any difference. Nor could he decide whether, thus relaxed, she was nearer to the natural Julie Hallam, or farther away. It was difficult to decide her true *métier*, and it was not in the least important, when she filled all of them so well. And, beyond all this, to have her exclusive company, at any level, in any circumstances, was still a rapturous surprise, disarming completely the subtleties of preference.

They were picnicking, as she had said by way of excuse: the boat was a borrowed sailing-dinghy, which was taking them, before a light breeze, from Hunter's Quay to the head of Holy Loch. The early September afternoon could not have been lovelier: as sometimes happened in these bleak northern waters, the relenting sun shone down with spring-like fervour, warming the water, bathing the whole estuary of the Clyde in a comforting glow. Their tiny boat ran between brown and purple hills, leaving far astern the busy anchorage, making for the peace and solitude which were promised them at the head of the loch. Lapped in a lazy quiet, they seemed to be deserting the normal world, whose demands they knew too well, for a private realm which they could fashion to their own liking. He was proud to be taking her there – proud, and happy, and something else as well, something gently beckoning which he could not define, and did not want to. The occasion had, he could not help realizing, all the elements of a 'party'; she was a beautiful girl in a boat, they were alone on a picnic, he was already much aware of her as a woman. But like that first time, when he had not kissed her, so now the moment was not necessarily that moment, and need not become so.

What they shared between them – the boat, the ripples that chattered under their prow, the sunshine, the hills – were clearly enough for her, and were thus enough for him.

Presently, breaking the companionable silence, she said:

'About Nelson.'

He smiled, recognizing in her a wayward but questing attention, and in himself a delight to be talking to her, on any subject under the sun, so long as her voice still linked him to her by its lovely clarity.

'About Nelson,' he repeated after her.

She leant back on the thwart, and the drops of water from her leg fell in-board again. 'I should say,' she remarked thoughtfully, 'that he would have liked my hair, whether it was officially approved or not. He would have made any allowances for a woman, surely? Look at Lady Hamilton.'

Lockhart stiffened, in spite of himself, in spite of the moment. 'What about Lady Hamilton?'

Julie was glancing up at the sail, whose shadow had just touched her face as the boat heeled. 'Didn't he come rather near to giving up everything for her – or at least, neglecting a lot of things which were really a great deal more important?'

'Nelson?' Lockhart drew in his breath. 'He would never have done anything of that sort, never in his life.' There was something in his tone which made her turn and look at him, and something in his face which surprised her when she saw it. 'He wouldn't have done so for anyone,' Lockhart repeated. 'He loved three things – the Navy, England, and Lady Hamilton. He loved them all very much – overwhelmingly, sometimes – but he always loved them in that order.'

'Oh ...' Julie smiled, still watching him. 'I only asked ...' But her curiosity continued. 'I didn't know he was a hero of yours. In fact, I didn't know you had such things as heroes.'

He smiled back at her. 'Certainly, I like dogs, too. And football matches, and beer, and life insurance. Every Sunday we put the nippers in the side-car ——'

She held up her hand, rather firmly. 'Just you go back a bit.'

'Yes, ma'am ... He's very much a hero of mine, as a matter of fact – a wonderful seaman, a wonderful leader, a kind man, a brave man, a lover whose mistress was perfectly content to bear his child, in or out of wedlock.' Lockhart, in his turn, looked up at the sail, as if he might find there the words he wanted to use. 'You know, there was a time when he held all England in the palm of his hand, and all Europe too: a single mistake at Trafalgar – the difference between saying "port" and "starboard" – might have been the difference between winning and losing, and could have changed the map of the world – and he knew it, and he was equal to it. He didn't lose sight of that, and he didn't lose sight of the rules he fought by, either.' Lockhart paused. 'If I were to give you the words of his last prayer, would you laugh at me?'

She shook her head. 'Tell.'

' "May the great God whom I worship grant to my country and for the benefit of Europe in general, a great and glorious victory: and may no misconduct in anyone tarnish it; and may humanity after victory be the predominant feature of the British Fleet." '

Now she nodded. 'That really covers everything, doesn't it? Right up to date, too. Were those the last words he wrote?'

'No. As far as I remember, he wrote to Lady Hamilton the last thing of all, just before Trafalgar, when he knew the French fleet was coming out and was going to fight. At least, he started the letter, and then stopped and said that he hoped to be able to finish it after the battle.'

'What was it about?'

'He just sent his love.'

After a moment, Julie said: 'She must have been beautiful.'

He shook his head. 'Not even that. Most people loathed her on sight: she had a lot of enemies – partly jealousy, partly because she was rather too candid and downright, and she was an easy person to sneer at – even her friends agreed that she wasn't attractive to the eye by the time she met Nelson. Undistinguished, fat, rather blowzy.'

'What, then?'

Lockhart shrugged. 'She had something for him. She was the other half of him, emotionally, the person he had to have, to make up for the difficulty and strain of what he was doing. You know, it doesn't really matter what a woman looks like, where a loving relationship is concerned. She's either desirable, or she is not: if she is, her looks and her manners don't matter, and if she isn't, no amount of small talk and smart-alec stuff will make any difference.'

'Pity,' said Julie despondently.

'You should complain ...'

'But if he was so exceptional a person,' she said, 'I wonder why he needed a woman, anyway. People like that are usually entirely self-sufficient.'

'I think it's reasonable,' said Lockhart after a moment. 'He was a complete man – a man of action, a man of imagination, a man capable of love. England provided half of what he needed to fulfil himself, she gave him the other half.'

'And they never overlapped, or got in the way of each other?'

'No. That was the admirable part. He was dedicated to both, and there was room for both.' Then he paused, and frowned. 'I've an idea,' he said after a moment, 'that all this contradicts completely something I've said to you already.'

She nodded, and smiled, and sat up suddenly. 'But I'm certainly not going to remind you, on this lovely day ... Are we nearly there?'

They were nearly there; and presently the boat grounded on the rough shingle beach, and slid forward a few feet, and came gently to rest. As they lowered and stowed the sail, they looked about them at the strange secret world they had reached. They were five miles up the still water of the loch, and almost out of sight of its entrance; they, and the boat, were dwarfed by what lay all round them, but it was a benevolent dwarfing, as if they were held within some capacious natural embrace that would never press too hard on them, never fail to cherish. Behind them was the deserted stretch of water, before them a curved beach, a single pine tree, and a ring of silent hills; the sun was warm on their faces, the whole air enchanted. Their voices when they spoke seemed to fall into deep silence, challenging it for a moment, and then becoming lost for ever.

They slipped over the side of the boat, and paddled ashore. He might have carried her, he thought suddenly, but it did not seem a necessary thing to do: her body which he had never touched, her perfume which he knew only faintly, were not appropriate to the innocent moment they were sharing. But perhaps this thought of his had also reached her, for when they had spread their rugs and unpacked the picnic basket, and settled down side by side, there was an unusual constraint between them. It was the first time that their isolation had been so complete, so unguarded: it was the first time, also, that they had seen each other out of uniform, and the simple clothes they were wearing somehow made it easier for them to think of each other as a man and a woman, bringing nearer to the surface a sensual awareness of their proximity, associating, for the very first time and with the utmost significance, her loveliness, his masculinity.

They talked desultorily, but it had no flow, no ease: they lay silent, enjoying the sun, but it was a restless enjoyment: they looked fleetingly at each other, but the looks were complicated and unreal. At last she frowned, and sat up straight, and said:

'This is quite different from any other time. Why is that?'

He might have guessed that she would thus present the problem for their joint inspection, promptly and candidly ... He said:

'It's being alone, I think. In complete isolation. It hasn't happened to us before.'

'But surely' – she paused, and frowned again – 'why should we be shy, or ill at ease, over that? It's not as if we were babies.'

Babies, he thought – why have I now only one image when she says 'babies' like that? What is happening to us so quickly? – or is it only to me ...? He spoke almost at random:

'Julie, we've met five or six times in the past eight months. Each time we come to know each other a little better, and I think we enjoy it a little more.' She nodded in agreement. 'It's been a process of exploration – very sweet, too. But it's been progressive all the time.'

'So it should be. That's been the best part of it.'

He was becoming shy now, and, he noticed with faint alarm, rather breathless. Surely he should be past that sort of nervousness ... I want her, he thought in confusion, looking at her breast and shoulders under the thin shirt: I knew that I would, but it isn't as simple as that, after all – I want her in so many different ways, apart from the breast, the mouth that promises to be soft. I want her and must have her, on any terms she chooses. But the more closely bound, the better ... He drew an uneven breath.

'It's still progressive,' he said with difficulty, 'but now we've come to the point when – you're so lovely – I am a man ——'

She said: 'Oh!' suddenly, and then: 'I know very well that you are a man.' He was aware of tension in her manner also: she was looking away, she might even have coloured slightly. Presently, she asked: 'Couldn't that be postponed a little longer?'

'It doesn't feel like it.'

'No, it doesn't, does it?'

'You know that I love you.'

She nodded her head. 'Now I do.'

'And you?'

'Wait for a few moments.' She was staring at the water, undecided, troubled as he had never seen her before. But already the air was lighter, the honest day more beautiful, because of what they had said. Now they knew, at least, where the margin of their delight was set.

She was silent for a long time, while the small waves lapped the beach and the sun blessed them; but when she spoke it was in a happier, more confident voice, as if she too were glad that the plain words and thoughts were now before them.

'I wish,' she said, turning towards him, 'that there could be a straightforward "yes" to that question, but it wouldn't be an accurate answer. We share a lot, don't we? – that's been true from the very beginning: we've seen it and we've felt it happening, and parts of it have been lovely.' Her eyes, grave and tender, were now regarding him with every sort of honesty. 'It began during that very first walk home from your party, when we came together at last after having to be apart for the whole evening. Probably we knew that this was the way it would go. You said' – she smiled vividly – ' "the walk made the party", and then we said goodnight.'

'I thought of kissing you, and then I thought not.'

'That was the first thought we shared ... Now we are here, suddenly peaceful in the middle of war: you love and want me, and I ——' She paused, and afterwards her voice was stronger. 'Look,' she said, 'people are always asking me to marry them, or sleep with them.' From her, in that firm and honest tone, it did not sound crude or awkward. 'In a war, in my job, surrounded by lots of people, it's bound to happen: no special merit is attached. Sometimes I think about the proposition, quite seriously, and then there is a false note, or the man is too quick, or the day is too dull, and I walk away from it again.' For some reason, she leant forward at that moment, and touched his bare arm: her soft fingers were immensely comforting, so that the bleak and terrible thoughts of other men making love to her, which had started to devour his brain, melted away on the instant. 'Now there is you,' she went on, 'and you are none of those bad things. There have been no false notes, you have matched my own pace, my own will, and no day with you is dull.'

He covered her hand with his own, and felt it move slightly. He looked up and said: 'As long as we *both* tremble a little, I don't think we need tell anybody about it.'

'Oh, I can tremble for you . . . Look,' she said again, 'with you I am on the edge of love, the very edge. There are things about you I like, things about you I respect, things that I love already, other things that are surprising. This afternoon, we've discovered something else – or almost discovered it.'

As she paused again, he nodded, and said: 'A new thing, but in line with the rest. The senses, the first stirring. It has been sweet.'

'It has been frightening . . . I don't mean that I've been afraid of suddenly looking up and finding you lying on top of me: I mean that it is altogether a new thing, and I have never felt it so strongly before.'

'And with all that?'

'With all that, the edge of love still.'

He got up, crossed the two paces between them on the rugs, and deliberately sat down again, close to her.

'You mean, I spoke too soon?'

'Not quite – it had to be said.' She leant towards him. 'When you are near to me, I *know* it had to be said. But as far as my answer is concerned, perhaps it *is* too soon – perhaps one single meeting too soon.'

'When you are near me,' he said unsteadily, 'I have to say: "May I kiss you?" '

'And I,' she answered, not hesitating, 'have to say: 'Oh yes, the situation certainly covers *that*''.'

Her lips were wonderfully soft, her cheek and hair fragrant, her body as compliant and as ravishing to his senses as he had known it would be. He murmured: 'Julie . . .' between two kisses, and he felt a trembling of her lower lip which might have been nervousness, could have been desire. The sky seemed to turn over as he opened his eyes again, to find her looking at him with a gentle, delighted surprise.

She said: 'You have all the talents.'

Smiling, taking from her the cue for a cooler moment, he asked: 'The edge of love, still?'

She nodded, laughing with him now. 'But the edge is nice, too.' She leant forward, kissed him briefly and assuredly once again, and then said, with infinite composure: 'Were you asking me to marry you?'

He stared at her. 'What else?'

'Kissing you put all sorts of other things into my mind.'

He realized that she had suddenly been made immensely happy, and deeply moved at the same time, and he wanted to match that mood with his own. He said, slowly:

'I was asking you for that, too . . . Of course I want you, in all the ways there are, including being your lover as soon as possible. But marriage seemed the way for us.'

'And dedication? The war?'

'Sweet,' he said – the first endearment between them seemed to constrict his throat – 'I just don't know the answer to that, any more. The war's still there to be fought, and we both still have to fight it. Long ago, it seemed to me that one could only do that by concentrating all the time, and excluding every other distraction. Now that seems – long ago.'

'We'll talk,' she said, watching his face. 'It doesn't matter now. The edge of love,' she murmured. 'How patient are you?'

'With hope, very patient.'

'No hurry for an answer?'

'No hurry in the world.'

'But you said "Lovers as soon as possible".'

'That was because I'd just kissed you. Kissing you means wanting you, on the instant. There were indications that – I don't think there's any polite way of putting this – it seemed to me that you are turning me into a very effective lover, just with two kisses and an arm round my shoulder.'

She smiled faintly, colouring again. 'I felt something like that, too.'

'It's all right for you,' he grumbled. 'No one can tell.'

She laughed. 'I suddenly know you very well. It's a tremendous relief.'

'How lovely,' he said, touching her cheek, 'to have someone who always understands what I'm talking about . . . And now I *really* want a drink.'

. . .

They held hands all the way back. Sometimes he said 'Julie', sometimes he leant over and kissed her: she seemed, on that slow return journey, to be exquisitely tender and near to him, as if they had already become lovers. At the foot of the loch they turned and set course for Hunter's Quay; and there, coming through the boom, a reminder of something which was not yet resolved, was a line of escorts – two frigates, four corvettes – punching the tide as they hurried for home after delivering their convoy. The two of them watched the ships in silence: they passed quite close, and the successive waves of their wash set the little dinghy dancing. When they were past, Julie said:

'You are thinking, "There is *Allendale*'s group", and I am thinking, "There is the war again".'

'We've managed to escape it for a long time.' He pressed her shoulder. 'Never leave me, Julie.'

As if she had not heard him, she said: 'I know where you're going tomorrow. Take care of yourself.'

Surprised, he asked: 'Something special?'

She inclined her head, very slowly. 'It's said to be the coldest journey in the world.' And she said again, her eyes on his face: 'Take care of yourself.'

CHAPTER 6

North Russia ... Chief Petty Officer Barnard, the bearded coxswain of *Saltash*, surveying the shoddy water-front of Murmansk, decided that this place was right in line with most of the other places he had visited during the war – it was not worth the trip. A pale sun, peering like a froggy, myopic eye from the lustreless sky, picked out the length of the wooden quay, and the snow continually trodden to dirty slush, and the jumble of roof-tops that lined the harbour. Murmansk – from this view-point, at least – was simply another harbour, with its equipment a little less efficient, its armed sentries a little more obtrusive, and its air a damned sight colder; and to get there, they had endured everything that the enemy had to offer in the way of attack, and had lost, in the process, a dozen ships, three escorts, and upwards of twenty planes from their carriers. They had made, in fact, an expensive, tiring, and extremely noisy excursion, and it was to be hoped that the Russians were duly grateful for the effort.

Barnard stirred inside his thick hairy duffle-coat, and beat his gloved hands together, and stamped his feet on the iron deck. Murmansk was unspeakably cold – he had never been more glad of his beard – but then, the whole of the trip had been like Murmansk in that respect, inflicting on them a seeping, searing sort of cold which found its way everywhere. The convoy, 'evasively routed' as usual, had coasted past the thick pack-ice round Bear Island and North Cape: in these Arctic wastes, there was no night, no real darkness at all, and over them, all the time, was the same cold grey light, falling on a flat sea also cold and grey. *Saltash*, and her fellow-escorts, and the convoy, might have been a selection of scale-models, placed, for further effect, on a false glass ocean decorated with falling snow. All the drama had come from the enemy, and it had come thick and fast, in every imaginable and vicious form.

Presumably these convoys had to go to Russia, thought Barnard: but by God, the price was a stinger! Jerry had tried everything on this trip, and it had paid him a classy sort of dividend. They'd had U-boats, they'd had torpedo-bombers and dive-bombers, they'd had a destroyer-sortie from one of the Norwegian fiords, they'd had swarms of E-boats – and it was damned cheek *them* joining in the Battle of the Atlantic. At one time there had even been a threat that the *Scharnhorst* would come out of hiding and add to the fun. Of course, there had been bags of escorts round the convoy – three groups altogether, with *Saltash* in charge of the lot. The skipper must have had something to carry in his head, all right ... And there had been a big-ship escort as well, three cruisers and a battleship, mooching about to the north of them, ready for trouble. But imagine the *Scharnhorst*, with four turrets of fourteen-inch guns, getting in among the merchant-ships before their own battleship could come within range. The German destroyers had been quite bad enough, when it came to ships being out-gunned by other ships.

Perhaps, thought Barnard, the destroyers had been worst of all. They'd come roaring down from the north-eastwards, three of them in line ahead, big as bloody cruisers, and then turned outwards, and began to pour hell into the ships nearest to them. One of the corvettes had bought it straight away – she'd steamed straight towards the leading destroyer, plucky little bastard, and been blown out of the water for her trouble, before she even got within range. There was nothing that corvettes could do about destroyers, and nothing much that frigates could do either – though *Saltash* had come streaking across to join in, with everyone on board soiling their pants on the way. Destroyers – six-inch guns ... Luckily the skipper must have sent a signal straightaway, as soon as the destroyers were sighted, because before anything else could happen, two of the cruisers had popped up over the horizon, and the destroyers had mucked off, without waiting to be told. They'd done enough damage, anyway – a corvette sunk, and three merchant-ships set on fire; but it might have been a lot worse, and they didn't come back for more, on that or any other day.

Perhaps, thought Barnard, the destroyers weren't as bad as the torpedo-bombers: they were both new weapons to *Saltash*, as well as to everyone else, but the bombers came over every day, for eleven days at a stretch, and in the end it got you down. Sometimes it was ordinary bombing, with the planes high up, and nothing much happening until the bombs arrived and the whole sea jumped, and the ships went up in smoke; sometimes it was dive-bombing, and the planes came screaming down, pointing straight at you, and flattening out at the very last moment; but usually it was torpedoes. The torpedo-planes were the hardest of all to spot; they came in low over the water, little specks of things hard to see in the grey light: then they started weaving, so that you couldn't keep them in the gun-sights, and then they dropped their torpedoes, almost within touching distance, so that there was no time to dodge, and then they got to hell out of it, while you were waiting for the bang ... *Saltash* had shot one of them down with her two-pounder, but one plane hardly made a dent; because the torpedo-attack went on for eleven days, and it happened four times a day – just as quickly as the planes could nip back to Norway and re-fuel – and they came over in droves from every bloody angle in the compass, twelve of them, twenty of them at a time, dropping their fish all round the convoy so they were bound to hit something. And when the ships were hit, and went down, there wasn't much chance for the poor sods on board, because of the cold.

Perhaps, thought Barnard, the cold was worse than the destroyers and the torpedo-bombers put together. The cold was everywhere, inside the ship as well as out: you *couldn't* get warm, not if you stretched yourself out on top of the galley stove. They must have shovelled tons of snow off the upper deck: they must have thawed out the guns a dozen times, using a steam hose that damned nearly got frozen up itself. Near to the ice, when *Saltash* was level with North Cape, and a bit of wind got up, the cold was like a scraper running over your raw face. One of the seamen, who'd taken off his gauntlets to open an ammunition locker, had torn off the whole of the skin of one palm and left it stuck to the locker like half a bloody glove, with him staring at it as if it was something hanging up in a shop. But that wasn't as bad as what happened to the poor bastards that got dropped into the drink.

There, you couldn't last more than a few minutes – the cold got you as soon as the water touched your body. There was one time that Barnard remembered specially, because it topped the level for the whole trip. One of the Seafires from a carrier, trying to intercept some high-level bombing, had got into trouble, and the pilot had to bale out ahead of the convoy. While the parachute was still in the air, *Saltash* had her whaler down and rowing towards the spot where he was going to fall – about a mile away. But even a mile had been too far, in that sort of weather. The pilot had waved when he landed in the water, and the coxswain of the whaler had waved back: it took them not more than three minutes to get to him, but in those three minutes he was stone-cold dead – frozen as stiff as a bloody plank. That was how you could die, up in these parts – in three minutes, between waving and rescue, between a smile and a fixed-for-ever grin.

Barnard, lost in his not-too-happy dream, became aware of a

movement by his side, and found that he had been joined at the rail by Lieutenant Allingham, the gunnery officer. The two were good friends, and they smiled at each other, and then without a word ranged themselves side by side, leaning over the taut wire rail of the fo'c'sle, staring down at the quay. Below them, a Russian sentry, bristling with weapons, came to a halt at the end of his beat, turned, and met their gaze unblinkingly, his hand on the butt of his revolver – an armed man in an ambiguous trance, a man standing stock-still at the tip of a fabulous continent, tethered to the end of his tracks in the snow ... They both watched him for a moment: then Allingham sighed, and straightened up a little, and said:

'Looking at Russia, Coxswain?'

Barnard nodded. 'That's just about it, sir. And Russia's looking at me, as usual.' He indicated the armed sentry, who still eyed them fixedly from under his strange steel helmet, as if daring them to come ashore, or to move *Saltash* one inch nearer the fatherland. Barnard, bored with that stare, waved to the man, who fingered his rifle instead of answering. 'Cheer up, *tovarich!*' called out Barnard, not to be rebuffed. The man below them looked to the right, then to the left, then jerked his head up again. 'Churchill!' he answered, conspiratorially. But he still did not smile.

'Churchill!' repeated Barnard, with great readiness. But then he shook his head. 'They're a queer lot, sir. Can't get on with them at all. Some of the lads have had rows already, over at the canteen. They just don't want to know ...'

'It's nothing like what I thought it would be,' said Allingham non-committally. He too had developed some strong views on Russia during the past few days, but the need for Allied solidarity prominently featured in confidential directives from the Admiralty, had to be borne in mind. 'You can't really expect them to be the same as us, though.'

Barnard nodded. 'Long way from home ... Specially from your home, sir.'

'I'll say ... Think of coming all this way, just to get a lot of dirty looks and an air-raid every morning and evening.'

'*And* what we ran into on the way here.' Barnard drew in his breath sharply. 'I reckon the skipper must be just about clapped out.'

'I could have slept for a week. In fact, if it weren't for these bloody air-raids all the time, that's just what I'd be doing.'

'I hope we don't have to do too many of these trips.' The sentry frowned up at them, as if he had been able to tune in to this disparaging thought. 'Do you honestly think they're worth it, sir?'

'I reckon so. The Russians need the material, and they're putting up the hell of a fight, you know. It's the only country, so far, where the Germans are really taking a knock.' Allingham waved his arm round, embracing the trodden slush of the quay, the mean ice-bound town, the single man watchful in the snow. 'It's difficult to realize it, looking at this little scrap-heap. But down there' – he pointed vaguely southwards – 'all sorts of big things are going on. If the Russians can stage a few more Stalingrads, and if we can help them via the back door here, then the war will start to peter out. That's worth a few trips like this one.'

'As long as they realize what these convoys have to go through to get here. I wonder what it is makes them so cagey.' He pointed once more the snow-bound sentry. 'Look at that chap. He either hates our guts, or he's scared stiff of being caught fraternizing. And they've all been like that. Whichever way you look at it, it's not much of a welcome.'

'Perhaps it's because they *are* fighting so hard, and what we've done so far doesn't show on the map. The only thing they want to hear is that we've started our second front, and until they read about that in the newspapers, they're inclined to think we're loafing.'

'But still ...' Barnard frowned. 'They're a queer lot, sir,' he repeated. 'Remember how we wanted to shift that wire, when we first came alongside? They wouldn't even let us land a couple of seamen, before one of their officers had been aboard to check up. Bloody cheek, considering the sort of trip we'd made to get here.'

Allingham nodded, in spite of himself. 'Yeah, it's queer ... If these chaps landed up in Sydney, we wouldn't exactly kiss them, but at least we'd say hello, and ask them along for a drink.'

'What do they drink in Sydney, then?'

'Beer, and plenty of it.'

'Tried the vodka yet, sir?'

'Yes – anything once. Perhaps it's no wonder these chaps are so bad-tempered.'

The air-raid sirens sounded, for the third time since daylight. *Saltash's* own alarm-bells followed, a moment later, and the ship sprang to life, forfeiting, as on so many other days, her afternoon siesta. The man on the quay retreated to a small sand-bagged sentry-box, a few yards away, but he continued to watch them warily, alert for sabotage or the display of secret weapons. Near to, some guns started firing, and from the grey lowering sky came the steady beat of aircraft engines. As usual, they would have to fight an extra round with the enemy, when they should have been in shelter and at peace.

'Murmansk!' said Allingham disgustedly. 'No sleep on the way up, and no sleep when we get here. The sooner we start back, the better I'll like it.'

'But we can't do it twice without a rest in the middle,' said Barnard, grinning.

'Coxswain,' said Allingham, completing the joke, 'that's what all the girls say ...' Then, the edge of laughter still in his voice, he began to marshall his guns' crews and bring them to readiness, while the man on the quay watched and listened to these antics from another world, and guarded closely his own.

. . .

Lockhart had already been in collision a number of times with the Russian interpreter, a small fiery individual who seemed to regard every request for stores or facilities as yet another example of the top-hatted capitalists milking the simple proletariat. On their last morning, an hour before sailing, there developed between them a row so furious and so all-embracing that it was difficult to remember that it had started with a complaint about the quality of the fresh meat supplied to *Saltash* for her return journey. When it had ranged widely, from a comparison of the Russian and the British standards of living, to an analysis of their respective war efforts, and fists had been shaken on both sides – for Lockhart found this habit of emphasis infectious – the interpreter took a stormy departure. At the head of the gangway he turned, for a final blistering farewell.

'You English,' he said, in thunderous accents and with extraordinary venom, 'think we know damn nothing – *but I tell you we know damn all.*'

. . .

Scene Two: A Storm at Sea. Enter a Ship, hard-driven, labouring . . . But even that simple directive could not be obeyed, because no ship could enter, no ship could make a foot of headway onto any stage like this. The storm-scene itself would have to move to meet the ship – and that, thought Ericson, when the fifth dawn in succession found his ship still fighting a fantastic battle to force her way even as far south as Iceland, that reversal of nature was not impossible; for here must be the worst weather of the war, the worst weather in the world.

It was more than a full gale at sea, it was nearer to a great roaring battlefield with ships blowing across it like scraps of newspaper. The convoy no longer had the shape of a convoy, and indeed a ship was scarcely a ship, trapped and hounded in this howling wilderness. The tumult of that southerly gale, increasing in fury from day to day, had a staggering malice from which there was no escape: it was as if each ship were some desperate fugitive, sentenced to be lynched by a mob whose movements had progressed from clumsy ill-humour to sightless rage.

Huge waves, a mile from crest to crest, roared down upon the pigmies that were to be their prey; sometimes the entire surface of the water would be blown bodily away, and any ship that stood in the path of the onslaught shook and staggered as tons of green sea smote her upper deck and raced in a torrent down her whole length. Boats were smashed, funnels were buckled, bridges and deck-houses were crushed out of shape: men disappeared overboard without trace and without a cry, sponged out of life like figures wiped from a blackboard at a single imperious stroke. Even when the green seas withheld their blows for a moment, the wind, screaming and clawing at the rigging, struck fear into every heart; for if deck-gear and canvas screens could vanish, perhaps even men could be whipped away by its furious strength ... For the crew of *Saltash*, there was no convoy, and no other ships save their own; and she, and they, were caught in a mesh of fearful days and nights, which might defeat them by their sheer brutal force. Normally a good sea-boat, *Saltash* had ridden out many storms and had often had strength to spare for other ships that might be in difficulties; now, entirely on her own, she laboured to stay afloat, wearily performing, for hour after hour and day after day, the ugly antics of a ship which refused, under the most desperate compulsion, to stand on her head.

Throughout it all, the ship's relay-loudspeaker system, monotonously fed by a satirical hand, boomed out a tune called *Someone's Rocking My Dream-boat*.

Each of them in the wardroom had problems of a special sort to cope with, over and above the ones they shared with the rest of the crew – the problem of eating without having food flung in their faces, of sleeping without being thrown out of their bunks, of getting warm and dry again after the misery of a four-hour watch: above all, the problems of staying unhurt.

Scott-Brown, the doctor, was kept busy with this human wreckage of the storm, treating from hour to hour the cuts, the cracked ribs, the sea-sickness that could exhaust a man beyond the wish to live. His worst casualty, the one which would have needed all his skill and patience even if he had been able to deal with it in a quiet, fully-equipped operating-theatre ashore, was a man who, thrown bodily from one side of the messdeck to the other, had landed on his knee-cap and smashed it into a dozen bloody fragments.

Johnson, the engineer officer, had a problem calling for endless watchfulness – the drunken movements of the ship, which brought her stern high out of the water with every second wave, and could set the screws racing and tearing the shaft to bits unless the throttle were clamped down straight away.

Raikes, in charge of navigation, was confronted by a truly hopeless job. For days on end there had been no sun to shoot, no stars to be seen, no set speed to give him even a rough D.R. position: where *Saltash* had got to, after five days and nights of chaos, was a matter of pure guess-work which any second-class stoker, pin in hand, could have done just as well as he. Ill-balanced on the Arctic Circle, sixty-something North by nothing West – that was the nearest he could get to it: *Saltash* lay somewhere inside these ragged limits, drifting slowly backwards within the wild triangle of Iceland, Jan Meyen Island, and Norway.

The ship's organization was, as usual, Lockhart's responsibility; and the ship's organization had become a wicked sort of joke. Between decks, *Saltash* was in chaos – the wardroom uninhabitable, the messdecks a shambles: there could be no hot food, no way of drying clothes, no comfort for anyone under the ceaseless battering of the storm. Deck-gear worked loose, boats jumped their chocks and battered themselves to bits, water fell in solid tons on every part of the ship: after facing with hope a thousand dawns, Lockhart now dreaded what might meet his eye at the end of his watch, when daylight pierced the wild and lowering sky and showed him the ship again. An upper deck swept clean, a whole batch of thirty seamen vanished overboard – these were the outlines of a waking nightmare which might, with a single turn of fortune, come hideously true.

As *Saltash* laboured, as *Saltash* faltered and groaned, as *Saltash* found each tortured dawn no better than the last, he, along with the rest, could only endure, and curse the cruel sea.

No one cursed it with more cause and with less public demonstration than Ericson, who, self-locked into one corner of the bridge, was fulfilling once more his traditional role of holding the whole thing together. After five days and nights of storm, he was so exhausted that the feeling of exhaustion had virtually disappeared: anchored to the deck by lead-like legs and soaked sea-boots, clamped to the bridge rail by weary half-frozen arms, he seemed to have become a part of the ship herself – a fixed pair of eyes, a watchful brain welded into the fabric of *Saltash*. All the way north to Murmansk he had had to perform the mental acrobatics necessary to the control of twenty escorts and the repelling of three or four different kinds of attack: now the physical harassing of this monstrous gale was battering at his body in turn, sapping at a lifetime's endurance which had never had so testing a call made upon it, had never had to cope with an ordeal on this scale.

Assaulted by noise, bruised and punished by frenzied movement, thrown about endlessly, he had to watch and feel the same things happening to his ship.

The scene from the bridge of *Saltash* never lost an outline of senseless violence. By day it showed a square mile of tormented water, with huge waves flooding in like mountains sliding down the surface of the earth: with a haze of spray and spume scudding across it continually: with gulfs opening before the ship as if the whole ocean was avid to swallow her. Outlined against a livid sky, the mast plunged and rocked through a wild arc of space, flinging the aerials and the signal halyards about as if to whip the sea for its wickedness. Night added the terrible unknown; night was pitch-black, unpierceable to the eye, inhabited by fearful noises and sudden treacherous surprises: by waves that crashed down from nowhere, by stinging spray that tore into a man's face and eyes before he could duck for shelter. Isolated in the blackness, *Saltash* suffered every assault: she pitched, she rolled, she laboured: she met the shock of a breaking wave with a jar that shook her from end to end, she dived shuddering into a deep trough, shipping tons of water with a noise like a collapsing house, and then rose with infinite slowness, infinite pain, to shoulder the mass of water aside, and shake herself free, and prepare herself for the next blow.

Ericson watched and suffered with her, and felt it all in his own body: felt especially the agony of that slow rise under the crushing weight of the sea, felt often the enormous doubt as to whether she would rise at all. Ships had foundered without trace in this sort of weather: ships could give up, and lie down under punishment, just as could human beings: here, in this high corner of the world where the weather had started to scream insanely and the sea to boil, here could be murder: here, where some of *Compass Rose*'s corpses might still be wandering, here he might join them, with yet another ship's company in his train.

He stayed where he was on the bridge, and waited for it to happen, or not to happen. He was a pair of red eyes, inflamed by wind and salt water: he was a brain, tired, fluttering, but forced into a channel of watchfulness: he was sometimes a voice, shouting to the helmsman below to prepare for another threatening blow from the sea. He was a core of fear and of control, clipped small and tight into a body he had first ill-treated, and then begun, perforce, to disregard.

.   .   .

No gale of this force could last for ever, or the very fabric of the globe would long ago have been torn to bits; and presently, as a grudging act of grace, the weather took a turn for the better. The sea was still jumbled and violent, but it was no longer on the attack: the wind still sang on a high note, but it had lost its venom: the ship still rolled and staggered, but she could, at least, now steer a single fixed course. There came a day when the upper deck began to dry off, and a start could be made with cleaning up the shambles below: when a hot meal could be cooked and eaten in comfort: when a man could climb from the fo'c'sle to the bridge without running a gauntlet of green seas that might toss him into the scuppers, or straight overboard: when the Captain could leave the bridge for more than half a watch, and sleep for more than an hour at a stretch ... The sun pierced the clouds, for the first time for many days, and set the grey water gleaming: it warmed the shoulders of their duffle-coats, and sent up a small haze of steam from the drying decks. It also showed them exactly three ships in sight, over a space of a hundred square miles of ocean which should have held fifty-four vessels in orderly convoy formation.

But perhaps that was too much to expect ... The process of rounding up the convoy took *Saltash* nearly forty-eight hours, steaming all the time at an average of twenty knots on a dozen different schemes of search: it was not eased by the fact that each individual escort was doing this same thing simultaneously, trying to marshal whatever merchantmen were in their immediate area, and that there were at one time six of these small convoys of half a dozen ships each, all trying to attract fresh customers to the only true fold, and all steering different courses. On one occasion, *Saltash*, coming across the frigate *Streamer* with five ships in company, signalled to her: 'The convoy is 200 degrees, fourteen miles from you,' only to receive the answer: 'The convoy is here.' It was, for a tired Senior Officer on the edge of irritation, a pregnant moment which Ericson longed to exploit.

But for him there could be no such delaying luxury: the crisp orders which went to *Streamer* were neither brutal nor sarcastic, simply explicit and not to be argued. They formed a pattern with all the other crisp orders of the last two days, and presently, as a result, things were under control again; presently, *Saltash* could station herself at the van of what really looked something like a convoy – straggling, woefully battered, but still a body of ships which could be honestly reported to Their Lordships as Convoy R.C.17. Ericson made this report, and disposed of his escorts in their night positions, and handed over to Allingham, who was Officer-of-the-Watch; and then, with a drugged thankfulness, he took his aching body down the ladder, in search of the shelter of his cabin, and of longed-for rest.

The weather was still wild; but with the convoy intact and the main chaos retrieved, the hours ahead seemed bearable and hopeful, and above all suitable for oblivion.

Then, not a mile astern of *Saltash*, a ship was torpedoed.

Ericson had just passed the first sweet margin of sleep when the alarm-bells clanged: for a moment he could not really believe that they were ringing, and then, as he felt the loathed sound drilling deep into his brain, he had such a violent upsurge of rage and disappointment that he came near to childish tears. It was too much altogether, it wasn't fair . . . He heaved himself out of his bunk, and followed the many other running feet up the ladder again, conscious only of an enormous weariness, and a brain suddenly and brutally robbed of the sleep it craved. How could a man, or a ship, cope with this? How could they be expected to fight anything except the weather?

It seemed that they would have to: it seemed that, as soon as the weather gave a foot of ground, the other enemy, ready in the wings, stepped in with fresh violence, fresh treachery. The scene that greeted Ericson had a pattern made familiar by a hundred convoys: it showed the ships in station, the dusk gathering round them, the heaving sea, and then the ugly deformity which meant disaster – the single winged ship sagging away out of line, already listing mortally, already doomed. She was a small ship: she must, as a prelude to her defeat, have had a special form of hell during the last week of storm ... Ericson looked at Allingham.

'What happened, Guns?'

'She just went, sir.' The Australian accent, as usual in moments of excitement, was thick and somehow reassuring. 'Fired a distress-rocket, about a minute ago. But how the hell could they hit her, in this sort of weather?'

'M'm.' Ericson grunted. The astonishing question had already occurred to him, but it was useless to speculate. Probably there was yet another new weapon: probably U-boats could now fire a torpedo vertically from the bed of the ocean, and hit a ship plumb in its guts. One could think of a nice expressive name for it. But it was no use being surprised at anything in this bloody, this immensely long war ... 'Who's the wing escort?'

'*Pergola*, sir. She's making a sweep to starboard.'

Ericson grunted again. That was all that could be done, at the moment: *Pergola* could sweep the suspect area, the stern escort could pick up the bits. *Saltash* could plod along at the head of the convoy, he himself could think it all out, with cutting logic, using an ice-cold brain ... He saw Allingham looking at him with a rough sort of compassion in his glance, taking in his inflamed eyes, half sunk in sleep, his swollen face, the twitching of his cheek-bone – all the marks of exhaustion which Ericson was aware of himself and which could not be disguised. He smiled ruefully.

'I'd just got my head down.'

'Bad luck, sir.' Allingham paused. 'Shall I go along to the fo'c'sle, sir? Or stay up here?'

Ericson smiled again, acknowledging the line of thought. 'You go down, Guns. I've got the ship.'

When he had gone, there was silence among the men now gathered at Action-Stations on the bridge. Ericson watched the convoy, Lockhart watched the sinking ship. Holt and the signalmen watched *Pergola*, the look-outs watched their appointed arcs, the bridge-messenger watched Ericson. It was a closed circle, of men in danger doing nothing at a moment when active movement would have been a relief, carried in a ship which might herself be doing the wrong thing for want of a single clue. When Ericson said, suddenly and aloud: 'We'll wait,' it was as much to bridge the dubious pause in his own mind as to inform the men round him.

But the pause was not long. There was an exclamation from Holt, the midshipman, and then he said excitedly:

'*Pergola*'s got a signal hoisted!' He stared through his glasses at the corvette, rooting away to starboard like a questing terrier. 'Large flag, sir.'

The yeoman of signals called out: '*Pergola* in contact, sir.'

I wonder, thought Ericson; but he did not say it aloud. *Pergola*, young and enthusiastic, was always ready to depth-charge anything, from a clump of seaweed to a shoal of sardines, but he did not want to discourage her. Depth-charges were cheap, ships and men were not ... Now all of them, save the stolid look-outs dedicated to their arc of vision, turned to watch *Pergola*. Three miles to starboard, she was steering obliquely away from the convoy: she was rolling and pitching drunkenly, and her increased speed sent the spray in great clouds over her bridge. Steaming full ahead, thought Ericson appraisingly: she must be going to drop some for luck. And as he thought it, and wished that *Saltash* might have an excuse for doing the same, another flag fluttered up to *Pergola*'s cross-trees, and the yeoman of signals called out:

'*Pergola* attacking, sir.'

Now they all watched with fresh attention, wondering how good the Asdic contact was, knowing with professional insight just how difficult it must be for *Pergola* to get her depth-charges cleared away and ready for dropping, while steaming full ahead in this immensely troubled sea. *Compass Rose* used to do this sort of thing, thought Lockhart, as *Pergola* gave an especially vicious lurch and shipped a green sea on her quarter: *Compass Rose* used to sweep into action balanced inelegantly on one ear and one leg, while poor old Ferraby danced a jig round the depth-charge rails as he tried to get his charges ready, with a bunch of ham-handed stokers to help him, and plenty of caustic comment from the bridge. It was nice to have graduated from corvettes ... Lockhart watched *Pergola* reminiscently: Holt and the signalmen watched her with a professional eye to her signals: below on the plotting-table, Raikes the navigator watched her with the searching beam of the Radar-set; and Ericson watched her with a proprietary interest. For him, she was simply an extension of his own armament, a probing steel finger sent out from *Saltash* to find and hit the enemy. The torpedoed ship had been his, and *Pergola* was his too: if the one balanced the account of the other, it would not be so bad, it would justify the escort-screen, it would appease the sense of failure that nagged his tired brain, it would let him sleep once more.

Pergola went in like an express train somehow diverted onto a switch-back railway. They saw her charges go down, they saw her sweep round to port as soon as they were dropped: then, after a few moments, the huge columns of grey-green water were tossed into the air by the explosion. When the spray settled, they waited again, their glasses trained on the place of execution; but the surface of the sea was innocent, the expected black shape did not appear. *Pergola*, now at half-speed, headed back towards the explosion area, uncertainly, like a small boy who has made far too much noise in his mother's drawing-room and wishes he were safely and anonymously back in the nursery. There was a pause, and then a third flag went up from her bridge.

'From *Pergola*, sir,' said the yeoman of signals promptly. ' "LOST CONTACT." '

'Call her up,' said Ericson. 'Make: "CONTINUE TO SEARCH YOUR AREA. REPORT NATURE OF ORIGINAL CONTACT".'

The lamps flickered between the two ships.

'CONTACT WAS FIRM, MOVING LEFT, CLASSIFIED AS U-BOAT,' came *Pergola*'s answer.

'WHAT IS YOUR ESTIMATE NOW?' was Ericson's next signal.

'I STILL THINK IT WAS A U-BOAT,' said *Pergola* manfully. Then she added, as if with an ingenuous smile: 'IT WAS WHERE A U-BOAT OUGHT TO HAVE BEEN.'

Now, there, thought Ericson, there I agree with you. The attack had certainly come from that side, the U-boat would naturally have tried to move away to starboard, she would have been steering the course that *Pergola* indicated; she might well have been just about where *Pergola* had dropped her depth-charges. That being so, it was worth while *Pergola* staying where she was, and continuing the hunt: in fact, he thought with sudden vehemence, it was worth while staying there himself, and organizing the hunt on a two-ship basis. He would be taking a chance if he detached two escorts from the screen; but it was very unlikely that the U-boat was one of a pack: in this weather, the convoy could only have been sighted by chance, from close to, and there would have been no time to assemble other craft for a concentrated attack. She was therefore a lone wolf, sinking her fangs once, swiftly, and then slinking off into the forest again. Lone wolves of this sort deserved special attention, special treatment. The chance was worth taking.

The pattern of action emerged new-minted from his brain, as if, however tired he were, he had only to press a button marked 'Detach two escorts for independent search' in order to produce a typed schedule of operational orders. The necessary directions were dictated in a smooth series which kept all three signalmen busy at the same time. Signals went to the Admiralty and the commodore of the convoy, to tell them what was happening: to *Harmer*, to take over as Senior Officer: to *Pergola*, to continue her search until *Saltash* joined her: to *Rose Arbour*, to take *Pergola*'s place on the screen: to *Streamer*, to despatch the sinking merchant-man by gun-fire, and then rejoin: and to the other escorts, to station themselves according to the new diagram. Then Ericson summoned Lockhart and Johnson, the engineer-officer, to the bridge, to explain what he proposed to do: he conferred, lengthily and technically, with Raikes at the plotting-table; and then he took *Saltash* round in a wide sweep to starboard, and, coming up on *Pergola*'s quarter, started sending a final long signal beginning: 'We will organize our search in accordance with two alternative possibilities.'

Lockhart had never admired the Captain more than during the

twelve hours that followed. In the end, he thought, for all these new machines and scientific stuff, war depends on men ... He knew that Ericson must have been desperately tired, even before the new crisis arrived: if the exacting trip north-bound to Murmansk, and the last five days of battering weather, did not suggest it, then his grey lined face and humped shoulders supplied a reliable clue. And yet there was in all his actions, both now, and during the subsequent long, intricate, and determined hunt for the submarine, no trace of tiredness or of readiness to compromise: he rose to the moment, and kept at the required pitch of alertness, as if he had come to the task fresh from a six weeks' holiday; and the result, in addition to being a remarkable physical effort, was, in the realm of submarine detection, a tactical masterpiece as well.

Ericson must have been very sure, thought Lockhart, that the submarine was there, and that *Pergola* – the happy-go-lucky *Pergola* – had for once been on the right track and might well have damaged her: he must have conquered his tiredness with this knowledge that the quarry was immediately to hand. For it was not enough to keep in mind that a ship had been sunk, and men killed in the process: that was a commonplace of the Atlantic, and the revengeful energy it bred soon petered out. It was the professional sense which was now the mainspring of every sustained effort of will: the feeling, present all the time, that senior officers of escorts were specifically hired to sink U-boats, and that for this reason U-boats must never be allowed to go to waste.

Certainly, Ericson clung onto his quarry, or the hope of it, as if he would have been personally ashamed to forfeit the chance of a kill ... It was six o'clock in the evening when *Saltash* and *Pergola* separated, to start their different schemes of search: it was midnight before any results rewarded either of them. Earlier, down in *Saltash*'s plotting-room, Ericson and Raikes had made a detailed appreciation of the prospects, involving three different suppositions. Firstly, the U-boat might have been slightly damaged by *Pergola*'s attack, in which case she would dive deep and stay there, in the hope of fooling the pursuit and patching herself up in the meantime. Alternatively, she might have been badly damaged, and would need to start creeping for the shelter of the nearest home-port as soon as she could. Lastly, she might have escaped damage altogether – or have been outside the area of attack in the first place: she would then probably decide, after the initial scare, to follow the convoy at a distance and come in for a second helping later that night. There were variations latent in all these possibilities; but thus the broad outlines had confronted Ericson as he started his reasoned, highly technical guesswork on the plotting-table.

The last possibility – that the U-boat would continue to follow the convoy – was something which *Saltash* must now disregard: if the U-boat were going to try again, *Harmer* and the rest of the escort-screen must cope with it themselves. That left the other two alternatives: the lurking in the deep, or the immediate creep for home. Lurking meant, for the hunting escort, a long and patient period of waiting up above: it might involve circling the area slowly for as long as twenty-four hours, all the time on the alert for any sign of a break-out. If, on the other hand, the U-boat had already started for home, the journey might be eastwards towards Norway, or south-east to the German coast, or due south to one of the Biscay ports: it meant in any case a rapidly extending range of search, becoming more like a needle-in-the-haystack proposition with every hour that passed.

Of the two, Ericson finally chose for himself the patient, stalking wait, above the spot where the U-boat ought to be: it was the one he thought most likely, and *Saltash*'s superior Asdic and Radar would give her a decided advantage if the U-boat tried to run for it. The other – the cast for home, in an ever-widening arc – was a somewhat forlorn venture: in assigning it to *Pergola*, he tried not to feel that he was giving the junior ship a dubious chance of distinguishing herself . . . Something of the sort must have occurred to the irrepressible *Pergola*, who, on taking her leave, signalled:

'DON'T FORGET IT WAS ORIGINALLY MY BIRD.'

Ericson, hovering between the alternative answers. 'We'll go fifty-fifty on the medals,' and 'Confine your signals to essential traffic', finally sent none at all. All that he really wanted to say to *Pergola*, as she drew away and the darkness thickened between them, was that she carried his blessing with her. But there was really no official version of this.

The next six hours had not the smallest excitement for anyone aboard *Saltash*: they had, in fact, a deadly sameness, an unrewarding monotony, the hardest thing of all for tired men to support. Ericson remained on the bridge the whole time, hunched in his chair, wide-awake, while *Saltash* quartered the suspect area at half-speed; for hour after hour her Asdic recorded nothing at all, and her Radar simply the diminishing speck of light which was *Pergola* sweeping deeper and deeper to the south-east. Ericson ate a scratch meal at eight o'clock: relays of cocoa reached him at hourly intervals: the moon came up, and then left them again: the sea flattened as the wind died. It was cold: the cold attacked not only the body, it chilled the mind as well, so that to keep alert, to believe that what one was doing was right, became more and more difficult.

At times Ericson's thoughts wandered so far that the effort to bring them back was like a physical ordeal, a cruel tug on some stretched sinew of the brain. I am very tired, he thought: I have this pain of tiredness in my legs and across my shoulders and under my heart: that thing inside my head is starting to flutter again. This search may go on for hours, this search may go on for ever: we are probably doing the wrong thing, we have probably guessed wrong in every respect, from the very beginning:

there were probably a pack of six or eight U-boats in this area all the time, and they are preparing to fall upon the convoy at this moment, while we fool about, fifty miles astern of it. I have weakened the escort-screen at this crucial time, I have taken away two ships out of eight, I have been, by one quarter, unforgivably stupid and rash, I am ripe for a court-martial . . . The Asdic pinged away, like a nagging insect: the tick-tick of the motor on the plotting-table reached Ericson continually up the voice-pipe, like some infernal metronome reminding him that everything he did was out of joint. The hours crept past, and the change of course which came every fifteen minutes seemed a futile break in a pattern already futile.

Now and again he spoke to Raikes, the navigator, who had the first watch; and Raikes answered him quietly, unhurriedly, without turning from his place at the front of the bridge. But these exchanges never contained what Ericson really wanted to say, and never what he wanted to hear, either: they simply featured a comment on the weather, a query about the distance run, a neutral remark on any neutral subject that occurred to him. For his own comfort, his own hunger, he wanted to say: do you think we are right, do you think we are wasting our time: is the U-boat here at all, or have I, in diluting the escort-screen by a quarter, made what may turn out to be a murderous mistake? But none of these were captain's questions, and so they remained unasked, prisoners in the brain; while *Saltash* covered the same square of ocean once every hour, and *Pergola* gradually faded out of range, and the black and empty sea, deserted even by the moon, offered to *Saltash* only a cold derisive hissing as she passed.

But the change of watch at midnight marked a change of fortune as well; Allingham and Vincent had hardly taken over from Raikes – indeed, Raikes was still writing up his meagre entry in the deck-log – when the pattern of the night quickly flowered, in the only way that could bring any pleasure to the senses. The Asdic-repeater, which could be heard all over the bridge, and which had been sounding an identical, damnable note for six hours on end, suddenly produced an astonishing variation – a solid echo, an iron contact in a featureless ocean . . . Ericson jumped when he heard it, as did everyone else within earshot: the bridge sprang to life as if the darkness had become charged with an electric fervour that reached them all instantly.

'Sir!' began Allingham.

'Bridge!' called the Asdic-rating.

'Captain, sir!' said the yeoman of signals.

'All right,' said Ericson, slipping down off his chair. 'I heard it . . . What a nice noise . . . Hold onto it . . . Sound Action-Stations . . . Yeoman!'

'Sir?' said the yeoman of signals.

'Make to *Pergola*: "RETURN TO ME WITH ALL DESPATCH".'

That's a guess, he thought as he said it – but the echo, loud and clear, confirmed him in the belief that this, the blank stretch of ocean which had suddenly blossomed, was now the place for all available hunting escorts to be. Only U-boats sounded like that, only U-boats could produce that beautiful metallic ring; and this U-boat, which had struck once and then lain in hiding for so long, must now be finally cornered. It would take *Pergola* over two hours to get back from her search, even 'with all despatch' – the Navy's most urgent order; but she deserved to be in at the kill, and she could play a useful supporting role if the U-boat were elusive ... The Asdic echo sharpened: Lockhart, now stationed on the set, called out: 'Target moving slowly right': Vincent, from aft, reported his depth-charges ready: *Saltash* began to tremble as the revolutions mounted, and the range shortened down to striking distance.

But this was to be no swift kill: perhaps indeed, it was to be no kill at all. During the next hour, *Saltash* dropped a total of sixty-eight depth-charges without, apparently, the slightest effect: the echo remained constant, the U-boat still twisted and turned and doubled back, with limitless cunning. It seemed as if no attack, however carefully calculated, was sufficiently accurate to bring her up short; they might have been launching snowballs into the fire, they might have been dropping cotton-wool bombs on the nursery floor, for all the difference their efforts made. Time and again *Saltash* swept in for the assault: the depth-charges went down, the surface of the sea leapt and boiled astern of her; but when she came round again, in a tight circle, she found that her searchlight still shone on a blank sea, and presently she would pick up the contact again – always there, always solid, but never to be grasped, and seemingly unaffected by the fury of the attack. Sixty-eight depth-charges, thought Ericson wearily: most of them had been pretty close: the men down there in the U-boat must be going through hell: why doesn't something happen, why doesn't it *work* ...? He shaped up for yet another attack, on a contact which was as firm as ever; and then he suddenly lifted his head, and sniffed.

'Number One!' he called out.

'Sir?' said Lockhart.

'Smell anything?'

After a pause: 'Yes – oil,' said Lockhart.

Oil. The hateful smell, which to them had always meant a sinking ship, could now mean a sinking U-boat instead ... Ericson, walking to the wing of the bridge, sniffed violently again, and the smell of oil came thick and strong to his nostrils: taken at its face-value, it meant damage, it meant, at least, a crushed and leaking bulkhead inside the U-boat, and it could mean total success. He ordered the searchlight to be trained right ahead, and there, where they had dropped their last charges, they presently saw the patch of oil itself – glistening, sluggish, reflecting the light most prettily, and spreading outwards in a heartening circle. They dropped another pattern of depth-charges as they rode over the area; and then, as they turned in again, the Asdic faded, and Lockhart reported 'Lost contact'.

The silence that fell on the bridge seemed to be a self-congratulatory one, but it was not so for Ericson. He would have liked to believe in that patch of oil, and that fading contact which everyone else took to be the U-boat slowly sinking beneath the beam of the Asdic; but he suddenly found that he could not believe it. Oil, for his private satisfaction, was not nearly enough: he wanted wreckage, woodwork, an underwater explosion, bits of men weaving gently to the surface. Oil could come from a minor leak, oil could even be a subterfuge; the U-boat might have released some on purpose, and then crept away, leaving the feeble English sailors to celebrate their kill in feeble English beer. Oil, like wine, could be a mocker ... She has gone deep again, he thought, with sudden, illogical conviction: maybe she is damaged, but she is not yet done to death: she will wait, and then come up again. We will wait too, he told himself grimly, with a new access of determination which must have come from the very core of his brain; and then aloud to Lockhart, he called out:

'Carry out lost-contact procedure. I'm going to go on with the attack.'

To his tautened nerves, it seemed as if the bridge-personnel and indeed the whole tired ship had sighed as he said the words. I do not care how sick of it you are, he said, almost aloud, instantly angry: if I am the last man to keep awake in this ship, if I am the last man left alive, I will drive her, and you, and myself, for just as long as I want to ... But no one had sighed, and no one had spoken, save Lockhart who repeated: 'Lost-contact procedure' to his Asdic operator; and *Saltash*, settling down to her steady half-speed progress, began again her interminable search, as if the past six hours now counted for nothing, and they were starting again from the beginning.

The trouble was that, ludicrously, there was nothing to start on. For the second time the U-boat, with her leak or her oil-decoy, with her shaken or exultant crew, with her dubious amount of damage, had vanished.

Surveying the fact dispassionately, Ericson found it hard to believe: continuing to survey it, his dispassion gave way to the beginnings of a blind rage. When Lockhart had reported 'Lost contact', he imagined that it was because of the disturbed state of the water, and that they would pick the U-boat up again in a matter of minutes, as had happened before; but when those minutes went by, and added up to five, and then ten, and then twenty, without a single trace of an echo on the Asdic, he found himself face to face with the fact that they might have lost her. After seven hours of trying, after nearly eighty depth-charges, after this enormous and sustained effort which was eating into the last reserves of his endurance ... He stood over the two operators at the Asdic-set, and looked down at the backs of their stupid doltish heads, and wanted above all else to take a revolver from the rack and put a bullet through the pair of them. *This could not happen to him* – the U-boat was *there* – they had had her almost in their hands, and now Lockhart and his two bloody fools of operators and his rotten set had let her slip away again ... When Lockhart reported, for the tenth time: 'No contact,' and added: 'She could have been sunk, don't you think, sir?' Ericson, with a spurt of anger, answered: 'I wish to Christ you'd mind your own business and get on with your job!' and strode out of the Asdic-compartment as if he could bear the infected air no longer.

But: I should not have said that, he thought immediately, leaning against the front of the bridge: it comes of being tired, it comes of losing the U-boat when we were so close ... He turned round.

'Number One!'

Lockhart came out of the Asdic-hut, and walked towards him in the darkness. 'Sir?' he said, with extreme formality.

'Sorry I said that,' grunted Ericson. 'Forget it.'

'That's all right, sir,' said Lockhart, who could rarely resist an apology, and certainly not one so promptly offered.

'I don't think she was sunk,' went on Ericson. 'Not enough evidence for it.'

'No sir,' answered Lockhart. He did not agree, but this was not the moment to say so.

'I'm going back to that square search again. We'll keep at Action-Stations.'

'Aye, aye, sir.'

Not Action-Stations, but sleep, thought Lockhart, returning to the set: that's what I want, that's what he wants, that's what we all want: and we're none of us going to get it, because the obstinate old bastard won't listen to reason ... He was quite sure, as was his leading Asdic-rating, that the U-boat had been destroyed, crushed, or battered to bits by the cumulative effect of seventy or eighty near-misses: she had probably collapsed, and was going down slowly, leaving that trail of oil which had so cheered him when he caught sight of it. But since it seemed that the slightest hint to this effect was enough to start a riot, it was better to carry on, without comment ... He shut the door of the Asdic-compartment, and said, in a non-committal voice:

'Normal sweep. We're doing a box search again.'

The senior rating on the set repeated: 'Normal sweep, sir,' and then sucked his teeth in unmistakable reproach.

'Don't make that filthy noise!' snapped Lockhart. 'Without comment' covered that sort of thing as well.

'Hollow tooth, sir,' said the man rebelliously.

'Get on with your work.'

The rating, now breathing heavily, bent over the set and made an adjustment to it, as noisily as he could. They were all of them a bit short-tempered, thought Lockhart: it's catching, it's an inevitable product of tiredness. He smiled to himself as he looked at the Asdic-rating, who was normally one of his favourites: he could have quoted with reasonable accuracy most of the thoughts and phrases that were going through the man's head. (*All you get is threats and abuse . . . The skipper gives him a rocket and he passes it onto me . . . Bloody officers . . . Roll on my twelve . . .*) With just enough friendliness in his voice to bring things back to normal without surrendering his point, Lockhart said:

'We'd better have another brew of cocoa. This is going to take a long time.'

It took a very long time indeed; and as the hours went by, without change, without significance, it began to seem as if the futile hunt might well continue to the end of time itself – or until, for some reason unrelated to their private effort, the war came to a finish, one side was declared the winner and the other not, and *Saltash*, receiving a postcard about the result, would be able to set course for home, in reasonable time to claim her old-age pension . . . *Pergola* joined them at three o'clock, coming up from the south-east at a speed which seemed to spurn the wasted hours of her diversion: her arrival enabled Ericson to extend the scope of the search, to guard the back door as well as the front, but she was no more successful than *Saltash* in picking up the scent again. The watch changed at four, the sky began to lighten from the eastwards, illuminating a sea as grey and flat and worthless as a washed-out water-colour: it showed also the two ships, five miles apart, seemingly intent but scarcely convincing – in fact, plodding to and fro like a couple of myopic old women making the rounds of the dust-bins, not knowing that these had been emptied hours before.

To Ericson, the dawn, and the outlines of his ship, and the grey faces of the men on the bridge, brought a sudden bleak doubt. He could be wrong, he could be wasting his time, for two reasons which now began to appeal irresistibly: the U-boat might be many miles away, or she might have been sunk by their original attack. At this, the lowest hour dividing night and day, when *Saltash* had been hunting for eleven hours on end, and he himself had been on the bridge the entire time, he was assailed by the most wretched sense of futility he had ever known; the temptation to call the thing off, to take the oil patch at its face value and claim a victory which no one would seriously deny them; this nagged at him like a cat mewing endlessly outside a door, his own door which sooner or later he would have to open. It would stop the noise; it would please the neighbours. And it would bring, for his own relief, the prospect of sleep ...

He was aware that all round him were men who had long ago made up their minds on these very lines: that Lockhart thought the U-boat had been sunk, that the hard-driven Asdic operators were sulky and sullen for the same reason; that *Pergola*, reading the report he had given her, to bring her up to date when she arrived, must have wondered why on earth they had not packed up and joined the convoy hours before, signalling a definite kill to the Admiralty as they did so.

The doubt and uncertainty increased his weariness: slumping in his chair, with nothing to break the monotony and no glimmer of success to sustain him, he found himself in mortal fear of falling asleep. He felt his whole brain and body being lulled into a delicious weary doze by the sounds round him – the noise of the Asdic, the slice-slice of *Saltash*'s bow wave, the men washing down the upper deck: even the movement each half-hour, as the look-outs changed and the helmsman was relieved, could be strung together as part of the same sleep-inducing chain. To resist it was agony, not to resist it gave him a feeling of sick foreboding: if he stayed awake he would begin to weep, if he slept he would fall off his chair, and then they would all think he was cracking up, and it would be true ...

Lockhart, who now had the watch, came out of the Asdic-hut, for the twentieth time, and said:

'Nothing on the recorder, sir.'

Involuntarily, Ericson's nerves began to jump. 'What about it?'

Lockhart stared. 'Nothing, sir. Routine report. It's the end of another sweep.'

'What do you mean, *another* sweep?'

Lockhart swallowed, as he had had to do many times during the past twelve hours. 'I thought you said, sir ——'

'Jesus Christ, Number One –' began Ericson, and then stopped. His heart was thudding, his brain felt like a box with a little bird fluttering about inside it. He thought: this won't do at all – I really will crack up, I'll be shooting somebody in a minute ... He stood up, and flexed his shoulders, sharpening and then easing the pain that lay across them. His head swam with the effort. But he knew now what he had to do next.

Two minutes later, down in his cabin, he confronted Scott-Brown, the doctor. The latter, routed out of his sleep as a matter of urgency by a startled bridge-messenger, was dressed in a pair of pyjama trousers and an inflated lifebelt; he still maintained, unimpaired, his Harley Street air of complete dependability. He took one look at the Captain, and said, in a tone of reproof which Ericson did not mind:

'Time you turned in, sir.'

'I know, Doc. But I can't.'

'How long have you been up on the bridge?'

'Since that ship went down.'

'It's too long.'

'I know,' repeated Ericson. 'But I've got to stay there. Can you fix me up with something?'

Scott-Brown frowned at him. 'Is it necessary? What's this all about?'

Ericson flared: 'Christ, don't _you_ start –' and then, his heart thudding again, he sat down suddenly. 'There's a U-boat here,' he said quietly, trying to conserve every effort, every urge of feeling. 'I know damned well there is, and I'm going to get her. I want something to keep me awake while I'm doing it.'

'How long for?'

'Another night, maybe ... Can you do it?'

'Oh, I can do it all right. It's just a question of ——,'

Ericson's nerves were starting to jump again. 'Well, do it then,' he interrupted roughly. 'What does it involve? An injection?'

Scott-Brown smiled, recognizing the point where medical prudence succumbed to the lash of discipline. 'Just a pill or two. Benzedrine. You'll feel like a spring lamb.'

'How long will it last?'

'We'll start with twenty-four hours.' The doctor smiled again, turning for the door. 'After that you'll go out like a light, and wake up with the hell of a hangover.'

'Is that all?'

'Probably. How old are you, sir?'

'Forty-eight.'

Scott-Brown wrinkled his nose. 'Benzedrine isn't a thing to play with, you know.'

'I wasn't intending to make a habit of it,' said Ericson sourly. 'This is a special occasion.'

Another two minutes, and Scott-Brown was back again, with two grey pills and a glass of water. Ericson had disposed of the first one, and had the second poised upon his tongue, when the bell at the head of his bunk began to ring.

He bent to the voice-pipe, swallowing as he did so, and called out: 'Captain.'

'Bridge, sir!' came Lockhart's voice, off-key with excitement. '_Pergola's_ got a contact.'

He felt like saying 'I told you so', he felt like shouting 'Nuts to all of you ...' He caught Scott-Brown's eye, expectant, slightly amused: he said, 'Thanks, Doc,' and started for the door. Behind him, the doctor said: 'In theory, you ought to lie down for ten minutes, and then ——,' and

then the measured voice was lost as he turned the corner of the passage-
way and began to race up the bridge-ladder.

Whether it was the benzedrine, or the feeling of eleventh-hour
reprieve, or *Pergola*'s activity, or the heartening effect of full daylight, he
felt like a king when he stood on the bridge again, and looked round him.
Now it was a different sort of scene ... Five miles away across the flat sea,
Pergola was turning under full helm and at full speed: the water creamed
at her bow as, coming obliquely towards *Saltash*, she roared in for her
attack. She flew the two flags which meant: 'I have an under-water
contact', and 'I am attacking': she looked everything a corvette, viewed
at dawn after a long and exhausting night, should look ... Ericson called
to Lockhart in the Asdic-hut: 'Have you got anything?' and then there
was a pause, and Lockhart answered suddenly: 'In contact – starboard
bow – bearing one-nine-oh!' and the Asdic repeater began to produce a
loud clear singing echo, on a cross-bearing which could only be the U-
boat which *Pergola* was attacking.

· *Pergola*'s charges exploded half a mile ahead of them: *Saltash*, weaving
in at right angles to complete a lethal tapestry, dropped her own not
more than twenty yards from the discoloured, still frothing, patch of
water. Then the two ships turned together, heading back towards the
fatal area, ready to do it all again, but this time, this time there was no
need. There came a sudden dull under-water explosion, clearly audible
all over the ship: a great gout of oily water burst upwards from the heart
of the sea, and it was followed by other things – bits of wood, bits of
clothing, bits of things which might later need a very close analysis ...
Ericson called for 'Stop engines', and *Saltash* came to a standstill,
surrounded now by a bloody chaplet of wreckage; the crew crowded to
the rails, the curious debris thickened and spread, a working-party aft
got busy with buckets and grappling-hooks. This was a victory which
called for trophies ... It took us twelve hours, thought Ericson, leaning
against the front of the bridge, hugely exultant; but we did it, she *was*
there all the time, I was right ... He turned and caught Lockhart's eye –
Lockhart, whose last attack must have been accurate to within five yards
– and Lockhart smiled ruefully and said: 'Sorry, sir!' to cover the past
night of disbelief, and the bad judgement which had prompted it. But it
did not matter now, and Ericson sat down in his chair, himself sorry for
only one thing – the benzedrine which he need not have taken, which he
should have saved for a really exhausting occasion ...

The bell rang from the quarter-deck aft, and Vincent said, in the voice
of a man facing grisly reality rather too early in the morning:

'We've got lots of wood-work, sir, and some clothes, and some other
things as well. Two buckets full.'

'What other things, Sub?'

After a pause: 'The doctor says, sir, they're clearly in his department.'

The ring of men standing round the two slopping buckets, sipping cocoa and staring, were talkative in victory.

'What's the skipper want with this lot? Bloody-minded old bastard!'

'It's evidence. Got to take it home with us. They won't believe us otherwise.'

'Only kind of Jerry I ever want to see.'

'Looks more like tripe and onions.'

'Don't let onto the cook, for Christ's sake.'

'Must be a month's meat ration here. Wait till I tell the wife.'

.   .   .

'Coxswain,' said Ericson, later that day, 'where are those buckets stowed?'

'In the galley, sir.'

Ericson swallowed. 'I think we'll have them in the sick-bay for the rest of the trip.'

.   .   .

'Sir,' said Lockhart, 'that looks like the Admiral waiting on the quay.'

'Oh.' Ericson, who was much preoccupied with bringing *Saltash* alongside, against a breeze blowing her off-shore and a brisk tide under her stern, merely grunted. Then he said: 'Stop starboard, slow astern port,' and then: 'I wonder what brings him here?'

'It could be us.'

'Stop port,' said Ericson. 'Hurry up those heaving-lines, or she'll blow out into the stream again . . .' He took a quick look through his glasses at the quayside, and nodded. 'Yes, it is us,' he said. 'That's really very nice of him . . . Slow ahead port . . . I hope we don't do any damage as we come alongside.'

'Stern-wire ashore, sir . . . I think he'd be prepared to forgive us, in the circumstances.'

The water between the quay and the ship began to boil as it was squeezed outwards: the wash of their screws surged and sucked at the oily wooden piles. *Saltash* edged nearer, cheating the wind, using the tide skilfully; the windlass on the fo'c'sle started a solid clanking as the head-rope came in. The Admiral, catching sight of Ericson on the bridge, waved cheerfully, and Ericson saluted.

'Better have a piping party, Number One,' said Ericson. 'This looks official.'

'Will you meet him, sir?'

'Yes. In fact I'll go down now, in case he does something athletic without waiting for the gangway. Take over here, and finish it off.' He smiled. 'Don't disgrace me, will you?'

It was a good ten minutes before *Saltash* was securely berthed, and Lockhart could give the crossed hands signal which meant 'Wrap up your mooring wires', and then ring off the engines. He delayed some moments longer on the bridge, savouring the fact of homecoming; watching the signalmen stowing away their flags and books, and the men on *Saltash*'s fo'c'sle talking to other men on the quay, and the tide running past their hull, and the fair estuary of the Clyde which they had not seen for six long weeks. It was nice of the Admiral to come down to meet them, though after the rough convoy, and the U-boat at the end of it, they did perhaps deserve a little cherishing. Lockhart had watched the Admiral come aboard, while the pipes shrilled, and had seen him shake Ericson's hand, and talk smilingly for a moment, and then go below with him; he himself might be sent for presently, to share in the congratulations, but it did not matter either way – they had their U-boat, they were home again, *Saltash* was secured alongside after yet another convoy, they were due for a boiler-clean ... He called down to the quartermaster, still in the wheel-house: 'Pipe leave to the port watch from seventeen hundred to oh-eight-double-oh,' and then he gathered his belongings together and made his way down the succession of ladders to his cabin. He was tired, and there was an ache in his legs, and he felt grimy and unshaven; but a hot bath and a couple of quick gins would cure most of that, and there was, at last, the blessed night for sleep.

From the passage-way he saw a shadow move within his cabin, and he thought: 'Oh God, what is it now?' and he pulled aside the curtain, and there, standing by his desk, was Julie Hallam.

They looked at each other for a long moment, he smiling, she grave and shy. Finally, she said:

'Your steward is shocked. But he let me in.'

He shook her hand and pressed it. 'Of course he did. No rules apply to you ... Julie, how lovely to see you, and how lovely of you to be here at all.'

'The Admiral came down to congratulate you, so I thought I'd come too.'

'I didn't see you on the quay.'

'I was hiding behind a crane. My congratulations are different.' Suddenly she put her arms right round his neck, and said: 'Oh, darling, I'm so glad you're back.'

He could not remember that she had ever called him 'darling' before, and his arms closed round her he felt weak with surprise, and with emotional reaction. How incredible to come back to this ... He said: 'I'm afraid I'm rather bristly,' but he kissed her nonetheless, and her lips met his warmly. Then he pushed her away with gentle hands, so that he could look at her face, and he said: 'Are you really Julie?'

She laughed, giving him a complicated, confederate look, and said: 'Well, anyway the uniform is the same.'

'You seem different – you even feel different. What have you been doing?'

'Waiting for you – watching the plot – wondering what was going to happen next ... Oh, darling,' she said again, 'what an awful convoy! Those aircraft all the time – and the destroyers – I thought you'd never get there. And then the weather on the way back, and that U-boat to finish up with. We must find you a shore job after this,' she said, suddenly grave. 'I can't go through all that again.'

Now what is this, thought Lockhart – but he did not really want to know: the wonderful change was enough. To have Julie in his arms cured all his tiredness, and made the bare cabin unbelievably warm and bright: to have Julie in his arms, renewing the sweet past so willingly and adding so much to it, was a moment already overflowing. He kissed her again, and this time it was not a short kiss; and presently she turned in his arms and began to murmur into his ear:

'I didn't know anything about loving anyone, until a little time ago. I didn't relate things like parting or danger to you at all. The war was just the war, a convoy was just a collection of ships. You were you – everything was separate and manageable ... It was when I read your signal: "Engaging enemy destroyers", that I started to know all about it, and you and I were suddenly right in the middle of the pattern, and you were in frightful danger from it. I've never felt involved before, but from that moment I was terribly involved, and it was all you – you were the convoy, you were everything.' She pressed him closely to her, rubbing and smoothing the rough surface of the duffle-coat. 'You suddenly became very precious to me,' she went on, in a low, gentle voice, 'and I knew I couldn't bear it if anything happened to you, and after that there was just the endless waiting for you to come back – four weeks, nearly five ...' She smiled. 'You see? – the uniform may be the same, but inside, inside ...'

'You're sweet,' he said, 'and I love you. What happens now?'

'Anything you say – anything you want.'

'Are you really Julie?' he asked again.

'New model,' she answered. Her face looked especially lovely as she said this, her eyes were full of tender readiness. 'I feel like a woman now, and it's totally new, and I don't mind who knows it or what it involves. Say what you want us to do.'

'I'm due for leave,' he said, hesitating.

'When?'

'As soon as I've got things clewed-up here – in about four days.'

'Where will you go?'

'Anywhere.'

'Somewhere with me,' she said.

A shaft of sunlight, traversing the open porthole, moved gently on the cabin floor; but they did not see it. For now they were looking at each other, and their looks were no longer complicated, but charged with a simple need, a simple relief. He said: 'I love you, Julie,' and she answered: 'That is now a very two-sided arrangement,' and held up her mouth to be kissed.

CHAPTER 7

It was a cottage, lent to them by a school-friend of Julie's whose work had taken her to London. It was a cottage not without drawbacks.

It lay deep in the wilds, at the foot of a glen near Loch Fyne: it was served by a single daily bus, and there were no shops nearer to it than five miles away. The place was old, stone-built, draughty: its wood fires smoked, its oil lamps, romantically dim, gave to every room a profound reek of paraffin. The roof over the kitchen leaked, and the kitchen itself boasted a villainous old cooking-range, from which food emerged either crisped to a cinder or stone cold. There were low, head-cracking beams in all the passages, and a staircase well designed for the twisting and wrenching of legs and ankles. The plumbing was primitive, the hot-water system uncertain and often mutinous. It was damp. There were clearly mice. There was no one to look after them.

It was wonderful.

It was not wonderful all at once, but it became so within a little while, as soon as the main astonishing margin of their meeting had been crossed. When they got off the village bus, self-conscious with their suitcases, it was still early afternoon; before them was a half-mile walk up the deserted glen, and the half-mile seemed to take them deep into constraint and uncertainty. It will be all right as soon as I kiss her, Lockhart thought, opening the garden gate and standing aside for Julie to enter; everything will come out straight, she will be just as she was in the cabin. But why then was this not a kissing moment? ... When they started to explore the house, they did so almost in silence: Julie mounted the stairway alone, while Lockhart, listening to her footsteps and knowing that she was entering what was perhaps to be their bedroom, stood below and wondered if, after all, this was going to be a success.

Presently he heard her coming down the stairs again, and then she stood standing in the doorway, watching him, gauging his mood. Then she said:

'What next?'

After a moment he answered: 'It's damp. I'm going to light lots of fires.'

'Do that ...' Then she smiled, equally at herself and at their joint embarrassment, and crossed nearer to him, and said: 'We can't expect to step into this all at once,' and then, more certainly: 'You can take it for granted that I *do* want to be here with you;' and after that it was, for the next few hours, all right.

But there was still the evening, and then the night.

Darkness came early on that November day; soon after sunset, the glen filled with shadows, the small house merged gradually with its background, and the frosty night descended, holding them hidden in its firm hand. They ate, they talked, they listened to music on the old battery radio; the house was now warm, their setting seemed private and unassailable. But to Lockhart, the darkness brought back with it straightaway the constraint of the afternoon. It was new and moving to be with her alone, in this enclosed world on which he had been fixing all his thoughts: she looked lovely – her hair loosely bound, her eyes dark and large in the lamplight: she wore a house-coat so feminine, so gracefully accented to her body, that it made her seem another person altogether. But against the implication of desire, there was tension between them, the sweet defeating tension of uncertainty: perhaps she had caught it from him, perhaps hers was of her own making, but on his side it sprang from a doubt as to whether, even now, they were to be lovers. Certainly, the right true end of love was there for them, but he could not decide whether they were due to reach it, or whether it was something she did not really want.

He sensed in her the same continued change which had brought them together – not dependence, but a readiness to give the lead into his hands: he sensed it, he could see it often in her glance and hear it in her voice, and he was mortally afraid of misusing it, of crossing too soon or too robustly the frontiers of her will and compliance. Worse things than diffidence sprang from this fear. Perhaps he had even made the whole thing up, he thought, with something like panic lest he should commit himself upon false ground: perhaps she had never meant that they should be lovers, but just that they should spend their leave together. Perhaps he did not deserve so beautiful a woman, perhaps he would be no good anyway.

It was she who cured the foolish moment of uncertainty, and she cured it with a single swift stroke which recalled, on the instant, the old Julie, the capable and competent person who disposed decisively of ships and people, and always looked round for more. Though this disposing was on a somewhat different plane ... They had been listening to the radio, he standing by the fire, she lying back on the sofa; and seemingly on an impulse she got up and walked across and kissed him. It seemed natural now that, as they stood clasped gently together, still listening to the music, the beating of their hearts should begin to overlay it ... A woman's voice on the radio sang a song with the phrase: 'To hold you close to my eager breast', and at the words he felt Julie's body stir under the thin material of her dress, and then she lifted her head and said softly:

'Did you hear that? – that's exactly what it feels like.'

Lockhart said: 'That is what it feels like to me, too,' and she smiled lovingly, and, as if to explain beyond question the urgency which now began to flow from all her body, she answered: 'I think I am wooing you,' and after that it came all right once more, and it came all right for ever.

.   .   .

Perhaps it was the contrast which was most moving: the tender refuge after strife and slaughter, the softness welcoming his hard body. It was, indeed, a contrast for both of them: he had come from the rough demanding school of war, she from her astringent dedication in the same field. They had been preoccupied, and therefore celibate; it had suited them until they met, and then it suited them no longer. But the surrender of this celibacy was overwhelming: it did all things: it astonished by its sweetness, it drowned in sensual fervour, it cleared magically the brow ... There had been nothing in their previous meeting, nothing indeed in their lives so far, which had promised or pointed to such a tempest of feeling and such a relief thereafter.

Lockhart awoke some time before dawn on that first night, after the deep drugged slumber which had claimed them both; and when he felt her stir near him, and heard her murmur: 'You should be still asleep,' he answered: 'There are other times for sleep,' and he struck a match and lit the candle by the bed-side, for the pleasure and comfort of seeing her again. What he now found in her was as moving as all the offering of the previous night, all the ready tumult. Her face on the pillow was tenderly relaxed, framed by the dark wayward crown of hair: her eyes, large and soft, now regarded him as if he were a beloved child which had done something especially pleasing, especially to be rewarded. Her eyes had been lovely before, on a cool plane of perfection: now, having seen and answered his ardour, and then softened to release and sleep, they had a residual contentment which caressed him, and the air between them, with grateful recognition, with warmth and a happy languour she need not deny.

She reached out both arms in greeting, uncovering for him her bared breast; and as he slipped within her embrace, and they continued to stare at each other, her look as for a beloved child changed into a look of a different sort – welcoming, acquiescent, humble and assertive within the same fervent pattern.

He took her in an intent trembling silence which neither wished to break.

After that they did not sleep: it was as if their second love-making, unravelling the sweet, strange fact of the first, released them now to enjoy all the rest of what they could give each other. They talked, unhurriedly, till morning, while the grey light, filling the glen again, seeped gently into their room: of all the countless dawns of the war, thought Lockhart, this was the first tranquil one, the first one where nothing could harm him, the first one with the lovely label 'Julie' ... They talked of many things: of loving and being loved, of what attracted them in each other, of their nervousness the previous evening: the process of bringing themselves and each other up to date within their small corner of history was easeful and exciting by turns, and deeply healing to all past fears and ordeals. I have won her, thought Lockhart, looking beyond Julie to the window-square of light that announced the day: I must keep her also – it is not just those eyes, and the body that is cool and hot at the same time, pure and shameless, her own and then mine, by quick turns, as I wish it and as she wishes it: this is the *person* for me – she makes sense of it all ... He turned on his elbow, looking down lovingly at her, and she met his glance with clear pleasure, and said:

'You are pale ... What are we going to do today?'

'Well – this,' said Lockhart, with little hesitation.

'It has my vote also.' She eyed the ceiling speculatively. 'But wasn't there some talk, a long time ago, of your being a Puritan?'

'That I am,' he answered determinedly. 'Who are you to doubt it?'

'I am a girl to whom a lot of nice things have been happening, almost continuously ... What is your brand of Puritanism, and why do you tell me all these terrible lies?'

'They aren't lies,' he said, with seriousness. 'I'm not a sensual person at all, really. You make me so, but then you are you ... There's been nothing like this in the war for me – nor ever, for that matter. It's a complete change, a complete break.'

'A break with what?'

'With reality, I suppose.'

'Look,' she said decisively, 'I do not like to be in that category.'

'I mean,' he said, floundering a little, 'that there's the war – you've come as a lovely surprise in the middle of it – I wish to God you could alter it for ever – but it's still there——'

'And you'll just go back to it afterwards?'

'I can't go back the same, but I have to go back. We both have. Julie,' he said, seeing in the half-light the hint of a smile on her face, 'you don't have to try to put me in the wrong. I do it quite well myself ...'

'My Puritan,' she murmured, 'how can I make you love me?'

'There are three ways,' he said with energy, steering away from the doubtful ground. 'You must look as you do now, you must feel as you did a couple of hours ago, you must talk as you do always. Even separately, they are irresistible. Together——' He stopped.

'Was it really two hours ago?' she asked innocently.

'Yes.'

'Puritanism indeed ...'

'I refuse to be put in the wrong over *that* ...' Attracted by a new and delicate sound, he turned towards the window. 'Do you know,' he asked after a pause, 'that it is snowing?'

She raised herself to look out of the window, showing her breast and shoulders a warm glowing white against the coarse sheets. 'How lovely!' she exclaimed. 'Now no one can reach us for days ...'

'For ever,' he said. 'Snow on – we have eggs, we have many things in tins, we have a large ham from Canada ...' The isolation which had threatened to be an embarrassment on the previous night, now seemed the prime blessing of their lives. 'Snow on, snow us up completely. Leave us here in peace.'

'And your war?'

'*The* war,' he corrected, 'need never reach Loch Fyne, and we need never see it again ... My darling,' he said, lying back once more, 'it is now seven o'clock, it is snowing hard. You said, "What shall we do today?" and I said – what did I say?'

She leant over him, confidingly close again, swiftly warm and alive, as if what she had heard in his voice were linked to something deep within her. 'I seem to remember,' she murmured, 'that you said: "This".'

'What is "this"?'

'This.'

.   .   .

She had beckoned him sensually, that first night, and she never ceased to do so, whether it was by a smile or a look or a movement, whether by a motionless ecstasy or some candid intonation of her voice – as when she said, stroking the smooth skin of his chest: 'You must light lots of fires again – I can't tell you how few clothes I'm going to wear, during the next nine days ...' For it had a deep, an astonishing strength for her, too. Occasionally, she would surprise him by her wildness in love-making, the tender and tormented clenching of her body. 'My storm,' he would whisper at the end – and as if that were a signal, he would feel the engulfing wave of her passion begin to break under him, and as if *that* were a signal, his own would break with hers, surging together upon the shore of their delight.

During all those days and nights, the dream-like haze in which they moved seemed to grow deeper, transfixing, submerging them both. Her eyes, her voice, her cordial body all ravished him; and she also, guiding and submitting at the same time, seemed able to make of his body a weapon for an extreme private rapture.

They often became, for each other, special people not alive before.

CHAPTER 8

When, back on the Clyde, they had to part – Julie to her austere office, Lockhart to sea again – he wrote her in farewell a letter of love and deep gratitude, marked here and there by a tender reminiscent carnality – the sort of thoughts he was bound to have, after so moving an interlude. It ended:

> *I don't think there is anything more to write except that you have become incalculably dear to me, and that the things it is grounded in are the things I want above all others. They are* NOT *all centred round that region of your body, for which I am sure there is some startling piece of Wren's slang; but it's idle to deny that they include it, as closely and as happily as it, last night, included me. I now adore you.*

PART SIX

CHAPTER 1

1944: WINNING

Buckingham Palace was not looking its best on that wet January morning: the bare trees dripped without ceasing, the Royal Standard clung forlornly to its pole, and the fallen masonry and boarded-up windows in the forecourt showed that His Majesty shared with his subjects not only their exposure to the hazards of war, but also their inability to get the after-effects repaired in anything under two years. On Grace Ericson and her mother, however, none of this could have the smallest effect: the day for them was indestructibly bright. They were both decked in every kind of finery: they were there by invitation of the Lord Chamberlain himself; and they were to see their nearest and dearest not only shaking hands with the King, but possibly even talking to him as well. For this Investiture was a personal occasion, arranged (it seemed) almost specifically on their behalf: to it, Commander George Eastwood Ericson, D.S.O., D.S.C., R.N.R., had been bidden, in order to receive the first-named decoration from the King's own hand.

It was very crowded: the ante-room was thronged with people, and the queues making for the main Audience Chamber recalled a successful film show. 'I thought you said there was only two relatives allowed,' grumbled Grace's mother, hemmed in by the slowly-moving mass. She looked round her belligerently, standing on her rights as a hero's mother-in-law. 'It's my belief there's been some shinnanakin'.'

'Hush, Mother,' said Grace, not for the first or the last time. 'You must behave yourself, really – think of what George would say!'

The old lady snorted. 'George wouldn't like us to be pushed and pulled about like this, that I do know ... Are you sure you've got the tickets?'

Grace did not reply: for her, though she was as gratified to be there as her mother, this was a different sort of occasion altogether. It was not just a show, not something you queued up for and complained about: it was a triumphant moment and a devout one – and she wasn't going to share that feeling with anyone and she wasn't going to have it spoilt either. She was immensely proud of what her husband had done, the more so because she knew what it had cost him: he *deserved* his medals, he *deserved* to have the King pin them on himself – and the meeting between him and the King was the sign she had long hoped for, a solemn ceremony to mark their compact, and to acknowledge the fact that George was working himself nearly to death, and was often in terrible danger, and never thought twice about it because the King was party to the bargain ... She hoped that, behind the scenes, they were already making a real fuss of him. This was his second medal, after all.

At that moment, as it happened, a very gentlemanly fellow in black breeches was saying briskly to Ericson and the others:

'D.S.O.'s and above, fall in, in two lines on the left.'

The ceremony got under way with precise formality. The audience settled itself, the King appeared on the dais, the vanguard of those who were to be honoured appeared in the doorway, while others pressed behind them. They were a mixed contingent, here and there contrasted in a somewhat moving way: among the leaders, a young airman with a cherubic face received the Victoria Cross, an old grizzled Admiral got some superior sort of knighthood, a soldier with scarred face and dark glasses groped his way forward to receive the George Medal. They came in procession, four deep, rank upon rank of accomplishment and valour and distinction; there were nervous young servicemen whose bravery had clearly petered out far short of this personal appearance, elderly colonels with the ribbons of many other wars upon their breasts, prosperous old Knights recalling Falstaff at his most expansive ... What a lot of different people, thought Grace Ericson – and why were so many of them in front of George?

'Where is he?' the old lady grumbled by her side. 'They're keeping him back, you mark my words.'

'Hush, Mother, do,' said Grace. 'He'll be here in a minute.'

As she spoke, Ericson appeared round the edge of the doorway, moving forward between an R.A.F. squadron-leader and a red-haired, red-faced leading-stoker who was blinking and sweating as if he had just run a hundred yards under bright hot lights. George looked tired and old, thought Grace, staring at him avidly; she felt prouder still now that she saw him standing in the King's presence, and the D.S.O. and the D.S.C. showed that other people were proud of him too; but the price of her pride was etched all too plainly in his lined face and greying, thinning hair, and she felt like crying as she marked them. For the trouble was that, caught in this endless war, he might go on and on, getting older and older, more and more tired, until – until ... Even now, there was no final figure set to this price he was paying: the total, the moment of quittance, seemed to recede whenever it was sighted, mocking them both every time the calendar came round again. The hard years of the war still followed one upon the other, with no respite in view: George was getting on for forty-nine, and he looked sixty – and now it was the start of yet another year – twelve more months to test and drain him. Perhaps this year would be the last one, perhaps not: they said that D-day was coming soon, but they'd been saying that for a long time, and nothing happened except the same war, the same bitter struggle which was using up people like her husband, making them old men a score of years before their time . . . She turned away, blinking, and whispered to her mother:

'Isn't he getting old?'

The old lady reacted with strange fierceness. 'I'm sure he's got a right to! Think of all his worries, and so much to do all the time. And then his brother being killed like that, and the Palace being bombed, on top of it all.'

After a moment, Grace whispered: 'I mean George, Mother.'

'Don't talk about the King like that,' returned her mother, more tartly still. 'You ought to be ashamed!'

Grace dropped the subject. Other people besides her husband were getting old. And the moment was at hand when neither of them should speak a word.

They both held their breath as Ericson was honoured.

CHAPTER 2

The ship worked for some months of the new year, the fifth in the dreary succession of the war; and then, for *Saltash* and her crew, there came a strange and sudden holiday. They were at St John's, Newfoundland, waiting between convoys, when the news reached them; the brief signal told them that they were to have a refit, with the long leave that went with it. But they were not to return home for the occasion; they were to dock on the opposite side of the Atlantic, in the Brooklyn Navy Yard in the heart of lower New York, and there enjoy a two-months' rest.

'New York!' said Lockhart, when Ericson showed him the signal. 'What's wrong with the Clyde?'

'Too crowded, probably,' answered Ericson. Then he smiled. 'You can't have all the luck all the time, you know.'

Lockhart met the smile, ruefully acknowledging what had been in his mind. 'I won't see her for ages,' he said glumly.

'War is hell,' said Ericson, with cheerful conviction. He welcomed the prospect of the refit, wherever it was to take place, and the news that they were to spend it in novel and attractive surroundings had put him in a holiday mood already.

'America,' grumbled Lockhart again, frowning down at the signal. 'Never heard of the place. What do they know about repairing ships?'

But that criticism, at least, did not survive their arrival, four days later, off Long Island Sound, and their sailing past the Statue of Liberty, up to the fabulous sky-line of New York and the entrance to the East River, and into the teeming maw of the Brooklyn Navy Yard. Not less than anyone on board, Lockhart found himself reacting to the first impact of America. The country might, from the English point of view, be rather a long way from the centre of affairs; but, judging by the evidence so far, going by size and noise alone, these people *must* be able to do things ... The impression of efficiency was presently confirmed, when *Saltash* came alongside and was invaded by a horde of quick-moving entirely silent men who paid no attention to anyone on board, but simply set to work tearing things to bits.

'Now just you take a rest, Commander,' said one of the dockyard officials, when Lockhart asked some questions about shore-lighting. 'We'll fix your ship up real pretty ... Know what I'd do, if I were you?' he added, with no alteration of his expression. 'I'd get to hell out, and come back around six weeks from now.'

'It's so difficult,' said Lockhart later to Scott-Brown. 'You don't even know whether they're being rude or not ...'

'It works both ways,' said Scott-Brown judicially. '*They* don't know whether our feelings are hurt.'

As soon as they were docked, and before any shore-leave was granted, Ericson addressed his crew on the quarter-deck.

'We're here,' he began, 'primarily because the shipyards at home are too busy to take us for refit, but that doesn't mean that we'll do badly out of the exchange. I'm quite sure that this shipyard will look after us just as well as one on the Clyde or at Liverpool – and if anyone thinks otherwise, I want him to keep it to himself. There are two or three things,' he went on, 'that I want to say about our stay here. First is that, as soon as we go ashore, we are guests of this country – and guests have to behave themselves especially well, they have to fit into their host's house and into his habits, even though they don't find it easy. Anything else is bad manners – and don't forget that people here will judge England by the way you behave. If you are noisy and rude, that means that England will get the same reputation ... Secondly, no matter how differently things are done here, don't criticize them out loud – and above all don't laugh at them until you're quite sure that Americans are prepared to laugh at them too. It's even possible that they do some things better here than they do in England – and even if that's not true, it doesn't do any good to make comparisons about different methods and different standards.' He paused. 'The other thing I want to mention is your own personal behaviour. I hope you'll make lots of friends. But don't try to overdo it, especially where women are concerned. Just because you're in a foreign country, that doesn't mean that every woman you meet is a potential prostitute, and that you can treat her like one. Treat women as you would at home – because they *are* the same as the women at home: there are the good ones and the bad ones, and they're in exactly the same proportion as they are in London or Glasgow. You'll find,' he ended, 'that the beer here is rather weak, but the whisky's rather strong – and cheap. If you want to get drunk, do it in private. Don't fall flat on your face in Fifth Avenue, because that's liable to get into the newspapers, and' – he became briefly stern – 'no one in Royal Navy uniform, and especially no one from this ship, is going to get into the newspapers, in that connection or in any other.'

CHAPTER 3

The radio building was large, shiny, and bustling: the studio where Lockhart was being interviewed resembled an aquarium, through whose glass walls other men and women, ridiculously silent, moved their mouths like suppliant fish.

'Just a short talk,' said the programme organizer, a grey man with a look about him of secret and permanent torture. 'But plenty of action, of course. Let's see, now ... Have you sunk a lot of submarines?'

'Only two,' said Lockhart.

'Gee, that's too bad. But we'll think of something ... Have you worked with the U.S. Navy at all?'

'We've run across one or two of your destroyers. We haven't worked in a group with them.'

'It'll come, it'll come,' said the other man, with a faint flicker of encouragement. 'Just as soon as you get yourselves organized ... How long have you been on combat duty?'

Lockhart hesitated. 'What do you mean by combat duty, exactly?'

The radio man stared. 'Gee, Commander, you're out of touch aren't you?'

'Yes,' said Lockhart, 'I'm terribly out of touch.'

'Well, I want to do this programme, anyway. It's a cinch from the Allied solidarity angle. And they said you gave them a right smart talk yesterday, at – where was it?'

'Women's Section of the Bundles for Britain organization.'

'Sounds like Mother's Day in hell ... Well, let's get something down on paper.'

. . .

In a corner of the huge popular restaurant on Times Square, Scott-Brown, the doctor – correct, austere, self-sufficient – was enjoying a singularly tender steak. At his side the waitress, a buxom young woman dressed in frilly apple-green, watched him intently, hand on hip. Each time he conveyed anything to his mouth, her interest seemed to reach a new crescendo.

When he became aware of the scrutiny, Scott-Brown turned and smiled. The waitress answered the smile, with a ready twist of shoulders and hips.

'You a Britisher?' she asked, after a pause.

'Yes,' said Scott-Brown politely, 'I'm from England.'

The waitress nodded, enormously pleased. 'Can tell you boys a mile away, just as soon as you start on the meat dish. Know why?'

'No,' said Scott-Brown. 'How do you recognize us?'

The waitress pointed at his left hand, then at his right. 'Knife and fork stuff,' she answered. 'Both hands together, like you was driving a team or something. No one else does that. Kills me every time.'

. . .

Midshipman Holt stepped into the automatic elevator behind a large tough-looking woman with blue-white hair. They were alone in the elevator, and there was silence as it began its descent. Then the woman, who had been eyeing the two red patches and the twisted braid, denoting his rank, which marked Holt's lapels, said suddenly:

'Say, can you tell me something?'

'Certainly, madam,' said the midshipman, who had dined well for his age.

'It's those things on your jacket.' She pointed to the red collar-patches. 'What's it mean?'

'I'm not really allowed to tell anyone,' said the midshipman.

'No kidding?' said the woman. 'I think you British are the cutest things.'

'But I'll tell *you*,' said the midshipman, with an alarming leer. 'It means the secret service – M.I.5.'

'No kidding?' said the woman again. She beamed at him. 'So young, too.'

. . .

The man, a United States marine corporal with a sodden face and two rows of medals, stood in Allingham's path, swaying slightly. The crowds on the sidewalk moved past them, carefully indifferent to what was going on. There were plenty of such scenes on the streets of down-town New York, and they were good scenes to avoid.

The marine tapped Allingham on the chest.

'What the hell sort of uniform is that?' he asked thickly. 'Where you from, bud?'

'Australia,' said Allingham. He moved to get past.

'That's a kind of Limey country, ain't it?' said the marine, detaining him.

'It's part of the British Empire, yes.'

' "Part of the British Empire",' mimicked the marine savagely. 'Why you all talk like a bunch of whores?'

Allingham said nothing.

'God damn Limeys,' said the marine. His sweating face gleamed in the lamplight from the nearest shop-window. 'Reckon we'll have to clean you up next, after the Japs.'

Allingham said nothing.

'No talk, huh? Guess you're right, bud. No fight, either. That's what I heard. Come all this way in a pretty uniform, just to eat good American food and lay a lot of our dames. When you going to start fighting?'

'Not this evening,' said Allingham.

'Not any evening,' sneered the marine. 'Leave it all to the Americans – the world's top suckers.' He swayed forward against Allingham, who gave way a pace, his fingers twitching. 'If you won't, you won't,' went on the marine. 'But don't get in my way again, or I'll beat the hell out of you, wherever you come from and however fast you're running.'

'I'm not running,' said Allingham hardly. 'But I'm not scrapping in the street, either.'

'Christ!' said the marine, 'they've started drafting the fairies ...' He turned suddenly, and rocketed through the nearest doorway, leading to a large, brassy bar. The quick disappearance, cancelling the ugly crisis, came as a relief, dissolving some of Allingham's anger. It was a good deliverance, from most points of view ... Something unusual about the entrance to the bar attracted his attention, and presently he saw that it was the ornate illuminated sign over the door.

'WELCOME ALL U.S. HEROES!' it said. And underneath: 'THROUGH THESE PORTALS PASS THE FINEST FIGHTING MEN IN THE WORLD.'

. . .

Ericson stood on the bridge of the new American destroyer, saying nothing, watching how they did it all. He was very glad to be on board, making the trip down the Sound as a guest on one of the ship's working-up exercises; a day at sea, after he had been so long tied to the land, was exactly what he wanted.

The American captain bent to one of the voice-pipes. 'What are you steering?' he asked his quartermaster below.

'Two hundred degrees, sir,' came the answer, in a ripe New Jersey accent.

The American captain turned to Ericson, smiling in a vague and friendly way. 'Fine day,' he said. 'Glad you came along ...' Then, forgetful, he bent to the voice-pipe again. 'What are you steering down there?'

'Jesus, Captain!' came the same voice in answer. 'I just told you.'

. . .

'They're not a bit like us,' said Johnson, the engineer-officer, looking round the wardroom dinner table, reproof in his voice. 'No discipline at all.'

CHAPTER 4

My darling one [Julie wrote], *I'm starting a baby – at least I think I am, and the frogs will say yes or no tomorrow. I'm sorry. I thought of not telling you, and then I thought how close we've become, and so I'm telling you after all. But even so it is nothing to worry you with. It hasn't happened before, because we haven't been lovers before, but it isn't the end of the world: I'll take a quick trip to London, where (you once told me in a lordly sort of way) they under-stand these things.* You are not to worry.

But come back soon: it is lonely, it is dull, it is a little ache of missing you, all the time. New York women may have everything else to commend them (you must make me a list of what they have) but they haven't got this heart that beats and warms for you. I will show you what I mean as soon as we are together again: and please make that as soon as possible.

Lockhart held the letter for a long time, without moving; it was as if her heart were lying in his hand. Swift pictures of her multiplied, just behind his eyes: feelings of shock and of tenderness strove within him, making him guilty and deeply loving at the same time.

The letter was so exactly like her. There was no panic, no reproach, no query of any sort; she had accepted the situation, and was about to deal with it competently. Perhaps she had done so already. In any case she seemed in no doubt that he would agree to what she had in mind.

Her ready acceptance, her competent planning, hurt something deep within him. She was accepting the situation, taking for granted her next step and his endorsement of it, because of his own clumsy manoeuvring; because he had said, or implied, many times, that they could not think of marriage until the war was finished with, that their love and their loving had been 'a break with reality'.

He remembered the crass words with shame and disgust.

He knew now that they were not true. She was the person he must have, not some time in the future, but now: he needed her – to love and be loved by, to salve the dreary war, to keep intact the bright warm promise that lay between them, whether they were together or apart.

The child would be the occasion of their marriage, not the reason for it. That reason was something deeper, stronger, more moving alto-gether. They had found it when they became lovers – perhaps a moment before – and it was not to be lost again. Not by his act, not by hers.

The simple fact was that she had become a precious part of his life, always to be cherished and now to be made sure of; and behind this need of her loomed his huge regret, and the hideous idea of her body being tampered with.

He cabled: 'HAVE IT,' and then sat down to write to her all that was in his heart.

CHAPTER 5

'It's an absolute fact,' Scott-Brown told them, wonder still lingering in his voice. 'There were these two people sitting at the next table to mine: an old chap with white hair, the kind you see in *Esquire*, and a young person with all the bosom in the world, and a mink coat to match it. They were talking of this and that – I couldn't help overhearing – and then suddenly the old chap leant across – it was lunch-time, mind you, and bright sunshine as well – and he said, in a very respectful way: "Little lady, I sure would like to po-sess you".'

'What was the answer?'

'She said' – and here Scott-Brown's voice reached an extreme pitch of disbelief – 'she said: "Honey, I'm just brushing and combing my hormones".'

.   .   .

'Of course,' said the man in the bar, 'we Americans take a different view of women altogether, from what you folks do.'

'I understand that is so,' said Raikes, the navigator, who had been in the bar longer than most people.

'Yes, sir,' said the other man, who had been there almost as long. 'We put them right high up on a pedestal.'

'Very wise,' said Raikes. 'Best way of seeing their legs.'

'And then,' said the man, who wasn't listening, 'we bring them tributes of candy and flowers, and we respect them.'

'That ought to do the trick,' said Raikes.

'That's why,' said the man, 'America is the only country in the world where women are one-hundred-per-cent safe all the time. Our young American girls,' he went on, developing his theme with relish, 'are clean and decent, without a wrong thought in their heads – and that's particularly so in the State of Missouri, where I come from. Our American homes are sacred, our American mothers are honoured throughout the land, and our American womanhood is universally held to be the purest in the world.'

'Good show,' said Raikes.

'Did you say something about legs, Captain?' asked the man presently.

'Yes,' said Raikes.

'I'm a tit man myself.'

. . .

'What have you been drinking?' asked Lockhart curiously.

'Peppermint frappé,' answered the midshipman.

'A whore's drink,' commented Lockhart.

'Is it, sir?' said the midshipman, surprised. 'It was her suggestion.'

. . .

'I love my husband,' said the girl, rising on one lovely arm from the pillow, 'but I'm *in* love with you. You see?'

'That's fine,' said Allingham.

'But, honey, you do understand, don't you? It's important.'

'Sure I understand. Just lie still.'

. . .

'It was between dances,' said Raikes modestly. 'We went out into the garden, and she said "You're welcome", and I was.'

'I noticed that it didn't seem to take you long,' said Scott-Brown austerely.

'She seemed to have some sort of quick-release gear round her waist. No trouble at all.'

'As long as it doesn't harm Anglo-American relations.'

'Huh!' Raikes snorted. 'It's nothing to what the Yanks are doing to ours.'

. . .

'They're not a bit like us,' said Johnson severely. 'No morals at all.'

CHAPTER 6

Lockhart wrote to Julie, from the New York hotel where he was spending a week's leave:

I've been playing poker most of the night, with some newspaper men. What good company they are – and how grand all the Americans have been to us; and, after nearly two months, how I long to get back to you! Now it is Sunday, Sunday dawn: the birds are tweeting, the cards fall from the nervous hands, the Regency scene dissolves. I love and think of you, even in this cold untender hour on the fourteenth floor of a New York hotel: I think of being married to you soon, I think of the child you are guarding for me.

But are you with me, in this dawn? Are you sleeping, are you restless, do you think and dream of me also? Is our cottage, where we were lovers, in your dream? Are there seagulls crying, is there wet heather to walk through, do we hold hands, is there a stirring somewhere in both our bodies: does love live, does it grow, does it move for us? What are your eyes like, your trembling lips, your breast that stroked my own? What is there for us in your dream, in your waking?

No, the hour is not cold, not untender: you are ever wanted, ever missed: you are Julie always, my sensual sister and child and loved one. I reach out for you now: we have shared many dawns, we said goodbye on one, many weeks ago: we share this one again, horribly divided – but the same birds sing, the town stirs, the light comes through the curtain, I touch you and hope you will wake. Wake, sweetheart: that was a kiss, that was a hand on your shoulder. But how warm you are. What were you dreaming of? Was it of this?

Oh, sweet, dawns are still like that, even masculine ones when the room is wrecked by empty glasses and cigar-ends and smoke and stale water in the ice-bucket. Perhaps it is bad to write like this, bad to send it to you; but it is no cruel reminder – these things are there for both of us, all the time, and soon, very soon, we will find them again. And now, in this belated dawn, you are kissed and bidden farewell.

CHAPTER 7

'Halt!' said Chief Petty Officer Barnard. 'Off caps! Signalman Blake, sir.'

'What's the charge, Coxswain?'

'Did leave a piece of chewing-gum adhering to the signal-projector, sir.'

'Oh ... You must keep your equipment clean, Blake, whether we're likely to go to sea or not. Otherwise you'll get into trouble. Caution!'

'Caution, sir. On caps! About turn! Double march!'

'Chewing-gum, Coxswain? How revolting!'

'We've been here too long, sir.'

. . .

'Don't come down to breakfast,' Ericson's host had said, when wishing him goodnight. 'We none of us do on Sundays. Get your sleep, and I'll have it sent up to you.'

Now, lying in bed on a bright Sunday morning, listening to a far-off radio and to some vague farm-noises below, Ericson waited for the promised breakfast. Physically he was at ease, but his thoughts did not match his body; this bed, this comfortable and cheerful room, this kindly welcome should have been all that he wanted, but they were not – they had a sour taste of guilt about them which he could not dismiss.

It was the fault of the war, of course, the war they were escaping. *Saltash* had now been out of action for two months, and she would not be ready to go for another fortnight or even three weeks: though the Brooklyn Navy Yard had proved efficient and co-operative, the delay was due to engine-room spares which could not be conjured out of the air.

Ordinarily, nothing would have been more pleasant than this lazy holiday. But the times were not ordinary, and the holiday could not be accepted save shamefacedly: while they lived on the fat of the land, the war went on, and other people carried it, people who had not had breakfast in bed for five years, and who usually had a rotten breakfast anyway ... In their welcome, the Americans had been kindness itself – witness the present invitation, a surprise approach by a complete stranger; but Ericson and his ship's company had been in debt to that kindness for too many weeks, and it was sapping and destroying all the hard, built-up training of the war. The waiting had put everything out of gear – men as well as machinery: *Saltash* now seemed to him a useless run-down hulk, shirking the battle, and her crew, strangers to the sea, were becoming in the process strangers to all but the most negative aspects of discipline.

The plain reason was that they had been there too long, and there was no cure except to go away and start being serious again, and that was still out of his hands.

There was a knock on the door, and a pretty child of ten or eleven, wearing bright red dungarees, came in, bearing a piled-up tray.

'Good morning, Commander,' she said, with the utmost self-possession. 'How did you sleep?'

'Very well, thank you.'

'I'll bring you the funnies just as soon as I can, but' – she explained seriously – 'in this family it's very hard to get hold of them before noontime.'

'There's really no hurry.'

'Dad says, eat a good breakfast, and then maybe you'd feel like playing a little golf.'

'I haven't played for a long time,' said Ericson, 'but I'd like to walk round.'

'That's fine ... Dad also said,' she went on, eyeing him gravely, 'that I wasn't to say anything about your accent. But it sure is cute.'

'Thank you. What's your name?'

'Ariane. For my grandmother. It's kind of French.' She looked down at the tray. 'Here's breakfast. Is it enough?'

Ericson's eyes followed hers. Breakfast consisted, besides coffee, of one large oval-shaped dish; and on it, neatly arranged, was a composite meal which was difficult to take in at a single glance. Its basic items were bacon, sausages, two eggs, some kedgeree, a piece of fish, four things that looked like scones, mustard, marmalade, a tomato, a fried banana, three slices of toast, and a waffle with a load of maple syrup.

'It's enough,' said Ericson. 'But stay and talk to me.'

'I'd like to. I mustn't stay long, though – I've got work to do.'

. . .

Disputes, sometimes small, sometimes big. Disagreements about how to do things, how to run countries, how to win wars. Arguments with workmen on board, with waiters ashore, with men in bars and women in bed. Slow grumbling in the messdecks, quick flare-ups at parties: stately or sulky anger when other people would *not* see the point of view. Leave-breaking, coming aboard drunk: a row with a dock policeman, a complaint about molesting which came near to rape. Recollection of what things were like in England; resentment against ease, against luxury, against an undeserved, opulent comfort in the midst of war.

Gratitude to Americans for being so kind, changing to so-they-bloody-well-ought-to-be when the mood sickened. Laughter, not kindly, at Yanks talking big. Yanks complaining about their rationing. Yanks with rows of medals simply for travelling from A to B, Yanks thinking they were wonderful and saying so out loud.

Remembering, sometimes mentioning, those first two years of neutrality, while Britain took it and bled and went broke. Fights, arguments, futile comparisons, bitterness, boredom. All part of the stagnation period, the waiting to get on with it.

'Sounds to me like you British are kinda burned up because Patton's troops are going ahead and yours are stuck down somewhere.'

'It isn't that. It's just that we don't like noisy generals.'

'The trouble with these people,' said Vincent, the quiet soft-spoken young sub-lieutenant who had been in corvettes since 1939, 'is that they don't take the war seriously. Even now – in 1944 – they've still only got one leg in. Their rationing's a joke, though they could hardly make more noise about it: you can still get all the meat you want, all the butter, all the petrol – particularly if you know the man behind the counter, or the man who fixes the priorities, or the man at the garage; and it's *still* considered a bit of smart operating if you get away with more than your share. But the thing that struck me most is their call-up system. There was a man at a party the other night, sticking his chest out because he had a wife and four children, and he'd got his call-up deferred again because of having them. It doesn't make sense . . . Anywhere else in the world – in Russia or England or Germany – having a wife and four children is a reason *for* fighting, not for getting out of it: it means you've got something special to defend, instead of being free and on your own, it's the best argument of all for not hanging back. But when I said that, I might as well have been playing the bagpipes . . . They don't see the war as a fight at all, they don't see it as something essential to win: for them, it's still in the nuisance category, an accident that interrupts the Great American Plan – but if you're smart you can keep clear of it, you can leave it to the next man to fight or overwork or go short of his comforts.

That's not the way to fight a war ... Damn' lucky for them we were there to take the first shock.'

'You've got it all wrong,' said Raikes. 'It may not be the way to fight a war, but it's the way to come out the winner.'

. . .

'The trouble with these people,' said Scott-Brown, 'is that they take the war too seriously. They see the whole thing as a personal tragedy: if you're drafted it's terrible, if you leave home to go to camp it's torture, if you have to go overseas it's bloody murder ... Wars should be taken in the stride, not inflated to ten times life size till everyone's crying their eyes out. The newspapers play it up, of course, now that America's started fighting: everything's a disaster, everything's the biggest victory since Bunker Hill, everyone's a hero, even if he just puts on a dirty-looking pink uniform and bullies a lot of mess-waiters at the nearest canteen. I wonder what would happen if they had a real air-raid on New York? All the reserves of bravery have been expended already, on waving goodbye to Joe when he leaves for his basic training; and as for the papers, they haven't any adjectives left to use ... They're not a great nation at all. There are just a lot *of* them.'

. . .

'The trouble with these people,' said Lockhart, 'is that you can't help liking them, even though you know you oughtn't to ... Do you remember what it was like, back in the middle Thirties? They lectured and screamed at us for years on end about stopping Mussolini, stopping Franco, stopping Hitler: it was a pretty safe lecture to give, three thousand miles away across the Atlantic. When war did break out, they waited over two years before they came into it: waited while we were Dunkirked and bombed to hell and lost nearly two thousand ships and Christ knows how many men: while we bankrupted ourselves, while we gave them almost all our overseas investments to buy arms, while we signed away British possessions like Bermuda and Antigua, in exchange for fifty rotten destroyers that were never out of the repair dock. Then they did decide to come in themselves. With a rush? Like hell ... They came in because they were attacked by the Japanese, and for no other reason: if it weren't for that attack, we'd still be waiting – and so would Hitler. If ever there's another war,' he said dreamily, 'I shall stay out of it for at least two and a half years – that's the average period of American neutrality, so far: in the meantime, I'd send plenty of instructions on being brave and standing firm, and I *might* start an organization called "Bundles for Both Sides" – it would depend on how nice people were to me ... But when this one is over, the thing to be will be an American – and at that point I wouldn't trade my own nationality for all the gold in Fort Knox. But they'll be running the world, because we'll be broke and exhausted: they'll be in charge of everything – these

dunderheaded children who can't see round the very first corner of
history, these products of a crapulous chauvinism——'

'Steady!' said Allingham. 'Fighting words. What do they mean?'

'They mean that I still like the Yanks, but I miss my soap-box. Have a
rum 'n coke, bud.'

. . .

'The trouble with these people,' said Johnson gloomily, 'is that
they've no common sense. They're not a bit like us.'

CHAPTER 8

He began to read it again, without understanding it at all – the terrible
letter from a friend.

> *You will have heard about Julie Hallam* [it said], *horribly sad, and the worst
> luck in the world. She would never have been in the picket-boat at all if she
> hadn't been standing in for another girl who was ill. I gather it wasn't anybody's
> fault: they were making the long trip back from Hunter's Quay, late at night,
> and a bad squall blew up which no one could warn them about. Perhaps the engine
> failed as well. None of us here knew anything about it for hours, and then a man
> rang up to say he'd seen the picket-boat's lights disappear, and was it important?
> ... By that time, even if they'd been able to swim round at all, they couldn't
> have survived the cold long enough to get ashore. We got all the bodies in the end –
> seventeen, mostly liberty-men, but four Wrens among them. I thought you'd like
> some details, as I knew you were a friend of hers. We miss her here very much.
> When do you and* Saltash *get back to the war?*

Better, perhaps, to hear it like this – almost accidentally, from a man
who thought you knew already, a man not fumbling for the first foolish
phrases. But drowning ... The fearful images slipped readily before
Lockhart's eyes, because he knew Julie so well, because he knew
drowning by heart: he saw the spread of hair round her lolling head, the
murky river rolling her over, the embryo child growing cold under her
breast. Ophelia, he thought immediately: something about 'poor
wretch'; and with sick apprehension he recalled the exact phrase – 'and
dragged the poor wretch down to muddy death'. Mud in Julie's eyes and
nostrils, mud clogging her livid throat: icy cold attacking her, and then
the sucking currents where the river met salt water.

It was like *Compass Rose* again, though this time it was a single sword.
But the same enemy had robbed him: a small wave of the cruel sea had
taken her for ever.

Better to hear like this, pierced unawares as by an ill-chancing thrust in the dark. But drowning, Julie, drowning ...

. . .

He was walking alone among tall buildings, buildings which crowded in but failed to crush him, leaving the top of his brain fatally free to think and feel. Men have never cried on this street, he thought: no tears on Eighth Avenue – but what did the rules matter, when every rule in earth and heaven had been broken at one stroke? He had lost the immediate picture of Julie dead: now it was the ache, the grip of bereavement, and the wild self-reproaches that went with it – how he should never have left her, how he should have married her straight away, how perhaps he had killed her, by betraying his dedication, and hers ... She had even been dead when he sent his last letter: he had been writing to a wraith, a spirit, a poor pale Julie who, when he tried to reach her, could only whisper and fade and leave him cold and alone, as he was now: stricken and shivering, among the crowds and the traffic and the buildings that would not fall.

Suddenly, up the street, he saw her coming towards him: Julie herself, with her dark hair piled up, Julie walking with that odd economical gait which was still the most feminine thing about her. Weak with shock and with longing, he waited for her to reach him: it *was* she – no one else walked like that, no one else had that lovely hair, that shape of head. It was she: the letter must have been wrong; even the countries had got mixed up.

When she had only a few more steps to go, he reached out an uncertain hand, and with it the crazy spell broke and his brain cleared agonizingly.

The stranger passed him, staring.

Something about 'another country', he thought. Some man from the grave once more sharing the shroud of his thoughts. Julie had died to such thoughts, such words, such mournings ... 'But that was in another country, and besides, the wench is dead.'

. . .

Now it was not the vile image of death, nor the ache of loneliness: now it was a wild desire to be away, to work, to do something to kill time and memory.

Up on the fo'c'sle, coiling down a wire, a man had made a clumsy job of it. 'Look,' Lockhart began, in a mild rebuke, and then he had remembered, and turned away, unable to finish the sentence, leaving the man puzzled and relieved. But 'Look' had been Julie's phrase, whenever she wanted to claim his attention. 'Look,' she had said, 'you don't know what love is,' and 'Look – if you want *anything* from a woman, it is to be from me.' To stumble thus upon the word 'Look', upon the very voice and touch of her wrapped in an innocent phrase, was enough to destroy him; it seemed that it might do so utterly, unless he could somehow exorcize the past. For now, pinioned by misery, he was the target of every stray dream, every longing which before had been thankfully referred to her.

'Dry sorrow drinks our blood,' he had thought; and presently, down in Ericson's cabin, appealing almost wildly, 'Can't we get away? Can't we start?'

'Soon,' answered Ericson, watching him with compassion that was very nearly love. 'Just as soon as we can. You know I'll do my best.'

CHAPTER 9

It was, cruelly, a good time to be dedicated, a good time to flog the body and the brain; for when *Saltash* did return, it was to a wonderful moment – the beginning of winning.

It was not yet victory: the enemy still had snapping teeth, and still used them when he could; but it seemed that success could now be sighted, far away at the end of the enormous tunnel of the years, and that *Saltash* was returning to a conqueror's ocean. They had been away only two and a half months, but already it had happened, already the wonderful change was apparent. Another colour seemed to have been added to the Atlantic, another blue to the sky; at night, the stars pricked a heaven full of the balm of victory. For after four and a half years of deadly struggle, when both sides, locked in combat, had stung themselves to a vicious and mortal fury, the enemy had begun to crack.

It showed itself in small things, it showed itself in big. It showed in the number of U-boat sinkings – ninety of them were sent to the bottom during the first five months of the year: a single escort group on a single twenty-day cruise accounted for six at one stroke. It showed in the huge convoys that went unharmed across the Atlantic, pouring the stuff in for the last assault; in March, for example, only one merchant-ship was sunk, out of the enormous total that crossed and recrossed the ocean. It showed in U-boat tactics, which had become a pale shadow of what they had been in the past: now, cautious and indecisive, they broke off the battle as soon as resistance was met, and they exhibited no sort of readiness to come back for more.

It showed in an ignominious surrender at sea, with the U-boat captain the first to start swimming towards the ship that had attacked him. It showed in a signal which came from *Rose Arbour*, one of the corvettes, when *Saltash* rejoined and took over command of the group.

'Glad to see you back,' ran the message. 'We were afraid you'd miss the last act.'

May, 1944, was not *quite* the last act, but it was near enough for the signal to make cheerful sense. The lights were brightening for the final scenes: there could not be many of them, and the play was now too far advanced for there to be any chance of a surprise ending.

But before that ending could be reached, the soldiers had one more thing to do.

CHAPTER 10

On the bright and awful morning of D-day, *Saltash* found herself, for the first time for many months, in unfamiliar waters. She was one of a number of support groups, patrolling in a wide ring across the mouth of the English Channel: they were there to intercept any U-boats that might be tempted to leave the dubious shelter of the Atlantic and make for the invasion beaches. They were, in fact, on guard at the back door, and Ericson, for one, felt very glad that he was doing a job connected, however loosely, with the main fabulous assault. On June 6th 1944, there was only one piece of land and water worth concentrating on; and any soldier, sailor, or airman who could not join in was missing an irretrievable moment of history.

Stretching far out of sight on either side of them, the lines of destroyers and frigates and corvettes wove a search-pattern that covered five hundred miles of water. It needed patience, that endless patrol – with the news coming over the wireless every half-hour, with the knowledge that, one step beyond the horizon, the huge armada had just delivered its first thrust. Viewing the battle from afar, knowing what was involved, they could only hope and pray: the men in the escort ships stood on guard at a distance, but others, fighting and dying as *Saltash* circled peacefully, were making this the most solemn and moving moment of the war, in which an outsider must take a truly humble part.

'I'm glad we got as near as this, anyway,' said Ericson, standing on the bridge and watching out of the corner of his eye the rest of his group turning at the limit of their search-area. 'It's not exactly spectacular, but at least we're part of the main operation.'

'I wish we could have gone across with them,' said Lockhart wistfully. '*Some* frigates did . . .' He looked out-board, where far away to the north-east the outline of Land's End and the Scilly Isles lay like a purple shadow on the horizon. 'It's funny that, in all these years, this is the only time we've ever been anywhere near the Channel.'

'Good moment to make the trip,' said Allingham, who was also up on the bridge, drawn there by the feeling they all shared – that this was not a day for being alone, or shut off from one's friends. He looked at his watch. 'Midday already. Wonder how it's going.'

'It's *got* to be all right!' said Lockhart, almost violently. 'This is the whole point of the war ... It's just our luck to be on the wrong side of the wall.'

It was the first time any one of them had felt involved in any theatre of war except their own. But on this day, the great Atlantic was nothing: all the sea war and all the land had shrunk down to a few miles of beach, a few yards of shallow water, and nothing else counted at all.

. . .

Saltash guarded the back door. Northwards to Land's End, eastwards up the Channel to Plymouth Sound, south-west towards Brest – the area altered daily, but the intention and the drill were the same. As a safety measure, the patrol proved well worth while; the U-boats *were* leaving the Atlantic, to try (as they thought) the rich and easy pickings waiting for them off the Normandy coast, and the dozens of escorts that barred their way were in a position to score decisively. The U-boats never did get through, save in negligible strength, and they never came to grips with any of the cross-Channel convoys: in trying to do so, they suffered losses as heavy, proportionately to their numbers, as any of the war.

Saltash herself, with *Streamer* in attendance, added one to the quota of loss: she cornered her quarry close inshore, off Start Point on the Devon Coast, and blew it to the surface with astonishingly little trouble. But it was odd, and faintly alarming, to be hunting a U-boat to its death and at the same time keeping a sharp eye on the depth of water under their keel, and the rocks lying off-shore: it was the first time they had ever had to worry about lack of sea-room, and it seemed as if they had left their proper element altogether and were splashing about, naughtily chasing gold-fish in a pond. The crowds of people waving to them from the nearest headland were the final disturbing item. This was not the Atlantic pattern at all ...

But it was good to justify their existence at such a time, when others were doing so in such brutal and bloody measure. Otherwise, thought Ericson, they hardly counted in the main tide of war at all: they remained on the outside, looking in. Even his own son was more closely involved. *His* ship had gone in on D plus 3 ...

. . .

Back, soon, to their Atlantic beat, which now seemed like patrolling the streets of a dead town, which everyone had deserted in favour of something more interesting. Now it was, in truth, a victorious ocean: scarcely a U-boat was to be seen, and huge convoys – one of them a record one of 167 ships – made the journey unmolested, bearing the vital supplies which the expanding battlefields of France must have. Some of

Saltash's charges were now routed direct to Cherbourg – a strange turn of fate, compared with the old days, when they had, with enormous difficulty, under constant air and sea attack, crept mouse-like into Liverpool Bay . . . But that was the way of it now, and so it continued to the end of the year: the U-boats, denied their bases in the Bay of Biscay, were being pushed back to Norway and even to the Baltic – and the Baltic was a very different matter, when it came to trying to keep up the pressure in the Western Approaches.

There were plenty for the Navy to do, because the needs of the cross-Channel shuttle service meant that there was a chronic shortage of escorts; and there was always a chance that German strategy might change, and try to strangle the supply-line at the Atlantic end. But it was mostly hard, montonous sea-time, with nothing to brighten it and no crises to cope with: it was rather like the first months of the war, when there were not enough U-boats to make a show, and what few there were had not yet worked out a plan of campaign.

Now they had had their campaign, and it was five years later, and for all the good it had done them, they might have saved themselves the trouble, and spared many ships and men.

But perhaps it had to be proved, thought Ericson, bringing *Saltash* up, for the twentieth time, alongside the quay at St John's, Newfoundland, with a featureless fourteen-day crossing behind her, and the ship needing nothing except fresh stores and a lick of paint. Perhaps it had to be proved, and there was no other way of doing it, no other way of sleeping peacefully in their beds, save at the fearful cost that lay in their wake.

CHAPTER 11

Christmas in home waters, Christmas at anchor in the Clyde.

They all felt that it was the last Christmas of the war, but the thought was never phrased aloud, for fear of reprisals from history. They had a wardroom party, but it was just like other wardroom parties: they drank a lot, Ericson joined them and then left at a discreet moment, the stewards got mildly drunk and upset the brandy-butter sauce on the turkey. At the head of the table, Lockhart presided, observing custom automatically: this was like last Christmas, and the Christmas before that – part of the war, part of the job that never ended. Last year there had been Julie, this year there was not: it was sad if you thought about it, so you didn't think about it: you ate and drank and chaffed the midshipman about *his* girl . . .

That afternoon while the ship slept, he had paid a visit to the hideous mass grave where she lay. But there was no special feeling, even about that; it was just a cold day, and an ache inside him, and being alone instead of being together. The usual empty thoughts, the usual hunger and wretchedness.

'Number One!'

'Sorry.' He jerked to attention. 'What did you say, Mid?'

'I've got the bachelor's button out of the pudding.'

He made an appropriate comment.

Presumably things would get better, after a time.

PART SEVEN

CHAPTER 1

1945: THE PRIZE

'And that is why,' said Vincent, plodding to the end of his lecture, 'it was absolutely essential to go to war in the first place, and why it's even more important to make sure that we do a proper job of winning it now.'

He shut his notebook with an unconvincing snap, and put on top of it the *Army Bureau of Current Affairs* booklet, on which his lecture had been based. Then he looked up, facing uncertainly *Saltash*'s lower messdeck, and the rows of stolid men who were his audience. The serried eyes looked back at him unblinkingly, with very little discernible expression: a few of them were bored, a few hostile, most of them were sunk in a warm stupor: they were the eyes of men attending a compulsory lecture on British War Aims. As on so many previous occasions, thought Vincent, the heady magic of ABCA had not worked ... He cleared his throat, sick of the whole thing, knowing only one way to play out time.

'Any questions?'

There was a pause, while silence settled again; many of the eyes dropped or turned aside, as if fearful of establishing contact with Vincent at this crucial moment of demand. The dynamos hummed loudly; *Saltash* swung a point to her anchor, and the shaft of sunlight through the porthole moved across the deck and over the feet of the men in the front row.

A man at the back cleared his throat, and spoke at last.

'Sir?'

'Yes, Woods?' It was bound to be Signalman Woods: Woods always asked the first question, sometimes the only one. Woods was hoping for a recommendation for Leading Signalman, and Vincent was the only man who could give it to him.

'Sir, if we get rid of all the Nazis, who'll run the country? Germany, I mean. Who'll be the government?'

I should really encourage him, thought Vincent, I should say: Now that's a very interesting question. But it's not, it's a bloody silly one, because it means he simply hasn't been listening at all.

'*As I mentioned*,' he said, with just enough emphasis to make the point, 'we are quite sure that there are enough non-Nazis in Germany to form a proper government. All they have to do is come forward, and——' he finished lamely, 'that is what will happen.'

'Thank you, sir,' said Woods politely, his effort accomplished. 'I just wanted to be sure.'

Silence settled again. This should be a brisk and lively discussion, thought Vincent sadly, but it isn't working; there ought to be a quick series of questions, a little argument, a fresh approach by some highly intelligent sailor, a great up-surge of speculation on this crucial question ... Most of the failure was his own fault, he realized; the matter interested him, but he had not been able to communicate that interest to any of them; it had been just another lecture period, filling in the time between 'Stand-Easy' and 'Hands to Dinner' – preferable to gun-drill or painting ship, not as interesting as playing tombola or doing nothing.

But here was someone else with a question, one of the stokers for a change. 'Sir,' said the man haltingly, 'when you said about fighting for a better world ...' But had the phrase sounded as appalling as it did now? 'Did you mean the League of Nations, like? No more war?'

A better world, thought Vincent – now how could he sum it up in terms which would mean something to a second-class stoker who had been a boiler-maker's apprentice before the war? He knew in his own mind what it involved – the Four Freedoms, the rule of Law, an end to tyranny, the overthrow of evil; but he had listed all these things in the course of his lecture, and explained them as best he could, and gone into detail whenever detail was worth while – and clearly it had meant absolutely nothing to his questioner, it hadn't made a single ripple ... I can't go through it all again, he thought despondently; there isn't time, and there's no point either, if the words and phrases that mean so much to me are meaningless to this man, this roomful of men like him.

'The League of Nations, or something of the same sort,' he said, 'will certainly be part of the post-war world. One of the things we've been fighting for is that international law should become strong again – that is, if one nation wants to start a war, the rest of the world really will combine to stop them. But when I talked about a "better world"' – he swallowed – 'I meant a better world for everyone – freedom from fear, no big unemployment, security, fair wages – all those sort of things.'

Silence again. Had his words meant anything to them, Vincent wondered: did they kindle any spark? – was there indeed a spark to be kindled?

Another man spoke, simply, doubtfully. 'Is it all going to be different, then?'

What was the answer to that? I hope so. 'I hope so,' he said.

A third man spoke, scornfully, out of some personal political copy-book he carried for ever in his head. 'There'll always be the bosses. Stands to reason.'

That's outside this discussion, thought Vincent – and yet, should *anything* be outside this discussion? If this man has been fighting for a world without 'bosses', why shouldn't he say so? If he thinks that his particular fight has been a failure, why shouldn't he say that as well? But it isn't really a fight about bosses – not in the sense he means; and I very much doubt whether he gave that aspect of it a single thought when he enlisted, or was conscripted. Yet 'bosses' or 'no bosses' *was* a post-war problem: it could even be true that the war, obscurely, was being fought to end the whole range of boss-tyranny – big bosses like Hitler, little bosses like the foreman with the rough tongue. If that were true, then it was a dangerous subject: the pamphlet hadn't said anything about the master-and-man relationship, it had treated with oppression at the international level only ... And that was what he had failed to interest them in – the large-scale pattern, the moral issue: those things had rung no bell at all.

He was about to answer non-committally when Signalman Woods came through again, this time in prim reproof.

'It's got nothing to do with the bosses. That's a lot of talk. It's war aims – what to do when we've won.'

At that there was a final blanketing silence: the moment of spontaneity was lost for ever. Last week's lecture had been so much better, thought Vincent; but then, that had been on venereal disease ... He cast about him for some phrase which might stimulate further questions, and found none; the subject had been dealt with, the potent leaven distributed, and the result now confronted him, unalterable, totally defeating. Then, far away, came the sound of a pipe: the audience brightened and shuffled: the pipe came nearer, and with it the quartermaster's voice: 'Hands to dinner!' There was movement at the back of the messdeck, a stirring, a heightened receptivity towards the first attractive idea of the morning. Vincent picked up his papers.

'That's all,' he said. 'You can carry on.'

Back in the wardroom, Allingham looked up when he came in.

'What's the matter, Vin? Brassed off?'

'Yes,' said Vincent. He went to the sideboard and poured himself a drink. 'I don't think these lectures of mine are much use.'

'What was it this time?'

'War aims – post-war prospects ...' He swung round. 'It ought to be interesting. It *is* interesting to me. But it doesn't seem to raise a single spark, for anyone else.'

'For some of them, surely,' said Allingham helpfully.

Vincent shook his head. 'No ... It's so difficult to make it sound convincing, or even to explain it properly. And morally speaking, people shouldn't really be called upon to fight, if they don't understand the real issues and wouldn't believe in them if they did.' He looked at Allingham with curiosity. 'Do *you* think it matters?'

'That we should explain – dress the war up a bit, make it a matter of conviction?'

'Yes.'

Allingham considered, frowning. 'I used to. I started the war like that, anyway. Now I'm not so sure. We've got to win the bloody thing, whatever material we use – willing or not . . . Perhaps it doesn't make a hell of a lot of difference, either way, when it comes to action – fighting, danger. Able-Seaman Snooks doesn't shout "Another blow for democracy!" when he looses off a couple of rounds at an aircraft: he says "Got the bastard!" if he hits and "——it!" if he misses. He just doesn't want to get killed, and he doesn't need any special inspiration or moral uplift for that.'

'But you feel the need for it yourself?'

'I don't even know that. I came a long way to fight this war, and I thought it was some sort of crusade then – but maybe I'd have come anyway . . .' He smiled, and rose, and came towards the sideboard and the gin-bottle. 'No good being left out, you know, even if you're an Australian.'

'But if it's just a *war*,' said Vincent despondently, 'it's not worth winning, it's not worth all the trouble.'

'It's even less worth losing,' said Allingham, with conviction. 'That's one thing sure . . .' He raised his glass, and drank deep, as if toasting the prospect of victory and survival. Then he smiled again. 'Cheer up, kid! It's too late to worry about it now, anyway.'

CHAPTER 2

Now there was a lull – but it seemed a friendly, not a foreboding lull: this was the pause before going on holiday, not the halt on the edge of the grave. The transatlantic convoys went on, unceasingly, but convoys were different now – once again, they were like the convoys at the very beginning of the war: ships and men occasionally ran into trouble, but they were always other ships, other men – strangers who had had bad luck, amateurs who had probably made some silly mistake . . . For the most part, the U-boats held off, for a variety of reasons which could only be guessed at: it might be fear, it might be insufficient numbers, reorganization, the saving of strength for some huge final effort. Whatever it was, the spring of that year gave them what all springs should give – ease, hope, and promise, in abundant measure.

For Ericson, it was a lull that he needed – he and *Saltash* together. One could perhaps divine more of the past history of strain from looking at *Saltash* than from looking at Ericson; but that did not mean that Ericson was not feeling it just as strongly . . . His men had become used to his grey hair, his gruff manner, his stern face which looked with an equal indifference upon a sinking ship, a dead man, a defaulter with a foolish excuse, a pretty visitor to the wardroom. This mask hid his tiredness; *Saltash* had no such camouflage. She had now been running for over two years, hard-driven years with little respite from the weather or the enemy: she was battered, salt-streaked, dented here and there – a typical Western Approaches escort, telling her whole story at a single glance. Ericson, surveying his ship as he put off in the motor-boat, sometimes found himself wondering what *Compass Rose* would have looked like, if she had still been alive and afloat. Not as pretty as he remembered her, certainly; for some of the original corvettes, which had seen it through in the Atlantic since 1939 – *Trefoil, Campanula,* their own *Petal* – looked like tough and battered old women who had been street-walking too long. So do I, by God! thought Ericson grimly. It was his fiftieth year, and he looked and felt every hour of it.

'I'm thirty-two,' Lockhart told him on one occasion, in answer to his question. 'The best years of my life have vanished . . .' But that was not really true, Lockhart knew well enough: for him, they were not lost years, in spite of the futility and wastefulness of war. He had grown up fast in the meantime, he was a different person from the twenty-seven-year-old, goalless, motiveless, not very good journalist who had joined up in 1939. War had given him something, and the personal cost was not a whit too high: he had missed five years of writing and travel, but he had gained in every other way – in self-discipline, in responsibility, in simple confidence and the rout of fear . . . I should be all right after the war, he told himself sometimes: because they can't muck me about any more, and I can't muck myself about, either.

For him as well as for Ericson, the lull in action was welcome, the more so since he saw it as an appropriate part of the pattern; it was the way things ought to be going, at that stage, to ensure that they should have the hoped-for outcome. If I were writing the story of this contest, he thought, this is where the book would tail off, because we've reached the moment when nothing happens – we're just winning the war, and that's all there is to say. That would be the whole point of the story, really – that in the end nothing happened, and it petered out into silence. The petering out was their victory.

' "And enterprises of great pith and moment",' he quoted to himself vaguely, 'de dah, de dah, de dah, "and lose the name of action".' But thank God the enterprises had done so: thank God for being alive on a fine spring morning in 1945, when he had never really expected to be, and when lots of people, who for five years had been trying to kill him, were dead themselves. Now in truth nothing was happening, and nothing was just what they had been aiming at, all along.

If only Julie had been alive as well, to share the moment with him, to give it warmth and happiness as well as its cold satisfaction.

CHAPTER 3

April ... April, in the Atlantic, brought the last few strokes of their war; and one of them, involving a homeward-bound convoy which *Saltash* was taking in to Liverpool, gave them the most unpleasant surprise they had had for many months. After the lull, the recent weeks had been startlingly and dangerously active. The enemy still had about seventy U-boats able to keep at sea, and though the brief and violent flare-up cost thirty-three of them sunk, it cost many merchant-ships as well. On one of these occasions, *Saltash* lost a ship on the very front doorstep – inside the Irish Sea, within sight of home. The ship was hit close to the bows, and she sank slowly, with little likelihood that any lives would be lost; but even so, the sudden mischance, at that late hour of the convoy and the war, had an evil element of shock.

They watched *Streamer* counter-attacking, on the other side of the convoy, but they could still scarcely believe that it had happened: it was the end of the war, the U-boats were virtually defeated – *and no U-boats operated in home waters anyway*. They had been aware that April was proving a bad month at sea, and that the enemy seemed to be making a last vicious effort to avert defeat; but it had never been brought so close to them, they had never seen it proved in so violent a fashion. It induced a sense of discomfort, a nervous foreboding, which lasted long after the situation had been set to rights. If this sort of thing could still happen, it not only restored the wicked past – it threatened, in an extreme degree, the promised future as well.

'You silly bastards!' said Raikes, aloud, when the flurry was over – the U-boat neatly despatched by *Streamer*, the merchantseamen rescued from the water: 'You silly bastards – you might have killed some of us.' He echoed all their thoughts at that moment; their hopes of staying alive, their prickling haste to get the thing over before they ran into any more danger or took any more chances. In the whole of the rest of the war, there might only be two or three more convoys for them to escort: in the whole of the rest of the war, it was possible that only one more escort-ship was going to be sunk. Make it not us, they thought – not at this stage, not so late in the day when we have very nearly finished, very nearly survived ...

Raikes, up on the bridge, had spoken for all of them; and later, in the wardroom, they returned to the subject, with a readiness which showed how deep an impression the torpedoing had made on everyone in the ship.

'It gave me the shock of my life!' said Allingham, downing one drink very quickly and reaching out for the next one. 'U-boats in the Irish Sea – at this stage? They must be stark staring crazy!'

'Crazy or not,' said Scott-Brown, 'it happened, and it can happen again. Particularly, if it's their last chance, and they know that it is. They'll go all out, and they won't care what happens as long as they do some kind of damage. That was a suicidal attack, this afternoon – but they made it, all the same. We've probably got to expect that sort of thing, and worse, in the future.'

'All I hope is that we don't get in the way of the next one,' said Raikes. 'I haven't lived as long as this, just to stop a torpedo when we're nearly home and dried.'

'It would certainly spoil my war aim,' said the midshipman, with decision.

'But it's the end of the fighting!' said Allingham, violent emphasis in his voice. 'We're over the Rhine, we've nearly joined up with the Russians, Hitler himself may be dead by now. What do they hope to gain by it?'

'Perhaps nothing.' Vincent, who had been sitting quietly by the stove, spoke suddenly. 'They're just going on fighting, that's all . . . If it were we who were near defeat, wouldn't we do the same thing, however hopeless it looked?'

He glanced round the wardroom, waiting for an answer.

'I should do exactly what I was told,' said the midshipman, modestly. 'But I don't think I'd volunteer for anything special . . .'

'But if it were really hopeless——' Allingham began, and then stopped. After a moment he smiled at Vincent. 'You're right, Vin – it *is* the only thing for them to do, and I hope we would do the same. They've got bags of guts, you know – you've got to hand it to them.'

'They can have any sort of testimonial they like,' said Scott-Brown, 'as long as they don't try to earn it by sinking *Saltash*.'

Raikes nodded. 'That's just what I thought this afternoon. It may sound a bit selfish – but this is such a bloody silly time to be killed.'

CHAPTER 4

May – and now, surely, now at last nothing could go wrong nothing could steal their victory, nor take their lives.

Saltash, divorced from the rest of her group, had been on independent passage from Iceland when she received the unusual signal: 'REMAIN ON

PATROL IN VICINITY OF ROCKALL'; and there she now was, steaming in a five-mile square round the isolated, inexplicable pin-point of rock which was really the tip of a mountain in mid-ocean – Rockall, rising from the depths of the Atlantic to break surface, by a few feet only, 300 miles from land: Rockall, the unlighted, shunned graveyard of countless ships, countless U-boats. But, Ericson wondered, why Rockall? – unless Their Lordships wished to place a finger on *Saltash* in case of need; and why 'on patrol'? – unless she were waiting for something which did not require an escort-group, something which one single ship could do.

'I think this is the end of it,' said Ericson privately to Johnson, when they were discussing the fuel situation. 'How much oil have you got in hand, Chief?'

'About two hundred tons, sir. Say fourteen days' steaming, at normal speed.'

'I don't think we'll be moving very fast. We're just hanging around, at the moment.'

Johnson looked at him curiously. 'How long for, sir?'

'I don't know, Chief. Till the bell strikes.'

Saltash steamed her slow circle. There were no ships to be seen, there were no convoys in her area: it was just a stretch of grey, flat-calm sea, with the gaunt rock in the middle, the horizon round them, the dull sky overhead. The Radar-screen was blank, the Asdic probed an endless empty sea: *Saltash* turned ninety degrees to port every half-hour, and in between times traced an uneven zigzag course, in case anyone were watching them. We've done this before, thought Ericson – in this ship, and in *Compass Rose* as well: once when we were hove-to with a damaged merchantman, once when we did a box-search for survivors, once when we were too early at a rendezvous. It had always been the same sort of exercise – waiting patiently, searching endlessly, keeping on the move in case of surprises. Now they waited, in the same way, but this time not knowing what it was they waited or searched for. They turned their ordained circles, first under a grey sky, then under a black, then under a grey again; they sweated out the successive watches, steaming at a steady ten knots and getting nowhere, doing what they were told and hoping the answer would come soon, before something went wrong, before this simple merry-go-round turned to wicked witchcraft, on the authentic Atlantic pattern.

Ericson told no one what it was about, because he did not know himself, and there was therefore nothing to tell; there was just the bare signal-log, which anyone could see, and the order 'Remain on patrol'. In his private mind, he knew that they were waiting for the end of the war – but that was guess-work, not to be shared because it had no backing from authority. The signal-log, the last explicit order from the Admiralty, was all they had to go on.

Once Raikes, when he was Officer-of-the Watch, said:
'I hope they don't try any tricks. It's a rotten time to be killed.'
Ericson frowned. 'That hadn't struck me,' he said, somewhat coldly.
'But it'll be a rotten time for anyone who tries to kill *us*.'

The expected signal came at dawn, on a dull calm morning which saw
Saltash still circling the rock, still occasionally weaving a cunning
variation of her course, still plodding along as ordered, and serving three
meals a day, and remaining keyed up for any danger, any last attack.
'Hostilities terminated,' it said. 'All U-boats have been ordered to
surrender by German High Command. The surrender-signal is a large
black flag. You should take appropriate precautions against individual
enterprise. The two U-boats which are presumed to be still in your
immediate area should be escorted to Loch Ewe.'
'Immediate area?' said Ericson. 'It's a libel ... We'll wait for them to
show up.'

. . .

The beaten foe emerged.
All over the broad Atlantic, wherever they had been working or lying
hid, the U-boats surfaced, confessing the war's end. A few of them,
prompted by determination or struck by guilt, scuttled or destroyed
themselves, or ran for shelter, not knowing that there was none; but
mostly they did what they had been told to do, mostly they hoisted their
black surrender flags, and said where they were, and waited for orders.
They rose, dripping and silent, in the Irish Sea, and at the mouth of
the Clyde, and off the Lizard in the English Channel, and at the top of
the Minches where the tides raced: they rose near Iceland, where
Compass Rose was sunk, and off the north-west tip of Ireland, and close to
the Faroes, and on the Gibraltar run where the sunk ships lay so thick,
and near St John's and Halifax, and in the deep of the Atlantic, with
three thousand fathoms of water beneath their keel.
They surfaced in secret places, betraying themselves and their
frustrated plans: they rose within sight of land, they rose far away in
mortal waters where, on the map of the battle, the crosses that were
sunken ships were etched so many and so close that the ink ran together.
They surfaced above their handiwork, in hatred or in fear: sometimes
snarling their continued rage, sometimes accepting thankfully a truce
they had never offered to other ships, other sailors.
They rose, and lay wherever they were on the battlefield, waiting for
the victors to claim their victory.
Two rose to *Saltash*, off Rockall.

. . .

They saw them on the horizon: the two hard shapes topping the sea-
level stood out like squat battlements: they could only be U-boats – the

hated and longed-for targets which were now part of the rubbish of defeat.

'Two submarines in sight, sir,' said the starboard look-out, stolidly submitting the most unusual report of the war; and *Saltash* began to speed towards the meeting, coming to Action-Stations as she did so. 'Keep her weaving, Coxswain!' Ericson called down to Barnard, and *Saltash* listed sharply as the wheel was put hard over, and the ship began to trace a swaying corkscrew pattern – the precaution Ericson had decided on, as soon as the present occasion arose. No desperate last-minute torpedoes for him ... When they drew near, they saw that the two U-boats were side by side, and stationary: their black flags drooped at the masthead, their decks were crowded with men – as were *Saltash*'s own, *Saltash* swept round them, moving at twenty-two knots in a tight, high-speed circle, listing heavily, following the U-boats with all her guns; the frigate's solid wash set the smaller craft rocking, and the men on the decks clung on as best they could, and occasionally shook their fists.

'What do we say to them?' said Ericson, who was clearly enjoying himself.

'Herr Doktor Livingstone, I presume,' said Lockhart.

'How about a warning shot, sir?' suggested Allingham hopefully.

Ericson laughed. 'I know your finger's itching, Guns, but I don't think there's anything to warn them about.' He considered. 'Perhaps a depth-charge would be a good plan, though – not too near, not too far away – just close enough to shake them. I want them to behave properly on the way home. Tell Vincent the idea – one charge only. He can drop it whenever he's ready.'

The depth-charge exploded at about the same distance from *Saltash* as from the U-boats; there was thus no possibility of damaging the latter's pressure hulls. But the single heavy charge, detonating with a crash somewhere near the surface of the sea, had a marked effect on all concerned. The mountain of water which shot upwards cast a dark shadow over the U-boats: the fine spray, falling slowly back, moved across them like a damp and drifting curtain. When it cleared, it was as if those on board had been through some sort of moral shower-bath as well: most of them raised their hands over their heads, there was some confused shouting on a querulous note, and a man climbed up the mast and spread out the black flag, so that it could be better seen.

'They've got the idea,' said Lockhart, who was watching through his binoculars.

'Glad they can take a hint.' Ericson picked up the loud-hailer microphone, and spoke through it. 'Can you understand English?'

Affirmative waves and nods came from both U-boats.

'University types,' said Raikes.

Ericson raised the hailer again. 'That was a depth-charge,' he said hardly. 'I have nearly ninety more of them ... You give no trouble, otherwise –' he gestured ferociously – '*donner und blitzen!*'

'Damned good, sir,' said Lockhart. 'Make 'em sweat.'

'Could you spell it, sir?' asked the hard-pressed signalman whose duty it was to write out whatever messages left the bridge.

'We are going to Loch Ewe in Scotland,' continued Ericson, making it sound like a father's unalterable curse. 'What is your speed on the surface?'

Faintly across the water came an answering hail: 'Ten.'

'It'll take us about two days,' said Ericson aside to Lockhart. 'I think we'd better steam in line abreast – I don't want these bastards pointing themselves at me, however subdued they're feeling...' He spoke into the hailer once more. 'Get your men below decks. Form up one on each side of me. The course is one-oh-five degrees – one hundred and five ... Do you understand?'

More waving, more acquiescent nods.

'Off we go then,' said Ericson. 'Do not alter your course for any reason. Do not signal to each other. Burn navigation lights at night. And don't forget those depth-charges.'

. . .

'Isn't this a mistake, sir?' asked Holt later that afternoon. He pointed to something on the signal-log. 'This signal addressed to the Admiralty. "I HAVE COLLECTED TWO EWE-BOATS" – spelt E-W-E.'

'We're taking them in to Loch Ewe,' explained Ericson. 'It's a joke.'

After a moment the midshipman said: 'It's a jolly good one, sir.'

'All right, Mid,' said Ericson, looking at him. 'I won't make any more.'

. . .

But the curious convoy was not to have a quiet run home; their holiday mood suffered a last disturbance, and the jovial toughness which had prompted Ericson to give the U-boats the full benefit of *Saltash*'s wash, and then to shake them up with a depth-charge, was brought into action once more, this time with crude anger to back it up.

It happened on the afternoon of the second day, when they were nearing the Butt of Lewis, the northernmost tip of the Outer Hebrides which marked the entrance to the Minches – the front drive to their home. The two U-boats had behaved themselves with perfect propriety during the past thirty hours: their courses could not have been straighter, their navigation lights at night had been models of brilliance. As a matter of precaution, however, Ericson had kept his Asdic operators at work, though there seemed little chance that they would have anything to report; when in fact they *did* get a contact, and a strong one at that, dead ahead of *Saltash*, the resulting flurry cancelled the whole end-of-the-war feeling at the first shrilling of the alarm-bell.

Ericson brought his ship immediately to Action-Stations; whatever the echo was, he was taking no chances, and if it were in truth a U-boat which was disobeying the order to surface, it was either still fighting the war or else playing the fool. He felt in the mood to punish both those things ... He signalled to his two prisoners: 'STOP INSTANTLY, AND STAY WHERE YOU ARE,' and as the U-boats obeyed, and their way fell off, *Saltash* increased to 'Full Ahead' and went in, prepared to attack. Lockhart said: 'It feels like a U-boat, sir, on the same course as us,' and Ericson answered: 'We'll drop a pattern, Number One. They may not have heard the news.'

The 'Stand by to drop!' warning had already gone to the depth-charge crews aft, when the U-boat rose a hundred yards ahead of them, breaking surface in a sluggish, take-it-or-leave-it manner which seemed designed to indicate that it was only doing so because it chose to.

'Stop both!' ordered Ericson. 'Port twenty!' *Saltash*, losing speed, came round in a circle under the U-boat's quarter, while Ericson looked at the wet grey hull through his binoculars. 'I suppose,' he said grimly, 'this is meant to show that they haven't really been beaten. It would serve them right if——'

He did not finish the sentence, but within his own mind he found that he was wrestling with a violent temptation. He wanted above all else to continue with the attack – the absence of the black surrender-flag gave him legitimate excuse; he wanted to ram or to shoot it out, or to toss a depth-charge right alongside the target; he wanted to show them that the war *was* over and the U-boats defeated, and that a British frigate could send them to the bottom any time she felt like it. He wanted, at this last moment, to prove how easy it was, by increasing his total war-score from three U-boats to four ... He stood stock-still in the centre of his bridge, recalling an old anger – the way he had felt when the U-boat captain, down in his cabin, had started throwing his weight about. Bloody Germans ... Now a man in a high-peaked cap appeared in the conning-tower of the U-boat, looking about him with leisurely care, and then stared through his glasses at *Saltash*. Another man climbed up by his side and stood there, doing nothing in an unconcerned sort of way.

'Still playing the fool,' grunted Ericson. 'Guns!'

'Sir?' said Allingham, from his place at the gun-control microphone.

'Fire a shot over his conning-tower. As close as you like.'

Allingham spoke his orders: B-gun roared: the shot fell with a great tawny spout of water, fifty yards beyond the U-boat.

'That must have just about parted his hair,' said Holt.

It seemed that it might well be the last shot of the long war. The two men lost their air of indifference on the instant, and waved energetically; others began to climb alongside them into the conning-tower, and then to overflow onto the fore-deck. A black flag jerked upwards on the short ensign-staff, and a signal-lamp started to wink with frenzied speed.

'Signal, sir,' said *Saltash*'s yeoman presently. '"I WILL NOT FIGHT YOU."'

'I don't mind if you do,' said Ericson, in prompt and stentorian tones over the hailer. He waited for an answer to the challenge, but none came. Some more men, leaving the conning-tower, now ran along the deck of the U-boat, their hands high above their heads.

'That's more like it,' said Ericson. And over the hailer crisply, finally: 'Take station with the others, and follow me.'

CHAPTER 5

So their battle ended, and so, all over the Atlantic, the fighting died – a strangely tame finish, after five and a half years of bitter struggle. There was no eleventh-hour, death-or-glory assault on shipping, no individual attempt at piracy after the surrender date: the vicious war petered out in bubbles, blown tanks, a sulky yielding, and the laconic order: 'Follow me.' But no anti-climax, no quiet end, could obscure the triumph and the pride inherent in this victory, with its huge cost – 30,000 seamen killed, 3,000 ships sent to the bottom in this one ocean – and its huge toll of 780 U-boats sunk, to even the balance.

It would live in history, because of its length and its unremitting ferocity: it would live in men's minds for what it did to themselves and to their friends, and to the ships they often loved. Above all, it would live in naval tradition, and become legend, because of its crucial service to an island at war, its price in sailors' lives, and its golden prize – the uncut life-line to the sustaining outer world.

CHAPTER 6

Their U-boats had been taken under guard, by a trio of bristling motor-gunboats which shot out of Loch Ewe and came snarling towards them at approximately forty knots. The newcomers had turned in a welter of foam and spray, loosed off a burst of machine-gun fire for absolutely no reason at all, and then settled down ahead and astern of the prisoners, with the contented air of men who had done the whole thing themselves. Their only signal had been: 'We have them.'

Saltash, feeling as if she had been rescued in the nick of time, was free to go to her anchorage.

The big frigate moved up the quiet sheltered waters of the loch towards the collection of shipping which lay at its head. It was past sunset, and cold: home from the sea, they were still muffled with strange caps and helmets, still duffle-coated still stamping feet which were heavy with sea-boots and thick grease-wool stockings. A strange quiet lay over *Saltash*, though her decks were crowded: there must have been a hundred and fifty men on the upper deck, lining the rails or sitting inboard on ammunition-lockers and hatches, but they watched in silence the calm water round them, the lovely hills still orange-tipped by the sun, the white cottages on the fringe of the loch, and the anchorage they were making for. It was the end of their day, and of the battle, but it was a subdued moment all the same: at such a time a man could not easily speak, he could best stand and stare.

As they drew nearer to the ships ahead, they saw that with the exception of a corvette, an oiler, and some small craft, all the rest were U-boats – sixteen of them, moored in a compact group under the eye of a battered trawler.

There was a murmur at that, and then silence again. The men of *Saltash* edged slowly across to the port rail of their ship, and gazed down on the surrendered U-boats as they steamed past them. They saw that the U-boats were already empty grey shells – their crews taken off, their guns shrouded: they lay silent and useless – but they were still the enemy, still the things that *Saltash* and the others had fought and defeated. There was about them much to look at, much to note, but the single detail which drew every man's eye was the big white 'U' on each conning-tower. The captive letter, repellent symbol of a hated warfare, now summed up the whole struggle for them: they had been chasing that 'U' for years on end, and now here it was, fought to a standstill and safe under guard – U for unsuccessful, U for undone, U for everything that meant victory for one side, final defeat for the other.

Saltash moved on past them: Ericson rang for 'Dead Slow': Raikes busied himself taking cross-bearings from the shore. On the fo'c'sle, the windlass clanked and hissed as the first shackle of cable was run out: Allingham, standing in the eyes of the ship, faced the bridge and waited for the signal to let go the anchor.

Raikes called out: 'Coming on the bearing now, sir.'

'Stop both!' said Ericson. While *Saltash* drifted to a standstill, he glanced round him. It was a good anchorage, the best they could wish for – sheltered, no shallow water nearby, no other ships to crowd him if *Saltash* started swinging. And the U-boats were within sight ...

'On, sir!' said Raikes.

'Slow astern, both!' Ericson called out, and then, as *Saltash* gathered gentle stern-way, enough to lay out the cable in a straight line on the sea-bottom, he said: 'Stop both ... Let go!'

Allingham raised his hand in acknowledgement, and repeated the order to his leading hand. There was a clunk as the stopper was knocked off, and the anchor plunged down with a rattle and a roar, waking the echoes all round them, making the sea-birds chatter and cry. The ripples spread, and faded: *Saltash* came to a stop, tugging gently.

'Got her cable, sir!' Allingham called out to the bridge.

Ericson drew a deep breath, stretching a little under his duffle-coat. That was all ... Over his shoulder he said:

'Ring off main engines.'

CHAPTER 7

Though the rest of the upper deck had long been deserted, Lockhart was not surprised to find Ericson up on the bridge: the big figure, looming suddenly out of the darkness, did not startle him at all. He might have guessed where the Captain would be, at this closing hour ... Ericson turned when he heard his step, and said: 'Hello, Number One,' as if he too were unsurprised. They stood side by side in the cold darkness, saying nothing for a space, sharing the moment of relaxation and the grateful calm round them.

It was still early evening, but by now it was almost dark; the moon was already entangled in the rigging, and one by one the shore lights were coming on – the stars of peace, the first lights since the beginning of the war. The edge of the loch could be seen, and the shadowy hills above it: astern of them, the clutch of U-boats lay silent and immovable – solid black patches on the restless water. Outside their sheltered haven the wind moaned, as if still greedy for *Saltash*, and in the far distance the cruel sea beat and thrashed at the entrance to the loch.

Lockhart knew why they were standing there together, leaning against the side of the bridge under the frosty open sky, though he was not sure that the moment could be adequately honoured. They were there because it was the last day of the war they had shared: the Atlantic battle was done with, and secretly they wanted to review it, even if it were by vague allusion only, even if no word were spoken. It was a time to draw the threads together – but perhaps, thought Lockhart, there were too many threads to this story: perhaps there was too much to be said, and to say it would entail a foolish babbling which the moment did not deserve ... But then this man, for whom he had such an enormous affection, would not babble, would not cheapen.

'Five years, it's taken,' said Ericson suddenly. 'Getting on for six ... I wonder how far we've steamed.'

'I added it up for *Compass Rose*,' said Lockhart, grateful for the lead.

'Ninety-eight thousand miles ... But I never did it for *Saltash*. It seemed to be unlucky.'

The noises of the ship rose vaguely to them: as was usual in harbour, somewhere a radio was playing, somewhere a small wave curled and broke against their hull, somewhere a heavy-stepping quartermaster made his rounds. Now the U-boats, the black shadows with no more fear in them, were caught in the track of the moon, and held there for their pleasure.

'I wish some of the others could have seen this,' said Lockhart, presently. 'John Morell. Ferraby.'

Ericson nodded. 'Yes, they deserved it.'

Lockhart, drawing some lost names from the shadows of his mind, murmured aloud: 'Tallow. Leading-Seaman Phillips. Wells.'

'Who was Wells?' asked Ericson.

'The yeoman in *Compass Rose*.'

'Oh yes ...'

'He used to say to his signalmen: "If you get worried, just sing out and I'll be up straight away" ...'

'This is the time that you miss them.'

'M'm ... But perhaps there are really too many people, to remember them properly. The names are just labels, in the end. Young Baker. Rose. Tonbridge. Carslake. All those chaps in *Sorrel*. And the Wrens we lost, on that bad Gibraltar convoy.'

'Julie Hallam,' said Ericson suddenly, trying it for the first time.

'Yes, Julie ...' For Lockhart's surprised heart, a twinge, and then nothing again. Perhaps, after a year, she really slept now, and he as well. It had been much the same with *Compass Rose*: there must be a special kind of war-memory – showing mercy in fading quickly, drowning for ever under the weight of sorrow.

'You didn't get any medals,' said Ericson inconsequently. 'But I did my best for you.'

Lockhart smiled in the darkness. 'I can bear it.'

'You deserved something, Number One.'

'I can still bear it ... Remember when we had that lunch in London, and I said I wanted to stay with you in *Saltash*?'

'Yes. Made a lot of difference to me.'

'Same here.'

One thread, at least, was tied: one of the things they had not been going to say was happily said after all.

Ericson sighed again. 'And we only sank three U-boats. Three, in five years.'

'We worked hard enough for them, God knows.'

'Yes.' Ericson brooded, leaning heavily against a corner of the bridge where he must have spent many hundreds of hours. Out of the deep dusk he said – and after sixty-eight months it was still a shock to hear him use the words:

'I must say I'm damned tired.'

Hermanus, Cape Province – Johannesburg, Transvaal
April 1948 – May 1950

THE END

The Ship

C. S. FORESTER

Dedicated
with the deepest respect
to the
OFFICERS AND SHIP'S COMPANY OF
H.M.S. PENELOPE

With half a million men in the Royal Navy at the time
this story was written, it is inevitable that there should
be some coincidence of names and ranks between
characters in this book and officers and ratings now
serving. This is so inevitable that the author has made
no attempt to avoid any such coincidence; all he can do
is to assure the reader that he has attempted neither
portrait nor caricature of any living person.

CHAPTER 1

FROM THE CAPTAIN'S REPORT

... and at 1130 the attacks ceased, although enemy aircraft were still occasionally visible ...

Paymaster Commander George Brown put his fountain-pen back into his pocket, put on his cap and got up from the table where he had been ciphering.

'I'm going for a prowl,' he told the petty officer beside him.

He slid his rather rotund bulk out through the narrow door and down three successive ladders, turning each corner and making each steep descent with the careless facility of long practice, even in the darkness that prevailed with the doors all shut. Emerging on the deck he stood and blinked for a moment in the sunshine, clear, sparkling sunshine which gave less warmth than might be expected in the Mediterranean in March. The sky was blue and the tossing sea was grey, the two colours blending exquisitely, the white caps and the white stretch of the wake completing the colour scheme to an artist's satisfaction.

The Paymaster Commander took a step or two farther into the waist, and stood and blinked again. He was not wasting time, nor idly taking the air; he was, as he might have expressed it himself, engaged in out-thinking Mussolini. The guns' crews at the four-inch guns, at the pom-poms and at the .50 calibre machine-guns were standing at their stations; as *Artemis* rolled in the heavy sea the brass cases of the ammunition expended in beating off the last attack jangled on the iron decks on which they lay heaped like autumn leaves.

The men at the guns were vigilant and yet relaxed; they would lose no time, not one-tenth of a second, in opening fire should another attack be launched, but they were not wasting their strength in staying keyed up unnecessarily. These men were veterans of nearly three years of war, three years during which at any moment death might swoop at them from the skies, and every movement they made showed it. The weapons they handled were part of their lives by now; not toys for formal parade, nor wearisome nuisances to be kept cleaned and polished in accordance with a meaningless convention; those cannons were of the very essence of life, as was the long rifle to the frontier pioneer, the brush to the artist, the bow to the violinist. In a world where the law was 'kill or be killed' they were determined to be the killers and not the killed – the tiger stalking his prey lived under the same law.

The Paymaster Commander had finished out-guessing Mussolini; his experience of aerial attacks told him that another was unlikely in the immediate future. And at the same time what he knew from the signals he had been deciphering made him certain that the respite was only a respite, and that more desperate work lay ahead even than beating off Italian dive bombers. He turned into the galley, where the Chief Petty Officer Cook, burly and competent, stood waiting for orders – the only man in the ship (until the Paymaster Commander decided to take his stroll), apparently, not engaged in the business of making the ship the complete fighting machine; and yet he, too, had his part to play.

'Half an hour to send food round,' said the Paymaster Commander. He picked up the telephone. 'Wardroom.'

In the wardroom the telephone squealed plaintively and the Surgeon Lieutenant Commander answered it.

'Wardroom.'

'Hullo, P.M.O. Purser here. Let's have some of my boys back. You can spare 'em.'

The Surgeon Lieutenant Commander looked round him. When H.M.S. *Artemis* was at action-stations the wardroom ceased to be the officers' mess and became the Medical Distributing Station. Here the wounded were brought for treatment – the sick bay, forward under the bridge, was both too small and too exposed to be used as anything other than a dressing station. The two casualties were quiet now, and the stretcher-bearer force was squatting on the deck. The Surgeon Lieutenant Commander carried grave responsibility in yielding to the Paymaster Commander's request. A sudden attack might leave twenty – fifty – wounded on the decks; a score of lives might depend on prompt collection and treatment. Wounded left lying were bad for discipline, bad for morale, apart from the guilty conscience which would torment the Surgeon Lieutenant Commander if his job were not properly done. But he had been shipmates for two years with the Paymaster Commander, and could appreciate his cool judgement and sober common sense. Pay was not the kind of man who would make a frivolous or unnecessary or ill-timed request. He could trust him.

'Right-o, Pay. I'll send 'em along.'

He looked along the row of squatting forms.

'You eight. You're all galley party? Report to the Paymaster Commander at the galley.'

The eight queerly-dressed men – between them all they hardly bore a single trace of uniform clothing – scrambled to their feet, and doubled forward into the sunshine which illuminated the waist and halted at the galley. The Surgeon Lieutenant Commander watched them go. Perhaps it was the sight of the ragged group running which started a train of subconscious memory, starting with the recollection of an inter-hospital cross-country race; the Surgeon Lieutenant Commander suddenly found before his mind's eye a picture of the interior courtyard at Guy's – the green grass, the dribbling fountain where pigeons tried to wash off London grime, the nurses, white aproned, in blue or lilac uniforms, first-year students carrying microscopes, third-year men lounging, pipe in mouth and comically manly, out from the gloomy entrance to the dissecting-room, the youthfulness and eager anticipation of the best in life. All bombed to hell now, he had heard. The Surgeon Lieutenant Commander shook the vision from him as though it were water out of his eyes when he was swimming; he turned back to take a fresh look at the rating with the head wound. There was a chance that the wounded man might live and be none the worse for his experience.

In the galley the Paymaster Commander was ready with the scheme he had long mapped out, and tested in a dozen engagements. He had six hundred men to feed, and none of them had eaten for six hours. The Paymaster Commander thought of the hungry six hundred with a queer tenderness. He was a man born for parenthood, for self-sacrifice, to think for others. If Fate had made him a millionaire, he might have been a notable philanthropist; if Fate had given him children, he might have been the much loved father of a family, but Fate had ruled that he should be a childless man and a poor one. And as the senior officer of the paymaster branch in a light cruiser his inborn instincts had play in other directions. At present his thoughts were queerly paralleling those of the housewife planning what would be best for her menfolk getting in the harvest or working at the mill – it was only common sense that they should be given the best available, and it was pleasant that that should be what he liked doing anyway.

There was no flame in the range by which cooking could be done – the oil fuel for the range had all been safely drained away below where it was less likely to start a fire – but there was a steam jet, and superheated steam, not the flabby vapour that issues from a kettle's spout, but steam at four hundred degrees, live, active steam, can do remarkable things in the quickest time. The cook was already putting the ingredients into the cauldron. No economy soup this, but the best the ship could provide, the best the limited imagination of the Admiralty could encompass for the men who fought the battles. To make the forty gallons of soup necessary the cook was ripping open four dozen vast tins of tomatoes; stacked round him were the sixteen tins of corned beef which would go in next. The Paymaster Commander, without wasting time, took the fourteen pounds of cornflour and began to mix it into a paste with water so as to make it smooth for admixture with the soup. While he was doing so he issued his instructions to the men who came panting up to the galley at the Surgeon Lieutenant Commander's orders.

'Get going on those sandwiches,' he said. 'Hopkins, open the tins. Clarke and Stanton, cut the meat. The rest of you see to the spreading.'

The men fell naturally into the parts they had to play, like actors in a well-rehearsed performance. The long loaves which the cook's crew had made and baked during the night were run through the slicer, the slabs of corned beef were slapped on the buttered slices, and the completed sandwiches were stacked aside; the knives flickered with the speed at which they worked, and they had no time for speech except for brief sentences – 'Let's have another tin here, Nobby'; 'More butter here!'

Cornflour, meat, vegetables, all had gone into the soup cauldron, and now the Chief Petty Officer Cook dropped in the three pounds of sugar and the handfuls of herbs which were his own contribution to the formula for producing appetizing soup. He stirred with his vast ladle, and then moved the lever of the steam valve round its pipe. Only a slight crackling and tremor indicated that steam from the ship's boilers – steam as hot as red-hot iron – was heating up the cauldron.

The Canteen Manager and his assistant came to attention before the Paymaster Commander.

'We've been sent to report to you from the wardroom, sir,' said the Canteen Manager.

'Very good. Start on the cocoa. Murchie, get those pickles opened.'

The Paymaster Commander swept his gaze round the galley. The soup was nearly hot, the forty gallons of cocoa were preparing, the mass of sandwiches nearly completed. He checked the other tubs – they were full of fresh water, in accordance with his standing orders. The Paymaster Commander had fought in another battle, once, in a cruiser which had filled with water nearly to the level of her maindeck. Desperate determination and brilliant seamanship had brought her in tow back to harbour after forty-eight hours of struggle against wind and sea, submarines and aircraft; but those forty-eight hours had been spent without drinking water, thanks to the holing of some tanks and the submersion of the others. The Paymaster Commander remembered the insanity of thirst and fatigue, and never again would he allow his men to suffer that agony as far as it was in his power to mitigate it. These tubs held half a gallon for each man of the ship's company – men could go for days on two pints of water if necessary.

His final inspection completed, the Paymaster Commander stepped out again on deck, balancing against the roll and heave of the sea. The horizon was still clear; there were no planes in the sky. On the port quarter the convoy still rolled along over the grey surface. Mussolini, the Paymaster Commander decided, was not going to cause any more trouble immediately; so he took up the telephone again and said 'Commander.' The Commander answered from his Damage Control Station on the boat deck.

'Pay here, Commander. Dinner's ready to serve. May I pipe to that effect?'

'Yes, carry on,' said the Commander.

The Paymaster Commander made his way forward and heaved himself up over the prodigiously high coaming to the foot of the ladder leading to the bridge.

'Bosun's-mate,' he ordered, 'pipe "cooks to the galley".'

The Bosun's-mate switched on the loudspeaker, and the eerie squeal of his pipe went echoing through every corner of the ship.

He was a North Country man, and his years in the Navy had not eliminated the North Country tang of his speech. He drew out the double O of the word 'cooks' until it was a treble or quadruple O, and he made no attempt to pronounce the 'the' sound in the 'the'.

'Cooks to t'galley,' he said into the loudspeaker. 'Cooks to t'galley.'

The Paymaster Commander went back to the galley. In the hundreds of years of the history of the British Navy this meaning of the word 'cooks' had suffered a change. They were no longer the men who actually cooked the food of their respective messes; they were merely the men who, each on his appointed day, carried the food from the galley to the mess. Already they were assembling there; men from the six-inch turrets and men from the four-inch H.A. guns; men from the magazines and men from the engine-room – in every quarter of the ship one man knew that it was his duty, as soon as he heard 'cooks to the galley' piped, to come and fetch food for his mates who could not leave their stations. The Paymaster Commander watched the food being served out, from A mess right through the alphabet to Z mess; from AA to ZZ, and then from AAA to EEE – food for five men, food for seven men, food for nine men, according to the number in each quarter; for each mess the food was ready stacked, and the Paymaster Commander nodded in faint self-approval as he saw how smoothly the arrangements were working over which he had sat up late on so many evenings. This was his own special plan, and he thought it improved on the system prevailing in other ships. It called for forethought and organization to feed six hundred men in half an hour, men who could not leave their guns, their gauges, or their instruments even for a moment while death lay only just beyond the horizon.

'I want those mess-traps brought back,' said the Paymaster Commander sharply, 'don't leave them sculling about on the decks.'

It was his duty to fill the bellies of his men, but at the same time it was his duty to safeguard Navy property. Just because a battle was being fought was no excuse for exposing crockery – even crockery of enamelled iron – to needless damage. The cooks had all left, and the Paymaster Commander picked up a sandwich and stood eating it, looking down at the galley party squatting on the decks spooning up soup into their mouths. Five minutes more of this let-up in the battle and everyone in the ship would have food inside him, and be fit and ready to go on fighting until nightfall or later.

He finished his sandwich and pulled out his cigarette case, and then stood with it unopened as a further thought struck him. He looked down fixedly at the Canteen Manager and his assistant.

'The boys'll want cigarettes,' he said. 'I expect half of 'em are short already.'

The Paymaster Commander was of the type that could use the word 'boys' instead of 'men' without being suspected of sentimentality.

'I expect so, sir,' said the Canteen Manager.

'Better take some round,' said the Paymaster Commander. 'You and Murchie see to it.'

'Aye aye, sir,' said the Canteen Manager, and then he hesitated. 'Shall I issue them, sir?'

'Issue them? Good God, no.'

The Paymaster Commander had visions of the endless reports and explanations he would have to make if he gave cigarettes away free to the Navy on the mere excuse that they were in action. And he had been in the service long enough to see nothing incongruous in the idea of sailors having to pay for their cigarettes in a ship which might during the next ten minutes be battered into a shapeless wreck.

'Half of 'em'll have no money, not after Alex., sir,' said the Canteen Manager.

'Well,' said the Paymaster Commander, the struggle between regulations and expediency evident in his face, 'let 'em have credit. See that every man has what he wants. And some of the boys'll like chocolate, I expect – take some round as well.'

The Paymaster Commander really meant 'boys' and not 'men' when he said 'boys' this time – there were plenty of boys on board, boys under eighteen, each with a sweet tooth and a growing frame which would clamour for sweetmeats, especially after the nervous strain of beating off aerial attack for four hours.

The 'mess-traps' about which he had worried – the 'fannies' of soup, the mugs and the plates – were already being returned to the galley. Things were going well. The Canteen Manager and his assistant filled mess-cans with packets of cigarettes and packets of chocolate, and began to make their way from action-station to action-station, selling their wares as though at a football match. Like the Paymaster Commander, neither the Canteen Manager nor the men saw anything incongruous in their having to put their hands into their pockets to find the pennies for their cigarettes and their bars of chocolate. It was a right and proper thing that they should do so, in fact.

'You men return to your action-stations,' said the Paymaster Commander to the galley party.

He looked round the galley once more, and then turned away. He walked forward, stepped over the coaming, took one last glance backward at the blue sky and the grey sea, and then set himself to climb the dark ladders again back to the coding room. Even if he did nothing else in the battle he had supplied the food and the strength to keep the men going during a moment in the future when history would balance on a knife-edge – his forethought and his training and his rapid decision had played their part.

CHAPTER 2

FROM THE CAPTAIN'S REPORT

... At 1205 smoke was sighted ...

Ordinary Seaman Harold Quimsby sucked a hollow tooth in which a shred of corned beef had stuck apparently inextricably. He ought to have reported that hollow tooth at least a month ago, but Quimsby was of the type of man who crosses no bridges until he comes to them. He did not let anything worry him very much, for he was of a philosophical nature, filled with the steady fatalism to be expected of a veteran of so much service, even though Quimsby was merely an enlistment for hostilities only. Some men would be uncomfortable up here in the crow's nest – not so Quimsby, whose ideal existence was one something like this, with a full belly and nothing particular to do. As H.M.S. *Artemis* rolled and corkscrewed over the quartering sea the crow's nest swung round and round in prodigious circles against the sky, but Quimsby's seasoned stomach positively enjoyed the motion and untroubled went on with the process of digestion.

Cold meat and pickles; that made a meal fit for a king. Quimsby liked nothing better than that. His portion of pickles had included no fewer than four onions, and Quimsby breathed out reminiscently, conscious of, and delighting in, his flavoured breath. He had swallowed down his soup and his cocoa, but they were only slop, unworthy of the name of food. Cold meat and pickles were the food for a man. He sucked at his tooth again, and breathed out again, sublimely contented with the world.

Everything seemed to be designed for his comfort. The chair in which he sat certainly was – the padded seat and back held him in exactly the right position for keeping the horizon under continuous observation through the binoculars laid upon the direction finder before his eyes. As

Quimsby rolled and circled round in the crow's nest he automatically kept the horizon swept by the binoculars; long practice had accustomed him to do so. A thrust of his feet one way or the other kept his stool rotating from port to starboard and back again, while his right hand on the lever kept the elevation in constant adjustment to correspond with the roll of the ship. Thanks to many hours of practice Quimsby was able to watch the whole horizon forward of the beam without allowing any of his automatic movements to break into his internal chain of thought, from the shred of beef in his tooth to the comfortable state of his inside and from that to unholy memories of that little bint at Alex. who had made his last shore leave so lively.

And from there his memories went back to his first arrival at Alex., his first glimpse of the East, and from there to his first voyage to sea back in the almost unbelievably distant days of 1939. He had been up in the crow's nest then, too, he remembered and his forehead wrinkled in faint bewilderment at the certainty that the scared, seasick, self-conscious youth at the direction finder in those days was, unbelievably but beyond all doubt, the same man who sat there so self-assured and competent now. That first report he had to make, when his binoculars picked up the dot on the distant surface and he had rung down to the bridge, his stomach heaving with excitement and seasickness.

'Something over on the left,' he had spluttered, all his previous instruction forgotten.

The unhurried voice of the First Lieutenant had steadied him.

'Where are you speaking from?'

'Headmast – I mean masthead, sir.'

'Then that's what you say first, so that we know down here. And you don't say "over on the left", do you? What do you say?'

'On – on the port bow, sir.'

'That's right. But it's better to give a bearing. What does your bearing indicator read?'

'Twenty-one, sir.'

'And how do you say it?'

'I – I've forgotten, sir.'

'Port is red, and starboard is green,' said the First Lieutenant patiently. 'Remember that port wine is red, and then you won't forget. And twenty-one isn't plain enough, is it?'

'No, sir – yes, sir.'

'Now let's have your report. Remember to say where you're speaking from first.'

'M – masthead, sir. Object in sight. Red two-one.'

'Very good, Quimsby. But you must say it twice over. You remember being told that? If the guns are firing we might not hear you the first time.'

'Yes, sir. I mean aye aye, sir.'

He had been a very green hand at that time, decided Quimsby. He felt self-conscious all over again at the thought of how Number One had coaxed him into making his report in the proper form so that it could be instantly understood. The subject was almost unsavoury to him, and his thoughts began to drift farther back still, to the time when he was selling newspapers in Holborn – the evening rush, the coppers thrust into the one hand as with the other he whipped the copies out from under his arm.

Then he looked more attentively at the horizon, blinked, and looked again with his hand on the buzzer of the voice-tube. Then he rang.

'Forebridge,' came the reply up the voice-tube.

'Masthead. Smoke on the starboard bow. Green one-nine. Masthead. Smoke on the starboard bow. Green one-nine,' said Quimsby ungratefully, all memory of that early training passing from his mind as he said the words.

CHAPTER 3

FROM THE CAPTAIN'S REPORT

... and a signal to this effect was immediately made ...

In H.M.S. *Artemis* a high proportion of the brains of the ship was massed together on the bridge, Captain and Torpedo Officer, Navigating Lieutenant and Officer of the Watch, Asdic cabinet and signalmen. They stood there unprotected even from the weather, nothing over their heads, and, less than shoulder-high round them, the thin plating which served only to keep out the seas when the ship was taking green water in over her bows. Death could strike unhindered anywhere on that bridge; but then death could strike anywhere in the whole ship, for the plating of which she was constructed was hardly thicker than paper. Even a machine-gun bullet could penetrate if it struck square. The brains might as well be exposed on the bridge as anywhere else – even the imposing looking turrets which housed the six-inch guns served no better purpose than to keep out the rain. The ship was an egg-shell armed with sledge-hammers, and her mission in life was to give without receiving.

Was it Voltaire who said that first? No, it was Molière, of course. Paymaster Sub-Lieutenant James Jerningham, the Captain's secretary, was sometimes able to project himself out of the ship and look down on the whole organization objectively. It was he who was thinking about

Voltaire and Molière as he squatted on the deck of the bridge eating his sandwich. Even after three years in the Navy he still had not learned to spend several hours consecutively on his feet the way these others did – they had learned the trick young (for that matter, save for the Captain, he was at twenty-seven the oldest officer on the bridge) and could stand all day long without fatigue. In the delirious days before the war he had written advertising copy, spending most of his time with his heels on his desk, and to this day he only felt really comfortable with his feet higher than his head.

One way of thinking of the ship was as of some huge marine animal. Here on the bridge was the animal's brain, and radiating from it ran the nerves – the telephones and voice-tubes – which carried the brain's decisions to the parts which were to execute them. The engine-room was the muscles which actuated the tail – the propellers – and the guns were the teeth and claws of the animal. Up in the crow's nest above, and all round the bridge where the look-outs sat raking sea and sky with their binoculars, were the animal's eyes, seeking everywhere for enemies or prey, while the signal flags and the wireless transmitter were the animal's voice, with which it could cry a warning to its fellows or scream for help.

It was a nice conceit, all this; Jerningham summoned up all his knowledge of anatomy and physiology (he had spent hours with a medical dictionary when he wrote advertising copy for patent medicines) to continue it in greater detail. The ratings detailed as telephone numbers on the bridge and scattered through the ship, with their instruments over their ears, were the ganglia which acted as relay stations in the animal's nervous system. The rating who had just brought him his sandwich was like the blood vessel which carried food material from the galley – stomach and liver in one – to the unimportant part of the brain which he represented, to enable it to recuperate from fatigue and continue its functions.

The lower animals had important parts of their nervous systems dotted along their spinal cords – large expansions in the dorsal and lumbar regions to control the limbs. The Chief Engineer down in the engine-room would represent the lumbar expansion; the Gunnery Lieutenant in the Director Control Tower would be the dorsal expansion – the one managing the hindlimbs with which the animal swam, and the other the forelimbs with which it fought. Even if the brain were to be destroyed the animal would still move and fight for a time, just as a headless chicken runs round the yard; and, like the very lowest animals, like the earthworm or the hydra, if the head were cut off it could painfully grow itself a new one if given time – the Commander could come forward from his station aft and take command, the Torpedo Gunner take the place of the Torpedo Lieutenant. And, presumably, young Clare would come forward to take his place if he, Jerningham, were killed.

Jerningham shuddered suddenly, and, hoping that no one had noticed it, he pulled out a cigarette and lit it so as to disguise his feelings. For Jerningham was afraid. He knew himself to be a coward, and the knowledge was bitter. He could think of himself as lazy, he could think of himself as an unscrupulous seducer of women, he could tell himself that only because of the absence of need he had never robbed the blind or the helpless, and it did not disturb his equanimity. That was how he was made, and he could even smile at it. But it was far otherwise with cowardice. He was ashamed of that.

He attributed to his brother officers a kindly contemptuous tolerance for the fear that turned his face the colour of clay and set his lips trembling. He could not understand their stolid courage which ignored the dangers around them. He could see things only too clearly, imagine them too vividly. A bomb could scream down from the sky – he had heard plenty that morning. Or from a shadowy ship on the horizon could be seen the bright orange flare that heralded a salvo, and then, racing ahead of the sound they made would come the shells. Bomb or shell, one would burst on the bridge, smashing and rending. Officers and ratings would fall dead like dolls, and he, the Jerningham he knew so well, the handsome smiling Jerningham whose good looks were only faintly marred by having a nose too big for the distance between his eyes, would be dead, too, that body of his torn into fragments of red warm flesh hanging in streamers on the battered steel of the bridge.

Closing his eyes only made the vision more clear to Jerningham. He drew desperately on his cigarette although it was hard to close his lips round the end. He felt a spasm of bitter envy for the other officers so stolid and impassive on the bridge – the Captain perched on his stool (he was a man of sense, and had had the stool made and clamped to the deck to save himself from standing through the days and nights at sea when he never left the bridge), Torps and Lightfoot, the Officers of the Watch, chatting together and actually smiling. They had been unmoved even during the hell of this morning, when planes had come shrieking down to the attack from every point of the compass, and the ship had rocked to the explosion of near-misses and the eardrums had been battered into fatigue by the unremitting din of the guns.

Part of the explanation – but only part, as Jerningham told himself with bitter self-contempt – was that they were so wrapped up in their professional interests that their personal interests became merely secondary. They had spent their lives, from the age of thirteen, preparing to be naval officers, preparing for action, tackling all the problems of naval warfare – it was only natural that they should be interested in seeing whether their solutions were correct. And

Jerningham had spent his years rioting round town, drinking and gossiping and making love with a gang of men and women whose every reaction he had come to be able to anticipate infallibly, spending first a handsome allowance from his father and then a handsome salary for writing nonsense about patent medicines. He had always felt pleasantly superior to those men and women; he had felt his abilities to be superior to those of any of the men, and he had taken to his bed any of the women he had felt a fancy for, and they, poor creatures, had been flattered by his attentions and mostly fallen inconveniently in love with him. It was humiliating to feel now so utterly inferior to these officers round him, even though war was their trade while he was merely a temporary officer, drifted into the rank of Paymaster Sub-Lieutenant and the position of Captain's secretary because for his own convenience he had once studied shorthand and typewriting. Those were happy years in which he had never felt this abasement and fear.

Jerningham remembered that in his pocket was a letter, unopened as yet, which he had picked up the day before when they left Alex., and which he had thrust away in the flurry of departure without bothering to open. It was a letter from that other world – it might as well be a letter from Mars, from that point of view – which ought to do something to restore his self-respect. It was in Dora Darby's writing, and Dora was nearly the prettiest, certainly the cleverest, and probably the woman who had been most in love with him of all that gang. She had written him heartbroken letters when he had first joined the Navy, telling how much she missed him and how she longed for his return – clever though she was, she had no idea that Dorothy Clough and Cicely French were receiving from him the same attentions as he was paying her. It would help to bolster up his ego to read what she had written this time, and to think that there were plenty of other women as well who would as eagerly take him into their arms. Only a partial compensation for this fear that rotted him, but compensation and distraction nevertheless. He opened the letter and read it – nearly six months old, of course, now that all mail save that by air was being routed via the Cape.

Dearest J. J.,

I expect you will laugh at what I have to tell you. In fact, I can just picture you doing so, but someone has to break the horrid news to you and I think I am the right person. The fact is that I am married!! *To Bill Hunt!!! I suppose it will seem odd to you, especially after what I've always said, but marriage is in the air here in England, and Bill (he is a First Lieutenant now) had a spot of leave coming to him, and we didn't see why we shouldn't. What will make you laugh even more is that Bill has been doing his best to get me with child, and I have been aiding and abetting him all I can. That is in the air too. And honestly, it means something to me after all these years of doing the other thing. And another thing is I shouldn't be surprised if Bill's efforts have been successful, although I can't be sure yet –*

Dora's letter trailed off after that into inconsequential gossip which Jerningham made no effort to read. That opening paragraph was quite enough for him; was far too much in fact. He felt a wave of hot anger that he should have lost his hold over Dora, even though that hold was of no practical use to him at the moment. It touched his pride most bitterly that Dora should have even thought of marrying a brainless lout like Bill Hunt, and that she should never have expressed a moment's regret at having to accept Bill as a poor sort of substitute for himself.

But this sort of jealousy was very mild compared with the other kind that he felt at the thought of Dora becoming pregnant. This simply infuriated him. He could not, he felt, bear the thought of it. And the brutal phrase Dora used – 'to get me with child' – why in hell couldn't she have worded it more gently? He knew that he had always coached Dora to call a spade a spade – not that she needed much coaching – but she might have had a little regard for his feelings, all the same. Those pointed words conjured up in Jerningham's mind mental pictures as vivid as those of bombs dropping on the bridge. Dora and he and the others of his set – Bill among them, for that matter – had always assumed an attitude of lofty superiority towards people who were foolish enough to burden themselves with children and slack-fibred enough to lapse into domesticity; and in moments of high altruism they had always thought it selfish and unkind to bring a child into the sort of world they had to live in. And yet if anyone were going to 'get Dora with child', he wanted to do the job himself, and not have Bill Hunt do it. Up to this minute he had hardly even thought of marrying, far less of becoming the father of a family, and yet now he found himself bitterly regretting that he had not married Dora before *Artemis* left for the Mediterranean, and not merely married her but made her pregnant so that there would be a young Jerningham in England today.

He had never been jealous in his life before, and it hardly occurred to him that he had had almost no cause to be. He had always thought that he would smile a tolerant smile if one of his women before he had quite done with her should transfer her affections to someone else. But this was not the case, very much not the case. He was hot with anger about it, and yet the anger about this was merely nothing compared with his anger at the thought of Dora being made pregnant by Bill Hunt. His jealousy about this was something extraordinary. Jerningham found time even in the heat of his rage to note with surprise the intensity of his feelings on the subject; he had never thought for a moment, during the blasé Twenties of his, that he would ever feel the emotions of uncultured humanity. For a harrowing moment he even began to wonder whether all his early cynicism had been quite natural to him. This was certainly the third instance of primitive emotion overcoming him – the first was way back in 1939, when he suddenly realized that Hitler was aiming at the enslavement of the world and he had found himself suddenly determined to fight, willing to risk even death and discomfort sooner than be enslaved; the second was when he had known physical fear, and this was the third time, this frightfully painful jealousy, this mad rage at being helpless here at sea while Bill Hunt enjoyed all the privileges of domesticity with Dora Darby. Self-analysis ceased abruptly as a fresh wave of bitter feeling swamped his reason.

He got onto his feet – he, who never stood when he could sit – because he simply could not remain physically quiescent while emotion banked up inside him. A buzz from the voice-tube behind him made him swing round, and he took the message.

'Masthead reports smoke, green one-nine,' he sang out, his voice harsh and unwavering, as it would have been if it had been Dora Darby he had been addressing.

'Very good,' said the Captain, 'Chief Yeoman, make that to the flagship.'

CHAPTER 4

FROM THE CAPTAIN'S REPORT

... Action was taken in accordance with the orders previously issued ...

'So that's that,' said Captain the Honourable Miles Ernest Troughton-Harrington-Yorke to himself.

The signal flags were already racing up the halliards – the Chief Yeoman had begun to bellow the names of the flags before the last words of the order had left his lips. It would be the first warning to the Admiral that the possible danger which they had discussed previously was actually materializing. The Italian fleet was out, as the reconnaissance submarines had hinted; and if it was out it could be trusted to be out in full force. How many battleships they had managed to make seaworthy after Taranto and Matapan no British officer knew quite for sure, but now he would know. He would see them with his own eyes, for the Italians would never venture out except in the fullest possible force.

He twisted on his stool and looked round him over the heaving sea. Ahead of the *Artemis* stretched an attenuated line of destroyers, the destroyer screen to keep down possible submarines. Away to port lay the rest of the squadron of light cruisers; the light cruiser silhouette had altered less than that of any type of ship since Jutland, and the ships looked strangely old-fashioned and fragile – mid-Victorian, to exaggerate – in their parti-coloured paint. The White Ensigns with the gay block of colour in the corner, and the red crosses, seemed somehow to accentuate this effect of fragility. Flown by a battleship the White Ensign conveyed a message of menace, of irresistible force; but in a light cruiser it gave an impression of jauntiness, of reckless daring, of proudly flaunting itself in the face of peril.

In the centre flew the Rear-Admiral's flag, beside the signal acknowledging that of the *Artemis*. The Captain wondered faintly what the Rear-Admiral was thinking about at this moment. Away over the port quarter wallowed the convoy, the fat helpless merchant ships, with a frail destroyer screen round them and the anti-aircraft cruiser in the centre. Helpless enough they looked, and yet they bore within them cargoes of most desperate urgency. Malta was threatened with every danger the imagination could conceive – the danger of attack from the air, of attack from the sea, of pestilence and of famine. A civilian population of a quarter of a million, and a garrison of God-only-knew how many were on short rations until the food these ships carried should be delivered to them. The anti-aircraft guns which took such toll of raiding aircraft were wearing their rifling smooth – here came new inner tubes to line them; and the barrages which they threw up consumed a ton of high explosive in five minutes – here were more shells to maintain those barrages. Here were heavy guns of position, with mountings and ammunition, in case the Italians should venture their fleet within range to cover a landing. Here were bandages and dressing and splints for the wounded, and medicines for the sick – the sick must be numerous, huddled below ground on meagre rations.

If the convoy did not get through, Malta might fall; and the fall of Malta would mean the healing of a running ulcer which was eating into the strength of Mussolini and Hitler. And to escort the convoy through there were only these five light cruisers and a dozen destroyers – the convoy *had* to get through, and if it were reckless to risk it with such an escort, then recklessness had to be tolerated. The man over there whose Rear-Admiral's flag fluttered so bravely could be relied upon to be reckless when necessary; the Captain knew of half a dozen incidents in which the Rear-Admiral had displayed a cold-blooded calculation of risks and an unwavering acceptance of them. Wars could only be waged by taking chances; no Admiral since history began had ever been able to congratulate himself upon a prospective certainty. The Captain knew how the Admiral proposed to neutralize the chances against him, to counter overwhelming strength with overwhelming skill. The next few minutes would show whether his calculations would be justified.

'You can see the smoke now, sir,' said the Chief Yeoman of Signals. There is was, heavy and black, on the horizon.

'Green one-o, sir,' said the forward look-out on the starboard side.

The big difference in the bearing proved that whatever it was which was making the smoke was moving sharply across the path of the squadron so as to head it off. The Captain turned and looked up at the vane on the mast, and at the smoke from the funnels of *Artemis*. It was only the slightest breath of smoke, he was glad to see – not the dense mass which the Italians were making, revealing their course and position half an hour before it was necessary.

He doubted if his smoke were visible even yet to the enemy, but it sufficed for his own purpose, which was to show him in what direction the wind was blowing. It was only a moderate breeze – last night's gale which had kicked up the present rough sea had died down considerably – and it was blowing from nearly aft. It was a strange turn of the wheel of fortune that the captain of a modern light cruiser on his way into action should have to bear the direction of the wind in mind and manoeuvre for the weather gauge as if he were the captain of one of Nelson's frigates. But the weather gauge would be of vital importance in this battle, and the squadron held it. The Italians had lost the opening trick, even though they held all the cards in their hands. And this moderate breeze was ideal for the laying of a smoke-screen – not strong enough to disperse it, and yet strong enough to roll it down slowly towards the enemy. It was a stroke of good fortune; but the squadron needed all the good fortune there was available if it had to face the whole Italian navy. If the wind had been in any other direction – but yet the Admiral's orders had envisaged that possibility. There might have been some interesting manoeuvring in that case.

The Chief Yeoman of Signals was standing with his binoculars to his eyes, sweeping back and forth from the destroyers ahead to the flagship to port, but his gaze dwelt twice as long upon the flagship as upon all the other ships put together. For the Chief Yeoman, during the twenty-eight years of his service, had been in battles before, from the Dogger Bank to the present day, and he felt in his bones that the next signal would come from the flagship. The discipline and training of twenty-eight years, in gunboats on Chinese rivers, in battle cruisers in the North Sea, were at work upon him to catch that signal the moment it was hoisted, so that it did not matter to him that in addition his life might depend on the prompt obedience of the *Artemis*. He had stood so often, in peace and in war, ready to read a signal, that it was natural to him to ready himself in this fashion, as natural to him as breathing.

The wife he loved, back in England – the service had kept him apart from her during twenty of the twenty-five years of their married life – had been twice bombed out of her home, and all the furniture they had collected and of which he had been so modestly proud was now nothing but charred fragments and distorted springs; he had a son who was a Leading Seaman in one of the new battleships, and a daughter who was causing her mother a good deal of worry because she was seeing too much of a married man whom she had met in the factory. He was a living, sentient human being, a man who could love and who could hate, a man with a heart and bowels like any of his fellows, the grey-haired head of a household, an individual as distinct as any in the world, but at this moment he was merely the eye of H.M.S. *Artemis* – less than that, a mere cell in the body of the marine creature which Jerningham had been visualizing, a cell in the retina of the creature's eyeball specialized to receive visual impressions.

'Signal from the Flag, sir,' said the Chief Yeoman of Signals, 'K for King.'

'Acknowledge,' said the Captain.

The cell in the retina had done its job, had received its visual impression and passed it onto the brain.

The Captain had open on his knee, already, the typewritten orders which laid down what each ship should do in certain specified circumstances, and he had foreseen that the present circumstances were those which would be covered by scheme K – moderate wind abaft, enemy to leeward. A pity in some ways, from the artistic point of view; there would have been some pretty work if it had been necessary to manoeuvre the Italians into the leegauge.

'Signal's down, sir,' said the Chief Yeoman.

'Port ten,' said the Captain. 'Two-one-o revolutions.'

'Port ten,' said the Navigating Lieutenant into the voice-pipe, 'two-one-o revolutions.'

The moment when a signal is to be obeyed is the moment when it is hauled down; the squadron was moving out to defend the convoy from the Italian navy in the way that had been planned. The Captain swung his glasses round him; the convoy was executing a wheel to port under full helm, the cruisers were turning more gently and increasing speed so as to remain interposed between it and the enemy, and the destroyers in the advanced screen were doubling round, some to reinforce the immediate escort of the convoy in case of simultaneous aerial attack, some to clear the range for the light cruisers. It was a beautiful geometrical movement, like a figure in some complicated quadrille.

'Midships,' said the Captain.

'Midships,' repeated the Navigating Lieutenant into the voice-pipe.

He broke the word into two, distinctly, for Able-Seaman Dawkins was at the helm, perhaps the most reliable quartermaster in the ship's company, but once – during that night action – Dawkins had misheard the word and the Navigating Lieutenant was taking no chances in the future. The ship was steady on her course now.

Deep down in the ship, below the water-line, where there was the least chance of an enemy's shell reaching him, Able-Seaman Dawkins stood with his hands on the wheel and his eyes on the compass before him. With his legs spread wide he balanced himself with the ease of long practice against the roll of the ship; that had to be done automatically down here with no stable thing against which the movement could be contrasted, and with his eyes never straying from the compass. It was only a few minutes back – at noon – that he had come down here and taken over the wheel. He was comfortably full of food, and at the moment his cheek was distended and he was sucking rhythmically. A few years back one would have guessed at once that he was chewing tobacco, but with the new Navy one could not be sure – and in the present case one would have been wrong, for Dawkins was sucking a lollipop, a huge lump like yellow glass which he had slipped into his cheek before going below. He had a two-pound bottle of them in his locker, bought in Alexandria, for as Dawkins would have explained, he was 'partial to a bit of sweet'. One of those vast things would last him during nearly the whole of his trick at the wheel if he did not crunch down upon it when it began to get small.

At the time when he left the deck full of soup, cocoa, and sandwich, and with his lollipop in his cheek to top up with, the aerial attacks had ceased, and convoy and escort had been rolling along at peace with the world. While he had been eating his sandwich Brand had told him that there was a buzz that the Eyety navy was out, but Dawkins was of too stable a temperament to pay much attention. He was a man of immense placidity and immense muscle; in fact, as he stood there sucking on his lollipop one could hardly help being reminded of a cow chewing the cud. It was hard, studying his expressionless face and his huge hairy arms and hands, to credit him with the sensitive reactions necessary to keep a light cruiser steady on her course in a heavy sea. He stood there at the wheel, the two telegraph men seated one on each side of him; he towered over them, the three of them, in that small grey compartment, constituting a group which in its balance and dramatic force seemed to cry out to be reproduced in sculpture.

Above his head the voice-pipe curved down at the end of its long course through the ship from the bridge; it, too, had a functional beauty of its own.

'Port ten, two-one-o revolutions,' said the voice-pipe unexpectedly in the Navigating Lieutenant's voice; the sound came without warning, dropping into the silence of the compartment suddenly, as on a still day an apple may fall from a tree.

'Port ten, two-one-o revs, sir,' echoed Dawkins instantly, turning the wheel. At the same moment the telegraph man beside him spun the handle of the revolution indicator to two-one-o, and he was at once conscious of the faster beat of the ship's propellers.

A sudden change of course; a sudden increase of speed; that meant action was imminent, but Dawkins had no means of knowing what sort of action. It might be dive bombers again. It might be torpedo bombers. A submarine might have been sighted and *Artemis* might be wheeling to the attack, or the track of a torpedo might have been sighted and *Artemis* might be turning in self-defence. It might be the Eyety navy, or it might be trouble in the convoy.

'Midships,' said the voice-pipe.

A man of less placid temperament than Dawkins might be irritated at that pedantic enunciation; the Navigating Lieutenant always pronounced the word that way, but Dawkins was philosophic about it, because it was his fault in the first place; once when he had had to repeat the word he had been caught transferring his lollipop from one cheek to the other and had spluttered in consequence, so that the Navigating Lieutenant believed his order had not been correctly heard.

'Midships,' repeated Dawkins; the ship was lying now much more in the trough of the waves, and he had to bring into play a new series of trained reactions to keep *Artemis* steady on her course. Those minute adjustments of the wheel which he was continually making nipped in the bud each attempt of wind and sea to divert the ship from the straight line; a raw helmsman would do nothing of the sort, but would have to wait for each digression to develop before recognizing it so that the ship would steer a zigzag course infuriating the men controlling the guns.

The guns were not firing yet, perhaps would not fire in this new action, but it would not be Dawkins' fault if they were incorrectly aimed, just as it would not be his fault if there were any time wasted at all between a decision to change course forming itself in the brain of the Captain and its being executed by the ship. He stood there by the wheel, huge and yet sensitive, immobile and yet alert, eyes on the compass, sucking blissfully on his lollipop, satisfied to be doing best the work which he could best do without further thought for the turmoil of the world outside.

CHAPTER 5

FROM THE CAPTAIN'S REPORT

... an Italian force of two heavy cruisers of the 'Bolzano' type and four cruisers of the 'Regolo' type and 'Bande Nere' type.

Another signal ran to the masthead of the flagship, fluttered to await acknowledgement, and then descended.

'Starboard ten,' said the Captain, with the Navigating Lieutenant repeating the order, 'Midships'.

The squadron now was far ahead of the convoy, and lying a little way distant from a straight line drawn from the convoy astern to the tell-tale smoke ahead, ready at a moment's notice, that was to say, to interpose as might be necessary either with a smoke-screen or with gunfire. Italians and British were heading directly for each other now at a combined speed of more than fifty miles an hour. It could not be long before they would sight each other – already the smoke was as thick and dense as ever it would be.

The masthead voice-pipe buzzed.

'Forebridge,' said Jerningham, answering it, and then he turned to yell the message to the Captain. 'Ships in sight!'

As Ordinary Seaman Quimsby's binoculars picked out more details he elaborated his reports with Jerningham relaying them.

'Six big ships!' yelled Jerningham. 'Six destroyers. Two leading ships look like battleships. Might be heavy cruisers.'

The crow's nest where Quimsby swayed and circled above the bridge was twenty feet higher than the bridge itself. It was an easy calculation that Quimsby's horizon lay one and a half miles beyond the Captain's, and that in two minutes or a little less the Italians would be in sight from the bridge. In two minutes they shot up suddenly over the curve of the world, climbing over it with astonishing rapidity. Visibility was at its maximum; they made hard, sharp silhouettes against the blue and grey background, not quite bows onto the British squadron, the ships ahead not quite masking the ships astern. Jerningham heard the voice of the rangetaker begin its chant, like a priest of some strange religion reciting a strange liturgy.

'Range three-one-o. Range three-o-five. Range three-double-o.'

There were other voices, other sounds, simultaneously. The ship was rushing towards a great moment; every cell in her was functioning at full capacity.

'Port fifteen,' said the Captain, and *Artemis* heeled over as she executed the sudden turn. 'Revolutions for twenty-seven knots.'

The squadron had turned into line ahead, and was working up to full speed to head off the Italians should it become necessary. As Jerningham watched the Italian ships he saw the leader turn sharply to starboard, revealing her profile; some seconds later the next ship turned to follow her, and then the next, and the next. Jerningham was reminded of some advertising display or other in a shop window. The vicious bad temper which Dora Darby's letter had aroused still endured within him, keying him up. The gap between imaginative fear and sublime courage, in a highly strung person, is only a small one; the residuum of bad temper sufficed to push Jerningham into boldness. He saw those six sharp profiles; the wind, blowing from the British to the Italians, kept them clear of smoke, unsoftened and undisguised. Jerningham went back through his memory, to those hours spent in his cabin of careful study of the pictured profiles of hostile ships, study carried out in a mood of desperate despair, when he knew himself to be a coward but was determined to be a coward deficient in nothing. He had the splendid memory which goes with a vivid pictorial imagination, and he could recall the very pages on which he had seen those profiles, the very print beneath them. He stepped forward to the Captain's side.

'The two leading ships are *Bolzanos*, sir,' he said. 'Nine thousand tons, eight-inch, thirty-two knots.'

'You're sure?' asked the Captain mildly. 'Aren't they *Zaras*?'

'No, sir,' said Jerningham with unselfconscious certainty. 'And the last three light cruisers look like *Bande Neres*. I don't know about the first one, though, sir. She's like nothing we've been told about. I suppose she's one of the new ones, *Regolos*, and the Intelligence people didn't get her profile right.'

'I expect you're right,' said the Captain. He had turned a little on his stool to look at Jerningham; he was surprised to see his secretary thus self-assured and well poised, for the Captain had seen his secretary in action before and had struggled against the suspicion that Jerningham had not all the control over his emotions which was desirable in the British Navy. But the Captain had learned to control his own emotions, and not the slightest hint of his surprise appeared in his expression or his voice.

'I think I am, sir,' said Jerningham, dropping back again.

In the Long Acre office he had had the ideal secretary, Miss Horniman, always at hand, always acquainted with the latest development, ready to remind him of the appointment he had forgotten or the copy he had to deliver, sympathetic when his head ached in the morning, and wooden faced and unassuming when she put forward to him an idea which he had not been able to produce, content that her boss should receive the credit that was rightfully hers. Jerningham always modelled his behaviour towards the Captain on Miss Horniman's behaviour towards him. The Captain might possibly have been wrong in his report of what he had seen if his secretary had not put him right, and the Captain would have the credit and the secretary would not, but that was the destiny, the proper fate of Captains' secretaries. He could grin to himself about that; the irony and incongruity of it all appealed to his particular sense of humour.

The Captain was a Captain R.N., thought Jerningham, only a few grades lower than God; out of a hundred who started as naval cadets only very few ever reached that lofty rank – he was a picked man, with Staff College training behind him, but here was something his secretary could do better than he. It was a very considerable help to think about that; it saved Jerningham from some of the feeling of intense inferiority which plagued him.

But he respected the Captain none the less, admired him none the less. Jerningham looked at him in profile, with his glasses trained out to starboard on the Italian squadron. Those black eyebrows were turned up the tiniest trifle at the corners, giving him a faintly Mephistophelian appearance. It was a slightly fleshy face; the big mouth with its thick lips might well have been coarse if it had not been firmly compressed and helped out by the fine big chin. There was something of the artist about the long fingers which held the glasses, and the wrists were slender although muscular. Jerningham suddenly realized that the Captain was a slender man – he had always thought of him as big, powerful, and muscular. It was a surprise to him; the explanation must be that the Captain must have so much personality and force of character that anyone talking to him automatically credited him with physical strength.

It made more piquant still the sensation of discovering that the Captain had been in doubt of the identification of those Italian cruisers. Otherwise it would have been almost insufferable to see the steady matter of fact way in which the Captain looked across at the heavy odds opposed to him, the inhuman coolness with which he treated the situation, as if he were a spectator and not a participant, as if – what was certainly the case, for that matter – as if his professional interest in the tactics of the forthcoming battle, and his curiosity regarding what was going to happen, left him without a thought regarding his own personal danger.

Jerningham felt intense envy of the Captain's natural gifts. It was an envy which blended with, and fed, the fires of the jealousy which Dora Darby's letter had aroused in him.

CHAPTER 6

FROM THE CAPTAIN'S REPORT

... At 1310 the enemy opened fire ...

Captain Miles Ernest Troughton-Harrington-Yorke kept his glasses trained on the Italians. Jerningham was undoubtedly right about the identification of them. The six best cruisers the Italians had left; and that was a Vice-Admiral's flag which the leading ship was flying. They could not be more than a few hundred yards out of range, either, with those big eight-inch guns of theirs. The Captain looked to see them open fire at any moment, while the British six-inch still could not drop a shell within three thousand yards of them. With the very detailed reports which must have reached them from the air they could be in no doubt of the situation; they could fear no trap, have no doubt of their superiority of strength. It was possible – likely, in fact, in view of the other intelligence – that this Italian force was only a screen for a still stronger one, of battleships and more heavy cruisers, but there was no need to wait for reinforcements. They were strong enough to do the business themselves, two heavy cruisers and four light against five light cruisers.

Only two months ago the situation had been reversed, when *Artemis* and *Hera* had come upon that Italian convoy escorted by the two Italian destroyers. The disproportion of strength had not been very different. If the Italian destroyer captains had been realists they would have simply run away, and by their superior speed they could have saved their own ships while abandoning the convoy to destruction. But they had stayed to fight, like a couple of fools, advancing boldly towards the British cruisers, and endeavouring to lay a smoke-screen. The first broadside of six-inch from *Artemis* had hit one of the destroyers – the Captain still felt intense professional pleasure at the recollection – and the third from *Hera* had hit the other. The two destroyers had been blown into flaming, sinking wrecks before even their feeble 120 mm guns had had a chance to fire; the British cruisers rushing down on them destroyed them in the few seconds which it took to cover the distance representing the difference in range. So the destroyers expended themselves uselessly, not having delayed for a moment the destruction of the transports they were escorting. Very foolish of them indeed.

If the Italian admiral over there – I wonder who he is? Nocentini, perhaps, or is it Pogetti? – knows his business he will turn two points to port and close with us and finish us off. And if we knew our business we would run like hares and save ourselves, and let the convoy go, and let Malta go.

The Captain's tightly-shut mouth stretched into a dry grin. That was logic, but logic was not war. If it were, Hitler would be dining in Buckingham Palace this evening, and Napoleon would have dined there a hundred and forty years ago. No, that was a slipshod way of putting it. War was perfectly logical, but to grasp all the premises of war was very difficult and it was as fatally easy to draw incorrect conclusions from incomplete premises in war as in everything else. A mere count of the tonnage and the guns of the opposing sides was insufficient; it was even insufficient to include an estimate of the relative excellence of the training and discipline of the personnel on the two sides. There were other factors – the memory of Matapan, of Taranto, of the River Plate; the memory even of the defeat of the Spaniards of the Armada or of the defeat of the Italians at Lissa eighty years back.

The Captain had read somewhere of an unpleasant child who used to find amusement in chasing the slaves round the compound with a hot poker. The child found out quite early that it was unnecessary to have the poker actually red hot; it would serve just as well if it were painted so that the slaves thought it was hot. The slaves might even suspect that it was only painted, but they would not take the chance involved in finding out. So it was at the present moment; the British Navy had a record of victory over odds, and the Italians one of deafeat by inferior numbers. This time the Italians might suspect that the odds were too heavy, the numbers too inferior, for history to repeat itself. But it might call for more resolution than they possessed to put the matter to the proof. It was going to be interesting to see.

Something beautiful showed itself at that moment in the field of the Captain's binoculars, a tall, lovely column of water, rising gracefully out of the sea like the arm clothed in white samite, mystic, wonderful, which rose from the mere to catch Excalibur. The Captain had vague theories of beauty; he had often wondered why one curve should be more beautiful than another, one motion more graceful than another. But he had never tried to crystallize his theories, to give definition to what he felt might be indefinable. Hogarth had once attempted it, with his 'Line of Beauty' on the palette depicted in the corner of his self-portrait, and he had tried again, and failed disastrously, when he wrote his 'Analysis of Beauty'.

But for all that, it might be worth someone's while to try to analyse why the column of water thrown up by an eight-inch shell should be so beautiful. The rate of its rise (and the mathematics of the relative velocities of its constituent particles had their own charm as well), the proportion of height to girth, the very duration of its existence, were all so perfectly related to each other as to give pleasure to the eye. The faint yellow tinge that it possessed (that meant high explosive shell) was an added charm against that sky and sea. And farther away, to left and to right, rose its fellows at the same moment, each as beautiful as the other; they were widespread, and even allowing for the fact that those eight-inch were firing at extreme range that meant that the gunnery control instruments in the Italian ship were not lined up as carefully nor as accurately as they should be.

The leading ship was altering round towards the enemy. That was the way to deal with them; if they won't come and fight, go in and fight them.

'Starboard ten,' said the Navigating Officer into the voice-tube, as *Artemis* reached the position where each of her four predecessors had made their two-point turns, and the cruiser heeled again as the rudder brought her round.

CHAPTER 7

FROM THE CAPTAIN'S REPORT

... the enemy withdrew ...

All down the line of Italian cruisers ran a sparkle of light, bright yellow flashes competing with faint success against the sunlight. Leading Seaman Alfred Lightfoot saw the flashes in the cruiser upon which he was training his rangefinder; he saw them double, because the range-finder presented two images of the cruiser, just overlapping. That double image was something like what he had seen once or twice halfway through a binge, after the seventh drink or so. For a few minutes, then, the lights behind the bar, and the barmaid's face, duplicated themselves in just the same fashion, just as substantially, so that one could swear that the girl had two faces, one overlapping the other by half, and that each electric bulb had another hung beside it.

Lightfoot twirled the controlling screws of the rangefinder, and the two images moved into each other; in the same way, when Lightfoot was getting drunk, he could by an effort make the two images of the barmaid's face run together again, so that they would click into sharp unity instead of being hazy and oreoled with light. He read off the scale of the rangefinder.

'Range two-seven-ho,' he announced, his Cockney twang flavouring the dry tone in which he had been trained to make his statements; the vowel sound of the word 'range' was exactly the same as he would have used in the word 'rind'.

The sharp image at which he was peering was obscure again at once; two shadowy cruisers were replacing the single one – there were two red, white and green flags flying aft, a muddled double mass of funnels. With his Cockney quickness of thought Lightfoot could, if he had wanted to, have drawn the obvious conclusion, that the two squadrons were approaching each other rapidly, and he could from there have gone on to the next deduction, which was that in a very few seconds they would be pounding each other to pieces. But Lightfoot did not trouble to think in that fashion. Long ago he had told himself fatalistically that if a shell had his name on it he would cop it, and from no other shell. His job was to take ranges quickly and exactly; that was to be his contribution to the perfect whole which was the fighting ship, and he was set upon doing that without distraction. Just once or twice when he had strayed into self-analysis Lightfoot had felt a little pleased with himself at having attained this fatalistic Nirvana, but it is hard to apportion the credit for it – some of it was undoubtedly due to Lightfoot himself, but some also to the system under which he had been trained, some to the Captain for his particular application of that system; and possibly some to Mussolini himself, who had given Lightfoot a cause in which to fight whose justice was so clearly apparent.

Lightfoot twisted the regulating screws again to bring the images together. It was twenty-one seconds since he had seen the flashes of the guns of the cruiser at which he was pointing, and Lightfoot had already forgotten them, so little impression had they made upon him. And during those twenty-one seconds the eight-inch shells had been hurtling towards *Artemis* at a speed through the air of more than a mile in two seconds because their path was curved, reaching far up into the upper atmosphere, higher than the highest Alps into the freezing stratosphere before plunging down again towards their target. Lightfoot heard a sudden noise as of rushing water and of tearing of sheets, and then the field of his rangefinder was blotted out in an immense upheaval of water as the nearest shell of the broadside pitched close beside starboard bow of *Artemis*. Twenty tons of water, yellowed slightly by the high explosive, came tumbling on board, deluging the upper works, flooding over Lightfoot's rangefinder.

'Ringe hobscured,' said Lightfoot.

He reached to sweep the lenses clear, and darkness gave way to light again as he stared into the instrument. For a moment he was still nonplussed, so different was the picture he saw in it from what he had seen just before. The images were double, but the silhouettes were entirely changed, narrow instead of broad, and the two flecks of colour, the double images of the Italian flag, were right in the middle of each silhouette instead of aft of them. Lightfoot's trained reactions were as quick as his mind; his fingers were spinning the screws round in the opposite direction at the same moment as he realized that the Eyeties had turned their sterns towards the British and were heading for the horizon as fast as they could go.

The spectacle astonished him; the surprise of it broke through his professional calm in a way in which the prospect of danger quite failed to do.

'Coo!' said Lightfoot; the exclamation (although Lightfoot did not know it) was a shortening of 'Coo blimey', itself a corruption of 'God blind me'.

'Coo!' and then instantly training and professional pride mastered him again, and he brought the images together with a deft twirl of the screws 'Range two-nine-ho.'

Paymaster Sub-Lieutenant James Jerningham saw the Italian ships turn away, and he gravely noted the time upon his pad. One of his duties was to keep a record of any action in which the ship was engaged, because experience had proved that after an action, even with the help of the ship's plot which was kept up to date in the chart-room, and with the help of the various logs kept in different parts of the ship – signal logs, engine-room logs, and so on – it was difficult for anyone to remember the exact order of events as they had occurred. And reports had to be written, and the lessons of the action digested, if only for the benefit of the vast fleet in all the oceans of the world anxious to improve its professional knowledge.

The Captain slid down from his stool and stretched himself; Jerningham could tell just from his actions that he was relieved at not having to sit for a while – the lucky devil did not know that he was well off. Jerningham's feet ached with standing and he would have given something substantial in exchange for the chance to sit down. The Captain walked briskly up and down for a while, five paces aft and five paces forward; the bridge was too small and too crowded with officers and instruments to allow of a longer walk. And even during that five-pace walk the Captain kept shooting glances round him, at signalmen and flagship and look-outs so as to maintain himself in instant readiness for action.

It might be said that while the ship was at sea the Captain never went more than five paces from his stool; at night he lay on an air mattress laid on the steel deck with a blanket over him, or a tarpaulin when it rained. Jerningham had known him to sleep for as much as four hours at a stretch like that, with the rain rattling down upon him, a fold of the stiff tarpaulin keeping the rain from actually falling on his face. It was marvellous that any man could sleep in those conditions; it was marvellous that any man bearing that load of responsibility could sleep at all; but, that being granted, it was also marvellous that a man once asleep could rouse himself so instantly to action. At a touch on his shoulder the Captain would raise his head to hear a report and would issue his orders without a moment in which to recover himself.

The Captain was tough both mentally and physically, hard like steel – a picked man, Jerningham reminded himself. And no man could last long in command of a light cruiser in the Mediterranean if he were not tough. Yet toughness was only one essential requisite in the make-up of a cruiser captain. He had to be a man of the most sensitive and delicate reflexes, too, ready to react instantly to any stimulus. Mere vulgar physical courage was common enough, thought Jerningham, regretfully, even if he did not possess it himself, but in the Captain's case it had to be combined with everything else, with moral courage, with the widest technical knowledge, with flexibility of mind and rapidity of thought and physical endurance – all this merely to command the ship in action, and that was only part of it. Before the ship could be brought into action it had to be made into an efficient fighting unit. Six hundred officers and men had to be trained to their work, and fitted into the intricate scheme of organization as complex as any jigsaw puzzle, and, once trained and organized, had to be maintained at fighting pitch. There were plenty of men who made reputations by successfully managing a big department store; managing a big ship of war was as great an achievement, even if not greater.

Jerningham, with nearly three years of experience, knew a great deal about the Navy now, and yet his temperament and his early life and his duties in the ship still enabled him to look on the service dispassionately as a disinterested observer. He knew better than anyone else in the ship's company how little work the Captain seemed to do when it came to routine business, how freely he delegated his power, and having delegated it, how cheerfully he trusted his subordinates, with none of those after-thoughts and fussinesses which Jerningham had seen in city offices. That was partly moral courage, of course, again, the ability to abide by a decision once having made it. But partly it was the result of the man's own ability. His judgement was so sound, his sense of justice so exact, his foresight so keen, that everyone could rely on him. Jerningham suspected that there might be ships whose captains had not these advantages and who yet were not plagued with detail because officers and men united in keeping detail from them knowing that the decisions uttered would not be of help. Those would be unhappy ships. But the kind of captain under which he served was also not plagued with detail, because officers and men knew that when they should appeal to him the decisions that would be handed down to them would be correct, human, intelligent. In that case officers and men went on cheerfully working out their own destiny, secure in the knowledge that there was an ability greater than their own ready to help them should it become necessary. That would mean a happy, efficient ship like *Artemis*.

Jerningham's envy of the Captain's capacity flared out anew as he thought about all this. It was a most remarkable sensation for Jerningham to feel that someone was a better man than he – Jerningham's sublime egotism of pre-war days had survived uncounted setbacks. Lost games of tennis or golf, failure to convince an advertising manager that the copy laid before him was ideal for its purpose, could be discounted on the grounds of their relative unimportance, or because of bad luck, or the mental blindness of the advertising manager. In this case there was no excuse of that sort to be found. Jerningham had never yet met an advertising manager whose work he did not think he could do better himself; the same applied to office heads – and to husbands. But Jerningham had to admit to himself that the Captain was better fitted than he was to command a light cruiser, and it was no mitigation that he did not want to command a light cruiser.

To recover his self-respect he called back into his mind again the fact that he had been quicker than the Captain in the identification of the Italian cruisers, and he went on to tell himself that the Captain would not stand a chance in competition with him for the affections of the young women of his set, with – not Dora Darby (Jerningham's mind shied away from that subject hastily) – but with Dorothy Clough or Cicely French, say. That was a comforting line of thought. The Captain might be the finest light cruiser captain, actual or potential, on the Seven Seas – Jerningham thought he was – but he was not to compare with Jerningham in anything else, in the social graces, or in appreciation of art or literature. The man had probably never seen beauty in anything. And it was quite laughable to think of him trying to woo Cicely French the way Jerningham had, finding her in a tantrum of temper, and subtly coaxing her out of it with womanish sympathy, and playing deftly on her reaction to win her regard, and telepathically noting the play of her mood so as to seize the right moment for the final advance. The very thought of the Captain trying to do anything like that made Jerningham smile through all his misery as he met the Captain's eye.

The Captain smiled back, and stopped in his walk at Jerningham's side.

'Was it a surprise to you, their running away like that?' asked the Captain.

Jerningham had to think swiftly to get himself back on board *Artemis* today from a Paddington flat three years ago.

'No, sir,' he said. 'Not very much.'

That was the truth, inasmuch as he had had no preconceived tactical theories so as to be surprised at all.

'It may be just a trick to get us away from the convoy,' said the Captain. 'Then their planes would have a chance. But I don't think so.'

'No, sir?' said Jerningham.

'There's something bigger than cruisers out today, I fancy. They may be trying to head us into a trap.'

The Captain's eye was still everywhere. He saw at that moment, and Jerningham's glance following him saw too, the flagship leading around in a sixteen-point turn.

'Starboard fifteen,' said the Navigating Lieutenant, and the deck canted hugely as *Artemis* followed her next ahead round. She plunged deeply half a dozen times as she crashed across the stern waves thrown up first by her predecessors and then by herself, and white water foamed across her forecastle.

'Flagship's signalling to convoy, sir,' said the Chief Yeoman of Signals, ' "Resume previous course".'

'We're staying between the Eyeties and the convoy,' remarked the Captain, 'and every minute brings us nearer to Malta.'

'Yes, sir,' said Jerningham. He cast frantically about in his mind for some contribution to make to this conversation other than 'Yes, sir,' and 'No, sir.' He wanted to appear bright.

'And night is coming,' said Jerningham, grasping desperately at inspiration.

'Yes,' said the Captain. 'The Eyeties are losing time. The most valuable asset they have, and they're squandering it.'

Jerningham looked at the Satanic eyebrows drawing together over the curved nose, the full lips compressed into a gash, and his telepathic sympathies told him how the Captain was thinking to himself what he would do if he commanded the Italian squadron, the resolution with which he would come plunging down into battle. And then the eyebrows separated again, and the lips softened into a smile.

'The commonest mistake to make in war,' said the Captain, 'is to think that because a certain course seems to you to be the best for the enemy, that is the course he will take. He may not think it the best, or there may be some reason against it which you don't know about.'

'That's true, sir,' said Jerningham. It was not an aspect of war he had ever thought about before; most of his thoughts in action were usually taken up by wondering what his own personal fate would be.

Ordinary Seaman Whipple was climbing the difficult ladder to the crow's nest to relieve the lookout there. The Captain allowed himself to watch the changeover being effected, and Jerningham saw him put back his head and inflate his chest to hail the masthead, and then he relaxed again with the words unspoken.

'And the next commonest mistake,' grinned the Captain, 'is to give unnecessary orders. Whipple up there will keep a sharp lookout without my telling him. He knows that's what he's there for.'

Jerningham gaped at him, wordless now, despite his efforts to appear bright. This was an aspect of the Captain's character which he had never seen before, this courteous gentleman with his smiling common sense and insight into character. It crossed Jerningham's mind, insanely at that moment, that perhaps the Captain after all might be able to make some progress with Cicely French if he wanted to.

CHAPTER 8

FROM THE CAPTAIN'S REPORT

... the enemy's cruisers were then joined by a fresh force consisting of two battleships of the 'Littorio' class and another cruiser of the 'Bolzano' class ...

Ordinary Seaman Albert Whipple was a crusader. Like most crusaders he was inclined to take himself a little too seriously, and that made him something of a butt to his friends. When he took over from Quimsby the latter grinned tolerantly and poked him in the ribs while pointing out to him the things in sight – the smoke of the Italian cruiser squadron, and their funnels just visible over the horizon, the distant shapes of the convoy wallowing doggedly along towards Malta.

'An' that thing in the front of the line is the flagship,' concluded Quimsby with heavy-handed humour. 'Give my regards to the Admiral when you get your commission.'

For one of the theories that the lower deck maintained about Whipple's seriousness was that he wanted promotion, aspiring to the quarter-deck, for Whipple had a secondary school education. The lower deck was wrong about this. All that Whipple wanted to do was to fight the enemy as efficiently as was in his power, in accordance with the precepts of his mother.

Albert was the youngest of a large family, and his elder brothers and sisters were quite unlike him, big and burly, given to the drinking of beer and to riotous Saturday nights; they had all gone out to work at fourteen, and it was partly because of the consequent relief to the family finances that Albert had been able to set his foot on the lower rungs of the higher education. The brothers and sisters had not objected, had shown no jealousy that the youngest should have had better treatment than they; in fact, they had been mildly proud of him when he came home and reported proudly that he had won the scholarship which might be the beginning of a career. Albert was white-faced and skinny, like his mother, and desperately serious. The brothers and sisters had never paid any attention to their mother's queer behaviour; their work in the tannery and the toy factory had made them good union members, but they had no sympathy with her further aspirations, with her desperate interest in the League of Nations, in the Japanese invasion of China and Franco's rebellion in Spain. They had laughed, as their father had learned to do before they were born. Their father could remember as far back as 1914, when the eldest child – George – was on the way, finding her standing on the kerb watching the soldiers of the new army marching down the street, bands playing and people cheering, and yet she had tears running down her cheeks at the sight of it. Mr Whipple had clapped her on the back and told her to cheer up, and as soon as George was born had gone off and joined the Army and had done his bit in Mespot. And when he had come back, long after the war was over, he had found her all worked up about the Treaty of Versailles, and when it was not the Treaty of Versailles it was some new worry about the Balkans or the militarization of the Rhine or something.

She had tried to capture the interest of each of her children in turn regarding the problems of the world, and she had failed with each until Albert began to grow up. He listened to her; it was a help that during his formative years he came home to dinner while the rest ate sandwiches at the factory. Those *tête-à-têtes* across the kitchen table, the skinny little son listening rapt to the burning words of his skinny little mother, had had their effect. Albert had it in mind when he was still quite young that when he grew up it would be his mission to reform the world; he was a little priggish about it, feeling marked out from the rest of humanity, and this conception of himself had been accentuated by the fact that unlike his brothers and sisters he had started a secondary education, and that he passed, the summer in which war began, his school examination a year younger than the average of his fellows and with distinctions innumerable.

The brothers had joined the Air Force or the Army, but with pitiably small sense of its being a sacred duty; they did not hold with Hitler's goings on, and it was time something was done about it, but they did not think of themselves as crusaders and would have laughed at anyone who called them that. And Albert had stayed with his mother, while his father worked double shifts at the tannery, until after a few months Albert and his mother talked over the fact that now he was old enough to join one of the Services at least – a poster had told them how boys could join the Royal Navy. Mrs Whipple kept back her tears as they talked about it; in fact, she jealously hugged her pain to her breast, womanlike. At the back of her mind there was the thought of atonement, of a bloody sacrifice of what she held dearest in the world, to make amends for her country's earlier lethargy and indifference. She was giving up her best-loved son, but to him she talked only of his duty, of how his call had come to him when he was hardly old enough for the glory of it. And Albert had answered the call, and his confident certainty in the rightness of his mission had carried him through homesickness and seasickness, had left him unspotted by his messmates' spoken filth and casual blasphemies. He had endured serenely their amused tolerance of his queer ways and priggish demeanour, and he devoted himself to the work in hand with a fanaticism which had raised the eyebrows of the petty officers of H.M.S. *Collingwood* so that now he was Ordinary Seaman in *Artemis* and noted down in the Commander's mental books – and in those of the Captain, too – as certain to make a good Leading Seaman in time.

Sea service weathered his complexion to a healthy tan, but neither good food nor exercise had filled him out at all. Perhaps the thought of his mission kept him thin. He was still hollow-cheeked, and his comparatively wide forehead above his hollow cheeks and his little pointed chin made his face strangely wedge-shaped, which intensified the gleam in his eyes sunk deep under their brows. All his movements were quick and eager; he grabbed feverishly at the binoculars resting in their frame before his face, so anxious was he to take up his duties again, to resume his task of avenging Abyssinia and hastening the coming of the millennium. Lying in a hospital at that moment, her legs shattered by the ruins that a bomb from a German aeroplane had brought down, his mother was thinking of him, two thousand miles away; either through space or through time it was her spirit which was animating him.

Whipple searched the horizon carefully, section by section, from the starboard beam to right ahead and then round to the port beam and back again; there was nothing to report, nothing in sight beyond what Quimsby had pointed out to him. He swivelled back again to the Italian squadron; his hatred might have been focused through lenses and prisms like some death-dealing ray, so intense was it. There were only the funnels of the cruisers to see, and the pall of smoke above them stretching back behind them in a dwindling plume. He swivelled slowly forward again, and checked his motion abruptly. There was a hint of smoke on the horizon at a point forward of the Italians, almost nothing to speak of, and yet a definite trace of smoke all the same, and clearly it was no residual fragment of the smoke of any of the ships which Whipple had in sight. For five seconds Whipple watched it grow before he pressed the buzzer.

The Captain's secretary answered it – a man Whipple had never cared for. He suspected him of he knew not what, but he had also seen him drunk, only just able to stagger along the prow back into the ship, and Whipple had no use for a man who let himself get drunk when there was work to be done, while there was a mission still unfulfilled. But Whipple did not allow his dislike to interfere with his duty. If anything, it made him more careful than ever with his enunciation, more painstaking to make an exact report of what he could see.

'Forebridge,' said Jerningham.

'Masthead. More smoke visible on the port bow,' said Whipple pedantically. 'Beyond the enemy cruisers. Green three-eight.'

He repeated himself just as pedantically. Back through the voice-pipe, before Jerningham closed it, he could hear his report being relayed to the Captain, and that gave him the comforting assurance that Jerningham had got it right. He swept the horizon, rapidly and thoroughly, before looking at the new smoke again; it was always as well to take every possible precaution. But there was nothing further to report except as regards the new smoke. He pressed the buzzer again.

'Masthead,' he said. 'The new lot of smoke is closing us. The same bearing. No, green three-nine.'

A bigger wave than usual, or a combination of waves, lifted *Artemis* ten feet vertically at the same moment as beyond the horizon another combination of waves lifted the Italian battleship *Legnano* ten feet also. In that crystal clear air against the blue sky, Whipple caught a glimpse of solid grey – funnel tops and upperworks, the latter apparently the top storey of a massive gunnery control tower. It came and went almost instantaneously, but Whipple knew what it was, and felt a wave of fierce excitement pass over him like a flame. Yet excitement could not shake the cold fixity of his purpose to do his duty with exactitude.

'Masthead,' he said down the tube, dryly and unemotionally. 'Battleship in sight. Green four-o.'

The blood was pulsing faster in his veins. A bibliophile finding in the twopenny box a long-sought first edition would know nearly the same thrill as Whipple felt, or a knight of the Round Table at a vision of the Grail. There were thousands of Italians there to be killed, ships which were the pride of the Italian navy were there to be destroyed. 'The thicker the hay,' said Alaric once, when the odds against his army were being pointed out to him, 'the easier it is mown.' 'The bigger they come,' said Bob Fitzsimmons, 'the harder they fall.' Whipple thought along the same lines. The appalling strength of the hostile force meant nothing to him, literally nothing, from the point of view of frightening him. He was merely glad that the enemy were presenting themselves in such numbers to be killed. If at that moment some impossible chance had put Whipple without time for reflection in command of the English squadron, the light cruisers would have dashed headlong into action and destruction. But Whipple was not in command. He was perfectly conscious that he was merely the masthead look-out in H.M.S. *Artemis*, and as such a man with a definite duty to perform to the best of his ability.

'Two battleships and a heavy cruiser,' he reported down the voice-pipe, 'heading a little abaft our beam. On the same bearing now as the other ships. The other ships are turning now astern of them.'

Whipple was reporting the development of the Italian fleet into line of battle, and in exactly the same tone as he would have used if he had been reporting sighting a buoy. That was the contribution he was privileged to make to the cause his mother had talked about to him over the midday dinner table in Bermondsey. Ordinary Seaman Albert Whipple, aged eighteen, was a prig and a self-righteous one. A cynic might well define *esprit de corps* as self-righteous priggishness – the spirit which inspired Sir Richard Grenville or Cromwell's Ironsides. From the yardarm close beside Whipple fluttered the signal flags which he had set a-flying.

CHAPTER 9

FROM THE CAPTAIN'S REPORT

... the behaviour of the ship's company was most satisfactory ...

The Italian fleet was up over the horizon now, their upperworks visible under the smoke, and the British squadron had wheeled about once more. The Italians were heading to interpose between the convoy and Malta; if it were not for that slow, lumbering convoy, crawling along at its miserable eleven knots, the light cruisers could have circled round the Italian battleships like a hawk round a heron. As it was the British squadron was like a man with a cannon ball chained to his leg, crippled and slow, forced to keep its position between the convoy and the Italian warships – those battleships were designed for twenty-nine knots and even when mishandled were quite capable of twenty-five. They could work steadily ahead, until they barred the route, forcing the British to attack to clear the path – as if a man with a penknife could clear a path out of a steel safe – and if the British sensibly declined the attempts and turned back, they would be pursued by the Italians, whose superior speed would then compel the light cruisers either to stay and be shot at or move out of the Italian path and leave the convoy to destruction.

It was all perfectly logical, positive, and inevitable when the data were considered – the eleven-knot convoy, the thirty-knot battleships, the Italian fifteen-inch guns, the British six-inch; the four hours remaining of daylight and the extraordinary clearness of the air. Fog might save the English, but there was no chance of fog in that sparkling air. Nightfall might save the English, too, for it would be most imprudent for battleships to engage in a night action with cruisers – that would be like staking guineas against shillings in a game of pitch-and-toss. But it was still early afternoon, and no more than half an hour would be needed for the Italians to reach their most advantageous position. Then five minutes of steady shelling would be sufficient to sink every cruiser in the British line; less than that to destroy the helpless convoy. Then Malta would fall; the running ulcer in Italy's side would be healed; Rommel in Africa, the submarines in the Atlantic would feel an instant lessening of the strain upon them; the Vichy government would be informed of one more step towards the German conquest of the world; the very Japanese in seas ten thousand miles away would be aware of a lightening of their task.

So obvious and logical was all this that the inferences must be clear to the rawest hand anywhere in the ship. It was not necessary to have studied Mahan, or to have graduated from the Staff College, to understand the situation. The ship's company of *Artemis* might not stop to think about Vichy or Rommel or the Japanese; but they knew the speed of the convoy, and the merest whisper of the word 'battleships' would tell them that their situation was a perilous one. And a mere whisper – with implied doubt – would be far more unsettling than any certainty. Not one man in ten in *Artemis* could see what was going on, and in a ship at action-stations it was hard for information to filter through by word of mouth.

In the Captain's opinion distorted news was dangerous. He knew his men, and he believed that his men knew him; if they heard the truth he could rely upon them whatever the truth might be. A crisis in the battle was close at hand, and he could spare not one moment from the bridge to tell them himself. He turned a little on his stool, caught Jerningham's eye, and beckoned to him. Jerningham had to wait a second or two while the Captain brought himself up to date again regarding the situation, looking at flagship and convoy and enemy, before he took the glasses from his eyes and turned a searching glance at his secretary. Jerningham was acutely conscious of that glance. He was not being sized up for any trifle; it was not as if he was a mere applicant for a job in a City office. The business he was to do was something touching the whole efficiency of the ship – the safety of Malta – the life or death of England. The Captain would not have trusted him with it if he were not absolutely sure of him. In fact, the Captain was faintly surprised at finding that he *was* sure of him; he wondered a little whether he had previously misjudged his secretary or whether the latter was one of those people who had moods, and was sometimes reliable and sometimes not. But whether he had misjudged him or not, and whether he had moods or not, this was the right time to impose responsibility upon him and to make amends if he had misjudged him, or to give him confidence in the future if this was merely an exalted mood.

'Go down,' said the Captain, 'and tell the ship about the situation.'

Jerningham stood a little startled, but the Captain already had his binoculars to his eyes again. He had given his order, and an order given by a Captain in a ship of war is carried out.

'Aye aye, sir,' said Jerningham, saluting as he jerked himself out of his surprise.

He turned away and started down the ladder. He was an intelligent man, accustomed in his private life to think for himself, accustomed to selling ideas to advertising managers, accustomed to conveying ideas to commercial artists, accustomed to telling the public truths or fictions in the fewest and clearest words. The Captain might easily have expanded the brief order he gave his secretary, telling him what to say and how to say it, but the Captain knew that it was not necessary; and also that to leave the responsibility to his secretary would be good for him.

Jerningham's mind was feverishly turning over words and phrases as he descended the ladder; he did not have time to assemble any, but, on the other hand, he did not have time in those few seconds to become self-conscious, nor had his weakness time to reassert itself.

'I've a message for the ship from the Captain,' he said to the bosun's-mate beside the loudspeaker bolted to the bulkhead.

The petty officer switched on and piped shrilly, the sound of his call audible in every part of the ship.

'The Captain has sent me to tell you,' said Jerningham to the mouthpiece, 'we've got the Eyety navy in front of us. Battleships, heavy cruisers, and all. They've run away from us once, the heavy cruisers have. Now we're going to see if the battleships'll run too. Three hours of daylight left, and the convoy's *got* to reach Malta. Good luck to us all. There's none like us.'

Jerningham opened his mouth to say more, but his good judgement came to his rescue and he closed it again. He had said all there was to say, and in an illuminated moment he knew that anything he were to add would be not only superfluous but possibly harmful. Men of the temper of the crew of *Artemis* did not need rhetoric; a plain statement of the facts for the benefit of those men below decks who had no idea what was happening was all that was needed.

He turned away from the unresponsive instrument, not knowing whether he had done well or badly; in the days of wooden ships, before public address systems had even been heard of, his words might have been received with cheers – or boos – which would have been informative. The ludicrous thought crossed his active mind that it was just like an advertising problem. How often had he devised ingenious methods by which to 'key' advertisements to discover which had the greatest pulling power?

His eyes met those of the bosun's-mate, and then travelled on to exchange glances with the other ratings – messengers and resting lookouts – stationed here. One or two of the men still wore the expression of philosophic indifference which so often characterized the lower deck, but there was a gleam in the eyes of the others, a smile at the corners of their mouths, which told him that they were excited, and pleasurably excited. That telepathic sympathy of his, which had assisted him to the downfall of so many young women, made him aware that the men were feeling the same inconsequent exhilaration as he felt – inconsequent to him, and novel and strange, but something they had known before and recognized. A climax was at hand, the climax to months and years of training and forethought, to the unobtrusive mental conditioning for which the Mephistophelian Captain on the bridge was responsible, to the life's mission to which men like Ordinary Seaman Albert Whipple had devoted themselves, or to the long line of fighting ancestors, which had generated them – like A.B. Dawkins down at the wheel, whose great-great-grandfather had run with powder charges over the bloody decks of the *Téméraire* at Trafalgar. It was the prospect of such a climax which exhilarated them, just as, ridiculously, it exhilarated him, and left them all careless of any possible consequences to themselves. He ran up the steep ladder again to the bridge, disregarding the way in which it swayed and swung to the send of the sea.

CHAPTER 10

FROM THE CAPTAIN'S REPORT

... increasing speed and at the same time making smoke ...

Back on the bridge, Jerningham looked round him to see that there had been no radical change in the situation during the short time of his absence. There were the minutest possible dots on the horizon below the Italian funnel smoke which showed that the Italian fleet was now actually in sight. A new string of flags was breaking out on the halliards of the flagship.

The Captain knew this was the moment. The Admiral had led them round until they were properly stationed with regard to the wind which now blew in a line from them to a point ahead of the Italians – that blessed wind, of such a convenient strength and from such a convenient quarter – and he had timed his arrival in this situation at the very moment when the Italians would be almost within range with their fourteen-inch guns. And so far the Admiral had shown none of his hand, except to display a determination to yield nothing without fighting for it, and the Italians must have been expecting that at least, as was proved by their caution in bringing up their battleships only behind a heavy force of cruisers.

The Chief Yeoman of Signals interpreted the flagship's signal, and the Captain was ready for it – the plan which he held on his knee laid it down as the next step.

'Revolutions for thirty-one knots,' he ordered. 'Make smoke.'

The Navigating Lieutenant repeated the order, and the Officer of the Watch pressed the plunger which ordered smoke.

Down in the engine-room the Commander (E) stood on the iron grating; being a tall man the top of his head was no more than a few inches below the level of the sea. He stood there with the immeasurable patience of his breed, acquired during countless hours of standing on countless gratings, and with his feet apart and his hands clasped behind him in the attitude he had first been taught as a cadet eighteen years before. He was the supreme lord of this underworld of his, like Lucifer, and he seemed marked out as such by the loneliness of his position, without a soul within yards of him, and by the light-coloured boiler suit which he wore, and by the untroubled loftiness of his expression. The very lighting of the engine-room by some strange chance accentuated the fact, glaring down upon his face and figure with a particular brightness, specially illuminating him like a character on the stage. He was a young man to have the rank of Commander and to carry the responsibilities of his position, to have hundreds of men obedient to him, to have sixty-four thousand horse-power under his control, to be master of the pulsating life of a light cruiser, but it would be a hard task to guess his age, so deliberate were his movements and so unlined and yet so mature was his face.

All the Commander (E) had to do was to stand there on the grating and do nothing else. A crisis might be at hand, but it could not affect the Commander (E) unless some catastrophe occurred. His work was done for the moment; it had been accomplished already during the years *Artemis* had been in commission. He had trained the engine-room complement into complete efficiency – the Engine-room Arificers and the Mechanicians and the Stokers; the Lieutenants and Sub-Lieutenants (E) who were his heads of department and his subordinates – not so many years younger than he – loved him as if he were their father, and would have found it hard to explain why if called upon to do so. None could appreciate the magic serenity, that endless patience, who had not served under him. Because of the love they bore him they knew his will without his expressing it, and they laboured constantly to anticipate it, to perfect themselves in their duty because he wished it, so that the organization and routine of the engine-room ran as smoothly and as efficiently as did the turbines at that moment.

And the turbines ran smoothly because of the previous labours of the Commander (E) – the sleepless vigilance which had watched over material and supplies, had read every engine-room log, had studied the temperatures of every bearing, the idiosyncrasies of every oil jet. There had been the endless desk-work, the reports written to the Admiralty (the strange gods of Whitehall whose motives had to be guessed, and who had to be propitiated by exact and complicated paper ceremonial, but who, once propitiated, were lavish like the savage rain gods of Africa), the statistics to be gathered and studied, the plans that had to be made against future contingencies. In time of war a light cruiser repairs and reconditions when she can and not when she should; and the Commander (E) had had to use forethought, and had had to display prompt decision, deciding what should be done, what opportunities snatched at, what might safely be postponed, anticipating future needs, doing today what would have to be done anyway during the next two weeks, leaving until some uncovenanted future doing the things which were not immediately essential.

As a result of all this the Commander (E) had nothing to do now; everything was being done by itself. Even the Senior Engineer, Lieutenant (E) Charles Norton Bastwick, felt a lack of anything to do, and came lounging up to take his stand beside the Commander (E), hands behind him, feet apart, in the 'at ease' position; it would be some minutes before he would once more feel the urge to walk round again, reading gauges and thermometers, and thereby debarring the Commander (E) from doing the same. It would only be if an emergency arose – if some near-miss shook up a condenser so that it leaked, or if a torpedo hit flooded a compartment, or some similar damage was inflicted – that they would have their hands full, improvising and extemporizing, toiling along with their men to keep the ship afloat and the propellers turning. And if the ship were to meet her death, if the sea were to come flooding in and the scalding steam – steam as hot as red-hot iron, steam that could roast meat to a frizzled brown – should pour into boiler-room and engine-room, and the order 'abandon ship' should be given, they would be the last of all to leave, the last to climb the treacherous iron ladders up to sea level and possible safety.

The engine-room was hot, because the ship had been going twenty-seven knots for some time now. The thermometer on the forward bulkhead registered 105 degrees, but for an engine-room, and according to the ideas of men accustomed to working in one, that was not really hot. And the place was full of noise, the high-pitched note of the turbines dominating everything – a curious noise, in its way an unobtrusive noise, which sounded as if it did not want to call attention to itself, the loudest whisper one could possibly imagine. The ears of a newcomer to the engine-room would be filled with it, all the same, so that he could hear nothing else. Only after long experience would he grow so accustomed to the noise that he could distinguish other noises through it, and hear human voices speaking at their normal pitch. Until that should come about he would see lips move and not be able to understand a word.

Bastwick and the Commander (E) were aware that above them, on the surface of the sea, some sort of action was taking place. All through the forenoon they had heard the four-inch and the Oerlikons and the pom-poms firing in savage bursts, and they had known that the convoy and escort were under aerial attack; but then the guns fell silent over their heads, and food had been brought to them, and there had been a brief moment of tranquillity. But then the bridge had rung down for twenty-seven knots, and they had had to switch over from the cruising turbines to the main engines (that blessed fluid flywheel which made the changeover so rapid and easy!) and the ship had begun rapid manoeuvring. Since then course had been altered so often that it was hard to reconstruct the situation in the mind. And once the ship had rolled and quivered to an explosion close alongside – God only knew what that was, for not a gun had been fired in the ship since the morning.

The squeal of the bosun's pipe suddenly made itself heard through the loudspeaker in the engine-room, attracting everyone's attention to Jerningham's voice which followed it. 'We've got the Eyety navy in front of us ... now we're going to see if the battleships'll run too ...' Jerningham's voice came to an end, but the Commander (E) and Bastwick still stood at ease on the iron grating, unmoved and unmoving. At any moment a fifteen-inch shell might come crashing through the deck above them, to burst in the engine-room and rend the ship apart while dashing them to atoms. Around them and beneath them a thousand-odd tons of fuel oil awaited the chance to burst into flame and burn them like ants in a furnace. A hundred tons of high explosive, forward and aft, needed only to be touched off.

But it was of the essence of life down here below the protective deck that destruction might come at any second, without any warning at all, and – more important from the point of view of mental attitude – without any possibility of raising a hand to ward it off. There was nothing to do but one's duty, just as the comic poet once declared that he had nothing to eat save food. Down there Jerningham's announcement on the loudspeaker had the effect of making everyone feel a little superior to the world above them, as the white settlers in Africa in time of drought might watch the natives sacrificing chickens or dancing wild dances to bring rain; the whites could feel contemptuous or compassionate – but they could not make it rain any more than the natives could. Above decks, Jerningham's announcement was like a stone dropped into a pool, sending a ripple of excitement over the surface; below them it was like a stone dropped into treacle, absorbed without any apparent reaction. The Commander (E) and Bastwick were watching Engine-room Artificer Henrose making the routine test of the boiler water, making sure that under the stress of continuous high speed the sea water pumped through the condenser to cool the used steam and to make it available for re-use was not leaking through any one of the thousand joints. Henrose, balancing against the roll of the ship, held the test-tube of boiler water in his left hand and poised the bottle of silver nitrate over it, letting the reagent fall into it drop by drop. Jerningham's announcement made itself heard, but Henrose might just as well not have heard it as far as any apparent reaction was concerned. He levelled the bottle of silver nitrate, squinted at the test-tube, and shook it, and squinted again. There was not the slightest trace of the white precipitate of silver chloride which would indicate that there was salt in the boiler water – salt which would eat through joints and tubes and cripple the ship in a few hours. Henrose went swaying back along the heaving grating to spill out the test-tube of water and replace the silver nitrate bottle. Italian dreadnoughts might be within range; that was interesting, just as was the fact that Henry VIII had six wives, but there was no salt in the boiler water, and it was that which mattered.

To starboard and port the needles of the revolution indicators moved sharply round the dial; the Commander (E) from where he stood – he stood there because although he had ostensibly nothing to do he could see from there everything of importance – could see that the number of revolutions ordered would give the ship thirty-one knots, full speed save for a knot or two in hand for emergencies. The Commander (E) was serenely aware that there was ample pressure available to satisfy this demand; it was because he could foresee such demands and plan economically for them ahead of time that he held the rank of Commander.

The four ratings who stood at the valves admitting steam to the four turbines began to spin the valves open, turning the horizontal wheels while watching the restless needles – two black and one red – of the dials. The note of the turbines began unbelievably to rise, unbelievably because the ear would not have believed that there could be a note higher than the previous one. More and more steam poured into the turbines, a tremendous torrent of steam, steam with a strength of sixty thousand horse-power. The beat of the propellers quickened, the needles crept farther round the dials until they caught up with and rested upon the others. The orders from the bridge were obeyed; the ship was making thirty-one knots, and in the engine-room it felt as if she were leaping like a stag from wave to wave over the lively sea.

A fresh noise broke through the whine of the turbines; this time it was a loud imperious clatter that none could mistake. A red light glowed high up on the bulkhead, and an indicator hand moved across from 'Stop making smoke' to 'Make smoke'. Bastwick moved forward leisurely towards the boiler-room. He knew that the signal was being repeated there – during the night before he had personally tested every communication – and he knew that Stoker Petty Officer Harmsworth was perfectly reliable, but he knew, too, that nothing is certain in war. As he went through the double door his ears clicked with the rise in pressure; at thirty-one knots the furnaces burnt in a few minutes enough oil fuel to warm the average house for a whole winter, and the air to consume that oil was a rushing mighty tempest dragged into the boiler-room by the partial vacuum set up by the combustion.

Harmsworth was completing the adjustment of the valves admitting just too much oil and shutting off just too much air to allow of complete combustion in this furnace. Bastwick stooped and peered through the glazed peephole. Normally it gave a view of a white-hot whirl of flame, but now it showed a hideous gloomy blackness; some of the oil was being burnt, but only just enough to break down the remainder into thick black greasy hydrocarbons whose sooty smoke was being caught up in the draught and poured through the after-funnel.

'Very good,' said Bastwick, straightening up.

The heat in here was oppressive, and the temperature would rise still higher with this increase in speed; there were trickles of sweat down Harmsworth's bull neck and among the hairs of his bare chest. Bastwick looked round the boiler-room, nodded to Sub-Lieutenant (E) Pilkington, and got a grin back in return. Pilkington was a brilliant youngster; one of these days he would be an Admiral. Bastwick completed a brief inspection and found everything satisfactory as it would be with Pilkington there. Then Bastwick made his way back to the engine-room, where the Commander (E) still stood on the iron grating, his handsome ageless face lit up by the harsh electric bulbs like that of a marble saint. But Bastwick knew that the Commander (E) had taken note that he, Bastwick, had recently inspected the boiler-room. The rudder indicator on the bulkhead, below the smoke telegraph, showed that the ship was changing course, and the two red lights beside it confirmed it by showing that the steering engines were at work. Bastwick knew, too, that the Commander (E) had noted this fact as well, and was making deductions from it regarding the battle. The saint might appear lost in contemplation, but when, or if, an emergency should arise he would be as prepared to deal with it as he could be, as any man could be.

CHAPTER 11

FROM THE CAPTAIN'S REPORT

... I found the smoke-screen to be extremely effective ...

Artemis was flying through the water now; at that speed with the wind abeam and the sea nearly so she lurched savagely and with unremitting regularity, hitting each wave as if it were something solid, her forecastle awash with the white water which came leaping over her port bow. Last of the line, she tore along over a surface already whipped creamy white by the four ships ahead of her; the mountainous waves thrown up by five hulls each of nearly six thousand tons travelling at that speed diverged on either side of her and broke into white water where they crossed the waves thrown up by the destroyers racing in a parallel line. The five cruisers went tearing along in their rigid line. Smoke began to pour from the after-funnel of the flagship in the van, a wisp or two at first, and then a thick greasy never-ending cloud; within two seconds of the first wisps there was smoke pouring from the after-funnels of all five of them – five thick cylinders of smoke, each so dense as to appear liquid rather than gaseous. They drooped down to the surface of the sea, and rolled over it, pushed gently by that convenient wind towards the enemy, and hardly dissipating at all, spreading just enough to blend with each other in a wide bank of smoke diagonal to the squadron's course so that even the second ship in the line, to say nothing of *Artemis* at the rear, was completely obscured from the sight of the Italians. And the thirty-one knots at which the squadron was moving was far faster than anything the dreadnoughts could do, so that although the Italian fleet was faster than the convoy the smoke-screen was being laid between the two; to attack the convoy the battleships would still have to come through the screen – they could not work round the end of it.

But to lay a smoke-screen and to hide behind it was a mere defensive warfare of the most pusillanimous kind. The enemy must be smitten, and smitten again, even though the smiting was with mere six-inch guns against twelve inches of armour-plate. Even though the enemy could not be hurt, his resolution must be broken down, his nerve shattered; he must be taught the lesson that he could not venture out to sea without submitting to vicious attack. And *Artemis* was last of the line of cruisers; abeam of her the smoke lay thickest, and it would be her movements that would be the most unpredictable to the enemy. It was her duty to smite, even though to smite she must expose those eggshell sides of hers to the sledgehammer blows of the enemy, and run the gauntlet of one-ton shells hurled with the velocity of a meteor, with an accuracy which could hit a tennis court from ten miles' distance.

The Captain sat on the stool which bucked beneath him like a playful horse; the motion was unnoticed by him even though the reflexes developed during years at sea were continually at work keeping him steady in his seat. He was thinking deeply, but on subjects so logical, and with such a comforting ingredient of mathematics, that his expression gave no sign of it. The Mephistophelian eyebrows were their normal distance apart; and although the plan he was to carry out called for the highest degree of resolution, the firm mouth was no more firmly compressed than usual, for the plan was a part of the Captain's life, something he was going to do, not something he wished to do or did not wish to do; something the advisability of which was not in doubt even though the details of execution had had to be left to this last moment for consideration because of possible freaks of weather or possible unexpected moves on the part of the enemy.

Three minutes of smoke meant a smoke bank a mile and a half long, far too wide for the enemy to watch with care all along its length. And with the smoke being continually added to at one end, the other end would probably not be under observation at all. And the smoke bank, allowing for spread, would be a quarter of a mile thick, but *Artemis* would be going through it diagonally, and it would take her (the Captain solved a Pythagorean problem in his head) fifty-five seconds to emerge on the other side, without allowing for the drift of the bank before the wind. This fifteen-knot breeze added a refreshing complication to the mathematics of it. It would take over two minutes to traverse the smoke bank; two minutes and ten seconds. The Captain turned to the voice-pipe beside him.

'Captain – Gunnery Officer,' he said. The Gunnery Lieutenant answered him.

'I am turning to starboard now, Guns. It will take us two minutes and ten seconds approximately to go through the smoke. You'll find the Eyeties about red five when we come out, but I shall turn to port parallel to their course immediately. Open fire when you are ready. All right? Goodbye.'

Artemis was the last ship in the line, and consequently the first to take action independently of the rest of the squadron.

'Turn eight points to starboard, Pilot,' he said to the Navigating Lieutenant.

'Starboard fifteen,' said the Navigating Lieutenant down the voice-pipe; *Artemis* leaned far over outwards as she made the right-angle turn – full speed and plenty of helm. 'Midships. Steady!'

'Stop making smoke,' ordered the Captain; he wanted the range clear for the guns when he emerged, and the signal went down through five decks to Stoker Petty Officer Harmsworth in the boiler-room.

So far the wind had been carrying the smoke solidly away to starboard, but now *Artemis* was heading squarely into it. One moment they were out in the clear sunshine with its infinite visibility. The next moment they were in reeking darkness. The stink of unburnt fuel oil was in their nostrils and their lungs. It made them cough. And in the smoke it was dark, far darker than the darkest coloured spectacles would make it; the Captain looked round, and he could only just see the white uniform of the Navigating Lieutenant two yards away. It was most satisfactory smoke as far as he could tell – he looked aft towards the masthead and could see nothing. But there was just the chance that the mast was protruding through the smoke and betraying the movements of the ship to the Italians.

'Call the masthead and see if the lookout is in the smoke,' ordered the Captain, and Jerningham obeyed him.

'Masthead lookout reports he is in the smoke and can't see anything,' he called into the darkness when he had received Ordinary Seaman Whipple's reassurance.

The duty had been useful to him. When they had plunged into the smoke his heart had seemed to rise in his throat, and it was only with an effort that he had seemed to swallow it down. It was beating fast, and the beating seemed to find an echo in his finger tips so that they shook. But the distraction of having to speak to Whipple had saved him, and he was able to recapture his new found sang-froid.

'Thirty seconds,' said the Torpedo Lieutenant. He had switched on the light at the hooded desk and, stooping with his face close down, he was reading the movement of the second-hand of the deck-watch.

'Forty-five seconds.'

It was strange how silent the ship seemed to be, here in the smoke. The sound of the sea overside was much more obvious than out in the sunshine. Within the ship as she pitched over the waves, vibrating gently to the thrust of the propellers, there was a silence in seeming accord with the gloomy darkness that engulfed them. The Captain knew that darkness did not necessitate absence of noise; it was a curious psychic phenomenon this assumption that it was quieter. No, it was not. In the smoke or out of it the wind was still blowing, and the turn which *Artemis* had just made had brought the wind abaft when before it was squarely abeam. That accounted for it; the ship really was quieter.

'One minute,' said the Torpedo Lieutenant.

That was interesting, to discover that it had taken him fifteen seconds to make that deduction about the wind. The opportunity of honestly timing mental processes came quite rarely. And the study of the speed of thought was an important one, with its bearing on the reaction times of officers and men.

'Seventy-five seconds,' said the Torpedo Lieutenant.

He must remember, when he thought about this later, that at the moment he was keyed up and as mentally active as he well could be. Perhaps the brain really did work more quickly in those circumstances, although it was hard to imagine the physiological and anatomical adjustments which such a theory could postulate.

'Ninety seconds,' said the Torpedo Lieutenant.

Presumably the R.A.F. doctors had been on a similar track for years. He must remember at some time or other to find out how much they had discovered; but they would of course be more interested in split seconds than in reactions lasting a quarter of a minute.

'One-o-five seconds,' said the Torpedo Lieutenant.

Not long to go now. But the smoke was just as thick as ever – extremely good. He must remember to put that in his report. The Captain shifted in his position on the stool, poising himself ready for instant action. It seemed to him as if the smoke were thinning. Just possibly the Italians could see by now the shadowy grey form of the *Artemis* emerging.

'Two minutes,' said the Torpedo Lieutenant.

Yes, he could see the Navigating Lieutenant plainly now. There was a second of sunshine, and then darkness again, and then they were out of the smoke, blinded a little by the sun, but not so blind as to be unable to see, full and clear, within six-inch gun range, the massive silhouettes of the Italian battle line almost right ahead of them, every detail plain, the complex gunnery control towers, the tripod masts, the huge guns, the reeking funnels.

'Port fifteen,' said the Captain, and *Artemis*, beautiful in the sunshine, swung round to turn her broadside upon that colossal force, like Ariel coming out to combat a horde of Calibans.

CHAPTER 12

FROM THE CAPTAIN'S REPORT

... fire was opened ...

The Gunnery Lieutenant wore the ribbon of the D.S.C. on the breast of his coat. *Artemis* had won victories before, and, under the Captain, it was to the Gunnery Lieutenant's credit that those victories had been so overwhelming. There was the daylight action against the Italian convoy, when the first broadside which he had fired had struck home upon the wretched Italian destroyer which was trying to lay a smoke-screen, had blown the destroyer into a wreck, and had enormously simplified the problem of the destruction of the convoy. The night action against another convoy had in certain respects been simpler, thanks to the Italians. They had not been so well trained, and because of their long confinement in harbour they had not had nearly as much experience at sea as the British. They had failed to spot *Artemis* in the darkness, and the Captain had been able to circle, to silhouette the Italians against the declining moon, and to creep up to them with guns trained and ready until they were within point-blank range at which no one could have missed. Two broadsides for one destroyer – the sheets of flame which engulfed her must have killed the men running to their guns, for she never fired a shot in return – and then a quick training-round and another broadside into the other destroyer. The latter actually fired in return, but the shells went into the sky; apparently her guns were trained ready for anti-aircraft action and some startled person just fired them off. Then nothing more from that destroyer after the second broadside crashed into her; only the roaring orange flames and the explosion of shells and torpedoes as the fire reached them and her crew roasted.

But at least *Artemis* had hit, with every broadside she had fired, and the loftiest gunnery officer in the British Navy could not have done better than that. It was proof at least that her gunnery was efficient, her gun crews fully trained, her infinite instruments properly adjusted, her gunnery officer steady of nerve and hand. In itself that was in no way enough to merit a decoration – it was no more than was expected of him – but the Admiralty must have decided that there was something more of credit to be given him, so that now he wore that blue-and-white ribbon.

Today the Gunnery Lieutenant's heart was singing. He was big and burly and fair. Perhaps in his veins there coursed some of the blood of a berserker ancestor; always at the prospect of action he felt this elation, this anticipation of pleasure. He felt it, but he was not conscious of it, for he was not given at all to self-analysis and introspection. Perhaps if someone whom he respected called his attention to it he would recognize it, this rapture of the strife, although years of schooling in the concealment of emotion would make the discovery a source of irritation. He was clear-headed and fierce, a dangerous kind of animal, employing his brain only along certain lines of thought. The men who swung the double axes beside Harold at Hastings and the reckless buccaneers who plundered the Spanish Main in defiance of odds must have been of the same type. With a Morgan or a Nelson or a Wellington or a Marlborough to direct their tireless energy and their frantic bravery, there was nothing that could stand against them.

It was tireless energy which had brought the Gunnery Lieutenant his present appointment. Not for him was the profound study of ballistics, or patient research into the nature of the stresses inside a gun; more clerkly brains than his could correlate experimental results and theoretical data; more cunning minds than his could devise fantastically complicated pieces of apparatus to facilitate the employment of the latent energy of high explosive. For the Gunnery Lieutenant it was sufficient that the results and the data had been correlated, that guns had been built to resist the stresses, that the apparatus for directing them had been invented. Dogged hard work – like that of an explorer unrelentingly making his way across a desert – had carried him through the mathematics of his gunnery courses and had given him a thorough grounding in the weapons he was to use. He knew how they worked – let others bother their heads about why they did. He had personality and patience enough to train his men in their use; the fiddling tiny details of maintenance and repair could be entrusted to highly-skilled ratings who knew that their work was to stand the supreme test of action and that in the event of any failure they would have to face the Gunnery Lieutenant's wrath. Endless drills and battle practice had trained both the Gunnery Lieutenant and his men until he and they and the guns worked as a single whole, the berserker now instead of with the double axe was armed with weapons which could strike at twelve miles, could pull down an aeroplane six miles up.

He sat in the Gunnery Control Tower which he had not left since dawn, one knee crossed over the other and his foot swinging impatiently. His big white teeth champed upon the chocolate with which he stuffed his mouth; he was still hungry despite the vast sandwich which the Paymaster Commander had sent up to him, and the soup, and the cocoa. Indeed, it was fortunate that the Canteen Manager had made his way up to him and had sold him that chocolate, for the exertions of the morning had given the Gunnery Lieutenant a keen appetite, partly on account of the irritation he experienced at being on the defensive. Beating off aeroplane attacks, controlling the four-inch A.A. fire, was strictly defensive work and left him irritable – and hungry.

The opening moves of the battle on the surface mollified him to some extent. He admired the neat way in which the Admiral had parried the first feeble thrust of the Italians, and reluctantly he agreed that it was all to the good when the Italian cruiser screen withdrew after having done nothing more than pitch a few salvoes into the sea alongside the British ships. His ancestors had been lured out from the palisade wall at Hastings in a mad charge which had left them exposed to William the Conqueror's mailed horsemen; but the Gunnery Lieutenant, as one of the Captain's heads of department, had been for some time under a sobering influence and had been kept informed as to the possibility of

Italian battleships being out. And he was aware of the importance of the convoy; and he was a veteran of nearly three years of life and death warfare. He had learned to wait cheerfully now, and not to allow inaction or defensive war to chafe him too much. But all the same the laying of the smoke-screen, which (after all those careful conferences) he knew to be the first move in a greater game brought him a great upsurge of spirits. He listened carefully to what the Captain told him on the telephone.

'Aye aye, sir.'

Then *Artemis* leaned over outwards as she turned abruptly and plunged into the smoke-screen.

In the Director Control Tower it remained bright; the smoke found it difficult to penetrate into the steel box, and the electric bulbs were continuously alight. The Gunnery Lieutenant's steel and leather chair was in the centre of the upper tier; on his right sat the spotting officer, young Sub-Lieutenant Raikes, binoculars poised before him, and on his left Petty Officer Saddler to observe the rate of change of range. In front of him sat Chief Petty Officer O'Flaherty, the Irishman from Connaught, at the director, and below him and before him sat a whole group of trained men, the pick of the gunnery ratings – picked by the Gunnery Lieutenant and tried and tested in battle and in practice. One of them was Alfred Lightfoot, his brows against the rubber eyepiece of his rangefinder; in the other corner was John Oldroyd, who had spent his boyhood in a Yorkshire mine and was now a rangetaker as good as Lightfoot. Behind them were the inclinometer operator and the range-to-elevation-and-deflection operator; the latter was a pop-eyed little man with neither chin nor dignity, his appearance oddly at variance with his pompous title, but the Gunnery Lieutenant knew him to be a man who did not allow himself to be flurried by danger or excitement. He was of the prim old-maidish type who could be trusted to keep his complex instrument in operation whatever happened, just as the Gunnery Lieutenant's maiden aunts kept their skirts down come what might. Even the telephone rating, his instrument over his head, had been hand-picked; in the ship's records he was noted as having been a 'domestic servant', and he found his present task of keeping track of telephone calls a little like his pre-war job when as a bachelor's valet he had had to converse over the telephone with creditors and relations and women friends and be polite to all of them. He had acquired then a rather pompous manner which stood him in good stead now in action – he had learned to recall it and employ it at times of greatest stress.

'We shall be opening fire on the enemy,' said the Gunnery Lieutenant into the telephone which connected him with the turrets, 'on a bearing about green eight-five.'

Long ago the Transmitting Station had passed the order 'all guns load', and before that the guns' crew had been in the 'first degree of readiness'. The team in the Director Control Tower, the marines stationed in the Transmitting Station, the men at the guns, were like men down on their marks waiting for the pistol before a sprint race. They would have to be off to a quick start – it would be on the start that everything would depend, because they must hit the enemy and get away again before the enemy could hit them back. Everybody in the ship knew that. Everybody in the ship had contributed something to the effort of making the thing possible, and now it was up to the gunnery men to carry the plan to completion.

Sunshine flicked into the Director Control Tower, flicked off again, and then shone strongly.

'Green five,' said the Spotting Officer as he caught sight of the Italian fleet, but the bearing changed instantly as *Artemis* swung round on a course parallel to the Italians.

'Fire at the leading ship,' said the Gunnery Officer, coldly brave. That was a battleship, least vulnerable of all to *Artemis*'s fire, but she flew the flag of the Italian Admiral. The three rangefinders in the ship were at work on the instant: Lightfoot and Oldroyd and their colleague Maxwell at the after-rangefinder spinning the screws and, as the double image that each saw resolved itself into one, thrusting with their feet at the pedals before them. Down in the Transmitting Station a machine of more than human speed and reliability read off all three recordings and averaged them. Each of the other observers in the Director Control Tower was making his particular estimate and passing it down to the Transmitting Station, and down there, by the aid of these new readings, the calculation having been made of how distant the Italian flagship was at that moment, other machines proceeded to calculate where the Italian flagship would be in fifteen seconds' time. Still other machines had already made other calculations; one of them had been informed of the force and direction of the wind, and would go on making allowance for that, automatically varying itself according to the twists and turns of the ship. Because every gun in the ship had its own little peculiarities, each gun had been given its individual setting to adjust it to its fellows. Variations in temperature would minutely affect the behaviour of the propellant in the guns, which would in turn affect the muzzle velocities of the shells, so that one machine stood by to make the corresponding corrections; and barometric pressure would affect both the propellant and the subsequent flight of the shells – barometric pressure, like temperature, varied from hour to hour and the Transmitting Station had to allow for it. And the ship was rolling in a beam sea – the Transmitting Station dealt with that problem as well.

'Table tuned for deflection, sir,' said the telephone to the Gunnery Lieutenant.

'Broadsides,' said the Gunnery Lieutenant coldly again. That was the way fighting madness affected him, so that he would take the wildest risks with the calmest manner.

All the repeaters before him had stopped moving now, and at this moment the last 'gun ready' lamp came on. There was no need to report to the Captain and ask permission to open fire; that had already been given. In those infinitesimal seconds the observations and calculations had been completed which were necessary to the solution of the problem of how, from a ship moving at thirty-one knots, to throw a quarter of a ton of steel and high explosive at another ship moving at twenty knots nine miles away.

'Shoot!' said the Gunnery Lieutenant loudly and still calmly, and then, as O'Flaherty pressed the trigger, he gave his next order, 'Up ladder, shoot!'

CHAPTER 13

FROM THE CAPTAIN'S REPORT

... and hits were observed ...

Chief Petty Officer Patrick O'Flaherty had been born a subject of the United Kingdom of Great Britain and Ireland, and for a short time he had been a subject of the Irish Free State before he enlisted in the British Navy and took the oath of allegiance to His Majesty the King of Great Britain and Northern Ireland. In the early days a few ill-mannered and stupid individuals among his shipmates had questioned him teasingly or casually as to the reason for his enlistment, but not one of them had asked him twice; even the stupidest could learn the lesson which O'Flaherty dealt out to them.

There had been wild times and black doings in Ireland in those days, and O'Flaherty as a child in his early teens had been through scenes of horror and blood; he may possibly have made enemies at that early age, although it is hard to imagine O'Flaherty even at fifteen being frightened of human enemies. One turn or another of Irish politics and of Irish guerrilla warfare may have resulted in O'Flaherty being deemed a traitor by his friends. In that fashion the boy may have found himself alone; or it may have been mere chance, some coincidence of raid and counter-raid that threw suspicion on him. There may have been no suspicion at all; the blood on O'Flaherty's hands may have called for the vengeance of someone too powerful or too cunning for the boy to oppose.

Perhaps, on the other hand, when peace descended upon Ireland, O'Flaherty may have joined the Navy out of mere desire for adventure, out of mere yearning for the sea that he knew in Clew Bay and Blacksod, possibly with the thought at the back of his mind that if he were ready to desert he would find in the British Navy endless opportunities of making a start in a fresh country without having to pay his fare thither.

But whatever was his motive, the British Navy had absorbed him. Its placid routine and its paternal discipline had been able to take a hold even on the wild Irish boy with the nerves of an unbroken colt. The kindly tolerance of the lower deck, where tolerance is the breath of life because there men have to live elbow to elbow for months together, won him over in the end – it cloyed him at first, sickened him at first, before he grew to understand it, and then to rely upon it. He came to love the breath of the sea, under equatorial stars in the Indian Ocean or freezing spray in the North Atlantic, as he had loved the soft air of Joyce's country. There had been black periods when the exile went through the uncontrollable misery of homesickness, but they had grown rarer with the years, as the boy of fifteen grew into the man of thirty-five, and providence, or good luck – or conceivably good management – had saved him during those times from breaches of discipline serious enough to ruin him.

Twenty years of service is a long time. Once he had been a pink-cheeked boy, in the days when, ragged and hungry, he had been a thirteen-year-old soldier of Ireland, sleeping in the hills, hiding in the bogs, crouching behind a bank with half a dozen of his fellows waiting to pitch a bomb into a lorryload of Black-and-Tans at the point where a bend in the road hid the felled tree. Now his cheeks were blue-black, and he was lantern-jawed; there were a few grey hairs among his wavy black ones, although the blue eyes under the black brows were as bright as ever, and the smile of the soft lips was as winning as ever. All the contradictions of Ireland were embodied in his person as in his career, just as obviously as they had been in the old days when the 'fighting blackguards' of Wellington's Connaught Rangers had stormed the castle of Badajoz in the teeth of the flailing musketry of Napoleon's garrison.

Today Chief Petty Officer O'Flaherty faced odds equally dreadful with his fighting blood as much aflame. His Irish sensitiveness and quickness of thought would not desert him, even when the Irish lust for battle consumed him – so that he reached by a different path the same exalted mental condition as the Gunnery Lieutenant who had entrusted him with his present duty. He kept the director sight upon the Italian flagship, holding it steady while the ship rolled, deeply to starboard, deeply to port, sighting for the base of the foremast and easing the director round millimetre by millimetre as *Artemis* head-reached upon the target ship. And with every microscopic variation of the director sight the six guns moved, too, along with their three turrets, five hundred tons of steel and machinery swaying to each featherweight touch upon the director, as miraculous as any wonder an Irish bard had ever sung about over his harp.

'Shoot!' said the Gunnery Lieutenant, loudly, and O'Flaherty pressed the trigger, completing the circuits in the six guns.

They bellowed aloud with their hideous voices, their deafening outcry tapering abruptly into the harsh murmur of the shells tearing through the air. And the shells were still on their way across the grey sea when the 'gun ready' lamps lit before the Gunnery Lieutenant's eyes.

'Shoot!' said the Gunnery Lieutenant.

O'Flaherty pressed the trigger again; the sights were still aligned upon the base of the Italian flagship's foremast.

'Shoot!' said the Gunnery Lieutenant, and again, 'Shoot!'

Twelve shells were in the air at once while the fountains raised by the six preceding ones still hung poised above the surface. This was the moment when heads must be utterly clear and hands utterly steady. Gunnery Lieutenant and Spotting Officer and Sub-Lieutenant Home forward in 'B' turret were watching those fountains, and pressing on the buttons before them to signal 'short' or 'straddle' or 'over'. Down in the Transmitting Station the signals from the three officers arrived together; if they were in agreement, or, if not, in accordance with the majority, the elevation of the guns was adjusted up or down the scale – the 'ladder' which the Gunnery Lieutenant had ordered – and to every round fired there were also added the innumerable other corrections: with an additional one now, because the guns were heating up. Yet every ten seconds the guns were ready and loaded, and every ten seconds the shells were hurled out of them, and the point where they fell, every ten seconds, had to be carefully noted – any confusion between one broadside and its predecessor or successor would ruin the subsequent shooting. The Gunnery Lieutenant could, when he wanted to, cut out completely the signals of the Spotting Officer and of 'B' turret officer, and rely entirely upon his own observations. But Raikes and Home were old and tried companions in arms. He could trust them – he stole a glance at Raikes' profile, composed and steady, and was confirmed in his decision. The Gunnery Lieutenant looked back quickly at the target. The next broadside raised a single splash this side of the target, and along the grey profile of the battleship a sparkling yellow flash, minute in the sunshine – another hit. Four hits with six broadsides was good shooting. That yellow flash was the consummation of a gunnery officer's career. It was for the sake of that that he endured the toil and drudgery of Whale Island, the endless drills, the constant inspection of apparatus; years of unremitting labour in order at the end of them to glimpse that yellow flash which told that the shells were hitting. The Gunnery Lieutenant stirred uneasily in his seat as within him surged the fighting spirit clamouring to hit and hit and go on hitting.

Now those bright flashes from the Italian flagship's sides were not hits. It was three seconds before the fall of another broadside was due. The Gunnery Lieutenant knew what they were. He spotted the fall of the next broadside and signalled it as 'short', and the fall of the next as 'straddle'. His finger was still on the button as the surface of the sea between him and the target rose in mountains, the incredible masses of water flung up by fifteen-inch shells.

'Shoot!' said the Gunnery Lieutenant.

With the bellow of the broadside sounded another tremendous noise, like that of a tube train hurtling through a tunnel – the sound of big shells passing close overhead. The Italian navy was firing back now. There were bright flashes all down the line; sea and air were flung into convulsions.

'Shoot!' said the Gunnery Lieutenant, and he marked up the next fall of shot.

And O'Flaherty at the director still kept the sights steady on the base of the Italian flagship's foremast, pressing the trigger as he was ordered, while the shells roared over him or burst in front of him and the guns thundered below him. That sensitive mouth of his – there was a girl in Southsea who still dreamed about that mouth occasionally – was smiling.

CHAPTER 14

FROM THE CAPTAIN'S REPORT

... until I turned back again into the smoke-screen ...

On the bridge the sudden crash of the guns made Jerningham jump, the way it always did. He told himself that if he had any means of knowing just when that crash was coming he would not jump, but up here on the bridge there was no warning. He felt the hot blast of the explosion, and looked towards the enemy to see if he could spot the fall of the shot; so the crash of the next broadside caught him off his guard again and made him jump and miss it. He hoped none of the ratings on duty up here had seen him jump – that second time he was sure his feet had left the deck. The third crash came at that moment and he jumped again. The din was appalling, and with every broadside he was shaken by the blast of the guns.

He straightened his cap, which had fallen perilously lopsided: and tried to stiffen himself against the next broadside. It was hard to think in these conditions; those explosions jumbled a man's thoughts like shaking up a jigsaw puzzle. He felt envy, almost hatred, for the Officer of the Watch and the Torpedo Lieutenant and the Navigating Lieutenant standing together like a group of statuary. By the time he pulled himself together half a dozen broadsides had been fired; *Artemis* had been out of the smoke bank a full minute, Jerningham looked again to starboard in time to see the first Italian salvo fling up the sea before his eyes; then he heard another rumble terrifyingly close over his head. He saw the whole Italian line a-sparkle with gunfire. Every one of those ships was firing at him.

He gulped, and then with one last effort regained his self-control, panic fading out miraculously the way neuralgia sometimes did, and he was left savouring, almost doubtingly, his new-won calm, as, when the neuralgia had gone, he savoured doubtingly his freedom from pain. Remembering the notes he had to take regarding the course of the battle he took out pad and pencil again, referring to his wristwatch and making a hasty average of the time which had elapsed since his last entries and now. When he looked up again he saw the sea boiling with shell-splashes. It seemed incredible that *Artemis* could go through such a fire without being hit.

But the Captain was turning and giving an order to the Navigating Lieutenant, and then speaking into the voice-pipe; the din was so terrific that Jerningham at his distance could hear nothing that he said. *Artemis* heeled and turned abruptly away from the enemy, and the gunfire ended with equal abruptness. Only a second or two elapsed before they were back again in the comforting smoke and darkness and silence; the smoke bank took the ship into its protection like a mother enfolding her child.

'God!' said Jerningham aloud, 'we're well out of that.'

He heard, but could not see, another salvo strike the water close alongside; some of the spray which it threw up spattered onto the bridge. He wondered if the Italians were purposefully firing, blind, into the smoke, or if this was a salvo fired off by a shaken and untrained ship unable to check its guns' crews; as it became apparent that this was the only salvo fired it seemed that the second theory was the correct one.

The smoke was beginning to thin.

'Hard-a-starboard!' said the Captain, suddenly and a trifle more loudly than was his wont.

Artemis leaned steeply over, so steeply that the empty ammunition cases went cascading over the decks with a clatter that rang through the ship. The Navigating Lieutenant was saying the name of God as loudly as Jerningham had done, and was grabbing nervously at the compass before him. Jerningham looked forward. Dimly visible on the port bow were the upperworks of a light cruiser, and right ahead was another, old *Hera*, the companion of *Artemis* in so many Mediterranean sallies. The ships were approaching each other at seventy miles an hour.

'Je-sus!' said the Navigating Lieutenant, his face contorted with strain.

Jerningham saw *Hera* swing, felt *Artemis* swing. The two ships flashed past each other on opposite courses not twenty yards apart; Jerningham could see the officers on *Hera*'s bridge staring across at them, and the set faces of the ratings posted at *Hera*'s portside Oerlikon gun.

'Midships,' said the Captain. 'Steady!'

Artemis went back to a level keel, dashing along the windward edge of the smoke bank away from the rest of the squadron. The Navigating Lieutenant put two fingers into his collar and pulled against its constriction.

'That was a near thing, sir,' he said to the Captain; the calmness in his voice was artificial.

'Yes, pretty close,' replied the Captain simply.

It must have been very shortly after *Artemis* had turned into the smoke to attack the enemy that the Admiral had led the rest of the squadron back again on an opposite course, so that *Artemis* turning back through the smoke had only just missed collision with the last two ships in the line. But because of good seamanship and quick thinking no collision had taken place; that was the justification of the risk taken.

The Captain smiled, grimly and secretly, as he reconstructed the encounter in his mind. When ships dash about at thirty knots in a fogbank surprising things are likely to happen. A twenty-yard margin and a combined speed of sixty-two knots meant that he had given the order to starboard the helm with just half a second to spare. As a boy he had been trained, and as a man he had been training himself for twenty years, to make quick decisions in anticipation of moments just like that.

Back in 1918 the Captain had been a midshipman in the Grand Fleet, and he had been sent in his picket-boat with a message to the Fleet Flagship one day when they were lying at Rosyth. He had swung his boat neatly under *Queen Elizabeth*'s stern, turning at full speed, then, going astern with his engines, had come to a perfect stop at the foot of *Queen Elizabeth*'s gangway. He had delivered his message and was about to leave again when a messenger stopped him.

'The Admiral would like to see you on the quarter-deck, sir.'

He went aft to where Acting-Admiral Sir David Beatty, G.C.B., commanding the Grand Fleet, was pacing the deck.

'Are you the wart who brought that picket-boat alongside?'

'Yes, sir.'

'Did you see my notice?'

'No, sir.'

'You've flooded my damned cabin with your damned wash. The first time the scuttles have been open for weeks. I go to the trouble of putting out a notice to say "slow" and the first damned little wart in his damned little picket-boat that comes alongside sends half the damned Firth of Forth over my damned furniture. My compliments to your Lieutenant, and you're to have six of the best. Of the *best*, remember.'

The midshipman displayed quickness of thought and firmness of decision to save himself from the pain and indignity of a beating. He stood his ground stubbornly.

'Well?' snapped the Admiral.

'That notice isn't hung so that anyone can see it coming under the ship's stern, sir. It's quite invisible from there.'

'Are you arguing with *me*?'

'Yes, sir. If the notice had been visible I should have seen it.'

That was a downright statement of fact, addressed boldly by a sixteen-year-old midshipman to the Commander-in-Chief. Beatty looked the boy up and down keenly, realizing that in this particular case a midshipman was sure of what he was saying. If his statement were to be put to the test, it would probably prove to be correct; and to make the test would be a most undignified proceeding for an Admiral.

'Very good, then. I'll cancel my order. Instead you will report to your Lieutenant that you have been arguing with the Commander-in-Chief. I'll leave the verdict to him. Carry on.'

That was Beatty's quickness of decision. He could not be guilty of an act of injustice, but discipline might suffer if some unfledged midshipman would be able to boast of having bested him in an argument. He could rely on the Lieutenant to see to it that discipline did not suffer, to administer a beating for the purpose of making sure that the midshipman did not get too big for his boots. And in the end, the midshipman had escaped the beating by simply disobeying the Admiral's order. He had made no report to the Lieutenant, thereby imperilling his whole professional career and running the risk of dire punishment in addition; a big stake. But the odds were so heavy against the Commander-in-Chief enquiring as to whether a midshipman had made an obviously trivial report to his Lieutenant that it was a safe gamble which had succeeded.

In the mind of a boy of sixteen to argue with an Admiral and to disobey an order was as great a risk as it was for a captain to face the fire of the Italian navy and to charge through a smoke-screen at thirty knots. There was risk in exposing a light cruiser to the fire of battleships. But, carefully calculated, the odds were not so great. *Artemis* emerged from the smoke-screen ready to open fire. The Italians had to see her first, and then train their guns around, ascertain the range, open fire. Their instruments would not be as carefully looked after, nor as skilfully handled. It would take them much longer to get onto the target. And the more ships which fired upon *Artemis* the better; the numerous splashes would only serve to confuse the spotters and gunnery officers – a ship that tried to correct its guns' elevations by observing the fall of another ship's shells was lost indeed. The greatest risk to be run was that of pure chance, of a fluke salvo hitting the target, and against that risk must be balanced the utter necessity of hitting the Italians. The Captain had calculated the odds to a close approximation.

CHAPTER 15

FROM THE CAPTAIN'S REPORT

... I then returned to continue the action ...

'That was a near one,' said Leading-Seaman Harris. He sat in the gunner's seat at the portside pom-pom and swung his legs as *Hera* tore past them. He grinned hugely, for Harris was of the graceless type that refuses to be impressed.

'Wonder 'ow old Corky's feeling,' said Able Seaman Ryder. 'D'you remember old Corky, Nibs? You know, the crusher. I 'eard 'e was in *'Era* now.'

A crusher is a member of the ship's police, and Ryder was a seaman familiar with those officials, like the majority of the pom-pom's crew. The ship's bad characters seemed to have gravitated naturally to the pom-pom. Leading-Seaman Harris had been disrated more than once, and only held his responsible position because of a special endowment by nature, for Harris was a natural marksman with a pom-pom. To handle the gun accurately called for peculiar abilities – one hand controlling elevation and the other hand traversing the gun round, like playing the treble and the bass on a piano. And it had to be done instinctively, for there was no time to think when firing at an aeroplane moving at three hundred miles an hour. The complex four-barrelled gun, a couple of tons of elaborate machinery, had to be swung forward and back, up and down, not to keep on the target but to lead it by fifty yards or more so as to send its two-pound shells to rendezvous with the flying enemy. Even with a gun that fired four shells in a second, each with a muzzle velocity of unimaginable magnitude, and even with the help of tracer shells, it was a difficult task – the gunner had to be a natural shot and at the same time flexible enough of mind to submit to the necessary artificial restrictions of the training gear, lightning quick of hand and eye and mind – with the more vulgar attribute of plain courage so as to face unflurried the appalling attack of the dive bombers.

In *Artemis*, as in every ship, there was courage in plenty, but the ship had been combed unavailingly to find another pom-pom gunner as good as Leading-Seaman Harris. He handled that gun of his as though it were a part of himself, looking along the sights with both eyes open, his unique mind leaping to conclusions where another would calculate. And experience had improved even Harris, because now he could out-think the bomber pilots and anticipate with equal intuition just what manoeuvres they would employ to throw off his aim. He was a virtuoso of the two-pounder pom-pom; this very morning he had increased his score by five – five shattered aeroplanes lay a hundred miles back at the bottom of the Mediterranean torn open by the shells Harris had fired into them.

So his crew were in higher spirits even than usual, like a successful football team after a match – it was a matter of teamwork, for the crew had to work in close co-ordination, supplying ammunition and clearing jams, like the half-backs making the openings for Harris, the gifted centre-forward who shot the goals. Exultation rose high in their breasts, especially as the starboard side pom-pom could only claim one victim, and that doubtful. If the opportunity were to present itself before the exultation had a chance to die down, the success would be celebrated in the way the gang celebrated every success, in indiscipline and lack of respect for superior officers – along with drunkenness and leave-breaking, these offences kept the portside pom-pom crew under punishment with monotonous consistency.

'Convoy's copping it,' remarked Able-Seaman Nye; a sudden burst of gunfire indicated that the convoy and its depleted escort were firing at the aeroplanes which had renewed the attack now that the cruisers' and destroyers' screen was out of the way.

'They won't come to no 'arm,' said Ryder. 'We got the cream of the Eyeties 'smorning.'

'Remember that one wiv the red stripes on 'is wings?' said Nibs. 'You got 'im properly, Leader.'

Harris nodded in happy reminiscence.

'How're you getting on, Curly?' he asked, suddenly.

Able-Seaman Presteign smiled.

'All right,' he said.

Presteign was the right-handed loader of the pom-pom, his duty being to replace regularly the short heavy belts of shells on that side, a job he carried out accurately and unfailingly; that goes without saying, for if he had not he would never have remained entrusted with it, Harris's friendship notwithstanding. It was odd that he and Harris were such devoted friends. It was odd that Presteign was so quick and efficient at his work. For Presteign was a poet.

Not many people knew that. Jerningham did – one evening in the wardroom the Gunnery Lieutenant had tossed over to him one of the letters he was censoring, with a brief introduction.

'Here, Jerningham, you're a literary man. This ought to be in your line.'

Jerningham glanced over the sheet. It was a piece of verse, written in the typical uneducated scrawl of the lower deck, and Jerningham smiled pityingly as he first observed the shortness of the lines which revealed it to be lower-deck poetry. He nearly tossed it back again unread, for it went against the grain a little to laugh at someone's ineffective soul-stirrings. It was a little like laughing at a cripple; there are strange things to be read occasionally in the correspondence of six hundred men. But to oblige the Gunnery Lieutenant, Jerningham looked through the thing, reluctantly – he did not want to have to smile at crude rhymes and weak scansion. The rhymes were correct, he noted with surprise, and something in the sequence of them caught his notice so that he looked again. The verse was a sonnet in the Shakespearian form, perfectly correct, and for the first time he read it through with attention. It was a thing of beauty, of loveliness, exquisitely sweet, with a honeyed rhythm; as he read it the rhymes rang in his mental ear like the chiming of a distant church bell across a beautiful landscape. He looked up at the Gunnery Lieutenant.

'This is all right,' he said, with the misleading understatement of all the wardrooms of the British Navy. 'It's the real thing.'

The Gunnery Lieutenant smiled sceptically.

'Yes it is,' persisted Jerningham. He looked at the signature. 'Who's this A.B. Presteign?'

'Nobody special. Nice-looking kid. Curly, they call him. Came to us from *Excellent*.'

'Hostilities only?'

'No. Joined the Navy as a boy in 1938. Orphanage boy.'

'So that he's twenty now?'

'About that.'

Jerningham looked through the poem again, with the same intense pleasure. There was genius, not talent, here – genius at twenty. Unless – Jerningham went back through his mind in search of any earlier recollection of that sonnet. The man might easily have borrowed another man's work for his own. But Jerningham could not place it; he was sure that if ever it had been published it would be known to him.

'Who's it addressed to?'

'Oh, some girl or other.' The Gunnery Lieutenant picked out the envelope from the letters before him. 'Barmaid, I fancy.'

The envelope was addressed to Miss Jean Wardell, The Somerset Arms, Page Street, Gravesend; most likely a barmaid, as the Gunnery Lieutenant said.

'Well, let's have it back,' said the Gunnery Lieutenant. 'I can't spend all night over these dam' letters.'

There had been three other sonnets after that, each as lovely as the first, and each addressed to the same public house. Jerningham had wondered often about the unknown Keats on board *Artemis* and made a point of identifying him, but it was some time before he encountered him in person; it was not until much later that this happened, when they found themselves together on the pier waiting for the ship's boat with no one else present. Jerningham was a little drunk.

'I've seen some of your poetry, Presteign,' he said, 'it's pretty good.'

Presteign flushed slightly.

'Thank you, sir,' he said.

'What started you writing sonnets?' asked Jerningham.

'Well, sir——'

Presteign talked with a restrained fluency, handicapped by the fact that he was addressing an officer; also it was a subject he had never discussed before with anyone, never with anyone. He had read Shakespeare, borrowing the copy of the complete works from the ship's library; he gave Jerningham the impression of having revelled in Shakespeare during some weeks of debauch, like some other sailor on a drinking bout.

'And at the end of the book, sir——'

'There were the sonnets, of course.'

'Yes, sir. I never read anything like them before. They showed me something new.'

' "Then felt I like some watcher of the skies",' quoted Jerningham, ' "When a new planet swims into his ken".'

'Yes, sir,' said Presteign respectfully, but with no other reaction that Jerningham's sharp glance could observe.

'That's Keats. Do you know Keats?'

'No, sir.'

'Come to my cabin and I'll lend you a copy.'

There was something strangely dramatic about introducing Presteign to Keats. If ever there were two poets with everything in common, it was those two. In one way Jerningham regretted having made the introduction; he would have been interested to discover if Presteign would evolve for himself the classical sonnet form of octet and sextet. Presteign had undoubtedly been moving towards it already. But on the other hand there had been Presteign's enchanted enthusiasm over the 'Odes', his appreciation of the rich colour of 'The Eve of St Agnes'. There was something fantastically odd about the boy's beauty (there was no other word for it) in the strange setting of a sailor's uniform; his enthusiasm brought more colour to his cheeks and far more sparkle to his eyes. From the way his cropped fair hair curled over his head it was obvious how he came by his nickname.

And it was basically odd, too, to be talking about the 'Ode to a Nightingale' to a man whose duty it was to feed shells into a pom-pom, when England was fighting for her life and the world was in flames; and when Jerningham himself was in danger. Yet it was charming to listen to Presteign's intuitive yet subtle criticism of the Spenserian stanza as used by Keats in 'St Agnes'.

It was all intuitive, of course. The boy had never been educated; Jerningham ascertained the bald facts of his life partly from his own lips, partly from the ship's papers. He was a foundling (Jerningham guessed that his name of Presteign was given him after that of the Herefordshire village), a mere orphanage child. Institution life might have killed talent, but it could not kill genius; nothing could do that, not even the bleak routine, the ordered timetable, the wearisome drill, the uninspired food, the colourless life, the drab clothing, the poor teaching, the not-unkind guardianship. Sixteen years in an institution, and then the Navy, and then the war. The boy could not write an 'Ode to a Grecian Urn', he had never read an ode nor seen a Grecian urn. He had never heard a nightingale, and the stained glass in the institution chapel could never have suggested to him nor to Keats the rose-bloom falling on Madeline's hands.

He wrote about the beauties he knew of – the following gull; the blue and silver stern wave which curved so exquisitely above the stern of a fast-moving cruiser, as lovely as any Grecian urn; the ensign whipping stiffly from the staff; and he wrote about them in the vocabularies of the institution and the Navy, gaunt, exact words, transmuted by him into glowing jewels. Keats would have done the same, thought Jerningham, save that Milton and Byron had given him a freer choice.

And it is humanly possible that Navy discipline – Whale Island discipline – played its part in forming that disciplined poetic style. Jerningham formed the opinion that it had done so. That interested Jerningham enormously. Outwardly Presteign – save from his hand-some face – was as typical a *matelot* as ever Jerningham had seen; if the institution had not taught him how to live in a crowded community the Navy certainly had done so. There was nothing of the rebel against society about Presteign; he had never come into conflict with rules and regulations – he wandered unharmed through them like a sleepwalker through bodily perils, carrying his supreme lyrical gift with him.

Yet in addition Jerningham came to realize that much of Presteign's immunity from trouble was due to his friendship with Harris – a strange friendship between the poet and the hard-headed sailor, but very real and intense for all that. Harris watched over and guarded Presteign like a big brother, and had done so ever since they first came into touch with each other at Whale Island – it was a fortunate chance that had transferred the pair of them simultaneously to *Artemis*. It was Harris who fought the battles for him that Presteign disdained to fight, and Harris who planned the breaches of the regulations that smoothed Presteign's path, and who did the necessary lying to save him from the consequences; Harris saw to it that Presteign's kit was complete and his hammock lashed up and stowed, reminded him of duties for which he had to report, and shielded him from the harsher contacts with his fellow men. Presteign's poetic gifts were something for Harris to wonder at, to admire without understanding; something which played no part in their friendship, something that Harris accepted unquestioning as part of his friend's make-up, on a par with the fact that his hair curled. And it may have been Presteign's exquisite sense of timing and rhythm which made him an efficient loader at the portside pom-pom, and that was the only return Harris wanted.

Up to the present moment Jerningham had only had three interviews with Presteign – not very long in which to gather all these facts about him, especially considering that he had spoilt the last interview rather badly.

'And who is Miss Jean Wardell?' asked Jerningham, as casually as he could – casually, but a sullen frown closed down over Presteign's sunny face when he heard the words.

'A girl I know,' he said, and then, as Jerningham looked further questions, 'a barmaid. In Gravesend.'

That sullenness told Jerningham much of what he wanted to know. He could picture the type, shopworn and a little overblown, uneducated and insensitive. Jerningham could picture the way a girl like that would receive Presteign's poems – the raised eyebrows, the puzzlement, the pretended interest for fear lest she should be suspected of a lack of culture. Now that they came by post they would be laid aside pettishly with no more than a glance – thrown away, probably. And Presteign knew all this about her, as that sullen glance of his disclosed; he was aware of her blowsiness and yet remained in thrall to her, the flesh warring with the spirit. The boy was probably doomed for the rest of his life to hopeless love for women older and more experienced than him – Jerningham saw that with crystal clearness at that very moment, at the same time as he realized that his rash question had, at least temporarily, upset the delicate relationship existing between officer and seaman, poet and patron. He had to postpone indefinitely the request he was going to put forward for a complete collection of Presteign's poetical works; and he had to terminate the interview as speedily as he decently could. After Presteign had left him he told himself again that poetry was something that did not matter, that a torpedo into a German submarine's side was worth more than all the sonnets in the world; and more bitterly he told himself that he would give all Presteign's poetry, written and to come, in exchange for a promise of personal immunity for himself during this war.

'How're you getting on, Curly?' asked Leading-Seaman Harris, swinging his legs in the gunlayer's seat.

'All right,' said Presteign.

Something was forming in his mind; it was like the elaborate gold framework of a carefully designed and beautiful piece of jewellery, before the enamels and the gems are worked into it. It was the formula of a sonnet; the rhymes were grouping themselves together, with an overflow at the fifth line that would carry the sense on more vividly. That falling bomber, with the smoke pouring from it and the pilot dead at the controls, was the inspiration of that sonnet; Presteign could feel the poem forming itself, and knew it to be lovely. And farther back still in his mind there were other frameworks, other settings, constituting themselves, more shadowy as yet, and yet of a promise equally lovely. Presteign knew himself to be on the verge of a great outburst of poetry; a sequence of sonnets; the falling bomber, the Italian navy ranged along the horizon, the Italian destroyer bursting into flames to split the night, the German submarine rising tortured to the surface; these were what he was going to write about. Presteign did not know whether ever before naval warfare had been made the subject of a sonnet-cycle, neither did he care. He was sure of himself with the perfect certainty of the artist as the words aligned themselves in his mind. The happiness of creation was upon him as he stood there beside the pom-pom with the wind flapping his clothes, and the stern wave curling gracefully behind the ship; grey water and white wake and blue sky; and the black smoke-screen behind him. The chatter of his friends was faint in his ears as the first of the sonnet-cycle grew ever more and more definite in his mind.

''Ere we go again,' said Nibs.

Artemis was heeling over on the turn as she plunged back into the smoke-screen to seek out her enemies once more.

CHAPTER 16

FROM THE CAPTAIN'S REPORT

... further hits were observed until ...

The smoke-screen was only a little less dense this time; it was holding together marvellously well as that beautiful wind rolled it down upon the Italian line. The ventilating shafts took hold of the smoke and pumped it down into the interior of the ship, driving it along with the air into every compartment where men breathed. Acrid and oily at the same time, it dimmed the lights and it set men coughing and cursing. In 'B' turret, forward of the bridge and only just lower than it, the guns' crews stood by with the smoke eddying round them; their situation was better than that of most, because the ventilation here was speedier and more effective than in any other enclosed part of the ship. The guns were already loaded and they could feel the turret training round. Every man of the guns' crews had a skilled job to do, at some precise moment of the operation of loading and firing, and to keep a six-inch gun firing every ten seconds meant that each man must so concentrate on doing his work that he had no time to think of anything else; after a few minutes of action they would find it hard to say offhand on which side the turret was trained, and unless the loudspeaker or Sub-Lieutenant Home told them they would know nothing about the damage their shots were doing. Their business was to get the guns loaded every ten seconds; the Transmitting Station would do their calculation for them, the director would point the guns and fire them. But they knew what the return into the smoke-screen implied. It was hardly necessary for Sub-Lieutenant Home to tell them quietly:

'We shall be opening fire again in two minutes' time.'

Most of the men in 'B' turret were at least five years older than Home, and most of them, too, were still devotees of the beard-growing fashion which had swept the Royal Navy during the opening months of the war. There were black beards and fair beards and red beards in 'B' turret; the men could well have passed for a pirate crew instead of seamen of the Royal Navy. Most of them were dressed in soiled and ragged clothes, for, very sensibly, none of them saw any purpose in exposing their smart uniforms to damage in battle, especially as the majority of them spent a proportion of their pay in making their clothes smarter and better fitting than when issued by the Government.

A devotee of discipline of the old school would have been just as shocked to see the easy way in which they attended to their duties; a man did not spring to stiff attention when he had completed the operation for which he was responsible. He took himself out of the way of the others and stood poised to spring forward again. There was no need for the outward show of discipline, of the Prussian Guard type, with these men. They understood their business; they had worked those guns in half a dozen victories; they knew what they were fighting for; they were men of independent habit of thought working together with a common aim. They did not have to be broken into unthinking obedience to ensure that they would do what they were told; thanks to their victories and to the age-long victorious tradition of their service they could be sure that their efforts would be directly aimed towards victory.

It was true as well that every man knew that the better he did his work the better would be his chance of life, that for every Italian he helped to kill in this battle there was one less Italian who might kill him, but that was only a minor, a very minor reason for his doing his best. Love of life did not have nearly as much strength as did the love for the service which actuated these men, the love for the ship, and especially the artistic desire to do perfectly the task before them. They were in that way like the instrumentalists in an orchestra, playing their best and obedient to the conductor not through fear of dismissal but solely to produce a good performance. This state of mind of the men – this discipline and *esprit de corps* in other words, which would excite the hopeless envy of admirals not fortunate enough to command such men – made anything possible in the ship save cowardice and wilful inefficiency. The martyr at the stake refusing to recant to save his life, the artist unthinkingly putting his whole best into his work, were actuated by motives similar to those actuating these gunners – although anyone who rashly told those gunners that they were martyrs or artists would at best be answered only with the tolerance extended by the Navy towards an eccentric. They were masters of their craft, balancing easily on the heaving deck, ready for instant action although relaxed, the jokes which were passing among them having nothing to do with the situation in which they found themselves.

The ship passed out of the smoke-screen; sunlight came in through the slits, and the smoke within began to dissipate under the forced ventilation. The deck under their feet took up a steep slant as *Artemis* turned; the pointer moved on the dial, and the turret rotated its heavy weight smoothly as Gunlayer Wayne kept his pointer following it. As the pointers coincided, with the guns loaded, the circuit was closed which illuminated the 'gun ready' lamp before the eyes of the Gunnery Lieutenant in the Gunnery Control Tower. And when Chief Petty Officer O'Flaherty pressed the trigger of the director, the little 'bridges' in the ignition tubes heated up, the tubes took fire, the detonators at their ends exploded into the cordite charges, the cordite exploded, and the guns went off in a smashing madness of sound, like a clap of thunder confined in a small room. The solid charges of cordite changed themselves into vast masses of heated gas, so much gas that if expanded at that temperature it would form a volume more than equal to that of the five-thousand-ton ship itself, but confined at the moment of firing into a bulk no bigger than a large loaf of bread under a pressure a hundred times as great as the heaviest pressure in any ship's boiler. The pressure thrust itself against the bases of the shells, forcing them up the twenty-five-feet guns, faster and faster and faster. The lands of the rifling took hold of the driving bands of the shells – that rifling was of the finest steel, for the pressure against the sides of the lands, as the shells inertly resisted rotation, was as powerful as that of a hydraulic press. Up the guns went the shells, faster and faster forward, and spinning faster and faster on their axes, until when they reached the muzzles twenty-five feet from the breech, they were rushing through the air at four times the speed of sound, having each acquired during that brief twenty-five feet an energy equal to that of a locomotive engine travelling at thirty miles an hour. And the recoil was exactly of the same amount of energy, as if each turret had been struck simultaneously by two locomotives moving at thirty miles an hour; but these two enormous blows fell merely on the recoiling systems of the guns – those recoiling systems over which so many ingenious brains had laboured, which represented the labour of so many skilled workmen, and which 'B' turret crew had kept in high condition through years of warfare. Unseen and unfelt, the hydraulic tubes of the recoil systems absorbed those two tremendous shocks; all that could be seen of their activity was the guns sliding slowly back and forward again. The two locomotives had been stopped in two seconds, as quietly as a woman might lean back against a cushion.

Number two at the right-hand gun was Leading-Seaman Harley – the bearded seaman with the appearance of a benevolent Old Testament prophet; as the recoil ceased he opened the breech, and by that action sent a huge gust of compressed air tearing up the bore of the gun to sweep away the hot gases and any possible smouldering residue. He flicked out the old firing tube and pushed in a new one, closing the venthole. Numbers four and five were Seamen Cunliffe and Holt; they already had hold of the new shell, taken from the hoist, and they thrust it into the hot chamber of the gun. Cunliffe pushed with the rammer until the shell rested solidly against the rifling.

'Home!' shouted Cunliffe.

Able-Seaman James was ready with the charge, and as Cunliffe withdrew the rammer James slid the charge into the breech and sprang back. Harley swung the breech shut, and the forward swing of the screw plug converted itself into a rotatory motion which interlocked the screw threads on breech and plug. As its motion stopped, Harley flicked over the interceptor which had up to that moment been guarding against accidents.

'Ready!' shouted Harley.

Wayne's pointer was exactly above the director pointer, and Harley had scarcely spoken when the guns crashed out anew, and the shells left the muzzles of the guns exactly ten seconds after their predecessors. Sub-Lieutenant Home looked through the glasses that were trained through the narrow slit under the roof of the turret. His gaze was fixed on the Italian flagship, but he was conscious, in the vague outer field of his vision, in the blue sky above the battleship, of a mysterious black line that rose and fell there, erasing itself at one end at the same time as it prolonged itself at the other. What he could see was the actual track of the shells winging their way through the air at two thousand feet a second; his position directly behind the guns gave him the advantage of following them with his glance as they rose three miles high and then descended again. The guns crashed out again below him, but he did not allow that to distract him, for he was looking for splashes. Just after this new explosion of the guns he saw the tiniest white chalk marks against the blue sky, appearing here and there behind the upperworks of the battleship – hard to tell whether before or behind, but these had no visible roots, he was certain. Home snicked the 'over' button decisively, but this was no time to relax, for the next broadside was already on its way, writing its black line against the sky.

A single splash whose root he could see, white against the dark grey of the battleship; two more tiny white tips beyond, and a reddish-yellow gleam, at the base of the foremost funnel.

'Straddle,' muttered Home, marking it up.

He had to keep his head clear despite the din and the excitement. *Artemis* might have the most perfect instruments, the finest guns, the best ammunition ever made, but they were useless without clear heads and steady hands and keen eyes. It took a keen eye to see an 'over', so that it usually called for a bold decision to mark it up, and the three buttons were temptingly close to each other; a nervous man or a clumsy man or a shaken man could easily signal 'over' when he meant to signal 'short'. Home was only twenty years old; a mature man would smile at the idea of buying a house on Home's recommendation, or investing his money on Home's advice, or even backing a horse that Home might fancy. The women who might meet him in drawing-rooms or at cocktail parties would think of him – if they thought of him at all – as a 'nice boy'; even the girls younger than him would hardly bother their heads about a penniless sub-lieutenant – someone they could dance with, a convenient escort on an otherwise empty evening, perhaps, but not someone to be taken seriously. Moreover, Sub-Lieutenant Home was not a young man with social graces, and he had an inborn tendency to mild stupidity; hostesses found him heavy in the hand.

He was not a man of active and ingenious mind, and people who knew him well would predict for him only the most undistinguished future – retirement from the Navy in twenty years or so with the rank of Lieutenant-Commander, presumably. It might in consequence be considered strange to find him in such a responsible position as captain of 'B' turret, but there was really nothing strange about it. Home was a man with all the dogged courage of the society whence he came. He could be relied upon to die where he stood – where he sat, rather – sooner than desert his post. His quiet unimaginative mind was unmoved by fear or by fear of responsibility; as he pressed those buttons he did not dwell mentally on the consequences of pressing the wrong one – the broadside that might miss, the defeat that might ensue from that, the fall of Malta as a consequence of the defeat, the loss of Egypt as a result of the fall of Malta, the victory of Germany, the enslavement of the world. Home may have been worried a little at the thought of a 'ticking-off' from the Gunnery Lieutenant, but beyond that his imagination did not stray. He merely made sure that he pressed the right button and observed the fall of the successive broadsides in their proper sequence. He would go on doing that until the end of time; and if evil fortune should wipe out the Gunnery Control Tower and the Gunnery Lieutenant he was perfectly prepared to take over the direction of the three turrets from where he sat and carry the responsibility of the whole ship's armament.

The bearded ruffians who manned 'B' turret accorded him the respect due to his rank and the devotion they were ready to give anyone who could be relied upon come what might to direct their endeavours to destroy the Eyeties. They knew him well after all these months of service, could predict with complete certainty what would be his attitude towards any of the usual crimes or requests. Even though he still only had to shave alternate days while their beards had grey hairs in them, he wore a gold stripe on his sleeve and he could (with discreet aid from tables) work out problems in ballistics or navigation which they never had any hope of solving – the two attributes were very much on a par with each other in their estimation; in other words they knew him to be a major cog in the complex machine in which they were minor cogs, but they also knew that the major cog would never break under the strain or jam through some unpredictable flaw.

CHAPTER 17

FROM THE CAPTAIN'S REPORT

... a hit started a small fire ...

Artemis was shooting superbly. The Captain could see that, with his own eyes, as he turned his binoculars upon the Italian flagship. With the shortened range it was possible to see not merely whether the splashes fell this side or the other of the target, but how close they fell, and they were raining so densely round the battleship that there must be many more hits being scored than were revealed by the fleeting gleams of the bursting shells which he could see; others were being obscured by the splashes or were bursting inside plating. It was impossible that they could do any serious damage to the big battleship with her vitals encased in twelve-inch steel, but they must be discommoding, all the same. The Captain experienced a feeling of elation which was extraordinarily pleasant. He was a man who was profoundly interested in the art of living. Rembrandt gave him pleasure, and so did the Fifth Symphony; so did bouillabaisse at Marseilles or southern cooking at New Orleans or a properly served Yorkshire pudding in the north of England; so did a pretty girl or an elegant woman; so did a successful winning hazard from a difficult position at billiards, or a Vienna coup at bridge; and so did success in battle. These were the things that gilded the bitter pill of life which everyone had to swallow. They were as important as life and death; not because they were very important, but because life and death were not very important. So the Captain allowed himself to enjoy both the spectacle of shells raining down upon the Italian flagship, and the knowledge that it was his own achievement that they should rain down like that.

The enemy's salvoes were creeping closer; it was nearly time to retire again. A mile away *Hera* had emerged from the smoke-screen, spitting fire from all her turrets. It seemed for a moment as if she were on fire herself, for during her passage through the smoke-screen she had breathed the smoke in through her ventilators, and now her forced ventilation system was blowing it out again in wreathes that curled round her superstructure so that she looked like a ghost ship. *Artemis* must have presented the same appearance when she came through the screen; the Captain was a little annoyed with himself for not having thought of it and borne it in mind – it would be of some importance in hampering the Italian rangefinders and gunlayers.

But with *Hera* out of the screen, and the other cruisers beginning to show beyond her, it was for *Artemis* to withdraw and leave the Italians to their weary task of getting the range of these new elusive targets. It would be ideal if the English ships were only to show themselves for so long that the Italians had no chance of firing on them at all, but that was a council of perfection, and impractical; what was to be aimed at was to strike an exact balance between rashness and timidity, to stay out as long as possible so as to do the most damage and yet not to run undue risks from the enemy's fire.

'Port ten,' said the Captain, waiting until a broadside did not drown his voice, and *Artemis* plunged back into the protecting smoke.

'Gawd!' said Leading-Seaman Harris down at the portside pom-pom, 'back in the smoke again! Slow, I call it.'

Not many of the ship's company of *Artemis* would have called her proceedings slow, but Harris had something of the spoilt prima donna about him. He wanted to be in action with his gun against dive bombers, and he faintly resented the main battery of the ship having a turn at all.

'It's this blasted smoke I can't stand,' grumbled Nibs. 'It makes me feel filthy under my clothes.'

An Italian salvo rumbled overhead and plunged unseen into the sea beyond.

'Wouldn't call it slow meself,' said Ryder.

'Where's Curly?' asked Harris. 'You all right, Curly?'

'Yes,' said Presteign. He was all right. The sonnet on the falling bomber, plummetting in flames into the sea, was nearly fully shaped in his mind, and he knew it to be good. 'I'm all right, Leader.'

Then it happened. No one can explain it. Fifty salvoes had been fired at *Artemis* without scoring a hit, and now, when she was invisible in the fog, a chance shell hit her. It struck full on the portside pom-pom, smashing it into jagged splinters of steel as swift as rifle bullets, plunged on and down, through the deck, and there it burst. On the edge of the huge crater it opened in the deck lay what was left of Presteign and Harris, and their blood mingled in the scuppers, so that in their deaths they were joined together.

Artemis staggered under the blow. In the engine-room, in the turrets, on the bridge, men grabbed for handhold to preserve their footing. That shell had struck *Artemis* with the force of an express train travelling at sixty miles an hour, with nothing to cushion the shock, nothing to resist it save the frail plating. But a trifle had saved her from utter destruction; the fact that in its plunging course the shell had struck the heavy pom-pom, five feet above the deck. The gun had been smashed into unrecognizable fragments by the blow, all its tons of steel torn into splinters, but on the other hand the fuse of the shell had been started into action. The ingenuity of man has progressed so far that as well as being able to throw a shell weighing a ton at a speed of two thousand feet a second, he can divide that second into thousandths, and arrange for the shell to explode either on impact or one two-hundredth of a second later, when it might be expected to be inside any armour plate it might strike. Having struck the pom-pom, the shell burst only just beneath the upper deck; had it not done so, it would have burst below the main deck, and it would have torn *Artemis* in two.

What it did was bad enough. It tore open a huge crater in the deck – a vast hole ringed round with a rough edge – long jagged blades of steel, blown vertical by the explosion. It tore huge holes in the ship's side, and drove red-hot fragments here, there and everywhere, forward through the frail bulkheads, down through the main deck, aft through the plating into the handling-room of 'X' turret. The mere force of its impact, the conversion of its energy of motion into heat, was sufficient to make steel white hot, and within the shell were hundreds of pounds of high explosive which turned the middle of the ship into a raging furnace. Below the upper deck, at the point where the shell burst, was the wardroom, where were the Surgeon Lieutenant Commander and his men, and two casualties hit by bomb splinters earlier in the morning. One moment they were alive, and the next they were dead, one moment they were men, and then the shell burst right in their midst, and they were nothing – nothing.

The heat of the explosion was like the heat of an oxy-acetylene flame, like the heat of an electric furnace. The paint on the bulkheads of the wardroom was only the thinnest possible layer – kept thin with this particular emergency in view – but it burst into raging flames, as if the very plating had caught fire. The scant covering of linoleum on the deck burst into flames. The padding of the chairs caught fire. The bulkhead forward, dividing the wardroom from its stores, had been torn open, and the stores caught fire, all the sparse pitiful little things which brought some amenity into the lives of the officers: tablecloths and table-napkins, newspapers and spirits, the very bread and sugar, all blazed together. On the starboard side of the ship beside the wardroom were the senior officers' cabins. They blazed as well – bedding and desks and clothing, paint and woodwork, and photographs of their wives and children, hockey sticks and tennis rackets. From side to side of the ship, from 'X' turret aft beyond the warrant officers' mess forward, the ship was a raging furnace, with flames and smoke pouring out of her riddled hull. Cascading into the flames fell the ammunition of the shattered pom-pom – deadly little shells, bursting in a devil's tattoo of explosions and feeding the flames which blazed luridly in the gloom of the smoke-screen.

The Commander – Commander James Hipkin Rhodes, D.S.O., D.S.C. – had been squatting on the boat deck aft, complaining bitterly to himself. When he had been a young lieutenant it had appeared such an unattainable apotheosis to become a Commander even when he attained the unattainable and won the vital promotion – the most difficult and most significant in a naval officer's career – from Lieutenant Commander to Commander it had been delightful and gratifying. But to be Commander in a light cruiser in action was to be a fifth wheel to a coach: it meant squatting here on the boat deck doing nothing at all, waiting merely for unpleasantness – waiting in case the Captain should be killed (and the Commander would rather be killed himself, with no sort of pose about that option) and waiting for the ship to be hit (and the Commander loved *Artemis* more dearly than most men love their wives).

On active service it was hard enough to keep the ship at all clean and presentable, the way any self-respecting commander would have his ship appear. He groaned each time *Artemis* dashed into the smoke-screen – he knew too well the effect that oily vapour would have on paint and bedding and clothing. A commander's duty in a big ship is largely one of routine, and after two years of that duty it can be understood that Rhodes had become too deeply involved in it, was liable to think too much about details and not about the broad outline of the fact that England was fighting for her life. As *Artemis* went into action he had been wondering what damage would be done to his precious paint, just as a woman's first reaction when she and her husband receive an invitation to some important function might be to wonder what she should wear. Rhodes, in fact, was in grave danger of becoming an old woman.

The shell burst, and the blast of the explosion flung him from his seat sprawling on the deck. His chin was lacerated, and when he got to his feet blood poured down his chest, but he paid no attention to it. He staggered to the rail, sick and shaken, and gazed down at the ruin six feet below him. The heat of the flames scorched his face. Then he rallied.

'Hoses, there!' he bellowed; the crew of the starboard side pom-pom – those who had not been mown down by the splinters – were picking themselves up out of the fantastic attitudes into which they had been flung, and the light of the flames lit them vaguely in the artificial darkness of the smoke. The voice of an officer pulled them together. Without knowing what they did they got out the hoses, going like automatons through the drill that had been grained into them. *Artemis* came out of the smoke-screen, and the flames paled almost into invisibility against the sunshine, masked by the thick grey smoke pouring up through the deck – foul, stinking smoke, for many things were burning there.

Rhodes half fell, half ran down the ladder to the upper deck, calling together the fire-fighting parties in the waist. The pumps began to sing; the prescience of the Commander (E) had provided ample steam for them. Rhodes plunged down to the mess flat below; it was full of smoke both from the screen and from the fire, and pitchy-black with the failure of the electric circuits – so dark that he could see, as he looked aft, the afterbulkhead glowing lurid red with the heat beyond it.

Rhodes was an old woman no longer. The explosion of a fifteen-inch shell had been sufficient to shake him at least temporarily out of his old womanishness. He organized the fire-fighting arrangements here, and then dashed up again to the boat deck where he could have the clearest view of the damage. There was no way of getting aft from here direct – the ship was ablaze from side to side – and the only way left would be to go down into the boiler-room and aft from there, under the fire. That would take a long time. He caught sight of Richards on the quarter-deck; he was in charge of damage control in the after part of the ship, and as Richards was alive and had a working party with him there was no urgent need for Rhodes' presence. He turned to the telephone.

'Forebridge,' he said, and then when Jerningham answered, 'Commander to Captain.'

The two brief waits, of a second or two each time, gave him time to get his breath and steady himself. For Rhodes there was some advantage about being old-maidish and fussy about detail. Being deeply immersed in his job shut out other considerations from his mind. He had to make a formal report, and it had to be done exactly right.

'Yes, Commander?' said the Captain's voice.

Rhodes reported what he had seen and done.

'Is it a bad fire?' asked the Captain.

The Commander let his eyes roam back aft, to the smoke and flame. From a commander's point of view it was a very bad fire indeed, but Rhodes still had some common sense left to save him from exaggeration. He made himself look at the flames with a dispassionate eye, the eye of a fighting man and not that of the ship's head housemaid.

'No, sir,' he said. 'Not a bad fire. It'll be under control directly.'

He put back the receiver and the instrument squealed at once so that he took it up again. The damage reports were coming in from the different compartments – a small leak here, a shattered bulkhead there. Nothing to call for a serious transference of his damage-control strength. Jerningham showed up beside him, a little white about the gills, but his manner was quite composed. Jerningham and the Commander disliked each other for a variety of reasons, and there was no pretence of cordiality as they spoke to each other. The Commander hastily recapitulated the reports which had come in to him, and Jerningham made notes on his pad, before they turned back to look at the fire.

A score of hoses were pouring water into the flaming crater; one or two pom-pom shells were still exploding down below, each explosion sending up a torrent of sparks like some vast firework. Another hose party came running down the waist on the portside; the man who held the nozzle dragged Presteign's dead body viciously out of the way. The jets would have mastered the fire soon enough, but a more powerful agency came into play. *Artemis* put her helm over, and as she heeled the hole torn in her side was brought below the surface, and the sea rushed in. Even on the upper deck they could hear the crackling as the water quenched the red-hot surfaces, and steam poured in a huge cloud up through the crater, enwreathing the whole stern of the ship. Then she righted herself as she took up her new course, then leaned a little the other way as the rudder steadied her, sending fifty tons of water washing through the compartment into every corner and cranny before it poured down in sooty warm shower-baths through the few holes torn in the main deck by the shell fragments. Only a little steam and smoke came up through the deck now; Richards stood on the jagged edge of the crater and looked down, while a petty officer beside him jumped down into the wrecked wardroom amid the unspeakable mess inside. Richards with his hands to his mouth bellowed the result of his inspection to the Commander – the holes in both sides of the ship above the water-line, the minor holes in the deck.

'I'll get those holes patched in a jiffy,' said the Commander to Jerningham. 'Report that to the Captain.'

'Aye aye, sir,' said Jerningham, remembering the need to salute only in the nick of time as he turned away.

The Commander promptly forgot Jerningham in the happier business of organizing. He was calling up in his mind where he had stored the rubber slabs, the battens and timbers that he would need for patching the holes, the ratings whom he would detail for the work. He had in his mind a clear picture of the things he had to do and the order in which he would do them as he ran down to the upper deck and set about the work, while Jerningham made his way back from the boat deck to the bridge and delivered his message to the Captain.

It had been rank bad luck that *Artemis* had been hit at all, but on the other hand the bad luck was balanced by the good luck that dictated how little damage had been done. A shell in the wardroom, with only the most minor damage below the main deck, would do the ship less harm practically than if it had burst in any other spot. No damage had been done to the ship's main armament, and the casualty list was small. The wardroom flat would flood and flood again as *Artemis* manoeuvred, before the Commander could get his patches into place, but (the Captain worked out the problem roughly in his head) her stability would not be greatly endangered by the weight of that mass of water above the water-line. She had plenty of reserve to deal with that, despite the shifting of weights as a result of firing off thirty tons of shells. A pity about the Surgeon Lieutenant Commander and his men.

'The portside pom-pom's crew's wiped out, you say?' said the Captain.

'Yes, sir.'

'Then Harris has gone.'

'Yes, sir.'

So *Artemis* had lost her phenomenal pom-pom gunner. Probably he was irreplaceable – the ship would never see his like again.

Jerningham thought of Presteign. He knew – he felt in his bones – that the Gravesend barmaid had crumpled up and thrown away each of those sonnets as they had reached her. And he had never got from Presteign that complete copy of his work. Something had been lost to civilization. Jerningham had been shaken by the explosion into a numbed state of mind; that part of him which had been trained into a naval officer was functioning only dully and semi-automatically, and it was strange that the other part of him should have this piercing insight and feel this bitter sense of loss. He would tell the Captain about Presteign some day if they ever came out of this battle alive.

Four destroyers were racing alongside of *Artemis*, overhauling her as they dashed to head off the Italian line. Signal flags went fluttering to the masthead of the leader, and the Chief Yeoman of Signals began to bellow his interpretation of them.

CHAPTER 18

FROM THE CAPTAIN'S REPORT

... without serious damage ...

The ship's company of *Artemis* knew the Torpedo Gunner's Mate to be a misanthrope – they had suffered for long under his misanthropy – and it may have been that which led the lower deck to believe him to be a bigamist. Certainly the most circumstantial stories were told about the Torpedo Gunner's Mate's matrimonial affairs, of the grim wife he had in Pompey, a wife apparently as repellent as himself, and of the charming young girl he was reputed to be bigamously married to in Winchester. Some went as far as to say that this new wife was his first wife's niece, or some blood relation at least, and there was always much speculation about the occult power by which he had contrived to win her affection and induce her to be an accessory in that particular crime of all crimes. He was an old man, too, as sailors count age, called back into service after retiring on pension, and the wags would raise a laugh sometimes by wondering what Nelson had said to the Torpedo Gunner's Mate when they last met.

Whatever might be the Torpedo Gunner's Mate's matrimonial vagaries on shore, at sea he was a single-minded man, a man with only one interest, which probably accounted for the ship's company's jests – a single-minded man is a natural butt. He was engrossed, to the exclusion of all other interests, in the ship's electricity supply and distribution. All his waking thoughts and most of his dreams dealt with electricity, as a miser can only think of his hoard. According to the Torpedo Gunner's Mate, no one else in the ship knew anything worth knowing about electricity; the Torpedo Lieutenant might be able to work out the textbook problems about inductance and hysteresis, but that sort of theoretical nonsense was of no use to a man confronted with the necessity of supplying electricity to every nook and cranny of a ship in every condition. The Torpedo Lieutenant certainly could not shut his eyes and count slowly along the main portside distributing main, ticking off one by one every branch, every fuse-box, and every switch, but the Torpedo Gunner's Mate could do that, and he could do the same for the accessory portside distributing main, and then pass over to the starboard side and do it all over again.

The Torpedo Gunner's Mate had the loftiest contempt for anyone who could not do that, which meant that he had the loftiest contempt for everyone in the ship. And because nothing in the ship could operate properly without electricity everybody on board, the Captain, the Commander, whose word was law, the Commander (E), the Torpedo Lieutenant, the Gunnery Lieutenant whose guns' crews considered themselves the most important people in the ship, every man Jack of them, in the Torpedo Gunner's Mate's mind, was a mere puppet dependent upon him for everything beyond the mere breath of life – and, considering the number of electrically-operated fans, they were dependent on him for that as well. He knew, even although no one else knew it, that he was lord and master of H.M.S. *Artemis*; that by opening or closing a few switches he could cut the thread of her life just as the Greek Fates cut the thread of the lives of mankind. He hugged that knowledge to himself secretly, as passionately as he hugged to his bosom the fair-haired charmer of Winchester. It was a constant source of secret gratification to him, not realizing in his blindness that at the same time the power was quite useless to him in consequence of his fixed determination to keep the electricity supply of *Artemis* functioning perfectly – he could no more have flouted that determination than he could have cut off his own nose.

The Torpedo Gunner's Mate's action station was beside the great switchboard, deep down in the bowels of the ship, and that was the place where he would rather be than anywhere else in the world – with the occasional exception of Winchester. He could feast his eyes on the dials and the indicator lights, run them once more over the huge wiring diagram, enjoying every moment of it – like a miser with his hoard again, fingering the coins and adding up the totals for the thousandth time with as much pleasure as the first. He took a glance at the specific gravity of the acid in the storage batteries; there was enough electricity there to fill the demands of the whole ship for three hours if necessary should the generators be damaged, and in three hours either the poor fools could get the generators working again or the damage must be such that the ship was lost. He was checking over the switchboard again when the shell struck and burst, and the deck beneath his feet heaved and flung him crashing down. He was on his feet again directly, disentangling himself from the rating who was stationed there with him to take his place if he became a casualty – as if the miserable ignoramus could possibly take his place! – and turned his eyes at once to the switchboard, to the dials and the indicator lamps. His assistant got to his feet beside him, but the Torpedo Gunner's Mate jealously elbowed him back; no man while he was on duty would touch that switchboard except himself.

Some of the lamps were out; some of the needles on the dials were back to zero. The Torpedo Gunner's Mate ran his hands over the switches like a pianist trying out a piano. He played a scale on them, switched over to the alternative main, and played the scale again, never having to take his eyes from the indicators as he did so – he could lay his hands blindfolded on any switch he chose. The lighting circuit to the after-mess flat was broken, and the Torpedo Gunner's Mate restored it; he did the same for other parts of the ship, for all except the wardroom flat. The indicator here remained obstinate. Nothing he could do could restore the flow of electricity in the wardroom flat. As far as the Torpedo Gunner's Mate was concerned, the wardroom flat had ceased to exist. He grunted as he reached this conclusion; not even his assistant, who was looking now at him instead of at the board, and who had borne with his moods for two and a half years, could tell what that grunt meant, or could interpret the stony expression in his face.

The Torpedo Gunner's Mate grunted again, and let his hand fall from the switchboard. He walked forward, rolling a trifle stiffly with the motion of the ship – he was a little troubled with rheumatism in the knees – and passed through the door into the telephone exchange. Here he surveyed the scene with a jealous eye, for only very partially was the telephone exchange under his charge. He supplied it with electricity, but Seamen Howlett and Grant who manned the telephone switchboard were not under the orders of his department, and the Torpedo Gunner's Mate strongly believed that they would be more efficient if they were. He did not like the fact that men who dispensed electricity – even in the minute quantities necessary to actuate a telephone receiver –

should not be under his supervision, and the work they were doing now, of testing the circuits and ascertaining which ones were still functioning, was so like the duty he had just completed as to rouse his jealousy still further.

He watched their deft motions for a brief space – he knew as much about their duty as they did themselves – and ran his eye over the telephone switchboard to check what they were doing. Here and there the board was spanned criss-cross by wires plugged in for the duration of the action, completing circuits which enabled the Gunnery Lieutenant to speak at will with his turrets and magazines, the boiler-room with the engine-room, and so on. The Torpedo Gunner's Mate was a little disappointed to see that the permanent circuits were correct; he could tell by the set of their shoulders that Howlett and Grant, despite the earphones on their ears and their preoccupation with their duty, were aware of his entrance and of the fact that he was brooding over them.

A light glowed on the switchboard and Howlett plugged in.

'Exchange,' he said.

The Torpedo Gunner's Mate could not hear the murmur in Howlett's earphone, but he saw where he plugged in the connection. Forebridge wanted to speak with sick bay – nothing very remarkable about that.

'One of you lads get me the Damage Control Officer,' said the Torpedo Gunner's Mate, picking up the telephone receiver beside him. 'This is a priority call.'

That was a gratifying thing to be able to say; during his brief watch over the switchboard he had been able to see how much in demand was the Damage Control Officer's telephone, and the fact that he could claim priority and insist on his own call being put through next, was a most satisfactory tribute to the importance of electricity. He heard the Commander's voice, and proceeded to report the result of his tests at the main switchboard.

'Very good,' said the Commander. 'Yes. Yes, the wardroom flat's been burnt out.'

The Torpedo Gunner's Mate put back the receiver and eyed again for a moment the unresponsive backs of Howlett and Grant. He was jealous of these two. They could listen to the telephone conversations, and even if they were too busy to do that they could still guess, from the origins and destinations of the calls coming through, what was going on in the ship. They shared his knowledge about the wardroom flat, and it was not fair – it was actually indecent – that it should be so. What he knew and ought to know by virtue of his position as dispenser of electricity they knew because they could take advantage of the duty to which they happened to be assigned. It was not consistent with the dignity of the Torpedo Gunner's Mate, in charge of the main switchboard – no, much more than that, it was not consistent with the dignity of electricity itself –

that he should not be solitary on a pinnacle of exclusive knowledge. He saw Howlett dart a glance at Grant, and he read amusement in it, something almost approaching insolence; what mollified the Torpedo Gunner's Mate and distracted him from taking instant action in defence of his dignity was the sight of the left side of Grant's face – so far he had seen only the back of Grant's head. Grant's left eye was blackened and puffy, the lid swollen and gorged. There was a contusion on his cheekbone which would probably turn black as well, and the cheek itself showed a faint bruise which reappeared lower down over the jawbone in more marked fashion.

'That's a rare shiner you've got there, Grant,' said the Torpedo Gunner's Mate.

'It is an' all,' said Grant, who despite his name, was born and bred in Manchester. Another light glowed on the switchboard, and Grant plugged in. 'Exchange.'

The explosion of the shell must have lifted Grant up from his chair and dashed him, face foremost, against the switchboard.

'Exchange,' said Grant and Howlett simultaneously, plugging in.

It was a trifle of a pill for the Torpedo Gunner's Mate to swallow for him to acknowledge to himself that the telephone switchboard was being properly looked after without his supervision, that these children of twenty or so would do their duty whether he kept his eye on them or not. The Torpedo Gunner's Mate had little faith in the young. He sighed and turned away, walking out of the telephone room back to his own treasured switchboard; his rheumatism gave him an old man's gait. He ran his eye over the dials and indicator lights; all was still well here; even his fool of an assistant rating had not managed to do anything wrong. The Torpedo Gunner's Mate continued to walk aft, through another door and into the most secret part of the ship.

He closed the door behind him and looked round. This was the Transmitting Station; the Torpedo Gunner's Mate knew that any foreign power, even in time of peace, would pay a King's ransom for the chance of having one of their experts stand for half an hour where he stood now. All about him were the superhuman machines upon which the best brains of the Navy had laboured for years in search of perfection, the machines which solved instantaneously the differential equations which would occupy a skilled mathematician for a couple of days or more, the machines which correlated half a dozen different sets of data at once, the machines which allowed for barometric pressure and for gun temperatures, machines that looked into the future and yet never forgot the past.

It was comforting to the Torpedo Gunner's Mate to know that these superhuman things were dependent on him for the supply of electricity which alone allowed them to function; the only crony he had in the ship,

Chief Electrical Artificer Sands (another man with proper ideas regarding the importance of electricity), spent most of his waking hours adjusting them and tuning them, pandering to their weaknesses and being patient with them when they turned obstinate.

In the centre of the room, ranged round a table large enough for a Lord Mayor's banquet to be served on it, sat the Marine band. In the old days travelling theatrical companies expected their players to do a double job, and take their places nightly in the orchestra preliminary to appearing on the stage; there would be advertisements in the theatrical papers for a 'heavy' who could 'double in brass'. Similarly, in *Artemis*, the musicians had a double duty, and the provision of music was the less important. The time they spent rehearsing 'Colonel Bogey' and 'A Life on the Ocean Wave' was only the time that could be spared from rehearsals of a more exacting piece of teamwork. The machines all round them, the superhuman machines, even when the Torpedo Gunner's Mate had supplied them with electricity and Chief Electrical Artificer Sands had tuned them to perfection, were still dependent upon human agency to interpret and implement their findings. Under the glass top of the table there were needles which moved steadily and needles which moved erratically, needles which crept and needles which jumped, and each needle was watched by a bandsman who had his own individual pointer under his control which had to keep pace with it, creep when it crept, jump when it jumped, utterly unpredictably. At the Transmitting Station table every item the Marine band played was unrehearsed and without score; the instrumentalists could never look ahead and find that some individuals among them had been allotted twenty bars' rest by the composer. There was no looking ahead, and each bandsman was obeying a different baton which might at any moment leap into activity and summon him to action.

At the head of the table, sitting on a higher chair which gave him a view over the whole expanse, sat the Commissioned Gunner, Mr Kaile, his telephone instrument clasped over his head, the other telephones within reach. In one sense, Mr Kaile was conductor of this mad hatter's orchestra. He had no control over what air should be played, nor when it should begin or end. He was rather in the position of a band leader who may find his instrumentalists suddenly striking up together at any moment without agreeing on the tune. He had to see that at least every instrument was in the same key and kept the same time, and, in accordance with the orders that came down from the bridge and from the Gunnery Lieutenant, and guided by the triple reports of the spotting officers, he was also expected – to continue the analogy – to swell or diminish the volume of sound as might be considered necessary; in other words, to send the range up or down the ladder, deflect to right or to left, as the direct observation of the fall of the shells might dictate.

However perfect the machines, war in the last analysis is fought by men whose nerves must remain steady to direct the machines, whose courage must remain high when they, as well as their machines, are in danger; whose discipline and training must be such that they work together. Every improvement in the machines does not dispose of this problem, but only pushes it one remove farther along. The Palaeolithic man who first thought of setting his flint axe in a haft instead of holding it clumsily in his hand still had to face and fight his enemy. Nelson's gunners had their ammunition brought to them by powder monkeys instead of by an automatic hydraulic hoist like the gunners in *Artemis*, but in either case the gunners had to stand by their guns to achieve anything.

So similarly round the table of the Transmitting Station it was necessary that there should be discipline and courage. Trembling hands could not keep those pointers steady, nor could minds distracted by fear be alert to follow the aimless wanderings of the guiding needles so that the guns above could continue to hurl forth their broadsides every ten seconds. Down here, far below the level of the sea, the men were comparatively protected from shell fire, but not far below their feet was the outer skin of the ship, and around them were the bunkers of oil fuel. Mine or torpedo might strike there, engulfing them in flame or water. Other compartments of the ship might be holed, and the sea pour in as the ship sank slowly; in that case it would be their duty to remain at their posts to keep the guns firing to the last, while above them there were only the difficult iron ladders up which they might eventually climb to precarious life.

The Marine bandsmen were perfectly aware of all this – they were far too intelligent not to be. It was discipline which kept them at the table; it was even discipline which kept their hands steady and their heads clear. Intangible and indefinable, discipline might perhaps be more clearly understood by consideration of one of its opposites. Panic can seize a crowd or an individual, making men run for no known reason in search of no known objective; in panic men shake with fear, act without aim or purpose, hear nothing, see nothing. Disciplined men stay calm and steady, do their duty purposefully, and are attentive to orders and instructions. The one is a state of mind just as is the other, and every state of mind grows out of the past. A myriad factors contribute to discipline – old habit, confidence in one's fellows, belief in the importance of one's duty. Roman discipline came to be based on fear of consequences; it was axiomatic in the Roman army that the soldier should fear his officers more then the enemy, and Frederick the Great used the same method with the Prussian Guard. An enthusiast will charge into danger, but, once stopped, he is likely to run away, and, running away, he is as hard to stop as when he is charging. Fear and enthusiasm are narrow and precarious bases for discipline. Perhaps the principal element in the Marines' discipline was pride – pride in themselves, pride in the duty entrusted them, pride in the cause in which they fought, and pride in the Navy in which they served.

The Torpedo Gunner's Mate indulged in none of these highly theoretical speculations. His glance round the Transmitting Station told him that the men were doing their duty, and gratified his curiosity; and a glance at Mr Kaile told him that all the apparatus was functioning correctly, thanks to the electricity which he was supplying to them. In reply to the Torpedo Gunner's Mate's lifted eyebrows, Mr Kaile gave a nod, and, having no more excuse to linger, the Torpedo Gunner's Mate withdrew to his action-station.

'Nosey old bastard,' said Mr Kaile; he said it half to himself, but the other half into the telephone, and he had to add hastily to the Gunnery Lieutenant who heard it, 'Sorry, sir, I wasn't speaking to you.'

The telephone gurgled back at him with the information that *Artemis* was turning again to the attack.

'Yes, sir,' said Mr Kaile.

Mr Kaile's war experience went back twenty-eight years. At the Battle of the Falkland Islands as a very young Ordinary Seaman he had played an undistinguished part, being merely one of the hands in H.M.S. *Kent* who had been used as living ballast, sent aft with every man who could be spared from his station to stand on the quarter-deck so as to help lift the bows a trifle and add to the speed of the ship in her desperate pursuit of *Nürnberg*. Mr Kaile had stood there patiently while *Kent* plunged through the drizzling rain of that dramatic evening, and he had cheered with the others when *Nürnberg*, shot to pieces, had sunk into the freezing South Atlantic.

He had married a girl when at last *Kent* reached England again, Bessie-Bessie had been no oil-painting even then, as Mr Kaile politely described her looks to himself, but it was largely owing to Bessie that Mr Kaile now held his present exalted rank, with a 'Mr' before his name and a gold stripe on his sleeve. Oil-painting or not, Mr Kaile had loved Bessie from the first, and had never ceased to love her, with her gentleness and sympathy and her unbounded faith in her husband. Nothing was too good for Bessie. On Bessie's account Mr Kaile had become a man of towering ambition, with dreams that he hardly dared admit even to himself; even he had never ventured so far into the realms of the wildly improbable as to imagine his holding commissioned rank, but some of his dreams had been almost equally fantastic – he had dreamed of Bessie living in a house of their own, a house bought and paid for with the money he earned, and filled with furniture, *good* furniture, on which all the instalments were paid. It was too lofty a dream that Bessie should have a maid in the house, wearing cap and apron, but Mr Kaile certainly had aspired in those old days to Bessie's having a charwoman to do the rough work of the dream house – a respectable old body who would call Mrs Kaile 'Mum'. Mr Kaile as a young Leading Seaman had thrilled to the idea of someone doing that, but when he spoke of it to his wife she had only smiled tolerantly and stroked his hair as if he were a child telling about fairies.

And Leading Seaman Kaile had gone back to sea with the ambition rooted more deeply still, to earn his first medal by the way he handled a machine-gun on the deck of the old *Vindictive* when she lay against Zeebrugge Mole with her upperworks being torn to splinters by the German artillery. The ambition had stayed with him when the war ended, and sustained him through the years of the peace, while he slaved to supplement an elementary education and master the complexities (complexities which grew even more complex) of the technical side of gunnery. Mr Kaile was not a brilliant man, but he was a man willing to go to endless effort, and under the stimulus of his ambition his mind grew more and more retentive in its memory for elaborate detail, and more and more orderly in its processes. He fell naturally into the discipline of H.M.S. *Excellent*, and when the textbooks that he read went beyond his comprehension he turned patiently back again to page one and started afresh analysing each sentence until he had cleared up the difficulty. He acquired the most complex assortment of rule of thumb knowledge, from the temperature at which cordite should be stored in a magazine to the breaking strain of chain cable. There was no gun in use in the British Navy which he could not repair or serve. He made orderly thinking an efficient substitute for the higher mathematics which he could never hope to learn, so that he could deal with muzzle velocities and trajectories in a workmanlike fashion. And he had risen from Leading Seaman to Petty Officer, and from Petty Officer to warrant rank, until at last he was what he had never hoped to be, a Commissioned Gunner, Mr Kaile; and Bessie lived in her own house – Mr Kaile deeded it over to her the day he paid the last instalment – full of her own furniture, and two days a week, before the war began in 1939, she had a charwoman in who called her 'Mum' to do the washing and the rough work. Mr Kaile did not know whether after the war there would be any servants again who would wear cap and apron, but so many unbelievable things had happened to him in his career that he had even thought this might be possible some day, and that he might have the last, ultimate pleasure of sitting in Bessie's own sitting-room hearing Bessie give instructions to her own servant.

Even without that prospect, merely to keep Bessie in her own house and surrounded by her own furniture, Mr Kaile would fight every Wop in the Eyetie navy. He had realized so many of his ambitions, with Bessie undisputably leader of society in the circle in which she moved as wife of a Commissioned Gunner she could queen it, if she willed, over the wives of Chief Petty Officers and Sergeants of Marines. In point of fact, Bessie did not queen it very obviously, as Mr Kaile had noticed just as he noticed everything nice about Bessie. The pleasure for Mr Kaile lay in knowing that she could if she wanted to. Mr Kaile's present position, sitting at the head of the table in the Transmitting Station, was closely enough related in Mr Kaile's mind with the continuance of that pleasure.

Mr Kaile was fully aware that the Eyeties had good machinery of their own. He had read with the utmost care the confidential notes which had been circulated to gunnery officers in the Royal Navy regarding the discoveries made in captured Italian ships. Captured submarines had contributed a little – the submersible six-inch gun mounting was a most ingenious adaptation of an idea which the Navy had been (in Mr Kaile's mind) a little premature in discarding – and the destroyer captured in the Red Sea had told much more. Reconstructing in theory the Italian system of gunnery control in big ships from what could be seen in a destroyer was a sort of Sherlock Holmes job, like guessing a man's height from the length of his stride between footprints, and it was just the sort of thing Mr Kaile was good at. In his pocket at that moment there was a nice letter from the Lords Commissioners of the Admiralty thanking Mr Kaile for some suggestions he had made on the subject. One of these days the English would lay their hands on an intact Italian cruiser, or even a battleship – Mr Kaile hoped when that happened he would be there to see. It would be pretty good material, Mr Kaile was sure, but Mr Kaile was not so wrapped up in materials as to be unaware that the best of material is still dependent on men to be handled properly. He looked down the double row of serious faces along the Transmitting Station table and was satisfied. These kids were sometimes inclined to a frivolity which needed restraint. They were well enough behaved; when the big explosion had come, and the ship had jerked as if she had struck a rock, the lights had gone out instantly. But when they had come on again (Mr Kaile gave grudging credit to the Torpedo Gunner's Mate for the promptitude with which the circuits had been restored) they were still all sitting in their places, and each had reported quietly that the pointer each was observing was still functioning. They were quite steady, and Mr Kaile was human enough to realize that they might not be so in that atmosphere, for some freak of the ship's ventilation was dragging into the Transmitting Station a horrible stench – of burning paint, perhaps, but with other elements added; possibly burning meat. Mr Kaile could be single-minded and ignore that stench, and he could control his thoughts so as not to speculate about what might be happening elsewhere in the ship to cause that stench, but he knew that might not be the case with these lads. He was glad to see that it was.

'Enemy in sight. Green four-o,' said the telephones to Mr Kaile.
'All guns load,' said Mr Kaile to the turrets. That was an automatic
reaction. The Transmitting Station was as quiet as a church, save for the
curt sentences passing back and forth. Band Corporal Jones at his
telephone was receiving, and repeating aloud, the enemy's course and
deflection, as the Rate Officer announced it. The marvellous machines
were making their calculations. Mr Kaile swept his eye over the table.
'Table tuned for deflection, sir,' he reported.
'Broadsides,' said the telephone back to him.
'Broadsides,' repeated Mr Kaile to the turrets.
A gong pealed sharply, and then *Artemis* heaved beneath their feet to
her own broadside, and the rigid steel of her structure transported the
din and the shock of the explosion into the Transmitting Station,
astoundingly. And the new data began to pour into the Transmitting
Station, and the pointers moved, tracked steadily by the Marine band,
while every ten seconds came the crash of the broadside, and the stench
from the burning wardroom flat seeped down into the Transmitting
Station, polluting their nostrils.

CHAPTER 19

FROM THE CAPTAIN'S REPORT

. . . so that the ship was ready to attack again . . .

The battle was approaching a climax. The wind had steadily rolled the
smoke-screen down upon the Italian battle line, and the British ships had
advanced with it, nearer and nearer to the Italian ships. The Captain on
the bridge of *Artemis* was considering the possibilities and potentialities
of an attack by the destroyers with torpedoes. A destroyer is even more
fragile than a light cruiser, and her attack must be launched only after
careful preparation of it to be successful. At more than five thousand
yards her torpedoes are running too slowly to have much chance of
hitting a well-handled target, and the longer the range the more difficult
it is to send the torpedo near the target. Fired at a line of ships, a salvo of
torpedoes nominally stands a chance of hitting with one torpedo in
three, because between each pair of ships there is an empty space twice
as long as any ship, but slow torpedoes and alert handling makes this
chance far slighter.
A forty-knot torpedo fired at a range of three miles at a ship advancing
at twenty knots reaches its target in three minutes having only travelled

two miles; but if the ship is retreating instead of advancing the torpedo must run for nine minutes, travelling six miles, before it overtakes its target. So a torpedo attack must always be delivered from ahead of the enemy's line, and it must be pressed home to the farthest limit in the teeth of the enemy's fire. That Italian battle line mounted over a hundred guns, which each fired a shell big enough to cripple a destroyer, over ranges at least three times as long as the maximum efficient torpedo range; if the destroyers were to launch a simple attack they would have a long and perilous gauntlet to run before they could fire their torpedoes with any hope of success. In fact, if even one of the six available destroyers got within torpedo range it would be surprising. And if, more surprisingly, that one destroyer had the opportunity to send off six torpedoes the chances would be against scoring two hits, and even two hits would probably not sink one of those big fellows over there. So the net result would be the loss of six destroyers in exchange for a temporary crippling of one or two major Italian units – a very bad bargain in the beggar-your-neighbour game of war.

The Captain had no need to recapitulate all this in his mind; his reasoning processes started at this point, up to which the facts were as much part of his mental equipment as a musician's knowledge of the number of flats in a scale. For the destroyers to stand any chance of success in the attack which the leader's flag signals were proposing to him the Italians must be distracted, their attention diverted and their aim divided. That meant launching another attack with the cruisers through the smoke-screen so that they could attract the Italian fire to themselves, and then the destroyers could slip round the end of the screen ahead of the Italians and charge in. The Italian reply to this would be to keep their big guns firing at the cruisers and turn their secondary armament against the destroyers; but the Captain doubted whether in the stress of action the Italian fire control would be effective enough to master this added complication. And when the Italians attempted it they would be under the rapid fire of the British cruisers, shaken by hits and blinded by splashes. Some of their secondary armament, behind thin armour, might be put out of action – by some good fortune perhaps even the secondary gunnery control in some of the ships might be knocked out by lucky shells. That would make all the difference in the world. Another attack of the cruisers would increase the stake thrown on the board – exposing them again to the Italian fire at ever-lessening range – but it increased the chances of success to a far greater proportion. It made a good gamble of it.

The Captain pulled himself up sharply; his thoughts were running away with themselves. He was allowing himself to be carried away by his emotions. The realization was thrust upon him by the discovery that he was pleased with the prospect of plunging once more through the smoke-

screen, of being deafened again by the guns of *Artemis*, of seeing the shells
he fired striking the Italian line. There was pleasure in the thought, and
that meant danger. The Captain was a man of violent passions,
although no mere acquaintance would ever have guessed it. People said
that 'Methy' – Captain the Hon Miles Ernest Troughton-Harrington-
Yorke – had ice water in his veins instead of the blue blood one would
expect of the son of the tenth Viscount Severne, but the people who said
so did not know him, however close their acquaintance with him. The
fact that he had a nickname should have warned them of the contrary,
for even when their initials run together so conveniently, nicknames are
not given to men who are as cold and hard and unemotional as they
thought the Captain to be. As a boy and a youth Methy had indulged
and indulged again in the rich dark pleasure of insane evil temper. He
had revelled in the joy of having no bounds to his passion, of every
restraint cast aside – the sort of joy whose intensity not even the
drunkard or the drug-addict can know. One of Methy's brothers carried
to his grave the scar across his scalp which resulted from a blow Methy
dealt him – a blow not dealt to kill, for in his rage Methy never stopped
to think of the possibility of killing, but a blow that might have killed.
Methy's brother carried that scar to his grave, the unmarked grave
amidst the shattered ruins of Boulogne where he fought to the last with
the Guards.

Methy's wife knew about the frightful passions that could shake the
man, for she had seen something of them. She could remember the
young Lieutenant about to sail for the East Indian Station, frantic with
jealousy that duty was taking him to the other side of the world while his
rival stayed in England. He had been brutal, violent, demanding that
she swear to be faithful to him, and she had been cold, aloof – concealing
her fright – reminding him that they were not married or betrothed and
that she had no intention of being either as long as he behaved like a
madman.

That had been a very late manifestation of passion, called forth by his
love for a woman; long before that he had come to realize the insidious
danger of a lack of self-control, and the insidious habit that could be
formed by self-indulgence, more binding even than a drunkard's. He
had mastered his passions, slowly and determinedly. Luckily he had
matured early; luckily the discipline of the life of a naval cadet had been
reinforced by the discipline of the life of a poor man's son – the tenth
Viscount Severne had no money to speak of, and his three elder sons
were in the Army. When Gieves' agent came on board at Gibraltar and
displayed shocked disapproval of jacket or cap, Methy had to smile and
refuse to take the easy step of ordering new ones; when his rivals thought
nothing of dinner at the Savoy or the Berkeley he had to suggest Soho.
And he had come through without becoming either embittered or

inhuman. Only a very few people knew that the Captain, good
humoured, easy going in everything unconnected with the Service,
witty and reliable and even tempered, had been compelled to learn to be
each of these things; and most people who were in that secret thought the
change was absolutely permanent. They looked upon Methy as an
extinct volcano; but he himself knew, only too well, that he was only a
dormant volcano, that mad rage could still master him – like some half-
tamed animal it would still rise against him the moment he took his eye
off it.

So the Captain regarded with suspicion his decision in favour of
attacking the Italians again; warned by the surge of fighting madness in
his brain he waited to cool off before reconsidering. He turned on his
stool and looked about him at the homely and familiar surroundings, at
the Torpedo Lieutenant and the Navigating Lieutenant and at
Jerningham, at the compass and the voice-pipes and the hasty afterthought of the Asdic cabinet. That had been hurriedly knocked together
of three-ply; the Captain clairvoyantly foresaw a day when peace-time
warships would have Asdic cabinets beautifully constructed of teak,
elaborately polished and varnished. Three-ply was good enough for a
light cruiser which might not be afloat by evening.

The fighting madness passed, his emotions under control again, the
Captain reconsidered the idea of covering the destroyers' attack with the
cruiser's fire. It was sound enough; the balance sheet of possible losses
weighed against the chances of possible gains showed a profit. It was
worth doing. Yet before deciding on a plan, it was as well to think about
the enemy's possible plans; the Italians the other side of the smoke-screen
might be making some movement which could entirely nullify the
destroyer attack, and they might also have up their sleeves some
counter-move which could bring disaster on the cruiser squadron. The
Captain thought seriously about it; if the Italian Admiral had any
tactical sense he would have turned towards the smoke-screen so that
when the British ship emerged again they would find him not ten
thousand yards, but only five thousand yards away; at that range the
Italian salvoes could hardly miss. In a five-minute advance the Italians
could reach the smoke-screen, and in another minute they could be
through it, with the convoy in sight and in range of their heavy guns.
There might be a mêlée in the smoke-screen at close quarters, where
chance could play a decisive part, and where a light cruiser would be as
valuable as a battleship. But chance was always inclined to favour the
bigger squadrons and the bigger ships. The Italians could afford to lose
heavily if in exchange they could destroy the British squadron first and
the convoy, inevitably, later. Malta was worth a heavy cruiser or two or
even a battleship. Far more than that; Malta was worth every ship the
Italians had at sea, whether the island fortress were considered as the

bastion of defence of the Eastern Mediterranean – as it was today – or as the advanced work from which an attack could be launched upon Italy – as it would be tomorrow.

It was only logical that the Italians should plunge forward into the attack – even if there were no other motive than the maintenance of the morale and the self-respect of the Italian crews, shaken by Matapan and Taranto and doomed to utter ruin if once more the Italian high command refused action with a greatly inferior force. That was all logical; the Captain reminded himself, smiling bleakly, that in war logic can be refuted by new arguments, and courage and dash on the part of the light cruisers could supply those. Time was passing, and the sun was sinking lower towards the horizon. The Italians had frittered time away. Even if now they made up their minds to attack there was a bare chance that a well-fought rearguard action might save the convoy – the British ships that survived the smoke-screen action might lay another screen, and, when that was pierced, another yet, and so on, until sunset. A bare chance, but it was a chance.

The flagship astern, re-emerging from the smoke-screen, was flashing a searchlight signal to *Artemis*, and the Captain heard the Chief Yeoman read off the letters one by one. By the time the message was one-third completed the Captain could guess what the end of it was going to be. The Admiral had reached the same decision regarding the destroyer attack as had the Captain, and this was the order putting into effect the plans discussed so long ago in contemplation of this very state of affairs.

'Acknowledge,' said the Captain to the Chief Yeoman of Signals, and then, to the Navigating Lieutenant, 'We'll attack again, Pilot. Starboard ten.'

CHAPTER 20

FROM THE CAPTAIN'S REPORT

. . . and the attack was made . . .

'X' turret was not under the command of a commissioned officer. The Gunnery Lieutenant had found a kindred spirit in his chief gunner's mate; Allonby was one of those inspired fighting men – the Gunnery Lieutenant was another good example – that England produces in such numbers. At twenty-four, with his profound gunnery experience and his powers of leadership, Allonby had a career before him. Chief Petty

Officer now, he was obviously destined to be commissioned Sub-Lieutenant shortly and Lieutenant immediately after, as soon as he should fill in the gaps in his technical education. The Captain had his eye on Allonby as a future Admiral. 'Aft through the hawse hole' the expression went, for describing the promotion of a man from the lower deck. Allonby would start with a handicap of six years in age, but prompt promotion would soon remedy that. No one could ever be quite sure how a man would react to promotion and added responsibility; Allonby might be a disappointment, but the Captain did not think it probable. On the contrary, he confidently expected that Allonby would clear all the hurdles before him and that one of these days Rear-Admiral Allonby would hoist his flag in command of a squadron. But that was part of the problematical future. In the pressing, concrete present, Allonby was in command of 'X' turret. He was a hard man and a good-tempered man simultaneously, with no mercy for any lazy or careless individual who came under his orders; a martinet despite his ease of manner and his unconstrained good humour. The energetic men of 'X' turret's crew liked him and admired him; the lazy ones admired him equally and liked him nearly as much despite themselves. It had not been easy for Allonby; the man promoted from the lower deck to a post of great power and responsibility has to face a certain amount of inevitable friction with his subordinates. His good temper was only partly responsible for his success with his men; the most potent factor was his consistency. The man who smarted under Allonby's reprimands or who went under punishment as a result of his charges could see clearly enough that Allonby was not gratifying his own ego, or asserting himself in beggar-on-horseback fashion. There was nothing moody about Allonby. He worked steadily for the efficiency of 'X' turret, and he worked for it in the same way every day. He might rule 'X' turret with a rod of iron, but it was always a rod of iron, not a rod of iron one day and a rod of clay the next.

Even Ordinary Seaman Triggs could appreciate that fact, dimly and without understanding. Triggs was the ship's bad character, careless, lazy, drunken, stupid, dirty – possessed, in other words, of all the qualities likely to get him into trouble. Most likely Triggs was of an intelligence well below standard, having slipped through the Navy's tests by misfortune or oversight. In civil life he would have sunk to the lowest levels of society, or rather have stayed there, among the shiftless drunken dregs which gave him birth. As it was, the Navy could feed him and clothe him, build up his physique and keep him at work which was not too exacting, but even the Navy could not give him the intelligence to profit by all this. His limited brain was almost incapable of grasping an order – the sharpest punishment could not impress upon him the necessity for listening to what he was told to do and then doing it. 'In at one ear and out at the other' as his exasperated shipmates said, and some would add that this was because there was nothing between his ears to act as an impediment. Five minutes after the six-inch guns' crews had been told to fall in for exercise the ship's loudspeaker would always say 'Ordinary Seaman Triggs, close up,' and it might even be two or three times that Ordinary Seaman Triggs was ordered to close up before he came tumbling aft to 'X' turret, his usual inane grin on his face, while Chief Petty Officer Allonby fumed and seethed. Time and place meant nothing to him. As a confirmed leave-breaker he rarely could be trusted ashore; when, after months on board perforce, he had at last purged himself of the sin of leave-breaking and was allowed ashore, it was only to be brought back by the naval police, hideously drunk and long overdue, to begin the weary cycle over again. There was always something of Triggs' in the ship's scranbag – lost property office – it was always Triggs who had to be told to get his hair cut or his nails cleaned. Captain and Commander had learned to sigh when they saw his name among the ship's defaulters and had him brought up before them, the silly smile on his face and his fingers twining aimlessly as he held his cap. The Captain had set in motion the official mechanism which would bring about Triggs' discharge from the Navy as unlikely to become an efficient seaman, but in time of war, with every man needed, and a personnel of a million men to be administered, the mechanism moved slowly, and Triggs was still on board *Artemis* when the battle was fought which decided the fate of the Mediterranean.

Allonby had stationed Triggs down in the magazine of 'X' turret, along with the officers' steward and the other untrained men, where he could do no harm. It was odd to think of Triggs put among tons of high explosive deliberately, but it was perfectly correct that he was harmless there, for cordite is a stubborn material. It will burn readily enough, but nothing save high pressure or another explosive will induce it to explode. As long as there was no chance of their catching fire the big cylinders of high explosive which Triggs handled were as harmless as so many pounds of butter. In the magazine with Triggs was Supply Assistant Burney, with more brains and reliability, and what Triggs and Burney had to do when the guns were in action was to take the tin boxes one by one from the racks in the magazine, extract the cordite charges from the boxes, and pass the charges through the flash-tight shutter in the bulkhead into the handling-room. Every ten seconds the two guns fifty feet above their heads each fired a round; every ten seconds two cordite charges in the magazine had to be stripped of their tin cases and passed through the shutter. That was all that had to be done; possibly in the whole ship when she was in action there was no duty calling for less practice or intelligence. Supply Assistant Burney may have felt himself wasted in the after magazine, but his routine duties in the ship made it hard to train him for a more exacting task, and his friends told him cheerfully that he could devote any attention he had to spare to seeing that Triggs did not strike matches down there. How Burney actually spent his time during the long and dreary waits while the guns were not firing was in squatting on the steel deck, with a couple of tons of high explosive round him and the sea just outside, reading *Economics in Theory and Practice*, for Burney's hobby was economics and he had vague ideas about some sort of career when he should leave the Navy. And Triggs would whistle tunelessly, and fidget about the steel cell that enclosed them, and, possibly, think vaguely whatever thoughts may come by chance into such a mind as Triggs possessed. He would finger the telephone, and peer at the thermometer, and drum with his fingers on the bulkhead. It was always a relief to Burney when the gong jangled and the guns bellowed atrociously overhead and he and Triggs had to resume their task of passing cordite through the shutters.

Down here in the magazine the forced ventilation was always hard at work, for cordite is peculiarly susceptible to changes in temperature, and if the after magazine was ever warmer or colder than the forward magazine the six guns would not shoot identically, the broadsides would 'spread', and all the skill of the spotters, all the uncanny intelligence of the machines, all the training of the guns' crews, would be wasted. So the ventilators hummed their monotonous note as air from the outside was forced down, and with it came the greasy smoke of the smoke-screen, and the sickening stench from the burnt-out wardroom flat. For the fifth time now the oil smoke was being drawn into the magazine, as *Artemis* made her third attack, but Burney and Triggs had not troubled to count, and could not have guessed at the number of times; they were probably vaguer about the course of the battle than anyone else in the ship. Petty Officer Hannay, in the handling-room, had not much chance of telling them, during the brief seconds the flash-tight shutter was open, the news he heard over the loudspeaker. Burney had learned to be fatalistic about his ignorance, and Triggs did not care.

CHAPTER 21

FROM THE CAPTAIN'S REPORT

... in support of the attack made by the destroyers ...

The Captain made himself ready to meet any emergency as *Artemis* shot out of the smoke-screen. Anything might be awaiting him on the other side. He might find himself right under the guns of the Italian battleships and heavy cruisers if they had moved forward to anticipate the attack. The Italian destroyers might be lurking in ambush beyond the smoke-screen, ready to send in a salvo of torpedoes. It was hard to believe that the Italian battle line would remain on the defensive under the repeated goading of these attacks.

The smoke wreaths thinned, the blue sky overhead became visible, and there ahead was the Italian line, nine thousand yards away, still fumbling to find an unopposed path round the smoke-screen that lay between them and their prey. The Captain kept his glasses on them as he gave his orders. It was the same line of battle – the two elephantine battleships in the van, massive and menacing, their silhouetted upper-works showing no sign of damage at that distance, and the heavy cruisers in their wake, smoke coiling greasily from their funnels. The second cruiser in the line had other smoke leaking from her upperworks – clear proof that a shell had got home somewhere in her.

Artemis came round on a parallel course, and her guns crashed out, the hot blast from them eddying over the bridge, the unbelievable noise of them beating against the eardrums of officers and men, and the faint smoke from the muzzles whirling by alongside. Through his glasses the Captain saw the long stout silhouettes of the leading battleship's big guns against the horizon. Slowly they shortened as the turrets trained round. They disappeared behind a screen of splashes as *Artemis*' broadside struck – through the splashes the Captain saw the gleam of a hit – and then when the splashes were gone the guns were still no longer visible, and the Captain knew that they were pointed straight at him. *Artemis* had fired two more broadsides, and at this range the shells reached the target a second before the next was fired. Splashes and flashes, smoke and spray made the battleship's outline uncertain, as the Captain held her in the field of his glasses, countering the roll and vibration of his own ship. But then the Captain saw, through all the vagueness, the sudden intense flames of the battleship's salvo. She had fired, and in that second the Captain was aware of four momentary black dots against the blue above her silhouette, come and gone so quickly that he could hardly be quite sure of what he had seen. It might be a subjective illusion, like the black spots that dance before the eyes in a bilious attack. This was no bilious attack; the Captain knew that what he had seen were the four big shells of the Italian's salvo on their way towards him, travelling faster than the speed of sound and charged with destruction and death. The Captain faced their coming unabashed and impersonal. A hundred yards from *Artemis*' starboard side rose the massive yellow columns of water; surprisingly, one big shell ricocheted from the surface, bouncing up without exploding, turning end-over-end and travelling slowly enough for the eye to follow it as it passed fifty feet above *Artemis*' stern. Everything was happening at once; a broadside from *Artemis* reached its target while the flash of the Italian salvo still lingered on the Captain's retina, and another was fired at the very moment that shell was passing overhead.

'Turn two points to starboard, Pilot,' said the Captain to the Navigating Lieutenant.

In response *Artemis* sheered towards the enemy's line, shortening the range. The Italian salvo had fallen short; they would lengthen the range for the next. The Captain saw the gleam of it, saw the black spots dance again before his eyes, and then he heard the rumble of the shells overhead, high-pitched for a moment and then dropping two tones in the musical scale as they passed to fling up their vast fountains a hundred and fifty yards to port; *Artemis* had ducked under the arc of their trajectory like a boxer under a punch.

'Four points to port, Pilot,' said the Captain.

The Italians would shorten their range this time, and *Artemis* must withdraw from the blow like a boxer stepping back. All this time her guns were bellowing in reply; the erratic course she was steering would make the Gunnery Lieutenant's task harder, because the range would be opening and closing for her just as much as for the Italians; but the Gunnery Lieutenant, and the machines in the Transmitting Station would be kept informed of the alterations of course, and would not have to guess at them – over in the Italian ships the Captain could imagine the inclinometer operators at work, peering at their smoke-wreathed, splash-surrounded target and trying to guess whether the vague image they saw was growing fatter or thinner. If *Artemis* zigzagged while the Italians maintained a steady course it would be to *Artemis*' advantage, therefore, and she would have more chance of hitting than the Italians had; while if the Italians should decide to zigzag, too, it would merely make it harder for everyone so as to give the British superiority in training and discipline more opportunity still.

The Captain was handling his ship, watching the Italian gunnery and observing the effect of his own. He turned and looked aft; the other cruisers had broken through the smoke-screen and were blazing away at the Italian line, a chain of Davids attacking Goliaths. He turned his attention forward again; that was where the destroyers would launch their attack as soon as the Italians were fully distracted by the light cruisers. It was a matter for the nicest judgement on the part of the destroyer leader, for the cruisers could not be subjected for too long to the fire of the Italian battle line. In the very nature of things, by pure laws of chance, one or other of those innumerable salvoes must strike home at last; he ordered a new change of course, and a sudden flash of thought set him smiling grimly again as it crossed his mind momentarily that perhaps, if the Italian spotters were rattled and the Italian gunnery officers unskilful, the 'short' might be corrected as if it were an 'over' and he might be steering right into the salvo instead of away from it. There was no predicting what unnerved men might do. But still it certainly could not be worse than pure chance, and the sea was wide and the spread even of an Italian salvo was small; the Captain's sane and sanguine temperament reasserted itself. Despite that tremendous din, with *Artemis* rolling in a beam sea, and with a dozen factors demanding his attention and his calculation, and in face of appalling odds it was necessary that he should remain both clear-headed and cheerful.

Jerningham behind the Captain felt physically exhausted. The noise and the nervous strain were wearing him down. This was the third time *Artemis* had emerged from the shelter of the smoke-screen to run the gauntlet of the Italian salvoes. How many more times would they have to do this – how many more times would they be able to? He was tired, for many emotions had shaken him that day, from terror under the morning's bombing attack to exasperation at reading Dora Darby's letter, and thence to exultation after the first successful attack. Exultation was gone now, and he only knew lassitude and weariness. He felt he would give anything in the world if only this frightful din would stop and the terrible danger would cease. The hand which held the rail beside him was cramped with gripping tight, and his throat was so dry that although he tried to swallow he could not do so. His eyes were dry too, or so they felt – his lids wanted to droop down over them and seemed to be unable to do so because of the friction with the dry surface. He was caught between the upper millstone of the Captain's inflexible will and the nether millstone of the Italian invulnerability.

It was a six-inch shell that hit the cruiser eventually, fired perhaps from the Italian flagship's secondary armament, or maybe a chance shot from one of the cruisers. The chances of dynamics dictated that it did not deal the *Artemis* nearly as severe a shock as the previous hit had done, although it caused far more damage. It struck the ship's side a yard above the water-line abreast of 'X' turret, and it penetrated the main deck as it burst, flinging red-hot fragments of steel all round it. Beneath the main deck there was No. 7 fuel tank containing fifty tons of oil fuel, and the shell ripped it open as it set everything ablaze. Oil welled up into the blaze and blazed itself, and the heat generated by the fire set more and more of the expanding oil welling up to feed the fire. The roll of the ship sent the burning oil running over the decks, turning the afterpart of the ship into one mass of flames.

It was not merely the oil which burnt; it was not merely No. 7 fuel tank which was ripped open by the flying red-hot steel. Inboard of where the shell struck was 'X' turret, and from 'X' turret downwards to the bottom of the ship extended the ammunition supply arrangements for the turret – the lobby below the gunhouse and the magazine below the lobby. Fragments of the shell came flying through that thin steel of the bulkhead of 'X' turret lobby, and with the fragments came the flame of the explosion. The rating at the shell ring, the rating at the ammunition hoist, fell dead at their posts, killed by the jagged steel, and the petty officer in charge of the lobby, and the other ratings survived them only by a second. They died by fire, but it was a quick death. One moment they were alive and hard at work; the next, and the cordite charge in the hoist had caught alight and was spouting flames which filled full the whole interior of the lobby. One quick breath, and the men who took that breath fell dead. It was their dead bodies upon which the flame then played, so hot that the bodies were burned away in smoke and gas during the few seconds that the ammunition blaze lasted. Lobby and crew were wiped out; of the crew nothing remained – nothing – and of the lobby only the red-hot steel box, its sides warped and buckled with the heat.

On the bridge the shock of the blow passed nearly unfelt; the crash of the explosion nearly unheard. Jerningham saw the Chief Yeoman of Signals, on the wing of the bridge, looking anxiously aft. Where Jerningham stood the funnels and super-structure blocked the view astern, and he walked to the side and leaned over, craning his neck to look aft. Dense black smoke was pouring out of the side of the ship and was being rolled by the wind towards the enemy, and as Jerningham looked he saw massive flames sprouting at the root of the smoke, paling as a trick of the wind blew the smoke away, reddening as the smoke screened the sunshine from them. It was a frightening sight.

'Turn two points to starboard, Pilot,' said the Captain to the Navigating Lieutenant; he was still handling his ship to avoid the shells raining round her, unconscious of what had happened. Jerningham saluted to catch his attention, and the Captain turned to him.

'Ship's on fire aft, sir,' said Jerningham. His voice quavered, and was drowned as he spoke by the roar of the guns. He repeated himself, more loudly this time, and the need to speak more loudly kept his voice steady. It was two full seconds before the Captain spoke, and then it was only one word, which meant nothing.

'Yes?' said the Captain.

'Pretty badly, apparently, sir,' said Jerningham. Exasperation at the Captain's dullness put an edge to his voice.

'Very good, Jerningham, thank you,' said the Captain.

The guns bellowed again, their hot blast whirling round the bridge.

'The reports will come in soon,' said the Captain. 'Pilot, turn four points to port.'

On the instant he was immersed again in the business of handling the ship. The destroyers were at this very moment dashing out of their ambush round the end of the smoke-screen, and this was the time for them to be given all possible support. As long as the guns would fire, as long as the ship would answer her helm, she must be kept in the fighting line – for that matter she must be kept in the fighting line anyway, if for no other reason than to attract to herself as much of the Italian fire as possible. The fact that she was a mass of flames aft did not affect the argument. Whether she was doomed to blow up, or whether eventually she was going to sink, had no bearing on the present. She would or she would not. Meanwhile, there went the destroyers.

The Captain fixed his glasses on them. The attack had been well judged, and the destroyers were racing down to meet the Italians on a course converging at an acute angle. They were going at their highest speed – even at this distance the Captain could see their huge bow-waves, brilliant white against the grey; and their sterns had settled down so deep in the troughs they ploughed in the surface as to be almost concealed. The White Ensigns streamed behind them, and the thin smoke from their funnels lay above the surface of the sea in rigid parallel bars.

The Captain swung his glasses back to the Italian fleet, and from there to the other cruisers streaming briskly along with their guns blazing; for the first time he saw the dense smoke which was pouring out of *Artemis'* quarter. He saw it, but his mind did not register the sight – the decision to take no action about the ship being on fire had already been made. He changed the ship's course again to dodge the salvoes and looked once more at the destroyers. His glasses had hardly begun to bear on them when he saw the sea all about them leap up into fountains – the Italians had at last opened fire on them. For a full minute of the necessary five that they must survive they had been unopposed. The destroyers began to zigzag; the Captain could see their profiles foreshortening first in one sense and then in the other as they turned from side to side like snipe under gunfire. Evasive action of that sort was a stern test of the gunners firing on them. Not merely was the range decreasing but the bearing was constantly altering – traversing a big gun back and forth to keep the sights on a little ship as handy as a destroyer, zigzagging under the unpredictable whim of her captain, was a chancy business at best.

It was important to note whether the Italian fire was accurate or not. The whole surface of the sea between the destroyers and the Italians was pockmarked with splashes, and far beyond the destroyers too. There were wild shots which threw up the sea hardly a mile from the Italians' bows, and there were wild shots falling three miles astern of the destroyers; over the whole of that length and making a zone a mile and a half wide, a hundred guns were scattering five hundred shells every minute, but the splashes were clustered more thickly about the destroyers than anywhere else – that much at least could be said for the Italian gunnery.

There were flashes darting from the destroyers, too. They were banging away with their 4.7-inch popguns – peashooters would not be much less effective against the massive steel sides of the Italian battleships, but there was always the chance of a lucky hit. The leading destroyer vanished utterly in a huge pyramid of splashes, and the Captain gulped, but two seconds later she emerged unharmed, her guns still firing, jinking from side to side so sharply that her freeboard disappeared as she lay over.

Jerningham was at the Captain's side again, with a report received by telephone.

' "X" turret reports they have flooded the magazine, sir,' said Jerningham to the Captain's profile.

'Thank you,' said the Captain without looking round.

If the after magazine was flooded, it would mean that the two guns in 'X' turret would be silent, that was all. There were still the four guns of 'A' and 'B' turrets in action, and four guns fired a large enough salvo for efficiency. *Artemis* would not blow up yet awhile, either; but as the Captain would not have varied his course of action even if he had been utterly certain that she was going to blow up in the next minute that did not matter.

The leading destroyer disappeared again in the splashes, and reappeared again miraculously unhurt. The second destroyer in the line swung round suddenly at right angles, her bows pointed almost straight for *Artemis*. A cloud of white steam enveloped her, and then a moment or two later her black bows crept out of it and she began to crawl slowly away, steam and smoke still pouring from her as she headed for the shelter of the smoke-screen. It was the first casualty; some shell had hit her in the boiler-room presumably. The other five were still tearing towards their objective; the Captain swung his glasses back at the Italian line in time to see a bright flash on the side of the Italian flagship – indisputably a hit and not gunfire, for it was a single flash – but he did not know enough about the broadsides *Artemis* had been firing to be able to credit it either to his own ship or to the destroyers. 'A' and 'B' turrets were still firing away, but, amazingly, the ears were so wearied by the tremendous sound that they took no special note of it unless attention was specially directed upon the guns.

By now the destroyers must be nearly close enough to discharge their torpedoes. The Captain tried to estimate the distance between them and their objective. Six thousand yards, maybe. Five thousand, perhaps – it was difficult to tell at that angle. The officers in command had displayed all the necessary courage and devotion. And the Italian destroyers were creeping out ahead of the Italian battle line to meet them now – they had been left behind when the Italian fleet turned about to try and work round the smoke-screen, and had been compelled to sheer away widely to get on the disengaged side, and had then had to waste all those precious minutes working their way up to the head of the line where they should have been stationed all along. At the first hint of a British destroyer attack they should have been ready to move forward to fend it off, engaging with their own class beyond torpedo range of the battle line. The Captain fancied that there was a bad quarter-hour awaiting the senior Italian destroyer officer if ever he made port; he would probably be unjustly treated, but a naval officer who expected justice was expecting too much.

The leading British destroyer was wheeling round now, and the others were following her example, turning like swallows. Presumably at that moment the torpedoes were being launched, hurled from the triple tubes at the Italian line. Thirty torpedoes, the Captain hoped, were now dashing through the water, twenty feet below the surface against the Italians – sixty thousand pounds' worth of machinery thrown into the sea on the chance that five pounds' worth of T.N.T. might strike home; that was as typical of war as anything he knew; the dive bombers he had beaten off that morning were a hundred times more expensive still.

He kept his glasses on the Italian line so as to make sure of the effect of the torpedo attack, even while, in the midst of the deafening din, he continued to handle his ship so as to evade the enemy's salvoes. He was wet through from the splash of a shell close overside, and his skin kept reporting to his inattentive mind the fact that it was clammy and cold, just as in the same way he had been listening to reports on the progress of the struggle to extinguish the fire aft. This was the crisis of the battle, the moment which would decide the fate of Malta and of the world. Whatever happened to that fire aft, he must keep his ship in action a little longer, keep his four remaining six-inch guns in action, not merely to cover the retirement of the destroyers but to out-face and out-brave that line of Italian capital ships.

CHAPTER 22

FROM THE CAPTAIN'S REPORT

. . . the ship sustained another hit . . .

When that six-inch shell struck *Artemis'* side they were hardly aware of it forward on the bridge, but aft in 'X' turret there could be no misunderstanding of what had happened – they heard the crash and felt the jar of the explosion, smelt the suffocating stench of high explosive and burning fuel, and saw the red flames that raged round them. Beneath their feet in the gunhouse they felt the whole structure stir uneasily, like the first tremor of an earthquake, but the guns' crews could not allow that to break the smooth rhythm of loading and firing – sliding shells and charges from the hoist to the breeches, inserting the tubes and masking the vents, closing the breeches and then swinging them open again. Yet something else broke that rhythm.

'Hoist's stopped working, Chief,' reported Number Two at the right-hand gun.

'Use the ready-use charges,' said Allonby.

Three rounds for each gun were kept in 'X' turret in contemplation of such an emergency – enough for half a minute's firing. There is no point in keeping ammunition below the surface of the sea in the magazine and yet maintaining large quantities of high explosive above decks behind a trivial inch of steel. And when dealing with high explosive – with cylinders of cordite that can spout flame a hundred feet long a second after ignition – thirty seconds is a long time.

Allonby bent to the steel voice-pipe beside him which led down to the lobby beneath his feet. A blast of hot air greeted him, and he hastily re-stoppered the pipe, for actual flame might come through there. The turret walls were hot to the touch – almost too hot to touch; the gunhouse must be seated at that moment in a sea of flame. It was just as well they were firing off those ready-use rounds and getting rid of them the best possible way. The turret was filling with smoke so that they could hardly see or breathe. They could be suffocated or baked alive in this steel box; the party in the lobby below must have been killed instantly. The instinct of self-preservation would have driven Allonby and the guns' crews out of 'X' turret the moment those red flames showed through the slits. It would be hard to believe that flight was actually the last thought that occurred to them, except that our minds are dulled by tales of heroism and discipline. We hear so many stories of men doing their duty that our minds are biased in that direction. The miracle of men staying in the face of the most frightful death imaginable ceases to be a miracle unless attention is directly called to it. Undisciplined men, untrained men, would have seen those flames and felt that heat; they might have halted for one paralysed second, but the moment realization broke in upon them they would have fled in the wildest panic that nothing would have stopped – possibly not even the threat of a worse fate (if one could be imagined) than being baked to death in a steel box. In 'X' turret under Allonby's leadership the thought of flight occurred to no one; they went on loading and reloading. Allonby had to take the decision that would make his turret utterly useless, even if the lobby and the hoist could be repaired; he had to relegate himself from being the proud captain of 'X' turret into the position of being a mere passenger at the same time as he put one-third of the main armament of *Artemis* out of action for good. He had to bear all the responsibility himself; with that fire blazing there was not even time to ask permission from the Gunnery Lieutenant.

Allonby seized the voice-pipe to the magazine, and to his intense relief it was answered; Allonby knew Burney's voice as he knew the voice of every man under his command.

'Flood the magazine,' said Allonby.

'Flood the magazine?'

There was a question mark at the end of the sentence – it was not the usual Navy repetition of an order. The crash of the firing of the next round made Allonby pause for a second before he repeated himself, slowly and distinctly, making quite sure that he was understood. The last round was fired from the guns as he plugged the voice-pipe.

'Clear the turret,' said Allonby to his men, and they began to scramble out, leaping through the flames to safety as if it were some ceremonial worship of Moloch.

Allonby applied himself to the telephone. The Gunnery Lieutenant and the Transmitting Station must know at once that 'X' turret had ceased to fire; otherwise both the control and the spotting of the other guns would suffer. When he had finished that it was too late to escape from the turret, which was ringed with fire now and whose steel plates were red hot.

And down below the main deck, below the water-line, Ordinary Seaman Triggs and Supply Assistant Burney came out from the magazine into the handling-room crew. The elaborate mechanisms which had been specially designed for this emergency had played their part in saving the ship from instant destruction. All the way along the chain of ammunition supply, from magazine and shell-room to handling-room, from handling-room to lobby, from lobby to turret, there were flash-proof doors and shutters. At Jutland twenty-six years ago, similar hits had resulted in the destruction of three big battle cruisers; the roaring flames of one ignited charge had flashed from one end to the other, from turret to magazine, setting off the tons of high explosive in a blast which had blown the huge ships to fragments. In *Artemis* only the lobby had been wiped out, and only two charges had added their hundred-foot flames to those of the burning fuel. The flash-proof doors had allowed time, had stretched the period during which safety action could be taken from one-tenth of one second to fifteen seconds – time for Allonby to give his orders, possibly time for Burney or Triggs to carry them out. The alleyway in which the group found themselves was a place of unimaginable horror. It was filled with dense smoke, but no smoke could be thick enough to hide the scene entirely. Through holes in the torn deck above long tongues of red flame were darting intermittently down from the blazing lobby. At the end of the alleyway the bursting shell had blown bulkheads and doors into a porcupine-tangle of steel blades which protruded from a burning sea of oil; and with every movement of the ship the surface lapped over them and the flames ran farther down the alleyway. The heat was terrific, and although the flames were distinct enough the smoke was so thick that only objects directly illuminated by them were visible – the men groped about blinded, their lungs bursting and their eyes streaming.

'Flood the magazine!' shouted Burney in the fog. He ran round to where the twin wheels were which operated the inlet valves, with Triggs behind him; they ran through thin fire. Burney laid his hands on the wheels.

He had been drilled as far as this. Among the innumerable gunnery drills, R.I. exercises and sub-calibre work, sometimes the order had come through 'Clear "X" turret. Flood the magazine,' and Burney had run to the valves, even as he had now, and laid his hands on the wheels, as he did now, with Triggs beside him. Mechanical arrangements for flooding magazines might as well not exist if a man were not detailed to operate them, and practised in what he had to do; and not one man, but two, for men may die in the Navy.

But in this case action was different from practice, for the wheels were too hot to touch. Involuntarily Burney snatched his hands back from them with a cry of pain. They were seared and burnt. A sluggish river of burning oil trickled towards them and stopped five feet from them. Burney put his hands to the wheels again, but when he put his weight on his hands to force the wheels round it was more than his will would endure. He cried out with pain, agonized. Blind reflexes made him put his charred hands under his armpits as he stamped with agony and the burning oil edged nearer to him.

Cordite is a touchy substance, impatient of bonds. Free from confinement it will submit to rough treatment; it can be dropped, or thrown or tossed about without resenting the indignity. It will even burn, two out of three times, without exploding – a block consuming itself in a second, which is its approximate rate of combustion, instead of in a hundredth of a second, which is its rate of explosion. But if it is compressed or confined it will resent it vigorously. A pinch of fulminate then will make it explode, the wave of exposion jumping from molecule to molecule through the whole mass with the speed of light. And cordite is touchy about the temperature at which it is kept, too – let that rise a few degrees, and it begins to decompose. Nitrous fumes begin to rise from it; strange, complex, unstable nitrous acids begin to form within it. It begins to heat itself up spontaneously, accelerating the process in a vicious circle. So that if its temperature is allowed to rise while at the same time it is kept confined a pressure is developed which increases by leaps and bounds, and the decomposing cordite, compressed beyond all bounds, will explode without waiting for a primer to set it off.

Within 'X' turret magazine temperature and pressure were rising rapidly as the magazine's bulkheads passed on their heat to the cordite within. Thick yellow fumes (although there was no human eye within to see them) were flooding into the magazine as the unstable molecules stirred restlessly. A blast was approaching which would tear the ship in two, which might wipe out every human life within her. Pressure was piling up. Ordinary Seaman Triggs heard Burney's cries; the flames from the burning oil dimly illuminated Burney's shadowy figure bowed over his charred hands. Drill and discipline had left a mark even on Trigg's vague mental make-up. He knew orders were meant to be obeyed, although it was so easy to forget them and so easy to be distracted from their execution. When he went on shore he never meant to overstay his leave; it was only that he forgot; only that drink confused and muddled him. When the order came over the loudspeaker ' "X" turret crew close up,' he would always obey it promptly except that he was so often thinking about something else. Here amid the smoke and flame of the alleyway, Triggs, oddly enough, was thinking about nothing except the business in hand. He saw Burney try to turn the wheels and fail, and without hesitation he took up the task. The pain in his hands was frightful, but Triggs was able to ignore it. He flung his weight on the wheels and they moved; again and again they moved, turning steadily.

Temperature in the magazine was high; there was a red danger mark on the thermometer hung within and the mercury was far, far above it. Pressure was high, too. Triggs turned the wheels, the steel rods rotated, the worm-gear turned, and the inlet valves in the magazine slowly opened to admit the sea. Momentarily there was a strange reluctance on the part of the sea to enter; the pressure within was so high that the twelve feet below water-line of the valves did not give enough counter-pressure to force the water in. Then *Artemis* rolled, rolling the valves three feet further below the surface, and that added pressure just sufficed. Two jets of water sprang up into the magazine, greedily absorbing the yellow nitrous fumes and cooling the heated gas so that the pressure within the magazine dropped abruptly; even when *Artemis* went back to an even keel the sea still welled up into the magazine, and when she heeled over the next time the jets spouted far higher, cooling and absorbing so that now the sea rushed in like a flood, filling the whole magazine.

Triggs knew now that his hands hurt him; the charred bones were visible where the flesh of his palms had been burned away. He was sobbing with pain, the sobs rising to a higher and higher pitch as the pain grew more intense and the realization of it more and more acute; wounds in the hand seem to be especially unnerving and painful, presumably because of the ample nerve supply to their surfaces. Burney mastered his own agony for a space, sufficient to lead Triggs forward to the sick bay where Sick Berth Petty Officer Webster was doing his best to attend to the wounded who were being brought in here now that the wardroom and the Surgeon Lieutenant Commander had been wiped out. Webster could at least bandage those frightful hands, and at least could give morphia to check those high-pitched sobs of Triggs'.

And meanwhile the Commander and his men, with 'X' turret's crew to help, and Sub-Lieutenant Richards with such of his men as the shell had left alive, battled with hoses and chemical extinguishers against the sea of flames that had engulfed the after half of the ship, reducing it bit by bit from a sea to a lake, from a lake to isolated pools, until at last the tons of sea water which the pumps brought on board had extinguished every spark.

CHAPTER 23

FROM THE CAPTAIN'S REPORT

... with moderate damage ...

When the crew of *Artemis* was at action-stations one of the loneliest men in the ship was Henry Hobbs, Stoker First Class. His station was in the shaft tunnel, aft, a watertight door behind him and a watertight door in front of him, cutting him off from the rest of the world, and his duty was to watch over the eight shaft-bearings and to see that they did not run hot. The shaft tunnel was an inch less than five feet in height, so that Hobbs walked about in it bent double; and it was lighted eerily by a few sparse electric bulbs, and when *Artemis* was under full power, as she had been during this battle, the tunnel was full of the incessant high-pitched note of the shaft, which in that confined space made a continuous noise of a tone such as to make the unaccustomed listener feel he could not bear to listen to it any longer. Stoker Hobbs was used to it; in fact, it might as well be said he liked the noise and that it was no hardship for him to be stationed in the shaft tunnel; it must be further admitted that when action-stations were being allotted Hobbs had looked so earnestly at Stoker Petty Officer Harmsworth so as to attract his attention and gain his influence in his favour in the matter. Harmsworth had cheerfully put forward Hobbs' name for duty in the tunnel because Hobbs was essentially reliable. It was unlikely that more than once in a watch an officer would come into the tunnel to inspect, so the stoker on duty there must be someone who could be trusted to do his duty without supervision.

The duty was not a very exacting one, because the main duty that Hobbs had to perform was to watch his eight bearings. He could tell by touch when one was running hot instead of warm, and he had exactly to anticipate this by opening the oil valve regulating the flow of lubricating oil to the bearing. The only other thing he had to do was to watch the bilge below the shaft – the ultimate lowest portion of the ship – and report if it began to deepen. The rest of the time Hobbs could spend in communion with God.

In Hobbs' opinion the shaft tunnel was the ideal place in which to address himself to God, and this opinion was the result of a large variety of factors. It was odd that the least potent of these factors was that he could be alone in the tunnel – solitude is something hard to find in a light cruiser crammed with a full wartime crew. The art of staying sane in a crowd, and of retaining one's individuality when living night and day shoulder to shoulder with one's fellows, has been perfected through generations of seamen since Drake in the give-and-take life of the lower deck, and a man has freedom enough to speak to God if he wishes to. The man who says his prayers is just another individual, as is the man who indulges in the almost forgotten habit of chewing tobacco, or the man who amazingly sleeps face downward in his hammock.

So solitude was to Hobbs' mind only the least attractive aspect of duty in the shaft tunnel – it was of some importance, but not of much. That continuous high-pitched hum was more important. Hobbs found that it led his mind towards the higher things of life. The finest organ playing in the world, the most impassioned sermons were less effective in this way than the note of the shaft as far as Hobbs was concerned. The vibration played its part, too; nowhere in the length and breadth and depth of H.M.S. *Artemis* was the vibration as noticeable as in the shaft tunnel. That vibration, intense and rapid, always set Stoker Hobbs thinking about the wrath of God – the connection could hardly be apparent to anyone else, but to Hobbs it was clear enough. It was important, for in Hobbs' mind God was a Being who was filled with implacable wrath – implacable towards Hobbs alone, as far as Hobbs knew or cared. It was none of Hobbs' concern how God felt towards all the other men who swarmed through the ship. The naked steel that surrounded Hobbs in the tunnel, and the dreary lighting – harsh patches of light and darkness – reminded Hobbs of God, too, and so did the cramped confinement, and the blind leaps and surges of the tunnel when the ship was in a seaway. And when the guns were firing the sound of them, by some trick of acoustics, was carried through the steel framework of the ship to a focus in the tunnel, so that it resounded like a steel drainpipe pounded with sledgehammers.

From this picture of the shaft tunnel can be drawn a picture, then, of the aspect of God which Stoker Hobbs thought was turned towards him, seeing that it was here, amid the din and vibration, among these repulsive surroundings, that he thought he was nearest to Him. Hobbs would have been the first to agree, on the other hand, that this was definitely only one aspect of God; just as only one face of the moon is visible to us on earth, however the earth rotates and the moon revolves, so God steadily kept only one side of Him towards Hobbs; there was another, beneficent side which other and more fortunate people could see – just as from another planet the back of the moon is visible – but they were not such frightful sinners, such utterly lost souls as was Henry Hobbs.

Close questioning of him, by someone whom Hobbs could not suspect of flippancy or irreligion, would have elicited from him the fact – not the admission – that all these dreadful sins of Hobbs' were at most venial, and the greater part of them were at least a dozen years old. At twenty Hobbs had kissed a girl or two and drunk a glass of beer or two too many. Possibly, he had even gone a shade further in both directions, but only a shade. As a boy he had stolen from his hardworking mother's purse, and once he had stolen a doughnut in a baker's shop. But Hobbs was utterly convinced that his childhood and youth had been one long orgy of sin, meriting eternal damnation a dozen times over; at thirty-two he was still paying for them in penance and submission to a God who might some day forgive and who meanwhile only deigned to acknowledge the sinner's existence in such places as the shaft tunnel.

When he had gone the rounds of his eight bearings and seen that they were all properly lubricated, and after he had tried the bilge and made certain water was not rising in the ship, Hobbs took off the little black skull-cap he wore on duty to cushion the blows his head was always sustaining in the tunnel when the ship rolled. He clasped his hands before him – his head was already bowed, thanks to the lowness of the tunnel – and he prayed once more to God for forgiveness for what had passed between him and Mary Walsh that evening in the darkened cinema.

The second hit on *Artemis* did not extinguish the lights in the shaft tunnel immediately. Hobbs felt it and heard it, but it was fifteen seconds later before the flames burned through the insulation of the wiring somewhere along its course and plunged the tunnel into complete darkness. Hobbs stood quite still, hunched over in the tunnel, with no glimmer of light at all. The shaft went on singing its vast song, and all about him was God. He was not afraid. 'X' turret guns above his head fell silent – he could distinguish between a full broadside and the fire merely of 'A' and 'B' turrets – but the framework of the ship transmitted a great many new noises to him, crashes and thumps and bangs, as the flames roared through the stern and the damage control party fought them down. He waited a while for the lights to come on again, but the fire was so far aft that the emergency circuit to the shaft tunnel was involved as well; there would be no more light in the shaft tunnel until – if *Artemis* ever came out of this battle – the wiremen could, under the instructions of the Torpedo Gunner's Mate, restore the circuit. Hobbs took his electric torch out of the pocket of his dungarees and made the round of the bearings again, turning the valves on and off, and when he finished he switched the torch off again. If there was no light there was no light, and that was an end to the business. He certainly was not going to waste the electricity in his torch, for no one – except God who shared the darkness with him – knew how long this action was going to last and how long it would be before he was relieved. God was all about him in the shaft tunnel. He could stand there, bent half double, and wait.

One moment he was alone with God in the darkness of the tunnel; the next, it seemed to him, he was knee deep in water, so suddenly it poured in. The surprising thing about the water was that it was *hot*. It had not come in direct from the sea – it was sea-water which had been pumped on the flames, had quenched areas of red-hot steel plating, and had thence found its way by devious routes – a fragile light cruiser after two heavy hits and two fires was likely to have many passages open in it – down into the shaft tunnel. As the ship rolled and pitched and water surged up and down the tunnel, almost carrying Hobbs off his feet and splashing up into his face when it broke against the obstacle of his body.

He groped his way through the darkness to the telephone and lifted the receiver. It was some seconds before Howlett or Grant at the telephone switchboard were able to attend to the red light which glowed at the foot of the board to show that the hardly-used telephone in the shaft tunnel was off its hook. During that interval the water rose suddenly again to Hobbs' waist – not hot this time but icy cold, for the red-hot plating was all quenched by now. When the ship rolled the water surged clear over Hobbs' head, throwing him down still holding the receiver. Howlett plugged in – Hobbs heard the welcome click – and said 'Exchange'.

'Engine-room,' said Hobbs, and when he heard the answer, 'Hobbs – shaft tunnel here. I want the officer of the watch.'

The water dashed him against the tunnel walls as he waited again until Lieutenant Bastwick answered him and he made his report.

'We'll pump you out,' said Bastwick. 'Open up the discharge valves.'

Hobbs put back the telephone – underwater – and felt his way to the valves. The motion of the ship sent the water up and down the tunnel; not merely did it wash over Hobbs' head, but when his head was clear it also compressed or rarefied the air at the end of the tunnel where Hobbs was so that his eardrums crackled and his breath laboured on those occasions when he had the chance to breathe. The water still flooded into the tunnel – overhead where the damage control party fought the flames it naturally occurred to no one that down in the shaft tunnel their efforts were fast drowning one of their shipmates – and there were twenty tons of it now, hurtling from end to end and from side to side. It picked Hobbs up and dashed him against the watertight door; the point of his shoulder took the shock, and he felt his collar-bone break. It was painful to raise his right arm after that, but he stuck his hand into the front of his dungarees as a substitute sling. The discharge valves were open now, and he hoped the pumps were at work.

The next rush of water up the tunnel was less violent, although it jarred him against the watertight door and hurt his collar-bone again, and the next one was weaker still, hardly over his waist. There were pumps at work all over the ship – some pumping water in as fast as possible to quench the fire, and others pumping it out again as fast as possible from those compartments down into which it drained in torrents, for watertight doors and watertight hatchways work only moderately well after a ship has been struck by heavy shells and has had a bad fire rage through a quarter of her length. Hundreds of horse-power were being consumed in this effort, and for hours now the engine-room had been called upon to supply the sixty-five thousand horse-power needed for full speed. The Commander (E) had had the responsibility of seeing to it that engines and boilers would produce more power than they had been designed to produce, and for a longer time than it was fair that they should be asked to do so: the fact that First Class Stoker Hobbs was not drowned miserably in the shaft tunnel was some measure of the Commander (E)'s success in his task.

Hobbs was still alive. His right hand was thrust into the breast of his dungarees, and his shoulder pained him. He was utterly in the dark, for his saturated electric torch refused to function. But he was alive, and he knew his way about the shaft tunnel, from one bearing to another, to the oil valves and back again, and his work which could be carried out one-handed. These were not circumstances in which he felt himself to be justified in asking for relief, and he made no such request; indeed, it did not occur to himself to do so. God was with him in the darkness, and as it happened Hobbs had never been in the shaft tunnel in darkness before. It seemed to him as if in the darkness God was not as inplacable, as remorseless, as he was when the tunnel was lit up – that may easily be explained by the harsh black-and-white lighting of the tunnel, for there were no soft tones about it when the bulbs functioned. Very deep down within him, very faintly, Hobbs may have felt that this experience, this being flung about by tons of water in a confined space, his broken collar-bone and his near-drowning, was an expiation of his goings-on with Mary Walsh, but Hobbs was a man of slow mental reactions and of morbidly sensitive conscience, and if this feeling was there at all it was very slight, even if later, after mature consideration, it grew stronger. It was just the solid darkness which was comforting to Hobbs, and his reaction to it was to feel as if God were not quite so angry with him. He felt his way round the eight bearings with his left hand, and as he did so he whistled between his teeth, which he had not done since first the conviction of sin had come upon him. It was a very faint little whistle, not audible at all through the high-pitched song of the shaft, and when Hobbs realized what he was doing he cut himself off, but not very abruptly.

CHAPTER 24

FROM THE CAPTAIN'S REPORT

... but firing was maintained ...

At some time during the few minutes – during the interval measured perhaps in seconds – following immediately after the launching of their torpedoes by the destroyers, a shell was fired from H.M.S. *Artemis* which changed the face of the war, altered the whole history of the world. Men and women in Nigeria or Czechoslovakia would feel the impact of that shell upon their lives. Headhunting cannibals in Papua, Siberian nomads seeking a scant living among the frozen tundra of Asia, toddling babies in the cornfields of Iowa, and their children's children, would all, in the years to come, owe something to that shell.

For the correct apportionment of the credit the history of that shell and the charge which sent it on its way should be traced back to their origins. There were, somewhere in England, women whose skin was stained yellow by the picric acid which entered into the composition of the bursting charge, who sacrificed strength and beauty in the munitions factory that filled that shell; their hair was bound under caps and their feet encased in felt slippers lest the treacherous material they handled should explode prematurely. There were women at the precision lathes who turned that shell until it fitted exactly, to the thousandth of an inch, into the rifling of the gun that fired it. There were the men that mined the iron and the coal, and the slaving foundry-workers who helped to cast the shell. There were the devoted sailors of the Mercantile Marine, who manned the ship that bore the nickel that hardened the steel from Canada to England, in the teeth of the fiercest blockade Germany could maintain. There were the metallurgists who devised the formula for the steel, and there were the chemists who worked upon the explosive. There were the railwaymen and the dockyard workers who handled the deadly thing under the attack of the whole strength of the Nazi air power. The origins of that shell spread too far back and too widely to be traced – forty millions of people made their contribution and their sacrifice that that shell might be fired, forty millions of people whose dead lay in their streets and whose houses blazed round them, working together in the greatest resurgence of patriotism and natrional spirit that the world has known, a united effort and a united sacrifice which some day may find an historian. Perhaps he will be able to tell of the women and the children and the men who fought for freedom, who gave life and limb, eyesight and health and sanity, for freedom in a long-drawn and unregretted sacrifice.

The miners and the sailors, the munition workers and the railwaymen, had played their part, and now the shell stood in its place in 'A' turret shell-room, and the charge that was to despatch it lay in its rack in the forward turret magazine. There were only humble workers down there, men like Triggs and Burney who worked in the after turret magazine. Harbord, the Captain's steward, was stationed in the forward magazine – a thin, dried-up little man, who was aware of the importance of serving bacon and eggs in the most correct manner possible when his Captain called for them. Harbord had come into the Navy from the Reserve, and had passed the earlier years of his life as a steward in the Cunard White Star. He had found promotion there, rising from steward in the second-class to steward in a one-class ship, and from there to steward in the first-class in a slow ship, and eventually supreme promotion, to steward in the first-class in a five-day ship, where the tips were pound notes and five-dollar bills, and where he waited upon film stars and industrial magnates, millionaires and politicians.

He gave them good service; perhaps the best service the world has ever known was that given in the transatlantic luxury liners in the Twenties and Thirties. He devoted his ingenuity to anticipating the wants of his passengers so that they would be spared even the trouble of asking for what they wanted – he learned to read their characters, sizing them up the first day so that during the next four they would perhaps not have to ask for anything. He could put a basin at the bedside of a seasick millionaire as he could serve a midnight supper for two – pork chops and champagne! – in the cabin of a nymphomaniac film star. He was unobtrusive and yet always available. When passengers tried to pump him about their fellow passengers he could supply what appeared to be inside information without disclosing anything at all. He knew the great, the wealthy, and the notorious, in their weakest moments, and to him they were not in the least heroic figures. Yet of his feelings he gave no sign; he was deferential without being subservient, helpful without being fulsome.

The trade agreement between the shipping lines regulated the fares charged so that the only way in which they could compete with each other was in the services they could offer – menus ten pages long, food from every quarter of the globe, masterpieces of art hanging on the bulkheads, orchestras and gymnasiums and swimming baths; the concerted efforts of ingenious minds were at work devising fresh ways of pampering the first-class passengers so that a thousand miles from land they were surrounded by luxuries of which Nero or Lucullus never dreamed, by comforts such as Queen Victoria never enjoyed. And the service which the stewards could give was an important part of this system. If by a particular manner and bearing Harbord could make his charges more comfortable, he was ready to display that manner and bearing – it was his job for the moment. The social system which permitted – encouraged – such luxury and waste, and which made him the servant of drunken ne'er-do-wells and shifty politicians was obviously in need of reform, but the reformation must start with the system, not with the symptoms. Meanwhile, he had work to do, and Harbord took pride in doing to the best of his ability the work which was to be done.

And when war came and the Navy claimed his services it was far easier to reconcile his prejudices with the type of work to which he was allotted. He was a steward, still, but the Captain's steward – trust the Captain to select the best available. The arts he had acquired in the Cunard White Star were of real use now, to serve a breakfast without breaking in on the Captain's train of thought, to attend to the trivial and mechanical details of the Captain's day so that it was only the war which made demands upon the Captain's reserves of mental energy. At sea when the Captain was day and night on the bridge, it was Harbord's duty to keep him well fed and well clad, and in port Harbord had to shield him from nervous irritation so as to allow him a chance to recuperate. His discretion and his trustworthiness were of real value nowadays; the desk in the Captain's cabin held papers which the German staff would gladly pay a million pounds to see – Harbord never allowing his mind to record the writing which his eyes rested upon. Visitors came to the Captain's cabin, officers of the ship, officers of other ships, Intelligence officers of the Army and Air Force Staffs, Admirals and Generals.

They talked freely with the Captain, and Harbord in his pantry or offering sherry and pink gin from a tray could hear all they said. Sometimes it would be things that would make the spiciest shipboard gossip – news as to where the ship was going, or alterations in routine, or promotions, or transfers, or arrangements for shore leave. Sometimes it would be matters of high policy, the course of the naval war, the tactics to be employed in the next battle, or the observed effects of new weapons or new methods. Sometimes it would merely be reminiscence, tales of battle with submarine or aeroplane or armed raider. Whatever it was bound to be of the most engrossing interest. An advance word to the lower deck on the subject of leave would make his confidants his grateful clients; when talking to his friends on shore Harbord could have been most gratifyingly pontifical about the progress of the war; and in every port there lurked men and women who would pay anything in money and kind for news of how such-and-such a submarine was sunk or what happened to such-and-such a raider. But Harbord was deaf and dumb and blind, just as he had been in peacetime when the newspaper reporters had tried to find out from him who it was who shared the politician's cabin at night.

When the hands went to action-stations his was a position of no such responsibility. He was like Triggs, merely a man who stripped the tin cover from the cordite charges and thrust the cardboard-cased cylinders of explosive through the flash-tight shutter of the magazine into the handling-room – his duties about the Captain allowed neither the time nor the opportunity to train him to do more responsible work. He was hardly aware of his unimportance; that much effect, at least, his previous experience had had on him. He handed the cordite with as much solemnity as when he offered sherry to a Vice-Admiral, although with a greater rapidity of movement. A lifetime of self-control had left him with little surface light-heartedness, just as the habitual guard he maintained over his tongue made the men who worked beside him think him surly and unfriendly. At his action-station he was in close contact with half a dozen men, because 'A' and 'B' magazines were combined into one, with a flash-tight shutter both forward and aft, the one opening into 'A' turret handling-room and the other into 'B'. During the periods of idleness when the guns were not firing the men could stand about and gossip, all except Harbord, who would not. His fellow workers – the queerest mixture, from Clay, the ship's painter, to Sutton of the canteen staff – had, as a result of their different employments, the most varied gossip to exchange, and Harbord's could have been a valued contribution. But he kept his mouth shut, and was repaid by his shipmates saying he put on all the airs of an admiral. Of all these it was Harbord who was privileged to be the man who handled the propellant charge that sent to its target the shell that changed history.

Forward in the shell-room it was Able-Seaman Colquhoun who handled the shell – a big curly-haired young giant from Birkenhead, whose worst cross in life was the tendency of the uninitiated to mispronounce his name and give the 'l' and 'q' their full value. It was always a ticklish job telling petty officers that he called himself 'Cahoon'; self-important petty officers were inclined to look on that as an impertinence. The six-inch shell that Colquhoun handled weighed one hundred pounds, which was why his youthful thews and sinews were employed here in the shell-room. In a rolling ship it called for a powerful man to heave as big a weight as that with certainty into the hoist.

Colquhoun was proud of his strength, and to put it to good use gratified some instinct within him. He smiled reminiscently as he bent and heaved. In the early days of the black-out in England, when his ship was under orders to sail, he had spent his last night's leave ashore with Lily Ford, the big blonde friend of his boyhood, who had repelled every advance made to her by every man she had met. She had kept her virginity as though it were a prize in a competition, not selfishly, not prudishly, but as if she looked on herself as if she were as good as any man and would not yield until she should meet one whom she could admit to be her better. But that night on the canal bank, under the bright moon of the first September of the war, Colquhoun had put out all his strength. It had been careless of Lily to let herself be lured by Colquhoun's tact to such a deserted spot as the canal bank, but it would really have been the same if there had been help within call – Lily would not have called for help to deal with a situation she could not deal with single-handed. She fought with him, silently, desperately, at first, and even when he was pressing her hard she would not do more than whisper hoarsely, 'Get away, you beast.' She writhed and struggled, putting out all the strength of her tough body, trained by the factory labours which had given her her glorious independence. Then she yielded to his overpowering force, breaking down suddenly and completely, her savage words trailing off into something between a sigh and a sob, her stiff body relaxing into submission, the mouth she had kept averted seeking out his in the darkness.

It was a succulent memory for the graceless Colquhoun; something to be rolled over the tongue of reminiscence, every detail just as it should have been, even to the walk back from the canal bank with Lily clinging to him, her boasted self-sufficiency all evaporated, and the fact that Colquhoun's ship was under orders to sail terrifying in its imminence and inevitability. She had clung and she had even wept, although the day before she would have laughed at any suggestion that she would waste a tear on any man. Well, that was two and a half years ago, and it was to be presumed that she had got over it by now.

'Come up, you bastard!' said Colquhoun without ill temper, for he was still grinning to himself; the arms that had clasped Lily Ford clasped the shell that was to change history, and slid it forward into the hoist.

At the same moment in the handling-room Able-Seaman Day, the man who lost his left forefinger as a result of a premature explosion at the Battle of the River Plate, took the charge that Harbord had thrust through the flash-tight shutter and pushed it into a pocket on the endless chain that ran up above his head through another flash-tight hatchway. The hoist rose, the endless chain revolved, the shell and charge arrived simultaneously in 'A' turret lobby.

The designer of a ship of war encounters difficulties at every turn. One school of naval thought clamours for guns, the largest possible guns in the greatest possible number, with which an enemy may be overwhelmed without the opportunity of hitting back. Another school demands speed, and points out that the best guns in the world are useless unless they can be carried fast enough to catch the enemy. A third school prudently calls for armour because, as Nelson once pointed out, a battle at sea is the most uncertain of all conflicts, and speed and guns may vanish in a fiery holocaust as a result of a single hit. And armour means weight, and guns mean weight, the one at the expense of the other and both at the expense of the weight that can be allotted to engines.

The designer reaches a compromise with these conflicting demands only to come against new incompatibles. Men must be able to live in a ship; the mere processes of living demand that they should be able to go from one part of the ship to another, and when she is in action it may well be that they have to do so with the greatest possible speed. But, once again, she may be struck by shells or bombs or torpedoes, and to minimize the damage of the hit she must be divided up into the greatest possible number of compartments bulkheaded off from each other, and those bulkheads must be free of all openings – except that there is the most urgent need for wires and voice-pipes and ventilating shafts to pass through them.

In the same way the gunnery expert insists that his guns should be placed as high as possible, so as to give the greatest possible command, and his insistence is met with the reply that guns and gun-mountings are the heaviest things in a ship and putting them high up means imperilling the ship's stability like standing up in a rowing-boat. Not merely that, but the gunnery expert, wise to the danger of high explosives, demands that although his guns should be as high above the level of the sea as possible the shells and the charges for the guns should be out of harm's way and as far below that level as possible; then, unreasonable as a spoilt child, he goes on to clamour for guns that will fire with the greatest rapidity and in consequence needing to be supplied every minute with a great weight of ammunition regardless of the distance it must be raised from shell-room and magazine. Even that is not all. The moment his wishes appear to be granted he baulks at the thought of a long chain of high explosive extending unbroken from top to bottom of the ship, and he insists that the chain be broken up and interrupted with flash-tight hatchways and shutters that must on no account delay the passage of the ammunition from the magazine to the precious guns.

Ingenious mechanisms solve this problem – so that when 'X' turret lobby in *Artemis* was set on fire the flames did not flash up into the turret nor down into the magazine – and then the designer is faced with a new difficulty, because the turret must, of course, be able to revolve, to turn from side to side, so that the belts and hoists are attached at one end to the stationary lobby, and at the other to the revolving turret; and this is the difficulty which designers for eighty years have struggled against. When Ericsson built *Monitor* he had a hole cut in the floor of the turret and another in the roof of the magazine below, and in order for ammunition to be passed up the turret had to be revolved until the two holes corresponded and the turret had to remain stationary until it was reammunitioned – a state of affairs no gunnery officer, intent on annihilating the enemy, would tolerate for a moment.

Even the apparently insoluble problem of the revolving turret and the stationary lobby has been solved now, so that whichever way the turret may be turning two shells of a hundred pounds each and two charges of cordite arrive in it every ten seconds to feed the guns, but the complication has forced another compromise upon the unfortunate designer. He is faced by the choice between employing men or machines – elaborate, complicated machines which may be disabled by a hit, or men who have to be fed, and given water to drink, and somewhere to sling a hammock, and who, in a nation exerting the last ounce of its strength, could be employed on some other urgent duty if not engaged in manhandling ammunition. Faced by this choice, the designer compromises, as he has compromised in his designs all through the ship. He makes the mechanisms as simple as he can without necessitating too great use of manpower, and he cuts down his manpower as far as he can without complicating the mechanisms too much. He ends, of course, by satisfying neither the Commander who is responsible for the men's living conditions nor the Gunnery Officer who is responsible for the guns, but that is the natural fate of designers of ships – the speed enthusiasts and the gunnery experts and the advocates of armour protection, the men who have to keep the ship at sea and the men who have to handle them in action all combine to curse the designer. Then comes the day of battle, and the mass of compromises which is a ship of war encounters another ship of war which is a mass of different compromises, and then, ten to one, the fighting men on the winning side will take all the credit to themselves and the losers – such of them as survive – will blame the designer all over again.

So the thews and sinews of Able-Seaman Colquhoun and the fussy diligence of Harbord were necessary to start the shell and its propelling charge on the way up from shell-room and magazine to 'A' turret lobby. Then Able-Seaman Mobbs tipped the shell out of the hoist into the shell ring; to him it was just one more shell, and not the shell on which the destinies of the world depended. With one shell arrriving up the hoist every five seconds he had no time for profound thought. He had to be as diligent as a beaver, and he was a man of full body, oddly enough. The stooping and the heaving which he had to do in the warm atmosphere of the lobby had no apparent effect on the waistline which week by week grew a little more salient as Mobbs left youth further behind and advanced further into maturity. He swept the sweat from his forehead with the back of his right forearm, avoiding the use of his hands, which were filthy from contact with the shells. But by now his forearm was nearly as dirty as his hands, and the sweat and the dirt combined into fantastic streaks diagonally across his pink face. On his cheeks and chin there was a fuzz of fair beard like a chicken's down, for Mobbs had been carried away early in the war by the revived naval craze for beards, and the poverty of the result had not yet induced him to reapply for permission to shave. The fuzz was dirty in patches, too, and there were little rivers of sweat running through it. Anyone in the lobby with leisure for thought would have smiled at the sight of him, his plethoric pink face and his ridiculous beard, his blue pop-eyes as innocent as a child's, and the streaked dirt over all. He moved the shell ring round for a quarter of a revolution to where Ordinary-Seaman Fiddler awaited it, and then he brushed his face and his left forearm and managed to streak it again in the diagonally opposite direction, thereby giving the finishing touch to his ludicrous appearance. No one had time to notice it, however. Another shell had come up the hoist, dispatched by Able-Seaman Colquhoun, and he had to deal with it – just another shell, no different in its appearance from its important predecessor now under the charge of Ordinary-Seaman Fiddler, no different from the scores that had gone before, or from the scores which, for all Mobbs knew, would follow after. It seemed to him as if he had been at work for hours tipping shells from hoist to ring and would go on doing so to the end of time. The thunder of the guns just above his head, the motion of the ship, made no impression on him; for that matter he was not even actively conscious of the stuffy heat of the lobby. Word had come through over the telephone system that 'X' turret lobby had been wiped out, and after magazine flooded, 'X' turret guns silenced. Mobbs heard the news as he toiled and sweated; some of his messmates were gone, and it must have been only by a miracle that he and *Artemis* together had escaped being blown into microscopic fragments. None of that was as important as this business of keeping the shell ring full and the hoist empty, not as important at the moment, at least.

Meanwhile, Ordinary-Seaman Filmore took from the endless chain the cordite charge that Harbord below him had put into it, and transferred it to the cordite hoist of the revolving structure – three neat movements did it all, in far less than the five seconds allowed him. It was an easy job for Filmore. He had time to think and talk. The empty pocket in the endless chain flicked out of sight through the flash-tight hatchway.

'Coo!' said Filmore. 'That means old Nobby's gone. *You* know. Not Nobby the Leading Cook. The other one wiv the red 'air. 'E owes me a couple o' pints, too. Last time——'

'Shut up,' snapped Petty Officer Ransome.

He should not have snapped; he should have given the order naturally and easily, as orders which must be obeyed under pain of death should be given, and he was conscious of his error the moment the words were out of his mouth. But he was newly promoted and not quite sure of himself, and the responsibility of 'A' turret lobby weighed heavily on him.

'Keep yer 'air on!' said Filmore to himself, very careful that he should not be overheard. By diligent testing he knew just how far he could go with every Petty Officer and Leading Seaman in the ship. He had the Cockney quick wit, and the Cockney interest in disaster and death. He felt about the death of the red-haired Nobby Clark in the same way as his mother in her Woolwich slum felt about the death of a neighbour. It was a most interesting event; although the daily miracles of sunrise and sunset quite failed to impress him, he was always struck by the miracle that someone he knew, had talked to and talked about, should now be something quite different, a mere lump of flesh destined to immediate mouldering and decay. It was not intrinsically a morbid interest, and certainly the death of Nobby Clark was something to be talked about, like a birth in the the Royal family. Petty Officer Ransome thought otherwise. If he had been a mere seaman he would gladly have entered into the discussion, recalling old memories of Nobby, and wondering how his widow would get along on her pension. But as a Petty Officer, responsible for 'A' turret lobby, and with an unjustified fear that it was bad for the morale of the men to dwell on the death of a shipmate, he cut the discussion short. As a distraction he gave another order.

'Keep it moving, Fiddler.'

'Aye, aye,' said Fiddler.

The shell vanished into the hoist in the revolving structure as a fresh broadside blared overhead. Ransome, in this his first action as a Petty Officer, was worried. From the time of going to action-stations he had felt a nagging fear lest his lobby should not be as efficient as the other two, lest a broadside should be delayed because ammunition was supplied more slowly to 'A' turret than to 'B' and 'X'. If that should happen there would be a sharp reprimand from Sub-Lieutenant Coxe over his head; even worse, the Gunnery Lieutenant, watching the 'gun ready' lamps, might – certainly would – be moved to enquire into the cause of the delay. It was not fear of actual reprimand, or of punishment or disrating, which Ransome felt, any more than the crew of a racing eight fears defeat as it waits at the starting point. It was mere nervousness, which sharpened his voice and led him into giving unnecessary orders, and it remained to be seen if time and experience would enable him to overcome this weakness. No man's capacity for command can be known until it has been tried in actual battle.

In point of fact, 'A' turret was easier to keep supplied than 'B' turret just aft of it. 'B' turret was superimposed, raised higher above the deck than 'A', so as to enable its guns, when pointed directly forward, to fire over it. Yet 'A' and 'B' turrets drew their ammunition from the same magazine, and from shell-rooms at the same level below the sea, with the result that 'B's' shells and charges had to be sent up on a journey a full seven feet longer that 'A's', enough to make an appreciable difference in the time of transmission and to demand a proportionate increase in efficiency on the part of 'B's' turret crew. Since his promotion Ransome had not begun to reason this out and comfort himself with the knowledge, which was a pity, for when nervousness begins to reason it ceases to be nervousness. Instead, he snapped, 'Keep it moving, Fiddler,' quite unnecessarily.

'Aye, aye,' grumbled Fiddler, a little resentfully, for he knew that there was nothing slow about his supervision of the shell ring. He was an old, old sailor who had seen Petty Officers come and Petty Officers go, who had been through battle and shipwreck and hardship and pestilence, sturdily refusing promotion despite the recommendations of Lieutenants and the suggestions of Commanders. The life of an Able-Seaman was a comfortable one, a satisfactory one, and he did not want the even tenor of his existence broken by the responsibilities of promotion. He did not look upon his experiences when the destroyer *Apache* was lost in a snowstorm in the Hebrides, and he had clung to a ledge of a cliff for a night and half a day with the waves beating just below him, as an interruption of his placid existence, nor the fighting at Narvik, nor the week he spent in an open boat when his sloop was torpedoed. Those were mere incidents, but to be even a Leading Seaman meant disturbing all the comfortable habits and daily routine acquired during twenty years of service. All he wanted to do was to go steadily along performing the duties allotted him, gaining neither credit nor discredit, neither promotion nor punishment, but reserving to himself the right to feel that he knew much more about seamanship and gunnery than did these whipper-snapper young Petty Officers whom they promoted nowadays. Ransome's order to him called forth the mechanical response to his lips, but did not quicken his movements in the least, for he knew he was doing his job perfectly, and probably a great deal better than Ransome could. The shell slid under his guidance from the shell ring to the revolving hoist, and soared up to the turret and out of his life, keeping pace as before with the cordite charge in the cordite hoist.

Sub-Lieutenant Coxe allowed his eyes to rest idly on the shell as it lay in its trough on its arrival, with its ugly distinctive paint on it, and ugly in its harsh cylindro-conical outline. There was not even a functional beauty about it, unlike most of the weapons of war, nor was it large enough to be impressive in its bulk. A six-inch shell, even one which is destined to free humanity, is unredeemingly ugly. Coxe never stopped to think for a moment whether it was ugly or beautiful. He was keeping a sharp eye on his guns' crews, watching each of their intricate movements. Coxe knew all about this turret and the principles that it embodied. He knew all the details of its mechanism, all the bolts and all the levers. If every six-inch turret in the Royal Navy, and every blueprint and every working drawing were to be destroyed in some unheard-of cataclysm, they could be replaced by reference to Sub-Lieutenant Coxe. When he was seasick (which was often) Coxe could forget his troubles by closing his eyes and calling up before him the obturator on the vent axial bolt or the tapered grooves in the recoil cylinder, but there was no need for seasickness to set him free thinking about gunnery. It occupied most of his thoughts; and in the same way that a man at dinner turns satisfied from a joint to complete the meal with cheese, so Coxe could turn from the comparatively simple mechanics of the gun-mountings to the mathematics of ballistics, and Henderson and Hasse's differential form of Resal's fundamental equation.

Coxe was an example of the mathematical prodigy, as his first-class certificates showed; at twenty his facility in the subject was striking. The fact that England was at war was at least postponing his specializing; a prolonged period of peace would almost inevitably have resulted in his being confined to desk work in a state of voluntary servitude, hugging his chains, respected, perhaps, in his own speciality, but unknown beyond a limited circle. In those conditions he would have been likely to forget that war is not a clash of mathematical formulae, but a contest waged by men of flesh and blood and brain. If anything would help to keep him human, to develop him into a wise leader of men instead of into a learned computer, it was his present command, where under his own eye he could see formulae and machinery and men in action together. The proving ground and the testing station could confirm or destroy theories about internal pressures and the toughness of armour plate, but only the proving ground of war could test men. The most beautiful machines, the most elaborate devices, were useless if the men who handled them were badly trained or shaken by fear, and there was the interesting point that the more complex the machinery, and the more human effort it saved, and the more exactly it performed its functions, the greater need there was for heroes to handle it. Not mere individual heroes either, but a whole team of heroes. Disaster would be the result of a weak link anywhere along the long chain of the ship's organization. A frightened rangetaker, a jumpy Marine bandsman at the Transmitting Station table, a shaken steward in the magazine, and all the elaborate mechanism, the marvellous optical instruments, the cannons that cost a King's ransom, and the machine which embodied the ingenuity of generations, were all of them useless. It would be better then if there had never been any development in gunnery, and they were still in the days when the gunnery handbook made use of the elastic expression, 'take about a shovelful of powder'. Euclid had pointed out that the whole is equal to the sum of all its parts, and it was dawning upon Coxe that there was not merely a mathematical application of that axiom.

With a new eye he saw Numbers Four and Five ram home the shell into the left-hand gun; he was familiar with the very abstruse mathematics involved in calculations regarding compensation for wear at the breech of the gun, and those calculations always assumed that the projectile would be firmly seated against the rifling. Some dry-as-dust individual at Woolwich made those calculations, some withered officer with rings on his sleeve and gold oak-leaves on his cap brim, but unless Number Five, there, the hairy individual with the crossed flags of England and France tattooed on his forearms, kept his head and wielded the rammer efficiently, those calculations might as well never have been put on paper.

Number Six was pushing in the charge. It had never occurred to Coxe before that the instructions which ordered this were no guarantee that it would be done. Number Six might drop the charge, or if his hands were shaking or he was not seaman enough to keep his footing, he might break it open against the sharp edge. Number Six might even become frightened enough to dash out of the turret and run below to take shelter under the main deck – that was a possibility that had never crossed Coxe's mind before, he realized, and yet it was a possibility. Number Six had a tendency to boils on the back of his neck; Coxe had never noticed that before either, but a man who could suffer from boils was a man and not a piece of machinery that shoved the propellant up the breech. Number Six – what the devil was his name? Stokes? Something like that. No, it was Merivale, of course – Number Six was a fallible human being. Coxe became guiltily conscious that it was even conceivable that Number Six would be less likely to run away when he should be pushing in charges if the officer of the quarters did not call him Stokes when his name was Merivale. That was not something that could be reduced to a mathematical formula. It was courage, morale, *esprit de corps*, discipline – of a sudden these were pregnant words for Coxe now.

He turned with a fresh interest to Number Two, who was closing the breech. Coxe was nearly sure that Number Two's name was Hammond.

He really must make an effort to remember. Hammond – if that was his name – was having trouble with his wife. The matter had come up when the Commander was interviewing request-men. Some neighbour, officious or well-intentioned or spiteful or over-moral, had written to Hammond telling him about nocturnal visitors to Hammond's home. White-faced and sick with despair, on the sunny quarter-deck, Hammond had admitted to the Commander that he would not be surprised if the accusation were true. 'She was like that,' said Hammond. Once she had promised that it would never occur again, and Hammond had believed her, but standing before the Commander, Hammond had reluctantly admitted that he had been an optimistic fool; yet clearly that had not made it easier for Hammond, his life in ruins, and only half-hearted even now in his desire to cut off his allotment of pay to the wife he was still, obviously, besotted about.

A man whose wife was being unfaithful to him was liable to neglect his business. Coxe was academically aware of that even though he could not conceive of anything, certainly not domestic unhappiness, coming between him and gunnery. He darted a glance to see that Hammond had inserted the tube and masked the vent. Hammond swung the breech shut and closed the interruptor.

'Ready!' he said quietly – Number Two at the other gun shouted the word excitedly. Hammond was cool; cold might be a better word for it. It might be merely the deadly coldness of an embittered man; but, on the other hand, it might be the effect of discipline and training. Coxe actually found himself wondering which it was.

Shell and charge were in the gun now. Magazine and shell-room and handling-room, lobby and turret, had all made their contribution. So had every man in the ship, from Hobbs down in the shaft tunnel to the Captain on the bridge and Whipple at the masthead. The fact that the shell now lying in the breech of the left-hand gun 'A' turret was going assuredly to alter the history of the world was something to the credit of every one of them. The whole is equal to the sum of all its parts.

'Shoot!' said the Gunnery Lieutenant for the hundredth time that day. His fighting blood was still roused; the long battle had not brought weariness or lassitude. He controlled and directed this broadside as thoroughly as he had controlled the first.

The elevation and deflection of the guns was fixed by the Transmitting Station; this broadside meant no more and no less to the men there than any other in the long fight. The Marine bandsmen followed their pointers and Mr Kaile handled his complex orchestra as always, and the fire gong rang for the hundredth time in the Transmitting Station as Chief Petty Officer O'Flaherty in the Director Control Tower obeyed the Gunnery Lieutenant's order and pressed the trigger, to fire the broadside that would decide the future of neutral

Ireland just as much as that of the rest of the belligerent world. The tubes heated, the charges exploded, and the four shells went shrieking over nine thousand yards of sea to their destined ends. Three of them missed, and the fourth one – the shell from the left-hand gun in 'A' turret – hit. The spotters in *Artemis* recorded 'straddle' and set themselves in ignorance of what that straddle meant to observe the next fall of shot.

CHAPTER 25

FROM THE CAPTAIN'S REPORT

. . . until the enemy turned away . . .

Kapitän-sur-See Helmuth von Bödicke stood on the signal bridge of His Italian Majesty's battleship *Legnano* with Vice-Ammiráglio Gasparo Gaetano Nocentini. They were out of earshot of their staffs, who stood decently back so as not to overhear the conversation of the two great men, who were talking French to each other; only when French failed them did they turn and summon Korvetten Kápitan Klein and Luogotenènte Lorenzetti to translate for them from German into Italian and from Italian into German. At the time when von Bödicke was young enough to learn languages it never occurred to any German naval officer that it might some day be specially useful to speak Italian, and Nocentini had learned French in the nursery and had never had either the desire or the intention to acquire the language of the barbarians of the north.

The signal bridge in *Legnano* was windy and exposed, but it was the most convenient place in the ship for the commanding admiral; the conning-tower was too crowded and its view too limited, while the signal bridge afforded the most rapid means of communication with the rest of the fleet. On the port side where Bödicke and Nocentini stood they had the best view of whatever was visible. Abeam of them was the immensely long black smudge of the smoke-screen which the English had laid down, and against that background, vague and shadowy, were the English light cruisers, screened from view during much of the time by the splashes thrown up by the Italian salvoes. Fine on the port bow were the English destroyers, just wheeling round like swallows on the wing, after presumably launching their torpedoes against the Italian line. Astern of *Legnano* came the other Italian ships, the battleship *San Martino*, the heavy cruisers and the light cruisers. What Bödicke and Nocentini could not see from the port side of the signal bridge were the Italian destroyers advancing too late against the English destroyers, but as they undoubtedly were too late it did not matter so much that they could not be seen.

The din that assailed the ears of the men on the signal bridge was enormous, frightful. Every twenty-five seconds the fifteen-inch guns let loose a salvo louder than the loudest thunderclap, whose tremendous detonation shook them like a violent blow, and, deep-toned behind them, *San Martino*'s big guns echoed those salvoes. These were intermittent noises; the din of the secondary armament went on without cessation, six-inch and four-inch and twelve-pounder all banging away as fast as they could be loaded and fired in the endeavour to beat back the destroyer attack. It was ear-splitting and made it hard to think clearly. And all round the ship were raining the broadsides from the English light cruiser, deluging the decks with splashes, or bursting against the armour with a piercing crash, straddling the ship so closely that the shells that passed overhead were audible through the detonations of the secondary armament.

Von Bödicke trained his glasses on the leading English cruiser. She was badly on fire aft, with thick smoke pouring out of her, and yet she was still firing superbly and fast. The rest of the line appeared to have suffered little damage, which was quite absurd seeing how much they had been under fire. These excitable Italians could never steady themselves quickly enough to hit an elusive target. Brave enough men, perhaps (presumably because of the infiltration of Nordic blood into their Mediterranean veins), but unsteady. He experienced a momentary feeling of helplessness when he thought of his mission; he had been sent here to crush the British fleet by the aid of the Italian, and now he was conscious of the weakness of the tool he had to employ. He was like a man setting out to move a heavy rock and finding his crowbar buckling in his hand.

He let his glasses hang by their cord from his neck, and he plucked at the torpedo beard he wore as a tribute to the memory of von Hipper. Naval warfare, a naval battle, was like a game of poker. A good hand was of no avail if it met a better; confronted with four of a kind a full house was as unprofitable as a pair of deuces; the winner scooped the pool and the loser had nothing. In land warfare, or in air warfare, the loser might hope for a profitable defeat, to gain so much time or to inflict so much loss as to nullify the other's victory, but at sea it was all or nothing.

It was all or nothing for him, von Bödicke, as well. Von Bödicke remembered receiving supplementary verbal orders at the Marineamt, and the thin lips and the almost colourless eyes of Admiral Fricke, the Chief of the Naval Staff. He could expect no mercy from Fricke if he were to fail, and it was no comfort to think that Fricke could expect no mercy either. Fricke was primarily a Nazi and only secondarily a naval officer, who had won his position through all the clashes and fierce jealousies of the Party. If the command of the Mediterranean were not achieved, other ambitious young men would pull Fricke down. And Fricke would die, of heart disease or a motoring accident, for a man who tried for power by way of the Party staked his life on the result; successful rivals would never run the risk of his regaining power and avenging himself, nor would the Führer. The blackguards of the Party acted on the principle that dead men knife no one in the back. Fricke would die, and old von Bödicke would merely be ruined, put on beggarly retired pay under police supervision. He would not even have enough to eat, for he would be a useless mouth, on the lowest scale of rations, and doomed to slow starvation because no one would help a man with no return favours in his gift to supplement his diet illegally. He turned to Nocentini beside him.

'We must turn towards the enemy, your excellency,' he said.

Nocentini looked down at von Bödicke, Nocentini tall and gangling and clean-shaven, von Bödicke short and stocky with a little bristling beard. Nocentini had received verbal instructions as well, and his came direct from the lips of Il Duce. Il Duce had been most explicit on the point that nothing was to be risked. An easy victory was to be grasped at eagerly, but only as long as there was no prospect of loss. The battleships with which Nocentini was entrusted were the only ones left serviceable in the Italian navy, and very precious in consequence. Il Duce had far-reaching theories about war; one was that it was most necessary to husband one's strength against the possible demands of an always dangerous future, and the other was that by biding one's time one always found opportunities to pick up highly profitable gains for almost nothing as long as one had not dissipated one's strength prematurely. Il Duce had been most eloquent about this, making his points one after the other with much slapping of his fat white hands on the table while the sweat made his flabby jowls shine in the lamplight. He preached caution in the privacy of his office with just as much fervour as he preached recklessness from his balcony. But the fervour had an unhappy ring, and the arguments were those of a beaten man, of a tired man. Il Duce was growing old.

That was one of the considerations Nocentini had to bear in mind. One of these days Il Duce would die, and no one could tell what régime would find itself in power; there might be prolonged chaos. A powerful fleet would be a potent factor in the struggle, and Nocentini had ideas about how to use it. So he was in complete agreement with the Chief of the State about the desirability of easy victories and the necessity to avoid crippling losses. He knew that it was only with the utmost reluctance that Il Duce had consented to risking the fleet three hundred miles from its base, even when the Germans, in their usual cocksure fashion, had assured him that the English had no capital ships whatever available in the Eastern Mediterranean. Nocentini fancied that the Germans had been using a great deal of pressure, threatening in the event of a refusal to cut down still further the tiny shipments of coal that just enabled Italian civilization to exist.

If he could wipe out this British squadron and its convoy it would add to his own prestige and that of the fleet, but it would restore something to the prestige of Il Duce as well. The wiping out would not be easy, for the English had already shown their readiness to fight to the last. Those early moves of his, cautious feelers to determine the British attitude, had proved this. To turn towards the enemy, to plunge into the smoke-screen, would mean a muddled battle, an undignified scuffle, and possible heavy losses in a close-range action. Nocentini simply did not believe the optimistic reports with which the Naval Intelligence kept bombarding him regarding the extremities to which Malta was reduced. He was not a natural optimist; and with regard to Malta, he had the unhappy suspicion that its fall would be just another chestnut pulled out of the fire for the benefit of the Germans.

Italy? Nocentini was not sure now what Italy was. Not Mussolini, assuredly. The vulgarian who had built up the Italian fleet, who had given it more men and more money than Nocentini had ever dreamed of, had something once to recommend him. But the frightened worn-out man, prematurely old, cowering in the Quirinal, pathetically pleading with Nocentini to be cautious, and with the haunting fear of the Nazis to be read in his face, was not a leader to be followed with devotion, and certainly not the embodiment of the Italy which Nocentini vaguely dreamed about.

The continuous crash of the guns, the constant arrival of reports, the very wind that whipped round their ears, confused Nocentini's mind and made thinking difficult. He stood and gazed down at von Bödicke, wasting precious seconds while the torpedoes were actually on their way towards them.

'Your Excellency,' said von Bödicke, 'it is absolutely necessary that you should give the order.'

Von Bödicke was in a desperate mood. He was disillusioned on every side. He suspected a policy of deliberate obstruction. In the opening moves of the battle heavy smoke had poured from the funnels first of this ship and then of that one prematurely revealing the position of the fleet. Any engineer ought to be ashamed of himself for permitting such a thing to happen; the lowest *maschinist-maat* in the German navy would know better. He had goaded Nocentini into signalling reprimands, and the replies that came back had been decidedly unsettling. One captain had blamed the oil fuel, and in the wording of his message had insolently suggested that the fuel's defects were due to the culpable carelessness of the German authorities who had supplied it. The worst of that suggestion was that it was possibly true; von Bödicke knew a little about Albert Speer, who made use of his position as Oil Fuel Controller to make profits for the dummy company which was really Albert Speer. With boiler-room crews as excitable as the Italians, it was too much to expect that they should keep their heads clear enough to deal instantly and accurately with crises like fluctuations in the quality of the oil in the pipes.

These damned Italians were all alike. They were jumpy and excitable. Most of them had had too little training at sea either to be able to master seasickness or to be able to carry out their duties in a crisis with a sea-way running. They had been firing away at the cruisers all this time and hardly scored a hit – when the action began he had visited turrets and gunnery control towers, to find officers and men chattering like apes and getting in each other's way. Von Bödicke suspected that half the salvoes they fired off had been unaimed as a result of inefficiency on the part of the guns' crews or the gunnery control crews; it was too much to expect that somewhere along the complicated chain there would not be at least one weak link – especially as the veteran seamen were being drained away from the ships to make good the steady losses in submarine crews.

Von Bödicke's desperation was being eaten away by a growing weariness. He hated Fricke for sending him on this thankless duty. Victory would confirm Fricke in his position; and Bödicke suddenly realized that bloody defeat might do the same. If he, Bödicke, were able to persuade Nocentini to make an attack, and this *Legnano* were to be sunk, and Bödicke along with her, Bödicke having done his best and the Italian navy proved to be obviously not up to its work, then no one could possibly blame Fricke. He would continue to lord it at the Marineamt. Self-pity came to soften von Bödicke's desperations as well. It was a frightful dilemma in which he found himself. This was no simple marine problem which he faced. It was a complex of political and personal factors intricately entangled. With a German fleet under his command, in German waters, he would not hesitate for a moment about what to do, but out here in the Mediterranean with these Italians it was quite different. The very name of the ship in which he found himself was an insult to Germany. Legnano was the name of the battlefield where der Alte Barbarossa had by chance met with defeat at the hands of the Lombard League. Mussolini had no business to recall to memory that unfortunate accident of seven hundred years ago. But it was just like the Italians; when they decided to call their battleships after Italian victories they soon found themselves running out of names. *San Martino* astern was named after a battle which was really an Austrian victory, terminated by an Austrian retreat merely because of the success of the

French on the other battlefield of Solferino. At Vittorio Veneto the decisive blow was struck by an English army, and then only after Austria had been stabbed in the back by the Jews and separatists. Von Bödicke remembered the sneer in which German naval officers so often indulged when they asked the rhetorical question why the Italians had named no battleship of theirs after Caporetto. The question was on the tip of his tongue as he looked at Nocentini, so bitter was his mood.

He had asked to have the Italian fleet turned towards the enemy, but he had no sooner said the words when he experienced a revulsion of spirit. He could not recall them, but he was in two minds about it. He simply did not know what he wanted. He was balanced on a knife edge of indecision, and Nocentini, looking down at him, knew it telepathically. He was just as undetermined, just as unsettled in his mind as was Bödicke. The minutest influence would decide him, like Bödicke, one way or the other.

'We must turn either towards or away,' said Nocentini slowly, groping with difficulty, in his dazed preoccupation, for the French words.

He would have liked more time to discuss it, so as to postpone the moment of decision, but he knew that was vain. It was twenty seconds at least since the British destroyers had launched their torpedoes. Nocentini looked over at the British squadron, at the smoke-wreathed silhouettes aflame with gun flashes. He knew much about the British Navy, and in that clairvoyant moment he visualized the disciplined sailors bending to their work, the shells quietly passed up from the magazine, the rapid loading and the accurate firing. And at that moment there was flung into the scale that factor that tipped it down and swayed the balance of von Bödicke's and Nocentini's hesitating minds. A six-inch shell struck full upon 'B' turret, below them and forward of them, and burst against the twelve-inch steel.

To the ship itself it did no particular damage. It did not slow the working of the turret; in fact, it left hardly a mark on the diamond-hard steel. Its fragments sang viciously through the air, ripping up planking here and cutting through a stanchion there, but they found no one in an exposed position, and they took no lives. The force of its explosion shook the group on the signal bridge, they felt the hot breath of its flame, and their nostrils were filled with the penetrating stink of its fumes, but they were unhurt. Perhaps of all the hits scored by *Artemis'* guns this one did the least physical damage, but for all that it was the one which turned the scale. All the other shells fired by *Artemis* had played their part, had leaded the scale so far, had worked upon the minds of Nocentini and von Bödicke, convincing them that here were no easy victims, no weak-minded enemies to be driven off by a mere show of force; but it was this last shell, which Colquhoun had lifted so casually, and which Mobbs and Filmore had sent up to 'A' turret with their minds occupied by Ransome's peevishness, and upon which Sub-Lieutenant Coxe had cast an unseeing eye while Merivale rammed it home, it was this shell bursting vainly against the turret that actually decided the history of the world.

Nocentini and von Bödicke looked at each other again as they steadied themselves after the explosion. Each was unhurt, each of them hoped breathlessly in his heart of hearts that the other was not. For one second more they hesitated, each hoping that the other would assume the responsibility for the next move, and during that second each of them read the added weakness in the other's face, and they both of them realized that there was no need to state formally what was in their minds. It would be better not to do so, they both decided; it gave each of them more chance to shuffle off the blame – if there was to be blame – upon the other. They did not meet each other's eyes after that; von Bödicke looked at Klein while Nocentini turned to Lorenzetti.

'Signal all ships turn together eight points to starboard,' said Nocentini. He was shoulder to shoulder with von Bödicke, and he did his best to convey by his bearing the impression that the two of them were in agreement on the decision, while von Bödicke, the moment he heard the decisive words, tried to put himself in an attitude of ineffective protest without attracting Nocentini's attention to it.

The flags ran up to the yardarm, flapped there in the smoke, were answered and were hauled down. Slowly *Legnano* turned her ponderous bulk about, her bows towards Italy, her stern to the British squadron.

'We had to do it,' said Nocentini. 'Otherwise we would have crossed the course of the torpedoes.'

Von Bödicke kept his mouth shut; he only just grasped the meaning of the Italian words, and he was not going to commit himself to anything that might later be construed as approval. He felt much happier in the probability that Nocentini could be saddled with the blame. He walked stiffly to the other end of the bridge, meeting no one's eye as the staffs made way for him, and for Nocentini at his elbow.

From the starboard wing of the bridge he could look down the long line abreast of the Italian fleet. The heavy cruiser on the far side of *San Martino* was still badly on fire. That would be part of his defence, if he should need defence. The guns had fallen silent, for the sudden change of course had disconcerted the trainers, and only half of *Legnano*'s armament could bear on a target right astern. And yet at that very moment another broadside from the British came crashing home as though the ship were suddenly struck by a Titanic sledgehammer. Some fragment hurled by the explosion rang loudly against the stanchion at his side. It was the last straw to von Bödicke that the British should persist in continuing the fight when he had allowed it to be broken off on the Italian side. He wanted to relax, to allow the tension to lessen, and yet the British were set upon continuing the action to the last possible moment. *Legnano*'s upperworks aft were riven into picturesque ruin, he saw. No vital damage done, but enough to make a deep impression on any civilian who might see it. That was all to the good. But Klein knew better. Klein, who had crossed the bridge and was standing at his elbow again, and whom he suspected strongly of being a spy on behalf of Fricke. Von Bödicke hated Klein.

'They are holding their course,' said Nocentini from behind his binoculars, which were trained on the British cruisers. He was speaking careful French, and von Bödicke realized that although the words were apparently addressed to him, Nocentini meant them to be recorded by Klein. 'They will not leave their smoke-screen.'

'That is clear,' said von Bödicke, agreeing speedily. He hoped as he spoke them Klein would not perceive the stilted artificiality of his tone; it was ingenious of Nocentini to suggest that the turn-away was really planned to lure the British cruisers away from their smoke-screen.

'We will re-form line ahead when the torpedoes have passed,' said Nocentini.

'Of course,' said von Bödicke. He had himself under control now. He kept his eyes steadily on the Italian and did now allow them to waver towards Klein for a moment. It was undignified and sordid, but defeat is always undignified and sordid. They were beaten men.

They were already out of range of the British cruisers, and the distance was increasing every minute. When they should form line ahead again and circle round to reopen the engagement it would be nearly dark, and no sane officer would court a night action with an inferior force. Someone was yelling madly from the masthead, his high-pitched voice clearly audible from the signal bridge, although von Bödicke could not understand the excited Italian. *Legnano* swung ponderously round again, under full helm, first to port and then to starboard – it was that, combined with the rush of the Italian officers to the side, and the way they peered down at the water, which told von Bödicke that the track of the torpedo had been sighted, and that *Legnano* was manoeuvring to avoid it. He caught his breath quickly. The gestures of the Italians showed that the torpedo had passed, and then directly afterwards there came the roar of an explosion to split the eardrums. The torpedo which *Legnano* had avoided had struck *San Martino* full in the side. An enormous column of water, higher than the funnel top, obscured the battleship momentarily before it cascaded back into the sea and revealed her with smoke pouring out of her side and listing perceptibly.

He caught Nocentini's eye again as the Admiral stood rapping out orders. The anxiety and strain had gone from the man's face. He was dealing with a familiar emergency, one with which he was competent to deal. Salving and protecting an injured ship was not like carrying the burden of the responsibility of battle. And not only that, but the problems of battle were solved for him. No one could expect him to leave an injured Dreadnought to shift for herself while he turned and re-engaged the enemy. No one could expect him to. A Nelson or a Beatty might take the risk, but no man could be condemned for not being a Nelson or Beatty. Nocentini actually smiled a little as he met von Bödicke's eye, and von Bödicke smiled back. Whatever happened now, they had at least an explanation and an excuse.

CHAPTER 26

FROM THE CAPTAIN'S REPORT

. . . and the action terminated.

The Captain had known temptation. With *Artemis* all ablaze aft, and one turret out of action, it was a strain to keep her in action, dodging the continual salvoes of the enemy. The very din of the continual broadsides was exhausting. Close at hand, on the port side, was the shelter of the smoke-screen. He had only to utter two words and *Artemis* could dive into it just as she had done before. There would be a relief from strain and danger and responsibility, and the thought even of relief that might be only momentary was alluring. And the whole principle of the tactics of the British cruisers was to make use of the smoke-screen as it rolled down on the Italian line; now that the destroyers had delivered their attack and turned back would be a fitting moment, ostensibly, for a temporary withdrawal. That was the temptation on the one hand, while on the other was the doubt of his own judgement that it was desirable to continue in action. That might be just fighting madness. He knew that his judgement might be clouded, that this decision of his to keep his guns firing might be the result of mere berserk rage. Yet his instinct told him that it was not so.

His instinct; something developed in him by years of study of his profession, of deep reading and of mental digestion of innumerable lessons, supplemented by his inborn qualities. That instinct told him that this was the crisis of the battle, the moment when one side or the other must give way. He knew that he had only to hold on a little longer – after that a little longer still, perhaps – for the battle to be decided. The whole series of thoughts, from the decision to cover the retreat of the destroyers to the momentary doubt, and then back again to the decision to maintain the action took only the briefest possible time, two or three seconds at most.

It was not to the discredit of the Captain that he should have experienced that two or three seconds of doubt, but to his credit. Had he not been tried so far as that it would have been no trial at all. War is something to try the very strongest, and it is then that those crack who are almost the strongest, the Nocentinis and the von Bödickes, oppressed by a complexity of motives.

The Captain was aware that his pipe was empty, and that he wanted to refill and relight it, but he did not want to take his binoculars from his eyes. The guns of 'A' and 'B' turrets roared out below him; the Captain did not know that from the left-hand gun of 'A' turret had flown the decisive shell. He saw the flight of the broadside, and he saw the yellow flash of the hit. Then, as another broadside roared out disregarded, he saw the long silhouette of the leading Italian battleship foreshorten and alter, the two funnels blend into one, the stern swinging towards him and the bow away. The Captain gulped excitedly. He traversed his binoculars round. Every Italian ship had her stern to him; it was a withdrawal, a retreat; the Italian flagship was not merely trying to disconnect the English gunners. This was victory.

He turned his gaze back to the Italian flagship in time to see the flash of another hit upon her. Good gunnery, that, to hit at that extreme range and with the range altering so fast. He dropped his glasses on his chest and took out pipe and pouch, feeding tobacco into the bowl with his long sensitive fingers, but his eyes still strained after the distant shapes on the horizon. They had turned away. They were refusing battle. The Captain knew in his bones that they would never turn back again to reopen the fight. A motive strong enough to induce them to break off the fight would be amply strong enough to keep them from renewing it; one way or the other they would find excuses for themselves.

His pipe was filled, and he was just reaching for his matches when the voice-pipe buzzer sounded:

'Director Control,' said the pipe. 'The enemy is out of range.'

'Thank you, Guns,' said the Captain. 'I have no orders for you at present.'

The Chief Yeoman of Signals saluted.

'I think I saw a torpedo 'it on the second ship from the left,' he said, 'while you was speaking.'

'Thank you,' said the Captain again.

He was about to take up his binoculars to look, but he changed his mind and felt for his matches instead. He could afford to be prodigal of his time and his attention now. Even a torpedo hit on a Dreadnought was nothing in the scale compared with the fact of the Italian turn-away. The tobacco tasted good as he drew the flame of the match down upon it, stoppered it down with the finger that long use had rendered comparatively fireproof, and drew on the flame again. He breathed out a lungful of smoke and carefully dropped the stump of the match into the spit-kid. The silence and the cessation of the enemy's fire were ceasing to be oppressive; the normal sounds of the ship's progress, the noise of the sea under the bows and of the wind about his ears, were asserting themselves.

So this was victory. The proof that the history of the world had reached a turning point was that he was conscious again of the wind about his ears. History books would never write about today. Even sober, scientific historians needed some more solid fact on which to hang a theme; a few ships sunk and a few thousand men killed, not a mere successful skirmish round half a dozen transports. Even in a month's time the memory of today would be faded and forgotten by the world. Two lines in a communiqué, a few remarks by appreciative com-mentators, and then oblivion.

Somewhere out in the Russian plain Ivan Ivanovich, crouching in a hole in the dusty earth, and looking along the sights of his anti-tank gun, would never know about *Artemis* and her sisters. Ivan Ivanovich might comment on the slightness of the aerial attack, on the scarcity of hostile dive bombers; it might even occur to him as a realist that a few well-placed bombs, wiping out him and his fellows, could clear the way into Moscow for Hitler, but even as a realist Ivan Ivanovich had never heard of *Artemis*, and never would hear.

To Hitler, Malta was a prize still more desirable than Moscow, and more vital to his existence. With the failure of the Italian navy to get it for him he would have to use his own air force; a thousand planes, and a ground staff scores of thousands strong would have to be transferred from the Russian front to Italy in the desperate need to conquer every bastion that could buttress his top-heavy empire. A thousand planes; planes that could blind the Russian command, planes that could blast a path through the Russian lines, planes that could succour isolated detachments and supply advance guards, planes that could hunt Russian guerilla forces far in the rear of the Germans or menace Russian communications far in advance. The Captain had no doubt whatever that as a result of todays's work those thousand planes would be brought south.

Whether they would achieve their object or not was more doubtful. The Captain had the feeling that the advocates of air power talked about today as if it were tomorrow. Tomorrow command of the air might take the place of command of the sea, but this was today. Today those half-dozen fat transports wallowing along on the far side of the smoke-screen were on their way to Malta, and it was today they had to be stopped, if at all. Today the convoys were still pouring in to English harbours, while across a tiny strip of water lay an enemy whose greatest ambition was to prevent them from doing so. It was sea power that brought them safely in. Tomorrow it might be air power; tomorrow the Captain might be an antiquated old fogey, as useless as a pikeman on a modern battlefield, but the war was being fought today, today, today. Rommel in Libya clamouring for reinforcement could have everything his heart desired if the British Navy did not interfere. The crippling of the American Navy at Pearl Harbor had put an eighth of the world's population and a quarter of the world's surface temporarily at the mercy of Japan and her twelve Dreadnoughts. Ships – ships and the men in them – were still deciding the fate of the world. The Arab fertilizing date palms at Basra, the Negro trading cattle for a new wife in Central Africa, the gaucho riding the Argentine pampas, did so under the protection of the British Navy, of which the Captain and his ship were a minor fraction, one of many parts whose sum was equal to the whole.

'Signal from the flagship, sir,' said the Chief Yeoman of Signals, reading it off through his glass: 'Resume – convoy – formation.'

'Acknowledge,' said the Captain.

He gave the order to turn *Artemis* back towards the transports, back through the smoke-screen which had served them so well. The revolution indicator rang down a reduction of speed, and peace seemed to settle closer about the ship as the vibration caused by full speed died away. Only a tiny bit of the sun was left, a segment of gold on the clear horizon – ten seconds more and it would be gone and night would close in. The Italians were already invisible from the bridge, and the Captain strode abruptly over to the masthead voice-pipe.

'Masthead,' said the tube to him in answer to his buzz. It was Ordinary-Seaman Whipple's voice.

'Can you see anything of the enemy?' asked the Captain.

'Only just in sight, sir. They're still heading away from us. They'll be gone in a minute.'

They were close clipped, incisive sentences which Whipple used. Whipple was conscious of victory, too. He was fighting for an ideal, and he was fanatical about that ideal, and this afternoon's work had brought that ideal a great deal closer. Yet Whipple did not indulge in idle exhilaration. The fact that he had to fight for his ideal, that the generation preceding his had once had the same ideal in their grasp and allowed it to slip through their fingers, had left him without illusions. Whipple was ready to go on fighting. He knew there was still a long bitter struggle ahead before final victory, and he guessed that after victory it would be another bitter struggle to put it to the best use, to forward the ideal, and he was ready for both struggles.

The Captain in his present clairvoyant mood could sense all this in the tone of Whipple's voice, and he drew once, meditatively, on his pipe before he turned away. One part of his mind was concerned in practical fashion with the future promotion of Whipple to Leading Seaman; the other was thinking how Whipple's generation, twenty years younger than his own, must take up the task of building the good of the new world as unfalteringly as they were applying themselves to the task of tearing down the evil of the old world, in each case facing random defeat, and unexpected disappointment, and peril and self-sacrifice, with selfless self-discipline.

As he looked up from the voice-pipe his eyes met those of his secretary.

'Congratulations, sir,' said Jerningham.

So Jerningham was aware of the importance of today, too. The rest of the ship's company, going quietly about their duties, had not yet attained to that realization. But it was to be expected of Jerningham. His civilian background, the breadth of his experience and the liveliness of his imagination, made him able – when he was not too closely concerned personally – to take a wide view of the war, and to realize how proper attention to his own duties would help Ivan Ivanovich in his hole in the ground, of Lai Chao tearing up a railway line in Shantung. There was a moment of sympathy between Jerningham and the Captain, during which brief space of time they were *en rapport*, each appreciative of the other.

'Thank you, Jerningham,' said the Captain.

This was no time to relax, to indulge either in futile congratulations or in idle speculation. The smoke-screen suddenly engulfed the ship; it was not nearly as dense as when it had first been laid, but with the rapid approach of night now that the sun was below the horizon the darkness inside the smoke-screen was intense. The Captain took three strides in the darkness to the end of the bridge and craned his neck to look aft. There was only the faintest glow to be seen of the fire which had raged there, and a few more minutes with the hoses would extinguish even that.

They emerged into the evening light again; the scant minute during which they had been in the smoke-screen seemed to have brought night far closer. There was just light enough to see how the fires and the enemy's hits had left the whole after third of the ship above water-line a tangle of burnt-out steel, a nightmare of buckled plates and twisted girders, desolate and dead.

Artemis under the orders of the Navigating Lieutenant was wheeling round to take the station allotted her by the standing orders for convoy escort at night. It was as well that the fires had been subdued, for otherwise the flames would be a welcoming beacon inviting a torpedo. The aeroplanes had attacked in the morning; in the afternoon they had beaten off the surface ships; tonight they would have to be on their guard against submarines, for the enemy, like the devil, was capable of taking many forms. One battle completed, one victory achieved, merely meant that *Artemis* and her men must plunge headlong into the next, into the long struggle of sea power against tyranny; the struggle that the Greeks had waged at Salamis, that the Captain's ancestors had waged against the Armada of Spain, against the fleets of Louis XIV and Napoleon and Wilhelm II, the long struggle which some day would have an end, but not now, and not for months and years to come. And even when it should end the freedom which the struggle would win could only be secured by eternal vigilance, eternal probity, eternal good will, and eternal honesty of purpose. That would be the hardest lesson of it; peace would be a severer test of mankind even than war. Perhaps mankind would pass that test when the time came; and when that time came (the Captain said to himself) he would fight to the last, he would die in the last ditch, before he would compromise in the slightest with the blind or secret enemies of freedom and justice. He must remember this mood; when he became an old man he must remember it. He must remember in time to come how nothing now was further from his thoughts than the least yielding to the open enemies of mankind, and that would help to keep him from the least indolent or careless or cynical yielding in that future.

The Captain suddenly tensed himself as his roving eyes caught sight of a twinkle of light ahead, and then he was able to relax again and even smile a little to himself in the twilight. For that was the evening star shining out over the Mediterranean.

THE END

Dive in the Sun

DOUGLAS REEMAN

CHAPTER 1

The night was moonless and very dark, and the black heaving water of the Adriatic moved uneasily in an oily, sullen swell. Occasionally the ebony water reflected a tiny pin-prick of light from one of the small stars, which seemed very high and aloof from the sea beneath, while from the invisible Italian coastline a small, hot breeze clawed weakly across the dull surface.

A watcher, had there been one, would have caught the briefest glimpse of a slender, stick-like object which rose rapidly out of the depths, throwing up a tiny feather of white spray as it cut through the water, like the antennae of a forgotten sea-monster.

The periscope vanished, as suddenly as it appeared, and for a short while the sea was again empty and desolate, then, with a surge of foam and spray, the sea was churned into a frightened torment, and the hard, streaming shape of the submarine rose gracelessly into view, the pressurized air hissing in a subdued roar, as water was forced from the ballast tanks, and the disturbed waves cascaded across the canting steel hull.

Within seconds, the confined space of the bridge above the conning-tower was filled with silent, purposeful figures, as the lookouts carefully scanned every inch of the surrounding area with their night-glasses, while on the casing below, the gun's crew stood huddled around their weapon, their hands reaching for the prepared shells, and smoothing away the dampness from the controls.

The Officer of the Watch relaxed slightly, as each man reported his horizon clear, and concentrated instead on adjusting the towel around his neck as a protection against the spray which drifted lazily over the squat bridge each time that the stem cut deep into the resisting waves. The electric motors died away, and were replaced instantly by the muffled thud, thud, thud of the powerful diesels, and he felt the air being sucked down into the open hatch behind him; air to feed the engines, which, in turn, would feed the starved batteries. In his mind's eye he could picture the too-familiar scene beneath his feet. The relaxing grins of the seamen, as they prepared to enjoy that first cigarette after surfacing. The watchful eye of the First Lieutenant, as he studied the compass, and passed his curt orders to the coxswain. The metallic clatter of countless pieces of intricate machinery, and the gleam of subdued lighting reflecting against the brass dials and greased periscopes. He stiffened automatically as another figure clambered over the hatch coaming and took his place beside him.

The captain glanced perfunctorily through his glasses, and checked the lookouts, before he squinted at the luminous dial of his watch.

'Just about time, Pilot,' he said at length. 'She'll be popping up any second now!'

They trained their glasses over the rear of the bridge, their eyes straining against the darkness, and trying to peer beyond the green and blue phosphorescence which danced crazily around the submarine's wake.

There was a strange air of tension on the bridge, and as the seconds ticked past, each man felt a rising edge of alarm.

Then, as they waited, the dark water took on a more definite shape, and slowly and painfully, the blurred outline of another craft rose quietly above the white track of their wake.

Occasionally, the tow-line tautened and whipped angrily above the wave-crests, and the other craft would veer round unhappily before being brought under control by its hidden helmsman.

The captain chuckled quietly. 'Well, there she is! Our midget submarine is still with us!'

He spoke lightly, but the other officer had watched him closely during the last six days and had seen all too clearly the immense strain on his captain's thin face. Six days of bitter anxiety as they had towed the tiny submarine and its deadly cargo across the war-torn Mediterranean, from Malta around the 'heel' of Italy, and steadily northwards up the hostile waters of the narrow Adriatic.

And now, nearly four hundred miles along the Italian coastline, his responsibility was practically over. It would soon be time to drop the tow and leave the little, fifty-foot miniature of his own boat to carry on with its dangerous mission.

He paused at the top of the hatch. 'Call me the second you sight anything,' he said unnecessarily, 'and watch the tow-line. We don't want anything to go wrong now!'

He clattered down the shiny ladder to the control-room, brushing past the next group of lookouts, who stood, their eyes covered with dark glasses, and smoking beneath the hatch, like a collection of blind men, and walked tiredly across to his First Lieutenant.

'All clear, Number One,' he nodded. 'The midget has surfaced quite well, and I'll be taking off the passage-crew any minute now. I'll just have a word with her operational crew before they take over, and go over the details again with her skipper.'

'I'd rather them than me, sir! People think *this* job is bad enough, but at least there's room enough to stand up!'

The captain yawned and stretched his cramped shoulders, his eyes resting momentarily on the pale, tired faces of his men, and his nose taking in the sour odour of oil and sweat, of damp clothing and stale food.

'It's a long war,' he remarked indifferently, 'and I'll never forgive Their Lordships for passing this towing job on to me. I've had to pass up several good targets because of it!' He frowned as he thought of his silent torpedoes lying peacefully in their tubes, and of the merchant-ships which had crossed his sights during the last few days. But his orders had left him in no doubt. He was to tow the midget submarine, *XE.51*, to a point thirty miles east of Rimini, and do nothing to arouse the enemy's suspicion, or give them cause to suspect any hostile activity in what was practically 'untried ground'.

'D'you think they'll have any luck, sir?'

The captain paused in his stride by the chart-table and leaned the faded elbows of his stained jacket on the chart. He checked the wavering pencilled line of their course and the small cross which marked the end of the journey.

'They must!' It was a flat statement. 'In twenty-four hours' time Italy will be invaded from the south and south-west by our chaps and the Yanks, and all hell will be let loose.' He tapped the chart with a pair of brass dividers. 'Here, the port of Vigoria – not much to look at, is it? But Intelligence and R.A.F. Recce have reported that the Jerries have got their biggest floating dock moored there. If the Allied invasion gets started all right in the south, it'll be their *only* floating dock which is big enough to handle their big stuff – cruisers and the like. If they got one whiff of what we're up to they'd tow the blessed thing across the Adriatic to Split, and could do all their repairs there. It could make a big difference to their surface forces.' He shrugged again. 'So, Number One, our little friend is going to take care of it!'

They stood looking at the chart in silence, visualizing the harbour defences, patrol boats, mines, and the inevitable uncertainty of Intelligence reports.

'We'll rendezvous with them afterwards, as arranged, and tow 'em back. Simple, eh, Number One?'

A shadow darkened the chart-table, and they turned to face the giant of a man who stood loosely beside them. All of six feet tall, he was powerfully built to the extent of clumsiness, but there was nothing awkward or slow in his square, unshaven face and cool, grey eyes, nor in the hard set of his jaw which jutted forward in a half-humorous, half-mocking grin. On the shoulder of his battledress blouse he carried the word 'Australia'.

Lieutenant 'Steve' Duncan, R.A.N.V.R., First Lieutenant of *XE.51*, eyed the two officers calmly, his big, square hands resting on his hips. He was most people's idea of the typical Australian, outspoken, tough, and seemingly larger than life. When he spoke, his voice was surprisingly low and well-modulated, and his hard, Queensland drawl made an incongruous note in the humid control-room.

'I've just been listening to you chaps,' he remarked slowly, 'and I'd like to point out that you're talking the sort of complete drivel which I'm beginning to believe is typical of everything in this war that I hate most!' He smiled gently, as if amused at the cold hostility in the submarine commander's eyes or by the look of alarm shown by the other officer, as he darted a quick glance at his captain's faded gold lace, which proclaimed him not only a regular officer, but two ranks senior to the Australian lieutenant.

The captain smiled thinly and pressed the palms of his hands against the edge of the chart-table.

'What is ailing our Colonial friend now?' He had got used to his imperturbable passenger during the slow passage, and had somehow avoided any definite argument, but on several occasions it had been a near thing. The trip was almost over. He felt he could now afford the luxury of tearing the man's arguments to shreds.

'Well.' Duncan rubbed his bristled chin pensively, his clear eyes staring hard at the dripping side of the hull, as if penetrating the metal, and already staring at his nearing objective. 'I think this is a duff trip! I reckon it won't matter a tinker's damn if we go after the dock or let it stay where it is!' He returned his steady gaze to each of the others in turn. 'Furthermore, I guess that if the Allied invasion of Italy depended on the sinking of a blessed dock, it'd be a pretty crook effort! No,' he shook his head slowly, 'it's just another small, crack-pot scheme that some joker has had in London or someplace, and it's snowballed into a "must", something that everyone now thinks is essential.' He guffawed deeply. 'Only thing is, they forgot it's going to be damn dangerous for some poor suckers to carry out!'

'You mean, you don't think you're capable?' The tone was cutting.

'Capable? Well, isn't that typical again? Just because some poor, ignorant Aussie has the effrontery to question the realism of his orders, you immediately take it as a personal insult!' He shook his head sadly, but the deep crowsfeet at the sides of his eyes revealed the hidden humour he was finding so enjoyable. 'We can do it all right! I've been in tougher spots than this before.' He waved his hands vaguely. 'All over the joint! Norway, up the Channel, and even down at Taranto. But those efforts were almost worth the sweat! No, we can do it all right, but I'm sick to death of being told to be a good boy, an' die for my country. Whose country, for Chrissake?'

'Now, look here——' began the other officer angrily, but the captain stopped him with a jerk of his head.

'All right, so you're capable. What does your skipper think about it? Does he think it's a waste of time, too?'

'Ralph Curtis? He's different.' A faraway look crept into his eyes. 'He's a natural, a born skipper. He can take a midget sub through the saloon bar of the "Royal George" an' no one would spot him. I've been on every operation with him right from the start. I'd not go with another. In fact, we've always been a team, up to the last job, when we lost our diver. But me an' the skipper, an' old George Taylor, the E.R.A., we've hung together like dung on a blanket!' He grinned broadly. 'Still, we've got a new diver for this job.' He looked at the captain cheerfully. 'A brand new sub-lieutenant, and the only regular officer in the crew. Still, he doesn't seem a bad cove for all that!'

There was a pregnant silence, and the shipboard noises seemed to move in on them. The clatter of a pump and the crackle of Morse from the radio-room, and in the far distance the sound of a plaintive mouth-organ.

A short, wiry petty officer, his body tightly encased in padded buoyant trousers and battledress blouse, with a pistol hanging from his hip, padded quietly down the control-room. He tried to side-step the three officers, but Duncan pulled him into the group with as little effort as a man picking up a dog.

'Say, George,' he said casually, 'the captain here says we're on to a real good thing! Isn't he just a smart one?'

Petty Officer George Taylor sighed deeply. He had been through all this before, in a dozen ports, with a dozen different kinds of results. Always Duncan had dragged him into one argument after another, seemingly for the pleasure of seeing the displeasure on the other officers' faces at having a ranker drawn into an intimate conversation.

Taylor was a Londoner, born and reared in Hackney, and until the war had called him had served happily, if not ambitiously, in a large garage and service station in Mare Street. Nothing had mattered much in those days, and the outside world had been something either to avoid or to ignore. He had contented himself with 'nights out' with the boys, beer and chips at the old Hackney Empire, and a good scrap at the Fascist meetings over in Dalston on a Saturday night. If anyone had told him that one day he'd be sweating in an engine-room of a midget submarine, a space with less room to move about than the back of an Austin Seven, while it slid silently under a watchful German warship, or played tag among the minefields, he would have told him to ' 'ave 'is 'ead tested!' He was a quiet, unimaginative man, but like so many of his breed, completely fearless and difficult to shock.

'I just bin with the blokes in the P.O.'s Mess 'ere,' he commented, as if he hadn't heard Duncan's remarks. 'Real nice little place it is, too, when there ain't so many blokes in it.' He cocked his head on one side. 'You called the skipper yet?'

'Nope. I aim to let him get all the sleep he can.' He turned to the submarine's captain. 'You ready to get rid of us yet?'

The man smiled. 'More than I can tell you.'

At that moment the loose green curtain across the tiny wardroom entrance jerked to one side and a slim, dark-haired figure yawned and stretched hugely in the opening. In his new battledress and spotless white sweater, Sub-Lieutenant Ian Jervis looked little more than a boy, and at nineteen his round, youthful face and smooth pink cheeks gave the impression that he was merely playing at some new game and was obviously enjoying every minute of it.

'Aha, our wayward diver!' grated Duncan. 'An' about time, too! All ready to leave this palatial scow, Ian?'

Jervis smiled readily, although he always felt uneasy and slightly nervous with this great Australian. After his Dartmouth training, and coming from a family which had boasted several admirals, including his father, he had never quite been able to accept the atmosphere of unreality and casual indifference which seemed to pervade the men of the newest arm of the Service. He was, as Duncan had pointed out, the only regular in the crew, and he couldn't help feeling that he didn't quite belong. Whether it was as simple as that, or whether it was because he was only a new replacement for the other diver who had been killed, he couldn't quite decide, but it was there all right. Then there was the skipper, Lieutenant Curtis. He remembered so vividly his first interview with him at Gibraltar when he had reported for duty.

The skipper had been sitting in his cabin on the submarine depot ship, apparently staring into space. Before Jervis could introduce himself, Curtis had sprung to his feet, his face white, his eyes suddenly alive and bright. He had stared for seconds at the startled Jervis, and then shaken him briefly by the hand and muttered something about being 'in a daze', and had been quite friendly. But several times since then, and especially on the towing trip in the submarine, he had caught Curtis staring at him bleakly, his eyes dark.

He had tried to tackle Duncan on the subject, but he had been unhelpful and had joked at his boyish fancies. Or had he just been evasive?

He had wanted to ask Taylor, who seemed to be a pretty level-headed sort of chap. But there was always the question of rank, and his own unwillingness to start something he couldn't finish.

He wrote regularly to his mother, and occasionally to his father, who, much to his own annoyance, was in charge of a shore-establishment, and had tried to describe his job and his companions. Duncan was an easy character to put in a letter, with his peculiar sayings which for the most part were quite above Jervis and seemed vaguely crude, and his rebellious attitude to the Service in general and regular officers in particular. But Curtis was different, and each time he tried to explain the man to his parents he realized that his words bordered on the most juvenile hero-worship that he would hardly have believed possible of himself.

He had heard about him when he had been under training as a diver for midget submarines. About the escapades in Norway, when he had won the Distinguished Service Cross, and about his daring and cool courage in pressing home his attacks to lay his two-ton explosive charges beneath the unsuspecting enemy. But it was more than the hearsay; it was the man himself. Tall and slim, his shoulders slightly stooped from the constant cramping confinement of the tiny hulls, he had a strange dedicated hardness in his otherwise calm face, which made him older than his twenty-six years. He had a friendly smile, and had always shown willingness to overlook Jervis' early discomfort, but in his eyes he seemed to hold a reserve, a strange barrier, as if he was watching, waiting for something to happen. It was obviously something new, because he had heard Duncan asking Taylor, the E.R.A., if he thought 'the skipper was goin' round the bend?'

He ran his fingers through his short wavy hair and grinned. 'I'm ready and willing!'

Duncan jabbed him in the ribs and leered. 'Don't talk like that in front of these two jokers; you know what they say about submariners!'

Jervis coloured and glanced anxiously at the captain. The latter had turned his back on them, however, and was staring at the chart.

'Shall I call the skipper, Steve?' Jervis asked hurriedly.

The captain suddenly stood up from the table. 'Yes, call him,' he said curtly. 'Tell him I'm going to put over the rubber dinghy to take off the passage crew.'

'Poor chaps,' chuckled Duncan. 'The towing crew have had the job of looking after the midget all the way here, an' now we take over for the best part!'

The captain eyed him coldly, a glint in his red-rimmed eyes. 'It's a pity it's all a waste of time then, isn't it?'

. . .

Lieutenant Ralph Curtis lay fully clothed on a bunk in the submarine's wardroom, his hands knitted behind his head, his eyes wide and sleepless, staring at the curved metal hull which rose over his body like the side of a tomb. The curtain which he had drawn along the length of the bunk allowed the harsh wardroom light to filter eerily across his tanned face and fair, sun-bleached hair, and beyond it he heard Duncan's booming laugh and the subdued mutter of con-

versation. On the other side of the steel plating he imagined he could
hear the swish of the Adriatic against the saddle tanks as the submarine
forged her way through the night, her small charge wallowing behind
her like a calf following its mother. He pressed his eyes shut for the
hundredth time, but although sleep had eluded him for days, he felt the
nervous tension running through him like an electric current, making
his heart and body throb with something like pain.

What had happened? What had changed his life from a breath-taking
adventure to a living nightmare?

He sighed deeply, and tried to stop himself from going over it all
again.

He gingerly allowed his mind to explore the future, and felt himself
pulling back, his stomach contracting violently. He touched his
forehead dazedly, feeling the cold layer of sweat which chilled his face
into a tight mask. He shuddered violently. Fear. Ice-cold fear. He could
almost see his father's steady, unwavering gaze across the wide, littered
desk.

'No guts, my lad! That's what's wrong with your generation!' Then
there would be a pause. 'Now, look at me. A self-made man. Built up this
business from nothing, just to give you the chance I never had!' His
father, even across the miles of invisible ocean, his words, his very soul
reached out to taunt and torture him.

Curtis thought of his father, probably sitting behind that same desk,
dealing with new orders for light machinery – or whatever he was
making now – drumming into his employees how important it was to
help the war effort, and, of course, to enlarge the business.

Beyond the curtain Duncan laughed again, and for a brief instant
Curtis felt the tinge of jealousy. Duncan, with his indomitable spirit and
unwavering strength. He had served with him long enough to know him
better than anyone he had ever met, and he had pictured so often the
huge Australian astride his pony on his vast farm, trotting through the
dust, exchanging jests with his father or his three brothers, and
planning, always planning some new improvement which in itself would
entail fresh labour and sweat before anything would show on the
shimmering, dust-blown wastes of his untamed country.

And Taylor, the E.R.A., did he envy him, too? He twisted his head on
the coarse pillow as if to banish the nagging fears in his brain. Taylor, the
personification of the British working class. Hard, shrewd, but gentle,
and with a strange contentment which left Curtis baffled.

Before it hadn't mattered. They had all been the closely-knit crew of a
midget submarine, the most lonely and the most dangerous section of
any navy in the world.

His mind ground remorselessly on. That had been before Roberts had
been killed.

His lips framed the unspoken words. 'Before *I* killed him!'

He opened his eyes suddenly, his whole body trembling, and stared hard the shining deckhead. He remembered that day on the depot ship, only a month ago, when young Jervis had arrived to replace Roberts. It had seemed impossible at the time, the cruellest stroke which fate could possibly have played. As the boy had stepped into his cabin, with the bright sun behind him, it was as if Roberts had come back from the dead.

He had questioned Duncan casually about the frightening likeness, but he had shrugged indifferently and said that there might be some likeness, but not so that you'd notice.

Curtis clenched his jaw tightly, his eyes watering. Some likeness! Were they blind? Or was he going mad?

A bell clanged in the engine-room and the beat of the engines slackened. It would be soon now. Soon he and the other three would be sealed in their little craft, and it would be too late.

He rolled over on to his side, biting at the pillow. Fear, when did it come to him? When did he first notice that the blood of courage had begun to freeze within him?

Soon it would be too late. The words beat like tiny engines in his skull.

This was the most dangerous escapade that they had attempted, and the most useless.

Before, it had been a mad, hit-and-run game, with no time to think, and the wild ecstasy of success to follow. But now, a floating dock in the middle of a hostile coastline, with little chance of survival however the attack turned out, and in addition, he was afraid. Desperately afraid – from his shaking hands, to the dry, bitter taste in his throat. He would refuse to go, and tell himself it was for the others' sakes and not for his own.

His father appeared again, mocking him with his smooth, shining face and well-clipped moustache. He knew what he would say all right. He remembered how he had fought desperately against the steady succession of planned moves which his father had called 'your future with the company'. The good school, mixing with boys whose only right to any future had been their birth, while he had had his bought in hard-earned money. Boys like Jervis, he thought suddenly, quiet, confident, decent chaps, who never spoke of money or business.

The war had been a blessing for Curtis, and he had fled from the factory and the board meetings, and the hard, probing tongue of his father, with something like relief.

It was that compelling urge to escape from his past of frustration and lack of purpose which had made him volunteer for midget submarines, and which had led him eventually to his own command.

He had looked then to his father for some small sign of faith, if not actual pride, but he had only written to complain of the time Curtis was wasting in the Service, time which the factory could not forgive or overlook.

When he had been awarded the D.S.C. after the Norwegian operations his father merely observed, 'Well, it might look all right on the company's notepaper, I suppose!'

That had been the last straw. Curtis had driven himself unmercifully, taking each operation with cold, calculated calm, and drawing closer to Duncan and the others for the comfort which had been denied him elsewhere.

Then it had happened, without warning, and like a stab in the heart. At Taranto, whilst attempting to lay the deadly charges beneath an Italian supply ship, they had become entangled in an anti-submarine net of a new, unknown pattern, which wrapped itself around the little submarine like a shroud.

Roberts, the diver, had given them a shaky grin and slithered into the Wet and Dry compartment and out through the hastily flooded hatch, and within seconds he was hard at work with the cutters, sawing his way through the slime-covered mesh of the net. Curtis watched him through the periscope, and saw his dim shape, with the pale blob for a face, twisting and turning, back and forth across the hull, barely visible in the dark gloom of forty feet of water. The patrol boat had found them just as the last strand was cut, and they heard the sharp ping of the submarine-detector echo against the hull as the invisible boat moved into the attack.

They had done this thing many times before, in many parts of the enemy's waters, but this time the diver was practically exhausted and had hardly the strength to pull himself back to the safety of the hatch.

Nearer and nearer thundered the racing engine of the attacking boat, and his scalp had tingled with the agony of suspense as he imagined the depth charges waiting to plummet down onto a trapped, unmoving target.

It was then that his last reserve had snapped and he gave Duncan the order to go ahead.

The midget submarine moved reluctantly from the pile of severed mesh, the ragged, knife-like ends clawing scratchily along the hull, screeching and moaning. Or perhaps it was Roberts crying out as the strands of wire ripped open his suit and carried his writhing body down to the bottom of the harbour.

The submarine had escaped, the supply ship blew up, and Curtis and the others were commended.

But somewhere at the bottom of that far-off harbour, between the twisted metal of the sunken supply ship and the tattered diving suit, Curtis' courage and confidence lay as surely as dead men.

There was a dull, metallic thud overhead, as the deck party prepared to lever the rubber dinghy out of the opened hatch, and Curtis heard the muffled bark of orders, and knew that at any second he would be required to show himself to the others.

As if in answer to his racing thoughts the curtain twitched to one side, and Jervis, his pink face gleaming with excitement, looked over the side of the bunk.

'All ready to go, sir,' his voice shook breathlessly. 'The captain says he's ready to put us across to our midget!'

Curtis swallowed hard and pressed his lips into a thin line in an effort to remove the loose feeling from his mouth. He tried not to stare at the boy's eager face, and instead began to fumble with his clothing and boots.

'Very good. I . . . I'll come at once.'

He watched Jervis' retreating back, and heavily lowered his body onto the deck. His legs shook, and he put his hand on the littered table to steady himself.

Fool, fool! He cursed desperately and silently, the hidden words welling up within him like a bursting flood. Go ahead and tell them you can't go! You're washed up – finished!

He looked round wildly and unseeing at the deserted wardroom with its abandoned belongings, garish pin-ups, and dirty crockery. Even that place seemed like a sanctuary.

The towing submarine's commander peered round the door, his eyes watching Curtis bleakly.

'All set? Anything I can do to help?' His tired voice was friendly, and Curtis pulled himself together with a tremendous effort.

'Thank you, I'm ready,' he heard himself answer. 'I'll leave now.'

As he followed the other officer across the gleaming control-room, he caught vague and disjointed glimpses of the silent seamen at their stations, the First Lieutenant beside the coxswain, and friendly, unspoken messages which were passed by their sleep-starved eyes.

He glanced round blankly. 'Where's my Number One and the others?'

'Already on deck by the dinghy.' The submarine commander's answer was short, and Curtis detected the urgency in his tone.

Wants to get rid of us, he thought bitterly. It was no joke for the other man to have his ship lying on the surface, with its main hatch open and unable to dive. He wanted to get down again, and sneak away from the coast.

Curtis lifted one foot to the bottom rung of the long brass ladder, which snaked straight up the tunnel of the dark conning-tower. His legs felt like lead, and the knuckles of his hands gleamed pale as he gripped the ladder with sudden desperation.

He lifted his head and stared up at the tiny oval sky and the few stars which swam back and forth across the gently rolling conning-tower. He wanted to cry out, to die – anything; but instead he just stared at the faint stars, realizing at that instant that everything had suddenly become hopeless.

'Are you all right, old man?' The voice was practically in his ear.

Curtis didn't turn his head. He dare not meet the other man's eyes. He nodded dumbly and began to climb.

The stench of diesel fumes faded, and the salt air bit across his face as he hauled himself onto the bridge.

He began to climb down the side of the salt-caked conning-tower onto the casing, where a huddled group of figures wrestled with the rubber dinghy.

'See you at the rendezvous! Good hunting!' The submarine commander's voice was distant and already belonged to another world.

Duncan's teeth gleamed in the darkness. 'Well, here we go again, Ralph! Four against the flamin' world!'

'Our gear has been sent across in the dinghy, Skipper.' Jervis was already slithering into the little rubber boat. 'I'm really bucked to be going back to our little midget again!' He laughed and jumped down into the boat.

Taylor followed him silently and with casual ease, his feet hardly touching the lapping water.

Duncan gripped Curtis' sleeve in the darkness. 'I'll tell you now, Ralph, I think this deal is crook! But as it's you I'm goin' with, well . . .' he shrugged expressively, 'I'm not too worried!'

Curtis followed him over the side, his body hunched and loose in the bottom of the dinghy. He hardly noticed their short journey, hand over hand along the tow-rope, and when he stared up at the small, slime-covered hull of his command, he shuddered, his mind still unwilling to accept the fact that he was beaten.

They scrambled up onto the tiny casing, pausing only for brief handshakes with the three members of the passage crew who had steered the little boat behind its big sister during the crossing, and then squeezed themselves through the circular hatch into their familiar surroundings.

Curtis remained on deck, and waited until the dinghy had been hauled aboard the other boat, and then slipped the towing wire. He heard the hatch shut, and then the thud of feet as the gun's crew ran below. With a roar like a sounding whale, the air hissed out of the big submarine's tanks as the hungry water surged in.

Curtis strained his eyes through the gloom, trying to capture the

picture of the diving, black hull. A gleam of phosphorescence danced
along her jumping wire and played briefly around the dripping gun
muzzle, and then she was gone. Not one ripple or tremor remained to
mark her passage, not even the probing periscope showed itself to ease
the ache of his loneliness and fear.

He staggered as a roller lifted the little boat under his feet, and he
groped his way towards the after hatch. As he lowered himself down he
allowed his gaze to fasten on the forward hatch. The diver's entrance
and exit. In his mind's eye he saw again the twisting figure and the
distorted face which he had watched through his periscope. It was the
same hatch, and this is the same boat, he told himself. Only I am
different.

The hatch thudded over his head. They had started.

CHAPTER 2

Duncan whistled softly to himself as he groped his way with practised
caution through the maze of equipment of the midget submarine's tiny
control-room and ducked his head tightly into his shoulders to avoid the
low, curving deckhead, which was already streaming with condensation, the rough paintwork glistening with a thousand tiny rivers.
Once aboard, some of his gnawing irritation and pessimism had
dropped away, and for a few moments he busied himself checking the
pumping system and hydroplane controls, his movements and observations automatic and thorough. He eased his powerful frame into his
seat at the rear of the control-room and allowed his eyes to wander for a
while over the small boat's nerve-centre, pondering on the fates and the
perversity of his own nature which had made him take such bitter
discomfort in exchange for the rolling freedom of his father's farm.

Taylor was already seated forward, his hands resting lightly on the
shining wheel, apparently studying the smooth dial of the gyro compass.
Heaven alone knew what he was thinking about. Duncan could only see
the back of his small head, but he could well imagine the man's quiet,
secret smile and dark eyes, as he sat waiting to steer the submarine on its
mission.

Jervis was grim-faced, his unformed features set in a determined
stamp as he leaned uncomfortably across the chart-table, dealing with
his additional duty of navigator.

Behind his back, Duncan sensed, rather than heard, the soft purr of the
main motor as it sent little pulse-beats throbbing through the toughened
plating.

Forward of the control-room, and separated by a watertight door was the tiny, cramped compartment known as the 'Wet and Dry', in which and from where, the diver left and entered the hull.

Duncan watched Jervis' tight lips musingly, and wondered how he would measure up to the job under actual working conditions. It would be a bit different from the training depot.

Beyond the 'W and D' compartment there was one further space, where the batteries were housed, and where one man could sleep in comparative comfort. Not much of a ship, he thought, but with two-ton amatol charges which were slung on either side of the hull, like saddlebags on a mule, she was a match for the biggest units of any navy, as the *Tirpitz* had discovered to her cost.

The hatch clanged shut as Curtis slithered down onto the deck and rammed home the clips.

Duncan watched him through narrowed eyes as he leafed quickly through the rough log left behind by the passage-crew.

Thank God old Ralph's aboard anyway, he mused. He smiled inwardly as Curtis ducked under the small periscope dome in the deckhead, the only place in the boat where a man could stand practically upright. The familiar, automatic motions took some of the edge from his mind, and made even the present risk seem almost commonplace.

Curtis caught his eye and smiled quickly, the corners of his mouth flicking upwards in a tight grimace. He's edgy, too, then. Or was that other business still worrying him? Duncan eyed his captain coolly.

'Here we go again,' he drawled. 'Another flamin' lesson in tactics!'

'Everything checked?' Curtis stared at him for several seconds as if weighing up his First Lieutenant's words to find some hidden meaning.

'Sure, Ralph, everything's all set. Let's go an' hunt for that little floating dock!'

Jervis twisted round at the chart-table. 'Do *you* think it's all a waste of time, Skipper? I mean about our going after the dock and everything. Steve says it's too late in the campaign to matter!'

Curtis spun round suddenly, his eyes blazing. 'For God's sake keep your crazy ideas to yourself, Number One! There'll be enough for all of us to do as it is, without you preaching about how the damned war should be won!'

The sudden flare of rage seemed to drag the energy from his taut body, and he staggered slightly to the boat's uneasy roll.

Duncan shrugged and stared woodenly at the deckhead. 'Sorry, Ralph. I didn't know you felt so strongly about it. Forget it!' He grinned, but inwardly the nagging feeling that Curtis had changed came back more strongly than before. So he *was* jittery. I'll have to keep an eye on him for a bit, he thought.

Curtis nodded vaguely, already thinking of something else. 'Right, let's get started!' His voice was dull.

He stared round the control-room, as if seeing it for the first time, and for a moment Duncan thought he was going to falter. When their eyes met again he saw that some of the old light had returned and the gaze was steady and resolved.

'Dive, dive, dive. Thirty feet. Eight-five-oh revolutions.' The orders rolled off his tongue as he stood in the centre of their little private world. They all depended on him from that moment until they reached safety again – or died.

'Check the trim, Steve. Let me know when you're quite satisfied.'

Duncan relaxed in his chair, his grin wider. 'Aye, aye, sir!'

He wrestled with the hydroplane control as Taylor eased open the main vent valves and allowed the water to surge into the tanks, forcing out the air with a subdued roar.

Jervis started, and then crouched down again across his chart, and as Curtis looked across at Duncan he nodded silently.

Duncan winked back. 'He'll do, Skipper,' he said cheerfully.

The Australian's big hands grappled again with the pumping controls until at length he was satisfied that the boat was perfectly trimmed and the tell-tale bubble of the inclinometer rested quiet and motionless. Until that operation was complete nothing could be attempted or carried out in safety by any of them.

'Craft trimmed for diving,' he said at length.

'Right. Take her back to periscope depth, Number One.' The boat rose easily and unhurriedly, and Curtis raised the slim periscope and tested it in every direction.

As he pressed his forehead against the cool pad, his eye projected over and across the black, silent wave-tops, he wondered how he had managed to get through the last few minutes. Minutes? It was like a lifetime.

It had been a near thing when Duncan had started to needle him, and what at any other time would have seemed the normal pre-operational banter had suddenly developed into something terribly important and infuriating. Supposing Jervis had been panicked by Duncan's words? Suppose it started to prey on his mind, as it was on his own? He felt a rivulet of sweat trickle down his neck, and he gripped the periscope-guide with sudden fear. The boy must be scared enough anyway, he thought, without being sparked into doing something foolish at the wrong moment.

He squeezed the button of the periscope hoist-switch and the thin tube hissed down into its well. He must keep going now. Must keep his mind on the present.

'Ninety feet, Number One.' He cleared his throat to disguise the harshness which had unwittingly crept into his tone. 'Steer three-five-oh.'

Taylor spun the wheel easily and watched the compass ticking round its case. 'Course three-five-oh, sir!'

Curtis leaned across the table at Jervis' side. He could feel the warmth of his body against his arm, and shuddered at the thought of his groping through the dark water in his skin-tight diving suit. He picked up the dividers and concentrated on the wavering pencilled lines and the craggy, uneven outline of the Italian mainland.

'Three hours to daylight,' he murmured, half to himself. 'We'll surface then and get our last good fix.'

'Where shall we hide up while we're waiting, Skipper?' Jervis' voice was also low, as if the enormity of their task had humbled him.

'Well, as you can see, the coastline up to the harbour approaches and main channel are pretty shallow, so I think we'll settle on the bottom about here.' He indicated a huddle of tiny figures on the chart. 'There's a sort of valley just there, carved out of the sandy bottom by the fast current which sweeps round the headland. The locals apparently call it *"il dietro del camello"*, the "camel's back". It's a good sixteen fathoms deep, so we should be fairly snug there until nightfall, when we shall make our first run-in.'

He felt Jervis shiver, and he glanced at him sharply. 'D'you feel all right about cutting the nets?' He tried to keep the fierceness from his voice, and added suddenly, 'We shall at least have surprise on our side.' And not much else, he thought bitterly.

Jervis smiled quickly, his face pale against the glare of the chart-light. 'I'm quite looking forward to it, Skipper! I was afraid the war would be over before I'd even finished my training. It all seems worth while now!'

Duncan groaned loudly behind them. 'For Chrissake! The war'll go on for ever! Years an' years! Don't you fret, son, you'll have plenty of time to be a ruddy hero!'

Jervis laughed uncomfortably and looked at Curtis, his eyes grave. 'Well, you know what I mean, Skipper. My father has always impressed it upon me that it's vitally important for an officer to have war experience. It's such a terrific help in later years,' he finished lamely.

Curtis looked away. It was amazing to think of this boy discussing the war so dispassionately and calmly, and to think that it might only be an interlude in his naval career, when in fact they were crammed together in this little steel shell, nosing through enemy waters with four tons of high explosive to keep them company.

His father, he thought . . . so he, too, had a father driving him on. Suppose the war did allow them all to survive? He almost groaned at the idea of such a possibility. But just suppose. What would happen to them? Duncan would be all right, and probably Taylor would be quick enough to adapt himself, but would Jervis really be able to settle down to the rigours of a peace-time Navy? And as for me, he thought, suddenly angry ... what would I do? Go back to my father's company, or try to break away on my own?

He remembered the last and only time he had tried to do just that. He had, through a few dubious contacts, managed to entangle himself with a group of young people in Chelsea. It had all seemed so different and vaguely daring. The loose talk, and midnight pyjama parties, and a few unsatisfactory meetings with trousered, overpowering girls who described themselves as either art students or models. It had been new, and for him, a glimpse of another life. But although they had been willing to accept his company, and had made him welcome, he had never been quite one of them. Always, behind him, lurked his father, and his background. In desperation he made the fatal mistake of trying to buy his popularity, and he still felt the quiver of complete shame he had experienced when one of the girls had said, 'Does your dear daddy know you're out so late, spending his cash?' He had driven home like a maniac, their laughter still in his ears.

He realized that Jervis had asked him a question, and the boy prodded the chart with his finger.

'... I mean, shall we leave the harbour the same way as we enter?'

'We'll have to wait and see what the exact situation is before I can answer that. According to reports there are at least two nets to get through. Then we'll have to creep right across the harbour, and that'll mean dodging the harbour traffic and hardly using the periscope at all, and then I'll try to get up alongside the main loading jetty.' He rubbed his chin slowly. 'The dock is apparently right alongside, and we should be able to duck underneath and drop the charges.'

'Here, Ian, come an' wipe down the flamin' boat!' Duncan's voice cut across their conversation like a saw. 'She's runnin' already!'

Jervis seized the big roll of old towelling and began to mop the streaming plates free of condensation. The air was still fresh, but the damp chill was already making itself felt, and they were all grateful for their extra clothing.

Curtis was glad to be left alone. He felt that by turning his body to the chart he could blot out the others, and by concentrating on his proposed attack he struggled to shut out their bantering conversation.

He tried to picture his boat as she must look to the fish. A small, whale-shaped object, thrusting her blunt nose through the dark water; blind, but for her instruments; helpless and lost, but for his calculations. Strangely enough, he felt a little calmer, but he had drained away so much of his energy that he found it difficult to decide whether or not that was a sign of hope or of resignation. He reached for his notebook and started again.

They would lie on the bottom for the following day and start to move in on the harbour defences just before nightfall. They ought to be at the first net before dusk, to allow Jervis a bit of practice before his real job started. If all went well they should be clear of the harbour and on their way out to the open sea by five in the morning. The charges would be set to explode beneath the dock at six, so they should be well clear before the pursuit started. The rendezvous with the towing submarine the following night. He began to sweat again. That was less than forty-eight hours away! Yet it was a life's span, an eternity!

He forced himself to think of the Allied armies crouching on the Sicilian shores, waiting to make their spring across onto the Italian coast. What would they be thinking? Not about this ruddy dock, he thought fiercely.

' 'Ere, can one of you gentlemen give me a break on the wheel?' Taylor glanced over his shoulder, his dark eyes gleaming. 'An' I'll get a nice cup of char goin'.'

'Sure. Take over, Ian. Old George'll show you how to mix a good brew.' Duncan laughed lazily. 'Perhaps that'll be some use to you in your career, too.'

Jervis grinned and slid into Taylor's seat, his hands gripping the brass spokes of the wheel. He was used to Duncan's humour, but somehow he couldn't bring himself to react to Taylor's casual acceptance of his companions. If they had all been officers it might have been different, he told himself, but each time Duncan shared a joke with the petty officer, at his expense, he felt a needle of resentment prodding him. I'll get used to it, he thought; we're just four men. He glanced quickly across at Curtis' shoulders, stooped over the table. Perhaps we're only three men, and a leader of men! He smiled at his own reflection in the compass, embarrassed by the complicated depth of his own thoughts. Must be going off my chump. He spun the spokes and started to hum to himself.

The electric kettle began to whistle shrilly and Taylor deftly busied himself with the tea.

He had never quite got used to the process of preparing food or drink on board. He always wanted to laugh at his own antics as he crawled and ducked about the tiny stove, going through the ritual which his mother had called, 'Wettin' the bed!'

Poor old Mum. It couldn't be much fun for her, with the old man away at the docks most of the time, or bending his elbow in the Bricklayer's Arms, and spending most of her nights in the shelter at the end of the road. He remembered the shock he had received on his last leave, when he had turned the familiar corner and stood stock-still to gape at the savage gaps in the shabby terraced houses. He had never really thought much about the air raids before. When it had been mentioned in the petty officers' mess the others had groused and grumbled about the 'bleedin' civvies', or had pointed out that the Jerries were getting a bit in repayment. But standing there on the corner, where he had grown up, had played about with the girls, and cheeked the coppers who came running and puffing after the street bookmakers, it had suddenly seemed very real, and very personal.

After that he had given his soul to the midget submarine's engines, and moulded himself into the framework of her small company. He smiled as he thought of Jervis' expression when he had first been introduced. Poor little bugger, he didn't seem to know whether to shake his hand or to put him in the rattle for not saluting!

He handed a mug of tea to Duncan, and for a second their eyes met. Good old Steve. Maybe I'll go out to his country after this lot's over. Mum'd probably kick up a fuss about leaving 'the street', but it'd do her good. It'd be a new chance for all of them.

He refilled the kettle methodically. We're all stark, bleedin' mad, he thought – drinkin' tea on the bottom of the bloody ocean, an' me dreamin' of home!

Duncan raised his mug. It looked like an egg-cup in his huge fist. 'Here's to yer! What a life!'

Taylor smiled his secret smile. 'Shouldn't 'ave joined if you can't take a joke,' he answered automatically.

Curtis took his mug of tea and lowered himself carefully into his metal seat, and cursed softly as a trickle of condensation found his neck. He sipped the tea slowly, and noticed that already it had attained the bitter taste which seemed to pervade the whole boat after it had been submerged for any time at all. He stared bleakly at the curved steel side and the quivering depth gauges. Somewhere beyond the toughened metal and the silent water lay the quiet, sleeping coastline, and he wondered vaguely what sort of a life the Italians would lead once the invasion had started, and which way their loyalties would lie. It was unlikely that their German masters would allow them much choice in the matter, he decided.

If only we could get on with the attack, and get it over, one way or the other. The waiting, and the probing, the constant watch over depth and speed, course and distance, only added to the constant worry and the twisting agony of fear.

He attempted to remember his reactions before his last operation, but he only succeeded in obtaining a few distorted images of the past. Like a flashback in an old film. He found he was squeezing the mug savagely, so he carefully stood it on the corticene deck covering, where it vibrated in mocking defiance to the tune of the motor.

It was with something like relief that he saw the hands of the brass bulkhead clock creep round, and he began to shift about in his seat in anticipation of doing something. Anything was better than listening to the others talking, and watching the instruments ticking and winking at him from each direction that he turned his sleep-starved eyes.

No orders were given, but each man moved quietly to his allotted place and sat waiting.

Curtis ran his hand slowly across the coarse material of his battledress, and felt the hard pressure of his stomach muscles. He had the overpowering urge to yawn and keep on yawning. With grim determination he gritted his teeth together and stared at the lowered periscope. He knew only too well that the urge to yawn was the most significant symptom of all. It was the open sign of fear.

He pulled himself together with a jerk, aware that Duncan was watching him and that they were all waiting for him to set the wheels in motion.

'I'm going up to have a look.' His voice was clipped but quite calm. 'How's the trim?'

'Craft trimmed for diving.' Duncan squinted at his gauges and juggled with the controls. 'Steady as a rock.'

'Right. Two-five-oh revolutions. Periscope depth.'

There was the barest tilt to the deck as the craft swam towards the waiting sun, and Curtis screwed his body into a ball, forcing himself down low against the deck, ready to use the periscope at the first opportunity.

'Nine feet, Skipper.'

He held his breath, and pressed the button of the periscope-hoist. He checked it slowly as it hissed out of the well, and then, with his face against the eyepiece, he continued to raise it until the bottom of the slender tube was just under two feet from the deck.

He watched, cold and fascinated, as the picture changed from a dark green, distorted jumble, to a sudden blinding light, as the lens broke the surface and cleared the friendly, glittering water. Scraping his knees, and heedless of the objects about him, he swung the periscope in a complete circle, from horizon to horizon and back again.

It was as if the stuffy, streaming control-room no longer existed. His body was still with the others, but his sight and his soul were free, and moving slowly and lazily across the clear green water.

He sniffed and licked his lips involuntarily, half expecting to taste the scent of the clean sea. But the oil and mustiness remained to remind him of reality.

After the darkness and the anxiety of transferring from the towing submarine, the waiting and the growing fear, the sight of the calm, deserted sea was breathtaking and somehow unreal.

He licked his dry lips, catching a brief glimpse as he did so of Jervis' face watching him questioningly.

He swore inwardly, and forced everything from his mind. Everything

DIVE IN THE SUN

but the winding strip of white sand and green trees which formed the full length of his vision. A few white buildings shimmered in the bright morning light, and across a sand-bar of a small cove he could just make out the shapes of some beached fishing boats. The periscope halted in its search as he fixed his eye on a tall, crumbling lighthouse.

He snapped the fingers of his free hand, and spoke from the side of his mouth, in short, brittle sentences.

'Ian, look on the chart. Viserba lighthouse. Has it got a sort of domed roof, like an observatory? If it has, stand by to take a fix!'

He felt the pad pressing against his damp forehead, and wanted to shout at Jervis to get a move on. Instead he peered quickly round at the open sea behind him. Still empty. Not even a white-capped wave to mar the glossy sheen of green glass.

'Yes, sir. Viserba lighthouse it is!' Jervis sounded excited.

He felt a surge of relief flood through him. They were at least on course and running to time. They had passed Rimini in the darkness, and somewhere over the shoulder of that green headland lay Vigoria, and the dock.

The handle of the periscope slithered under the sweat in his palm and a tremor of cramp explored his thighs, but he hardly noticed. His brain worked rapidly and coolly, and for a moment the sickness of his stomach subsided.

'Take a fix.' He watched the lighthouse drift across his sight. 'Lighthouse bears Red one-four-five. The stone beacon on the headland bears Red one-oh. Got it?'

'Ship's head three-five-oh,' chanted Taylor from behind the compass.

'Give me a fresh course for the next leg, Ian. We'll alter course in five minutes from the time of the fix.'

Duncan's slow voice broke in on his racing thoughts.

'Say, Ralph, aren't you keeping the stick up for a bit too long? I mean, some joker may be having a look-see with some mighty powerful glasses.'

Curtis bit his lip. He knew that Duncan was right. It was almost the first lesson he had learned, but something twisted inside him, making him keep the periscope fixed on the shore.

'You attend to your job, Number One, and then I can do mine.'

The words were an implied insult to Duncan's ability to keep the boat steady, but the voice still drawled across the control-room, slow and unperturbed.

'Just thought you ought to be reminded, that's all.'

'New course, three-five-nine.' Jervis' voice had gone suddenly quiet and troubled.

Curtis wanted to scream at them, to drive his fist into Duncan's face, anything to shut up their stupid voices once and for all.

The lighthouse passed out of his vision as he viciously jerked the handle round.

A tiny bird glinted in the sun's light and dipped towards him. The sea was lighter now, and he could imagine the first hint of the warmth to come. He shivered miserably. Soon the little cottages would be alive with people, and the narrow tracks down to the white beaches would be filled with chatter and laughter. It was a different world, where a man could live and be free, could love and find happiness. While he ... He shuddered again, and swung the periscope to search for the lonely sea-bird.

The whole lens suddenly filled, and he stared in chilled horror at the wide, silver wings and the flashing arcs of the twin propellers. The periscope hissed down into its well, and he stared blindly at the depth gauge.

'Dive, dive, dive! One hundred and twenty feet! Hard a-starboard!'

He listened helplessly to the water surging into the tanks, and felt the deck cant and stagger beneath his feet.

In a strange, harsh voice he said, 'Enemy aircraft overhead. Coming straight for us!'

He tried to shut out the picture which filled his aching mind, of the aircraft's bombs plummeting down into the crystal-clear water, of the one short moment of horror before their broken hull sank swiftly to the bottom.

You fool! You damned, bloody fool! He ground his teeth together to stem the anguish which was tormenting him, and tried to concentrate on the swinging compass.

'Meet her, steer oh-nine-oh!'

Still nothing happened. Perhaps the plane hadn't seen them. Perhaps it had been moving too fast and too close to the surface to spot the short shadow of the midget submarine.

'Captain, sir!' Jervis' strangled voice was shaking with emotion. 'Maximum depth here is one hundred feet!'

The words struck his mind like an ice-pick, and he swung round to stare at the boy's white face, the edge of the chart crumpled under his fist. Then, reading the despair on his face he wrenched his eyes to the gleaming dial of the depth gauge.

The long, slender needle crept remorselessly round. Eighty-five feet. Ninety feet. The boat plunged steadily towards the bottom.

'Hold her, Steve! Hold her!'

He saw Duncan's body stiffen as the man wrenched urgently at the controls.

The next few seconds lasted a lifetime. It was a race between the emergency air supply roaring into the tanks, and the deadly, wavering depth needle.

Some of the angle lessened in the deck, and the dive gradually slowed its pace. Then with a sickening lurch, which flung Curtis in a heap on the deck, the hull struck the first sand-bar. Like a mad porpoise she bounded across it, and struck again, the toughened metal scraping and jolting in protest. Curtis tried to regain his feet, and saw Jervis clinging desperately to the lockers, his eyes closed, his lips pressed into a thin line. The lights flickered and then recovered, as the boat bumped and heaved across the bottom.

Duncan's face was wet with sweat, and his normally calm eyes were wild. 'I'm holdin' her! Come on, old girl, steady now!' Another bump made him curse, and stagger in his seat.

Curtis' voice was flat and without emotion as he took over control once more, and with the blood pounding in his ears he settled the boat slowly on the bottom. The unbroken purr of the electric motor died away, and the shaken vibration of the hull settled into a pregnant stillness.

For a while no one spoke. The condensation began to drip heavily across their heads, yet nobody moved. They were like four stricken corpses.

Duncan slowly recovered and released his hands from the controls. He seemed to prise his fingers free, and as he drew in a long intake of breath the others began to move from their carved positions.

Curtis felt the weakness flooding through his trembling body, and wanted to vomit.

He said suddenly, 'Sorry, chaps. I'm afraid I made a muck of that.'

Taylor turned gingerly in his seat, as if afraid that any small movement would start the submarine on its mad capering once more. 'Bit er bad luck that! Just as well you spotted the bastard, sir!'

Duncan laughed softly. 'Yes, Ralph. A bit of luck.'

Curtis looked at him dully, aware of the stillness and the tension, but mostly aware of the contempt in Duncan's cold eyes.

Taylor glanced anxiously from one to the other. He sensed that something worse was about to happen. Something more dangerous and impossible than anything that the enemy could do. He must do something and damned quick. The captain had lost his nerve at the time, possibly. Didn't we all? And old Steve was looking a bit nasty, too, but something must be done before it got any worse and the strong link of their friendship and loyalty was broken.

'Er, d'you reckon they saw us, sir?' Taylor's voice was unnaturally casual. 'Will it make much difference to us if they did?'

Curtis fumbled blindly with the chart, his eyes misty. 'I don't know. Perhaps they didn't.'

'No, maybe they thought we was a whale.' Duncan crossed his legs carefully. 'Don't kid yourself, George. They saw us. They've probably got every damned Eyetie alerted from here to the Vatican! It'll be a really good do now! Too right it will!' He spat angrily on the deck.

Jervis ran his fingers across his damp face. 'Well, we knew it would be a risk coming up here at all.' There was a pathetic defiance in his voice, and Duncan's hard stare softened.

'Sure, kid. But we don't have to waddle about the surface like flamin' ducks, do we?'

Curtis turned wearily towards the forward door. The bunk in the tiny battery compartment seemed the only place to hide from the implied insults.

'We shall carry on as arranged.' He stared at each of them in turn, his eyes burning in their sockets with the effort. 'Try and get some sleep; we'll need all we can get. We'll start our run-in at eighteen hundred.' He looked lastly at Duncan, half hoping that the old, lop-sided grin would come back. but the Australian's eyes were indifferent, and without waiting for Curtis to say more, he yawned and began to search for the electric kettle.

In the stinking darkness of the battery compartment Curtis laid wide-eyed and stiff on the narrow bunk, each muscle and nerve stretched and taut.

He heard Duncan's laugh and Taylor's tuneless whistle, and as he laid staring at nothing he felt already excluded from their world, and so sudden and terrifying had been his complete collapse that even then he was unable to grasp the magnitude of the disaster.

.   .   .

As the rim of the sun dipped towards the edge of the hidden horizon the midget submarine encountered the first net. Although the speed of the boat was only a little above one knot, and even though they had all been tensely waiting for just such a moment, each man recoiled with the sudden shock, and waited breathlessly for the motor to slow even more and the harsh grating of the groping mesh to quieten sullenly as it sagged against the craft's blunt bows.

Jervis was already dressed in his tight diving suit, and sat uncomfortably in the 'W and D' compartment, his face white against the dark skin of the shining costume.

It had been terrible, waiting on the bottom for the coming of darkness, with his imagination torturing his thoughts and preventing the sleep which he craved so desperately. Coupled with that, the brittle atmosphere within the boat and unusual silence between his companions built up a fresh uneasiness, which the promise of action did little to dispel.

He grinned lamely as Duncan craned his body round to squint at him through the narrow watertight door.

'All set? Ready to have a go, kid?'

Jervis nodded stiffly, the suit already dragging on his body. 'Shan't be sorry to get out and stretch my legs!'

Curtis scrambled across the control-room, his face tight and grim. His eyes darted from the diving suit to the depth gauge, which stood steady at thirty feet. The slow turning screw of the boat kept her solidly against the net in the exact position required for her to burst through, as soon as the tough mesh had been cut.

Without speaking, Curtis connected the oxygen supply and gently fixed the boy's nose-clip in position. For a moment his blue, troubled eyes rested on Jervis' face, and a brief smile of encouragement softened his hard expression. He gripped his hand tightly, the only part of his body to be left uncovered, and when he spoke his voice was quiet but surprisingly strong and steady.

'Take it easy, Ian. If you find you can't manage it alone, one of us'll come out and give you a hand.' The grip of Jervis' hand tightened. 'Promise me you won't do anything crazy. We've got plenty of time for this job, and there's no need for heroics.'

Jervis nodded, and moistened his lips. 'I'll be careful, Skipper.'

Taylor, sitting straddle-legged at the wheel, called hoarsely, 'Good luck! Don't take too long outside!'

Curtis snapped the circular face-piece in position and clipped it tight.

Jervis watched the preparations, suddenly aware of the great silence and feeling of loneliness.

Without another glance Curtis closed the watertight door, and the diver was quite alone.

He perched his body carefully on the edge of the 'heads', and began to breathe in regular, steady gulps of canned air. The compartment was so small that it always reminded him of the cupboard under the stairs at school, where he had nearly suffocated when locked in for a prank. The sides brushed his shoulders and his head was only inches beneath the curved deckhead.

Shutting out the urge to panic, he reached out and twisted the valve which would flood his tiny compartment and enable him to escape to the outside.

The pump started, and within seconds he felt the water swirling across his feet in an angry torment. Up and up, pressing the suit against his legs in a cool embrace, the water was soon lapping his buttocks and exploring his thighs. Nervously he plunged his hands deep, to accustom them to its temperature and to be ready for the work outside the hull. It was warmer than he had expected, and he placed them on his knees and watched them sink into the rising water like two pink crabs. Over his chest, around his neck, and with a sudden flurry, over his head. He was completely submerged. He waited a moment longer, and then, satisfied that the pump had ceased and conscious of the pounding of his heart, he allowed one arm to swim upwards to release the clips on the hatch. Holding carefully to the rim of the hatch, Jervis rose smoothly through the circular opening.

Once clear, he twisted his body round, his limbs turning lazily to the pull of the water, until he faced the night-periscope, where he knew the skipper would be watching him, and gave the thumbs-up sign. A cloud of tiny silver air-bubbles, released from the folds of his suit, scattered towards the surface, and he lifted his face to watch them disappear above him. Already his fears were beginning to die, and in their place came the usual feeling of wild exhilaration which the very sensation of diving seemed to bring. He watched, wide eyed, the strange ceiling of the sea, less than thirty feet over his head, a vast, undulating sheet of green glass, speckled and spanned with long gold braids from the setting sun. Occasionally little groups of fish darted towards him, only to halt quivering in their flight before hurrying nervously away from the strange creature before them.

Jervis moved slowly and leisurely along the dark casing of the hull, fascinated by the huge, towering shape of the net which wavered towards the boat like a spider's web grappling with a fly. He released the powerful wire-cutter from its pocket inside the casing and gingerly took hold of the nearest mesh. Beneath him the submarine was poised and still but for the faint tremor of the slow-turning screw and the ribbons of weed which danced lazily from the hydroplanes.

Jervis felt almost sorry for his companions cooped up in their steel shell, and wondered briefly what they were talking about.

He checked the cutter and then laid the knife-edge on the first thick strand. Slowly and methodically he began to cut away the wire, snipping and sawing out the sections of the net in the shape of a giant inverted 'V', leaving the apex intact against the boat's snout. It began to get darker, the water above and around him changing to a dark, mottled blue, and he lost all sense of time. His life and his thoughts were concentrated on the net and the cutter, which grew heavier and stiffer in his aching grasp. The muscles in his back protested at every move, and his hands felt raw and ice-cold. Once, in order to grip the cutter with two hands, he lost his footing on the net, and the weight of the heavy instrument dragged him downwards past the boat, before he could pull himself against the rough wire and drag himself painfully back to the widening hole, his blood pumping in his skull.

Somehow he finished, and with a savage gulp at his air-supply, he hacked away the last strand. With a tired shudder the panel of wire folded over away from the boat, and their way was clear. He felt the boat begin to move, and slipping and sliding along the hull, he guided her through, holding the savage, torn wires clear of the hull until the net suddenly vanished astern in the gathering gloom.

He returned the cutter and wearily groped his way into the open hatch.

So weak was he by that time that he had to make several attempts to clamp down the hatch, and as he lowered his body onto the 'heads', he made the last effort and turned down the valve-handle.

Mesmerized, he watched dully as the water began to fall away and some of the pressure on his chest started to subside.

Still dazed, he saw the watertight door open and felt Curtis opening and removing his face-piece. He couldn't hold the cup of tea which was offered him, but sat, shaking like a child, as Curtis held it to his lips.

'Well done, Ian! Very well done!' Curtis sank back on his haunches as if removed from some terrible doubt.

The others called from the control-room, and Jervis gave a slow grin. 'Boy, it's damp outside!' was all he managed to say.

The next minutes dragged by as the boat moved cautiously across the wide harbour approaches. Each man concentrated on his job except Jervis, who lay back limply in his wet suit, eyes closed, his thoughts resting not on the last net, but the one ahead.

Curtis checked his notebook once more and glanced at the clock. 'Take her up. Periscope depth.'

Duncan eyed him quickly before turning back to his instruments.

He thinks I'll do the same again, thought Curtis, a sudden spasm of white-hot rage coursing through him. Damn him!

He lifted the periscope slowly, squinting frantically to accustom his eyes to the dusk and the distorted movement of the low wave-tops. For a while he could see nothing. Then, as he swung the thin tube in a narrow arc, he caught his breath sharply. The high side of a ship loomed darkly to one side, a mooring-buoy nodding gently at its stem. He lowered the periscope and waited until they had passed the silent ship. Probably a merchantman moored in readiness to leave by daylight.

The motor whined steadily, and at a painful crawl they moved deeper and further into the harbour. When he raised the periscope again he caught a glimpse of a tall, white tower shimmering eerily on the end of a long breakwater. He measured the distance and bearing rapidly, and waited for his next look before making a decision.

'Just coming up to the main entrance,' he spoke tersely. 'Steer oh-one-five! Keep her steady at periscope depth, the bottom's fallen to only five fathoms hereabouts!'

He raised the periscope once more and watched the white tower fading into the distance. A small, dark shape rounded the end of the breakwater, and the steady beat of her powerful diesels throbbed through the submarine's hull, making them stiffen into a fresh alertness.

Narrowly Curtis watched the boat swinging towards him. The white finger of a searchlight stabbed once, twice, and three times, casting

quick, furtive beams across the still hulls of sleeping ships alongside the
tangle of jetties and wharves.

'Patrol boat,' he said softly. 'Probably hasn't got any Asdic –' He bit
his lip, as a sharp, metallic ping echoed along the hull. The submarine
turned like a boxer to parry the thrust, so that her narrow beam was in
the path of the probing detector.

The patrol boat's engines faded away across the harbour, and Curtis
took another look. The traffic was getting thicker. Two small launches
putt-putted across his vision, and a lumbering coaster glided past
towards the harbour mouth, a low plume of black smoke darkening the
night sky.

Twice more they ducked to avoid anchored ships, and once they
sweated painfully as the hull scraped against a mooring-buoy.

The lens of the periscope suddenly filled with red light as a lamp
stabbed out ahead. Then, as he watched, the long shape of a destroyer
began to slide across the main harbour towards another ship, the one
which had flashed the light.

Curtis paused to dash the sweat from his eyes. This was a bit of
unexpected luck. They must be getting near the next net, and the
outward bound destroyer was having the gate opened for her.

'Get ready to give me full speed! As soon as the gate's opened, I'm
going to make a dash for it!'

Jervis sat up immediately, his eyes searching. 'Won't they pick up our
motor, at full revs?'

Curtis was pressing the hoist-switch again and shook his head briefly.
'No, the big chap'll drown ours!'

Suppose we can't make it before the boom-gate vessel closes the gap?
A cold chill ran across his neck. We *have* to make it!

The destroyer's engines thundered through the boat, making the
instruments chatter and vibrate like mad things. Curtis saw the long,
grey shape slide past, the froth already mounting at her stem.

'Full ahead! Steer oh-two-oh!'

He had said it. They were suddenly moving more rapidly towards the
narrow opening in the gate. The buoys which supported the nets bobbed
darkly, like the heads of tired swimmers, and the boom-vessel grew
larger and sharper in detail. He could see her long, spindly funnel and
the bulky shapes of her winches and hoisting gear. He heard clearly the
thud of her engine as she began to draw the buoys together again.

We're not going to make it! He watched in rising anguish, as the gap
became narrower and more distorted.

He could see the rust-dappled sides of the ship, and caught the glow of
a cigarette from her narrow bridge. Thirty feet, fifteen feet, there seemed
to be no entrance any more.

He saw the high, jagged stem rising over him like an axe, and wanted to hide his eyes from the impenetrable wall of metal which loomed across their path in a solid barrier.

'Hard a-starboard!' His voice was a sob.

He saw the vessel sheer away, and heard the grate of metal along the hull, as the casing ground against one of the buoys. A final jerk, which made Taylor gasp and cling more fiercely to the wheel, and then they were curving round, away from the net. They were through.

'In!' said Curtis. He couldn't trust his voice for more.

Duncan spoke from between his teeth, 'Well, there's no turning back now, is there?'

'Was there ever?' Jervis was massaging his raw hands and watching Duncan curiously.

Duncan laughed shortly. 'Could be, Ian. Could be.'

At minimum speed the boat prowled across the harbour, while Curtis hurriedly checked the chart and measured the distances between the piers and jetties. Jervis knelt at his side, studying Curtis' quick, skilful movements.

'You did that for *me*, didn't you, Skipper? You didn't want me to go out and cut another net?' He spoke very quietly and saw Curtis stiffen.

Curtis turned his face so that they were only inches apart. 'Questions! Nothing but damn questions! For Christ's sake shut up and let me get on with my job!'

Jervis coloured, and lowered himself shakily to the deck. Duncan glanced casually at him and shrugged. 'A hard life, ain't it?'

Curtis twisted a pencil between his strong fingers and closed his eyes tightly, forcing his reeling thoughts to grapple with the attack. Jervis, the young fool! Did he really think I wanted to make it easier for him? Hadn't it occurred to him that I can't stand the suspense of waiting any longer? Steve knew. He sees right through me. He knows I can't hold out much longer.

He crawled back to the periscope and raised it cautiously, thinking as he did so how quiet it seemed in the boat.

The long grey finger of the loading jetty lay before him, its sharp outline broken in places by the bulky shapes of moored vessels. They passed softly down the side of a high freighter, a dim arc-lamp giving him a quick view of some army lorries lashed across her decks. The lamplight filtered across the water in a pale silver sheen, too weak to endanger the tiny black stick which moved so purposefully through the uneasy, lapping wavelets.

They don't seem to be very worried about the blackout here, he thought absently; perhaps the Allied invasion has been delayed. Surely something must be happening in the south by now. 'Damn!' He pressed the button as another patrol boat chugged slowly amongst the ships.

Some uniformed figures squatted around a small gun on the boat's foredeck, their uniform buttons glinting under the arc-lamp.

He listened to the engine fading away, and Taylor began to whistle softly between his teeth.

Curtis took another quick look and edged the boat even closer to the nearest merchantman.

The submarine sank like a sounding whale, and dipped under the ship's fat bilge, scraping the sand and muck on the harbour bottom, and once, with a sharp metallic screech, actually colliding with the stonework of the jetty.

Silently the boat settled on the bottom and the engine died away.

'We there?' Duncan sat back heavily in his small seat.

'The dock is about fifty feet ahead of us.'

Curtis' words dropped like pebbles in a still pool. He waited while each of the crew digested them.

'What'll we do, Skipper?' Jervis suddenly checked himself, afraid that Curtis would turn on him again. But his captain merely looked at him unseeingly and bit his lip.

'There doesn't seem to be much water here.' Duncan spoke slowly, as if he, too, were being cautious. 'If that flamin' dock is a bit low in the water, we might find it a bit of a squeeze!'

'We're going in now! We've got to drop a charge at each end of the target, to make quite sure!' He turned to Jervis. 'Get into the "W and D", Ian; you might have to go out and assist things in a minute.'

The submarine moved forward once more. Curtis counted off the seconds, visualizing the giant, factory-shaped floating dock towering over them. There was a sharp metallic clang, and the control-room rocked violently.

'We're underneath,' he announced flatly.

'Christ, they must be bloody deaf up there!' The words were forced from Taylor's twisted lips. His whole face looked sunken and shone with sweat.

The boat stopped.

Curtis checked the fuse-settings of the charges and began to wind the big basket-wheel on the port side. They heard the charge fall away, and each man imagined the deadly shape falling like a giant leaf, to settle practically alongside the hull.

They began to bump their way along the bottom of the dock, Curtis checking the time and trying to estimate when they had covered about three hundred feet.

'Stand by!'

Curtis swung the starboard release wheel and held his breath. Overhead he could hear the steady beat of several engines, probably generators on the dock, or maybe some repairs being carried out.

'Charge gone!'

Curtis looked wildly around the control-room as a fresh grating on the hull cut the words from his mouth. The boat shivered and settled down again. There was a strange groan from the metal overhead.

Duncan sat bolt upright. 'Jesus! They're floodin' the dock! We'll be pinned underneath an' go up with the charges!'

Curtis pulled desperately at his jacket, as if stifling to death. 'Full ahead!' He tapped Taylor sharply on the arm, so that the man jumped in his seat. 'Use the wheel all you can to free us!'

The motor whined and shuddered on its bed, and as the sturdy little hull twisted under power and rudder they heard the clinging pressure of the massive dock on their casing, as it tried to hold and destroy its own killer.

Through the glass ports in the periscope dome Curtis saw a break in the black wall of disturbed mud and overhanging shadows. One more thrust. We've *got* to get clear!

Over his shoulder he said, 'Watch it, Steve! Don't let her break surface and give the whole game away!'

'Hark who's talking!' Duncan's voice sounded breathless with the effort of controlling the boat's savage motion. 'I guess I'm not in the mood for a ruddy sermon!' he added jerkily.

Curtis momentarily forgot the danger and the grinding of metal against the hull. A wave of sickness coursed through his taut limbs, and he stared wildly at the other man's intent and angry face.

'What did you mean by that?' He had to hold his stooped body close to the periscope to prevent himself from falling. 'What the hell are you implying?'

'Forget it till later!'

'Damn you! I'm asking you now!' His voice rose to a shout, and Taylor wrenched his eyes from the compass to stare miserably from one to the other.

Curtis reached out and gripped Duncan's shoulder. 'Come on, spit it out while you've got the chance! Tell me what you've been thinking all this time! Now's your chance to get it off your ruddy chest!' He glared round the boat, seeing only a misty picture of the wet, glistening plates and Taylor's bent shoulders at the wheel. Of Jervis' white face framed in the open door, and lastly Duncan's tight lips and lowered head. As the Australian remained silent, Curtis shook his shoulder and shouted even louder. 'You think I'm scared, lost my nerve, is that it? Or are you afraid to tell me that I'm a murderer, too?' He fell back weakly, his blue eyes suddenly dead.

Duncan's hands were rigid. 'I said forget it, Ralph. For Christ's sake get a hold of yourself.' His tone had changed and he sounded uneasy. 'Right now, I guess we have a job to finish. The rest'll keep.'

At that moment the submarine cleared the overhanging end of the dock and moved awkwardly towards the centre of the harbour.

Duncan licked his lips. 'Looks as if the Eyeties didn't get a tip that we were comin' after all,' he said slowly. 'I guess we're all born lucky.'

Curtis ran his palm along the periscope, heedless of the thick grease which clung to his skin. You finally did it, he told himself. You finally cracked. It was almost a relief. He was dimly aware of Jervis' quiet voice behind him, talking to Taylor.

'Steer one-five-five. We should be clear of the main jetties in about ten minutes.'

'Aye, aye, sir.' Taylor's answer was automatic and subdued. All the life seemed to have gone from him.

Curtis eyed them moodily. They already think I'm redundant, something to be tolerated until we get back. He watched Jervis moving uncomfortably by the chart-table, his shining diver's suit hanging on him like an obscene skin.

'I'll give the necessary orders, thank you.' His flat voice made Jervis start and move clumsily towards the diving compartment. 'When I've got the boat back to the rendezvous you can all do what you like. Until then,' he paused wearily, 'you'll obey orders. All of you!'

The boat slid silently through the water, and no roar of engines overhead, or the sudden crashing detonation of depth charges, pursued their slow and cautious passage. It had been a perfect attack. Curtis almost groaned aloud at the mockery of his thoughts.

As if reading his mind, Duncan stirred his cramped body. 'Pretty smooth, Ralph. I'd say there's not much wrong with your touch that a good rest won't cure. We've all been overdoin' things a bit.'

'Periscope depth!' Curtis fiddled impatiently with the switch and ignored Duncan's words. He felt strangely calm and resigned; it was a feeling which his self-made loneliness only helped to strengthen as he glared bleakly at the crouched figures grouped about him. Each man was wrapped in his own private thoughts.

The periscope hissed slowly upwards.

He searched the harbour eagerly, a feeling of crazy recklessness making his head swim. He saw a small motor boat moving like a shadow towards the top of the anchorage. With childish defiance he kept the periscope raised and looked back at the fading shape of the dock.

But for you everything might have been different. But the lie died in his brain as his eye turned back across the black water and fastened on a small bobbing float. He stared at it blankly, forcing himself to concentrate once more and aware of some rising sense of warning.

A thin grey streak probed faintly across the sky, and the outlines of the distant ships became harsher. Soon a new day would dawn in Vigoria, and with it would come disaster when the charges exploded. He watched the float bobbing towards him. We're on the right course for a quick exit. We should be up to the nets soon, but not as quickly as this. Then he saw another group of floats. He chilled. It must be another net.

'Thirty feet! Another net!'

The deck tilted obediently, but at the same instant they heard the clatter of wire across the hull. He realized he was still holding the periscope switch in his hand and he pressed it frantically. Even as the tube hissed down he heard the sharp groan of metal, and a thin trickle of water ran across his wrist. He stared at it for some moments before he could bring himself to realize that the periscope had been caught in the net. The scraping of the wire ceased and the boat skimmed under the net.

'Only an anti-torpedo net,' said Taylor quietly. 'Luck's still with us!'

Curtis wrenched desperately at the hoist. The periscope was jammed solid, and the water still seeped threateningly down the greased tube.

'Take her up. Surface!' He stood upright under the dome, his hair pressed against the rough metal.

Duncan eyed him strangely.

'Surface,' he repeated heavily. 'We're blind. We'll have to run out on the surface!'

He opened the hatch, gasping as the salt air struck him in the face and a stream of spray broke over the coaming. Heavily he climbed up onto the casing, leaving the others behind in the darkened control-room. Wearily he strapped himself to the twisted periscope standard and braced his feet on the slippery deck. He bent his head until his lips brushed against the speaking tube, his eyes on the white tower of the harbour entrance.

Why not just step over the edge? Finish the whole damned business once and for all? What was the point of trying to escape now? As soon as the dock blew up, every destroyer and aircraft for miles around would be looking for them.

The first line of net buoys loomed ahead, and he conned the boat round until the shape of the boom-vessel was lost in the gloom. The boat moved smoothly between the first two nodding buoys, while Curtis gritted his teeth and waited for the net to grip them. They passed cleanly over the top of the sagging net and he breathed again. It was a race now. The next net must be reached before it became any lighter. Already the sky had brightened alarmingly, and somewhere across the harbour he heard the scream of a train whistle.

He spoke carefully down the pipe. 'Give me full revs!' He was amazed at the calmness in his voice. 'Once over the next net we should be OK.'

'We over a net already then?' Taylor's voice rattled tinnily up the tube. 'Cor, fancy that!'

He heard Taylor pass the information to the others, and without

warning he began to tremble violently. He knew then that he couldn't
desert them whatever he had done, or whatever they thought of him.
  They passed over the last net, within two hundred yards of a sleeping
destroyer, and turned for the open sea.

CHAPTER 3

Curtis locked his fingers tightly behind his head and lay back uncomfortably on the small bunk across the chart-table. He tried to relax his
body and concentrate on the steady, monotonous pulse-beat of the
motor.
  The shaded light in the control-room seemed to have lost some of its
brilliance and shed a yellow, sickly glow across the instruments and
dials, and twisted Duncan's intent face into a mass of shadows, from
which his cold eyes stared fixedly at the depth gauge and the clock.
  Taylor was still at the wheel, while Jervis was trying to find sleep in the
forward battery compartment.
  Curtis again resisted the temptation to look at the brass clock. It must
be nearly six, he thought. Soon the charges would explode and turn the
peaceful harbour into a raging hell. He swallowed hard, tasting the
bitter coating of oil and grime in his throat.
  The submarine had dived as soon as it had cleared the harbour
approaches, and as the sun rose above the horizon like a solid gold ball
they had groped their way down to a depth of thirty feet and steered
purposefully across the open bay.
  He pressed his eyes shut and tried to calculate the situation more
clearly. They would have to lie on the bottom soon and rest. As soon as
the charges exploded he knew from past experience that every craft and
plane would be alerted, and their slightest movement in the shallow
coastal waters would invite attention and attack. He heard the wheel
creak, and he was reminded of his new worry. The gyro compass had
started to play up. Both he and Duncan had carried out the usual check,
but the rapid alteration and sudden deviation pointed to one thing. The
severe grinding which the boat had received beneath the floating dock
had caused more damage than any of them was prepared to admit. He
bit his lip hard. The boat was blind, and with a faulty compass as well,
the possibility of making a rendezvous with the towing submarine in the
middle of the night seemed hopeless. Apart from that, he knew that by
taking his time over his approach to the rendezvous, and by keeping the
other, larger craft helpless on the surface, he was doubling the risk to
their lives, as well as those of his own crew.
  His aching mind shied away from the obvious solution, from which

there was no real alternative. We shall have to ditch the boat, he told himself, and try to make it overland. He had heard of other crews doing the selfsame thing in the past. But that was in Norway, an occupied country, not in Italy. He shuddered.

'Damn!' Taylor spun the spokes again, and craned forward over the compass. 'She's not answerin', Steve!'

Duncan waited a moment before replying. 'Bring the cow round to due east again. Then ease 'er off to your course slowly. We've got to keep goin' for a bit, just to put a few miles between us an' the big bang.'

The wheel creaked, and Curtis felt his heart beginning to thud painfully against his ribs. Duncan knows, he thought. He knows we're going to ditch.

'Course steady on oh-nine-oh.' There was a pause. 'Oh, sod it! She's payin' off again!'

Curtis forced his eyes open and slowly eased his legs down to the deck. 'Keep trying,' he said quietly. 'I'm going to set her down on the bottom shortly. but keep trying for a bit longer.'

Duncan looked up, his eyes searching. 'Feelin' better, Ralph?'

Curtis nodded vaguely.

'Good. I reckon I was right about this bein' a crook deal.'

Curtis stiffened, but the other man shook his head briefly, a small smile breaking through his dirty, stubbled face.

'*We* were all right, Ralph. It was the job which was stupid! I reckon you did real well to get us out like that, and on the surface, too!' His grin broadened. 'I thought we was all goin' at each other's throats for a bit, eh?'

Curtis felt a tremor of emotion coursing behind his eyes, and he looked away.

'Sorry about that, Steve. It's all been playing on my mind a bit.' He groped for the right words. 'I've never forgotten how young Roberts died. It was my fault. I killed him as surely as if I'd shot him.' He found that the relief of confiding in someone was almost more than his mind could stand, and he slumped heavily against the useless periscope. 'And now all this happening.' He waved one hand around the boat. 'I don't mind telling you, we're in a jam.'

'You mean we're goin' to let the old boat go, is that it?' Duncan eyed him calmly. 'Reckon it's all we can do under the circs!'

A great tidal wave of sound engulfed the hull, a sullen, angry roar, like the crumbling of a distant dam. Together they looked at the clock, while Jervis scrambled through the open door, his eyes wide and enquiring. It was two minutes past six.

Silently Duncan reached across and gripped Curtis' hand. 'Well done, Skipper. You blew the bastard's bottom off! You got us in, and you got us out!'

They all shook hands, and Curtis wanted to cry out as each man looked him in the face and smiled. Jervis rubbed his hands across his pale face and looked from one to the other, as if amazed by the calmness of these experienced seamen, while Taylor turned back to the compass, a small secret smile of private satisfaction on his tight-lipped mouth.

'Shall we be able to pick up the towing sub all right?' Jervis seemed to suddenly come to life.

Duncan shot a quick glance at Curtis and rubbed his chin slowly. 'We'll be makin' the trip on foot, that is unless we can whip a boat off some damned Eyetie!'

Curtis hardly noticed the look of dismay on the boy's face; he was already reaching for the chart. Of course, that was the answer. Steal a boat and move down the coast by night. They should be able to find some sort of hide-out during the daylight, and if the Allied invasion had got into full swing they ought to be able to contact their own people within a week, maybe less, if all went well. He ran his eyes across the chart, his mind picturing again that quiet fishing village he had seen through the periscope. His finger paused over the markings on the roughened chart. Was that only yesterday? He shook his head wonderingly.

The towing submarine would wait at the appointed place, and then return to base. Signals would be made, and in due course the dreaded telegrams would be received in four homes. Four homes, separated not only by distance, but by completely different ways of life.

A small moment of cruel pleasure flickered through his mind as he thought of his father. No doubt he would even make capital out of his bereavement, he thought bitterly.

Jervis looked even paler, and Duncan reached out with his foot to kick him chidingly in the ankle.

''Ere, snap out of it, Ian. It'll do us good to stretch our legs.'

Jervis still stared straight at the side of the hull, his eyes dull. 'What would they do to us if they caught us? Would we be treated as prisoners-of-war and everything?'

Curtis eyed him levelly. 'They say they're going to hang every midget submariner, frogman, commando, charioteer, and what-have-you that they can catch, Ian. The German High Command say we're all saboteurs, and must be treated as such. So get it through your head – we're not going to be caught!'

'No, that's right, sport!' Duncan laughed only with his mouth. 'We're goin' to see that you get home to your dad, the Admiral, just so that you can tell 'im what a lot of scruffy jokers we all are in this outfit!'

Duncan turned back to Curtis, a look of careless ease on his face. Curtis' sharp words had somehow struck new life into him, and even Taylor looked more relaxed. 'Where you settin' us down, Ralph?'

'I'll go back to this deep underwater valley, you remember, "*il dietro del camello*", and as soon as it's dawn tomorrow, we'll slip ashore. We can sink the boat in deep water then.'

'What'll we take with us, Ralph? I guess we won't want to lug too much ashore, especially if we've got to swim for a bit!'

Curtis pulled the chart closer to the light.

'The beaches are pretty shallow for a long way out. I think it'll be more of a wade than a swim. We'll need the emergency pack and a good water container.' He rested his hand almost gingerly on the holster which hung on his hip. 'We shall need these as well. Although I don't aim to have to use them.'

'I wouldn't mind too much.' Duncan eased his depth controls, his eyes distant. 'You should see my old man. He can knock the eye out of a jack-rabbit at a hundred yards with a pistol.' He shook his head, marvelling at his own memories. 'He sure is quite a guy.'

'What did you say when you came over and joined the Royal Navy?' Curtis was suddenly curious about Duncan's father, although he had heard so much about him he sometimes felt he knew him better than his own.

Duncan gave his slow smile. 'We was out checkin' the wire one day, when we ran into old Dick Masters, the constable. He told us he'd just got the griff about the boys pullin' back to Dunkirk. I was so worked up about the mess the Pommies were makin' of it I said I wanted to make for Cairns and join up. My old man didn't even bat an eyelid.' Duncan grinned affectionately. 'He just waved his fist across our land – an' we've got quite a piece – and he said, "I built this up from nothing! I've worked hard all me life, an' I've seen drought, famine, death, good times, an' bad, an' I've made something for a man to be proud of. But d'you know, boy, the thing that still stands out most in my memory is the morning that me an' my cobbers hit the beach on the Dardanelles. So I'm not goin' to stand in *your* way now!"'

'He must be a fine man,' said Curtis quietly.

Duncan nodded. 'He's a bloodthirsty old bastard, that's for sure!'

Jervis was peering at the chart, his mind confused by the casual conversation. 'It's a long way from that village to the south coast. I wonder if we shall be able to contact the army all right.'

'I got a brother in the Eighth Army,' said Duncan slowly. 'Reckon we should spot him soon enough.'

'I didn't know that, Steve.' Taylor's voice showed rare surprise at the secret.

'Well, I didn't want you to think I'm always boastin'; I'm a modest guy, y'know!'

As the clock turned down the hours, Curtis found that the preparations for leaving the boat helped to settle his nerves, and now that he had made his decision he felt a new feeling of relief overriding his other fears. The compass got steadily worse, and once he surfaced the boat for the briefest period possible to try to fix his position.

He opened the hatch, half blinded by the dazzling sunlight, and more than apprehensive about what he might find.

The horizon was clear but for the thin white line of the distant headland. They were well off course, as he had feared, but still close enough inshore to pick out the twisted point marking the curve of the coast. Somewhere behind that line he knew he would find the village. As he swung his binoculars in a wide arc he saw a tell-tale wisp of smoke on the horizon, and even as he watched he saw three slim grey hulls scudding in a tight formation across the sparkling water. The sun beat down on his neck, warming his limbs and driving the stale, chilled cramp from his bones. Destroyers, and moving in fast. The hunt had started. In the far distance he could faintly hear the heavy drone of aircraft, probably taking off from the aerodrome at the rear of Vigoria.

The hatch clanged shut over his head, and the boat began to dive once more.

Duncan licked his lips. 'Man, did you smell that air, George? I just can't wait to get out of this can!'

Taylor nodded, and watched the compass closely. Outwardly calm, he was vaguely troubled by the new turn of events and the fact that he didn't feel the security he had hoped for. He had thought that the only thing that mattered was to get the skipper and Steve together again. They seemed to be hitting it off all right, and the skipper appeared to be something like his old self again, but – he fidgeted in his seat – there was something else. The danger? He scoffed at himself with disgust. What was danger anyway? You couldn't see it; you couldn't feel it; so what the hell!

I hope we get back soon, he thought desperately. I don't want Mum all worked up worrying about me. He sighed deeply, suddenly feeling his weariness. Everybody worrying about somebody else. Makes you sick! The compass swung lazily, mocking him, and he muttered obscenely under his breath.

'Want me to take over?' Jervis sounded strange, too.

'No. I'm not dead yet!' he answered shortly. Bloody regular officers, he reflected with sudden anger. Nice as pie when things were going wrong, but once out of a jam and they were trying to ram rank down your throat.

Jervis sank down on the deck, feeling lost and at the same time in the way. He sat heavily on the coaming of the diving compartment watching the other three as if he was looking in from outside the boat and their world. The cold excitement of leaving the boat and cutting the net, followed by the nerve-stretching attack on the dock, left him weak and limp, and what might have been the greatest moment in his life, and the conclusion to a great episode in his career, had suddenly widened into something frightening and unreal. He watched Curtis searching through the lockers, a lock of his fair hair falling across his grimy face as he tossed unwanted articles aside with little grunts of impatient irritation and built up a small pile of equipment beside him on the oil-smeared deck.

Duncan stared woodenly at his controls, his hands and shoulders moving slightly at each perverse swing of the little boat, but from the faraway expression in his eyes Jervis could tell that he was already scheming and plotting over the next few hours, which might well decide whether they would live or die.

Jervis shook his head jerkily as a wave of fatigue brought the damp ache into his bones to replace his fading energy. He stared round at the unheeded and dripping hull, all at once realizing just how important the tiny boat was to all of them. It was not just a weapon of war, another machine of destruction, but the very breath of their existence. Take it away, or just abandon it, and they were all naked and out of their element. He wanted desperately to burst out with his ideas to the others, but something akin to a hidden pride checked him, and he sat staring from one face to the other, and tried to fathom out the exact course which events might take.

He had considered most possibilities in the past, but all his ideas had included the Navy and everything that went with it. He had always been surrounded and protected by it, and had been brought up to rely on the strange tradition and comradeship of the Service, which was more like a religion. Everywhere he had been he had always been surrounded by others of his own mould, and he had imagined himself after this operation, stepping ashore in Malta or Alexandria, and finding himself right back amongst the safety of the only life he understood. He could not bring himself to realize, even partly, just what it would be like suddenly to find himself washed ashore on some unknown beach, like a piece of flotsam discarded by the sea, and to find a way through a country which hitherto had been merely a collection of superior holiday resorts in his own experience, and was now a sullen, alien territory, with every sort of danger and hazard to keep him and his companions from reaching safety.

He nearly screamed aloud when Duncan started to talk about his father, and Curtis had begun to question the Australian about his farm and that distant life. It was crazy and unreal, and as if they were two strangers passing the time on a long-distance train journey, especially when, a short time previously, the skipper had been almost on the point of striking Duncan while the enemy dock had groaned threateningly overhead. And what was all that about murdering the previous diver?

Jervis looked carefully at Curtis' set face and cold eyes as if he might find the answer there.

Curtis paused in his search and glanced up quickly, scanning the boy's face questioningly. 'Get out of that diving suit, Ian,' he snapped, 'and start smashing it up, and all the other diving gear. Got it?'

Jervis coloured and dropped his eyes, as if caught out in his thoughts, and began to struggle out of his suit. So there was no chance of a change of plans. It was all decided, and they were going to abandon the boat. He had held onto the forlorn hope that perhaps the damage wasn't quite so serious, and that there might still be a chance of making for the rendezvous.

As if in answer, Taylor let free a stream of curses as the compass danced madly in its case.

Jervis thought of the towing submarine's cosy wardroom and the smell of closely-packed, friendly bodies, and the buzz of casual but steadying conversation, which spelled safety and hope. He bent over his task, his eyes stinging with tears and loneliness.

Curtis sighed and sat back on his haunches to survey the pile of gear beside him.

'I think that's about all,' he was thinking aloud. 'Tinned food and chocolate. A torch, two escape maps, and a couple of grenades.'

Duncan smiled bleakly. 'Not exactly a campin' outfit, is it? Still, I daresay we'll get by.'

Curtis eyed him, his blue eyes troubled. 'I'm not looking forward to it myself, you know!'

He was amazed that he was able to think so clearly again, and that the ache of fear only lurked in his heart and not in his limbs. Perhaps it was because something outside his own will had taken over command of his actions, or maybe it was just the inevitability of disaster.

'Matter of fact,' continued Duncan calmly, 'I'm thinkin' it might be quite amusin'!' He released one hand from a lever to wave down the obvious protest. 'No, quite seriously, it'll be a sort of change for us.' He looked around the control-room, taking in the dirt and disorder, and the crumpled figures of the others. 'It's time we got shot of this for a bit. We ought to find the trip back quite interestin'!' He laughed impetuously. 'Say, Ralph, what a lark it'd be if we captured Mussolini or somethin' like that!' He chuckled and rolled his eyes. 'Might even latch onto some little Eyetie senorita, too! They say the sheilas round here are quite somethin'!'

He looked across at Jervis' stooped head, and his eyes crinkled into narrow slits. 'Why, the boy he'd be really learnin' a few things!'

Jervis smiled weakly, but didn't answer.

'See? He's thinkin' about it already.'

Jervis licked his dry lips. 'I was just wondering about the strength of the enemy around this part of the coast,' he said at length, his voice quiet and unsteady.

'Strength of the beer more like! Christ, what wouldn't I give for a dirty great pint of Tooth's beer right now!' Duncan smacked his lips noisily.

Curtis was watching Jervis with sudden interest, and waved the Australian into silence. The boy had changed. He looked as he himself had felt such a short time ago. And with Taylor already showing signs of strain, it was cutting down their slim chances even more.

'How d'you mean, Ian?' he asked casually. 'What have you got in mind?'

Jervis swallowed hard, his face pale. 'What I mean is, Skipper, do you think there'll be many German troops around here, or will the Italians be in control?'

'It doesn't make a lot of difference, surely? We have to avoid them all, that's the only certainty we have. Don't imagine that the Eyeties are soft, because they're not, and remember, it's their country we're messing about.'

'That's right,' said Duncan brightly. 'So long as they only outnumber you twenty to one, you'll find 'em pretty tough!'

Jervis looked across at Curtis with something like pleading on his round face. 'We're not cut out for this sort of thing, Skipper! We're sailors, not soldiers! We haven't got a clue about getting across open country and all that sort of thing, and living off the land!' The words poured from him like a flood.

'You speak for yourself!' Duncan wriggled in his seat. 'I've done it all me life till I was stupid enough to get mixed up with this caper!'

Curtis' mouth tightened and his eyes looked like twin pieces of blue glass. 'Look here, Ian. Lots of our blokes have had to ditch before now, and have made it! In Norway, for example, when the country was deep in snow and England across the other side of the sea. You must have heard or been told about it?'

'But, Skipper,' Jervis had committed himself, and seemed incapable of reading the warning in Curtis' face, 'that was a country where the people were all for the British——'

Curtis cut him short. 'Whereas, this country is warm and full of food and God knows what else, *and* with a bit of luck the army are waiting for us at the other end by now! If you weren't up to this sort of risk, you should have got your father to wangle you into something safer!'

He knew that his words were cutting the boy in half, but he knew, too, that everything depended on the others being ready to back him up when the time came. Without another word he crawled through the diving compartment and into the battery room, his mind already busy with his hazy plan.

Duncan breathed out slowly. 'Well, Ian, I'm not the one to brag, but I could have told you that would happen!'

'I – I'm not afraid! It's just, it's just . . .' he faltered helplessly, all his defences down, 'I've never experienced anything like this before.'

'Hmm. It's not exactly the kind of affair we want to dabble in every day, is it?' He leaned over and banged the boy's shoulder. 'Cheer up, cobber! D'you want to live forever?'

When eventually the motor died away, and the midget submarine settled on the soft sandy sea-bed, the Adriatic was dark and still and allowed the boat and her crew peace and time to dwell on their thoughts for the morning which was yet to come. A destroyer cruised seawards looking for the unknown marauder which had left its mark painted in the sky over distant Vigoria – a sullen, flickering red glow which refused to be quelled.

Somewhere in the darkness, beyond the destroyer and her consorts, the towing submarine's commander watched the glow in his periscope. 'There'll be no rendezvous after all, I'm thinking,' he said softly.

. . .

The thick, damp air of the control-room was tense and expectant as the small boat moved slowly and carefully towards the surface. Each of the four men stooped across the controls was thinking the same thoughts, and wondering what was awaiting them in the world above their heads.

The hands of the brass clock pointed at four o'clock, and even in the boat's confined space Curtis seemed to feel the chill of the dawn mingling with the foul, fume-laden air. He stole a quick searching glance at the others, noting their bulging pockets and rumpled battledress blouses. They had all discarded their waterproof clothing to give them some semblance of uniform should they run straight into an enemy patrol. Curtis shivered, in spite of his taut muscles. He had heard that the Germans had a quick way with suspected saboteurs.

We should be about a quarter of a mile offshore, he pondered; that'll enable us to sink the boat in deep water and still make it possible to swim to the beach fairly easily. He pictured the details on the chart which seemed burned into his brain, and wondered if they could make the trip to the small hill at the side of the village without being seen.

Duncan looked up from his controls, his face suddenly alert and strained.

Curtis tensed automatically, and bent his head as if expecting to hear the sound of engines overhead, but Duncan frowned and shook his head briefly.

'No, Ralph, it's not that,' he said slowly. 'The motion – d'you feel it? We're jerkin' a bit too much!'

Curtis bit his lip. Duncan was right; the boat was rolling far too much, and as the depth gauge crept backwards and the boat swam persistently upwards, the motion of the hull, normally steady and calm until the actual moment of surfacing, was extremely uneasy. That could only mean that the weather had deteriorated during the night, and one of the brief Adriatic gales had materialized to make their task even harder.

Taylor spun the spokes carefully and shifted in his seat. 'Bit of roughers!' he muttered. 'Just our bleedin' luck!'

'It'll make us more difficult to spot, if there's anyone watching.' Curtis kept his voice even. 'We shall have to make it quick though.'

The boat lurched, and he put out his hand to stop himself falling. The heavy automatic against his hip reminded him again of the uncertainty, and for an instant a tremor of panic coursed through him. He cursed himself. No second thoughts now. This was another point of no return.

'Ten feet, Skipper!'

Curtis was grimly reminded that this would normally have been approaching periscope depth before he had blinded the boat with his stupidity. He wondered vaguely if Duncan was thinking the same.

He slipped the clips on the main hatch and braced his shoulders beneath it. The motion was much worse and the whole control-room was swinging through a crazy arc, throwing pieces of loose gear from side to side, and making the hunched occupants cling onto the controls, or anything else, to prevent serious injury.

'Surfaced!' Curtis spat the word from between his clenched teeth, and heaved open the hatch. For a moment the blast of cold air which lashed him across the face made him gasp, but the sight of the high grey waves which seemed to dwarf the casing of the boat forced all other thoughts from his mind. Gasping painfully, he dragged himself over the coaming and crouched on the small, wave-swept deck. He had to cling to the broken periscope with all his strength to prevent himself from being tossed into the swirling, white-capped water, and with his eyes half-blinded by spray he peered anxiously towards the shore, or where it should have been. Overhead the scudding black clouds tried to disguise the feeble efforts of the dawn to break through, and he knew that unless he acted at once, daylight might surprise them helplessly tossing on the surface. As the boat lifted sluggishly beneath him he caught sight of a dull grey hump and a thin strip of beach. It looked miles away, and as the boat fell heavily into a trough he realized that it was going to be a difficult trip, and they would be in poor shape when they reached the protection of the shore. *If* we make it, he thought wildly.

A long, low roller, its jagged crest laced with blown spray, pushed the boat onto its side and sent a stream of water plunging through the half-open hatch. The boat felt heavier and was not answering to the helm. It could not be long now.

Curtis choked as his head ducked under the clawing seas, and leaned into the control-room. Water surged about the confined space, and already a necklace of blue sparks danced across the switchboard.

'Come on!' He had to yell to make his voice heard above the thunder of the breakers. 'Bale out!'

Taylor appeared beside him, his slight body distorted by his life-jacket, his unruly hair already plastered across his tanned face. As he scrambled up beside Curtis he looked at the sea and swore.

'Christ! Look at that bleedin' lot!' He forced a grin. 'Feel jus' ready for a swim!'

Curtis nodded and helped to pull Jervis over the coaming. The boy looked as white as death, and as a curtain of spray rose over the pitching hull he cried out and hung onto Curtis' arm.

'All got your life-jackets fixed?' He had already checked, but anything was better than just sitting in silence as the water pounded across their sodden bodies.

Duncan pulled himself up beside them, panting heavily. 'She's goin', Ralph!' The water streamed across his thick hair, adding to his wild appearance. 'No need to open the vents!'

'Right, lads!' Curtis spoke jerkily. 'Make for that hill and try to keep together! If we get parted, get there anyway, and watch out!'

Taylor stood up, his legs splayed on the slimy metal. ''Ere we go, blokes!' There was no humour in his eyes, as with a deep breath he stepped clear of the casing. In a second he was well away from the boat, his body buffeted by the waves, and his dark head and orange life-jacket showing only briefly over the surging water.

Duncan followed, making a huge splash as his seaboots kicked out behind him. 'Keep goin', George, I——' his words were drowned by the roar of the rollers cascading across the midget submarine's stricken hull.

Curtis gripped Jervis' arm savagely, so that their faces touched. 'Keep going, and don't look back!' It was suddenly terribly important that the boy should be safe. 'I'll be behind you. Now jump!'

Jervis stared mesmerized at the sea and sobbed, his face puckered up with fear.

The boat plunged again, but didn't seem to be answering her buoyancy tanks.

She's going, Curtis thought desperately. For a moment a twinge of regret crossed his mind. The plunging, waterlogged hull beneath his slipping feet had lost its power to kill and maim, it was somehow pathetic as it tried to lift above the waves yet fell each time deeper into their cruel embrace. The bull-ring lifted momentarily in defiance, and then he felt her begin to slide from under him.

'Jump, man!' He thrust his hand under Jervis' life-jacket and pushed. Together they fell spluttering and gasping into the spray. Curtis felt his ears sing, and tasted the bile in his stomach as he was sucked under. He emerged, choking and gasping, and turned, treading water, to watch

XE.51's propeller turning slowly in the air, as the small, cigar-shaped hull pointed skywards like a memorial. To us, he thought, with sudden fear.

Then it vanished, and with a groan he started to strike out towards the beach, all thoughts banished from his mind but for the cruel necessity to keep swimming, and not give in to the desire to let himself be dragged after his command.

Of the others there was no sign, but he did not seem to worry any more. Nothing mattered but to keep swimming. To keep swimming.

CHAPTER 4

The short, steep waves pounded along the beach, whipped into fierce breakers by the blustery wind. As the sky brightened, their colour began to change from a dirty grey to a deep, cold green, and their anger and strength seemed to mount, as if to vent their full fury upon the white sands before the sun rose to drive their passion back into the langour of a late Adriatic summer.

Duncan had lost sense of time, and until he felt the sand grate against his leaden boots he had begun to feel that his sense of direction had gone, too.

The water within two hundred yards of the tempting safety of the beach was shallow, and half swimming and half crawling, he made a slow and painful progress. Each time he tried to rise up to his feet in the waist-high water a breaker would smash him down from behind, and he felt the strong undertow pulling at his sodden clothes, and the treacherous sand sliding and sucking at his boots. The life-jacket was more hindrance than help, and several times he tried to slip from the harness, but each time he had to give his full strength to a fresh tussle with the waves, which dealt him unwavering body blows from every direction at once.

As he reeled once more to his feet, he half turned and saw a yawning crest bearing down on him, and wearily he kicked forward to save himself. He had a blurred impression of being hurled forward like a twig on a mill-stream, then his face and chest were crashing and scraping on the smooth sand, and he waited for his lungs to burst. He laid where he had been flung, vaguely conscious of the heaviness of his limbs and the receding roar of the water. Gingerly, he opened his eyes and winced. His eyes and mouth were seemingly filled with grit, but he realized that he was firmly on the beach, and a feeling of urgency drove his aching body to its knees and he crawled clumsily up the shelving sand, the sea creeping and hissing up to his heels, to claw and pluck in one final effort to claim him.

The buttons had been ripped from his blouse, and his trousers dragged at his hips as if anchored to the ground. His hair was matted across his streaming forehead, and he was aware of the grit burning in his left eye and the painful beat of his heart. He sat on his haunches in the puddled sand, glaring round with one eye, a wild, gaunt figure, dark against the lightening sky. The beach was empty, and not even a sea-bird challenged the disturbed fury of the water.

Suddenly his glance steadied on a small blue hump which ebbed and rolled across the other side of the sand spit.

With hidden energy Duncan staggered to his feet, and half shambling, half running, he hurried towards it. He kept shaking his head to clear the water and the deafness from his ears, and he held his face to one side to give his good eye a clearer view.

Taylor's body was limp, and in Duncan's hands it already seemed to have the frailty of death.

He pulled the man's head clear of the waves and began to drag him up the beach. Taylor's feet bobbed and nodded with each effort, and his heels cut two pathetic furrows in the virgin sand. As he laid him down, the water began to pour from his open mouth, and Duncan's heart bounded as he heard him begin to retch. Taylor vomited and groaned, and hit out feebly at the air. As his torn fingers touched Duncan's arm, they clutched tightly to the wet cloth and stayed motionless, while the remnants of his mind tried to convey the sense of safety to his half-drowned body. His eyes fluttered open, and Duncan gently wiped the sand and salt from his face.

'All right, cobber? Take it easy.' Duncan smiled sadly.

Taylor stared at him in a mixture of fear and disbelief. 'Steve? Steve?' he croaked vacantly. 'What you doin' 'ere?'

Duncan grinned broadly. 'Waitin' for a bus! What d'you think?'

He propped him carefully against a hillock of soft sand and peered round quickly with his awful, one-eyed stare. 'You stop here, chum, I've got to get after the others!'

Taylor groaned and lay back obediently. 'The others? Oh yes, the others!' He gingerly felt the firm ground under him, and suddenly smiled. 'Christ, that was close!'

Duncan moved down to the water's edge, his mind working furiously. He could now see the other side of the small cove quite clearly and the hill for which he had battled so painfully. Must look for the others, he thought, can't just take George and leave them to rot.

He broke into a run, his boots slipping and sliding, and his stinging eye making him stagger into the water in a drunken, zigzag course.

He halted, sniffing the air, some sense of warning flooding through him. In front of him was a small broken cliff, where one of the hills around the village had fallen into the sea. He heard a voice and then a few short footsteps.

He craned his head and fumbled for his pistol. His groping fingers found only an empty holster, and without even giving it further thought he doubled his huge fists and stepped slowly to the edge of the rocks.

A feeling of relief changed his caution to one of abandon as he saw Curtis swaying in the water knee-deep and staring out to sea. 'Ralph! You son-of-a-bitch! Am I glad to see you!' He reached him in a bound and gripped him by the arm.

Curtis shook at his hold, in a feeble, pre-occupied effort to free himself, never taking his eyes from the sea, and it seemed to Duncan that he was trying to walk back into the waves.

'Ralph! What's up? Have you seen somethin'?' He glared painfully over the water, but saw only the empty tossing whitecaps.

Curtis took another step and mumbled half to himself in a low, broken voice.

'I've let him go, too! I'm going back for him!'

'Who? Ian?' Duncan swung him round to study his face with sudden anxiety. 'I found old George; he's coughin' his heart up on the beach, but he's dinkum otherwise!'

Curtis didn't seem to hear. 'I let him down. He needed me, and I let him go!'

A thin watery beam of yellow light lit up their bruised faces, and Duncan trembled with suppressed urgency.

'Come on, Ralph! There's nothin' you can do. If he's gone, he's gone, an' that's that!'

Curtis turned drunkenly on the soft sand, his eyes blazing. 'I've killed him, too! Damn you, let me go! I'm going after him!'

Duncan looked back up the beach. Taylor might try to find him and get lost. The skipper was obviously done in, and in no condition to make decisions about Jervis or anything else.

'Ralph, come on, boy,' he spoke with deceptive gentleness. 'We've got to hit cover, but quick!'

'Must go and find him.' Curtis staggered weakly and started to wade into the water.

Duncan patted him on the shoulder, and as Curtis turned impatiently towards him, he drove his fist upwards in a short, vicious uppercut. Curtis didn't even touch the sand, as he was pitched across the other man's broad shoulder.

Breathing hard, Duncan plodded along the beach until he met Taylor swaying unsteadily by the hillock where he had left him.

'Cripes! Is the skipper dead? 'As 'e bought it?' Taylor trotted to meet them, his face strained and suddenly old.

'Nope! He's passed out!' Duncan measured up the distance to the hill and took in the mass of bushes which crowned its summit like a green wig. 'C'mon, we got to move, George, and get ourselves bedded down.'

The climb upwards was slow and painful. Every minute of the journey made Duncan's breath wheeze and sob, and each second he expected to hear a challenge or the crash of a shot. Taylor trotted beside him, muttering and cursing, oblivious to danger and still only half aware that he had survived.

They found a thick clump of bush and bracken on a small overhanging shelf of sandstone, and Duncan laid his burden thankfully under the shade of the leaves. 'Sit down, George,' he said patiently, as Taylor stood dazedly on the edge of their hideaway, 'you're a bit too old for shooting!' He sighed as Taylor slumped heavily beside him like a puppet which had had the strings cut from it, and peered over the top of the coarse grass at the side of the ledge. The village was smaller than he had imagined. Tiny, whitewashed, single-storied cottages scattered carelessly in the deep cleft between the hills and lining the rough track which led down to the beach. He could just see the line of brightly painted fishing boats pulled up on the far end of the sand spit, and licked his lips. One of those might do, he thought.

A dog barked, and he saw the shadows cast by the cottages begin to harden and darken as the sun filtered through the cloud, which already seemed to be fading.

Several of the dwellings had smoke drifting upwards from their chimneys, and Duncan was aware that he was ravenously hungry. The smoke was going straight up, he realized bitterly. The wind had gone as suddenly as a bad dream. But for its visit, their suffering might have been saved, and Ian might have been with them. A figure stepped from one of the doors, small and indistinct. It stretched, and Duncan imagined him yawning to greet the morning. It was peaceful and unreal. Untouched and all the more terrifying because of it.

Duncan sighed and rolled on to his side, feeling the water drain from his boots. A little of the sun's rays touched his cheek, and he felt very tired. He turned to speak to Taylor, but he was already asleep, sprawled on his back where he had fallen in the effort of pulling off his sodden jacket.

With a groan he turned onto his back and laced his fingers beneath his hair and felt the coarse mixture of sand and salt which it had collected.

His mind wandered aimlessly back to the midget submarine, and he imagined their control-room already being explored by the fish. It was to be hoped that too much oil had not seeped to the surface, he decided, it might make things more awkward. He heard a long intake of breath, and craned his head to watch as Curtis sat up slowly, rubbing his jaw.

The blue eyes moved vaguely around the bushes and the clear ceiling of the sky before they eventually settled on Duncan.

'Sorry about the poke, Ralph.' Duncan spoke guardedly. 'I guess it was 'bout all I could do.'

Curtis frowned as if trying to piece together what had happened, and then his eyes clouded and he drew up his knees to his chin, his arms wrapped round them.

'I was going after him.' It was more of a question than a statement. 'I remember him calling.' He shook his head. 'Perhaps I only imagined that I heard him.' He sat up with a jerk. 'Hell! Where the devil are we?'

Duncan grinned, and allowed his bunched muscles to relax slightly. 'On the goddamned hill! Right where you wanted us!'

Curtis raised himself on his knees, still rubbing his chin. 'You can still land a punch,' he commented, as he surveyed the village beneath them. 'No hard feelings, Ralph?'

'Not to you.'

'D'you want to go over what happened?' Duncan saw the crouched shoulders stiffen, and wished he could see his eyes.

'He was drowned,' he said flatly. 'What else is there to realize?'

Duncan sighed, and tried to open his left eye. 'What else, as you say. What a bit of damned bad luck.' He decided it would be prudent to change the subject. 'What now exactly?'

Curtis sat back on his haunches, the clean outline of his face turned towards the sun. 'We must wait until it's dark, and then have a scout round.' He eyed the fishing boats narrowly. 'Of course, if that lot shove off for the day, we might slip out during the day and get the lay of the land. We'll have to get some grub. We don't seem to have much left.' He pulled out his wet pockets. 'I've only got a grenade and this tin of meat.'

'I know which I'll have!'

Curtis smiled for the first time. 'Thanks, Steve,' he said simply.

He looked at Duncan's eye. 'Here, let me have a go.' He cut the tail off his shirt with his diver's knife, and after drying it in the warm air he began to dab the grit from the inflamed eyeball.

Every so often they watched the houses, waiting for some sign of what to expect.

A woman in a bright red dress left one of the nearer cottages and walked slowly towards the beach. The two officers stared at her curiously. She was short and fat, and her long black hair gleamed dully in the sunlight. She was a woman, nevertheless, and one of the potential enemy.

'What a bird!' Duncan blinked his eye and smiled happily. 'I feel ready for anythin' now. Even her!'

Some men and women had gathered at the top of the track, and Duncan's heart gave a leap as he saw the fishing nets that some of the men were dragging down the path. 'They're goin' out, I guess.'

'Good. There don't seem too many of 'em, do there?'

Duncan hissed sharply, 'Hold it, there's a car or somethin' comin'!' Taylor groaned and suddenly appeared beside them, scratching his stomach absently.

'Get down, George!' Duncan snapped. 'The big picture's just startin'!'

The villagers had nearly reached the sand spit, and they could hear their voices quite clearly as they chattered and laughed and stuffed their pockets with food which the women were carrying. They, too, were suddenly aware of the noise of the car engine. They all halted, and several more faces appeared at some of the doorways.

Curtis frowned. 'They're not used to cars here either, apparently!'

'Not surprised.' Taylor was watching the people as if he had never seen any before. 'What wiv them bleedin' roads I'm surprised they see anythink!'

'Nuts! I've driven over worse'n this,' began Duncan, but Curtis's frozen expression halted him.

A small, sandy-coloured scout car came labouring around the side of the end houses, and with its fat tyres skidding over the dirt track, drove straight for the centre of the village.

They gazed at the man who stepped from the back seat and stood tapping his boot impatiently until the villagers started to hurry towards him.

Duncan dug his fingers into the sand. It was not quite as he had expected it would be, and the man, rather than he and his companions, seemed out of place.

I've been fighting them for four years, he thought slowly, and this is the first proper German I've seen.

He had seen plenty of prisoners, but they were quite different. Sullen, beaten, they bore no resemblance to the slim, impatient figure who leaned negligently against the side of the car. He could see the pistol at his belt, and the long-peaked Afrika Korps cap with its silver eagle.

Curtis wasn't looking at the man any more. He stared fixedly at the bright orange life-jacket which the German officer had just pulled from the car and flung at the feet of the fishermen.

'D'you see that, Ralph?' Duncan whispered excitedly. 'The bastard's got Ian's jacket! What d'you think it means?'

Curtis shook his head, his eyes puzzled. 'Ian might have slipped out of it and the thing's been washed up somewhere, or,' he added harshly, 'Ian might have been in it when they found it.'

Duncan seemed even more excited. 'The wind, Ralph, don't you remember? It was agin us! He wouldn't have been washed up yet. He must have made it on his own!'

Curtis appeared to Duncan to grow in stature. 'Steve, you may be right!' They both turned their eyes to the German. 'But where the hell is he? I wish to God I could hear what that Jerry's saying.'

'They don't seem to like what he's said, anyway.'

Duncan was right. The villagers bowed their heads, and some started to shout from the crowd in high, protesting voices. But the officer raised his hand so that his watch glittered in the sun, and at the same time tapped his holster.

Then he turned his back and climbed into the car, and within seconds only a cloud of yellow dust remained to mark his visit.

'Well, what d'you make of that?' Duncan peered at the fishermen who were dispersing towards the boats.

There was no shouting or laughter any more, and Curtis saw one elderly woman dabbing her eyes with her black skirt.

'I imagine that Jerry has made some sort of threat.' Curtis spoke musingly. 'After the dock blowing up, and then finding a British life-jacket, they've come to the conclusion that there's a saboteur of some sort hiding in the vicinity. He must have warned 'em to keep their eyes peeled – or else! That makes it even more important that we should find Ian before someone else does.'

'I'll go,' said Duncan woodenly.

'We'll both go, separately,' said Curtis. 'George must stay here, just in case Ian shows up later on.'

Taylor screwed his face into a grimace. 'Wot, leave me all on me jack? Can't I come too?'

'No. Don't talk so wet.' Duncan eyed him cheerfully. 'You must keep the welcome mat down for us!'

They settled down to wait, watching the boats being warped down the white sand and into the calm water. There were a few waves and only a few shouts, and then the boats were moving slowly away, their tan-coloured sails hanging limp and the ancient diesel engines thumping noisily on the clean air.

The women and a few old men watched the boats depart, and then they moved back to the village and stood in small huddled groups, their hands and arms jerking expressively as they loitered together, apparently unwilling to be left alone.

Taylor produced a watertight packet of chocolate, and they ate it in quick, hungry gulps. They were all feeling the pains of thirst very badly, and when Duncan saw an old villager carrying a long-necked bottle into a cottage he ground his teeth angrily.

'Jesus! Just look at that joker! I'll go down an' have some of that if he waves it about any more!'

Curtis looked down at the empty beach. Empty but for a torn fishing net and a few nodding gulls. The boats were well clear now, small coloured smudges on the green sea.

'I'll work down along the beach, Steve, and try to get beyond the cove, where you found me last night,' he added with a thin smile. 'I think your best bet is to skirt the houses and try to find where the road leads. No tricks, and no risks. Got it?'

Duncan saluted with a coarse gesture and grinned, his teeth white against the stubble of his chin. 'Right! How long shall we all be?'

'Not too long. 'Bout an hour at the most.'

'Blimey! An hour?' Taylor scrambled up protestingly. 'What am I supposed to do then?'

Duncan forced him down again. 'Steady, George. Just sit tight and keep yer eyes peeled!'

Taylor huddled miserably under a bush and watched the two figures disappear round the side of the hill. It was bloody to be left alone. His eye fell on the sand-covered grenade which Curtis had left behind. The mechanic's brain took over from his fears, and with quick, deft movements he began to dismantle and clean the bomb, his face set in concentration.

Once down the hill and across the open sand spit, Curtis realized just how inadequate his plans were. He felt completely naked and unprotected as he pressed himself against the rocks and stones at the foot of the small cliff and stared wildly about him, as if he was already being hunted.

He had repeatedly put off thinking about the actual method and time of escape, and the admission of his failure to make some definite plan worried him. The thought of Jervis made him leave the cover of the rocks and hurry further along the side of the cove. It reminded him of Cornwall, with its deserted beach and impressive silence. But the suspense and the constant fear of discovery made him concentrate on each piece of cover in advance and stop to listen at every few steps.

Once he looked back for the hill, but it had vanished from his vision. That made him feel even more alone, and he had to force himself to move forward again until he reached the end of the cove where the hills and the beach met, and the only way forward was to climb. He studied the hills carefully and slowly. Sparse green grass, yellowed by the heat and the salt air, and some small clumps of trees. Here and there were a few haphazard plots or gardens cut into the hillside, as if the villagers had half-heartedly tried to cultivate the land and had given it up as a bad job.

Suppose I had come ashore at this point? he thought. Where would I go? The hill for the rendezvous was invisible, and with the sea at my back there was only the open sand of the cove or this range of hills.

He thrust his hands into his pockets. They were dry and stiff, and his fingers felt the familiar shape of his pipe. He had neither his pouch nor any matches, but the feel of the pipe gave him confidence. It was like an old friend, and he stuck it between his teeth, the salt taste reminding him of his thirst.

Suppose I meet someone? What do I do? Shoot him, or her, and just walk on? He felt the pistol suddenly heavy at his hip. This is madness. I must think of something. He found that he had started to climb the smooth side of the hill.

He froze as a dog barked shrilly in the distance, and he wondered how Duncan was getting on. Duncan would be better at this sort of thing, he thought bitterly. He was good at everything. If he had been in command none of this would have happened.

He looked back at the open sea. It was no longer hostile. It was home and refuge all in one. He was, as Jervis had said, out of place ashore. The sea shimmered and seemed to mock him.

A dark shape moved in the corner of his eye, and even as he turned, he saw the forepart of a ship begin to move slowly round the headland. For a moment panic gripped him. It was as if the ship was looking for him and had already moved round to trap him from behind. He calmed slightly when he considered that he must be invisible as he stood on the grassy slope, and as the ship slowly took shape the very idea of pursuit seemed ridiculous.

She was an old coastal schooner, and had once been very beautiful. Her slim hull still bore traces of white paint, and her long raked bowsprit and two lofty masts added to her appearance of past craftsmanship. Her dirty sails were furled, the canvas hanging from the yards in uneven, careless bundles. A blue cloud of exhaust gas hovered around her high counter, and he could clearly hear the rasping cough of an old engine.

There were plenty of similar craft plying their trade up and down the Adriatic, and the Germans had made full use of them for carrying supplies and troops, and thereby relieve the overworked railways and roads. A few figures were on her littered deck, but only one man appeared to be in uniform. The sun flashed on a white cap and drill tunic as a tall figure strode from one side of the poop to the other.

Instead of going about and making for the open sea, she altered course towards the cove, and he saw a group of figures gathering in the bows around the anchor.

Must know the water pretty well, thought Curtis, as he watched the ship feeling her way between the dark patches of the shallows. He remembered well enough how little depth there was outside the cove, and wondered if the little schooner was permanently based here.

He watched narrowly as a dinghy was lowered over the ship's side and

bobbed reluctantly against the hull, while the vessel continued to move
slowly towards the shore.

He heard a faint shout, and saw the splash under the bowsprit as the
anchor plummeted down.

A moment later the little schooner swung lazily at her hawser, and the
engine, after a few rasping coughs, fell silent.

Curtis sat in the grass, biting on the stem of his pipe and feeling the
warmth of the forenoon sun coursing through his whole body. A tiny sea-
breeze fanned his face, and he jerked back his head to shake away his
dry, salt-caked hair.

He found that he was able to concentrate more fully and his mind had
stopped jumping from one possibility to another. Somehow, he
knew that this schooner was the answer to his prayer, the avenue of
escape.

Thinking of the others brought his mind back to Jervis. They had to
find him before they could do anything else, before they could
contemplate any movement at all.

Then there was the problem of finding out about the Allied invasion.
Suppose it had been called off? That would mean a complete alteration
of plans.

He leaned forward as the dinghy shoved off from the schooner's side.
Two roughly-dressed seamen pulled at the oars, while two other men sat
in the stern.

Curtis snuggled down deep in the grass and made a small opening to
watch the boat's leisurely approach.

One of the passengers was a short fat Italian in a faded red shirt, and a
greasy peaked cap tilted over his eyes. Flabby and middle-aged, he had
only the cap to show his authority. Must be the captain, thought Curtis.
Yet the other man, who sat stiffly on the thwart, was obviously no mere
seaman.

The boat grated ashore and the fat Italian stood up and stepped easily
over the gunwale onto the firm sand. As he stepped clear of the dinghy
he revealed his slightly-built companion, whose white drill jacket and
well-creased trousers clashed with the rough appearance of the other
men. Curtis' heart quickened as the second passenger stepped carelessly
onto the beach and, after a brief word with the Italian, started to walk
up the cove, practically on the same track which Curtis had just taken.
As he walked he swung his uniform cap in his hand, his fair hair tilted to
the sun and tanned skin dark against the white drill.

The sun also reflected on the glittering shoulder straps of his tunic. As
he drew nearer Curtis realized what he had first feared, that the man was
a German naval officer, the two bright bars of gold lace proclaiming him
to be a lieutenant.

Must be in command of the schooner, he thought. It was common practice for the Germans to put their own officers in charge of the normal Italian crews.

The German was practically below him, and Curtis caught his breath as he stopped to examine the deep footmarks in the sand. Curtis' own footprints. But after a cursory glance round, the lieutenant carried on his way towards the end of the cove.

Curtis lost sight of him for a few minutes, and then saw that the German was climbing up the hill by a small narrow path, his legs moving in long rhythmical strides and his head thrown back like an athlete.

He waited until the other man had passed over the rim of the hill, and then, very slowly, his mouth dry, and not only from thirst, Curtis started to follow him.

The house which confronted him on the other side of the ridge was a surprise in itself. Two-storied and spacious, it stood in the middle of a vast, diamond-shaped flower garden. Small stone walls separated the various colourful sections from the wide circular drive which sur-rounded the house, and several large ornamental ponds, with gentle fountains playing on the dark water, were placed at intervals around the gardens.

The house, white-painted and cool, seemed to be all windows, and as he watched he saw the German run lightly up the steps to the deep, sun-shadowed porch and disappear into the house.

In the drive stood three cars – two large Fiats, and the dusty scout car which Curtis had seen earlier.

He licked his cracked lips as the sound of the hissing fountains penetrated his racing thoughts. He cursed himself for his weakness, and tried to peer round the small wall nearest him to see the other corner of the building. Probably a German officers' mess of some sort, he decided. Although a more un-military place would be hard to imagine. He glanced at his watch. Ought to be getting back soon. Taylor will wonder what the devil's happened to me.

There was a sudden grinding of gears and the sound of a labouring engine beyond the line of trees which framed the house, and then a long-muzzled armoured car, the black crosses clearly painted on the turret, drove into view and parked beside the scout car. After a few moments three soldiers in field-grey uniforms tumbled out of their vehicle and sat on the grass under one of the trees. He could hear their laughter, and watched enviously as one man, a corporal's chevron on his sleeve, held a chianti bottle high over his head and tried to catch the liquid with his open mouth as it splashed redly across the front of his tunic.

Curtis tore his eyes away and began to retrace his steps. Once clear of the ridge he started to run down the hill towards the beach, conscious of the need to get under cover and discuss his discoveries with the others.

He paused wearily at the foot of the small cliff and mopped his streaming face with his sleeve. As he lowered his arm he froze, and stared fixedly at the horse and rider which were cantering slowly and easily towards him.

At any other time the girl and her chestnut horse would have been a sight to make any man stand and gasp, but at that moment, as she turned easily in the saddle and shaded her eyes to watch the anchored schooner, Curtis was rooted to the spot with the sudden danger and menace which she represented. She was clad in a bright green shirt and well-cut jodhpurs, and her hair, which was woven into a long single plait, hung across her slim shoulders like a blue-black snake that rippled and shone each time her body jerked to the horse's motion.

A sudden desperate idea came to Curtis as he watched her drawing nearer and nearer to his position. The schooner was obviously a regular visitor to the cove, as was the German officer, so why shouldn't this girl take him for a German from the ship?

He already had his battledress trousers tucked into the top of his leather sea-boots, and with his fair, sun-bleached hair and blue eyes he looked more like the popular conception of the typical Aryan than did either of the officers Curtis had already seen.

The horse saw him and stopped, its huge liquid eyes watching him anxiously, while the front hooves pawed the sand in quick, agitated movements.

The girl swung round in the saddle, a look of brief annoyance flitting across her dark face. Then she saw Curtis, and her full red mouth tilted at the corners in surprise, and for a moment Curtis thought she would speak.

With his heart pounding against his ribs, Curtis nodded to her, his head bobbing forward in a neat motion which helped to hide his face from hers.

Keeping his eyes hard and cold, he allowed his mouth to smile briefly. *'Guten Tag, Fraulein!'* And then he had passed her.

He forced his eyes to stare dead ahead at the wavy line between sand and sea, and waited breathlessly for the girl to call after him, or hear her challenge his appearance on the lonely beach.

After a while he stopped and bent down to remove his boot. As he tipped an imaginary stone from it, he glanced quickly back up the beach. He was just in time to see the sun's reflection across a piece of green shirt and the horse's chestnut flank before both horse and rider vanished over the Ridge towards the hidden house.

A shiver ran through him, and he looked down at his filthy battledress and salt-whitened boots. His face felt rough and bruised, and his whole being throbbed with weariness and sudden frustration. His father's voice seemed to boom in his ears, probing, chiding, and sarcastic. All at once

Curtis began to realize just what his present position really meant. He was little better than a hunted animal. As a person he no longer existed. He thought of the proud girl on her horse, the look of surprise and contempt on her face. No doubt the mistress of one of the Germans, he thought, and he suddenly felt the old hatred begin to mount within him. It was as if his father had forced him to hate once more, had even provided the goading force to make him act. He ran blindly along the beach, only half aware of the rocks which he ducked around and the stunted bushes which afforded him cover.

He was breathless when he eventually reached the top of the hill, and fell gasping beside Taylor and Duncan, who eyed him with alarm.

'OK, Ralph? Did you find anything?'

Curtis lay propped on his sore elbows, his chest heaving painfully. For a few moments he could not speak, but he stared unbelievingly at the flask of water which Duncan proffered him. He grasped the slim, straw-bound bottle and lifted the neck to his lips. They watched him as he swallowed a mouthful of water and closed his eyes in silent ecstasy.

'Well, Ralph?' Duncan rubbed his hands together impatiently.

Curtis nodded slowly. He could still feel the water in his throat. It was like the fountains around the silent house. 'I saw some more soldiers,' he answered flatly. 'And the ship!'

A light gleamed in Duncan's eye. 'The ship? Ah, yes. We are thinking the same things, eh?' He grinned recklessly.

'Where did you get the water?' asked Curtis sharply, the bottle again catching his eye. It was like a piece of another world.

'Christ, never mind the bottle!' Taylor exploded, his face drawn. 'What about the bleedin' Jerries?'

Duncan ignored the outburst. 'Found the bottle outside a hut, and then tumbled on a stream. But, Ralph,' he leaned forward, his face urgent. 'I found out a few things, too! I think Jerry is movin' up troops all over the place, and look at this!' He handed Curtis a crumpled sheet of newspaper. On the front page was a printed map showing the southern half of Italy. The whole southern coastline was stabbed with huge arrows, each marked with a Union Jack. Curtis stared at it blankly, the glaring Italian headlines dancing before him like a weird code. 'Don't you see, Ralph, it's on! The boys have landed!' Duncan's voice was dangerously loud. 'The invasion's under way!'

Curtis handled the scrap of paper as if it was a precious document.

'Today's date on the paper,' he said at length, 'so they must have been fighting for a couple of days already.'

'Does that mean we're going to pinch a boat?' Taylor looked anxiously from one to the other.

Duncan eyed the schooner, which swung at her anchor like a small white toy, the distance masking her scars and adding to her graceful beauty. 'Too goddamned right we'll pinch a boat! Eh, Ralph?' He rubbed his hands together like sandpaper. 'There's only a Jerry officer an' a handful of flamin' dagos aboard! We can get aboard her easy, an' with the grenade and our two pistols we can take care of them easy!'

His jubilation and wild excitement was infectious, and Curtis rolled over to stare at the ship, his blue eyes cold and hard.

'We might, at that,' he said softly. 'We shall have to do it when she's due to sail, and not before.'

Duncan shrugged. 'Hmm, I guess so. It wouldn't do to give anything away to the locals. I don't reckon that old engine'd take us far enough before the high-fly boys came after us.' His eyes took on a dreamy look. 'Just think, George, a coupla days and we'd be reportin' to Admiral Cunningham in person. One flamin' dock blown up, and one little Eyetie schooner for a bit of yachtin'!'

Taylor looked unconvinced. 'It's a long way,' he muttered.

Duncan slapped him across the shoulder. 'Yeh! An' it's a damned long way to walk, too!'

Curtis was thinking hard; a plan was coming at last. All they had to do was find out when the ship was leaving, and be ready. He sighed, *and* find Jervis. He suddenly remembered the Italian girl. She had been beautiful, and he tried to picture her face, but he could only see her red mouth and the arrogant tilt of her head.

'Bitch!' he said savagely.

'How's that again?'

Curtis shook his head, irritated with himself for allowing the girl to intrude on his plan. 'Nothing. But I was just thinking, we'll have to get ourselves cleaned up a bit.'

Duncan's jaw dropped. 'We aimin' to go callin' on the local parson?'

'We may have to look like Germans,' answered Curtis slowly.

'Us?' Taylor was looking worse. 'We'd never get away wiv it!'

'I already have!'

He turned back to the ship. She was suddenly inviting and beautiful, like a lonely woman. He sighed wearily and rested his head on his hands. Where the hell was Jervis?

As if reading his thoughts, Duncan said quietly, 'If the boat's ready an' we haven't found Ian,' he paused, 'well, are we leavin'?'

'What d'you think?' He kept his eyes averted.

'I think we shall have to go. After all, he may have bought it already.' He shrugged. 'Still, you're the skipper.'

Curtis felt desperately tired. 'Yes, *I'm* the skipper,' he answered bitterly.

Taylor shifted uncomfortably in the sand. 'The crew of the boat ain't come ashore yet. Maybe they're shovin' off sooner than we think?'

'Nope. They've not taken on fresh water yet.' Duncan's voice was patient. 'I saw some of the locals gettin' the water cart filled, so they'll be in for tonight, I reckon.'

'Did you see her captain?' Curtis turned his mind back to the plan. 'What, the fat little bloke with the cap? Yeh, I saw him. He was gabbin' about the water, I think. He didn't look so hot, did he?'

It all seemed suddenly clear and urgent, and Curtis sat up with a quick, nervous movement.

'Look here, Steve, this is how I see it.' His voice was crisp, and Duncan eyed him with evident surprise.

'We'll get down to the village this evening, when it's nice and dark, and have another poke round for Ian. At the same time we'll get a wash and tidy up, so that we don't stand out as bloody scarecrows if we want to show ourselves. I think the Jerries will be worried at having a saboteur hanging around the place, and sooner or later they'll start putting the heat on the villagers. That's what our friend was doing this morning, I imagine. Right so far?'

Duncan nodded thoughtfully. 'Yeah, I think so. D'you think Jerry is worried about his gallant allies? I mean, d'you suppose he's wonderin' which way the cat'll jump when our fellas get a bit closer?'

'Well, wouldn't you?' Curtis smiled grimly. 'I'd like to get my hands on some of the bastards!'

'What in hell's got into you, Ralph? I'd have thought you'd done your share of blowin' 'em up!'

Curtis shrugged vaguely. He wondered at himself and why he was feeling so bitter again. Was it the girl's expression? Was it that she had seen him for what he was? He shook his head angrily to clear it of these stupid fancies.

'How's the other pistol?'

'S'okay,' said Taylor. 'I give it to Steve. 'E's more 'andy wiv it.' He held up the grenade with something like pride. 'This'll do me!'

'Right. Well, hang onto it.' Curtis surveyed them bleakly. 'It'll be quite something if we pull this off!'

Duncan tossed the pistol and caught it lightly in the air. 'We'll give the little Jerry lootenant something to write home about!' He tossed the gun again, his mouth set in a hard smile. 'I hope he's enjoying himself with the local sheilas tonight!'

Taylor looked across. 'Why, for Pete's sake?'

The gun landed with a sharp smack in Duncan's palm and pointed unwaveringly at the sea. ''Cause I don't think he'll get another chance, that's why!'

They settled down to watch and sleep by relays, each man taking a turn in the vigil over the dusty village and the little glimmering ship.

Each man saw them differently. Duncan watched the white cottages and followed the movements of the villagers narrowly, with the eyes of a hunter. He didn't feel either beaten or subdued, just the vague urge to get to grips with the future, and as soon as possible. A young girl walked down the path to the sea, leading a goat on a cord. He smiled secretly. A girl under the sun, with her mouth against your ear, and her body close to yours. That would be more like it.

Taylor saw only houses and vague shapes of people moving near them. They were all hostile and alien to him, and each untoward movement made him duck his head and curse the stupidity of leaving the submarine. Somehow he didn't feel it likely that he was going to live much longer, and the more he thought about it, the more the shadows seemed to close in.

Curtis saw many things, although few of them were there to see. Once the girl's face was there, shimmering in the sand, mocking him, like the girl in Chelsea. And then he began to sweat as he saw the twisting, distorted face of Roberts in the severed net. But as his body got nearer, Curtis saw that the face was different; this time it was Jervis, and the face was changing. It was no longer distorted and swollen, but sad and reproachful, and the dead lips said silently, 'I trusted you, and you failed me!'

Curtis ground his teeth and mopped the sweat from his eyes. The sun smote his neck like a fiery sword, and he groaned aloud with the thoughts which tortured him. Was that why he wanted action? To free himself from his guilt? He tried to concentrate on the schooner, which seemed to quiver in the heat-haze. Tomorrow. What would happen then, and how many of them would be left?

He glanced back at his companions, who were sleeping in the shade of the bushes – Taylor with his mouth open and his breath rough and uneven; Duncan sprawled like a dead man in the sand, the pistol protruding from his belt like a wicked steel eye.

Which of us will be next? He reached wearily for the flask, and remembered the house on the hill. She would be there. Cool, soft dress, and slim brown hands stroking that long plait of hair. Damn her! And all the others! But the strange yearning in his chest persisted and kept him company throughout his watch.

The sun crossed its summit and began to move graciously over the flat sea. Some of its rays fell on the schooner, and some lighted the sails of the returning fishing boats. And some caressed the dark green trough which hid the flooded submarine, where it lay empty and harmless, like a dead shark.

CHAPTER 5

Sub-Lieutenant Ian Jervis opened his eyes slowly and stared vacantly at the roughly-timbered roof above his head. For several long moments he lay quite still, as if waiting for life to re-start and events to fall into their proper perspective. He was aware instead of the throbbing pain which burned across his head like a branding iron, and the great feeling of weakness which made him groan again and move his head dazedly from side to side.

As his cheek brushed against the rough, dirty pillow under his head, he chilled, as the complete strangeness of the silent room brought the terrifying memories flooding back to him in a series of wavering pictures. Most of all, he remembered the sea. The great, black towering waves which dragged and beat at his body until he no longer held the breath to call out, and which filled his eyes until he could no longer look for the help which he knew could never come. He tried to wrinkle his brow, as if that might help to clear his brain, but the stabbing pain across his head made him cry out, and his eyes clouded with tears. Vaguely, he could remember the beach rushing towards and then beneath him, as a wave lifted him up and flung him like a rag doll on the shore. Then the blow, a second of flashing light which exploded in his skull, and then . . . he stared round . . . and then what?

Slowly the picture of his refuge became complete, as with short, painful twists of his neck he examined each section of the room. It was only about ten feet by ten, and appeared to be some sort of hut. The floor was bare, stamped earth, and the bright sunlight which filtered around the sides of the strips of sacking which covered each of the two tiny windows displayed, amongst other things, a pile of old, sea-washed bottles and a torn net, while against the broken brick grate was stacked a mass of old driftwood, a navigation lamp, and a stinking bundle of rags. A movement in the grate made him gasp, and he lowered his gaze to meet the curious, unwinking stare of a large grey rat, which sat perched on an upended tin can, slowly and methodically cleaning its whiskers.

'G'on! Scat!' Jervis tried to shout, but his voice was a mere croak, and he let his head fall back onto the sacking of his pillow. He tried to think and keep back the tide of misery which threatened to engulf him with each new discovery.

As he moved his head, his palm touched the warm skin of his thigh, and with quick nervous movements he found that beneath the evil-smelling blanket he was quite naked. The shock made him struggle up onto his elbows, and the realization of his nakedness brought the feeling back to his limbs. The roughness of the blanket against his skin, the pain in his head, and the fact that he was alone in some strange hut, told him that at least he was still free. But who had put him there, and where his rescuer had gone, was quite another thing. And where were his clothes? A cold chill ran down his spine. Suppose someone had found him, and hidden his clothes while he fetched the police or the soldiers? He struggled with the blanket, suddenly frantic. Must get out. Must get away. The messages hammered in his head as he scrambled over the side of the battered couch. As his bare feet took his weight, the hut seemed to swim around him in a mad whirlpool, and he reeled against the wall, trying to fight off the dizziness and the pain, his hands scrabbling weakly for support. The rat scuttled amongst the old bottles and vanished, and Jervis stood with his legs astride, as if on the deck of a heaving ship.

Another movement caught his eye from across the couch, and for a moment he was almost too frightened and sick to look.

It was a long strip of cracked and scored glass, probably taken from an equally old wardrobe, and as Jervis stared at his own distorted reflection he hardly noticed the bruises on his sunburned skin, or even the crude bandage which entangled his skull like a turban. As the blood pounded through his veins, and his fingers gripped the wall behind him, he found that he was staring, not at a proud, dependable officer, but at a shaking, frightened boy.

With a sob he leaned back against the warm stonework and closed his eyes. He was suddenly both ashamed and completely without hope. To be found like this ... He looked down at himself in despair. It was the final stab of failure.

Where were Curtis and the others, he wondered. Most likely dead, as he himself might have been but for all this.

He sensed that there was someone or something watching him, and he had to force his head round to look. The room was still and empty, the sun glinting on the old bottles and making his limbs shine against the filthy couch, like a statue. His eyes reached the heavy door and stopped. It was just the same as before, but for the cracks in the unplaned woodwork. They no longer allowed the sunlight to enter like little gold spears; they were black, covered from outside.

So they've come. He felt his limbs go slack, and a bitter resignation held him quite still and limp as he stood and watched the door. A small spark of defiance dared to lighten some of the blackness in his mind, and he tried to pull himself together, to get ready for whatever was to come.

The door opened with surprising quickness, and the strange figure stood black against the sunlight and the green hills, like a gaunt scarecrow.

The man stepped inside the hut with a queer, loping gait, and shut the door behind him. For a moment he leaned back against the door and stared fixedly at Jervis as the rat had done, without speaking or moving. Jervis clenched his fists and gazed, wide-eyed. The man was dressed in a greasy, ragged smock which hung almost to his knees, and from under which his thin bent legs protruded like sticks. His feet were encased in a dirty pair of sandals, and the skin of his bare feet was thick with grime and filth.

Jervis could only stare at his face. It could have been any age between twenty or fifty, encircled with a mass of wild, straggly black hair and a thick beard, which left only the large, vacant brown eyes and a patch of sun-wrinkled skin uncovered. It was his mouth which drew Jervis' fascinated eyes. It was wide and slack, and moved loosely with restless abandon, as if its owner neither possessed the will nor the wish to control it. Even as he watched, the creature's tongue lolled wetly across the rim of his beard and an unheeded stream of spittle ran downwards across the tattered smock. As Jervis stood against the wall he saw that the man was carrying what appeared to be his uniform, rolled in a tight ball, the boots and pistol belt protruding from the middle.

'I . . .' began Jervis slowly, his voice shattering the silence of the room. 'I must thank you . . .' he stopped. The man only rolled his eyes wildly and allowed his mouth to slip into a lopsided grin.

God, he groaned inwardly, a raving lunatic! A crazy hermit or beachcomber who had stumbled across his body by accident, and who was going to torment him even more. He held out his hands for his clothes, and waited for the man to snatch them away.

Instead, the grin faded, and for a brief moment he looked almost solemn, and then, with great care, he handed the bundle to Jervis.

Keeping one eye on the figure by the door, Jervis began to struggle into his crumpled uniform. It was a tremendous effort, and once he would have fallen but for a clawlike hand which darted out and held his elbow like a vice until the weakness had passed.

Eventually he had finished dressing, and only the pistol belt lay between them on the floor. As he bent to pick it up a look of indescribable pain crossed the other man's face, and he cowered back against the wall.

Jervis stood up, the heavy belt gripped uncertainly in his hand. For a moment he forgot his own pain and misery, and his heart filled with pity for the human wreck who had rescued him, bandaged his head, put him to bed, and dried his soaked clothing, and who now cowered with fear at the sight of the gun.

He tossed it onto the couch and grinned shakily. 'See?' He pointed at the gun. 'See? Friends, yes?' He stopped. It had sounded so ridiculous, and apart from the change of expression on the creature's face it was obviously useless trying to speak English. As Jervis watched, the grin reappeared, and the man nodded violently, his thick tangled hair falling across his forehead like a mane. From his mouth came a queer, spine-chilling gurgle, as if he was choking, and then more nods.

Jervis sat down weakly on the couch and followed the man's movements with his eyes, as he darted around the hut, searching and scratching amongst the piles of flotsam and junk.

An idea crossed his mind, and he waited until the man had his back turned, and then, mustering his strength, he called sharply across the room.

'Here, you! Stand to attention when you're addressing an officer! What's your blasted name?' He fell back on the couch, laughing uncontrollably and with something like hysteria.

What else can happen now? A deaf-and-dumb madman for company, and I don't even know where I am! He jumped as he felt a prod in the thigh. The man was holding a cracked cup out to him.

Jervis held it to his lips. It was strange that he felt no thirst, but this poor creature had probably been pouring water down his throat while he was unconscious. He sipped the brackish water slowly, aware that the brown eyes were watching him eagerly.

He handed the cup back, and received some fresh tomatoes in return. He offered some of them back, but immediately the man shrank away, and shook his head decidedly.

'All right, my friend, I'll eat, and I only wish I could tell you just how I feel about being rescued, and about your kindness.'

The tomatoes were delicious, and he handed back the empty plate, a smile of satisfaction on his lips. He hoped that would make up for the lack of words, and he was rewarded by the lopsided grin and a low grunting.

Jervis wondered what would happen next, and stood up to look from one of the windows.

The effect was instantaneous. He felt the clawlike hands on his arms, and as helplessly as a baby he was dragged back to the couch. The wild figure shook his head and waved his arms about in a frenzy, and once, stood against the window, crucified by the sunlight, and shook his head so violently that Jervis thought he was having a fit.

Jervis nodded slowly and tried to smile. 'All right,' he murmured softly, 'I get it. You're trying to tell me it's not safe to go out. So what'll we do? Stop here till the war's over?' He lay back on the blanket, the throbbing in his head again taking control. Can't think about it any more. Must rest. Must get my strength back. He watched through half-closed lids as his weird companion capered around the hut, his shadow looming and fading like a huge bat. He felt the strong fingers pulling off his battledress blouse and lifting his feet onto the couch, but he didn't care any more. In some strange way he felt safe, and allowed some of his defencelessness to fall more as a mantle than a scourge.

     . . .

When he awoke the sun had moved from the windows, and the squalid interior of the hut was deep in shadows. Jervis yawned and moved his aching head gingerly from side to side. He was once more alone, and for one instant he thought the meeting with the pathetic hermit had been part of a dream, but the stench of rags and the surrounding heaps of rubbish brought back his memory and made him wonder where his protector had gone.

His legs felt a little stronger, and after taking a few cautious steps around the hut, he went to one of the windows and peered through the cracked and grime-tinted glass.

He found that the hut was situated on the side of a gently sloping hill, which ran down to a wide span of beach, and which appeared to be completely deserted by both dwellings and trees alike. As he pressed his cheek against the blistered frame, he could just see the edge of a small village, two or three little white houses, slumbering against the grassy slopes of the neighbouring hills, their low walls bathed in deep blue shadows, as the sun passed slowly towards the horizon.

It must be late afternoon, he decided, as he gazed first at the sky and then at the strip of lighter skin across his wrist, where his watch had once been. I wonder if any of the others are safe, and whether he, or they, are waiting on the hill? He shook his head to clear away the throbbing pain. I must do something, or I'll go as mad as that other poor devil.

He pulled the pistol belt from under the blanket and gingerly drew the automatic from its holster. He weighed the weapon in his palm, and remembered the little red-faced petty officer who had instructed him and the rest of his class by the side of a Scottish loch.

'Now, gentlemen! All you 'as to do is point at 'is belly, an' squeeze the trigger! Got it?'

It had seemed so remote and vaguely theatrical at the time that probably none of the young officers had really considered the true implications. But now Jervis pulled back the slide and heard the top bullet in the clip snap into the breech. He applied the safety catch, and once more stared out of the window. What should he do first, he wondered?

I'll wait until my friend comes back and then try to make for the rendezvous. Suppose it's empty? He shivered at the thought. He would be no better off than before. In fact, here at least he was safely hidden. But suppose one of the others *had* survived, and lay injured or sick somewhere out there on the beach, or up in the hills? His mouth tightened, and he slipped the gun into his trouser pocket. He knew he had to go. It might be the skipper. The thought of Curtis, and how he had surfaced the submarine to save him the agony of cutting another net, decided him.

A lorry revved its engine in the distance, and a flock of sleeping gulls rose in a white cloud from the beach, screeching and mewing.

Jervis crossed quickly to the door and pressed his eye against one of the wide cracks.

He found that he could see right along the edge of the village and across the winding track which led away from the sea, and from which came the sound of yet another engine. As he watched, he saw the front of a heavy diesel lorry heave itself around the side of the hill, spewing thick dust and sand from under its fat tyres, and grind down the middle of the road. Another followed, and after a brief interval, two more. They were giants, their sides caked with old mud and their high canvas canopies torn and dirty. The engines whirred into silence, and from the cabs he saw the figures of uniformed drivers, they, too, dust-covered and worn, climb down and gather around their vehicles.

Italian soldiers, he thought, as he watched one stubble-chinned driver relieving himself at the side of the road. Didn't look like a search party. They had obviously driven a long way, and looked anything but warlike.

Jervis watched them keenly, his eye watering against the crack, but oblivious to his cramp or the pain in his head. This was the enemy, and he felt neither elated nor frightened. The little grubby soldiers were as he had always imagined them to be when he had heard and read of them surrendering by their thousands to the Eighth Army in the desert, in that first, far-off flush of victory.

A few of the villagers had started to move up the track towards the lorries, but the drivers waved them back, and one of them even unslung a machine carbine from his shoulder, as if to emphasize the point.

The villagers, mainly fishermen and their wives, hung back in a curious, chattering group, while from between the packed bodies a few children squeezed through and gazed wide-eyed at the visitors. One of the drivers, a tubby little man with a short pointed beard, walked slowly towards the rear of one of the lorries, and on tiptoes peered over the raised tail-board. He was shouting at someone inside, and occasionally shook his head. The crowd was silent now, and Jervis could feel the tension rising like a wave. The Italian soldier, he appeared to be a corporal, stamped his foot and angrily turned his back on the lorry, and strutted back to his men, who were watching disinterestedly from the side of the road. They all seemed to be waiting for something, or somebody. An officer probably, Jervis decided.

There was a sudden flurry of movement from the first lorry, and before any one of the soldiers could move a pair of legs slithered over the tail-board, and a man staggered out into the dying sunlight. There was a gasp from the crowd, and the corporal stepped angrily forward.

Jervis had gone cold, and he could feel the hair rising on his neck as he stared at the lone figure which stood swaying in the dust, his eyes blinking and staring round at the watching Italians. His khaki battledress was torn and stained with long patches of dried blood, and one arm was completely hidden under a great wad of dressings and rough bandages. His young red face was racked with pain and anger, and he shook his unruly hair from his eyes and swallowed hard.

'Fer Christ's sake,' his voice rose in a high cracked sound, 'are yer just goin' ter stand there?' He waved his uninjured arm at the lorries, his face torn apart with sudden desperation. 'My mates is in there! Some of 'em's dyin'!' The corporal had reached him by this time and pushed him roughly towards the lorry. A murmur of sympathy rose from the watching fishermen. The British soldier staggered against the tail-board, the fight already draining from his face. 'They're wounded! Don' you understand, you Wop bastards? Fer Christ's sake give us a drink of water!' But the corporal seized him by the belt and jerked him over the tail-board, and followed him into the hidden interior.

Jervis sank back, stunned and sick. Hearing that pain-racked Cockney voice, and seeing the misery on the man's face, had swept away his previous feelings and fears like a cold wind. He beat the dirt floor with his fist in impotent rage. A few yards from the hut were four lorries crammed with British wounded, and *he* had been worrying about his own plight. They must have been captured in the south, he thought wildly, and they had probably been driven non-stop, two hundred miles or so, to this miserable place. The swine! There were tears of rage running unheeded down his chin, as he thought of the horror such a drive would entail to wounded men fresh from the firing line. What were they doing here anyway? There had been no hospital marked on the submarine's chart, just a godforsaken fishing village. Sobbing with rage, he pressed his eye back to the crack. A small khaki scout car had arrived, and the Italian soldiers had pulled themselves into some semblance of attention.

Jervis stared with sudden hatred at the slim, dapper officer in the polished boots and Afrika Korps cap who stood listening to the excited explanations from the corporal.

The German nodded briefly and glared round at the soldiers and the villagers. He pointed at the lorries and waved his arm angrily over the village. Still nobody moved, until with a sudden crash the officer banged his fist onto the bonnet of his car. With a jerk everyone started moving at once, and Jervis saw the women passing jugs of water and fruit to the soldiers, who in turn carried it into the lorries.

It was at that moment that Jervis saw his new companion trotting vaguely along the side of the hill towards the hut. In the fading light, and set against the background of bustling villagers, he looked even stranger than before. But Jervis closed his eyes and groaned aloud, as he saw the German officer pause impatiently in the middle of his orders, to glance sharply at the passing figure. The strange, capering scarecrow was the same as before but for one thing. Over his smock he now wore Jervis' blue battledress blouse, the gold lace shoulder straps glinting and reflecting in the dying light.

The German frowned and turned as if to continue with his task, and none of the villagers seemed to take any notice of what was obviously a familiar figure, until with a jerk the officer flung up his arm and pointed excitedly, while his mouth struggled with the right words of Italian.

For a moment the soldiers gaped at him, but as the officer pointed again, they ran after the slow-moving figure, their boots clashing on the loose stones, and their faces both angry and mystified.

Within twenty yards of the hut, one of the soldiers overtook their quarry and pulled roughly at the man's arm. He and the soldier skidded to a breathless halt and stood staring uncertainly at each other. Jervis watched wildly as the German, followed by his own driver, came slowly up the hill to the waiting group, while the idiot gave his lopsided grin and stood beaming at each man in turn. The German pointed to the tunic with an impatient gesture, and one of the Italians reached out to pull it from the gaunt shoulders. Impatiently he shook the groping hand free and clutched the tunic more closely to his body with childish defiance. His eyes were screwed up with anxiety, but the grin remained, as if its owner was unwilling to believe that anyone could want to deprive him of his new possession.

The officer was obviously getting completely exasperated. Now that he was so close, Jervis could see the sharp, pointed features beneath the long-peaked cap, and the lines of irritation about the man's thin mouth.

He spoke sharply to his driver, a slow-moving giant of a man in grey tunic and dusty jackboots, who stepped forward with casual ease and drove his fist into the idiot's face. Like a puppet, he fell on his back, while the big German trooper bent laboriously over him and stripped off Jervis' jacket, as if he was undressing a stubborn child.

He handed it to the officer, who searched rapidly through the pockets and examined the shoulder straps eagerly, while the other soldiers looked from him to the still figure on the ground and shuffled their feet uneasily.

The Italian corporal shouted from the bottom of the hill and pointed to the hut.

Jervis chilled, as all the eyes turned up towards his hiding place. It was as if they could already see him through the crack in the door.

The officer tossed the tunic to the ground and slipped open the top of his long leather holster. Ignoring the Italians, and never taking his cold eyes from the hut, he jerked out his Luger and pointed it towards the door.

'*Guck mal, ob da noch jemand drin ist!*' he ordered, the sharpness of his voice falling on the human air like a knife. His driver snatched the machine carbine from the Italian corporal, and started slowly towards the door.

Jervis' eyes widened as he saw the man walking calmly, yet with obvious alertness, towards him. The grey uniform blotted out the other faces, and as he drew even nearer Jervis could see his fat, heavy face quite clearly, and the little beads of sweat which trickled from beneath the grey forage cap.

He shivered violently and groped for his own pistol. He stood back from the door and raised the gun slowly in front of his body. It seemed to be of terrible weight, and his hand shook, until he gripped the butt with such force that his wrist ached and his knuckles were white against his tanned skin.

Nothing happened, and he ground his teeth together to stop himself from shivering. He could feel the sweat running down the small of his back and was conscious of the great stillness which seemed to hang over the hut and beyond.

The crash of glass which shattered the silence made his body leap, and the sour taste of vomit pause in his throat as he spun round on the floor, his eyes seeking blindly, the pistol waving from side to side. He felt all the strain of the past day exploding in his brain, as he looked at the long black muzzle which lay across the sill of the small window.

'*Hände hoch!*' The fat German gestured with the carbine towards Jervis' pistol. A smile played across the fat lips with something like pity, but the eyes which peered through the broken glass were hard and devoid of all compassion.

Almost unconsciously, Jervis let the gun fall from his nerveless fingers and immediately hated himself for giving in so easily. As if reading his thoughts, the German pointed the carbine unwaveringly at the boy's stomach, and shook his head briefly.

'Still! Stand still!' The clumsy words were filled with menace.

The door jerked back on its hinges as a well-delivered kick brought the sunlight pouring into the hut, lighting the scene, and seeming to lay bare Jervis' shame.

The officer nodded curtly to the face at the window, and picked up Jervis' pistol. He tossed it to someone outside the door, and regarded Jervis with cold curiosity.

'You are a British officer?' The voice was as hard as the eyes, but the accent was almost flawless.

Jervis shrugged. 'Yes. Sub-Lieutenant Jervis, Royal Navy!' As he answered, he lifted his head and looked the other man straight in the face. A feeling of pride or despair made him draw himself to attention and lift his chin defiantly.

'Please spare me the heroics! You will need all those later!' He waved the pistol sharply. 'Outside! And do not be tempted to do anything stupid!'

Jervis blundered out into the sunlight and blinked at the circle of watching faces. At the bottom of the hill the soldiers raised their rifles threateningly, and drove the villagers away from the road and clear of the lorries.

Jervis walked down the hill to where the scout car stood, and where the idiot sat in the dust, rubbing his chin and moaning gently. Jervis stopped dead at the sight of him, and turned back to the officer. 'That man there,' he pointed, and the idiot caught his eye and smiled pitifully, 'he knows nothing about me. He's deaf and dumb!'

The German eyed him thoughtfully, his face in shadow. 'Then he will be no loss, will he?' He barked an order, and the Italian corporal sprang to attention, his little beard pointing out at a ridiculous angle, but his eyes fixed on the seated prisoner.

'He's mad!' continued Jervis, suddenly frantic. He had seen the look of hatred on the corporal's face. It was as if the man had been looking for someone to vent his temper on, and to clear the air of his own humiliation.

The German smiled. 'He was assisting you to escape. What does it matter who or what he is?' The smile faded. 'An example must be made; these people are swine, without backbone, they have to be taught a lesson!' He pushed Jervis' shoulder. 'Now, into the car, we have a journey to make!'

The driver slid into his seat without even a glance at his prisoner, and waited for his orders. Jervis gripped the armoured side of the car, and turned back to the hut. Over the officer's shoulder he saw the corporal beating at a writhing shape on the ground, whose wordless mouth twisted and mouthed in horrible contortions as the soldier stood astride him, a heavy steel rod in his fat hands. The other soldiers laughed and jeered, and one of them tore the old smock from the broken body, and waved it like a flag over his head. The movements ceased with awful suddenness, and the corporal looked down at the man, his streaming face split in an ingratiating smile. Jervis stumbled blindly into the car, heedless of the watching soldiers, and conscious only of the pathetic ragged heap at the corporal's feet.

The German officer nodded to his driver and the car began to move. 'Carrion!' he said, half to himself, and then settled down comfortably in his seat, the Luger resting in his lap.

Jervis drew his legs together and bunched himself into a tight ball in the corner of the open car. The very idea of bodily contact with the officer who sat so calmly at his side seemed at that moment to be unclean, and he felt his tight limbs trembling with helpless rage, and a new feeling, previously unbeknown to him, but which he now recognized as hatred.

He only half noticed the last of the white cottages slide past in a cloud of dust, and the crouching hills close in to blot out the laughing sea. He kept remembering his strange friend and helper, and seeing his awful silent pleas for kindness and mercy. And the British wounded; his mind vaulted painfully back to the sun-baked lorries and their loads of human suffering. What would happen to them? He forced himself to look sideways at his captor. He saw that the man was watching him quietly, his eyes darkened by the soft peak of his cap.

'You are no doubt wondering where we are going? What is going to happen to you, *ja*?'

Jervis shrugged with an indifference he no longer enjoyed. 'I suppose you intend to shoot me, isn't that the general idea?'

The German frowned, and then sighed with mock sadness. 'You are a prisoner, you will be treated accordingly. However, if you intend to co-operate with my superior officer, I have little doubt that you might be given more,' he paused significantly, 'preferential treatment!'

Jervis clenched his fists. 'Why did you let your men kill that poor creature? He didn't know or understand anything!' The words burst from him. 'Now I understand what is meant by German cruelty!'

'Silence! How can you understand anything?' His face was tight with rage. 'You are a mere boy, masquerading as an officer! I suppose you are going to tell me that when you blew up the dock at Vigoria, you did not know you blew up many innocent persons also, is that not so?' His mouth twisted into a bitter smile. 'Civilians, dockyard workers, all blown to hell!'

'The dock was a military objective, it was part of the war!' Jervis leaned forward until the muzzle of the Luger rested against his side.

'War! Of course it was war, and so was that business back in the village, so do not try to make black white!'

They both glared angrily at each other in silence, and Jervis became aware that the driver was whistling softly, his massive head sunk indifferently into his shoulders.

'What will happen to those wounded?' Jervis' voice was quiet and flat, the angry outburst had sapped away his strength.

'The wounded?' He appeared to ponder on the matter, but he, too, seemed to be regretting his sudden flare of temper. 'They will be looked after. At the moment we are a little short of medical staff, but never fear, they will be cared for. The Third Reich never abandons those who have fought bravely!' There was an imperceptible sneer in his tone.

Jervis ignored the implication, and stared down at his knees. 'How is the battle going in the south?' He tried to appear calm, but his heart was pounding with sudden eagerness to hear news of the outer world, *his* world.

The German laughed shortly. 'It is being won.' For a moment a smile passed across his cold features, and the years seemed to drop away. 'No doubt I shall be able to find out for myself very soon.' He stared past Jervis at the green hills. 'For four years I have been fighting the British, and always people ask, how goes the battle! But it still goes on. France, Holland, Egypt, and now Italy.' He shrugged, irritable with himself. 'It will be over one day. That is all I can say!'

The car halted at the side of the main road, and their voices were drowned by the thunder of vehicles. Jervis watched as lorry after lorry rumbled past, each jammed with stony, set faces and nodding coal-scuttle helmets. More lorries carrying tanks and guns thundered along the narrow road, shepherded by military police on motor cycles. To Jervis it was like a film. This was part of the enemy war machine, and next to him was a German officer. It was more like a nightmare. He glanced up at the sun and back to the road. They were going south. To the front. A cold thrill ran through him, and he remembered the wounded in the village. How many of these German soldiers would live to see the sun rise in a few more days? He pressed his lips together in a tight line.

I hope you rot in hell! It was like a prayer.

The car started again and swung into a tiny narrow lane between two crumbling white gateposts.

A German soldier saluted, and then they were speeding up a long gravel drive towards a proud rambling house on the top of a slope. As the car swung past a pair of gentle fountains and topped the rise, Jervis swallowed and bit his lip. Beyond and below the house lay the sea. He wished he could not see it. Each diadem of glittering green light seemed to mock him, as the smooth surface caught the last brilliance of the sun.

I shall never see it again, he thought. The car had stopped in front of the house, and the officer pointed to the entrance. 'The end of the road, *ja*?'

As he climbed wearily up the wide steps at the entrance to the house, the smell of fresh flowers and the cool cleanliness of the dark interior only added to the feeling of unreality, and he stood uncertainly in the majestic, marble-pillared hallway, only half taking in the ornate, gilt-encrusted decorations and the single chandelier, which hung like a huge ear-ring from the domed ceiling.

Tall doors of dark seasoned wood opened off from each side of the hall, and he stepped back involuntarily as two soldiers, hatless and with their sleeves rolled above their elbows, staggered past him, panting beneath the weight of a large metal trunk. He noticed, as his eyes became accustomed to the gloom, that the place seemed littered with pieces of luggage and packed equipment, and on a magnificently carved chest he saw an upended steel helmet and a pair of goggles perched incongruously alongside a tall, flower-filled vase.

The German officer grunted, and tapped Jervis under the elbow. 'Wait here. I will inform the colonel of your arrival.'

Jervis watched the thin, brisk figure cross the polished floor, his high boots clicking on the wood blocks, and pass through one of the doors. Jervis did not have to turn his head to know that the driver was standing close beside him, and he felt his spirit draining from him, leaving him in a daze of miserable uncertainty.

Somewhere in the house a telephone buzzed like a trapped fly, while from the sun-dappled drive came the staccato roar of motor cycles. The two soldiers returned and picked up more of the baggage from the floor.

One of them, a short, red-faced man, stopped for a moment and stared at Jervis in surprise. For a moment, a slow smile crossed his face, but immediately it vanished, and he hurried away with his burden, as the officer returned.

He stopped directly in front of Jervis and ran his eyes sharply over his crumpled trousers and stained jersey, as if he was carrying out an inspection.

Jervis coloured. 'Satisfied?' he asked with sudden anger. 'I'm afraid I didn't find time to change!'

The German's face remained impassive. 'The colonel will see you now. He has not much time. The regiment is leaving immediately.' He rubbed his sharp chin, his eyes thoughtful. 'The colonel speaks no English. I will translate the information you have to give.' He turned on his heel before Jervis could answer, but as he opened the door he said softly over his shoulder, 'Do not irritate the colonel, he is not in the mood for insolence!'

Jervis followed the officer into the wide, comfortable room, his heart pounding painfully, and his fingers clenched tightly against his sides. His captor halted, his boots coming together with a sharp click, which jerked Jervis' racing thoughts into readiness in spite of his misery, and made him glance round with chilled anticipation.

The long windows which looked out across the lawns to where the sea sparkled so invitingly covered the complete side of the room, while the other walls were lined with books and hung with large military maps.

The desk which dominated the room was also littered with maps, and several field telephones, which hung in their leather cases, ugly and out-of-place.

A tall, stooped officer stood behind the desk, while to one side, and sitting with his legs crossed in a comfortable chair, was a dapper, quietly dressed civilian.

The colonel straightened his back slowly, as if it was both an effort to tear his eyes from the maps and to find time for this interruption.

He listened to the short, barking sentences from Jervis' captor, his pale eyes moving restlessly around the room, and his long slender fingers beating a gentle tattoo on the top of the desk. Jervis wanted to scream as the voice droned on, while the colonel listened, and the civilian's head nodded slowly in either agreement or understanding.

The colonel held up his hand, his voice, which was surprisingly low and soft, was directed to the officer, although the pale eyes were now fixed on Jervis in a flat, unwavering stare.

'Herr Colonel wishes to know how your raid was carried out. Answer please!'

Jervis swallowed hard, and met the colonel's eyes. 'I am not obliged to answer. According to the Geneva Convention, I——' he got no further.

The colonel slammed his fist onto the desk, so that a pencil rattled noisily across the floor, and his voice, although still under control, was harsh.

'Herr Colonel says that you are not to be stubborn. You are not making it easy for yourself!'

The civilian spoke for the first time, and Jervis wrenched his gaze from the tall figure by the desk to the other man, who nodded encouragingly, his grey, clipped hair catching the reflections from the dying sun.

'I am Guilio Zecchi.' He dropped his dark eyes to study the pointed toe of his shoe. 'I am the Mayor and political liaison officer to the colonel here. Please do not disregard the colonel's warning, he is a dangerous man, and,' he shrugged eloquently, 'he has much to do!' He wriggled his plump shoulders more comfortably into the chair, and smiled gently. 'We know that you were responsible for the crime in Vigoria.' He waved a well-manicured hand, as if dismissing the whole incident as some unfortunate lapse of sanity. 'The Colonel wishes to know how you did it. Tell him!'

Jervis was thinking furiously. They had not caught Curtis or the others. They did not know about the submarine. He spread his hands in a movement of resignation.

'I was landed by submarine some days ago.' The lie came easily. 'I placed the charges beneath the dock, and went back to rendezvous with the boat before the explosion was due. My rubber dinghy sank, and I had to swim ashore. I struck my head ...'

At this point the colonel pointed to Jervis' bandage, and barked a question.

'The Colonel asks how you managed to treat your injury?' The officer's voice sounded strained.

Without turning his head, Jervis spoke from between his clenched teeth. 'Tell him about the poor wretch who helped me, and how your gallant soldiers taught these gutless Italians a lesson!' He darted a glance at the mayor, and was gratified to see a brief look of anger darken the smooth face.

The colonel looked from one to the other, and then at his watch. As if to add to the urgency of the proceedings, one of the telephones whirred impatiently.

The colonel spoke sharply into the mouthpiece, his eyes searching across one of the maps. With a grunt, he slipped the telephone into its case and bundled the maps together into a flat folder. He lifted his eyes quickly and stared at Jervis, his face tired and suddenly old.

'The Colonel says that you will be detained here for the night. Tomorrow you will be shot!'

Jervis staggered as if he had received a blow in the heart. He couldn't speak or even move his mouth, which had suddenly gone quite dry.

The colonel walked slowly around the desk, his eyes sweeping the room as if to ensure he had left nothing behind. He halted between Jervis and the door, and his tone was quiet, almost gentle. Then he nodded to the mayor who still sat in his chair, and marched briskly from the room.

Jervis turned to see the door close, and met the cold stare of the other officer. The man's face was expressionless as he said, 'Herr Colonel said it is better to die a brave man, than to be interrogated by the Gestapo!' His shoulders seemed to sag. 'He is right. Be thankful.' He gestured with the pistol. 'March! I will take you to your quarters.'

Jervis faltered, knowing that his face was ashen, but still he forced himself to speak to the mayor.

'There are British wounded in the village. What can you do for them? You must do something to help!'

'You do not think of yourself? That is good.' He studied Jervis closely. 'You are brave. Never fear, the wounded are being taken care of. They will go north by sea. The roads are filled with, er, military traffic. There is no room for anyone going the other way, I fear!'

Jervis tore his eyes away, and looked once more at the sea. I must hang on, can't break down now! His lip trembled.

'Thank you, sir. I feel better now!'

He crossed to the door, the German behind him.

There was a roar of engines, and he heard several vehicles crunching down the drive. He noticed that the luggage was missing from the hall, and only one soldier stood by the entrance.

He glanced involuntarily at the chest. The helmet and goggles had also gone. He walked blindly down a white-walled passage, the colonel's words ringing in his brain. Tomorrow you will be shot.

They reached an open door to one side of the long passage, and involuntarily Jervis stopped and drew back, the bare, stone-walled room which confronted him brought home the hopelessness and complete collapse of his final position.

The German's voice was crisp and alert, as if he, too, sensed the awful finality of the forbidding room.

'Inside,' he snapped, 'it would be stupid to resist!'

Jervis' shoulders slumped, and he walked slowly through the door. It had once been a storeroom of some kind, and the rough walls were lined with wooden shelves, empty but for scraps of old straw and torn paper. A camp bed stood in readiness in one corner, and a crude bucket in the other.

Jervis stared round unbelievingly, his trapped gaze taking in the bareness of the room, the lack of even a window, and the armed sentry who now stood watchfully behind the officer.

'Food will be brought shortly. I would advise you to eat, then try to sleep.' The German's tone was almost matter-of-fact. 'The sentry does not speak English, and he has been told to shoot, should you try to escape! Is there anything you wish to say?' One eyebrow lifted slightly.

Jervis clenched and unclenched his fists, and tried to clear his brain. 'How ... I mean when will it be?' His voice was hoarse, and in the confined space of the room his breathing sounded fast and uneven.

'First light. Five o'clock, I think.'

'I see.'

How unimportant he seemed to be to these people. He was already dead in their eyes. He remembered how the colonel had been impatient to leave with the regiment, the blowing up of the dock no longer important. Those details could be left to someone else to worry about.

The German looked at his watch and sighed. 'I am going. I wish you luck!' He smiled briefly. 'Perhaps I, too, shall be joining you soon!'

'I thought perhaps you might be staying to ...' Jervis faltered.

'I am a soldier – not an executioner! I will follow my regiment, and see how goes the battle.'

He spoke sharply to the sentry, who stood stiffly to attention, his eyes fixed on Jervis, his lips moving slightly as if repeating his officer's orders.

The officer paused in the doorway. 'Goodbye, *Herr Leutnant*, be brave!' With those words, he stamped away down the passage, his boots echoing mockingly back into the room.

Jervis looked at the sentry, who stood stiffly by the open door, his Schmeisser automatic pistol cradled across his forearm, its barrel moving slightly in time with the soldier's breathing.

He was little more than a boy, tall and gawky. His ungainly limbs were distorted by the huge boots and the heavy steel helmet which seemed to make his narrow face even more insignificant.

Younger than I am, he thought, and just hoping that I'll make a run for it. Almost without thinking, he stepped halfway towards the door. The Schmeisser rose a couple of inches, until it was level with Jervis' chest. The soldier's thin mouth split into a wide grin, the bared teeth giving him a slightly crazy look. 'Bang!' he said, and laughed delightedly at his joke.

Jervis turned his back, and forced himself to lie down on the bed. By twisting his head to the wall he was able to blot out the sentry, who still chuckled in the open doorway, and as he concentrated his aching eyes on the rows of uneven bricks, he thought again of the way in which he had already been forgotten. He rubbed the palms of his hands angrily across his eyes until the pain forced back the tears which threatened to lay bare his misery and fear to the watching soldier. God, why this way? Why didn't I fight it out in the hut? His tortured thoughts ran on in their haphazard groping for an answer, but only bricks were there to mock him.

The house seemed very silent, and he decided that it must be nearly dark outside. He darted a glance at the door. The gun was still rigid and unwavering. Perhaps he'll be one of the firing squad. Or maybe they don't do it that way. Wait until I fall asleep, and then ... a trickle of sweat ran coldly across his cheek, as he remembered the sentry's gun.

By an almost physical effort, he thought of his father, and the sun slanting across his mother's grey hair as she pruned the roses. His father had always seemed to be rather a forbidding man, but as Jervis closed his eyes to try to picture him more clearly, he could only see the kindness in the old man's face.

But, of course, he thought dully, they think I'm dead already. The submarine will have been reported missing, and I shall be merely remembered, as I am remembering them. The cold finality of it seemed to sober him, and he lay wide eyed, staring at the flaking ceiling. His breathing became calmer, and his limbs started to relax.

It's funny how death doesn't seem half so terrible, once you know it's inevitable, he thought, and I must make sure that I don't let myself down when the moment comes. The corners of his mouth drooped, and for an instant the sickness began to mount again inside him, so he turned his thoughts back again, it was useless anyway to look forward.

He stiffened, as the sounds of voices drifted down the passage. One, a woman's voice, called out sharply in Italian, and the other was swallowed up by the banging of a door.

The sentry drew his feet together, as the first voice drew nearer. It changed suddenly into fluent German, and the soldier nodded violently, his helmet jerking forward over his admiring eyes. Jervis stared at her coldly, a feeling of resentment and anger changing the girl who now stood inside the room from a creature of beauty to another part of a scheme to mock and degrade him.

She stood quite still, looking down at him, her bare brown arms silky beneath the naked light bulb. She was wearing a plain, dark green dress with a leather belt, the tightness of which helped to accentuate the rich curves of her body.

Her dark eyes were almost black with the contempt and hatred which she directed at Jervis, and her wide mouth trembled as she spoke softly over her shoulder in German. The sentry, who was peering round the edge of the door, tittered, and settled down comfortably to watch, as the girl moved slowly across the room, stooping slightly, as if to make quite sure she took in every detail of Jervis' face.

He sat up slowly, and was about to rise to his feet, when the Schmeisser motioned him to remain seated.

So that she can mock me to her heart's content, he thought bitterly. He stared fixedly at her slim, bare legs, and was half tempted to throw himself at her. Only a few feet separated them. He tingled at the idea. It would be one last gesture.

He went suddenly rigid. The girl continued pacing the floor, but her sneering voice had changed to English. He looked up, startled, and her eyes flashed with anxiety and sudden urgency.

'Keep your head down! There is little time, so do as I say, and I might be able to help you!'

For a moment his eyes held hers. She was no longer sneering, her mouth was trembling with desperation, and he lowered his head, so that neither she nor the sentry should see the faint hope in his eyes.

She breathed deeply, and carried on with her pacing. As she spoke, the sentry tittered happily, quite convinced that she was continuing her attack in English.

'Listen to me. I will help you to escape, if you will tell me where your friends are!'

Jervis' hope changed into a sudden cold wariness, and he sat forward on the edge of the bed, his eyes following her feet, but his mind again on guard.

'I know you lied to the colonel. I saw one of your friends on the beach this morning. Tell me where I can find them, and I will fetch them to you.'

Jervis shook his head. 'I am alone. I don't know what you are talking about.'

She darted her hand beneath his chin and jerked up his head so that her eyes held his in a silent plea. 'Please! I tell the truth, I saw one of them today!'

The shock of her smooth skin against his neck made him search her face with new interest. 'Describe the man you saw.'

She stamped her foot, but there was frustration not anger in her eyes. 'There is no time!' She saw his obstinate mouth, and she darted a quick glance at the door. 'He was tall and fair. He had two stripes on his shoulder, and he was carrying a pistol! Now do you believe me?' Jervis struggled with his emotions. It could be a trap to draw the others into the net. That must have been Curtis she saw. A little breath of warmth moved within him, but he forced himself to consider the girl's words. 'Why didn't you tell the colonel about this?'

'I cannot tell you that. You must trust me. Please!'

She stood over him, her hands clenched and her body trembling with emotion.

'It could be a trap.' Jervis watched her eyes, and saw the despair which followed his words. He knew that he was going to tell her, and he knew, too, that by so doing, he was risking more than just his own life, and the few hours left until dawn.

'The hill at the end of the beach. By the fishing boats. They might be there. I don't know.' As the short sentences jerked from him, he instantly regretted his outburst, and looked up at her with sudden fear.

But for a moment her wide eyes softened, and she nodded quickly. 'I will go, before someone suspects. I am going to hit you now, I am sorry!' With that, she struck Jervis a ringing blow on the cheek, and as he reeled back across the bed, she stepped quickly from the room.

He sat up, gingerly feeling his face. The blow had somehow cleared away his doubts about her, and he felt a tremor of excitement run through his body, which even the jeering laugh of the sentry did nothing to dispel.

He met the sentry's stare calmly. You wait, my lad. If the skipper comes you'll laugh the other side of your face.

He lay back on the bed and closed his eyes. The girl had been a link, no matter how frail, with the outside. And from the outside, help would come, he was sure of that. He had to be. It was all he had left.

CHAPTER 6

Curtis settled his elbows more comfortably in the grass, and craned his head as high as he dared to watch the first of the lorries as it trundled awkwardly down the track and onto the beach. As the front wheels tested the strength of the sand, the driver revved his engine impatiently, the blue diesel fumes hanging listlessly on the still air. The villagers followed the lorry in an anxious, silent crowd, occasionally pointing either at the beach or the lorry, but mostly watching the uniformed figures who waved at the driver, or shouted urgently whenever the wheels threatened to leave the narrow track.

Curtis had been on watch when he had heard the lorries halt at the top of the village, and after waking his exhausted companions, had fretted impatiently, and constantly changed his position to try to see what was happening. He had seen some of the returning fishermen run with their women up the track, ignoring their nets and showing an indifference to their boats which was completely alien to their kind anywhere.

'Somethin's up, Ralph.' Duncan had come completely awake, his eyes narrowed against the sun. 'Reckon it's a search party?'

They had felt for their scanty weapons, and Curtis had placed Taylor at the rear approach to the hill to watch for any new activity, but after what seemed like an eternity, a few uniformed Italians had sauntered down to the beach accompanied by the captain of the schooner. And now, the first of the lorries had started to move towards the sea.

'They're goin' to load some gear onto the ship,' said Duncan. 'Looks like they might be sailin' soon, eh?' He smiled slowly, the leathery skin about his eyes bunching into broad crowsfeet. 'We still goin' through with our plan, Ralph?'

Curtis studied the lorry, noting the travel stains across its broad bonnet.

'We'll take her whatever happens. Unless they're embarking a regiment of troops!' He smiled slightly, but inwardly he was already considering that such a possibility would smash his flimsy plans to nothing.

'Another truck on the way,' announced Duncan suddenly. 'An' there's some more behind that!'

The dust rose in a thick cloud as the four lorries manoeuvred into a ragged line on the edge of the soft sand and halted. The fishermen were listening to a tall officer in a dove grey uniform, who was waving a stick vaguely towards the boats and then at the schooner. The fishermen walked back to their boats and stood in a silent group, while the officer held up his stick like a sword and pointed at the lorries. He was smiling, his teeth gleaming whitely beneath a neat black moustache. He was apparently shouting some sort of a joke to the onlookers, but until the soldiers laughed, none of the villagers moved or spoke, and the tension could be felt by the three sun-baked figures at the top of the hill.

The tail-boards of the lorries fell with a series of dull thuds, and some of the soldiers climbed up inside the tall vehicles.

Curtis swore and squinted fixedly at the scene, wishing that they would finish their job, whatever it was, and leave the beach empty once more.

'Bloody Eyeties!' Duncan rolled his tongue across his lips. 'Always make such a shindy over everything, I shouldn't be surprised if——' He stopped, and Curtis felt his fingers dig into his arm.

Neither spoke as the first khaki figure half fell, half staggered down onto the sand. He stood swaying dazedly from side to side, feebly trying to support himself on a piece of boxwood. One of his feet was encased in a great wad of bandage, and he tried to hold it clear of the ground by leaning on the little piece of wood. His bent swaying shape threw a queer twisted shadow across the white sand, like a caricature of a man.

Another soldier climbed down and cannoned into him, and for a moment they swayed together, in a frantic embrace. This man was whole, but for the bandage across his eyes and most of his face. His hands gripped the other man and held on desperately, as the cripple fought to hold his balance and at the same time pacify his blinded comrade.

One of the drivers laughed and kicked away the wooden prop, and both of the tattered figures rolled over in the dust. Curtis drove his fingers into the grass until they were buried in the coarse dirt, the heat of his rage and anguish almost blinding him, as one by one the ragged, khaki scarecrows fell, or were dragged from the four lorries.

Duncan was crouched by a bush, his thick arms rigid, like a runner waiting for the gun, and his jaw moving silently as he cursed and swore under his breath in a savage chant.

There were altogether about thirty wounded men on the beach. Some sat dejectedly in the sand, their heads hanging practically to their knees, while others clung together for support, their bandages stained either with dirt, or by the bright red patches which marked the pattern of their combined suffering.

Some just laid where they had fallen, crumpled shabby forms, which had once been British soldiers.

A driver shouted hoarsely, and some of his comrades climbed back into one of the lorries and dragged two more figures down over the tail-board.

The officer shouted angrily and waved his stick, but the driver merely shrugged and prodded one of the bodies with his foot.

A figure suddenly detached itself from the khaki huddle and limped stiffly towards the officer. He carried one arm in a sling and only one eye was visible from beneath the massive dressing about his head. No one moved to intercept him, as with his good arm swinging in almost military precision, he marched up to the Italian officer, who stood swinging his stick idly against his polished boot, as if he had been hoping for and expecting just such an encounter.

The soldier halted, his head twisted on one side so that he could see the other man. A set of sergeant's stripes hung loosely from his sleeve, and as Curtis watched with sick horror, he could see the glint of campaign ribbons on the soldier's chest.

The sergeant pointed stiffly at his companions and then at his own injuries. His mouth opened and closed slowly, as if he was trying to explain his requirements in that peculiar pidgin English which British troops use when confronted with a foreigner.

The officer yawned elaborately, and in obedience, some of his men laughed. The sergeant's red face seemed to get redder, but he brushed the sweat away from his face and continued to speak and gesticulate. The officer was evidently getting bored, for he called to the men by the boats and turned on his heel.

The sergeant dragged himself painfully after him, anxiety giving him sudden energy.

'Christ! The poor devils are dyin'!' Duncan's voice shook as the words were dragged from him. 'That stinkin' bastard's makin' the guy crawl!' He half rose to his feet, one hand groping for his pistol.

Curtis dragged him down beside him, his face set in a bitter mask. 'Get down, Steve! We can't do anything for them yet!'

'Yet? You mean we're goin' down to have a crack at those yellow apes?'

Curtis nodded, his throat clogged, as the wounded men began to stagger to their feet. 'We'll help them, if it's the last thing we do!' He slammed his hands together. 'Look at them! God, why doesn't someone give them a hand?'

The officer walked away towards the sea, and one of his men pushed the sergeant towards the boats.

Duncan ran his fingers through his hair and pulled at his jacket, as if he could no longer breathe. 'All those blokes bein' packed into that one crummy ship? How long'll they be aboard for Chrissakes? They need medical attention, and quick!'

Curtis narrowed his eyes, as he looked towards the still forms which lay by the lorries. 'Not them,' he said softly. 'They're out of it.'

One of the watching women was cryinc 'nto her apron, and Duncan looked down at her, his face hard.

'Yes, cry, you bitch! When the Eighth Army comes through here, you'll remember all this!'

The boats pushed off from the beach, but as one of them bumped against a sandbank, weighted down with its heavy load, one of the khaki shapes half rose from his seat, and the silence was split by a terrible cry of pain.

In the bows of another boat a stocky figure scrambled precariously onto the gunwale, his head bandages gold in the sun. Curtis groaned aloud; it was the sergeant again. His groan faded into a sob as the sergeant's cracked voice floated across the painted water.

'Bless 'em all, bless 'em all! The long an' the short an' the tall!'

The schooner's captain waded after the nearest boat and climbed clumsily over the stern, while behind him, alone on the beach, the officer danced up and down with rage, screaming and waving his stick at the sergeant, *'Silenzio! Silenzio!'*

An old fisherman standing by his cottage door saluted with sudden gravity, and a woman pulled her child closer to her skirt.

Curtis watched the boats bump alongside the schooner, their shapes blurred and indistinct.

'We'll board her tonight,' he said quietly. 'Whatever happens now, we have to take that ship!'

Duncan stared down at the officer, his face tired and heavy. 'I hope he's around, when we go!'

They looked at each other, both aware of the new implication and the coldness which had enclosed them like a shroud.

They waited until the bodies had been removed from the beach, and the lorries had departed, and then settled down to wait for the darkness. The waiting had been made easier by the hatred which waited upon each of them with persistent greed.

. . .

The grass around the hilltop rustled uneasily as the cold breeze from the north tested its strength momentarily on the side of the slope, before passing on with mounting strength to fan out across the bay and bring the dark water alive with dancing whitecaps. Occasionally the moon showed itself in a feeble silver crescent, and tinged the edges of the black racing clouds with its fading brilliance, so that they looked angry and solid as they scudded purposefully across the late evening sky. As the moon darted an occasional ray upon the shoreline, the distorted shapes of the cottages shone like large lumps of sugar, before fading away into the blackness of the surrounding hills, and the sand spit seemed to rise from the sea in an effort to hold the passing light, before it, too, joined the shadows and the unsettled noises left by the wind.

Curtis stood up and stamped his boots in the dust, while he attempted to study the luminous dial of his watch.

Taylor stood at his side, his face an indistinct blob against the sky. He was buttoning his jacket, and carefully going through his pockets.

'We makin' a move soon, Skipper? There don't seem to be anybody about.'

'Yes, soon.'

Curtis stared towards where the schooner lay, but against the constant movement of the water and the rearing and falling of the short, white-crested waves, he could no longer see the vessel's hull. The nagging doubts persisted, and he had only half heard Taylor's question.

Suppose the ship pulled out without warning, and without waiting for the German officer to rejoin her? Until the last of the daylight had passed with the sun behind the headland, he had watched the movements in the village, and had waited coldly for the ship to show some sign of departing. Fresh water had been rowed out to the schooner's side, the operation being carried out in several laborious trips by the fishermen in their boats, but still nothing happened. Like the others, Curtis had expected that a doctor would arrive to attend to the wounded, but the village had gradually quietened, and the ship had become more and more indistinct in the gathering darkness. Perhaps they had a medical officer on board, he thought, and dismissed the idea as unlikely, the gnawing anxiety he felt for the wounded soldiers only adding to the uncertainty of his next move.

A stick cracked, and both men went stiff. They heard Duncan curse briefly from the ground below them, and Curtis moved to meet him.

'See anything?' His voice was low, but the urgency was clear in his question.

Duncan shook his head, and held up the water bottle. 'Just filled this in the stream, an' came straight back up. All quiet in the village though. 'Cept for a couple of Eyeties on motor bikes.' He jerked his thumb towards the main road. 'Police, I guess.'

Curtis pulled his belt tighter, and adjusted his holster with sudden care. 'Might as well get started then.'

'Yep.' Duncan handed over the bottle, its crude neck cold and wet. 'Pity about Ian,' he said slowly. 'But there's more to think about now.'

Curtis drank without feeling. 'Yes.'

Taylor shifted his feet and took the bottle with sudden eagerness. He drank deeply and wiped his mouth with his sleeve. 'Well, shall we go? I'm fair gettin' the wind up, standing about up 'ere!'

Curtis peered at their dark shapes, and wished that he could see their faces. 'Well, here goes.' His stomach contracted and he swallowed hard. 'We'll go down now and get one of the boats away. I'll just go over the drill again.' He looked at Taylor. 'You go straight to the poop, by the mainmast. I think the engine-room hatch is about there, so you'll be ready to get things started if we carry things the way we want them. Here,' he handed the pistol to him, 'take this. If anyone tries to enter or leave the engine-room, show him this.'

'S'pose he won't stop, what then?'

'Kill him!' Curtis was surprised by the chill in his own voice.

'I reckon there'll be about ten to a dozen in the crew, an' there are about three soldiers or coppers on board that we know of as well.' Duncan's hand rasped across his chin. 'We might be able to enlist a bit of support from the Tommies, too, eh?'

'Maybe.' Curtis hurried on. Now that he had shown his hand, he wanted desperately to get started. 'You, Steve, will stay with me. We'll make for the after hatch, the one behind the wheel, as I think the captain'll be in there. Once we've got him safe, well, we'll see.' He paused. 'Any ideas?'

'They only seem to have a short cable down, Ralph. We can slip the anchor completely, and get clear without any fuss at all, provided there's no bloody noise!' Duncan flexed his shoulders. 'If we can get out of this blessed place, we can be sixty miles clear by dawn!'

Curtis frowned. So many ifs, but there was no other way.

''Ere, wot a lark if we made it OK!' Taylor chuckled with something like his old humour. 'Won't the blokes be surprised, eh?'

Curtis gripped his arm tightly. 'We'll have a go, George. We'll feel more at home out there anyway.'

Curtis looked up warily, as Duncan's hand rose like a white glove. 'Don't move, blokes!' His voice was almost conversational. 'But I think we've got company!'

They all stood transfixed in attitudes of surprised watchfulness, each man straining his ears and eyes without moving his head.

Curtis was conscious again of his heart pounding with mounting persistence. 'Jervis? D'you think it's Jervis?' His voice was a mere hiss of breath.

Duncan's head turned slightly, and as the moon peeped over a cloud, his bared teeth gleamed like those of a cornered animal. 'No, it's not him,' he said slowly. Curtis saw him move his hand, and heard the metallic click of a safety catch. 'Stay 'ere!' Duncan sounded preoccupied and strange. 'I'm a bit more used to this sort of caper. I'll head the bastard off, whoever it is. Got yer knife, Ralph?'

Curtis nodded and slipped it from inside his blouse. It was still warm from contact with his own body, and he suddenly regretted giving his gun to Taylor.

'Now keep still. Give me time to get clear. P'raps he won't come up here, an' we won't have to do anythin'. But if he *does* ...' He left the rest unsaid, and as the others watched, his huge bulk seemed to melt into the bushes with hardly a sound.

Curtis leaned forward, his mouth half open, his eyes wide with concentrated effort. Then he heard it for the first time. The uneven swish of grass, and the soft crunch of sand, as cautious footsteps groped their way along the side of the hill.

He heard, too, the rasp of Taylor's breath, and the soft moan of the wind across the top of the bushes.

With the wind in his ears, Curtis repeatedly lost the direction of the footsteps, but with each lull he heard the sounds getting steadily louder and nearer, and he gripped the knife with sudden determination. Nothing must interfere with the plan now. Nothing and nobody.

If only he knew where Duncan had gone. He held his breath, realizing that the sounds had stopped.

Curtis raised his foot with elaborate care and stepped nearer to the bushes. His sleeve brushed against Taylor's taut body, and he moved his mouth against the man's cold ear.

'Right below us,' he whispered. 'Think I can hear his feet on those stones!'

'Let's get 'im fer Gawd's sake!' Taylor's voice shook with suppressed despair. 'I can't stand much more!'

Curtis nodded briefly and held the knife before him like a rapier. He tucked his chin into his chest and waited, eyes on the edge of the slope.

It was even darker and, but for the distant whitecaps, there was no division between land and sky, sand or sea.

Curtis took half a step forward as another twig cracked, and the footsteps started again.

From the corner of his eye he saw a slight hardening to the outline of the ledge and as he turned, the pale oval of a face rose cautiously over the long grass.

His feet moved with sudden fury and he flung himself down the slope, the knife lifting above his head, as with a sob he reached out for the wavering shape, which had halted, trapped on the loose edge of the final slope.

With a thud their bodies met, but even as they crashed down onto the ground, Curtis' fingers had found the throat, and savagely he forced backwards into the grass, the knife held poised and ready.

Taylor slithered down beside him with a grunt. 'Got 'im! Well done, Skipper!' he panted.

A cloud parted, and as their spreadeagled forms were bathed in the unearthly light, Curtis trembled, and allowed the choking throat beneath his fingers to relax.

Two terrified eyes stared up at him like black pools, and he felt the long hair across the back of his hand as the girl moved her head and retched weakly.

One bare leg was pinned beneath him, and the other was crooked against his chest in a pitiful defence, while from her parted lips her sobbing breath jerked in quick, painful gasps.

Duncan rose from the ground like a shadow, the moonlight giving his tousled hair a wild halo. 'All clear below!' he jerked. 'Nobody else followin'.' He motioned to the knife which still hovered uncertainly in the air. 'OK, Ralph, finish him off!' He dropped to his knees and gasped with amazement. 'Jesus! A dame! That's all we needed!' He continued to stare as Curtis sat back on his haunches and slipped the knife into his belt. 'What the hell's she doin' up here, eh?' He rubbed his arm angrily. 'Better finish her off anyway. Can't risk an alarm now!'

Before the moon disappeared, Curtis saw the girl's hand move gingerly to her throat, and for a moment there was a strained silence as she coughed and tried to speak.

'It's the girl I saw this morning on the horse,' Curtis said, and he reached out to touch the thick braid of hair. 'I didn't expect to see *her* again!'

'Please! Please listen to me!' Her voice was husky and strained, and the three men watched her with mixed emotions, caught off guard by the sound of their own tongue. It was a soft voice, yet full of strength and without fear.

'I was looking for you, I knew that you were here on the hill.' She broke off and coughed painfully for a few moments. 'I thought you were going to kill me,' she continued, the words directed at Curtis' dim shape, 'the ... the knife was ver' close!'

Curtis drew his hand away from her hair and stood up abruptly. 'How did you know where to find us?' His voice was flat and impersonal, as if he had not heard the tremor in her tone.

'Your friend, the young officer. He told me!'

There was another short silence. The wind moved amongst the leaves, and Duncan knelt closer to the girl, as if unsure of his hearing. It was Curtis who acted first, and with such speed that the others jumped back in surprise.

He reached down and seized her wrist, dragging her to her feet, until her face was almost against his, her teeth bared with pain.

'What did you say? *Who* told you?' His blood was pounding madly in his brain, and he was unconscious of her cry of protest, as he twisted her wrist savagely. 'Now be careful what you say, for if you're lying, I'll kill you with less feeling than stamping on a beetle!' His voice was dangerously calm, but the force of his words made her twisting body go suddenly limp and still.

'It is true! He told me! You must see that I speak the truth. He is a prisoner at my father's house. He was caught by the soldiers this afternoon.'

Curtis felt her body tremble, but he held his grip, and nodded curtly. 'Well, go on! What else?'

She dropped her face, and seemed all at once to shrink before him. 'They will shoot him at daybreak' – she cried out sharply as he twisted her arm further – 'unless, unless we do something to rescue him!'

'*We?* What's this then? Have you changed sides all of a sudden?'

'Steady on, Ralph!' Duncan was on his feet, his words casual. 'She may be trying to help. She didn't have to come here, did she?'

'It's a trap.' Curtis stared down at her bowed head, as if to penetrate her defences and find the thruth. 'They've made Ian talk, and have sent her out as the bait!'

'It is not so! I want to help him, and you!'

'Let's hear her story, Ralph.' The voice was more insistent. 'Can't do any harm.'

Curtis released her wrist with a jerk and she shrank away from him, rubbing the bare skin with her hand.

'All right. Talk. And make it quick!' Curtis turned his back and stared out to sea, breathing quickly.

She turned to the others, her hands outspread. 'We can go to the house,' she began eagerly, 'he is in a small storeroom at the side of the kitchen, you could——' She halted as Duncan waved his hand to interrupt. He still held the pistol, and the steel gleamed dully as it passed over her head.

'Hold on, sister. One thing at a time. Who are you anyway?'

'I am Carla Zecchi; my father is the mayor here and of the neighbouring villages.' There was a touch of pride in her voice.

'Big stuff, eh, George?' Duncan spoke thoughtfully, his eyes resting on her slim figure. 'Where does your father come into all this?'

She shrugged. 'Your armies have invaded my country, and the Germans are already worried about our government. They think we might not wish to remain their ally when it is inevitable that the country will be destroyed by continuing the fight. My father does not know I am here. No one does, except for your friend.' Her shoulders lifted slightly. '*He* trusted me!'

'He didn't have much choice maybe?' Duncan rubbed his chin, then irritably thrust the gun into his holster. 'How is he? Is he all right?'

'He is well. But time is short, we must act now!'

Curtis spoke sharply over his shoulder. 'Ask her why she is doing this!'

'Well? What's the answer to that?' asked Duncan.

'My father will be one of the first to be arrested if the Badoglio government tries to parley with your army commanders. He has supported the régime right from the start, and the Germans would try to make an example of him.' She shuddered. 'That must not happen. If I can help you now, perhaps you will be able to help my father to escape with you!'

'How exactly?'

'I know a house to the south of here, where you could hide, and when your army reaches that place, you can tell them how my father helped you to escape. They would not be ungrateful.' She stopped, breathing jerkily, her hand rubbing at her throat.

'Does he know about all this?' Duncan looked quickly towards Curtis, but his figure was unmoved.

'No! He would never agree. He is a patriot. He does not think our government will ask for an armistice. He is loyal only to them.' She tossed her head angrily. 'He is mistaken. I know it!'

'You could be right there!' He turned again to Curtis. 'Well, Ralph, what d'you think?'

Curtis jerked his head. 'Keep an eye on her, George, Steve and I will have a little yarn about this.'

She watched them quietly, her legs gleaming in the pale moonlight. 'I thought the British were kinder to their prisoners than this.' She said it with neither bitterness nor anger, and Taylor raised his hand anxiously.

'Quiet! D'you want to upset the skipper again!'

'So he is the captain? He is a hard and cruel man, I think!'

Taylor eyed her furiously. 'We seen some of your bloody Wop soljers behavin' like gents this afternoon, I don't bloody well think! You jus' keep nice an' quiet, an' maybe things'll work out as you say. OK?'

Curtis and Duncan stood side by side on the far edge of the hill.

'I think she's telling the truth anyway, Ralph. In fact, I'd stake my life on it!'

'You may have to!' Curtis shook his head impatiently. 'I believe her story up to a point. But there's a lot she's not told us yet. Still, the idea's all right. It's given me a new lease of life!'

'You mean we're goin' to this flamin' house and hide out till the pongoes arrive?' Duncan was incredulous. 'What about the ship? And the poor bloody soldiers aboard?'

'Shut up! Keep your voice down!' Curtis glared at him through the darkness. 'Of course my plan still goes. But there's no need to tell her about it. We'll make for her father's house now. I've already had a good look at it, I believe, and get Ian away. If that works, we'll get on to phase two, that suit you?'

Duncan gripped his arm. 'Sure, Ralph, you certainly are a crafty cove! You were a bit tough on her though. I thought you were goin' to bite her head off!'

'I've no time for any of them.' Curtis stared across at the two dark figures. 'But come on, we've got to pump her some more yet!'

The girl watched him apprehensively. 'You decide?'

'How many troops at the house?' Curtis ignored her angry intake of breath. 'Is that armoured car still there?' He watched her reaction to his words with cold satisfaction.

'German soldiers nearly all gone. Six are left in the house as guards, but most troops had gone by this afternoon. They have gone to the fighting in the south,' she added.

'I see. Nobody else then?'

'There are the local Carabinieri, but they are stationed at the other side of the village. Their officer is at the house, too, and of course Heinz ...' she faltered, 'I mean that *Leutnant* Beck is there also.'

'Heinz is it?' Curtis laughed softly. 'That's the German officer from the schooner, I take it?'

'Yes.' The answer was guarded.

'How long will he be there? He might upset things if we arrive unexpectedly.'

She shook her head. 'No, that is impossible. He is leaving on the ship at midnight. He is sailing with the wounded soldiers.'

'Midnight, eh?' Curtis answered casually, but he knew that Duncan had followed his train of thought.

'Right, you lead on, *signorina*, we'll get into position by the house now and spy out the land.'

Duncan was looking at his watch. 'Nearly nine o'clock. Things are gettin' interestin'! By the by, Ralph, how do we aim to spring Ian from this place?'

They all looked at the girl.

'He has one guard. You will be able to silence him, yes? The other soldiers are in a small lodge on the other side of the estate. It will be safe.'

'And the policeman? That *gentleman* we saw on the beach today?' Curtis eyed her bleakly.

'He will be going to the schooner. Some of his men are already aboard.'

'Well, well.' Duncan rubbed his hands together, and Curtis looked at him warningly, but the Australian merely smiled and continued to rasp his hands together.

'Let's go,' snapped Curtis suddenly, and with the girl's slim shadow ahead of them, they scrambled in single file down to the deserted beach.

Curtis glanced sideways as Duncan tapped him on the shoulder. 'Good about Ian, eh, Ralph? I know how you felt about leavin' without bein' sure!'

He nodded. 'I only hope he *is* still safe!'

They hurried on in silence, occasionally stumbling across a hillock or mound of sand, or halting to listen for any sounds from the village.

The sea seemed angrier now, and the water sloshed and gurgled into little runnels across the beach, whilst in the bay the waves crowded together in a disturbed fury of noise.

Curtis watched the girl narrowly as she twisted and turned along the edge of the beach, towards the steep hill at the end of the cove.

He felt no fatigue or weariness of any kind, all the anguish and pain of the last days dropping away like a cloak, and walked like a man possessed of some cold, terrible force which drove him forward, calm, and dedicated to the task in hand. It was like the old days, he thought, no time for regrets or hopes. Just the uncertain objective ahead.

They climbed the long, curving track, the girl's feet beginning to lag and falter with the effort of the pace. Once she stopped and looked back at him. 'Can we rest for a moment?'

He gestured sharply. 'Keep going! You said yourself that there's little time!'

Taylor sighed with astonishment when they reached the first of the fountains in the dark garden.

'Cor! Like 'Ampton Court!' His voice was normal, and Curtis was again grateful for the supreme standard of toughness required in the submarine service.

The house was totally dark, the blacked-out windows shining in the moonlight like great blind eyes.

They lay in a line behind a flowerbed, the girl between Curtis and Taylor. Her breath was painful, and she seemed near to collapse. Curtis tapped her on the arm, suddenly conscious of her smooth skin, cool beneath his fingers.

'Which way do we go in?'

She raised herself with an effort and pointed. 'That is the side where the kitchen is. The room where your friend is lies next to that archway.'

'Right, this is what I want done.' Their heads crowded together expectantly. 'Steve, get round to the rear of the house, that'll put you between it and the lodge where the guards are. Take one grenade with you, in case we're rushed!' He turned to the girl. 'George and I'll come in with you at the front. Can the sentry see us from his position?'

'No. But we are too soon yet! The other two are still there!' Her eyes flashed with alarm.

'Maybe they'll be with your father, eh?' He smiled calmly. 'OK, Steve, you get going!' Duncan slid away over the flowerbed and vanished.

She gripped his sleeve with sudden alarm. 'What are you doing? You said you would wait until they had gone to the ship!'

'*You* said that!'

She shook his arm, her voice frightened and angry. 'But, but it will be dangerous! They are too many for you!'

Curtis handed the remaining grenade to Taylor, and took the pistol in exchange. 'Come on!'

She still clung to him, pulling him down. 'You cannot do this, he will fight you! It will be a disaster!'

He dragged her to her feet. 'Who? Heinz? If he's sensible, he'll do as he's told! As *you* tell him!' He let the words sink in.

'You swine! You ... You ...!' She stood trembling with frustration and fury, but Curtis waved the pistol towards the house.

'Remember what I said earlier, and there's your father to think of now!'

The gravel sounded terribly loud as they crossed the drive and passed along the side of the house.

They reached a long french window, and Curtis pulled the girl to his side. 'What's this?' he whispered.

'The library.' She sounded lifeless and beaten.

From behind the drawn curtains they could hear the sound of voices and the soft purr of an Italian orchestra.

'Good, listening to the radio. Your father?'

She again nodded.

'Who's the other one? The German?'

'Yes.' It was only a whisper.

They moved onto the deep porch, and Curtis saw her hand rest hesitatingly on the door handle. He turned to Taylor. 'Keep close, and watch out for the other chap!'

Taylor showed his teeth. 'Right!'

The air which fanned their faces as the door opened was warm and scented with flowers, and Curtis glanced quickly from the dim hall-light to the long passage which curved away from the far end. All was quiet, and very still.

She crossed the dark floor to a pair of wide doors, her small feet making no sound. She paused and looked at Curtis' face imploringly. 'Please?'

But Curtis looked past her and moved the gun sharply. His heart seemed to have stopped, and he could feel Taylor's body crowding behind him in the doorway.

Taylor's unshaven face was drawn and wary, his grubby hand clutching the grenade in front of him like some kind of offering.

'Open!' Curtis hissed the words between his teeth.

The doors opened wide to reveal the soft lighted room, with its deep chairs and rows of leather-bound books, but Curtis had eyes only for the plump, unsmiling man who lay back in his chair, his fingers pressed together, his brow creased in a frown of concentration. He saw, too, the gleaming white uniform of the officer he had seen on the beach. In that split second he saw it all, and when they turned to look at the girl, Curtis thrust her to one side, the gun steady in his fist.

'Tell them to stay where they are, and keep still!' The words were harsh and without feeling, the impact of his voice and his sudden appearance making the two men freeze into positions of shocked dismay.

'My father understands.' She spoke hoarsely, and then continued in German. The young officer half rose from his chair, his expression slowly changing to one of fury.

Curtis smiled unpleasantly. 'Tell him to be sensible. I'd hate to dirty that uniform!'

The mayor gripped the arms of his chair and levered himself forward, his face pale but surprisingly calm. 'If you have harmed my daughter in any way I shall see that you suffer for it!' His dark eyes flashed defiantly, and Curtis shrugged his shoulders and pointed to the girl.

'She is well. See for yourself. Now,' his tone became sharper, 'where is the police officer?'

She ran to her father's side and dropped to her knees, while the German stared stonily at her and then back to Curtis. The mayor ran his fingers over her hair, as if to reassure himself, but said nothing.

'Tell him, Papa!' She looked up at her father, her eyes grave. 'It will be for the best!' She said something in German, her voice soft and pleading, but the lieutenant still stared in front of him with dulled eyes.

'He is in the room upstairs, *signore*. The one at the top of the stairway.'

Curtis hesitated. It had been easy so far, and he knew the danger of resting on his laurels. His eyes darted around the room, but he could see no further weapons.

'All right, George,' he said mildly, 'christen the Jerry.'

Taylor frowned uneasily, and then his dirty face split into a grin. 'I gotcher, Skipper!' And he walked briskly across the room towards the bookcase. As he passed behind the German's chair, he suddenly raised the grenade and brought it down viciously on the man's skull. The girl choked back a cry, and sat with her hands wrapped across her open mouth, her eyes on Curtis' face.

Taylor watched the man slump to the floor, and wiped the grenade on his sleeve.

'Well done, George!' To the two pairs of eyes across the room he said, 'He will be safer there. He might have been tempted.'

He beckoned the girl. 'We'll pay a visit upstairs.'

She kept away from him as they mounted the soft stair carpet. Curtis, his eyes watchful, halted in front of the bedroom door. He looked at her with tired gravity, suddenly realizing that he hadn't really seen her before in the light.

She was very beautiful, and with her eyes black with anger and fear she possessed the perfection of a wild animal. He shut his mind, and thought of Jervis. It was impossible to believe that he was somewhere on the floor below.

His fingers gripped the door handle. 'Wait here. Don't move.' He opened the door slightly and peered through the brightly lit crack into the soft-scented bedroom.

The Italian officer sat pensively on the edge of the bed, slowly pulling on his boots. His jacket hung open, and on his shining mane of greased hair he was wearing a hairnet. He whistled softly, and stood up to look at himself in the mirror.

Curtis remembered the limping, battered British sergeant on the beach, and felt the pity drain out of him.

He stepped across the carpet and rammed the gun into his spine.

Their eyes met in the dressing table mirror. The blue ones hard and uncompromising; the others popping out with sheer terror.

They left the room together, the Italian not even noticing the girl, and walking with exaggerated eagerness to show he was willing to co-operate.

Once inside the library again, Curtis tossed the Italian's small automatic to Taylor. 'They're all yours, George!' He grinned, but the sweat was pouring down his spine in a steady stream, while his stomach felt as if it was full of lead. 'So far, so good. Now for Ian!'

He walked to the door, but the girl held up her hand. 'I will go first, as I said I would.'

'I thought you had perhaps changed your mind?'

'We do not all break our promises, *Capitano*!' She spat the words at him.

They stood in the silence of the hall, she slim and defiant, and Curtis beginning to feel the first reaction of exhaustion.

He cursed inwardly. No time for that now. This is going to be the worst bit of all.

She brushed past him and walked confidently into the passage. Curtis waited a few seconds, then looked slowly around the curve of the wall.

Immediately, he saw the sentry. A young boy in German uniform, his small eyes fixed on the approaching girl. A shaft of light poured through an open door beside him, and Curtis licked his lips worriedly. It would be a close thing, he thought, and measured the distance along the passage.

She halted, and Curtis watched her hips move provocatively, as she casually leaned against the doorpost. She spoke loudly to someone inside the room, her voice filled with scorn, yet the words making Curtis raise his pistol and point wildly at the sentry.

'Hey, Englishman! Wake up! I have brought a friend, but do nothing yet! I will tell you when to do something!' She laughed, and Curtis saw the soldier's thin face split into a foolish grin.

Curtis breathed out slowly. What a chance the girl was taking, he thought, as he watched the wavering snout of the man's Schmeisser.

She turned lazily away from the room, so that she faced Curtis, her hands pressed against the wall behind her. Her breasts moved quickly beneath the soft green dress, and Curtis could well imagine the effect she was having on the sentry.

The man faltered, and for a brief instant Curtis felt almost sorry for him. The oldest trick in the world, he reflected.

Then, as the sentry's gun wavered, she reached forward and flung her arms around his neck. The next few seconds were filled with terror and hate, as Curtis jumped along the passage in a few bounds and pulled the man's steel helmet backwards from his head. The thick leather chinstrap

bit into the soldier's throat, and he dropped his gun with a clatter, as he
scrabbled furiously with clawing fingers to save himself.
Curtis was only half aware of what he was doing. There was so much
to see and understand. Jervis' pink, wildly excited face danced to meet
him, while over the soldier's writhing shoulder the girl leaned weakly
against the wall, her eyes closed.
'Skipper! Oh, Skipper! You came back! You're here!' Jervis babbled
incoherently.
The body gave a final gasp and slithered to the floor.
Curtis clapped his hand across the boy's shoulder. 'Good to see you,
Ian,' he muttered. 'Now pick up that Schmeisser and let's get
organized!'
Jervis looked at the girl, his high spirits giving way to concern. He
touched her arm gently, and she opened her eyes to stare at him, her
expression dazed and bewildered.
'Thanks!' Jervis faltered, unsure of himself. 'You were wonderful!'
Curtis glanced at them sharply, his mind already seething with the
urgency of his scheme, and fully alive to the increasing danger. 'Get the
clothes off him!' He jabbed his foot into the crumpled body at his
feet.
Jervis tore his eyes from the girl and looked at the dead soldier's
empurpled face with sick revulsion. 'What for, Skipper?' he asked in a
low voice. 'Do we need the uniform?'
'No. But I want it to look as if you killed the guard and escaped in his
clothes. We'll carry them down to the beach and bury 'em in the sand.'
He jerked his head impatiently. 'Get your clothes off as well, and chuck
them on the floor!'
Jervis coloured. 'But what do I wear if——'
'Just do as you're told, Ian. I'll have some other things ready for you by
the time you've finished. Now for God's sake get a move on!'
He gripped the girl's elbow and guided her forcefully along the
passage. He glanced back to see Jervis tearing with frantic haste at the
soldier's uniform, his face averted from what he was doing.
'What are you doing? What is it that you are planning?' She twisted in
his grip, her voice bitter.
'We're leaving. I told you!'
Curtis pushed into the library, to where the two Italians and Taylor
sat facing each other in uneasy stances of watchfulness.
'Is 'e all right, Skipper? You found 'im?'
'He's fine, George. Now listen. Strip the uniform off the Jerry here,
and take it along to Ian. Tell him to get it on immediately. It should be
just his size.'
He watched as Taylor stooped over the unconscious officer, his eyes
burning with sudden fatigue. 'What time was our friend due to leave for

the schooner?' He directed the question to the girl without turning his head.

'About eleven. I told you they were sailing at midnight.'

'They still are.'

Curtis eyed the well-muscled body of the German stripped to his underclothes, as Taylor gathered up the white uniform and ran from the room. A tough customer, he thought. Just as well we laid him out for a bit.

The Italian police officer who, Curtis noticed, had removed his hairnet, was sitting bolt upright on the edge of his seat, his pop-eyes fixed on Curtis' pistol. 'Plis, *signore*,' his words were slurred with fear, 'what you do? I not soldier! I give no trouble!'

Curtis eyed him coldly. 'You will leave for the ship as arranged, with one of my officers, d'you understand?' The Italian nodded with pathetic eagerness. 'Right, you behave yourself, and you might be allowed to live!'

The mayor had recovered his bland composure, outwardly at least, and frowned at Curtis' last words.

'What do you hope to do? You are playing a dangerous game!'

He eyed his daughter, his face suddenly grave. 'What made you act as you did, Carla?'

She shrugged defiantly, her tanned, heart-shaped face controlled and calm. 'I thought this officer would help you to go away from here.' She spoke in careful English, the words directed as much at Curtis as her father. 'You know what will happen if our government sues for peace. You have always known it!' The mayor did not interrupt her, but his eyes were sad and he stared vacantly at his hands. 'We would have been safe then. We could have waited in peace for a while!'

'I understand,' he said quietly, 'but I do not think that this officer will permit such an arrangement.' He lifted his eyebrows questioningly, and looked up at Curtis.

'We are all going in the ship!' Curtis stared at him, coldly angry. He ignored the gasp from the girl, and the flash of hatred in her eyes. 'We will sail tonight at the time which has been arranged. I cannot leave you here, obviously, so you will have to keep us company. I must warn you again, that as I have no choice in what I am doing, you will be advised to do as I say, or I will not answer for the consequences!'

Taylor spoke from the door. 'Right! I've done that, Skipper. What next?'

'Go and fetch Steve.' He glanced at the ornate clock over the fireplace. Ten to eleven. 'Keep your eyes peeled, George!'

'I must admire the way you are dealing with a difficult situation.' The mayor smiled thinly. 'You are a man of many parts, *signore*.'

The girl murmured beneath her breath, her eyes on Curtis.

'You must not think too badly of him, Carla. He will die if he is captured. He is desperate.'

'He is a cheat, and a liar!' She swung her shoulders round, her face hidden.

Her father smiled again and spread his hands defensively. 'You will not get far, *signore*, I am afraid. The sea will be alive with our ships!'

'Whose? Yours or the Germans?'

'What matter? We are allies!'

I wonder for how long, Curtis thought. He jerked round, startled, his gun swinging towards the door.

Jervis grinned with embarrassment, and held out his hands awkwardly. The uniform fitted him well. 'Steady on! I'm on your side!'

Curtis smiled. 'Go with this young lady, and get all the first aid gear you can lay your hands on – bandages, lint, anything. Be back here in five minutes!' He addressed the girl. 'Help him, please, and bring a small bag for your own things. *One* bag,' he added.

Duncan shouldered his way into the room, the light playing across his wild, unshaven face and crumpled uniform. 'Dinkum, Ralph? Good!' He nodded to the mayor and fastened his gaze on the other Italian. 'I thought we'd meet again,' he growled.

'Later!' snapped Curtis, his eye again on the clock. 'Did you see anything?'

Duncan dropped his voice. 'Don't tell Ian this, but I found something out in the field by the guardhouse. There was a nice new post driven into the ground, complete with ropes! And nearby there was a neat little open grave!'

Curtis looked grim. 'Near thing, eh?'

Duncan stared round the room. 'Sure thing. Say, didn't young Ian look a peach in his new outfit? What's the idea? When I met him with our girl friend just now, I thought the game was up!'

The German on the floor groaned, but remained motionless, and Curtis pointed at him briskly. 'Tie him up, Steve. You'll probably have to carry him to the ship, so make a good job of it.'

Duncan shook his head in admiration. 'You're a marvel, Ralph. I just don't know what's keepin' you on your feet, let alone holdin' your brain together!' He cut the silk cord from the curtains with his knife and knelt across the German.

The clock began to chime, and Curtis peered through a gap in the curtain. All was quiet, although the moon was much brighter and turned the hedges and buildings to patterns of blue and silver.

Jervis returned carrying a sack and a large case. 'A few personal things,' he explained defensively as Curtis' eye fell on the case. 'I've got a few bandages as well.'

'Right. You, Ian, go down to the beach now, and wait at the end of the sand spit. If anyone from the village speaks to you, just wave the Schmeisser at them. They won't stop to argue.' He indicated the police officer. 'Take him with you. When you leave by the front door, make sure that you hold it ajar for a minute or two. There's a sentry on the main gate, I understand, and I want to be sure that he sees you both leave. Everything must look quite normal.' He turned to Taylor. 'You take the mayor and his daughter and go out the back way. Keep to the path we came by, but keep out of sight. Make certain there's no trouble,' he added harshly.

Taylor licked his lips. 'Ready, mate?'

The mayor stood up and took the case from Jervis. He linked his arm through the girl's and followed Taylor through the door.

Jervis clicked his heels and smiled shakily. 'Gosh, it's like a miracle, seeing you both again!'

Glass clinked from the oak sideboard as Duncan slipped two bottles inside his blouse. 'Get crackin', Ian, an' keep an eye on this joker! I want to have a word or two with him later!' He looked threateningly at the shaking Italian.

Jervis put on the German cap, tucking his rough bandage under the rim. 'Lucky he's got a big head!' he grinned, as the German groaned again and twitched violently.

He slipped the machine pistol under his arm and beckoned to the police officer. 'Come on then. We're going home!'

Curtis and Duncan watched the two figures stand momentarily under the light from inside the porch and then stride across the drive and down towards the cliff path. In a few seconds they were out of sight. The house was suddenly quiet, and Curtis looked at Duncan wearily, his face grey with concentration and effort.

'Let's follow George, eh? We can leave this place now.'

Duncan smiled cheerfully and hoisted the German across his shoulder. 'I'm glad you decided to listen to the girl, Ralph. She'll be good company!'

'We're not in the ship yet, or out at sea either!' Curtis was instantly ashamed of the snap in his voice. 'Sorry, Steve, I'm about done in.' But he knew that the girl was the real cause of his irritation.

'Not bloody well surprised! Wait till we get back to Alex. I'll get you something to put you right!'

They crossed the lawn and started down the narrow track. Curtis stopped only once, and looked back at the deserted house. There'll be quite a panic in there shortly, he thought grimly.

CHAPTER 7

The wind was veering rapidly to the east, and some of its force could be felt on the beach, as the short rollers plunged unevenly along its length, throwing tongues of spray and spume across the moist sand.

Curtis peered at his watch and then across the dark, pitching water to where he judged the schooner was riding.

Duncan dumped the German's body on the ground and stretched his arms with relief. Curtis could hear the German biting and choking on his gag, but did not even spare the man a glance; he concentrated instead on the sea, and Jervis' white figure which stood stark against the black backcloth like a ghost.

He was dimly aware of the other figures huddled behind him in the overhanging shadow of the hill, and of the girl's lowered voice as she spoke to her father. Taylor was standing a little apart from the rest, his head turned towards the hidden village.

He saw Jervis raise his arm, and imagined that he could see the flash of his torch as he gave the awaited signal to the ship.

'It'd be a real joke if the perishers have shoved off without waitin' for the Jerry and his mate, eh?' Duncan chuckled without humour. 'We'd look a right lot of mugs then!'

'Signor Zecchi has informed me that this is the correct time for the schooner's departure, and he has also explained the signal that is normally given.' Curtis spoke shortly. 'I don't think we need disbelieve him at this stage.'

'Thank you.' There was a trace of sarcasm in the mayor's reply. 'I am honoured that you trust me so!'

Curtis moved his shoulders in a quick nervous gesture. 'I think you know better than to play games!'

They fell into an uneasy silence once more, and Curtis wondered what Jervis was thinking as he stood on the edge of the water with the tall Italian. Now that the first wave of violence and fury had passed from him, he felt a vague prickle of resentment and disappointment which he could not begin to understand. Coupled with the feeling of emptiness, he knew that in some way he was still blaming himself for everything which had happened.

He stiffened, and cocked his head on one side. Faintly at first, and then more persistently, came the squeak of oars and the slap of a boat in the trough of the waves.

'Ready?' He was awake again, and momentarily his fears moved into second place. 'George, watch this lot. Steve, you and I'll go down to the boat as soon as it beaches.'

'I'm with you!' Duncan blew into his cupped hands. 'Quite a lively sea for movin' about, I must say!'

They saw the boat slide sluggishly over a white-capped roller and slew carelessly across the shingle. Two humped figures bent over the oars, and their faces gleamed white in the moonlight, as Curtis and Duncan ran down into the water.

Curtis laid his hands on the gunwale and spoke slowly to the police officer, his words plucked from his mouth by the wind. 'Tell them that there are extra passengers,' he said. 'You can tell them that we are members of the German Navy if you wish!'

The officer's eyes rolled from Curtis to Duncan, who was standing with casual watchfulness behind him, one hand beneath his jacket, and then in quick, excited sentences, he spoke to the oarsmen. One of them shrugged obediently, while the other merely stared indifferently at the water which sloshed across the boat's bottom-boards.

Duncan steadied the boat as Taylor shepherded the mayor and his daughter down the beach.

The girl turned as if to make one last protest to Curtis, but as she stared at his set, shadowed face, she sighed and stepped lightly into the boat. Taylor followed them, his lips pursed in a silent whistle and, at a nod from Curtis, Duncan ran up the beach for the German.

One of the oarsmen looked up, startled, as the body was dumped behind them in the bottom, but Duncan glared and growled unintelligibly under his breath, and the man bent uneasily across his oar.

Jervis sat upright in the stern, his shoulders squared and his face shaded by the cap.

Before pushing the boat into deep water, Curtis examined the placing of everyone in it with silent care. He nodded to Jervis, satisfied that he was sitting in the most conspicuous position, and where any lookout was bound to see the German uniform, before realizing that anything unusual was happening.

He had done all he could, and with a grunt he pushed the boat clear.

The oars rose and fell, and the boat rose and plunged across the waves. With its extra load it was sluggish and unsteady, and the bottom was soon filled with water, which moved across their feet and splashed persistently along the worn gunwale. The land seemed to fade almost at once, and but for the glint of the moon along the sand spit and the dim hump of the hill, it had already lost its identity.

They saw the schooner's hull first, her smooth white side pitching angrily, as she tugged at the anchor cable, and then, as the boat moved slowly under her high stern, the tall, circling masts and the flapping, carelessly-furled sails loomed over their heads.

Across the stern Curtis could just see the vessel's name, *Ametisa*, scrawled in wide gilt lettering, which had once, no doubt, been the pride of her owner or captain.

The bow oarsman opened his mouth as if to hail the deck, but Duncan punched him in the arm and shook his head.

The boat scraped alongside and Curtis stood up, his limbs suddenly light, and reached for the schooner's rail. He heaved himself up and over in one quick movement, his boots skidding on the wet deck.

He glared round, his eyes searching desperately amongst the unfamiliar shapes and shadows of the darkened ship.

Duncan stood beside him, and then Jervis. Taylor's small figure rose and fell in the boat alongside, his shoulders stooped like a small idol, as he sat quietly watching the others in the boat, his pistol in his hand.

What the oarsmen thought, Curtis neither knew nor cared, and he rested momentarily against the scored gunwale of the ship, unsure of what to do next.

At that very moment, a figure seemed to rise out of the deck between the masts, his uniform buttons glinting in the circle of light which followed him through the opened hatch.

Duncan stepped easily forward and waited for the man to climb onto the deck. As he bent to refasten the hatch, Duncan drove his boot into the lowered head, and then caught his body before he could fall onto the wet planking.

'One less,' he said calmly, and pulled a pistol from the man's belt. Still holding the limp figure, he tossed the gun over the ship's side.

Curtis spoke quietly over the gunwale: 'Signor Zecchi! Up here quickly!' Turning to Duncan, who was busy tying up the policeman with his belt, he whispered: 'We'll grab the skipper now!'

The mayor arrived on deck, his eyes blinking around him.

'Come on,' snapped Curtis. 'Steve, stay on deck!'

He propelled the mayor to the after hatch, aware that Jervis was following behind, the Schmeisser pointing dangerously at his legs. He slid back the hatch and almost fell down the steep ladder beyond, and ducked beneath a swinging oil lamp, which cast an uncertain glow along the short passage with its three closed doors. Curtis paused uncertainly, the mayor pressed against him, and Jervis' white legs still on the ladder.

As if in response to his unspoken question, a door opened, and the fat stomach of the captain appeared in the passage. He was still wearing the greasy cap which Curtis had seen earlier, and his round, unshaven jowls dropped even lower as he stared at Curtis' gun and then at his face.

He opened his mouth to speak, his breath fanning across Curtis in a curtain of sour wine and tobacco, but the mayor shook his head authoritatively and held up his hand.

'Stay still, *Capitano,*' he commanded quietly. 'This is a British officer!' He waited patiently, but the Italian sailor merely goggled at Curtis, his throat moving and bobbing above his red shirt. 'He is taking your ship!'

'Do you speak English?' Curtis spoke sharply, aware of the time all this explanation was taking.

'*Si!* Ver' good English!' He glanced round desperately. 'Where you come from? I not understand what is happening!'

'Get on deck and call your men! And be quick about it!' Curtis stared at the fat, sweating face in exasperation. 'You are sailing at once!'

'But, *signore*——' he spread his palms appealingly.

The gun moved lower. 'Call them!'

Jervis squeezed back to allow him to pass, then ran up the ladder after him.

The captain peered worriedly at Jervis and shook his head, before reaching up to the bell, which hung on a bracket on the mast.

Duncan uncoiled himself from the rail, his eyes on the captain. 'He OK, Ralph?'

'We'll see! Any sign of the others?'

Duncan laughed shortly. 'They're up in the fo'c'sle, playin' dice, by the sound of it.'

'Where are the wounded?'

Duncan shrugged. 'Not a sign of 'em yet.'

The bell jangled loudly, and Duncan loped across the deck to halt beside the narrow door leading into the fo'c'sle.

Light spewed across the ship as the door swung open, and a blue cloud of tobacco smoke billowed up between the legs of the six men who stamped irritably into the cold air.

Three of them were uniformed Carabinieri and the others seamen, their ragged jerseys and dirty duck trousers clashing with the smart boots and belts of their companions.

There was an exclamation of surprise, and one of the policemen dived backwards to the door, which, just as suddenly, slammed hard into his face. He reeled back, his hand clamped across his bleeding mouth, as Duncan stepped from behind the door, the gun balanced in his hand like a toy.

'Stand still, you jokers! Unless you want to step off!' He grinned savagely at each of them and gestured towards the trussed figure on the deck. 'One of yer mates! See?'

They stared round the deck, drawing together as if for support, while Curtis spoke rapidly to the captain.

'Where are the rest? You should have a bigger crew than this!'

Counting the two oarsmen still in the dinghy, there were only five seamen.

'I am trying to tell you,' began the captain, his voice resigned and tired. 'These are all I have! My other boys desert, two . . . three days ago, I forget! They get worried 'bout the invasion, they wanna get home to their families! Me? I got no family, justa this boat!' He clenched his thick fists in sudden despair. 'Now you gonna take her away from me!'

'Where are the soldiers who were brought aboard?' Curtis made an effort to control his rising temper. 'Come on, man! Where have you put them?'

'They below, in the hold,' he answered sulkily. 'I was told to put 'em there!'

Curtis stared at him in disbelief. 'Wounded men? In the hold?' He seized the man savagely by the front of his shirt, and thrust his face forward. 'By God, you bloody Wops sicken me! If any more of them die, I swear you'll regret you were born!' He felt the fat body quiver. 'Now, prepare to get under way, just as you were ordered!'

'I do my best.' He moved his hands vacantly, his face twisting worriedly. 'Is a ver' difficult channel!'

Duncan's voice grated across the deck. 'You'll get us clear though, won't you, Captain? Just for us?'

The captain glanced at the hard, mocking eyes and swallowed unhappily. Then he jerked his hands at the stunned sailors and pointed to the capstan. One of the men started towards the hatch over the small engine-room, but Curtis shook his head.

'Come up, George, and get the engine started.'

Signor Zecchi coughed. 'You leave little to chance, I see.'

Curtis ignored him, his aching brain groped for possible flaws in his plan, and he tried to keep his mind away from the silent wounded below his feet, at least until they were clear of the anchorage. He watched dully, as the girl appeared on the deck and stood shivering beside her suitcase. The two sailors heaved the wriggling German after her, and then towed the dinghy round to the davits aft.

Curtis turned to the police officer. 'Get your men in a line, quick!' To Duncan: 'Search them, and make sure they're well locked up!'

Surprisingly, the captain said over his shoulder, 'There is a good storeroom down there.' He pointed to another hatch. 'They will be safe in there.'

When Duncan had herded the Carabinieri away, and the German had been dragged after them, Curtis eyed the captain thoughtfully. 'Aren't they friends of yours then?'

The captain shrugged and spat over the gunwale. '*Facisti!* They stink!'

The deck quivered, and there was a dull roar from the engine-room, but after a few coughing protests, the motor settled down to a confident rumble.

The captain spat on his hands and took the wheel, whilst from forward came the clink of cable as the capstan heaved in the anchor.

He leaned comfortably on the wheel and pouted his thick lips expressively. 'We won't get far, *signore*! Patrol boats! Bombers! No, we won't get far!'

He spun the wheel and peered at the compass, which danced loosely in its ancient brass binnacle. A thin spindly lever at his side protested as he pushed his bulk against it, until it squeaked level with a worn plate stating '*Velocita massima!*', and as the propeller churned a cheerful white froth beneath her counter, the *Ametisa* swung drunkenly into the wind and thrust her sharp stem over the first long roller.

Curtis watched for a few minutes, then beckoned to Jervis. 'You stay here on the poop, and watch the deck. Nobody is to go below until Steve has searched all the crew's quarters.' He glanced at the captain's squat shape, his fat straddled legs braced behind the wheel, and raising his voice, he added, 'And if we go aground, shoot him!'

He turned away from Jervis before he could answer, and stood for a moment against the rail, his hands resting heavily on its worn and grooved surface. The sudden realization that the ship was his – brought home to him by the steady beat of the engines and the swish of foam against the pitching hull – seemed to bring all conscious thought to an end. The weight of his body grew heavier on his arms, and his head sagged forward over the rail. He was shivering, and had to clench his teeth to withstand his weakness, which felt like real pain.

'*Signore?*' The mayor moved quietly at his elbow. 'May we go below now?'

Curtis levered himself away from the rail, his fingers slipping reluctantly from its support. He peered at the mayor through half-closed eyes, and nodded wearily.

The girl's voice was cold and unforgiving. 'Perhaps he wishes us to be locked in the store with the others!'

He stumbled past her and led the way down the steep ladder to the cabin flat. The lamp swung more jerkily than before, and the narrow passage leaped and staggered with the ship's lively movements. The hissing roar of the sea was muffled, and the air was thick and stale. He pushed open the first door and glared at the bare cabin, with its neat bunk and newly-painted sides. Another lantern swung crazily from a deck beam, casting strange shadows across the cabin's clinical bareness and the framed portrait of Adolf Hitler. A small safe was bolted to the bulkhead, but apart from a narrow wardrobe containing some more items of German uniform, there was nothing dangerous in sight.

'You can have this one, *signorina*. It was evidently your friend's cabin, so it's bound to be fairly clean!'

She looked at him without speaking, her slim body swaying to the motion of the ship. She placed the suitcase on the bunk, and with her eyes still on his face, she slowly ran her fingers along the black plait across her shoulder.

Curtis took the mayor's arm impatiently, and led him to the other cabin.

It was completely the opposite to the other. The captain's possessions were scattered across the bunk and on the deck, while on the rickety table stood two empty *vino* bottles and a half eaten sandwich. Over the bunk a series of voluptuous pin-ups smiled and reclined in crude abandon.

There was a pistol in one of the desk drawers, and a mountain of old letters and papers.

'Stay here!' he ordered curtly. 'I think you now understand our position well enough?'

The mayor inclined his head gravely, but Curtis had the impression that he was secretly amused.

'Don't touch anything. Go to bed, if you like.'

He lurched for the door, the air suddenly beginning to stifle him. More than anything else he wanted to lie down, and the sight of that filthy bunk tempted him more than anything he could remember. He paused for a second in the doorway and looked back at the plump, dignified Italian.

'I am sorry you have been caused all this inconvenience, and I appreciate your daughter's courage, whatever her reasons,' he faltered, and the mayor stared at him, his black eyes expressionless. 'Perhaps it will all turn out for the best for you, too.' He stopped, angry with himself, and ran up the ladder.

Duncan greeted him with an easy smile. 'All quiet, Ralph. I think the captain here has cottoned onto the general idea. I don't reckon his boys'll give any trouble now.'

'Good,' Curtis answered vaguely. 'Now for God's sake let's have a look at those poor devils below!'

Two seamen rolled back the hatch, their eyes on Duncan, and Curtis bent carefully over the high coaming, a feeling of nausea rising within him as the stench of closely packed bodies, sweat, and something worse hit him across the face.

The light in the hold was poor, but good enough to see in an instant the twin lines of crumpled figures which ran along both sides of the hold. Some of the soldiers lay on pieces of sacking in positions of sleep or even death, while others dragged themselves aimlessly between the lines muttering encouragement, or cursing each other as either a wounded limb or a careless boot started off another frenzied convulsion of pain.

Duncan followed close behind him, two lanterns adding to the picture of misery. His face was a mask, but the cold light in his eyes dimmed as he stared over Curtis' shoulder.

One of the soldiers rolled wildly onto his back, his fingers hooked into his sacking. 'Water! Fer God's sake give me a drink!' A chorus of cracked voices joined his plea in a terrible cry, whilst from the far end of the hold Curtis saw the red-faced sergeant stagger to his feet, his good eye darting around his men. 'Easy there, lads. Be all right soon.' He sounded tired, and his voice was no longer jaunty.

He peered down the dim hold, watching the two figures on the ladder. 'Come on, lads,' he pleaded. 'Don't let the bloody Eyeties see you're done in!'

A lump filled Curtis' throat, and he gripped the ladder fiercely. 'For Christ's sake,' he groaned, 'they'd have died down here! Look at them!' He swayed, and Duncan gripped his arm savagely.

His voice, close against Curtis' ear, was steady and very quiet. 'Come on, Ralph! Give 'em the shock of their lives!' He squeezed more insistently. 'You can do it! You know you can!'

Curtis tore his eyes from the hold and met Duncan's stare. The awful strength from the man's eyes seemed to run through his blood like brandy, and he bit his lip with sudden determination.

He stepped slowly down into the hold, his hands at his sides, and the light glittering and swaying across his fair hair and the tarnished gold lace on his shoulders.

He halted, praying that his voice would not let him down. He need not have worried, his words, amplified by the sides of the hold, and cutting through the sudden silence, were clear, and full of confidence.

'All right, you lazy lot! The convalescence is over!' He paused, his hands on his hips, his unshaven chin jutting forward. 'The Navy's here!' He stopped, unable to continue, and stared blindly back at Duncan, who nodded his huge head and grinned.

The effect of his words was instantaneous and electric.

The sergeant ran towards him, his arm-sling jerking and bobbing, as with his other groping hand he prodded the startled men and shouted with wild excitement.

'Hear that, Ginger? It's the bloody Navy! What did I tell you, Bert? It's them! It's all right!'

Curtis was stunned by the shouts and the pathetic capers of the sergeant, and could only stand in the middle of the whooping, hopping soldiers.

The blinded soldier sat bolt upright on the pile of rags in one corner, shaking urgently at the arm of the man next to him. His mouth moved in a white crescent beneath his bandages. 'Wake up, Ralph! We've been rescued!' He stopped tugging, and sat back, suddenly lost and silent, his fingers still holding onto his friend's tunic.

The soldier, Ralph, lay where he was, unmoved and indifferent, his glazed, unblinking eyes staring at the deckhead.

Curtis watched, suddenly cold. It was not only the feeling of loss which he seemed to share with the blind soldier; it was also that the dead man had been called Ralph.

He pointed desperately, and calmed the sergeant's excited shouts. 'Help him, Steve,' he called, 'and get some of the sailors down here quickly!'

The sergeant was speaking again, his boots together with something like his old smartness. 'Sarnt Dunwoody, sir! First Battalion, Middlesex Light Infantry!'

He stared at Curtis as if still unable to believe what he saw. 'By God, sir, I don't know 'ow you got 'ere, but by heaven it's a bleedin' miracle!' His red face seemed to crumple, and he fidgeted with his sling. 'I don't think we coulda managed much longer!'

Curtis nodded dumbly, aware that Duncan and three of the more able soldiers were passing round great mugs of fresh water.

'The buggers wouldn't give us anything to drink. Kep' sayin' we'd 'ave to wait!' continued the sergeant with abrupt fierceness, as he relived the whole nightmare over again. 'Wait! After bein' blown to 'ell an' then bein' cut about in a Jerry dressin' station, to say nothin' of twenty-four hours in a bleedin' lorry!' He stared round at his men with something like paternal pride. 'But they didn't give in!'

'You've been in charge all the time?' The question was a mere whisper, but the sergeant smiled sadly.

'Yessir. Y'see, our last officer died before we was patched up. 'E was a good kid, too!'

Curtis saw the campaign medals on the old soldier's chest. A generation and another war apart.

'I'll see that you're not forgotten either, Sergeant.' He swung round to follow Duncan, afraid that the sergeant might see his face.

Duncan's voice seemed to come from every direction at once. 'Come on, sport! Get this down you! It's only water I'm afraid, but I've got those goddamned Eyeties cookin' a month's rations up for you as fast as they can move their little selves!'

He bent over the blind soldier. 'Come on, young 'un, give me a hand with this water.' The soldier shrank away, but Duncan pulled him to his feet and thrust the big water jug into his hands. Then leading him slowly between the men, he manoeuvred him away from the other silent figure.

He caught Curtis' dull stare and winked. 'Think I'll join the Army, eh, Skipper?'

Curtis smiled. It was the first time Duncan had avoided using his Christian name. So he had noticed, too.

He caught sight of the stocky little soldier whom the sergeant had called Ginger. He was staring at the Italian seamen with undisguised hatred, his mouth quivering.

'Here, you!' Curtis beckoned across a prostrate soldier. 'Come here a minute!'

The man came quickly, his eyes feverish but alert.

'Are you fairly fit?' Curtis studied the man's single bandage about his throat. 'I mean, d'you feel you can give me a hand?'

The soldier grinned, his whole expression changing to one of eagerness. 'Sir! Just give me the word! I'm so keyed up, I think I'll go off my head if I can't do something!'

'Well listen, er, Ginger, go on deck will you? There's an officer there by the wheel dressed as a German. He's guarding, among other things, a pile of pistols we've taken off the guards. I want you to gather them up and pass them to any one of your chaps you think is fit enough to keep an eye on things. OK?'

'Yessir!' The man was already halfway up the ladder, his nailed boots clattering on the wooden rungs.

'And no reprisals!' Curtis called after him.

He halted, level with the deck. 'They're not worth a bullet, sir!'

Curtis took a deep breath and sought out the sergeant once more. 'How are your men now?'

Dunwoody sighed worriedly. 'Not too bad considerin', sir. Four dead and ten pretty grim.' He brightened slightly. 'But the other twelve seem to 'ave taken new 'eart since you arrived, sir!' He glared admiringly. ''Ow did you get 'ere, sir?'

Curtis eyed him glassily. 'Too long a story for the moment. But I can tell you this, we're not even half out of the wood yet!' He forced a weak smile. 'But if you can carry on here for a bit, I'll be very grateful.'

'Jus' tell me what to do, sir.' He, too, seemed to have taken on a fresh strength.

'Any more N.C.O's?'

'Bert's pretty good,' he answered slowly. ''Ead wound, an' gets a bit dizzy, but 'e'll last out a bit longer, sir.'

'Right, put him on deck behind the wheel. Let him sit on something, and see that he's armed.' The soldier, Ginger, reappeared with the guns, his face pale but determined. 'He's to watch the crew and see that there's no funny business. You can carry on down here and serve out the food when it arrives. I'll see if we can get a good hot drink too, if that's possible!'

The sergeant loosened his belt. 'Leave it to us, sir.'

Curtis climbed the ladder to the deck, pausing on the top rung to let the salt air sting his face. His weariness still closed in with relentless persistence, but stubbornly he forced himself onto the darkened deck. The moon had vanished altogether, and the weather was freshening. Overhead, the cloud banks scudded across the black sky like solid things, and the loose rigging moaned and creaked in monotonous liaison. A dim light flickered against the captain's fat face as he leaned over the compass bowl, and Jervis' white shape hurried to meet him.

'How are they, sir? Can I do anything?'

'There's a soldier coming to relieve you, Ian. I shall want——' He broke off as a thin corporal clambered unsteadily from the hold and peered at them from beneath his white bandages. He was wearing a khaki balaclava rolled over his dressing, and looked almost piratical. 'Ah, here he is! Know what to do, Corporal?'

'Yessir!' The man scrambled across the heaving deck and planted himself firmly on the after hatchway behind the wheel. He rested a small pistol on his knee, and began to rock to and fro, his arms folded in solemn concentration.

'Now,' continued Curtis, having seen that the captain had noted the new arrival, 'I shall want you get cracking on the chart, if there is such a thing aboard, and there's a safe which might prove interesting, too.'

He crossed to the captain and glanced at the compass.

'Clear of the sandbanks?'

'*Si, signore*, we are almost abreast of the headland I think.'

'Stay on course, due east until we're well clear, and then I'll give you a fresh one. Got that?'

The man shrugged. 'We will not get far, I think that——'

Curtis bent closer, his eyes cold. 'I don't give a damn what you think. Just do as I tell you!'

'*Si, Tenente.*' His tone was subdued.

'Do you ever get challenged when you pass the headland?'

'Not unless a patrol boat comes. Then we sometimes speak.' He squared his thick shoulders with something like pride. 'But they know that I, Fausto Macchia, am always reliable. I know this coast like my own mouth!'

'Where are your charts?'

'There are two in my cabin. I do not need such things on my trips.'

'Our journey will be somewhat different, I think,' said Curtis with cold irony. 'I'm going to have a look at them now, so call me if you are worried about anything.'

The captain laughed bitterly. 'Worried? On such a fine night?' He cursed silently as Curtis disappeared down the hatch.

The mayor was sitting on the edge of the bunk, his eyes half closed. Curtis hardly spared him a glance, but hunted about the cabin until he found the charts beneath a pile of old magazines. He swept the bottles from the table with the back of his hand, his impatience mounting when he saw the grease and various stains which almost covered the markings on the charts.

He tossed one to one side and studied the other, his legs braced and his elbows planted on the edge of the table. He swore beneath his breath and pulled the lantern closer.

'Out of date, not corrected, and not been properly used for years, I should think! Here, Ian, get cracking.' He found an ordinary ruler in the desk and an old pencil. 'Try and lay off a course from here.' He tapped the chart with his finger. 'That's where I think we'll be in about an hour. I want you to lay off a course to take us approximately east-south-east from that position. By daylight we should be well clear of the coast, and then I'll decide what to do.'

He looked at his watch and stared fascinated as the hands opened to one o'clock. Fantastic, he thought, only an hour, yet we're at sea and away. He caught the mayor's eyes flickering in the lamplight, and turned his back. A ship full of disabled men, and smouldering Italians. What were *they* thinking about? How long would it take them to realize and assess the position of their new masters?

'Can you cope, Ian?' he asked abruptly.

'I'll try, Skipper. It's a bit of a mess.' He rubbed his nose ruefully. 'But I'll have a go!' He gestured towards the mayor. 'He'll be watching me!' The boy grinned, and Curtis' mouth tightened into a hard line.

He held up his watch so that both could see. 'In four or five hours it'll be daylight. He'd have been watching you then, no doubt, if we hadn't got away!'

He slammed the door behind him, and stood breathing heavily in the passageway. He was wrong to use the boy like that. What the hell was the matter with him? He half turned to re-enter the cabin, but a shaft of light fell across his arm as the other door opened quietly. She stood looking at him in silence, the edge of the door pressed against her breast. His eyes wavered, but he forced himself to remember how she had ensnared the sentry at the house.

'Well, *signorina*?' he asked levelly. 'Can I help you?'

'I was just wondering what was happening.' Her voice was soft, and seemed to act as a caress on his burning brain. 'Is it getting rougher?'

'A little.'

'You look like death, Lieutenant. It is a great strain for you.'

He still stared at her, his eyes heavy with fatigue. She looked lovely . . . and yet. He shook his head as if to clear it. Yet . . . there was something hidden behind her wide eyes.

'You capture the ship; you kill a man with your bare hands; and still you go on. You are a remarkable man!' Her full lower lip glistened momentarily, as she smiled gently. 'What makes you keep driving on?'

Suddenly he wanted to forget the ship, and everyone in it, and just be able to bury his aching head on her breast. Just to stand together, and feel the protection of her soft warmth.

He opened and shut his mouth, unable to find any more words.

'My father admires you, you know.' She tossed her head and sent the long black plait dancing across her shoulder. 'I think you are fighting *two* wars, yes?'

Duncan skidded down the ladder, followed by two soldiers. Curtis eyed him dully, and braced himself for another onslaught of questions. Duncan merely nodded calmly and glanced quickly from him to the girl. Then he jerked his thumb at the other men, who stood staring at the girl in dull surprise.

'I've come to fix that safe, Ralph. I thought you'd like these two blokes to watch this end of the ship.'

One soldier had both hands encased in huge dressings, but the other seemed complete but for grotesque strips of adhesive plaster across his cheeks and neck. They both grinned self-consciously and continued to look at the girl.

'All right,' said Curtis tonelessly. 'Think you can manage it?'

Duncan laughed and with over-elaborate courtesy he took the girl's forearm and slid past her into the cabin.

'This ain't a safe, it's a sardine tin.' Duncan rubbed his hands. 'Soon have the back off that.' He looked up. 'Some of those lads need fresh bandages quick, Ralph. I don't like the look of a couple of them.' He lowered his eyes. 'They'll not last till mornin'.'

'I see.' Curtis opened the cabin door behind him and looked at the soldiers. 'Make yourselves comfortable in there. The food'll be down soon.'

'I will go and help with the wounded soldiers.' The girl stepped into the passage, so that the rolling of the vessel brought her shoulder against his chest. 'I will be happy to serve them.' Her eyes were dark and masked her thoughts from him.

'Very well.' He pressed his palms against his legs. 'Thank you.'

'Good girl, Carla! They'll sure get a kick out of that!' Duncan dropped to one knee, his hand on the safe, and Curtis felt a stab of resentment at the casual use of her name.

She smiled across at Duncan and then started up the ladder, her legs practically touching him.

He stared after her, until he realized that he was still looking at the empty swaying hatchway.

'We'll split into two watches, Steve,' he said vaguely. 'You and George first, and then I'll come on with Ian at dawn.'

'Lie down, Ralph,' commanded Duncan softly, 'before you bloody well fall down!' The safe dropped off its fastening, and Duncan examined the back intently. 'Huh, just tin. I'll soon fix that!' In the same tone he added, 'I can deal with things here, you're worn to a splinter!'

Curtis shook his head stubbornly. 'Lot to do. Must hang on a bit longer.'

'We'll need you more when it's daylight,' answered Duncan soberly, 'a whole lot more. Christ, man, we can manage now for a bit. What in hell's name are you tryin' to prove?'

Jervis looked round the door, his eyes watching Curtis unsurely. 'I've worked out the course, Skipper. What now?'

'Leave it with me, Ian,' Duncan said coolly. 'You an' the skipper are watch below for a bit.'

The boy looked at Curtis for confirmation, and he shrugged heavily. 'All right, Ian, hand over the watch. Get some sleep.'

Duncan's mouth twisted into a smile. 'That's it, Ian, get your head down while you've got the chance.'

Curtis looked at them as if he was going to add something more, but instead he pushed open the door of the captain's cabin, and blinked wearily at the small cluttered space, and at the two soldiers who squatted on the deck in one corner, one leafing through a tattered magazine, and the other leaning against the bulkhead, his eyes closed in sleep.

The soldier with the magazine grinned cheerfully. 'Everything OK, sir, Jim here's havin' forty winks.'

Curtis steadied himself against the table. 'Let him sleep. Call me if you need anything.'

Signor Zecchi was curled up in the one decent chair, his hands thrust deep into the pockets of his grey suit, and his tie loosened across his chest. His heavy lids fluttered uneasily, and he watched Curtis stare at the empty bunk.

Curtis could feel the man's eyes upon him, but he was conscious of the desire to sleep more than anything else. I mustn't give in, he protested inwardly, but the bunk swept to meet him, as he sprawled with sudden and complete surrender on the crumpled blankets.

The soldier dropped his magazine and moved slowly around the cabin, the heavy boots sliding with each roll of the ship. Deftly he lifted Curtis' sprawled legs over the side of the bunk, and unfastened his belt.

Without a glance at the mayor, he slithered down again onto the deck and reached for his book.

The mayor cleared his throat. 'I do not think private soldiers in the Italian Army watch over their officers so carefully.'

The man glanced at him sharply, but seeing the sadness in the mayor's eyes he grinned openly. 'Well, somebody's got to look after 'em, mate, and I reckon this one's worth it!'

Curtis groaned and dug his fingers into the pillow. The voices in the cabin were part of another world, and he did not even attempt to fathom out their meaning.

As the darkness closed over him, he could recall the girl's face and her voice saying: 'You are fighting *two* wars.' He rolled over onto his face and lay still.

Above the stuffy warmth of the cabin the wind sighed and moaned along the deserted deck, and as the ship lay momentarily to one side, a white sheet of spray hissed over the gunwale and broke angrily against the loose rigging.

Duncan prowled restlessly back and forth across the poop, his chin deep in his jacket collar, and his stomach burning contentedly with the whisky he had taken from the house.

The captain still lolled across the wheel, his thick legs braced and fluid as each wave lifted the poop behind him. Duncan smiled grimly and glanced quickly at the compass as he passed.

They were on their new course which, all being well, would carry them clear of the coast before dawn. Then, he halted as if to relish the thought, they could turn for the south. Two hundred and fifty miles at eight knots, that would be just over a day's steaming, and they should be within reach of some friendly forces.

It would be unlikely that the schooner would be missed for two days, he pondered, and by that time, well, anything might have happened. Then there was the girl, Carla. He glanced at the darkened hatch across the hold. She was still down there with the troops. Lucky devils, but there was plenty of time for him, too, he decided.

In his side pocket he carried the contents of the German officer's safe. A small book of recognition signals and local patrol areas. Ralph would find that very useful, but it'll keep until first light. He met the captain's face across the compass, and the man's mouth opened as if to speak. Duncan glared at him fiercely, and continued his pacing.

At the weather rail he paused and grinned into the teeth of the wind. They were all frightened of him, he knew that, and enjoyed the feeling of power it gave him.

He thought of Curtis, and marvelled at his stamina and will to keep going. He's changed all right; more than I'd have thought possible. He looked down at the dark water, fighting his own tiredness with sheer brute force. 'We've all changed,' he spoke aloud, 'and I'm not sure if it's for the better!' He laughed harshly, and two Italian seamen who darted past carrying the empty food tins from the hold, stopped rigid in their tracks, like rabbits caught in the glare of headlights, and waited until Duncan had crossed to the other side of the deck before they scuttled towards the fo'c'sle.

The steady beat of the engine pulsed life into the ship, and with each turn of the pitted and scarred screw, drove her onward into the night, leaving the darkened shoreline to sink into the storm.

Taylor climbed heavily around the shuddering engine, his filthy hands moving with strange gentleness across the rusted controls, as if to coax and wheedle the best effort from the ill-used cylinders, which had carried the ship heaven knew where in the past, and upon which they all depended at this moment.

He sank back at last, his boots lolling and nodding within inches of the giant flywheel's gleaming teeth. He was happy in his own peculiar way, and watched the wheel spinning with the inner satisfaction of a born engineer.

The hatch was shut, the air thick with fumes and the stench of cheap diesel oil, but to him the tiny engine-room was a refuge, and something he could understand. If anything went wrong with the bellowing engine, he could deal with it. He glanced sleepily at the tools which he had arrayed on the deck in readiness, knowing just how much the others depended on him. His head rested against the pulsating bulkhead, and he closed his eyes, leaving his ears to follow and check the gyrations of his charge. It shut out the sound of the storm, and hid the misery of the wounded in the hold. He did not even have to worry about the behaviour of the skipper, or what made each of them act so differently, now that they had been given a new role to play. His head lolled, and a gentle snore drifted into the racing engine.

Twenty feet behind Taylor, beyond the bulkhead and lying uncomfortably in the narrow passage, Jervis still stared fixedly at the swinging lamp, his troubled eyes following the darting shadows as if mesmerized. Overhead came the measured tread of Duncan's boots, and he wanted to join him and pour out his heart to him there and then.

What was different? He tried to think of all that happened, but already the German colonel and the sneering sentry had lost their firm outlines of reality. He touched the bandage around his head, hoping that he might be able to see more clearly the eager, pitiful expression of his strange, mad saviour. It was no good. Each time he was reminded instead of the present, and the uncertainty which the dawn would bring.

He flinched as a trickle of water filtered through the hatch and splashed across his face.

Curtis had made him feel as he did, he knew that, but he was still reluctant to consider the cause of his behaviour.

When he had burst into the house and dropped the sentry's lifeless body carelessly on the floor, that should have been the greatest moment of Jervis' life. But as he closed his eyes, he could only think of the overriding disappointment which had shown in the skipper's eyes. It was almost as if Curtis had expected to find someone else in the cell, someone for whom he had been searching for a long time.

He pillowed his head on his arm and sighed. Perhaps I'm going off my head, he thought unhappily. A large wave punched the side of the hull with sullen force, and Jervis swore aloud, and was more surprised at his own words than the anger of the sea. Must be getting like Steve, he thought, and with a ghost of a smile on his lips, he fell asleep.

The *Ametisa* seemed eager to do battle with her common enemy, and as her raked stem dipped into each trough, the long bowsprit slashed downwards like a sword, until, with the water cascading over the bow, she lifted skywards again, victorious and trembling. One of the furled sails billowed with sudden fury, as the searching wind found its way into its folds and puffed it out from the yard in a flapping, ungainly pocket.

The captain looked up from the deck, his eyes squinting into the darkness as he searched the night sky for the new sound. He half reached for his bell, and then shrugged and continued to wrestle with the wheel, as if one more disaster was not even worth his consideration.

The schooner plunged on, alone in the tormented water. Of her passengers and crew, some slept the sleep of the exhausted and the beaten, while others still clung to the last shreds of watchfulness and human cunning.

Some wondered about the dawn, and a few prayed for the strength to meet it.

In a corner of the streaming deck, covered by canvas and firmly lashed in place, four soldiers lay together. They were neither thinking nor hoping, and for them the dawn would never come.

CHAPTER 8

Duncan clattered noisily down the ladder, slamming the hatch behind him, and almost stepped on Jervis' sprawled form in the middle of the passage. He stood astride the curled body and yawned hugely, his raised fists brushing the low deckhead. With a grunt he stooped and shook Jervis' shoulder.

'C'mon then! Don't make a bloody meal of it!'

Jervis groaned and sat up blinking, his red-rimmed eyes staring round at first with shocked unfamiliarity and then with renewed weariness.

'Oh, it's you, Steve,' he answered dully. 'I wondered where the blazes I was.'

Duncan's eyes crinkled. 'Who the hell were you expectin'?' He gestured towards the girl's cabin. 'Or is that where you've been all night?'

'Steady on, Steve,' began Jervis hotly, his face flushing, 'you're wrong about her! She's a damned fine girl!' He struggled for words. 'Why, if it

wasn't for her, I'd be dead right now, and you'd have sailed without me!'
Duncan smiled grimly. 'Well, that's got that off your chest, hasn't it?
Now perhaps you'll call the skipper and tell him it's nearly dawn,
leastways it would be, but for the blasted clouds!' He turned heavily on
the ladder and reached for the hatch. '*I* think she's dinkum, too, Ian, if
that's of any interest to you.'

Jervis struggled to his feet and swayed against the door frame. 'I
know, Steve. It's just that I can't understand what's got into the skipper.
He keeps flaring up all the time. I just don't know how to cope with him
when he's like that.'

'Well, Ian, just put yourself in his place. How d'you reckon you would
have measured up to all this, eh?' He sighed and rested his elbow on the
ladder. 'It's just that we're not used to this kind of war. Up till now it's
been a pretty remote business for us.'

'How can you say that?' Jervis interrupted. 'Why you and he, and
Taylor have been right in the thick of it from the beginning!'

Duncan raised his hand patiently. 'Not in this way. As I said, it's been
sort of remote. This is the real war. Bein' able to see the enemy for once as
flesh and blood, not just a hunk of ruddy steel in your periscope sights!'
He opened and closed his hands, while Jervis watched them as if
fascinated by their power. 'Bein' able to see how they work, and act! And
knowin' what it's like to hunt and be hunted!' He slammed back the
hatch, and sniffed at the air. 'By the way, Taylor's name is George. You
might remember that, Ian!' His body clambered over the coaming, and
Jervis was left staring at the closed hatch.

'Damn!' he said fiercely.

The ship lurched and he smoothed the rumpled uniform with distaste.
The German eagle on his right breast seemed to mock him, and even the
uniform made him feel more than ever a man on the outside, looking in.

He wondered how it could all end, and whether the schooner was in
fact the real answer to their destinies, or merely a means to their ultimate
destruction.

He cleared his dry throat, and pushed his way into the stuffy cabin.
The lamp had burned lower, and he had to strain his eyes to make out
the distorted shape of Signor Zecchi sprawled open-mouthed in the
chair, his feet entangled with those of a sleeping soldier whose bandaged
hands stuck out in front of him, their hidden suffering marked on the
soldier's thin face. The other soldier stared up at him, his eyes glassy, and
forced a grin.

Jervis crossed to the bunk and laid his hand on Curtis' arm, which
hung over the side of the bunk like a dead thing. He jumped as Curtis
immediately sat up, his eyes bright and searching. He looked up at
Jervis, his face pale, almost grey in the lamplight, and for a few seconds
seemed to have difficulty in collecting his wits.

'Lieutenant Duncan's respects, sir, and it's just on the dawn.' He paused, stupidly aware of the formal naval speech and how out of place it sounded under these circumstances.

Curtis rubbed his knuckles savagely into his eyes and coughed. 'Well, Ian, no one can say that your training hasn't been thorough!' He sat upright, his hair tousled across his forehead, but with a smile on his lips. 'We'd better go on deck and see what's what, hadn't we?'

Jervis smiled gratefully and followed Curtis from the cabin. He watched Curtis' shoulders stoop as if from the shock, as the keen air met them on deck, and waited with all the alertness he could muster, prepared to justify himself in front of Curtis and all the others if necessary.

Duncan's shadow broke from the rail. 'Mornin', Ralph! You're lookin' a bit better.'

Curtis smiled with his teeth. 'Feel like death! I don't see much light yet.'

A tiny flicker of silver lanced at the black line where the horizon should have been, and occasionally the clouds seemed to lose their power as a growing glimmer crept over the sea's edge.

'Angry!' commented Duncan, and then pointed up at the masts. 'But you can see the topmasts now!'

Curtis lifted his head and stared up at the quivering spars and the billowing ball of loose canvas. 'What about that?' His voice was hard as he turned to the captain, who still leaned heavily across the wheel.

'S'not important, *signore*. We never use him.' The voice was tired, almost disinterested.

'It might be later on! Get your men to work on it as soon as it's light!' He looked down at the package which Duncan had thrust into his hand. 'What's this, Steve?'

'Baccy! Got it from forward. Thought it might interest you, seein' what a glutton you are for the old pipe!'

They watched as Curtis pulled out his pipe and slowly filled the bowl with rank Italian tobacco. It was a moment of peace, and nobody wanted to spoil it. It suddenly seemed terribly important that Curtis should have his smoke.

He ducked his head beneath the gunwale, and they heard the rasp of a match. He stood up, the reflection from the glowing bowl casting a small flush across his taut features. He blew out a cloud of smoke, and they watched it hover momentarily around his head, before being plucked away by the wind.

Curtis breathed deeply, his body balanced and relaxed on the wet deck.

'A forgotten ship,' he said slowly. 'No one knows where we are, or where we're making for!' He puffed out more smoke. 'Only *we* know anything! I only hope to God we're doing the right thing!' he ended fervently.

Duncan yawned. 'It's a right queer set-up all right. But I'll tell you now, Ralph, if we pull this off, it'll be really something. It may prove something different to each one of us,' he paused, his shadowed eyes on Curtis' face, 'but it'll be worthwhile!'

'I hope so!' Curtis looked across the tumbling water. 'Bed, Steve. I'll take her now.'

Duncan opened the engine-room hatch and peered into the foul interior.

'Good old George,' he chuckled. 'I'll leave him be!' He swayed across to the after hatch and yawned again. 'Just a couple of hours an' I'll be up again, lookin' for some grub.'

His head was level with the deck when Curtis called him.

'Yeah? What d'you want?' Duncan's voice was slurred.

'Thanks, Steve. Just thanks.'

They heard him laugh. 'Oh sure!' The hatch slammed.

Jervis trembled and checked his muscles angrily. 'I always thought it was warm in this part of the world, Skipper.' His voice was tinged with caution.

Curtis leaned back against the rail, his pipe jutting like an extension to his chin. 'A strange sea this,' he answered quietly, 'as unpredictable as a woman.'

'D'you think we shall see anything, I mean a ship or something like that?'

He shrugged. 'Hard to tell. Never has been a lot of enemy activity up here. It was a bit too remote for our ships to operate, except for submarines that is, and they don't like it either.' He shook his head slowly. 'No, we just can't be sure of anything yet. We must be on our toes the whole time.'

'I'll get some lookouts sorted out as soon as it's lighter,' began Jervis. 'The soldiers might be able to do that quite well.'

'Yes, the soldiers.' Curtis stared at the silent hump on the deck. 'We must bury those chaps, too. As soon as possible.'

He suddenly gripped Jervis' arm, and pointed across the sea. 'Look, Ian! D'you see that?'

He followed the pointing finger, half afraid of what he might discover. A pattern of gold light spilled across the horizon and splashed the distant waves to give them life and an angry splendour. The clouds above moved faster, as if to escape the full majesty of the dawn, which refused to give way to the storm and to the passing power of the night.

'It never fails to move me.' Curtis was quite sincere. 'It makes all this seem so fragile and unimportant.' He laughed, as if embarrassed. 'It's quite something, as Steve would say.'

Two seamen appeared on deck, scratching and yawning, and from the spindly funnel over the fo'c'sle a puff of smoke proclaimed that breakfast, of sorts, was on the way.

Curtis examined the long telescope which he had procured from the captain and tested it on the horizon.

'Not exactly a Zeiss, but it'll have to do,' he commented.

Jervis walked slowly across the sloping poop and stared back along the dim, uneven wake, following it until it was lost in the fading shadows and torn apart by the short, steep waves. Already the outlines of the individual white crests were becoming more clearly defined, while around him the ship seemed to grow larger, and more vulnerable.

He turned his back to the sea, and watched Curtis pacing briskly up and down across the poop. The wind ruffled his fair hair, and gave him back his boyish look, but the eyes which darted up to the masts, or scanned the lightening horizon, were neither young nor restful. Jervis sighed, and wished he understood what was going on behind those cold eyes, and whether any of Curtis' thoughts were directed at him.

There was a slight disturbance at the hold hatchway, and Sergeant Dunwoody stood swaying in the grey light. Seeing Curtis he stamped aft and halted by the wheel. His hand swung up in a smart salute.

'Mornin', sir! What orders, sir?' His eye studied the tired naval officer with interest, but his expression was calm and respectful.

'We must bury those four chaps of yours.' Curtis pointed with his pipe stem. 'It won't do the rest of them any good to see them lying there.'

Sergeant Dunwoody fidgeted with his sling. 'Another gone in the night I'm afraid, sir. 'E was done for before 'e got on the boat.' His tone, although matter-of-fact, did not disguise his sadness.

Curtis looked at the compass, his eyes distant. 'I see. Very well, we'll get on with it now. Before there's anything else to worry us.'

The sergeant hurried back to the hold, beckoning as he did so to two seamen.

Curtis stared at Jervis. 'Give him a hand, Ian.'

Jervis stood by the lee rail as the seamen unlashed the bodies and laid them in readiness. The extra one was hurriedly wrapped in a length of worn canvas, and an old seaman, his face a mass of tiny wrinkles, like a piece of hardened leather, began to sew the ends together with twine.

A bar of gold light mounted the ship's rail and spilled onto the deck, lighting the seaman's bent head and his thick mass of grey hair. There was little warmth in the gentle ray, yet already the decks had lost their coat of spume and spray, and even the sounds of the sea seemed lulled.

The sun glinted on the man's needle, as with a jerk he broke the thread and raised his eyes, their watery brilliance telling nothing to Jervis, who stared fascinated at the soldier's boots which still protruded from the end of the canvas.

He shook himself and looked quickly at the hold, aware that some of the soldiers had come on deck and were standing in a silent group by the hatchway, their bandages white against their sunburned faces, and their tattered khaki clothing clashing with the dark green and silver of the sea.

Sergeant Dunwoody glared round and nodded to Curtis. 'Ready, sir!'

Curtis stared in silence at the five bundles which had once been men.

'Have you a British flag aboard?' He faced the captain, suddenly angry.

'No, *signore*. We have just the usual signal flags.' He pointed at the locker by the mainmast. 'I am deeply sorry, but we have no use, you understand.'

Curtis walked quickly to the locker and wrenched open the lid. He could feel all eyes on him as he pulled the untidy bundle of flags onto the deck in a tangled mass of colour.

He had intended to drop the soldiers over the side during the night, but now that he had seen the sergeant's face and those of the other wounded, he was glad he had waited. Whatever lay waiting for them in the path of the sun, and however wasted his efforts might be, he suddenly felt that this thing was terribly important. His fingers closed over the International Code flag V. It was a white flag with a bright red diagonal cross. That would have to do, he thought, and beckoned to Jervis.

'Spread this over them,' he said, 'it's all I can find.'

Over his shoulder he said curtly, 'Stop the engine!' He heard the long lever grate over, and seconds later, the engine coughed and died away.

The engine-room hatch banged open and Taylor's heat-reddened face appeared over the coaming.

''Ere, what the 'ell d'you think you're doin'?' He glared at the captain, who pointed quickly to Curtis and laid a fat finger across his lips. Taylor blinked wearily. 'Sorry, Skipper!' He then leaned across the coaming, his chin on his forearms, his eyes distant.

Curtis looked round the watching faces, and wondered what he was going to say. He had never seen a sea burial before, let alone conducted one.

A squeaking block distracted him, but when he turned angrily towards the sound, he saw the captain hauling the Italian tricolour to the position of half-mast. He had removed his greasy cap and his bald head gleamed in the sunlight like a brown egg.

His eyes fell on the girl and her father, who had also appeared on the poop. Signor Zecchi looked old and crumpled, but the girl at his side stood proudly against the stiff breeze, her thin dress pressed against her slender body, her gaze fixed upon Curtis. He noticed vaguely that her hair was loose, and some of the severity seemed to have left her, as with each breath of wind she put up her hand to brush the hair from her face.

Curtis tore his eyes away. The ship lolled heavily in each trough, and started off a fresh set of noises. Ropes creaked and blocks clattered as the rigging bit at the spiralling masts, while at the waterline the water gurgled impatiently, as if hungry for what was to come.

'We came together by accident,' began Curtis, his gaze fixed on the wavering bowsprit, 'and I don't know these men as well as you do. But I know that I am speaking for all of you when I give them God's blessing.' He stopped. The words sounded foreign and stilted, and he looked quickly at the men. Their faces were set and grim, yet some of the tension seemed to have gone. 'We will now commit their bodies to the deep.' He finished, his mind empty. 'Carry on, Mr Jervis!'

The planks were hoisted by the seamen, and Curtis set his teeth, as one of the bodies began to slide towards the edge.

Suddenly the sergeant's voice crashed on his ears. ' "A" Company, 'shun!'

The soldiers lurched to attention, and Curtis was thankful, knowing that the sergeant and all the others had felt as he. They did not need his words. They were saying goodbye in their own way and tomorrow, if it came, they would speak with friendly ease of these five men.

The seamen placed the planks carefully on the deck, and one of them rolled up the flag. It was over.

'Thank you, Sergeant. You can carry on to breakfast now.'

'Sir.' He wheeled to leave and paused. 'A nice neat job, sir, if I may say so.'

Curtis nodded to Taylor. 'Full throttle, George!' His head vanished, and Curtis breathed with quiet relief as the engine rumbled into life.

The captain had put another seaman on the wheel, and wiped his hands across his trousers. 'I will see that my men carry out your orders. You can trust me, *signore*. I have never liked working for the Germans.' He spat accurately over the rail. 'They have no humour, you understand!'

Curtis smiled, and the captain spread his hands with obvious delight. 'See, *signore*, you at least agree with me on that!' He ambled forward, humming to himself.

Signor Zecchi turned up the collar of his thin jacket, and glanced from Curtis to the empty sea.

'Where are we this morning?'

The girl interrupted with a soft laugh. 'Does it matter, Papa? We are his prisoners!' She smiled sadly at Curtis, her teeth gleaming through the dark veil of her blown hair.

Curtis shrugged. 'What difference indeed,' he answered. 'You will be safe aboard this ship, but who knows what is happening on the mainland by now. Perhaps the Germans have started to shoot some of your countrymen by now!'

'Never! We hate war, but we are loyal to our allies!' But there was less conviction in his sunken eyes.

The girl shivered, and her father took her arm. 'Come below, Carla. There will be breakfast soon. You will become ill in this wind.'

Her eyes played across Curtis' face. 'I will wait a little longer, Papa. You go below now. I will watch the sun drive away the night.'

He sighed and left them together at the rail.

'I liked the way you spoke to your men, Lieutenant. It was a bad thing you had to do.'

'I've had to do worse. Thank God there weren't more of them.' He looked sideways at her firm chin and slender throat. 'If they had been left down there without attention, many more would have died.' He watched a small pulse beating beneath her throat. 'As it is, I can't be sure yet.' He left his fears unsaid.

'You have done what you thought you had to,' she said gravely. 'If you had followed my plan, you could have been safe in a good hiding place.'

'Then we could have waited with your father for the British Army; then he *and* his social position would be restored, is that it?'

She kept her face averted, but he saw her shoulders toss with impatience. 'Would you not do that for your own father?'

Curtis laughed aloud, and she stared at him in a mixture of rage and despair. 'You are mocking me, Lieutenant!'

He laid his hand on her shoulder and shook his head. 'I am sorry, *signorina*. I apologize for laughing, but I am afraid you do not know my father!'

He fell silent, and she lowered her eyes to his hand, which still rested across her shoulder. 'I think I will go below now.'

He dropped his hand, conscious of the warmth in his palm. 'Perhaps you will be good enough to help with the wounded again?'

'Is that what you really wanted to ask, Lieutenant?' She smiled at the discomfort on his face, and walked to the hatch. 'I will help.' With a wave to Jervis who hovered eagerly nearby, she ran lightly down the ladder.

'What a girl, Skipper! I've never seen anyone like her!' Jervis scratched his head, as if the right words would come from there. 'Why, she's lovely!'

Curtis examined his pipe and began to fill it. 'What would *your* father have to say about her, I wonder?'

Jervis drew himself up and inserted one hand melodramatically into his jacket. 'Looking at girls, Ian? Disgustin'! What's her phone number?' Jervis stopped the imitation and grinned with embarrassment. 'Well, something like that anyway.'

Curtis stared at him in amazement. It was as if the boy had suddenly taken on a new personality, or a fresh lease of life. 'Well done, Ian!' he said, knowing that if he had treated him better he would have behaved like this before. 'I'm sure your old man would say nothing of the sort!'

He loosened his jacket and ran his fingers through his hair. The air was humid, in spite of the wind, and the clouds seemed to be holding the heat steady over the sea, while the sun dipped and wavered across its surface, plunging it into dark shadow for one minute, and opening up the rollers into barriers of green glass the next.

He felt his rough chin as he watched a seaman place a tray of coffee and hot sausage on the deck by the wheel.

'After that, I'm going to have a shave, Ian, *and* a bath if I can manage it.'

'Shall I call Steve to relieve you, Skipper?'

He smiled briefly at the boy's pink face. 'You're the navigator. You can manage by yourself, eh?'

Jervis grinned. 'I think so, in fact, yes, Skipper!'

The morning wore on, the schooner's course taking her further and further from the mainland, until it seemed to all aboard that they had been sailing purposefully towards the horizon for days instead of hours.

Curtis had stripped to his trousers, and was busy shaving with the captain's razor in the cabin. His skin, washed and briskly towelled with a sheet from the bunk, glowed pleasantly, and he smiled at his reflection in the small mirror as he remembered the captain's own towel. It was hardly the thing to touch, let alone use.

Duncan sprawled in the bunk, snoring with relaxed ease, and from across the passage he heard the girl talking to her father.

He paused with his shaving and rested his hand on his own shoulder. He met his own gaze in the mirror, as he remembered how she had looked at him.

An urgent tapping overhead on the glass skylight made him glance up, ashamed of being discovered with his thoughts. Jervis was stooping over the sill, squinting through the dirty glass.

'Skipper! Another ship! Fine on the starboard bow!'

Curtis dropped the razor and kicked at Duncan's outflung arm. All the peace and security which had lulled him during the dawn fell away in a second, and he felt that he and the ship had been laid bare and open by his weakness.

Duncan rolled off the bunk and landed lightly on his feet, reaching automatically for his pistol belt, and glancing up at Jervis' face as he did so.

'What's up? A riot or somethin'?'

'A ship, Steve!' Curtis threw his jacket across his bare shoulders and wrenched open the door. 'Keep down as we go on deck, and make sure all our people stay hidden!'

'D'you aim to fight it out?'

Curtis paused at the top of the ladder and looked downwards, his face a mask. 'Fight? With what?'

Duncan grunted and pulled the belt tight around his waist. 'Well, I don't aim to end up in any stinkin' grave, not without a scrap, anyroad!' He glared belligerently.

Curtis laid the telescope on the hatch coaming as Duncan squeezed past him, and dropped uncomfortably onto his knees. 'Remember the wounded, Steve!' He hissed the words after Duncan's bent shoulders. 'D'you want to get them shot up, too?'

Duncan did not answer but ran crabwise towards the hold.

Curtis sighed and steadied the telescope against the pitch of the ship. The wavetops loomed distortedly in the lens, and with difficulty he trained it round until he saw the sudden movement of the other vessel.

Silver-grey in the feeble sunlight, it moved purposefully across his line of sight, a white bow-wave slashing from either side of the high sharp stem as it cut into each roller and sheared the green water into a seething chaos of spray.

He watched the ship's silhouette with practised eye, his heart heavy. A *Dardo* class destroyer, he thought, and one shell from her battery of four-point-sevens would put a quick end to all his hopes with no effort at all.

She was still about two miles away, yet even as he watched, she grew larger in the lens, until he could clearly discern the white caps on the high bridge, and the long, slender gun barrels on the fo'c'sle.

The captain padded up the ladder and paused uncertainly by the wheel, his eyes following the other ship.

Curtis snapped the telescope shut and looked up at him. 'Have you seen her before?'

The captain shrugged vaguely. 'Maybe, *signore*. Who can say? We often meet the patrol ships, but I do not come as far south as this in normal times!'

Duncan crawled along the deck, keeping his powerful body hidden beneath the bulwark. He slithered to a halt opposite the the wheel, and supported his chin in his hand.

'All snug an' quiet, Ralph. How's the visitor gettin' on?'

'She's moving in,' he answered slowly. 'She's bound to ask us who the hell we are.'

As he spoke, a light flickered from the destroyer's bridge, and some of the bow-wave dropped away, as the ship slowed down.

'She's flashing.' Curtis spoke in almost a whisper, his throat dry. 'Make your reply, Captain.'

Duncan tossed the small code book across the deck to land within Curtis' reach.

'It gives the recognition signals in there, Ralph, and all the right dates for this month.'

He pulled the long diver's knife from his belt and jabbed it into the deck. It quivered in the planking like an obscene crucifix, and Duncan smiled lazily at the watching captain.

'Make sure you give the right signal, sport! We don't want any accidents, do we?'

The captain tore his eyes from the knife and spoke quickly to the seaman at the wheel, who ran to the flag locker. He took over the wheel and jerked at the spokes uneasily, until two flags soared to the schooner's gaff and broke stiffly into the breeze.

Jervis stood in full view by the rail, his hands clasped behind his back, as if he was Officer of the Watch in a peacetime battleship. He stared fascinated at the graceful destroyer, feeling that each pair of binoculars was trained upon him, as it might well be, and tried to keep the appearance of bored irritation which he had already seen used by German officers.

A harsh metallic voice boomed across the water, the Italian words hardened and distorted by the loud-hailer, and the captain reached wretchedly for his battered megaphone.

'What's he saying?' Curtis barked, maddened by the stillness which had engulfed the schooner. 'What do they want to know?'

'They wish to know where we are bound. But I think they are otherwise satisfied!'

'Tell them we are making for Bari. To evacuate wounded personnel.'

He drummed his fingers on the deck as the captain yelled across the narrowing gap. It seemed fantastic that the patrol ship should be satisfied, and yet why not? He tried to put himself in the destroyer captain's place. No doubt they encountered countless schooners and other coastal craft in these waters, and there was enough to worry about already, what with the invasion and increased sea traffic, without bothering with a vessel so obviously under the control of the German Navy. He watched, holding his breath with relief as the other ship's screw whipped the sea into a fury, and drove her steadily on a diverging course.

Jervis stood stiffly at attention and saluted the tiny figures on her armoured bridge.

Duncan laughed. 'Well done, Ian! Proper little Nazi you are!'

Jervis looked down at Curtis and smiled shakily. 'Gosh, Skipper, that was a near thing!'

'We'll alter course as soon as the destroyer's hull is down,' answered Curtis thoughtfully. 'She may report our position by radio, although I doubt it. But we can't afford to take chances. Get below, Ian, and start on your chart. I want to keep more to the eastward if possible, though

668 DIVE IN THE SUN

it'll be a longer way round. We can't afford to cross swords with that sort of thing!'

Jervis watched the destroyer's shape shorten as she turned away, a soft plume of smoke drifting from her squat funnel. 'I wish we were in something like her, Skipper. Why, we might even——' He broke off, his eyes wide with alarm. 'Look out! Hold her, for God's sake!'

The girl burst through the hatch, her leg brushing away Curtis' hand, as he reached vainly to stop her. Before anyone could move to intercept her, she had reached the taffrail, and stood silhouetted against the sky, her long hair streaming behind her.

Even as Curtis hurled himself across the deck, she lifted her arms high and waved with wild desperation after the destroyer.

Curtis pinioned her arms to her sides and pulled her down to the deck, so that their faces were inches apart. He stared at her wild, blazing eyes and her lips parted yet soundless, as she met his gaze with all the fury and venom of a trapped animal.

'You little fool! What the devil are you trying to do?' He tightened his hold as she wriggled madly under his body. 'I should have realized that you'd try something like this!'

Duncan sprawled against one of the open wash ports, his eyes narrowed while he followed the other ship. He relaxed slightly and turned his head. 'She's still goin'. They didn't notice a damned thing!'

She suddenly went limp, and Curtis released his hold, his face a mixture of anger and weariness. 'Go below,' he ordered, 'I'll talk to you in a minute.'

She stepped slowly onto the ladder, her face turned towards the ship. It was already well clear, and its outline had begun to shimmer with indistinct beauty.

Curtis felt for his pipe, his thoughts racing angrily through his brain. It was his fault. He should have been more prepared for something like this. If only she'd speak. Anything would be better than the great emptiness which seemed to fill her dark eyes.

'I have my responsibility, *signorina*,' he said, his voice flat, 'just as you have yours.'

She looked at him with a long, calculating stare. 'You do not understand, Lieutenant. You are a hard man, yet,' she shrugged, as if dismissing him, 'you were not always so, I think. Why do you try to prove what is not there? Why must everyone suffer because you must satisfy your own soul?'

Curtis trembled. 'What the hell are talking about? We are at war, in case you have forgotten, and I don't intend to sacrifice the men under my charge to please you or any other damned——' He broke off, angry with himself, and frustrated by the small smile on her lips.

'Because of any damned Eyetie? Is that what you're trying to say?'

Her smile vanished and she dashed the loose hair from her face. 'You are like the Germans! You delight in this war! As if it was some sort of game!'

Curtis saw the expression of agony on Jervis' face as he reached the girl's side in two strides.

'Don't you ever say that to me again, *signorina*!' She moved back against the hatch, as if expecting a blow. 'I'm sorry I trusted you, that's all! And if the Germans are relying on your people as allies, I'm sorry for them also!' His eyes blazed with suppressed emotion. 'Now get to your cabin, and keep out of my way! See that she and her father understand what I mean!' He glared at Jervis. 'And then carry on with the navigation!'

He walked stiffly to the rail, trying to shut out the sounds of her feet on the ladder.

Duncan stood up and sat on the rail facing him. 'That was quite a potful, Ralph! Still, I reckon you can't blame her exactly. How would you feel under the circumstances?'

'For God's sake, stop it!' Curtis turned on him, his body trembling. 'I'm sick to bloody death of being told what I must do!'

Duncan took the weight of his body on his hands and leaned slightly forward. 'Take it easy, Ralph. I'm just sayin' that you can't blame the girl, that's all!'

'I'm not blaming her, or anyone else! I don't give a damn what she thinks, or how she feels, so long as she doesn't interfere with what we have to do!' Curtis' eyes swept furiously across the horizon. 'And if you want to start giving me lectures, you can think again!'

Duncan stood up, his face impassive. 'In that case, I'll leave you alone for a bit, an' go below. I'll be havin' a spot of shut-eye if you want me.'

He waited a while, watching Curtis' stiff shoulders black against the sun. He was about to add something more, but with a grimace, he lowered himself down the ladder.

What in hell's name is the matter with us? he pondered. It irritated him to feel this vague threat of discord between them, but it annoyed him still more that he was unable to root it out and destroy it.

All at once he wanted to be alone with his thoughts. Everywhere he looked in the ship he found either soldiers or seamen, and now as he entered his cabin, he found the mayor once more in the chair, sitting gloomily with his feet resting on a locker, his eyes staring into space. The two soldiers were asleep, and in the light which filtered through the skylight, their faces appeared grey with fatigue and shock.

Jervis looked up from the chart and smiled wanly. 'Hello, Steve. I've just laid off that course the skipper wanted.' He scratched his head with the ruler, his nose wrinkling with distaste. 'God alone knows if it's anywhere accurate. Even with the vaguest sort of dead reckoning it's pretty hopeless without any proper navigation instruments. I don't know how they've managed, I'm sure.'

Duncan fell heavily on the bunk and sighed. 'Don't give it a thought, kid. We're zigzagging all over the flamin' ocean, so I don't suppose it makes a blind bit of difference whether it's accurate or not!' He sighed again, and pulled a bottle from his inside pocket.

'Is that whisky?' Jervis stared with surprise.

'Sure is. Our little friend here left it lyin' on the table when we left his house.' He held it up to the light and frowned. 'Not enough to keep a dog alive! Want a lick?'

Jervis shook his head. 'Couldn't we give some to the wounded?'

'I've already given 'em the other bottle, and some brandy I found in the crew's quarters. 'Sides, I don't reckon they ought to have too much till they've been seen again by a doctor.' He took a long sip from the bottle and let his head fall back on the pillow. His creased face seemed consumed by inner thought and worry, which was so unlike his normal demeanour that Jervis squatted on the edge of the bunk and peered at him closely.

'What's the matter, Steve? Is there anything I can do?'

'I'm all right.' He glared over Jervis' shoulder at the silent figure in the chair, and lowered his voice. 'No, I'm damn well not all right! For once I'm out of my depth, and I don't feel . . . well . . . how shall I put it? . . . at home.'

'Everything's going well so far,' began Jervis cautiously, but was silenced by the gleam in the Australian's eyes.

'How can you talk like that, man? Anything might happen. Right now; this afternoon; or at midnight. Surely you realize that?'

'Yes, but that's a chance we have to take.'

Duncan gripped his wrist fiercely. 'Don't tell *me*! I know all that! I suppose it's this situation, and this flamin' ship. Before, it was better. Just the four of us.' He smiled with the nearest approach to sadness that Jervis had ever seen. 'Four against the world! That's how it was. Now look at us!' He snorted. 'All bits an' pieces hangin' together for mutual support. It's ragged, an' I don't like it. I like to be able to deal with anything I'm called on to meet. I'm useless at this sort of game.' He drank some more whisky and closed his eyes.

'What about the skipper?' Jervis asked cautiously. 'What does he plan to do if we're spotted again?'

Duncan smiled sourly. 'Ralph? He's so twisted up inside that he doesn't know whether to spit, or have a haircut! What with him an' that girl, well, I give up!'

'She saved my life, Steve.'

'Sure. I know that.' Duncan sounded completely weary. 'But what's she up to? Blow hot, blow cold! One minute she's a little heroine helpin'' us jokers, and the next she's yellin' for the Duce to come an' rescue her! Huh, women!'

'I don't know a lot about women, I'm afraid.' Jervis waited, half expecting Duncan to laugh at him, but he merely grunted, and lifted the bottle once more. 'But she's really lovely. I've never seen anybody like her.'

'Well, if that's how you feel, go an' have a yarn with her. It'll do you good.' He grinned crookedly. 'And it'll give me a chance to get some sleep!'

Jervis picked up the chart and moved quietly from the cabin. He paused outside the other door, then knocked.

She opened the door immediately and stared at him in surprise. 'Well? Have you come to taunt me?'

Jervis coloured and fumbled with the chart. She stood easily in the centre of the small cabin, her hands on her hips and her lips parted in an expression of smouldering resentment.

'I wanted to know if there's anything you need.' He swallowed and stumbled on. 'Please don't be upset about what has happened. I know how you feel. It's all such a beastly business.'

Her mouth softened and her slender body seemed to relax. 'Come and talk to me, Ian. You do not mind my using your first name?'

He lowered his face to hide his pleasure. 'No. No, of course not. Tell me what is worrying you.'

She shrugged and sat on the side of the bunk. Jervis' eyes strayed to her slim neck and the dark shadow at the top of her dress. She had not noticed, and seemed intent on watching a small beetle which explored the bulkhead opposite her.

'Well, Ian, I cannot tell you what happened to me. You will not believe me, because you are a man, but when I saw that ship, that Italian ship, I was so overcome that I acted without thought.'

'It was a dangerous thing to do, *signorina*.'

'For you, yes. I understand that well enough. And believe me, Ian, I would not wish anything to happen to you. But,' her mouth quivered momentarily, 'what about my father and I? What will happen when you reach your friends?'

'You will be well looked after. I can promise you that! We shall say how you saved my life, and everything else you have done.'

She smiled sadly. 'You are a good person to know, Ian, but I am afraid that you have forgotten that we are enemies. My father is a Fascist and loyal to the régime. When our country is overrun, as it will be, for the Germans will not try to hold such difficult territory, there will be a new government, with different ideas. When my father is released, it will be like returning to a foreign country. No one will want to remember him, or what he has helped to do!'

'Could it have been any different?'

She walked to the bulkhead and watched the beetle scurry into a crack.

'If we had gone to the hiding place I told you about, it might well have been different. My father has friends and certain property, which would help considerably.' Her eyes lifted to his face, bright and warm. 'You do see that, don't you? Please tell me that you at least can understand!'

'I think I do.' Jervis felt suddenly humble. It was true what she had said. There would be little warmth left for a pro-Fascist when the old régime had fallen.

Her eyes were moist but she smiled across at him. 'Thank you. I could not bear to think that I brought all this on my father without any reason at all. It has been driving me mad! But I know that the Germans would have killed him, just as they would you. When someone is useless to them, they destroy him, like cutting off an infected limb!'

She began to plait her hair, her hands moving with new life.

'Come, you must take me to the wounded. I will change their dressings.'

Jervis looked at the chart, aware that Curtis was on deck waiting for him.

'I'll tell him what you're going to do.' He grinned sheepishly. 'He ordered you below, remember.'

She patted the plait into place and tossed it over her shoulder. Jervis thought that at the moment she looked like a child, although he guessed that she must be at least four or five years his senior.

'Yes, you tell him. I will look after those men, no matter what he says! You go and tell him that, and I will tell my father that you have said all will be well!'

She ran past him, and instinctively Jervis caught her wrist. She halted, quivering like a doe in flight.

'Thank you for your confidence,' he said awkwardly.

Her look of surprise faded, and she regarded him gravely. 'You are good, Ian.' Rising on her toes, she kissed him briefly on the cheek, then with a smile, she had left him.

For some moments he stood staring at the door, his hand on his cheek. 'Carla,' he said softly, but only the beetle heard him.

He looked up anxiously as he heard Curtis call harshly from the deck, 'Ian! What the hell's taking you so long?'

Jervis blinked as he arrived on the poop, aware of the sudden change in the weather. Most of the cloud banks had broken, and the heat rose from the baked deck to greet him, like steam from a boiler. He turned his face from the sea, blinded by the millions of shimmering lights which stabbed from every dancing wave and from the white-hot stare of the sun.

Curtis studied the chart and compared the markings with those in the German's notebook.

Jervis stood back, watching his engrossed face with fresh curiosity. Remembering what Duncan had said, he felt a pang of uneasiness as he studied the young-old face with the cold eyes. Eyes which were now scanning the chart with fanatical eagerness, as if amongst the scrawled lines and symbols were the answers to his secret fears.

'It's the best I can do, Skipper.' Jervis spoke warily. 'The gear is pretty crude for this sort of thing.'

Curtis grunted and watched a wheeling gull, which like a lone watcher, swooped and dived across the wake.

'The girl is going to attend to the soldiers,' added Jervis after a long pause. 'Is that all right?'

Curtis nodded vaguely. 'Girl? Oh yes, of course.'

He squinted up at the masts and studied the uneven shape squatting on the yard. A leg swung easily with the motion of the ship, as the old Italian seaman scanned the horizon.

Jervis followed his gaze and gasped. 'Can he be trusted? I mean, do we have to rely on his lookout?'

Curtis eyed him slowly. 'Who else d'you suggest? One of the wounded perhaps? Or yourself?' His tone was deceptively mild, but Jervis had now learned to recognize the danger signal.

'Sorry, Skipper. I expect he'll be fine for the job.'

'That's a comfort to know.'

Curtis watched the girl's shadow cross the deck as she hurried past, carrying a roll of freshly torn cloth. She kept her eyes averted, but there was the hint of a smile on her soft mouth.

Curtis waited until she had vanished into the hold, his expression watchful.

'Alter course. Steer due east.'

He followed the captain's plump hands as they spun the worn spokes over to port. A ruby ring flashed incongruously on one finger, and Curtis stared at it, as if fascinated.

'How long will it be before we make towards the land again!' Jervis saw the shutter drop again in Curtis' eyes, as he brought his mind to bear on the question.

'Soon, I hope. I can't delay too long.' For a moment Jervis thought he would open up a little more, but he merely added, 'The wounded need attention badly.'

Sergeant Dunwoody clattered noisily towards them. His red face was beaded with sweat, and he had discarded his jacket. Jervis noticed that his khaki shirt was spotted with blood.

Curtis stiffened. 'What's wrong, Sergeant?'

'That other chap, sir. Lake. He's dead I'm afraid. 'E 'adn't a chance anyway. But it's something else as well, sir. The dressin's are pretty bad, an' I'm a bit worried about it. The lads need seein' to quick, sir.' He watched Curtis, squinting his good eye and plucking nervously at his sling.

'I see. I'll do my best, Sergeant.' Curtis bit his lip and nodded. 'I'll do my best.'

'I'm sure you will, sir.' Dunwoody forced a smile and stared round the empty sea. 'Cor, like Ramsgate, ain't it?'

'Go with the sergeant, Ian. See what you can do to help. I'll have the hatch taken right off so that they get a bit more fresh air.'

Jervis faltered. 'It's not your fault, Skipper. You've done more than anyone could expect.' He stopped, aware that Curtis was not listening. The pale eyes were on the move again, searching the horizon, watching and calculating.

'Are you comin', sir?' The sergeant fidgeted at his elbow.

Jervis still hesitated, feeling that he should try to explain his thoughts to Curtis. 'Perhaps we shall find it easier to miss the patrols than we thought.'

Curtis seemed to jerk himself together with a great effort. He glanced briefly from Jervis to the sergeant, and gestured towards the hold. 'Get to it, Ian. There's a lot to do yet.'

Jervis sighed and followed Dunwoody's broad back into the deep recess of the hold.

The sunlight swayed back and forth through the wide hatchway like the beam of a drunken lantern, as the ship rolled uneasily from side to side. The sea, driven by the short gusts of wind, was furrowed into long, lazy rollers, and the schooner's course took her broadside along them, making the very masts groan in their sockets.

Jervis steeled himself for the job he had to do, as he met the sour stench which was trapped by the high sides of the hold, and carefully avoided the still body at the foot of the ladder, with its face covered by a piece of blanket.

The first wave of joy and enthusiasm which had greeted Curtis and Duncan when they had boarded the schooner had spent itself on the shock and misery which had now made itself felt in the hidden menace of the soiled bandages and discoloured skin.

A soldier rolled painfully on his side and tried to vomit into a basin. Each time he turned, his injured legs thudded helplessly on the deck, and he fell back, retching and exhausted. There was a flurry of movement, and the girl hurried to his side, her feet stepping and dodging the sprawled limbs and torn bandages. Even in his wretchedness, the soldier feebly tried to push her away, unwilling for her to see him in his pitiable state. She brushed his hands aside and knelt down on the deck, the man's head firmly pillowed on her knees.

Her voice was low and husky, as she smoothed away the hair from his damp face. 'Come on, Tommy. Gently now.'

Jervis turned away and went after the sergeant, who was stooping alongside another man and talking in low tones with the corporal, Bert.

He looked up as Jervis joined them, and shook his head worriedly. 'Look at this lot, sir. I don't quite know what to make of it.'

They had removed the bandage from the man's thigh, and Jervis swallowed hard, the spittle thick in his throat. What had once been a mere flesh wound in the man's leg, had blossomed angrily into a savage mass of discoloured and weeping tissue.

'Er, what is it? Can we clean it up a bit?'

The corporal sucked his teeth and sat back on his haunches. 'Gone rotten, that's what! He'll lose that leg, I'm thinking!'

' 'Is leg? ' 'Is bleedin' life, you mean!' hissed Dunwoody fiercely. ' 'E needs penicillin an' transfusions,' he added vaguely.

The man in question opened his eyes and stared glassily at Jervis' uniform. His thin body began to shake with silent laughter, and the corporal gingerly covered up the wound.

'Can't you stop this bloody ship rolling about, sir?' The man's voice was a mere whisper. 'It's making me feel numb all over. Can't feel my legs at all.'

Jervis forced a smile. 'Won't be long now. We'll have you home soon.'

The sergeant followed him as he moved along to the next man, and tugged gently at his sleeve.

'It's miles an' miles yet, ain't it, sir? What chance do we really 'ave? We can't go on kiddin' these chaps if they ain't got a chance!'

Jervis looked woodenly at the man at his feet. Naked, and flat on his stomach, he was quite still, but for his fingers which were curled into a blanket in a desperate grip. Two of his companions were engaged in removing a soiled dressing from the small of his back by gentle strokes of a rag soaked in warm water. The bowl they were using was already slopping over with bloodstained water and pieces of skin. The man groaned, his neck muscles bunching with effort, and one of his hands began to pound at the deck.

'Steady, mate. Keep yer 'air on!' The sweating soldier with the rag glanced up at Jervis and shook his head. Aloud he said, 'Old Jim 'ere is a real card! Swinging' the lead proper 'e is!' But there were tears in his eyes as he spoke, and he seemed to Jervis to be trying to tell him something more. That no matter how bad they all felt, they would back Curtis to the end.

He beckoned the sergeant away from the others. 'How long, Sergeant? Just how much time d'you think we have?'

Dunwoody stared round helplessly, and then seemed to come to a decision. 'We can hold on, sir. None of 'em wants to give in, but they're livin' on borrowed time, as from now, I reckon!'

Jervis ran his fingers through his hair and felt the sweat running over his scalp. If the ship turned for the coast now, and right now, there was a chance that these men might be saved. A military hospital could never refuse to help men in this state, be it Italian *or* German. Then they would be able to lie in safety until the Allied armies reached them. And us? He shuddered. There would be no mercy for himself and the others, he decided.

A shrill cry from the far end of the hold made his teeth grate, and helped to decide him on his next action.

'I think we should consider the state of the worst case, Sergeant, and act in his interest first.'

The sergeant didn't answer. He was unused to sharing confidences with an officer.

He walked to a patch of sunlight, where the girl was busy rolling another bandage. She looked up at him, her lips pale.

'You're doing wonders, Carla. I don't know how you're sticking it out.'

'They are so helpless. It is all so ... so terrible for them.'

'I am going to tell the skipper just that.' Jervis watched her small hands manipulating the crude bandages. 'We must make for the shore now.'

Her eyes widened. 'But that is dangerous for you? You will surely be captured again?'

'We shall see.' He reached up for the ladder. 'Perhaps you will get your way in the end, *signorina*.'

She passed a hand across her brow, and picked up a basin. 'I must go to them, Ian. Be careful what you do. I am sure that your captain already has a plan. He may not be willing to give in to you.'

Jervis felt vaguely piqued by her remark. It was as if she did not consider him capable of making such a decision. He stuck out his chin and started up the ladder.

'I know what I'm doing, Carla!'

He found Curtis still by the wheel, as if he had never moved. His face turned towards him as he approached, and one eyebrow lifted questioningly.

'Well, how are they?'

Two seamen staggered from the fo'c'sle carrying a huge can of fresh water towards the hold, and Jervis waited until they had gone before answering.

He met Curtis' stare. 'I think they're in a damned bad way, sir. Some of the wounds are going septic.'

Curtis glanced towards the bowsprit and tapped his pipe into his palm. 'If we had not taken the ship, they would still be en route for Venice. By tonight they might have reached their destination, and from that time this ship will be missed and an alarm will go out. We will have to be very careful and make full use of the darkness. Tomorrow we might well be within close contact with our own forces, or the following night at least.'

Jervis quivered with exasperation. 'But, Skipper, half of them'll be dead by then!'

'If we hadn't arrived aboard, I expect most of them'd be dead by now.' There was no harshness in his voice. It was merely a plain statement of fact.

'How can you talk like that? Don't you care what happens? They're helpless, but so pathetically eager to prove their loyalty to *you*! Can't you do something for *them*?'

Curtis twisted the pipe between his fingers, his mouth tight. 'That's enough, Ian! I asked you to help the wounded, not start behaving like a child!' He stared angrily around the deck, his eyes blazing. 'Don't you think I know about all this? That's why I'm trying to get them back to their own people. I owe them that.'

'Or do you mean that *we* won't be captured?' Jervis let caution fly to the winds. 'Who are the more important? Us or them?'

Curtis let his arms fall limply to his sides, and Jervis thought he had given in. But his voice was calm and unhurried, as if he was speaking to a fractious schoolboy.

'I've given you your orders. Now kindly carry them out.'

Jervis stammered with anger. 'You won't turn for the coast then? You'll carry on with this scheme of yours?'

'I'll alter course when I'm ready. Not before. Now carry on, Mr Jervis!'

'Aye, aye, *sir*!' Jervis was trembling with suppressed rage and emotion. 'I hope you're satisfied!'

As he blundered towards the hold, Curtis' cold voice halted him in his stride.

'And another thing, I'll trouble you to discuss these ideas with me before you start holding council with everybody else!'

Jervis almost fell down the ladder, and stood weakly on the bottom rung, breathing heavily.

'You spoke to him, Ian?' She crossed quickly to his side. 'What did he say?'

'He refuses to budge.' Jervis' eyes filled with tears of humiliation and bitterness. 'He's as hard as iron! I wouldn't have believed it!'

Carla Zecchi watched him thoughtfully. 'He may be right, Ian. He has had much experience perhaps?'

'Experience? Of what?' He winced as another cry floated along the hold. 'He seems immune to personal suffering! He's like a man possessed!'

The wounded man cried out once more and Carla plucked nervously at her thin dress. Its hem was stained where she had knelt in the soldier's blood, and there was a bruise on her arm to mark the place Curtis had gripped her as he pulled her to the deck.

'Come on, Ian, we must stop him shouting, before the others get more upset.'

He followed her, dragging his feet, casting quick, sickened glances at the suffering and pain which bordered the sides of the hold.

The cry from the tormented man even penetrated the thick bulkhead of the engine-room, and clashed with the persistent rumble of the diesel.

Taylor jerked out of his doze and lolled his tongue across his dry lips. The thick haze which hung over the engine hovered like a group of conversing spirits, which changed their hues and shapes as the shafts of sunlight filtered through the deck grill and danced across the revolving shaft.

Taylor groaned and eased his cramped body onto his knees. Listlessly, he checked the gauges and the oil, and wondered what to do next. Overhead he knew that the sun was soaring to its noon zenith, and there would be little shade on the dried decks. Below it was stuffy and foul, but at least in the engine-room no one disturbed him. He had discarded his jacket and jersy, and sat bare to the waist, his spare body running with sweat, and his hair plastered against his forehead.

The skipper had peered down the hatch at him earlier, and had asked about the engine revolutions, but apart from brief, routine questions, he had seemed unwilling to talk.

That suited Taylor, who felt that by just concentrating on their jobs, they could somehow make the time pass more quickly, and with each turn of the shaft they would be thrust more speedily towards safety.

It was odd how the change of environment had altered them all. Without the hard shell of the midget submarine, with all its familiar pitfalls and discomfort, they seemed to move without purpose or confidence.

He felt disturbed and surprised at Duncan, who could always be relied upon for a jest or a bit of company. I expect he's more out of his depth than I am, he pondered.

There was little deck-space in the engine-room, merely a sort of planked catwalk which ran around the sides and provided a place for one engineer to watch over the diesel. Apart from that, the place was moulded into the hull, so that he could see the ribs of the ship running right down to the keel beneath and where the shaft vanished into its sleeve to join the thudding propeller.

He stared at the swilling and vibrating scum of bilge water, and watched it rippling around the ribs, to lap near the racing teeth of the giant flywheel. Once it reached that wheel, he knew he would be drenched, as it was picked up like a stream by a water mill. Never look after their bloody ships, he thought irritably, as he groped for the handle of the bilge-pump. I pumped the whole lot dry just after dawn, and here it is again. He cranked steadily and noisily, his breath wheezing in his throat.

Didn't join up to bugger about in this sort of floating ruin, he thought, as the ship rolled lazily, and forced him to put his hand on the hot exhaust pipe.

He pumped in an even, unhurried swing, his mind drifting wearily away from his task and the ship.

He thought of Madge, the girl who lived in the next street in Hackney. She was working on the buses now, and right good she looked in her uniform. He always went up to the garage by Hackney station when he was on leave, just in the hope he might be able to date her, before some other bloke got the chance. A grin split his grimed face. She was quite a girl! Kept changing the colour of her hair, but she was still smarter than all the little Yiddisher bits who hung around the town hall dances.

He yelped as a jet of slimy water cascaded out of the bilges and soaked his skin in a sheen of oil and filth. As he shrank to one side, the flywheel bit into the water and sent another small tidal wave sluicing up the side of the engine-room to cover him, and fall hissing on the engine casing.

He stopped pumping, his head cocked on one side. He shielded his eyes from the spray and peered down into the bilges. Instantly, his heart began to pound. There was no mistake, the lower rivets in the stout ribs were now covered completely, and he had been pumping all the time!

He forced himself to act calmly, and began to check the pump. It was working well and quite in order. The bilge-water was rising around the racing wheel in a steady stream now, and even as he watched, he saw the level rise over the engine bearers. Frantically, and fully awake, he began to pump with feverish haste.

Clank ... clank ... clank ... he watched mesmerized, as the pump handle jerked back and forth, conscious only of the water which surged and hissed against him and the engine.

'Christ! We're sinkin'!' he gasped aloud. 'Can't keep this up fer long! Engine'll seize up in a second!' The sentences jerked from his twisted mouth, but, nevertheless, he stayed where he was, and glanced quickly at the level of the water.

Nearly a third of the flywheel was under water now, and the noise in the confined space seemed like a giant waterfall. He realized that he was in the lowest part of the ship, and the leak must be somewhere forward. He'd have to attract someone's attention, so that a search could be made. It was queer that no one had noticed anything, it must be quite a large leak.

He gasped painfully and turned to change hands on the pump handle. As he did so, a savage burst of water struck him full in the mouth, and he slipped, spluttering on the catwalk.

'Gawd blast yer!' he choked, 'I'm gettin' out! S'like tryin' to bale a battleship wiv a chamber-pot!'

He stopped and rubbed his hand across his wet mouth with sudden disbelief. There was no taste of salt at all, and apart from the usual tinge of oil, it was quite fresh and cool. He reached blankly for the handle, his sodden brain wrestling with the problem. It wasn't possible, and yet, he cursed aloud and bent over his task.

The sun, like a triumphant warrior, had succeeded in driving away the last of the clouds and was able to concentrate its full strength on the lonely ship beneath. The deck-caulking, already in need of repair, gleamed wetly, and stuck to Curtis' boots as he moved restlesly about the shimmering deck.

The captain sat inert under the bulwark, his cap tilted across his eyes, and Curtis could not tell whether or not he was still awake; while the helmsman, a small wiry Sicilian, crouched across the spokes of the wheel, his scrawny neck protected by a length of faded bunting.

Curtis had to check himself from looking repeatedly at his watch and compass, and tried instead to concentrate on the bowsprit. He watched it rise sluggishly to point at the blue sky as the stem mounted a wave, and then as the schooner thrust her way forward, dip downward until it seemed to rest on the horizon like a pointer. He wished he had his cap, or something to help drive away the relentless throbbing in his head and neck.

A thin plume of smoke still rose from the galley funnel, as the huge pots of water were boiled for the business of cleaning wounds and dressings alike.

He had buried the last man to die before the heat had reached its maximum power, but apart from the sergeant and Giulio Zecchi, there had been few spectators this time.

He thought of Jervis and clenched his fists angrily. Young idiot. What the hell did he mean by getting so entangled with everything? He forced himself to relax. It was Jervis' first operational trip anyway, so perhaps this had to be expected. Still, his sort of reasoning was infectious. His predecessor, Roberts, would have acted differently, he thought, but immediately dismissed the idea. What was the use ... he was dead.

He squinted his eyes to look for the seagull, but it had vanished, and in some way he felt saddened.

We're all dead really. Given up as lost by everyone but ourselves. His thoughts returned persistently to Jervis. Young fool. Couldn't see further than himself.

He watched the bowsprit and wondered about the night. It seemed so far off, that it took real effort to continue with his plan for altering course. If the schooner was reported missing before nightfall, it would be the end anyway. But – and his pulse quickened at the thought – if they could keep clear of patrols until they were hidden by the darkness, there was a chance, and a good one at that, he could get them all to safety.

He frowned as he listened to the clank of the bilge-pump. Poor Taylor was obviously suffering, too. He could imagine what this ordeal was doing to the E.R.A's strength of mind.

The mayor had left the deck, and Curtis was glad. The man's strange, haunted eyes troubled him, and already he seemed to have aged considerably.

A shout from forward made him look up startled. One of the seamen was shouting excitedly and waving an empty bucket.

The captain stood up with ponderous dignity, his eyes dark and grave.

'What's he yelling about?' Curtis asked. 'Tell him not to disturb the people below!'

The captain moved slowly across the poop, his hands feeling his pockets as if uncertain what to do next.

He faced Curtis with watchful calm. '*Signore*, he says that the fresh water is no more!' He waited for the impact to show on Curtis' taut features, and hurried on, 'That is impossible of course, for we take on a thousand gallons!' He shrugged helplessly. 'But if he says so, then it is true!'

Curtis' face was still blank, yet already the shock of the captain's words was working furiously on his mind. The seaman placed the bucket on the deck with a hollow clang, and stood quietly watching the two captains with patient interest.

Curtis heard the captain fire a series of questions at the man, but knew from the definite way he answered, and the professional movement of his hands, that there could be no doubt about his findings.

The captain dropped his voice and moved still closer. 'It is very bad. The water has been allowed to drain away. The valve has been opened.' He met Curtis' eyes, suddenly enraged, as if he, too, had been betrayed. 'It was no accident, *signore*!'

At that moment the engine-room hatch banged open and Taylor emerged, his skin running with sweat and oily water, his eyes blinking in the glare.

'Strewth! I thought we was done for! I've just pumped the 'ole bleedin' ship aht! Some clumsy twit must 'ave upset something!' He groaned wearily. 'An' I thought we was sinkin'!' he added reproachfully.

He looked from one to the other, his quick mind already aware that his news held more impact than he had imagined.

'Where is the water valve?' Curtis' voice was calm, even distant.

'In the hold, *signore*. We use it when we drain the tank for cleaning.'

'I see.'

Curtis turned to Taylor. 'George, call Steve and the sergeant. I want all the people from the hold on deck. All those who have been fit enough to move about, and have had access to that part of the ship.'

'What's up then, Skipper?' Taylor scrambled towards the after hatch.

'We have a new enemy among us, George. It's too late to do anything useful about it, but I just want to meet the one concerned.'

The captain saw Curtis' face and shuddered.

CHAPTER 9

Jervis took a last look around the hold, noting the quiet which seemed to hang over the ship, and which surrounded the listless wounded men who lay in their various attitudes around him. Only two or three of the more capable soldiers remained to tend to their requirements as best they could, and Jervis felt his eyes straying to the large water-can which swung lazily from a deck beam. It was queer about the water giving out, he could not even begin to understand what had happened, and was almost too tired to contemplate it. Taylor had slithered down the ladder, his dark face angry, even sullen. He had muttered something about the water, and that the skipper wanted all the personnel from the hold on deck at once. Jervis had deliberately delayed his own departure after Carla, the sergeant and the others had left, partly because he wanted to make sure that the wounded were quiet and as comfortable as possible, and did not suspect that the sodden dressings on their wounds were the last they could expect, but mostly because he wanted to show Curtis that he, at least, was not impressed by this peremptory summons.

He sighed and climbed up to the deck. The sun hit him across the neck and seemed to sap the last energy from his body. He noticed that the group of assorted figures gathered around the poop were silent and watchful, and no one looked up as he walked aft and leaned heavily against the mainmast.

Curtis was standing apart from the group, his hair almost white in the glare, as he looked over the rail at the dancing wake.

Duncan and Taylor stood together by the hatch, the E.R.A's wiry body dwarfed by the other man's shoulders, as he leaned his elbows on the edge of the open door, his face dulled either by sleep or drink.

Curtis looked up, his eyes covering the group of weary figures and resting momentarily on Jervis. He cleared his throat, the sound drawing their attention to his face.

'You know that the fresh water has gone,' he began calmly, 'but you may not be aware of the cause, or,' he paused, his mouth hardening, 'the possible consequences.'

The girl moved closer to her father, who stared with passive eyes at the deck, the movement making Curtis turn briefly in her direction.

'Someone has deliberately opened the cock on the storage tank, while he, or she, was in the hold!' He waited while a babble of voices broke out on the poop.

Sergeant Dunwoody gestured fiercely with his hand, as if unable to find words. 'But sir,' he stammered, 'oo'd do a thing like that? I mean ter say, sir, we're bitched wivout water!' He glared with sudden suspicion at those nearest him and lapsed into silence.

Jervis watched the girl from beneath his lashes, conscious both of the meaning of Curtis' announcement and the sudden look of fear in Carla Zecchi's eyes. She had gone pale, and he could see her fingers twisting nervously into the back of her skirt. 'Or she', Curtis had said, and Jervis was moved both by anger and pity. He remembered her coming into his prison and risking her life to entice the German sentry to his own death. It must have been her, it was all dropping into place now. He understood what she had meant by her hints about saving her father and getting Curtis to change his plan. No wonder she was unworried by Curtis' scheme to sail the schooner all the way to the south coast, while he himself had fumed and cursed at Curtis' hardness. She had known about this all the time; in fact, she probably got the idea from his own concern for the wounded. He forced himself to think and shut his ears to the protesting voices and distorted faces. What did it matter anyway? He had wanted the ship to turn for the coast, and now Curtis would have to alter course. The reason was unimportant. She had save his life, and nothing else mattered any more.

Curtis held up his hand and the sounds died.

'Whoever is responsible for this stupid and dangerous act – and it is someone here right this minute – has committed himself and all the rest of us to one course of action only.' Jervis could see that Curtis was labouring to keep his voice under control. 'I shall have to turn immediately and try to find a way to the nearest port, where the wounded will be landed and handed over to the authority responsible for that area. Without treatment and proper care, clean dressings and all the rest of it, things were bad enough. Without water, and all that water means to injured men, there is no alternative but to give in.'

Duncan shook himself like a dog, and stared round with disbelief and amazement.

'Now listen, Ralph!' He moved his hands threateningly. 'You're not goin' to jag in without findin' out who did this are you?'

'Well, what d'you suggest?' Curtis sounded tired, almost distant.

'I've got ideas, by Christ I have!' He pointed suddenly at the girl. 'What about her? What's she been doin'?'

His eyes were slitted with fury, and Jervis forced himself to look at Carla, his suspicions immediately turned into reality as he saw her wide eyes dark with fear. She opened her mouth as if to speak, and Jervis stepped quietly in front of her.

They would shoot her or something, he thought desperately, the look on Duncan's face was enough to tell him that nothing Curtis would do or say could prevent it, even if he had wanted to.

He felt strangely calm, and his voice was almost conversational. 'As a matter of fact, *I* did it!'

The effect of his words was terrifying by its cool impact. Curtis stared down at him, his mouth quivering with shock. The others seemed to fade into indistinct shapes, and Jervis could only see Curtis' face and the utter disbelief which clouded his eyes, before the shutter dropped and his face became a cold, impersonal mask.

'Why?' One word, softly spoken, but as the ship lolled gently in a trough, it was like an axe falling on stone.

'Because . . . because it is useless to go on like this.' Jervis' elation had gone, he waited to be free from the others and be left in peace. 'You wouldn't alter your mind. So I tried to do what is best for all of us!'

Carla Zecchi sobbed quietly, and Jervis shrugged with sudden impatience. What the hell anyway, they had been dead before. This was just the beginning of reality for them.

He reeled against the wheel, his head dancing with pain as a fist thudded into his cheek.

Duncan caught him by the arm and swung him round, his face twisted with fury.

'Why you dirty little gutless bastard! We pulled you out of the grave, and now you go and louse on us!' He raised his fist again. 'I'll make sure you don't do anything else! At least you're in the right bloody uniform!'

Jervis twisted free, feeling the salt taste of blood on his lips, and ran blindly across the hatch.

He saw Taylor's body jerk from the rail, and tried to dodge his foot as it shot forward to trip him. He fell heavily on the deck and saw the rough planking with sudden clarity, as he lay panting and waiting for the next blow.

Instead, Curtis' harsh voice cut across his confused mind. 'That's enough, Steve!' Then as nothing happened, more quietly, 'Fetch the chart, and bring it on deck.'

Jervis stood up, shaking his head to clear the dizziness from his eyes.

Curtis regarded him slowly, with something like pity or shame on his set features.

'I'm putting you under arrest. I don't understand what happened to make you act like this, but you were wrong, and stupid!' Then in a louder voice, 'Sergeant Dunwoody, take this officer below, and see that a guard is mounted. An armed guard!'

Dunwoody rubbed his mouth, his eye blinking. 'Yessir. It'll be a pleasure!'

Jervis stumbled towards the gaping hatch, but darted a glance back at the girl. She was staring at him fixedly, but there was more surprise than relief on her face.

Taylor rubbed his bare arms and followed Jervis with his eyes. 'I dunno why you bothered to live!' he said softly.

Below it was quiet and cool, and Jervis was in the girl's cabin, with the door locked behind him, before he really understood what had happened, or what he had done.

He pressed his head against the smooth planking, and closed his eyes. What would his father think when the story became known? Of how he had sacrificed his comrades because of a girl's hidden promise. 'It doesn't matter!' He spoke aloud, as if repeating a lesson. 'This is ridiculous to act like this. I will explain what really happened when it's all over!' He flung himself down on the bunk, wretched and stunned, as the full realization crushed in on him like a crowd of screaming maniacs.

. . .

Curtis sat on the rail and watched the bowsprit once more. It was curious how the ship had changed its outline now that the sun was on a different side. He tried not to look back at the twisting wake, as if he was afraid he might see his hopes and his chance of freedom mocking him from the waves, as the ship swung round towards the invisible shore.

Jervis of all people. It was unthinkable, almost obscene.

Duncan sat hunched under the bulwark, his head resting on his chest. An empty bottle rolled unheeded in the scupper, and occasionally Curtis heard him mutter thickly to himself.

Giulio Zecchi appeared at his side, his small hands deep in his jacket pockets. He waited, like a plump bird, until Curtis turned to face him.

'A big disappointment for you, Lieutenant. I am sorry.'

Curtis did not answer, but waited listlessly, his gaze on the man's dark eyes.

'But it is time we had a talk, I think.' He squared his shoulders, and rocked forward on his toes.

He knows that he's soon going to hold the whip hand, Curtis thought, it was amazing how everything had collapsed, and how calmly he was able to view his failure.

'Well? What have you on your mind?'

The mayor pouted his lower lip. 'When we reach the coast, what will you do?'

'Surrender the ship. What else?'

'I will do what I can for you, Lieutenant.' His tone was almost gracious. 'I may be able to help quite considerably where your wounded are concerned. But I am afraid I can do little about you and your three colleagues. You are rather in a different category.' He smiled thinly. 'But who knows? Perhaps you will be kept as prisoners.'

Curtis stared at him coldly. 'Things have certainly changed for you, Signor Zecchi. Now you will be able to return to your fold as a hero, and one who has proved his worth to the Party and to his German friends! Very fortunate for you!'

He smiled. 'Shall we say that the hasty action of your young officer, for whatever reason he might have had, was an act of grace? It is life, Lieutenant.' He shrugged. 'I am afraid you have only yourself to blame, but, nevertheless, I thank you for your treatment of myself and Carla.' He drew a small cigar from his breast pocket and inserted it delicately between his teeth. 'If only one could always foresee the future!' His glance fell on Duncan's still form. He raised an eyebrow. 'And what of the gallant Australian?'

'He'll be all right,' Curtis answered quietly. 'You need have no fear.'

The mayor smiled and lit his cigar. 'I think that fear is now unnecessary for me. It might be unfortunate for the wounded men if anything was to happen to me, eh?' He walked away, humming to himself.

Curtis clenched his fists and stared wildly at the sun, until he could stand the pain no longer and his eyes were running with tears. Every movement and shipboard noise seemed more pronounced, and even the steady beat of the engine filled him with revulsion. Somehow and somewhere, he had allowed his purpose to be blunted and turned aside by his own over-confidence. He beat a slow tattoo on the rail with his palms, his body shaking with uncontrollable despair. To drive away the fear which had first held him in its grip, he had tried to prove his strength and determination in front of the others, and to justify his actions he had endeavoured to produce an unworkable plan, for which he had neither the training nor the stamina to complete.

For a few moments longer he tortured himself with the weapons of self-pity and frustration, and then tried to bring himself to contemplate the future.

It had been a flimsy enough plan, he knew that, yet with any small remaining spark of luck they might have reached safety, and some of the guilt and remorse would have been lost in the fulfilment of the voyage to the south.

The lookout called shrilly from the masthead, and without enthusiasm or interest, in fact with little feeling of any kind, he lifted the telescope and pointed it in the direction indicated by the man's arm.

A small coaster pushed her way northward along the lip of the sea, her squat bridge and funnel changing shape as she altered course laboriously on another leg of her zigzag. Still further distant, a mere shaft of silver in the sunlight, her escort prowled watchfully, no doubt listening for the unlikely presence of a submarine.

The captain coughed discreetly, and Curtis turned with impatience. 'Well? What d'you want?'

Curtis expected him to behave much as the mayor had done, and was surprised to see the intense expression in the man's small eyes.

'*Signore*, I think I have a part of an idea.' He darted a quick glance around the poop and sat down beside Curtis on the rail. '*Permesso*, but as I said, I think we might find a way out of this.'

Curtis eyed him searchingly. 'Why, Captain? Why should you want to help me?'

'Ah well.' He smiled uncomfortably. 'It is also to help myself you understand! But we Italians are not a warlike people, you must know that. And I think that my country will not wait to be stamped into the dust before it feels it necessary to' – he spread his hands with eloquent understanding – 'sign an armistice!'

'Go on.' Curtis was suddenly quite sure of the man's eagerness, and felt that he was being as sincere as he knew how.

'I have sailed this coast for many years, *signore*, and I know many people. For months now there have been rumours about what would happen if your armies land in our country.' He shrugged. 'Well, the time is near I think for the dreams to become real, whether some of us like it or not!' He leaned closer. 'We do not like the Germans, that you already know. It was very fine in the beginning, when our leaders gave us great things and promised us more. But when the German Army came to the south, and from the desert, things changed for all of us. They did not trust us, and made many regulations and laws to hold us down. Of course, the *Fascisti* thought it was wonderful,' he spat with his usual ease, 'but the rest of us grew to hate the strutting boots and endless orders. It was like,' he paused, trying to find the right words, 'like the barking of dogs! No, *signore*, the Germans will find themselves alone and unwanted!'

Curtis felt his spirits sink even lower. 'I know all this. It was the only thing that could happen.'

The captain laid a fat finger against his nose and watched Curtis sadly. 'Patience! I am trying to tell you what I, Fausto Macchia, would do, if I were in your feet!'

Curtis' strained face melted into a smile in spite of his misery. From the moment he had boarded the schooner this little captain had remained self-contained and yet comical.

'Very well, Captain. Please continue, although I do not think there is any choice left for me!'

'There is always a choice! Did you notice how little interest that ship and the destroyer took of us? And did you not think it strange that there was no signal?' He smiled, as if sharing a deep secret. 'They do not care any more. Why should they?'

'But what has all this——' But the captain silenced him with a frown.

'Please, *signore*, I am arriving at the end soon. It is ver' difficult for me in a foreign language.'

'You speak it well.' Curtis clasped his hands in his lap and tried to mask his impatience.

'Yes, I do,' he beamed. 'But this is what I have in mind. To the south is the Gargano Peninsular, you know of it?'

'Yes. I had hoped to be past that point by tomorrow morning. After that,' he shrugged wearily, 'but what does it matter now?'

The captain's eyes gleamed like black beads. 'We will make for the peninsular, we will not pass it!' He rocked back on his fat buttocks, until the waves seemed to reach up for him.

He was evidently amused by the perplexed expression on Curtis' face, and he gripped his arm with sudden familiarity.

'We are sailors, you and I. We know nothing of the ways of the land, and the people who live there.' He embraced the sea with an excited hand. 'Here, we are safe. *This* we understand. We will go to the Gargano Peninsular! Ask me why, *signore*!' He was unable to conceal the excitement which shone on his round face and made his chins bounce loosely across his crumpled shirt.

'You tell me. Why?' Curtis wondered how much longer he could put up with the man's behaviour.

'Because the Germans are gone from t'.. re!' He studied Curtis' face with relish. 'Yes, *signore*, all gone! They have gone to the fighting further south. The peninsular is a good place to be!'

Curtis was fully alert now. 'It's still a long way away. What about the wounded men?'

'Please, *signore*, I have thought of all that. We will drive the ship faster, the engine can give a little more I think.' He dragged his finger across his pendulous lower lip and held it up like a small child. 'The wind, you feel it? It is from the north! We will spread the sails! You give me the idea when you tell me about furling them correctly!' He jumped to his feet and stared down at Curtis. 'We can get there *before* morning! I have friends there, *signore*. Maybe we can get a doctor, and we can certainly get more water! What is there to lose?'

Curtis stood up and began to pace the deck with quick, nervous

strides. What is there to *gain*, I wonder? he thought. Aloud he asked,
'Why do you wish to help me?'

The captain sighed and moved his tongue in his cheek. 'If I help you,
signore, I keep my ship, and no doubt the British will not bother me? On
the other hand, if I go back to the Germans, what will happen? They will
use the *Ametisa* and her poor captain until they have no further use for us,
and then . . . Boom! Finish! They will leave nothing behind in Italy when
they go, that I know!'

Curtis halted in his stride and faced him thoughtfully.

'You really believe you can contact your friends?'

'But of course! I was born in Spigno, I know many people!' He
dropped his voice. 'What can be lost by it? If I am wrong,' he kissed his
fingers, 'Boom! But if all goes well, it is a ver' good plan, yes?'

Curtis grinned, his mind made up. He clapped the captain across the
shoulder. 'A *very* good plan! I'll get the chart!'

The captain smiled broadly. 'As you wish. For myself, I have little use
for such things!'

Curtis reached down and shook Duncan roughly by the arm. 'Steve!
Get up! On your feet, you drunken Aussie!'

Duncan stared at him with bleary eyes, unable to understand the
boyish elation on Curtis' face.

'Whassup? We arrived yet?'

'I'm going to have one last try, Steve!' He pulled the grinning captain
beside him. 'We had a genius in our midst and didn't know it!'

Duncan staggered to his feet and belched grandly. 'You nuts or
somethin'? How can things happen like this? Always when I'm
asleep!'

The captain chuckled, no longer afraid of Duncan. 'Me. I never sleep!
Only my body sleeps!' He punched the big Australian playfully on the
stomach. 'Your captain a good fella!' He beamed at both of them and
then hurried to the wheel.

Duncan shook his head and grimaced sourly. 'What in hell's name has
got into him?'

'He's given me an idea, Steve. In fact, I'm going to try and break out
after all. Whatever the damned consequences!'

Duncan listened unbelievingly, as the little captain screamed out a
string of orders at his depleted crew. Taking the wheel, he spun the
spokes with deft eagerness and watched anxiously as his men scrambled
up the sagging rigging. The ship veered round, and as the first patched
sail was unleashed, the captain gasped with pleasure. As he turned
briefly towards the two officers, they saw that this eyes were wet.

'For years I have waited to sail my *Ametisa*! Now for the first time since
this accursed war begins, she will fly like a bird!'

Soon the thin jibsails crept skywards from the bowsprit, while aft the poop was darkened by the impressive beauty of the swinging spanker, which even the stains and patches could not spoil. The schooner leaned over on her side and stayed there, as the wind thrust steadily at her new power.

Duncan leaned against the tilting rail and whistled with amazement.

'Well, can you beat that! These damned Eyeties! He makes the flamin' ship move an' now he's cryin'! That really beats everythin'!'

Curtis propelled him to the hatch. 'Get George and tell him the sky's the limit! I want every last bit of power! And you lay off a new course that'll take us to the north-east of the Gargano Peninsular!'

Duncan bit his lip and watched the new light which gleamed from Curtis' eyes.

'Don't bank too much on this, Ralph! It might not come off you know.'

But Curtis lifted his head with complete confidence and calm.

'What is there to lose now?' he asked simply.

Duncan shouted Curtis' instructions to Taylor's incredulous face above the roar of the diesel, and was only sure that he had understood when the little man seized his hand and danced dangerously on the oily catwalk.

He heard a series of disjointed yelps. '. . . another chance! Show the bleedin' . . .' and nodded in agreement.

He ran quickly to the after hatch, ducking his head beneath the long, unfamiliar boom, and glanced up at the towering sail. His craggy face creased into a reluctant smile.

'Good on yer, you little Eyetie sea-cook! But I'll believe it all when I see it!'

He was about to step into the cabin when he stiffened, as Jervis called through the opposite door.

'Is that you, Steve? Can I speak to you for a moment?'

Duncan's smile vanished, and he paused uncertainly in the sloping passage-way.

'Please, Steve. I want to try and explain!'

Duncan's eyes met those of the soldier who sat crouched outside the door. He was the one with half his hand missing. Duncan had seen him moving unsurely about the deck gazing dazedly at the fat dressing on the end of his arm. Duncan remembered the water, and his face hardened.

'It's me! Ian!' the voice called again.

Duncan patted the soldier's shoulder vaguely and moved towards the chart. Over his shoulder he called, 'Never heard of him!' He slammed the door behind him and stared down at the chart, his eyes angry. 'Blast the ruddy war!' he said.

True to the captain's promise, the *Ametisa* had taken on new life, and with her frayed rigging thrumming in the wind and her deck beams shuddering to the increased vibration of the engine, she flung herself joyfully across the water.

Curtis stayed with the vigilant captain, the chart folded beneath his arm and an unlit pipe clamped between his strong teeth. Never before, not even on the most hazardous operation, had he felt the agony of passing time. Each unfamiliar movement by one of the soldiers, or a change of expression on the captain's face, made him steel himself in readiness for a change of plans to meet a new crisis. A small fishing fleet, a mere cluster of black dots in the distance, passed with maddening slowness, and he thought it typical of fishermen the world over to carry on with their trade regardless of the world's happenings.

Signor Zecchi came on deck and sniffed the air with obvious satisfaction.

Curtis spoke softly to the plump man at his side. 'Not a word to him about what we're doing. Not yet at any rate.' He was not even sure himself why he felt such uneasiness at the mayor's presence, but something about the man's complete self-confidence and the bland lack of expression on his smooth face made him cautious.

'We are moving nicely, Lieutenant. It is making a great difference to set the sails so.'

'Yes. With the following wind we are getting another four knots out of her.'

'When do you expect to make a landfall?' The question was light, yet Curtis sensed the strain in his voice.

'It is hard to say exactly. We have drifted quite a bit. And of course the navigation is quite difficult under these circumstances.'

Signor Zecchi's eyes watched him closely. 'Perhaps we shall sight a patrol ship soon. It would be advisable to signal her if so. My daughter and I could transfer to more comfortable quarters, and you would receive better assistance for your charges.'

'Perhaps.' And we would be clapped in irons, he thought. 'I expect that all major war vessels will be congregating in the south.'

'It is a pity we have no radio aboard. It would be good to know what is happening down there.'

Curtis sensed a challenge being offered, and smiled briefly. 'There can be little doubt about the final outcome, surely? Whatever happens to us, nothing can stop the Allied armies now. If your country persists in its resistance, it will suffer much damage and misery.'

'The battle is not over yet, Lieutenant!' His voice was stiff. 'The Germans will not give up without a fight!'

'I see. You mean you've already thought that your people might give up?'

'Never!' The black eyes flashed with sudden anger. 'We are of one mind! One basic principle binds us in a common shield against the invader!'

Curtis grinned. 'Calm yourself, please! You're not addressing a political rally now!'

Behind him the captain chuckled, and the mayor glared fiercely towards him.

'You will do well to mind your manners, Captain! I have a good memory!'

The captain stared calmly at the sails. 'Forgive me, *signore*. I am only an ignorant sailor.'

The mayor snorted, and with hands bunched into his pockets, he stalked forward towards the fo'c'sle.

The captain watched him go. His eyes were narrow slits when he spoke.

'I think maybe it would be better if he did not reach our destination!'

'No. We cannot blame him for his opinions. Besides,' he smiled wearily, 'we don't know what is going on behind us. He has been missed by his friends, and for all we know, they might have seen through our whole scheme.'

'Hmmm!' He was unconvinced. 'Tell me, *signore*, did you see that dock blow up? The one in Vigoria?'

'No. We were clear by then.'

'It must be a terrible thing to carry out such destruction.' The captain studied Curtis curiously. 'Does it bother you at all?'

'It is war. It is never good to remember things like that.'

The captain laughed with sudden gaiety. 'You are not like the Germans! They would be boasting of their achievements by now, if they were in your position!'

Carla Zecchi walked quickly across the poop from the hold. She stood momentarily by the rail, breathing deeply, her head held upwards against the blue sky.

Curtis saw the dress tighten across her rounded breasts with each breath, and felt his heart beat with excitement which he was unable to control. She's lovely, he thought. So slim and yielding, and yet in some ways harder than all of us.

I wonder what she thinks about me? I practically accused her of sabotaging the water supply. It seemed the only explanation at the time. He walked slowly towards her, and stood just behind her at the rail.

As his shadow fell across her body she turned and looked up at him. He had expected animosity, or open hostility, but her eyes held only a strange sadness.

'How are the wounded, *signorina*?' His voice was almost gruff, and he felt clumsy beside her.

'The same. They are all very strong men, fortunately. I think they will survive the journey.'

'I see.'

Curtis stared at the water as it surged and gurgled along the wooden hull. He tried to think of something to say, but her unwavering eyes made thought difficult.

'In England you would talk about the weather?'

He darted a quick glance at her, expecting taunts or sarcasm.

She smiled gravely, her small teeth gleaming. 'What is it you wish to say to me? If it is an apology, I would rather hear about the weather!'

He laughed bitterly. 'Nevertheless, I *am* sorry about all that has happened to you. You have been a tremendous help right from the start. I am sure that had my duty permitted otherwise, things might have been very different.' He paused again uncertain of how to continue.

She turned her head away from him, and her tanned neck was close to his face. Painfully close it seemed.

'Will you try to escape again when we reach the land?' Her voice was soft. 'You will surely not allow yourself to be taken prisoner now that you have got so far?'

'I don't know yet what I shall do.'

She twisted round again to face him, her eyes puzzled. 'That I find hard to believe. You do not strike me as a man who fails to make preparations.'

Curtis grinned awkwardly. 'You forget. We are enemies.'

'Yes, that is so. I wish it could be otherwise.'

He studied her face with sudden intentness. 'I believe you meant that!'

'Perhaps. I have had much time to think on this ship. And I know you have done what you had to do. Just as my father has acted with devotion and loyalty in the past.' She shook her head angrily and the plait danced down her back. 'The past! It is the future which is so terrifying!' She looked straight into his eyes. 'For all of us!'

She moved as if to leave him, and he knew that he needed her to stay.

'Perhaps after the war we may meet again? Things might be different then.'

'Let us not even talk of the future, please!' Her eyes were filled with concern. 'But I will tell you one thing.' She was facing the sea once more, and he had to bend his head to catch the words. 'I am glad that I have known you.' She moved aside, as he half reached out to touch her. 'Let us leave it at that. For us there may be no future at all, so let us be content.' She almost ran back to the hold, and Curtis was left staring blankly at the empty deck.

It was the final twist of fate. If he had found such a girl before . . . in other circumstances. He halted his racing thoughts. There could be no other girl. But she had tried to tell him that hope was wasted. When the world shuddered in its torment, there was no longer any room for the little people and their desires.

Duncan swayed towards him, his boots thudding on the sloping deck.

'Hey, Ralph! What's into you?' He stood straddle-legged by the lee rail, his eyes squinting against the glare.

Curtis shrugged heavily. How could he even begin to explain?

'I'm tired, that's all. How's everything going?'

'Fair. There's another meal on the way, an' most of the pongoes are trying to get some sleep. If only we could give 'em a bit of professional treatment, they'd be fine.' He dropped his voice. 'D'you really think we've got a chance?'

Curtis hid the surprise which welled up inside him. It was odd to see the defeat on Duncan's face. He had always been the driver; the unbreakable rock around which their small team had been built, and now he had changed.

'Well, we've a chance of some sort. That's all I can tell you.'

Duncan smiled grimly. 'It's certainly done wonders for you anyway. You look like a new bloke. At one time I thought you were startin' to throw a fit of tantrums!'

'I was.' Curtis' voice was quiet. 'I think this business has been a real test for all of us.'

'Jesus! It's one I can do without!' He stared morosely at the sea. 'It's like we're not movin'. I wish to God we had a real boat!'

Taylor climbed out of his hatchway and nodded to them. 'Nice day, all!' He sauntered across, wiping his filthy hands on a signal flag. 'Why the glum faces then? I thought we was all fixed up.'

Curtis looked at them and pointed to the horizon. 'When that starts to darken, I'll feel a bit better. In any case, don't breathe a word to anyone about our idea. Not even to the soldiers. No need to raise their hopes unnecessarily.'

Duncan nodded his huge head. 'I was just thinkin'. It's queer without Ian. Sort of busted up the team, I mean.'

'Maybe there was more to it than we know, Steve. He's new to this sort of thing, remember.'

'We was all new once, Skipper!' Taylor's eyes gleamed with sudden fury. 'It was all wrong! I feel all let down like!' He waved the flag vaguely. 'No, 'e didn't 'ave ter do that!'

'We'll talk about it later.'

'Might not be time, Ralph.' Duncan rubbed his chin. 'If we run into trouble, I'm makin' a break for it.'

The others regarded him thoughtfully.

Taylor was the first to speak. 'Wivout us, yer mean?' He sounded incredulous.

Curtis smiled with a calmness he did not feel. 'When the time comes, we'll stay a team. Got that?'

Duncan sighed deeply. 'You're nuts, Ralph. But we'll see.'

Taylor relaxed, his thin face dark with indignation. 'An' I should fink so, too! We ain't in the blessed outback now yer know! This is the Royal bloody Navy, ain't it?'

Curtis strode back to the wheel, his heart pounding. For the first time in his life he knew what it was to feel a leader. They really *did* need him! Before this he had always regarded his position as a mere clause in an act, a signature on a piece of paper.

He looked towards the open hold, hoping to see the girl again, and suddenly began to whistle.

.   .   .

The darkness was so complete that the schooner was enclosed and encircled, a world apart, sharing the night only with the slender crescent of the moon, which hung cold and aloof over the main-truck. The wind had lost it persistent force, and came instead in short, blustery puffs, which whipped the black oily surface of the sea into a shimmering mass of dancing catspaws, and splintered the moon's faint reflection into a broken necklace of silver, whilst above the decks the limp sails billowed suddenly into shape, the coarse canvas booming and cracking with fury, before falling loose and useless as before.

The beat of the engine had softened into a slow confident rumble, and added to the general feeling of tenseness which hung over the vessel as it crept towards the as yet invisible shore.

Curtis shivered slightly and turned up the collar of his jacket.

'How long now, d'you think?' He spoke with quiet fierceness to the Italian captain, who merely shrugged his shoulders, his face hidden in the darkness.

'Half hour, maybe less. It is a long time since I was here.'

Curtis strained his eyes along the ship's length, as if by so doing he might suddenly see his objective. He was getting jumpy again, and tried to reason calmly with the problem which faced him.

'What sort of place is this anyway?' he asked, and immediately regretted the impulse. He had already examined the chart in great detail with Duncan, and had got a fairly clear picture from the captain, too. But now that supposition and planning had passed by and the whole operation was budding into a grim reality, he felt he wanted to be assured once more.

The captain sighed and glanced over the helmsman's stooped shoulder at the dim binnacle light.

'It is but a tiny place. 'Bout the size of the village where we all met.' He chuckled to himself. 'Nothing there except a bit of a jetty and a few fishing boats. Ver' poor place, forgotten, useless. But I think it will suit our purpose.' He lapsed into silence again.

Duncan padded out of the darkness of the half-deck and peered down at the compass.

'I've spoken to the pongoes an' told 'em what we're tryin' to do. Most of 'em seemed to think you're a mug for botherin' about em, but I think that they realize it's the only thing to do now.'

'How are our prisoners? Keeping quiet?'

'I went along to see that they were OK an' had been fed. That Jerry, Beck, or whatever his name is, kicked up a fuss of course, but I gave him one of his uniforms to wear, an' think that cheered him up a bit. The master race didn't take very kindly to sitting in his underpants in front of his friends!'

Another shadow glided silently along the poop, and Curtis caught the faint scent of the girl's hair as she crossed to his side.

'Soon now?' she enquired. 'I cannot keep still for wondering what will happen next.'

They all jumped as the captain grunted and pointed towards the bows with evident satisfaction. A light stabbed the darkness half-heartedly three times and then left them in darkness once more.

Curtis shook his head with admiration. 'That was Vieste Light? You certainly know this coast very well, Captain!'

'What did I tell you, *signore*? I do not need charts! I can smell my way!'

'Say, how come we've only just seen that light?' Duncan sounded irritable.

'Simple, my friend! It has been hid by the headland. Now we are running into a tiny bay, the one I showed you on the chart. North-west of Vieste.'

The light stabbed the night again. Three flashes apparently suspended in the curtain of night.

The old grey-headed seaman scuttled down from the fo'c'sle and called softly to the captain.

'He can see the coast. He had good eyes, that one!'

He rapped out an order and his men began to shorten sail, the noise of the clattering blocks and stiff canvas against the spars seeming to drown even the note of the engine.

Curtis felt the girl brush against his sleeve, and looked down at the pale oval of her face. When the light flashed its endless signal again, he saw the twin reflections in her dark eyes.

'What do you wish me to do?'

'You will stay aboard when I go ashore with the captain. I hope I shall not be long.' He wondered why he was telling her all this, but he realized that since she had joined him on the poop, he had ceased to worry about what he had to do.

He saw her bared teeth.

'I said that you would be a man to make plans! I was very right, yes?'

'I don't like this, Ralph!' Duncan interrupted hoarsely, as the dark shadow of the land seemed to grow out of the night itself. 'How can this joker know where he's goin'?'

Curtis shrugged. 'Well, it's too late now, Steve. No turning back.'

Duncan grunted and made his way forward to check the mooring lines.

Curtis could almost feel the weight of the land, which grew darker and larger and more menacing with each second that passed. Already he could see the faint arm of the bay reaching out on the port beam, and even the wind had lost them, muffled perhaps by the hidden hills and cliffs ahead.

The captain took over the wheel and peered watchfully over the rail as the ship glided evenly through the calm water. Everyone was silent, and conscious of the lap of water against the hull and the clank of chain as the captain eased the wheel a spoke one way and then back.

The girl gasped and involuntarily gripped Curtis' arm, as without warning, the white hull of an anchored boat loomed out of the night and passed eerily down the *Ametisa*'s side.

The captain spun the wheel and jerked the lever at his side. The engine died away into an uneven neutral, and they heard the swish of water under the stem as the schooner turned slightly in her course and dodged another moored vessel.

He grunted. 'Even less boats here than when I came before!' His tone was almost conversational and showing nothing of the strain of piloting the schooner into an unlighted cove amongst anchored fishing boats.

Curtis smiled, and was conscious of the fact that Carla Zecchi had not removed her hand from his arm. I must be mad, he thought. To think about her now, when at any moment we may be picked up in a searchlight and shot to pieces.

A thin grey finger of jetty loomed up practically under the bowsprit, and as the captain put the engine astern, and a rope fender was dropped between the hull and the crumbling stonework, one of the seamen vanished over the side and could faintly be seen running towards a stone bollard, dragging behind him the huge eye of the ship's head-rope.

Curtis felt a vague sensation of anti-climax, as another man secured the ship by the stern and the captain allowed the engine to shudder into complete silence.

The schooner creaked and groaned against her fenders, and the seamen stood in a group by the rail, staring curiously at their homeland.

'Well, *signore*? Here we are. No soldiers, an' no *Fascisti*!' He laughed. 'Now we go ashore, eh?'

Curtis felt Carla's hand slide away, and watched her as she walked to the rail. She was looking up at the dark shapes of the hills, only faintly visible against the starred pattern of the sky.

He drew Duncan aside and tried to see the expression on the man's face. 'You'll stay here as we arranged, Steve,' he began slowly, 'and make sure that nobody gets ashore. I've told the mayor to co-operate with you, so you won't have to use any force.'

'Have you any idea what you hope to do out there?'

'The captain and I will have a scout round and see if we can find a doctor. He says he's got plenty of contacts hereabouts, and I imagine from what he says that the locals are a pretty independent lot. It's obviously true that the Jerries *have* left here, they'd never allow such a slipshod sort of security!'

'Can't I come with you? I hate the idea of bein' cooped up with all these jokers!'

'Now we've already settled all that.' A slight hardness crept into his voice. 'If anything goes wrong, you'll be in charge, so you must be ready to act accordingly!'

The captain ambled over to them and gestured towards the jetty. One of his men was holding what appeared to be a glistening snake above his head and grinning broadly.

'The fresh water, *signore*! She is connected to the jetty by that hose!'

Curtis sighed with relief. 'Get cracking on that, Steve. Have the tank filled up, and I'll get going for a doctor.'

Sergeant Dunwoody saluted stiffly in the darkness. 'You off, sir?'

'Yes. My Number One's in charge now. Keep all our people off the deck, and see that all the hatchways remain covered. You can take the Schmeisser yourself, Sergeant, and station yourself up by the fo'c'sle.'

He turned back to Duncan, relieved to be moving. 'So long, Steve. I'll try not to hang about!'

There was a sudden disturbance by the aft hatch, and Signor Zecchi ran excitedly across the deck.

'What is the meaning of this, Lieutenant? Where are you going? I insist on going with you!'

Duncan growled warningly, but Curtis raised his hand calmly. 'Please be quiet! I came back to the coast as I promised. For the wounded, not for you, you understand?'

The man swayed and half stepped towards the darkened rail. 'But this is an outrage! I must get ashore now!' He dropped his voice to an unexpected tone of pleading. 'I will not make any trouble.'

His daughter moved to his side. 'It is all right, Papa! You must not get excited.'

Curtis was aware that the captain was waiting impatiently by the rail. 'I must go,' he said shortly. 'No one goes ashore without my permission, and that's final!' He nodded to the girl, and followed the captain onto the jetty.

The feel of the rough stones beneath his feet made him falter and glance back at the indistinct shape of the little schooner, but a hand pulled at his arm and the captain muttered urgently. 'Come! It is nearly two of the clock. We must hurry!'

They stumbled along the jetty's hundred yards and began to climb up a narrow winding roadway, the surface of which was pitted and scarred with wheel-ruts and deep pot-holes.

Overhead they heard the drone of high-flying aircraft, and Curtis glanced up in time to see the shadow of one flit across the moon like an evil bat.

Bombers, he thought breathlessly, as his boots tripped and stumbled across the road. Perhaps they were British planes, and the idea gave him an unreasoning comfort.

They climbed in silence, Curtis keeping his eyes on the road, or on the broad, sweat-stained back of the Italian captain.

The village was even poorer than the one he had already seen, and he was amazed at the flimsy, rough-boarded hovels which were hunched on the side of the hills, overlooking the inlet. A dog whined dismally in the distance, and once Curtis thought he heard a child cry out briefly in one of the dwellings. Nets and various oddments of fishing gear, all crude and much repaired, lay heaped between the low rooftops, and they had to climb and duck over several piles, before the captain could find his way onto the main road through the village. There were no motor vehicles of any kind to be seen, and only once did Curtis see any building constructed of concrete.

He stopped dead in his tracks and pulled the captain close. The building was smooth and grey, with small black slits for windows.

'Hold it!' he gasped. 'That's a pillbox, a gun-mounting, or something!'

With something like a swagger the captain walked over to the concrete emplacement and kicked it with his shoe. He chuckled. 'See? Empty, like their promises! They have all left, I tell you!'

They hurried on, and Curtis wondered what the captain might have said if some Germans had come out of the pillbox to see who was knocking at such a late hour.

'Ah! There it is!'

Curtis almost collided with the little man, as he halted and pointed ahead.

'For one second, *signore*, even I was beginning to think I had lost my way!'

The small church was almost invisible against the hillside, and only the small bell-tower broke its dim craggy outline.

They passed around the low side, and the captain pointed at a small extension at the rear.

'I must see the priest, you understand. Only he can help us.' He peered at Curtis with sudden eagerness. 'You trust me, *signore*?'

Curtis nodded wearily. 'Go ahead. But how d'you know it's the same priest who was here before?'

He shrugged. 'I do not. But we will try caution, and if that fails, we will try the revolver!'

He motioned Curtis back into the shadows of the church, and then began to pound gently on the door.

In the stillness of the night it sounded like a gun being fired, and Curtis tore his eye from the captain to look back along the roadway. There was only the pillbox, white in the moonlight, to remind him where he was, and but for the distant murmur of the sea, he could have been anywhere.

A light flickered beneath the heavy door, and Curtis heard the captain speaking softly through a small grille which was suddenly lighted by a lantern from within.

A chain clattered, and the door was opened slowly to reveal a tall, thin figure in the traditional black robe of a priest. His features were thin and yellow against the raised lantern, and the sparse hair on his narrow head stuck out above his ears like little tufts of white feathers.

The captain grinned with obvious relief. 'It is Father Bernucci! We are saved!'

Curtis felt the man's deep-set eyes watching him, as the captain rattled off a lengthy explanation, with many gestures at Curtis and towards the sea.

The old man nodded slowly and beckoned them both inside.

It was cold inside the unlighted porchway, and it was with amazement that Curtis found himself being ushered into a low beamed room, lit by candles and by the cheerful flicker of a dying fire. The walls were lined with old, leather-bound volumes and several faded pictures, and the plain, stone-flagged floor was comfortably decorated by two long woven mats.

The priest continued to question the captain, as he added a log to the fire and then laid cheese, wine and a dark loaf on the carved table.

Curtis sank into the high-backed chair and drank the wine with quiet relish. He was aware of the fatigue which hovered just behind his eyes and the difficulty he had in focusing on the long-stemmed glass in his hand.

The priest sat stiffly on a bench facing him, his bony hands resting in his lap. A large crucifix swung from his neck and glittered in the candlelight.

Curtis felt his eyelids drooping. Another squadron of bombers droned overhead, or perhaps it was the same group going back, their evil work done and their youthful crews returning to their beds.

The priest suddenly spoke, his voice soft and husky, and his English so perfect, that Curtis was startled into attention.

'I have listened to Fausto Macchia, and I think I understand what has happened.' The old eyes rested on Curtis' uniform in a brief appraisal. 'You are an ememy of this country, but,' he lifted a finger as Curtis leaned forward, 'I think it will not be so for long. Be that as it may, I will help you, and at once.'

'That is most kind of you, Father. The wounded soldiers need proper attention, and more than I can give them.'

'If you had not come ashore like this, how many of them might have died?' The eyes were unwavering.

The captain interrupted with a laugh. 'Less than half! Yet the lieutenant here has risked his own life and everyone else's for the sake of those few!'

'I was not prepared to take such a risk, that's all,' Curtis answered simply.

'Quite so, my son. It is strange what war will do to us as individuals. In war, the young often feel they have no real mission, and yet,' he fingered the gold cross thoughtfully, 'perhaps you, at least, have been allotted your task to perform.'

He wrote slowly on a sheet of paper, and when he had finished, he glanced at Curtis, his eyes enquiring. 'You would like to see what I have written? It is a message for my friend. He is the doctor.'

'I trust you, Father.' He found that he meant it. 'Will there be any Carabinieri on the roads tonight?'

The priest smiled sadly. 'They have been conscripted into the army. They left this morning!'

He handed the message to the captain. 'Take this to the doctor, Fausto. You know his house.'

The captain tucked it into his shirt. 'Have you still got your old bicycle, Padre?'

The priest nodded. 'Take it, Fausto. It will help to remove some of the signs of good living from you.'

The captain picked up his cap and walked to the door. 'This will not take long, Lieutenant. I shall be back to the ship with the doctor within an hour!'

'Right. I'll find my way back there now, and have the wounded prepared for immediate treatment.'

He took the priest's dry hand. 'And thank you, Father, for everything.'

'For everything?' The priest cocked his head on one side. 'For the help, do you mean? Or for the faith?'

He was still smiling as Curtis stumbled out into the darkness and started to feel his way down the road to the village and the sea.

CHAPTER 10

Duncan sat uncomfortably on the stone bollard opposite the schooner's bows and stared into the shadows at the far end of the jetty. An unlit cheroot hung from one corner of his mouth and his hands lay spread across his knees. Occasionally he looked across at the ship, as an unusual noise or movement caught his attention, but otherwise he remained wrapped in his own concentrated thoughts.

It seemed ages since the skipper had gone up towards the silent village, although he knew that it could not have been more than half an hour or so. At first, he had driven the Italian sailors like mad to get the water tank filled, and he had kept the others occupied with boiling water and preparing the more seriously wounded for inspection. He shifted his buttocks angrily on the cold stone. It was damned unlikely that any such doctor would be available. More likely a couple of platoons of Jerry soldiers.

The corporal, his head wrapped in a balaclava, crossed the jetty, his studded boots clinking on the stones, and halted beside him.

'Give you a break, sir?' The man stared over Duncan's shoulder with practised eye.

'Fair enough.' Duncan stood up and stretched. 'I'll go and give the ship a shake-up!'

He climbed over the gunwale and walked carefully to the hold. Removing the canvas which hid the lights beneath, he lowered himself into the too-familiar place, which to him had become a symbol of suffering and discomfort.

The girl was there he saw, and with Taylor was busy with one of the wounded. It was damned odd, the way that she and the skipper looked at each other.

Taylor glanced up and grimaced. He had washed his hands and arms free of engine filth, and compared to his body, they gleamed with unnatural whiteness under the lamplight.

'Skipper back?' he asked shortly.

Duncan shook his head and took a dirty dressing from the girl. He threw it quickly into a pail, aware of the sickly smell which seemed to pervade the hold.

Carla Zecchi sat back on her haunches and blew a loose strand of hair from her face. 'I am getting stiff!' She tried to smile, but the tiredness was too strong for her. 'I wish we had just one more helper.'

Duncan grunted. She probably meant Ralph, he decided. 'Well, perhaps the doctor *will* come,' he said. 'But we must be ready for the worst.'

'You're a cheerful one!' Taylor covered the soldier with a blanket and stood up. 'You'll 'ave me in stitches, you will!'

'I am sorry about Ian.' She looked at both of them anxiously. 'It was a strange thing to do.'

Duncan could see that she wanted to ask him something, but his face remained impassive.

'I s'pect he wanted to stretch 'is legs, miss!' Taylor said, and moved across to the next man. He stooped down, his sharp eyes moving despairingly from the bandages on the soldier's legs to the expression of glassy concentration in his eyes. He grinned. ''Ere, mate, let's 'ave a look at yer. Doctor's comin' to fix yer up!'

The soldier moved his white lips and a thin stream of saliva ran down his chin.

'What the hell d'you want to tell the poor joker that for?' Duncan hissed down at him, his eyes hard. 'You'll do him no good if the bloke doesn't arrive!'

Taylor continued to grin at the soldier. ''E'll come,' he said softly. 'Skipper'll get somebody.' Under his breath he added, ''E's *got* to!'

Duncan stood up and cursed as his head collided with a beam. He was now so much on edge that he felt he had to be doing something.

'I'm goin' on deck to have another prowl round,' he said. 'This hangin' about is drivin' me up the creek!'

As he swung round to leave the girl caught his arm, her eyes steady with resolve. 'I should like to speak to Ian, please. I think it might help. He must be very worried about all this.'

Duncan shrugged. 'Suit yourself. I don't suppose Ralph'd mind. And in any case, I'm in charge at the moment!'

'I'm sure he wouldn't mind anyway,' she answered softly. 'And thank you.'

Taylor watched them go. 'Can't do any more 'ere till we get some more dressin's,' he called, 'so I'll keep an eye on things 'ere!'

'You've been a wonderful help,' she said. 'You understand these men.'

Taylor moved his feet uncomfortably. 'That's right, miss. Proper Florence Nightingale I am!'

It seemed even darker on deck, and the moon had moved behind the hills at the back of the village.

They climbed down the aft hatch and the soldier outside the cabin door yawned and nodded companionably.

'How are you, digger?' Duncan peered at the man's bandaged hand.

'Could do wiv a drink, sir.'

'Nip off an' have one then. We shall be down here for a bit.'

The hatch closed and Duncan reached out for the key which protruded from the lock on the cabin door.

'Want me to come with you?' His tone was gruff, but the uneasiness was clear to her.

'I wish you would. It would make things easier for all of us.'

Duncan swallowed and slammed open the door with unnecessary violence.

Jervis jumped up from the bunk, his eyes startled.

'Carla! And ... and Steve!' He held out his hands, his mouth quivering. 'Thank God you've come down!'

'Her idea.' Duncan folded his arms and eyed him coolly.

Jervis turned to the girl. 'Where are we? What's happening? I've been nearly going mad in here!'

'We have arrived at some small place that the captain knows. We have got some water,' she dropped her eyes, 'and perhaps a doctor may be found also.'

Jervis stared at her incredulously. 'But what about the Germans?'

'They are not in this place apparently.'

'So your little bit of stupidity misfired, Ian.' Duncan's face was hard and unyielding.

'Why did you do it, Ian?' she asked gently. 'Why did you not trust your own captain? He is a strange man, but ... but ...' Her lashes dropped with sudden embarrassment. '... he has suffered much for all this.'

Jervis' jaw dropped. 'What are you saying? How can you of all people talk like this?'

'What do you mean, Ian?' She held her slender body erect, her small chin high. 'What are you suggesting?'

Duncan had tensed. 'Yeah, what in hell's name are you babbling now?'

'But I did this for you!' Jervis still stared at her. 'And now everything's changed!' He ran his fingers through his hair desperately. 'I didn't realize we were still going to try to get away!'

Duncan leaned his back against the door as someone moved quietly in the passage. These soldiers don't take long to get a drink, he thought.

'I am only a passenger ... a prisoner, call me what you like.' She tossed her head impatiently. 'But I understand what your captain is trying to do, and I think he is right. My father may think otherwise now, but later on he may be glad all this had happened.' She lowered her voice. 'You were wrong to do what you did!'

Jervis' face collapsed. 'But I did it for you, Carla! I didn't want you to be punished for ... for what you did with the water! But it was all wasted, I——'

She crossed the cabin and seized his hand. 'What are you saying? I did not touch the water! I did not even know where it was!'

Duncan breathed out explosively. 'Hold it! D'you mean, Ian, that you just admitted to this, to cover up for her?'

They both turned to him like defiant children.

'I was with the wounded all the time,' she said hotly, 'I could not have done it, even if I had wanted!'

Duncan rubbed his chin, his brain jumping madly. 'Well, if neither of you did it ...' He paused, his eyes suddenly anxious.

'Somebody else ...' Carla's voice trailed away, and the resistance seemed to drain from her.

They looked at each other. Jervis was the first to speak.

'You think it was your father?'

'Of course she does! Who else?' Duncan jumped for the door, his face wild. He twisted the handle, but nothing happened.

Carla and Jervis stared at Duncan's hand on the door. Neither spoke, and the silence in the cabin was complete and menacing.

They all heard the clatter of feet on the ladder and the sound of hurried steps across the deck.

'Here! Open the door!'

Duncan suddenly burst into life, the reality of the new danger making his eyes blaze with fury. He pulled the pistol from his belt, but with a shake of his head he threw his weight against the door.

'Can't risk the sound of a shot!' he gasped, as he drew back and hurled himself once more at the door. There was a splintering crash, and he burst out into the passage.

Followed by the others, but unaware of them, Duncan ran on deck, his eyes wide as he stared round at the silent shadows. He ran wildly along the deck, peering from side to side and over at the deserted jetty.

At that moment Jervis, who had run to the fo'c'sle, called out, his voice shaky.

'Here, Steve! Quick, the sergeant!'

They found Sergeant Dunwoody lying on his side in a crumpled heap, his bandages white against the blackness of the raised fo'c'sle.

'He's still breathing,' commented Duncan briefly as he stood up. 'I think he's had a crack over the head.' Duncan was thinking furiously. 'Call some help from the hold, Ian. I'm goin' to look for somebody!'

He stared at the girl's frightened face. 'I don't know how much you've had to do with this, but I promise you that——' He broke off, as a sudden burst of firing cut across the jetty.

'God! The Schmeisser!' Duncan pulled out the pistol and vaulted over the bulwark, to land crouching on the jetty.

He dimly heard the girl sob and say, 'He wouldn't, Ian! It *can't* be him!' before he started to inch his way along the lip of the stonework, his shoulders hunched and the pistol unwavering in his hand.

The corporal appeared to be asleep. One hand was beneath his bandaged head, and the balaclava lay unheeded by the stone bollard at his feet. Duncan stepped over him, his teeth bared as he searched the darkness at the end of the jetty. There was nothing he could do for the corporal, the burst of bullets from the automatic pistol had practically decapitated him.

Fired from behind, too, he thought coldly, as he ran on into the sandbank beyond the jetty. He halted, breathing fast. No sound, but for the gentle lap of water against the beach and the barking of a dog, came to his straining ears, although as he listened, his head bent forward, he imagined that he could hear a stone falling on the cliffs, far to his right.

Taylor panted out of the night behind him, his eyes dark blobs on his pale face.

'Get 'im? Where's 'e gone?'

Duncan shrugged. 'God knows!'

Taylor stared round the unfamiliar roadway, his shoulders jerking with pent up sorrow and rage. 'The bastard! The rotten, stinkin' bastard! The poor bloke never 'ad a chance!'

Duncan hissed, 'Steady! Someone's runnin' this way!'

They froze by the roadside and then Duncan stepped forward. 'It's the skipper,' he said quickly.

Curtis loomed up almost at their side before they could actually see his anxious features.

'What's happened? That shooting ...' He was breathing fast, and had obviously been running for some time.

They heard the laboured whine of a car engine, and then, as they turned towards the cliff road, an ancient Fiat bounced around the corner and drove recklessly towards the sea.

'It's the doctor, thank God!' muttered Curtis as he caught a glimpse of the Italian captain's fat face through the open window. He turned back to Duncan.

'Come on, man! Spit it out!'

'Zecchi's jumped us! Grabbed the Schmeisser and killed the corporal!' He waved towards the sloping hillside road. 'He's up there somewhere!' He turned to Curtis, his voice unnaturally earnest. 'I couldn't help it, Ralph! I never gave it a thought!'

'What about Carla, the girl?'

'Aboard. I don't think she had anythin' to do with it. He'd not have left her behind.'

The car skidded to a halt, its engine hissing. Curtis reached it in two strides. He saw a small, bird-faced man in a dark suit behind the wheel.

'*Medico!*' began the captain proudly, then catching sight of the others and the drawn guns, 'What 'appens, *signore*? Trouble?'

'Never mind that!' Curtis' voice was terse. 'Get to the ship.' He nodded briefly to the doctor. 'Very pleased to see you, sir. Please do all you can for those men.'

The doctor ducked his head and grinned. 'Pleasure!'

Curtis turned to the captain. 'That road, where does it lead?'

'That one? To Vieste. It is about ten kilometres from here.'

'Are there any police there, d'you think?'

'There could be,' he nodded quickly. 'It is likely.'

Curtis stood back. 'Go to the ship then. We must carry on and catch him before he reaches help.'

The car moved off, the captain obviously eager to know what was happening.

Curtis looked from Duncan to Taylor. 'Right, let's go. We've got to catch him, and that's all there is to it!'

'But, God, it'll be dawn soon! We've gotta get clear!' Duncan stared wildly as Curtis turned as if to go.

'And how far d'you think we'll get, once he's telephoned for assistance! Now come on. Move!'

They started to run along the road, their feet keeping a muffled rhythm in the dust as they turned the corner and pounded up the hill. Curtis' breath was strangely calm, and although he was outwardly alert and watchful, he kept thinking of the girl. She had nothing to do with it, Duncan had said. It was a small light in this terrible darkness.

'Wot's the use?' Taylor spoke between his set teeth. ''E might 'ave cut across the 'ill.'

Curtis shook his head and increased the pace. 'He's not cut out for this sort of thing, and we're supposed to be fit! And don't forget that he's armed!'

They ran on.

The road got narrower, and the countryside was completely open and windswept. There were no dwellings of any sort, and even the grass on the slopes was mere stubble and weed. There was no cover there.

The moon showed itself again as they topped the rise, and cast a feeble glow over the landscape, leaving the sea dark and shapeless, like a velvet cloak.

Taylor stumbled and fell, and for a few seconds lay winded and gasping on the dirt. He was aware of the sharp pain over his ribs, and rmembered the hand grenade inside his blouse. He saw the other two running on, Curtis merely glancing back to see that he was all right, and then beckoning sharply with his hand.

He staggered to his feet, cursing breathlessly. For a moment he was reminded of his rough childhood in the East End, and his endless search for manhood. Before he could join the gang in his street, he had been made to fight a boy much bigger than himself. It had been a terrible and bloody experience for him. He had found on that occasion that once his blood had become heated with fury he had fought blindly and viciously, like a madman, and even when his frightened opponent had run for home, he had pursued him, his mind blank but for the desire to destroy his enemy.

He started to run after the others, his rage still as fresh and compelling as the moment that he had discovered the dead corporal lying pathetically on the jetty. It was as if something else had him in its grip, something which he had only briefly controlled since that fight so many years before. Giulio Zecchi was no longer a mere enemy, he was the very pivot around which their lives revolved, and the one person who would bring all their hopes crashing to the ground.

Taylor was small and wiry, but his body was as hard as nails, and powered by his new fury, he overtook the others and ran purposefully down the centre of the road.

Duncan saw him shoot past and for a moment thought that the man had seen something. He groaned aloud and dashed the sweat from his eyes, as he half realized what Taylor was doing.

They topped another rise and Curtis called a halt. Duncan dropped onto one knee, trying to listen in the darkness, but heard only the savage pounding of his own heart. Taylor slithered to a stop and looked back impatiently at the others.

Curtis didn't know what had made him halt, but as he stood, trying to control his laboured breathing, his hands loose at his sides, he felt that they were very near their quarry. He tried to calculate how long they had been running and how far the other man might have got. It was too difficult, and he stared moodily at the black shoulder of the overhanging hillside. On his left the roadside petered out and after a small rocky fringe, dropped away steeply to the beach below. Nothing there, he decided, and looked back at the road. Perhaps, just a few yards ahead, Zecchi would be waiting. One final burst from the Schmeisser, and he would finish all three of them. He beckoned to Duncan.

'You take the hillside, Steve.' He noticed the listless droop of the man's shoulders and added easily, 'You're the only one who can manage that sort of thing. Try to keep level with us, but watch the road in front.'

Duncan shook himself and nodded. With a sudden burst of energy he jumped the loose rocks at the side of the road and was soon lost on the hillside.

Curtis gave him a few seconds to get started. 'Right, George, you keep on the left of the road and about twenty yards behind me. If anything happens, jump over the edge of the cliff and blaze away for all you're worth!'

Taylor digested this carefully. 'An' wot about you, Skipper?'

'I'm going to walk down the middle of the road,' answered Curtis calmly.

'Bit dodgy, ain't it?'

Curtis raised his hand. 'Listen!' They cocked their heads. 'I heard something! Come on!'

Taylor dropped slightly behind Curtis' tall figure and plodded forward along the edge of the road. He found it difficult to drag his eyes from the skipper's back. Alone, in the middle of the road, striding along as if on parade, he looked vulnerable and completely open for attack.

Curtis stepped briskly round the next curve, his breath momentarily halted as he waited for a shot to smash him down, but nothing happened. Perhaps Zecchi had found another route after all, but he dismissed the thought instantly. He was a stranger here, too, and he knew quite well that his only hope was to reach the nearest village or town.

Chasing a man in his own country, he thought suddenly. It only helped to add to the unreality he now felt. His foot kicked against a small metal object. He scooped it up in one movement and continued walking. He knew without looking at it that it was Zecchi's cigarette case, and the find gave him a cold sense of relief and loathing together.

His head was beginning to pound with his exertions, and inwardly he told himself to keep with Taylor, near the only available cover. Then it happened. A little above the road to his right there was a savage burst of orange flashes, accompanied by the short, harsh rattle of the Schmeisser.

He flung himself recklessly forward, aware of the bullets singing hotly past his face and snickering amongst the loose stones behind him. As he reached the edge of the road, he rolled over against the rocks and fired two shots indiscriminately into the darkness. Taylor fired, too, and Curtis sighed with relief. He realized that the rocks near him afforded no real cover at all, and should Zecchi have noted his position, another burst would finish him. He bared his teeth savagely. Go on, shoot away! Steve will get you in a minute, you murdering bastard!

Taylor called across the road, his voice hoarse. 'I gotta thirty-six in me pocket, Skipper! Shall I 'eave it at 'im?' He cursed horribly as two shots whined down from the slope and made him duck down the cliff.

'No! Remember Steve!'

He peered round the rocks. Nothing stirred. Zecchi had used only single shot that time. Of course! He almost cried out with excitement. There was only the one magazine with the gun.

His neck ached with concentration and anxiety. The shots might easily be heard a mile away on such a still night. Perhaps that was Zecchi's idea. He jumped, as Duncan's powerful voice shattered the stillness.

'Look out! He's off down the road again!'

Then they were all running again, caution thrown to the wind, like hounds after a stag.

Duncan grunted as he landed in the road and gathered speed towards the next bend, his head hunched in his shoulders.

'Soon now!' he gasped at Curtis. 'He can't manage much more!'

They rounded the curve together, and stopped.

The moon had risen above the hill again, and like part of a carefully dressed stage, the next fifty yards of roadway was bathed in eerie blue light.

Giulio Zecchi had stopped, too. They could just define his round pale face and short grey hair, as he stood in the middle of the road, his square figure heaving from exertion.

Curtis stared past him at the line of figures across the road. Dark, formless shapes, they might have been of stone, but for the gleam of moonlight on their levelled rifles. Even as the three of them watched, another slow-moving line of heads appeared along the top of the rise, closing the road into a silent arena.

'Well, that's that!' The bitterness in Duncan's voice was complete.

Giulio Zecchi rested a plump hand on his chest, fighting for breath. 'Nothing to say, Lieutenant?' He laughed wildly. 'What about the Australian? Nothing? Such a pity!'

'Oo are they, fer Gawd's sake?' Taylor stood loosely, his hand inside his blouse. He could feel the rough warmth of the grenade under his palm. One pull, and I'll blow all of us to hell!

Curtis' voice was cool. 'Some sort of Home Guard, I imagine. It doesn't matter I suppose, what it is!'

A man stepped slowly from the watching line of figures. He was small and lithe, his body distorted by the gleaming bandoliers of ammunition criss-crossed over his shoulders and the cape loosely hanging from his back.

He stood like a small rock, as Zecchi poured a torrent of Italian into his attentive ear. His eyes were fixed on the three figures at the other end of the road, but even across the moon-bathed track, Curtis could see the strange watchfulness of the man and the evident interest he was showing.

'Shall we make a run for it?' Duncan's voice was a mere whisper.

Curtis didn't turn his head. 'They're behind us, too. Don't look round!'

He stiffened, as followed by Zecchi, the little man started to walk slowly towards him.

He halted a few feet away and bowed mockingly. 'I speak English. Tell me who you are!' His voice was tired, almost caressing.

'Hasn't he told you? We are British officers.'

'Of course. I just wanted to hear you speak.' His thin face split into a grin. In the half-light his face looked evil. 'And this is Giulio Zecchi, I believe? He has told me about your strange journey, but enough of that.' He jerked angrily, as Zecchi grabbed his arm and pointed at Curtis.

'Seize them now! We will take the ship easily, there are only a few miserable wounded aboard!' He drew himself up, his composure returned. 'You were foolish to think we Italians could not fight, Lieutenant!' His voice trembled with excitement and contempt. 'I will order these men to take you to the nearest German outpost! They will be very glad to deal with you!'

The little man smiled again. 'I understand you have no radio on your poor ship, Captain?' His voice was even more silky.

'No.' Curtis sensed a slight movement from Taylor's hand, and steeled himself.

'So amusing to speak English again,' he remarked inconsequently. 'I was a law student in London, before the war.' He bowed again, the movement making a beam of moonlight dance along the path of his pistol. 'Allow me to introduce myself, Captain. I am Ludivico Fanali, once a lawyer, now District Commander of the People's Liberation Army!'

Curtis stared at him silently, the words not seeming to penetrate his racing thoughts.

He had turned away from Curtis and was regarding Zecchi with cold enjoyment. 'But for the unfortunate lack of a radio, you would have known that the Italian Government has sued for peace with the Anglo-American armies! There has been a big change here since you were last a lackey of the Germans!' The last words were harsh, like a lash. 'So now, Signor Giulio Zecchi, you are *my* prisoner!'

The mayor seemed to shrink. His mouth opened and shut, but nothing but disjointed sounds emerged.

Curtis saw the armed men begin to close in, as their leader continued. 'It is a fortune of war that you tried to destroy the ship's water supply. But for that, you would have been safe and comfortable in a British prison camp.' He shrugged. 'As it is, I now have in my possession one of the filthiest Fascists our poor country produced!' He laughed. It was a terrible sound. 'You should be honoured, *signore*! Even down here we have heard of your doings and of the people you have condemned to the forced labour camps to please your other Fascist friends!' He stepped back, as if unwilling to be infected by him. 'Say goodbye to the lieutenant! I am sure he has work to do!'

Taylor's hand trembled on the grenade. He could feel the sweat cold on his spine. Another miracle was happening, and he couldn't bring himself to understand it.

'Does that mean we're all right?' He stared incredulously as Curtis pulled out his pipe and placed it between his teeth. He had seen him do that many times, immediately after an underwater attack. When things had started to improve and the danger was passing them by. To Taylor it was like a sign from heaven.

'You are Partisans?' Curtis had not even realized that he had taken out his pipe, but knew only that he wanted to hug the weird little man who stood so patiently before him.

'I believe that is what we are called.' He laughed shortly. 'We are only just getting accustomed to the idea!' He became suddenly brisk. 'You must get back to your ship. At once! There are German patrols in the area, looking for us!' He smiled apologetically. 'Father Bernucci informed me of your plight. It is as well that I decided to come.'

'Why didn't the Father tell me about the armistice?' Curtis tried to remember the priest's sad face.

'It is as well to be careful. Now please go, Captain.' His voice was quietly commanding and full of authority. 'Time is short for all of us.' He turned to the quivering form of Giulio Zecchi. 'Especially for him!'

Curtis wavered, a feeling of pity in his heart, as he saw the dark, silent figures jostling closer to the mayor. There was a sudden movement from the crowd, and Zecchi whimpered as somebody emptied a can of liquid over his head.

The partisan leader gripped Curtis' wrist, his fingers hard and cold. 'Go now! It is better!'

Curtis wrenched his eyes away and pulled Duncan by the arm. 'Come on, let's go!' He had smelt the tang of petrol and knew what was going to happen.

'We'll run back to the ship,' he said harshly, and kicked viciously at Taylor's boots. He was standing mesmerized by the twisting, gibbering shape of the mayor, as he tried to duck away from the man with the lighted match.

'Forgive them,' said the leader simply. 'They have suffered much, and they have long memories!'

Sickened, the three men started to run down the road. But not before Curtis had seen the writhing figure, wrapped in flames, as it jumped screaming over the edge of the dark cliffs.

Once round the first curve in the road, they halted, and Curtis rubbed his eyes wearily. He heard Taylor retching, and was suddenly aware of the gleaming cigarette case in his bunched fingers. With a feeling of revulsion he hurled it from him and sent it skimming over the cliff edge towards the silent water.

'Ready chaps?' His voice was steady, but he was glad of the darkness.

'Fair enough.' Duncan fell in step beside him and with Taylor plodding silently behind, they started down the empty road towards the cove.

. . .

Jervis crossed the schooner's darkened deck in quick, nervous steps and hovered at the side of the coaming over the hold. Every available lantern had been placed there to help the funny little Italian doctor who, with the captain, was organizing the wounded soldiers with all the brisk efficiency one might have expected in a well-equipped field hospital. Jervis glanced anxiously over his shoulder at the dark bulk of the land. The glare of lights from the hold seemed to welcome attention from every direction, and more than once, his heart chilled as he imagined that he heard the sounds of vehicles from beyond the hills. He tried to laugh off his growing fear, when he discovered that the sounds were those of distant aircraft, but he found only the sick, empty sense of despair, which had kept him company since the skipper had left to look for the girl's father.

He walked stiffly to the rail and forced himself to stare along the deserted jetty. Try as he might, he could not avoid looking at the still shape by the mooring bollard, its head gleaming wetly in the moon's feeble gleam. He swallowed hard and gripped the rail with sudden desperation.

I'm the one, he thought wretchedly. I've caused all this. Just because I wanted to appear the big man in front of her. If I hadn't made such a stupid gesture, the skipper or Steve would soon have discovered the real culprit, and all this might have been avoided. He jerked upright, startled. A faint burst of firing echoed around the invisible cliffs beyond the cove, but before his reeling brain could be brought under control, the silence of the night closed in once more, and he was left listening to his heart.

He felt the sweat trickle across his scalp, and his nostrils quivered like those of a cornered animal. That was automatic fire. Perhaps the skipper was already dead, and Zecchi was on his way to the ship with soldiers. He closed his eyes and saw again the mocking smile of the German officer who had captured him.

'An example must be made!' he had said.

He strained his ears into the darkness, his eyes still pressed shut with concentration. There it was again. Some sharp shots, mingled with the heavy thud of another pistol. He forced himself away from the rail and stared round. If the skipper and the others had run into an ambush, then he, Jervis, was in charge of the whole venture. The ship creaked peacefully against the fenders, and beneath him in the hold, he heard a soldier laugh. It was a high pitched sound, and Jervis had to stop himself from running madly to the safety of the aft cabin. A slow, terrible thought began to penetrate his racing brain. Suppose the Italian captain had arranged all this. Or even the girl, Carla. It was possible, and quite within their power. After all, he thought wretchedly, the skipper had only the word of the captain, and a promise from the local priest, that everything was safe. He felt his hand on the smooth leather of his holster. He must do something. But what?

His legs quivered as he lowered himself into the hold and stood taking in the scene which shone beneath the lanterns like a crude tapestry. The little doctor was in his shirtsleeves, but still wearing his wide-brimmed black hat. Across his round paunch a huge watch-chain swung and jerked, as he ducked and pranced around the man who lay on a rough table made from odd boxes and covered with blankets. The soldier, naked from the waist down, watched fascinated as the doctor made a few final adjustments to the leg bandages and then sank back on the table, a small smile on his tight lips.

The doctor pulled off his glasses and polished them vigorously with his handkerchief. He frowned briefly, as the Italian seamen who were pouring boiling water into a small dish, allowed some of the steam to billow across the table, and then his eye fell on Jervis. He nodded and waved his hands around the hold.

'Ver' good!' He nodded again, and beamed at the soldiers. 'I think we do ver' well!'

He signalled with his finger to two of the soldiers who were acting as orderlies and, helped by the captain, they removed the man from the table and kicked the dirty dressings into a pail which was overflowing onto the deck.

Jervis watched the girl as she walked out of a darkened corner of the hold, leading the blind soldier by the arm. Her face was pale and strained, and he noticed the streaks of blood on her wrist and on the skirt of her dress, as she moved under the lanterns. She did not appear to see Jervis, and her eyes were dead and dull.

The doctor darted a quick glance at her and rose on tiptoe to speak in Jervis' ear.

'Ver' good girl, eh? She 'as been working like a, like a——' he broke off and shrugged. 'But I do not think she will last much more, eh?' He studied Jervis' taut features with professional interest, and then with a grunt he turned to the young soldier, who was sitting uneasily on the edge of the table.

Sergeant Dunwoody walked shakily across the littered hold, and stared at Jervis suspiciously. He had a further bandage across his forehead, and occasionally his good hand moved gingerly across his face, as if to assure himself that the damage was not more serious. The doctor had been quite angry with him and, aided by the captain, had forced him to sit and rest, but even then he had fidgeted with his pistol and stared round the hold, his eye gleaming with cold rage.

The girl released the soldier's arm and stepped back. Her elbow touched Jervis' tunic and she spun round startled, her eyes black with anxiety.

'Is there no news? Have they come back yet?'

Jervis thought about the shots, but shook his head. 'Nothing yet. Perhaps he got away.'

She studied him, her mouth slack. Jervis thought she was surprised at his remark, but he no longer trusted his judgement about anything.

'He killed that man!' Her voice was low and unsteady, and she spoke slowly, as if repeating a lesson. 'I cannot understand.' She looked searchingly at Jervis. 'All this has unhinged him, perhaps?' She waited, but he could only stare at her. 'I wish I knew what was happening!'

The captain joined them, wiping his fat palms with a piece of cloth. 'That boy is the last.' He glanced curiously at Jervis and then at the girl. 'I think I'll go on deck an' prepare to leave, eh?'

Jervis blinked and then tightened his mouth. 'No! Wait!'

The captain paused, a slight frown creasing the smoothness of his brown, egg-like head. 'For what? Your commander will return soon, an' we must be ready to go.'

Jervis dropped his hand onto his gun, and saw the captain's troubled eyes follow it down.

'What makes you so sure he'll be back?' He had to drop his voice to restrain the tremble which crept into it. 'Suppose you've been lying all the time?' He took a half step forward, and the captain swallowed.

'He will be back. He will do what he has to do!' He darted a quick, unhappy glance at the girl, but she was still watching Jervis. 'Please! Let me prepare the ship, eh?'

Jervis jerked his head towards the hatch. 'I'll come with you then.'

He waited until the captain had started up the ladder, and then turned to the girl. For a long moment they looked at each other, but he could see that she had already excluded him from her own thoughts.

The doctor had removed the bandages from the soldier's eyes, and was staring with bird-like intensity at the man's face.

Carla Zecchi moved automatically to the soldier's side and took his hand firmly between her own, as the man said in a small voice, 'I still can't see, Doctor. There's nothin' at all!'

She pressed his hand still harder, as if to force the rising panic from him, and by so doing, share with him her own private loss and misery.

Jervis blundered after the captain and found him giving orders to two of his men.

'Here! Wait a minute! What the hell are you doing?'

The captain halted and stood patiently waiting for Jervis to catch up. 'The mooring ropes, *signore*. We must slacken off the lines in readiness.' His dark eyes were watchful.

Jervis ran to the rail and listened. Nothing. Not even a gull broke the silence.

They're not coming, he thought wildly. They're dead, or perhaps only wounded, and lying up there helpless. He stared round at the menacing shapes of the sleeping hills. He imagined the stealthy footsteps of the soldiers, as they slowly surrounded the cove and lined up their sights on the pale shape of the small schooner. A nerve jerked in his throat, and he ran his tongue across his dry lips.

'Time? What's the time?' He snapped his fingers urgently, as the captain fumbled for his heavy pocket watch.

'Nearly three.' There was no help in the man's voice.

God, it would be dawn soon. He stared up at the gently spiralling masts and imagined that he could already see them more clearly. If we left now, we could be well clear, perhaps twenty miles out by first light. He bit his knuckle, as he tried to assemble his ideas in order.

'Well, *signore?* Can I get ready?' The voice was prodding him again.

'Very well. Carry on.' He waited, numbed, as the captain and his two men climbed onto the jetty and began to cast off some of the lines. A figure moved by the bollard, and he almost cried out. He tore at his holster as he saw the dim, shapeless form shorten, to kneel beside the dead corporal.

The captain moved with surprising agility. 'It is the priest! Father Bernucci! He will look after the body.'

'What about the soul? Will he look after that?' Jervis laughed crazily, and the man on the jetty looked up, his crucifix shining like a star against his dull robe. The captain shrugged and hurried away.

Jervis walked slowly to the high stern and looked past the bobbing shapes of the two moored fishing boats, to where he knew the open sea lay waiting.

The captain could handle the schooner, and he could navigate the vessel onto some sort of course which would eventually take them to a safe area. But only if they left at once. He stood upright, his arms rigid, as if he had just received an order.

'Start the engine, Captain!' he called sharply, all the pent-up fear released in that one, brief command.

The captain spoke to one of his men and strolled to the wheel.

'We are leaving?'

'Yes.' He wrenched his eyes from the kneeling priest. 'We cannot wait any longer.' His voice rose to a shout. 'Don't just stand there, man! Get ready to leave!'

'I will tell the doctor. He has finished anyway.' The captain loitered, as if to say more, but with a deep sigh he shuffled towards the hold.

The doctor appeared on deck, buttoning his coat. He breathed deeply and walked uncertainly to the rail. He paused, and spoke over his shoulder. 'I go, *Tenente*. They will do well for a day or two. I 'ave left bandages and a few drugs.'

Jervis nodded violently. 'Thank you, Doctor. Thank you very much.'

The little man shook hands with the captain. 'Who knows what the dawn will bring!' He sounded tired and frightened.

The captain darted a glance towards Jervis. 'Yes. The dawn.'

He watched as the doctor crossed the jetty to stand by the priest. The engine roared into sudden life, racing and spitting under the seaman's careless hand.

The captain grunted and swung the wheel experimentally in his hands.

'We will wait a little longer?' His voice was pleading.

All fall into a trap, thought Jervis, and smiled without humour.

'Ten minutes,' he heard himself say and wondered at his own behaviour.

A muffled thudding rose under the forward deck, and Jervis jerked his hand angrily at the captain.

'What the hell's that?'

'The prisoners! They are fighting, I expect.'

'Go and quieten them!' Then as he imagined he saw the eager light in the man's eyes, 'No, I'll go!'

He strode along the deck, his mind blank but for the ache of fear and anger. He almost collided with Carla Zecchi as she leaned limply against the foremast. He paused nervously. The thudding continued, but the girl seemed dazed and unaware of what was happening.

'Are you all right, Carla?'

She nodded. 'I was hoping they might be back.'

Jervis' nerves jumped as the thudding grew louder, interspersed with shouts. 'I must go!'

'I will come with you.'

She followed him along the deck, her slim shape close behind the pale outline of his uniform.

Jervis climbed down to the storeroom and banged angrily on the stout door. 'Quiet in there! Keep silent!' There was a pause, and then he heard a shrill, frightened voice, and he guessed it was the police officer.

'Please, *signore*! Take this man out of here! He is going mad!'

There was immediatedly a string of curses in German and more terrified shouts.

'It is Lieutenant Beck,' the girl said distantly. 'He has been quarrelling with the others.' Her voice was almost matter-of-fact.

'I'll fix him!' Jervis was almost glad to be able to release some of his pent-up despair, and he jerked impatiently at the heavy staple, his gun in his hand.

As the door swung back he saw the five policemen cowering at one end under a pile of boxes and crates. The German officer stood straddle-legged before them, a rough piece of timber in his fist. He glared at Jervis, but lowered the club, his chest heaving.

The police officer stepped forward, his dark eyes watchful. 'Please, *signore*! You take us to another place, yes? He will kill us!'

Jervis waved his pistol. 'Tie him up! Use that rope over there!' He gestured with his pistol, and the Italian's teeth gleamed with triumph.

At that moment the girl stiffened and raised her hand. 'What was that? I thought I heard a shout!'

Jervis' heart bounded, and he cocked his head to listen.

The German acted with sudden frenzy. He leapt across the store-room and kicked the Italian viciously in the groin. With a scream the man fell against Jervis, knocking him into a heap on the deck. As he fell, his head struck against the door-post, and he was only dimly aware of the gun being wrenched from his hand, and the terrified scream of the girl, as the German dragged her up the ladder, the gun covering his retreat.

Jervis staggered weakly to his feet, aware of the stamping feet across the deck, and the captain's excited voice. The police officer moaned softly on the deck, and Jervis slammed the door shut before he dragged himself up the ladder.

The captain shook his arm and peered into his face. 'What 'appen? That German has gone up the jetty! You let him escape?'

Jervis hung weakly to the rail. 'I know! I know! I'm going after him!'

Without waiting for a reply, he broke into a run. He had seen the German's uniform gleam momentarily at the end of the jetty, before disappearing round to the right, towards the village.

His fear was forgotten and he was so overwhelmed by what had happened, that he could only think of it being the final proof of his weakness. He was not even aware that he was unarmed, and as his footsteps thudded along the cobbled jetty, he was filled with the desire to revenge himself on the German, as if by so doing he could drive away some of the shame which was his.

He paused briefly at the foot of the old stone stairway at the end of the jetty and looked up towards the village. The overhanging hills masked any outline he might have been able to recognize, but as he watched he heard the girl cry out, her voice shrill with terror, and all the more chilling because of it apparent nearness.

'Go back! He is going to shoot!' Then there was a sharper cry, and silence.

Jervis sucked in his breath and started to climb the steps. For once, he thought, there was no clear way out, and no one to turn to. It would only be a gesture, he knew, and any second would bring the bullet from the darkness which would end everything. He prayed that it would be quick.

From the cliff road above the cove, Curtis watched the figures below him, his brain cold and clear in spite of the unexpectedness of the scene, which was made more unreal by the pale patches of moonlight and the dark, passive background of the water.

The German and Jervis, in their identical drill uniforms, were quite clear, but as he watched the third figure pinned down behind the low stone wall at the top of the steps, his inside twisted with unexpected anguish.

Duncan licked his lips. 'What the hell are we goin' to do? Ian's comin' straight up those steps. He'll never stand a flamin' chance!'

They heard the girl cry out, and Curtis moved quickly to the edge of the road. 'Come on!' Then cupping his hands, he yelled, 'Stay where you are, Ian! We're coming down!'

Jervis heard the sudden voice booming and echoing amongst the rocks, stood still on the steps, his fists clenched to his sides, and a cold relief flooding through his quivering body. He closed his eyes but felt the tears wet against his cheek. He was no longer alone.

Slithering and stumbling down the rock-strewn slope, Curtis kept his eyes on the German. When he had called out, the man had swung round involuntarily, shocked by the threat behind him. He recovered himself in an instant, and without another glance at Jervis, he pulled the girl to her feet, and before Curtis had even time to guess his intention, thrust her backwards over the wall. She gave a short scream and vanished. Curtis remembered clearly the long steep flight of rough stone steps and choked back a sob of pain and fury. The German had gained the lower road and was running strongly and easily towards the village.

Once Curtis' feet landed on the road he summoned up all his strength and, aided by the overwhelming madness within him, he ran purposefully down the middle of the track, the pistol tight in his hand. The white uniform vanished as if the German had disappeared into thin air, but as Duncan and Taylor panted on behind him, he waved them to a halt and stared narrowly at the pale hump of concrete that he had seen earlier.

'He's in that pillbox,' he said. His voice was flat and devoid of emotion.

Duncan tried to see his face. He guessed what was passing through Curtis' mind. He had know him long enough to appreciate what he was suffering.

'What'll we do?' Taylor dragged his feet uneasily and glanced down at the dark sheen of the cove.

Duncan spoke with soft pleading. 'Come on, Ralph. Let's leave him! We can't force our way in there. He'd pick us all off. Let's get back to the ship an' get the hell outa here!'

'He's in there all right.' Curtis spoke half to himself. 'He knows we can't get in after him, and yet we can't afford to leave him behind. He'd have every damned German he could find after us!'

'But we must go!' Duncan persisted. 'We shall have to chance it!'

Curtis faced him squarely, his eyes gleaming. 'Yes, you *would* chance it, wouldn't you? Bash on, and hope for the best!' He dropped his voice suddenly. 'Well, I'm not like that. I've got so far, and if you think I'm going to let that murdering bastard stand in my way, you'd better get back to the ship and wait for me there!'

Duncan was silent, appalled by the change which had come over Curtis.

'The grenade, George! Give it to me!' Curtis held out his hand and felt the serrated sides of the bomb warm on his palm.

He ran across the road and pressed himself against the tall side of the pillbox. He could faintly hear the German moving about inside, and lifting his head he called out sharply.

'Come out with your hands up!' He did not know if the man understood or not, but he heard him laugh, the sound amplified by the tomb-like interior of the emplacement, and seconds later a shot crashed from one of the narrow weapon-slits and whined angrily across the road.

Curtis pressed his back against the wall, his eyes on the moon. He knows he's safe, he though. We can either stay here and wait for him to come out, or go away and leave him to fetch help. Either way we're finished.

He didn't look down at the grenade as he gripped it in his right hand. He removed the pin and threw it from him.

Across the road Duncan heard the metallic rattle of the pin on the roadway and felt suddenly chilled by the finality of the sound. 'He's goin' to do it!' To himself he said, it's because of the girl.

Curtis released the lever on the grenade and seemed to feel it come alive in his hand. With two seconds to spare he spun round and lobbed it through the nearest weapon-slit.

He heard a grunt of surprise change to a spine-chilling scream, before the weapon-slits blossomed into fiery red eyes and the muffled crash of the grenade reverberated around the hills, flinging stone splinters and a choking cloud of dust across to where Taylor and Duncan watched in shocked silence.

Curtis stepped into the road and walked briskly towards the cove. Over his shoulder he said, 'Start the engine, George, we can't hang about here if there are patrols about!' To Duncan he merely remarked, 'Pity about the noise!'

Curtis hardly remembered speaking to either of them, and had to force his legs to remain steady as he approached the edge of the steps.

At once he saw a small group around her body at the bottom of the steps, Jervis' white uniform, the ghoulish shape of the priest, and the short figure of the doctor.

Carla Zecchi's body looked small and child-like, and for once Curtis did not care what the others thought as he dropped onto one knee and felt her cold hand in his.

The doctor smiled unexpectedly. 'Ver' good girl. She safe!'

'I broke some of her fall.' Jervis' voice died away as Curtis slid his arm under her shoulders.

She opened her eyes, as if she had been expecting him. She said one word. 'Father?'

Curtis shook his head, and she sighed heavily and closed her eyes. Duncan jerked his head at Taylor and Jervis.

'Stand by to shove off! Skipper says we must sail at once!'

They looked down at Curtis' bowed head and the girl's black braid across his arm and moved slowly away.

The doctor smiled. 'She will be OK but a bit painful, eh?'

Father Bernucci stood up, and to Curtis appeared gigantic and all-powerful. 'She can stay with me, my son. I will hide her. No one will know about her, or who she is.'

Curtis looked down at the soft, relaxed face, and remembered what had still to be done. Their real danger might still be ahead, and yet the thought of leaving her behind seemed an even greater risk.

There was a distant rattle of gunfire, and the doctor shuddered and ran towards his car.

The priest shrugged. 'That may be many miles distant.' His fine old head was raised to the stars, and Curtis thought he looked like a saint.

'Nevertheless, Father, I think it might be unwise to risk leaving her here.'

As if in answer, the girl's arm moved up slowly like a ghost and hung weakly across his shoulder.

The priest nodded gravely. 'Maybe it is better.' He rested his hands on them for a moment and, as another burst of firing awakened the echoes, he gathered his robe around his thin body and started off along the road. Once he called back, but Curtis could not hear his words.

Gently, and with infinite care, he gathered her up in his arms and walked slowly towards the pale shape of the *Ametisa*. Her hair was warm against his cheek and as he looked at her he saw a tear on her cheek, although she seemed to be smiling.

A tiny silver light caressed the horizon and the moon seemed to shrink away from the dawn's threat, but Curtis was unwilling to notice either as he stepped carefully onto the deck and made his way aft to the cabin.

The lines snaked aboard and with an urgent flurry of foam the huge screw churned the mud and sand from the bottom of the cove, as the little ship tore herself eagerly from the jetty and tacked round smartly towards the sea. The fishing boats bobbed and faded behind her, and the cove was soon lost in the gloom, but above, on the high cliff road beside the smoking pillbox, the priest watched them go. He saw the sails shake out and climb easily into place, and saw the ship heel over, like a sea-bird spreading its wings. Then she was gone.

He thrust his hands into the folds of his robe and, with the crucifix swinging against his chest, he plodded towards his church.

CHAPTER 11

An Italian seaman emerged from the fo'c'sle and walked stiffly to the lee rail, a bucket of scraps dangling from his hand. He sniffed the keen breeze, and without effort emptied the bucket over the side. For a moment he watched the rubbish twist and dance in the eddies of the bow-wave and then turned his lined face to the empty horizon, his lips pursed into a silent whistle.

Duncan stopped his restless pacing across the poop and watched him with dulled eyes. He felt strangely relieved when the man had returned to the fo'c'sle, and by keeping his back to the stooped helmsman, he was able to retain the impression of isolation. A stronger breeze ruffled the water, which in the early morning light had the solid surface of old pewter, and the sails boomed hollowly and made the slender vessel cant over even more onto her side, so that the hissing water creamed close to the dipping rail.

Duncan noticed none of these things, and merely stared vacantly at the sweeping bowsprit.

His eyes were tired and gummed up with strain and weariness. He no longer relied on his natural resistance to the elements, and it took conscious effort to refrain from shuddering each time a plume of spray spattered across the damp planking and doused his face with stinging salt.

He glared moodily around the ship, taking in the taut rigging and the worn billowing squares of the sails. The schooner had become part of their lives. In fact it had drawn all of them to its own service. They were no longer a team, and it even seemed that each of them was trying to keep away from the other.

He wrinkled his tanned forehead in concentration. It was useless trying to imagine what the future would bring, and the past was so mixed-up and confused, that he found it difficult to space out the events into separate periods. He stared fixedly up at the mastheads and cursed aloud. The skipper had been right about him. His mouth drooped as he recalled Curtis' cold eyes as they stood outside the deserted pillbox. It had been easy before. Routine; an objective; and the savage exhilaration of victory. He flexed his muscles, but it gave him no pleasure.

A sound behind him made him turn, and he saw Jervis walking slowly from the aft hatch, his dark hair rippling in the keen air. Jervis nodded and stood in silence beside him.

Now that the ship was serenely on her course again, he, too, was aware of the empty feeling of peace with foreboding; a calm spell of unreality, like a ship passing through the storm centre of a typhoon.

He cleared his throat and saw the seaman at the wheel raise his black eyes momentarily from the compass and stare at him, his face empty. 'Everything quiet?' He did not want to speak, and yet the silence was more threatening than the expression of loss on Duncan's face.

'Too damned quiet!' Duncan moved his shoulders beneath his rumpled battledress, and his stubbled chin rasped against the upturned collar.

'I haven't had a chance to speak to you about what happened,' began Jervis suddenly. 'I expect you're all thinking it was my fault?' He waited half-defensively for the other man to attack. Duncan did not answer, but merely grunted.

Jervis hurried on, 'I know I was wrong now! But at the time something made me act as I did. I felt out of place.' He faltered. 'How can I begin to explain? I saw the skipper and you acting as if you'd always been doing this sort of thing, and I just knew there was something lacking in me!'

Duncan sighed. 'I shouldn't give it a thought if I were you. It doesn't matter any more.'

Jervis stared at him and felt vaguely cheated. The reply was flat and indifferent, and he did not know how to continue, although every memory was a torment. 'Can't you understand?'

'Understand? What is there to understand? It wasn't your fault. I thought it was at the time, but now . . . ,' he paused and looked down at his boots, 'I guess it's just the way it panned out!'

'I didn't measure up to my own standards,' Jervis persisted.

Duncan smiled, his eyes strangely sad. 'All men are equal, I'm told. That doesn't have to mean they're all the same!'

Jervis bit his lip. 'Oh damn!' He had seen the round shape of the captain appear above the hatch coaming.

Duncan grinned at the captain but felt the effort almost cracking his face. He was pleased to see the man, if only to shut Jervis up. He felt irritated and ashamed that Jervis still looked up to him in the same stupid, trusting manner. He was too complicated, too stuffed full of tradition and values. What did they count out here in this damned old scow? He watched Jervis leaning on the rail, his face furrowed as if in pain.

'*Buon giorno!*' The captain scratched his stomach and pulled a pair of black cheroots from his shirt. He gave one to Duncan and jammed the other between his thick lips.

'We are making the good time, yes? Soon we shall see a beautiful ship maybe, an' then we will be safe an' treated like heroes!' His paunch shook with merriment. 'Good, eh?'

'What happens if it's a German ship?' Duncan answered sourly.

'I shall tell them you forced me to bring the ship here, an' maybe they give me the Iron Cross!' He laughed loudly, and the lookout in the bow turned his head to watch.

Duncan smiled in spite of the gnawing uncertainty in his bowels. 'A wooden one, more likely!'

The surface of the sea was split into long paths of different hues. The horizon was silver, and the grey pewter had give way to streaks of green and dark blue, whilst above, the sun had lost its first watery pallor and climbed steadily and confidently along its well-tried path towards the blue emptiness of the sky.

Some of the sun's early warmth seemed to penetrate the dirty glass panels of the cabin skylight and give new life to the dingy carpet and the stained, chipped furniture.

Curtis sat crouched on the edge of the bunk, his body swaying mechanically at each roll of the hull, his eyes heavy and sore with fatigue and concentration.

The girl on the bunk lay quite still, and it was some time before he realized that her eyes were open and watching him with quiet tenderness.

His brain summoned his body to life, and he leaned over her, his tired face anxious.

'Feeling better? Would you like something to drink?'

He supported her head in his hand and held a glass of wine to her lips. The warmth of her head coursed through his hand and seemed to give strength to his arm. Her head fell back on the rough pillow and she smiled up at him. He pulled the blanket up to her chin, and thought how strange had been the fate which had thrown them together.

'Tell me about it, please.' Her voice was soft and pitched very low.

'About your fall?' he asked lightly, knowing what she really wished to hear.

'About my father. How he died.' Her voice was without bitterness and her eyes were lacking in accusation, the sadness making them instead dark and strangely still.

'Not now, Carla.' He looked away. 'Later, when all this is over.'

Her hand moved from the blanket and found his.

'Did you do it?'

He squeezed her cold fingers. 'No. We ran into an ambush. Partisans.'

Some of the old fire flashed into her watching eyes. 'The carrion! It is what we can expect now!' But still the tears did not come.

'I am sorry.' he began simply. 'Things moved too fast. We were powerless.' He expected her to remove her hand, but it remained in his, growing warmer with the contact.

'The ship is quiet.' She spoke softly, and Curtis found he was conscious of the water rippling past the hull and the muted beat of the engine. They might have been alone together in the ship. Alone and at peace.

'We might be lucky today,' he said at length. 'We might meet a friendly ship. If only we had a radio! Or if we——' He stopped as she squeezed his hand.

'I shall be sorry to leave the *Ametisa*.'

He looked at her anxiously, but her face was quiet and relaxed.

'The future will be kinder, Carla.'

'There is no future, I think.' She moved restlessly beneath the blanket. 'What will become of us?'

Curtis looked desperately around the cabin. 'Well, we'll get away from all this. Find somewhere we can relax, and try to forget what has happened.'

She struggled up onto her elbows, her eyes pleading. 'Please do not say that! We are together here, and here only! If we get to safety, it will be good for the others, but you and I,' she sank back wearily, her throat trembling, 'we will be lost. We have no place together!'

He tried to speak with confidence. 'The war won't last forever! Why, it might be a matter of months! And then I shall take you away and make you see me as somebody different!' He grinned shakily.

She closed her eyes and moved her head from side to side. 'The war may also last for years. The Germans will go on fighting until they are all destroyed, or they have destroyed you. Then you will have to fight all the others – the Japanese, perhaps the Russians!'

Curtis smiled. 'They're our allies.'

'The Germans were our allies, too,' she answered quietly.

Curtis went cold. 'But suppose you're wrong, Carla? Surely it's not hopeless?'

She opened her eyes and smiled, but her mouth quivered. 'Be content with now!'

He sat in silence as she fell into another exhausted sleep, her hand small inside his own.

She was right, he thought bitterly. All his plans and dedicated self-made suffering seemed unimportant now. Even the nightmare which had robbed him of his courage and changed him into a haunted figure seeking an impossible penance for what he had done. He studied the girl's quiet face. She had once asked him what he was trying to prove. Now, none of that mattered, and he knew that his real atonement would be losing her.

He heard Duncan's hoarse voice above his head, and he gently released her fingers and covered her bare arm with the blanket. He stood up and looked round the cabin once more. The lamp swung peacefully from its bracket and the sunlight moved back and forth in shimmering reflection on the deckhead.

He did not want to leave the place, fearing what he might find outside, where reality could only bring more danger and misgivings.

Duncan was running for the hatch as he emerged, blinking on the warm deck. He saw the man's craggy features lined with something like the anger of one who has been cheated.

'Aircraft!' he shouted. 'Port bow!'

Curtis ran to the rail, his fair hair blowing across his forehead. At first he could see nothing, although the high-pitched whine of the engine cut into his brain like a knife.

It was low down, its thin, wafer-edged shape mingling with the fresh dancing water, as it weaved and curtsied over the wavetops, the silver arc of its propeller seeming to touch the spray which reached up to touch it.

Barely a mile from the schooner, it swerved aside and clawed its way lazily towards the sun, which flashed angrily across the perspex cockpit cover and lighted with fire the dull black cross on the fuselage.

Duncan watched it apprehensively. 'They finally found us!' he said.

Taylor squinted at the aircraft, as with effortless grace it climbed upwards, until it seemed to be pinioned by one of the schooner's tapering masts, and with his jaw set in a tight grimace, he ran lightly to the engine-room hatch. He swung one leg over the coaming and looked questioningly at Curtis.

'Full revs, Skipper?'

Curtis nodded, his eyes still on the enemy.

The old diesel thundered into renewed effort but, in contrast, the breeze suddenly died and the sails, suddenly stripped of their power, hung limp and steaming in the warm sunlight.

'Go to the hold, Steve,' he said quietly, 'and explain the situation to the soldiers. Keep them together and ready to leave the place quickly.'

Duncan ducked his head beneath the boom to follow the plane. 'What d'you reckon he's up to?' He sounded calm, almost relieved that the waiting was over.

'Having a good look at us, and probably wirelessing his base at the same time. We shall soon know.'

Duncan started for the hold, his eyes falling on the Italian captain's face. The man was not looking at the aircraft, but staring round at his ship with sudden fear.

'I'll be in the hold if you want me, Ralph. In case anythin' goes wrong,' he grinned sadly, 'well, it's been nice knowin' you!'

Curtis smiled at him. 'Thanks, Steve.'

Duncan jerked his hand towards the poop. 'What about the girl? Are you gettin' her on deck?'

He shook his head, his eyes clouding. 'No, I'll let her sleep. That doctor gave her some dope. It's better this way.'

Duncan nodded and looked up at the blue sky. The aircraft was a mere silver speck, so high up that it was difficult to recognize its shape. 'If only we had a flamin' gun of some sort! We could at least have a go!' He caught Curtis' eye and ran to the hold.

Curtis turned to Jervis, who stood stock-still in the middle of the poop, his lips moving soundlessly.

'You stand there, Ian. We can try the old deception trick again. It might work.'

Jervis looked down dazedly at his crumpled uniform. 'It's all up, isn't it?' His voice broke. 'We're so helpless!'

'Just keep calm,' answered Curtis patiently, 'and remember that I'm relying on you!'

Curtis stepped into the shadow of the big sail, as with an ear-shattering roar the aircraft plummeted out of the sky, to level off only feet from the sea. It flashed across the surface, so close to the schooner's stern that they could clearly see the goggled head of the pilot as he turned to study them, as a motorist might glance at a passing signpost. Curtis pressed his back against the mast, and to overcome his trembling limbs, examined the aircraft with professional detachment.

'Messerschmidt fighter,' he said calmly. 'Quite a nice looking plane!'

Jervis raised his hand weakly towards the plane and felt the rush of its passage across his face. He turned desperately to Curtis. 'Do you think he'll go away?'

Curtis did not answer, he had seen the fighter begin its slow turn, its wings fanning over like those of a drifting gull.

'Captain! Take the wheel yourself!' The terrified man gripped the spokes and shouldered the seaman out of the way. 'Ian, get flat on the deck, he's coming in!'

He glanced quickly along the quiet deck. When he looked back to Jervis he saw that the boy was still standing motionless, his pale face turned towards the fighter with disbelief.

'Get down!' he roared. 'He means business!' Then in a quieter voice, 'Plenty of other people have gone through this, Ian. This is the *real* war!'

He saw Jervis throw himself down, and as he turned to find the plane, he saw that it was cutting over the water and coming straight for him.

As he watched the thin edges of the wings, he saw them suddenly come alive in a line of rippling orange flashes. The harsh rattle of the eight machine-guns sounded like a giant tearing sheets of steel in half, and before his brain had recovered, the water near the ship's side boiled into a savage frenzy, and as the plane drew nearer, the hull shuddered and splintered under the barrage of bullets. He saw the deck planking clawed and torn, and a section of the bulwark rose into the air, as if detached by an invisible hand. With a deep-throated roar, the fighter pulled out of its attack and zoomed over the masthead. Before its shadow had left the deck, Curtis was across the poop and trying to judge the pilot's next move. The man was in no apparent hurry. He had, after all, all the time he needed.

Jervis swallowed and peered over the edge of the bulwark. He picked gingerly at the torn woodwork and followed the trail of destruction across the ship, over the sea, until he could see the tiny circling shape of the fighter.

Curtis stood close to the captain. He could almost smell the man's fear, and he spoke sharply.

'Alter course when I tell you! Put the wheel hard over, and at once! Hang onto yourself, man! I thought you had nerves of steel?'

The captain's eyes were wide with misery. 'My ship! My *Ametisa*! I am afraid for her!' His body seemed to shrink as the fighter's engine screamed across the sea once more.

Curtis gritted his teeth and dug his fingers into the boom. He waited, his breath stilled, counting the seconds.

Brrrrr! Brrrrr! The guns rattled and whined. He was getting better at it. This time the bullets clawed across the whole poop like a steel whip.

The seaman at the the captain's side spun round, his scream choked short as a heavy bullet smashed into his chest and flung him across the rail like a rag doll. For a moment he hung there, his sightless eyes filled with fear and hatred, and then he toppled slowly over the bulwark into the sea.

Splinters whirred through the air, torn in fantastic shapes from the planking, and Curtis heard the hiss of canvas, as the shots poured through the sails and severed the lamp rigging.

The captain squeaked, as with a clang the brass top to the binnacle, only a foot from his body, jumped from its clasps and rolled across the deck.

The air was full of noise and fear. Curtis shouted above the din of the engine, 'Hard a-port!' and saw the stricken schooner tack round with seconds to spare. The fighter was there again, its wings alive with chattering fury, as it plunged recklessly down, the wing tips seeming to brush the bowsprit.

Curtis realized suddenly that the ship's engine had stopped, and even as he tried to concentrate, he felt the ship slowing down and saw the bow-wave fading and growing more indistinct.

The planks at his feet jumped and shook, and he put his hand to his cheek to feel the warmth of blood where a flying wood splinter had caught him.

Taylor clambered over the coaming, cursing, and trying to tie his handkerchief around his wrist. Blood pumped steadily over his clawed fingers, and Curtis ran quickly to his aid.

Taylor leaned limply against the hatchway, his breath whistling between his teeth, as he watched the plane overhead.

Curtis fixed the bandage. 'Engine finished?'

He shrugged angrily. ''Fraid so. All the fuel pipes gone, and Gawd knows what else!' He watched the fighter with narrowed eyes. 'Nice bastard, ain't 'e?'

Curtis thrust Taylor down with his hand, shouting in his ear. 'Here he is again! Get down!' He felt Taylor's body shudder against his own, as the guns roared deafeningly. The shots seemed to come from all round them, and he winced as a heavy block, cut from the mast, struck him across the shoulders.

He blinked and scrambled to his feet. The fighter was growing smaller and smaller, as it tore towards the invisible mainland.

''E's packed up!' Taylor croaked incredulously.

'He's done what he came to do!' Curtis sounded weary and resigned. 'The ship's stopped and helpless. I expect there'll be a destroyer along soon to pick us all up!'

His searching eyes fell on the captain, and he ran across to where he sat awkwardly on the deck. He had his back against the wheel and one of his short legs was doubled beneath him.

He looked up at Curtis, his face grey. 'As I told you, *signore*! Boom! All finish!' He sagged lower, and Curtis saw the widening stain across his thighs. He knelt at the man's side, feeling helpless.

'Is there anything I can do?'

A bright scarlet thread wound its way from the corner of the captain's mouth and dripped off his chin. He shook his head jerkily. 'My ship! My little *Ametisa*!' He coughed, and a fresh flood ran from his mouth. 'Look what they do to her!'

His eyes were still wide with pathetic anger, as he stared up at the shattered masts and torn sails, when with a deep sigh his head lolled and his braided cap fell to the deck.

Curtis picked it up and gently replaced it on the man's head.

Jervis was shouting wildly. 'He shot us up deliberately! He only shot at the after part of the ship! Just wanted to hold us here to be captured!' He stared vacantly at the dead captain.

Curtis stood up. 'Yes, that's what he had in mind, I expect——' He broke off, suddenly icy cold.

The after part, Jervis had said. All at once he was running, tearing at the cabin hatch cover. He stumbled down the last few steps and wrenched open the cabin door.

'Carla!' He called her name as he burst in, and then found himself staring down at her upturned face. She was lying on the cabin floor, where she had pulled herself from the bunk. A trail of blanket had followed her across the deck, and Curtis' heart surged within him as he saw her eyes open.

As he dropped to his knees a shaft of sunlight hit him in the eyes, and he glanced up in surprise.

Across the side of the cabin was a line of neat round holes.

He stared unbelievingly at the bunk and at the deck. Beneath the blanket he saw the sunlight glitter on the bright red drops which marked the girl's progress towards the door.

With a sob he tried to gather her up, but she shook her head with sudden violence, her eyes dark with pain.

He kept his hand under her shoulders, feeling her life seeping over his wrist.

His eyes were misty, and he had to keep blinking to retain the picture of her pale face as she whispered against his cheek.

'*Sento un dolore – qui!*' She tried to move her hand behind her, but he held her wrist and tried to smile.

'You'll be all right, Carla! You'll be all right!'

She stared up at him, her eyes exploring his face with sudden intentness.

'We are together now!' She smiled as he smoothed her hair from her forehead. 'This is how we wanted it, yes?'

He waited, staring brokenly at her and feeling the warmth fading from her hand.

He bent lower, as her lips moved again.

'Do you remember seeing me on my horse? I saw you striding along the beach, trying to look like a German. You were not ver' good at it!' She bit her lip, and he tightened his hold on her.

'I remember. I thought how lovely you looked. And after you had passed, I turned to look back. I shall never forget!'

She moved her hand flat against his face, her fingers touching his eyebrows.

'Perhaps you will be safe, now that it is night again.'

Curtis glanced fearfully at the bullet holes in the torn planking. The sun was as bright as before.

'You see, we had no future? Only now ...'

He nodded blindly. 'Yes.'

She stiffened. 'Hold me! Now!'

But as he gripped her, she relaxed and smiled up at him. When he realized that the smile was fixed and unmoving, he prised her fingers from his hand and kissed her gently on the lips. Her perfume seemed to cling to him as he picked her up and laid her carefully on the bunk.

He closed her eyes and stood back against the bulkhead, unable to leave her. The smile remained, as if she was still holding onto the small moment of happiness.

His limbs were numbed and he stood quite still, staring down at her. Even his breath seemed to have stopped, as if by the slightest movement he might miss something, or if by waiting he might find he was still dreaming.

Duncan lurched into the cabin and stopped dead. His eyes darted from Curtis' stricken face to the still shape on the bunk, and he stepped forward, his hands half raised, as if he expected Curtis to fall.

'What is it?' Curtis' mouth moved slowly, and his voice seemed to come from far away.

'Would you like me to take over, Ralph?' His voice was gruff and very low. 'I didn't realize ...' He stared helplessly at the girl's body.

'No. I'll come. There are things we have to do.'

He paused by the door, and Duncan could almost feel the agony in Curtis' eyes as he looked back. There was an expression of complete loss on his drawn features, and something like pleading in his blue eyes. 'I shall come back,' he added.

Duncan was not sure if he was being spoken to, or whether the promise was addressed to the girl. He touched Curtis' elbow, and followed him up the ladder into the bright sunlight.

Curtis stared round the torn decks and only half heard the clank of the hand pumps forward. His glance passed over the soldiers, who were gathering silently amidships, as if they were no longer there, and moved restlessly across the smiling water to where he had last seen the aircraft.

Jervis was about to speak, his streaked face white and strained, but as he opened his mouth he frowned and glanced at Duncan.

Duncan shook his head quickly and turned his eyes away.

Only Taylor spoke. He walked slowly towards Curtis, rubbing his palms against his greased trousers.

For a moment he waited, until the empty eyes were turned towards him, then he cleared his throat, his mouth forced into a smile.

'I'm sorry, Skipper. Bloody sorry.' He waited, his face tense and anxious, but Curtis merely nodded and patted his shoulder.

'Yes, George. Yes.'

He looked quickly over Taylor's shoulder at the khaki figures who stared listlessly at the sea, or were helping their more badly wounded comrades find a little shelter by the bulwark.

'Why are these men on deck?'

Duncan seemed to jerk out of his trance and hurried to his side. 'Hold's makin' water a bit. The pumps are only just about holdin' their own.'

'I see.' Curtis tried to guess what all this could mean, and frowned because he could not bring himself to think of an answer.

'I've ordered a meal and some drink for the lads, Ralph. It may be some time before they get another.' He scanned the horizon in a quick furtive movement. The sea was still empty. But not for long, he thought. Curtis walked right aft to the worn taffrail and leaned back, so that his body hung suspended over the faded gilt lettering on the stern. The ship was already dead. With each sullen roll, her masts sagged and jerked and the broken rigging swung unheeded across the decks, blocks clattering, and the torn sails casting strange shadows with each uneven movement. The pumps worked steadily and monotonously, theirs the only sound, but for the slosh of trapped water in the hold and in the deep bilges.

He let his head drop onto his chest, and Jervis stepped closer. He saw the movement, but had already dismissed Jervis from his aching mind.

Waiting. We are always waiting. But this time not for me.

The ship lurched and settled deeper.

Some of the soldiers were getting restless, and one was heard to say, 'But there's no life-jackets or anythin'! What'll we do?'

Sergeant Dunwoody looked at the lone figure on the poop and licked his lips. 'This old ship's all right, lads! I expect the Jerries'll be soon now. They'll look after you OK!' There was no irony or bitterness in his voice. 'I'm almost past carin' meself!'

Curtis looked up suddenly, as a white gull swerved past the stern, and almost level with his face. It hung motionless, one black unwinking eye fixed on him.

He remembered the casual scrutiny he had received from the German pilot. Casual; indifferent; efficient.

He remembered how the floating dock had appeared through the periscope. Had he ever considered what was happening beyond the cold impartiality of the lens? He groaned and Jervis hovered nearer.

'Can't I do something, sir?' He fell back as the eyes followed the gull over the poop, and fixed his face with a flat stare.

'Well, Ian. Have you learned anything by all this? D'you think your father would call it useful experience?'

Jervis stammered, 'I don't know how to answer, sir! I – I'm too shaky to think of anything!' He turned miserably for Duncan, but he was at the other end of the schooner with the soldiers.

'Why are you always running away, Ian?' His voice was mild, and the boy found he could no longer meet those unblinking eyes.

'Why not just sit down like me, and think about it all?' He moved his hand vaguely to take in the ship and the sea. 'This is all experience, if you care to make use of it.'

Jervis shifted uneasily. 'How d'you mean, sir?' He prayed that Duncan would not be long.

'We started off as a well-oiled machine. Look at us now!' He hurried on as if he was afraid that Jervis might not understand. 'Somewhere, somehow, in the middle of all this efficiency, we find something real and precious. I suppose that it could happen to a soldier, too. He might be lying in a shell-hole, waiting for the shot to come which will kill him,' he smiled secretly, 'then he sees, right by his face, a small leaf, or perhaps a flower, which has been overlooked by the efficiency of man. What must he feel at that moment, eh?' He reached out with sudden force and gripped Jervis' tunic in a hand of steel. 'Tell me what he feels!' He was shouting.

Jervis tried to pull away, but he was quite powerless. He swallowed hard. 'Well, I suppose he feels that ...' He tried to think of an answer, but he was mesmerized.

'He feels that up to that single moment his life has been empty, and wasted, and beyond it there is nothing more!' He stared hard into the boy's eyes. 'Remember that, Ian!'

He unhooked his fingers and jerked the German eagle from the white tunic. He held it for a moment, then dropped it over the rail. When he looked up again, Jervis had gone, and he saw him talking to Duncan by the hold.

The warmth of the smooth rail caressed his hands, and he noticed that there was dried blood on his fingers and on the front of his jacket. He made a last effort to close his mind, to use it like a flood-gate against the torrent which at any moment would finally break him down. He looked up warily as a man shouted.

'There! There it is I tell you!' The voice was cracked and incredulous.

He saw that the others were looking across the rail towards the inviting water.

A muscle twitched in his cheek, but that was the only outward sign to show that he, too, had seen the movement beneath the surface.

A gasp rose from the soldiers, as with a terrifying roar, the submarine heaved itself out of the depths, water cascading from her evil slime-covered snout and from the squat conning-tower.

Duncan ran aft, his face hard. 'They're here!' He passed his hand over his face and stared at it dully. 'Nice timin', the bastards!'

Sergeant Dunwoody tore his eye away from the surfacing monster and turned briskly to his men.

'Well, come on there! 'D'you want to show 'em we're licked, eh? Come on there! Fall in! Two ranks, an' pick up yer dressin'!'

The weary men shuffled into line, while their friends who lay on the deck stared unseeingly at the sky, waiting for the inevitable.

Jervis walked to the rail, his limbs suddenly light and without feeling. He watched the water stream from the gunbarrel and dance like diamonds along the jumping wire. It was nearly over. The conning-tower blossomed into a moving flower of heads and white caps, and from behind the gun he saw another group moving briskly under the orders of a man with binoculars. The black gun-muzzle trained round until it was pointing straight at him, and he turned his eyes to Curtis. He was still sitting on the rail, his eyes resting on the submarine with something like disinterest.

A breeze came from nowhere and rippled eagerly across the calm water, making small catspaws dance along the submarine's ugly hull. It fanned across the conning-tower just as a seaman was hoisting a flag on the stumpy staff. It reached into the flag and blew it out stiffly, with sudden pride, over the heads of the men on her bridge.

A soldier started forward from the wavering ranks and pointed, his mouth working with inarticulate excitement.

'Look! Look at the flag!' He broke down, sobbing, as the White Ensign floated in front of their eyes.

The ship was alive with cheering and noise, as the submarine slowly manoeuvred alongside and the gun was trained away.

Before she ground against the wooden hull, seamen were already leaping aboard to take the heaving lines, and from the conning-tower the commander watched the shattered schooner in silent disbelief.

Duncan waved to him. It was the same submarine from which they had disembarked, so very long ago.

A young lieutenant landed on the deck at his side and shook his limp hand.

'It's good to see you! I still can't believe it!'

Jervis was shouting. 'How did you find us?'

The lieutenant grinned, his unshaven face alight with pleasure. 'Too long a story for now. We had a whisper from Intelligence that something was going on, but we never dreamed it would be you!'

The submarine commander scanned the sky with sudden urgency.

'Look alive there! Get those poor chaps aboard, Brian! And be sharp about it!'

The forward hatch of the submarine was already open, and more seamen were lowering some of the badly wounded men into the boat's bowels strapped like mummies in Neil-Robertson stretchers. As they swung down, many hands reached out for them, and bearded faces grinned encouragingly.

''Ere comes the bleedin' Army!' called one. 'Just in time for a tot!'

The schooner's deck was all at once deserted, and the little khaki flood had been completely swallowed up by the hatches, which were closed once more.

The lieutenant walked across to Curtis. 'Are you ready to leave, sir?'

Curtis stooped beside the Italian captain and tied the man's belt through the splintered steering wheel.

The schooner was already much more sluggish, and was no longer answering to the gentle movement of the water.

The lieutenant watched Curtis rise. 'Are you all right, sir?'

Duncan answered gruffly, 'Of course he is! What the hell did you expect?'

'I'm just going below, Steve. You get aboard the submarine.'

Jervis and Taylor clambered over the slippery casing and climbed onto the conning-tower to stand beside the commander and his lookouts. The powerful diesels throbbed impatiently, and the seamen on the casing flicked the lines expertly, ready to cast off.

The lieutenant stared down at the dead Italian. 'It must have been quite a party!' he murmured. 'All those soldiers, the five prisoners, *and* the crew to contend with!'

Duncan was not listening. He was remembering the strange gleam in Curtis' eyes as he had gone back to the cabin.

'S'cuse me! I'm just goin' below. I shan't be long!'

'Well, all right. But for God's sake don't hang about. We'll be in real trouble if the Jerry turns up!'

Duncan walked softly down the ladder, his heart pounding. The ship was quite still, and he was conscious of the eerie silence, which added to the impression of desertion and finality.

The cabin door was partly ajar, and he halted noiselessly outside. He could see the pale shape of the girl's face on the bunk, and framed against the white bulkhead he saw Curtis' tall shadow. He seemed to be saluting, but as Duncan peered around the edge of the door, he saw the pistol in his hand.

He darted across the deck, not daring to call out, and gently prised the gun from his hand.

'No, Ralph.' He spoke quietly. 'Not this way!'

Curtis looked at him momentarily, and then crossed to the bunk. Duncan couldn't see whether or not he was touching or speaking to her, but he saw the stooped shoulders shake violently.

Curtis stood up and walked from the cabin. This time he did not look back, nor did he remember how he came to be with the others on the conning-tower.

The schooner seemed to grow very small as the other vessel drew away, and as if in a dream he watched her slowly heeling onto her torn side.

. . .

The submarine commander spoke briskly into the voice-pipe. 'Diving stations! Stand by to take her down, Number One!'

He watched the four figures at the rear of the bridge, staring back at the sinking ship.

Duncan and Taylor stood side by side behind Curtis, and Jervis was gripping the steel plates with obvious emotion.

Duncan stepped forward just as the *Ametisa* dipped her bow under the caressing water and slipped his hand through Curtis' arm.

'You did well, Ralph,' he murmured.

Curtis smiled sadly and craned his head to watch as the white hull began to slide under the waves.

The lonely gull was still circling over the tall masts, and the Italian ensign made a small patch of colour against the torn sails.

He continued to smile, because he was still looking down at her face on the bunk, but as the masts vanished in a small flurry of foam, his floodgate burst.

For Ralph Curtis the single moment of peace was past.

THE END